I0831301

MAGIC, ACADEMIES & VAMPIRES

THE VAMPIRE VINCENT
BOOK TWO

BENJAMIN KEREI

1

NIGHTMARES

To misquote my wife's favourite novel, it is a truth universally acknowledged that a father in possession of children, must be in want of a good night's sleep. And though I was past the point where this should have been an issue, having become a vampire and slept through my children's teenage years, life finds a way. Sometimes, that *way* is painful. Sometimes, that *way* involves magic. And sometimes, that *way* leaves you broken as a father.

I went from sleeping peacefully in my grave to experiencing unimaginable agony, the kind that causes demons to shudder as they carve into a sinner's soul. My outsides were my insides, and my insides were everywhere except where they should be. My flesh folded through itself and over itself in an excruciating dance of loose muscle and bone as everything fought to reposition itself with agonisingly slow intent.

In the dark, flesh-filled prison of my body, my vampiric instincts woke from their slumber with one thought. One instinct. *Survive.*

My soul remained asleep, too weak to claw its way back to the world of the living through the ravenous survival instincts of the monster who had ransacked its home. There was no Vincent, no self-aware conscience to guide the monster that sensed it was far from home and the safety and peace it offered, no morality or control to restrain its intent.

Driven by survival, the monster lashed out, latching onto the nearest source of life that could save it from its misery. Teeth met flesh, and I learned the answer to a question I never wished answered.

Blood, that sweet elixir which made me salivate every time it tantalized my senses, had a flavour as close to pure joy as I could imagine. The best day of my life could be summed up by its taste.

Blood entered the monster's mouth, like the juices of forbidden fruit, curling its toes with happiness and delight. The monster drank without remorse, without thought, without pause to consider the consequences. The blood flowed down its throat, absorbing into its flesh without ever reaching the stomach, as its demonic parasites glutted themselves on the gift of life to recover from the mistreatment the soul called Vincent had subjected them to.

One by one, the parasites healed from their pain and mistreatment. The raging inferno of life force held within the corpse they'd reanimated, which was beyond their reach for months, became available, allowing them to recover.

Pain began to vanish as the demonic parasites restored their vampiric kingdom. The threat to their survival retreated. And strength returned to the soul called Vincent.

As the monster continued to feed, I began to wake. It was a gentle pull, a tug that was slowly returning me to the world of the living, without pressure or fear. It whispered that I was safe and happy.

And then a small voice, filled with pain, that sounded like my wife's when we met, whispered in my ear. "Dad, you're hurting me."

Those four little words, spoken by a voice that had matured over the past eleven years, were all it took to break me from my peaceful, indulgent haze.

My eyes snapped open as my fangs retracted. If I had a heartbeat, it would have raced. A wave of abject terror filled me, as the joy-filled taste remained on my tongue. Nauseous dread swept through me as I pulled my mouth from Kathrine's throat and stared with mounting horror at the ragged, fleshy wound I'd given my daughter.

Kathrine looked like her mother, with dark blonde hair and dimpled cheeks. Her shoulders were slim, and slightly wider than her mother's, because of her extra height. Tears sat in creases of her eyes as she looked at me with horror, fear, and hopeless confusion. Like she couldn't understand why her daddy was hurting her.

Her heartbeat fluttered, weak and erratic, as she gazed up at me from the ground, the way she had as a child when she had fallen off her bike and broken her arm. She wanted me to fix it. To make it better.

But I couldn't fix it.

I'd bit too deep.

I'd drunk too much.

She was dying.

Because of me.

Notifications appeared before me, driving home the reality of my actions.

You have mastered your Royal Vampiric Thirst skill.
Your Ancient Royal Vampiric Bloodline skill has increased to level 15.

The sound of her fluttering heartbeat pleased the monster but appalled the father I had been as I dismissed the notifications. The flesh missing from her throat looked like art to the monster but hurt my soul to see. And the joy her blood had brought me made the experience feel like a happy dream, instead of the living nightmare that it was.

The vampire could not deny the reality it saw, as my soul screamed its way into madness. Without any effort, it forced the madness to accept this reality, freeing me to react with cold dispassionate logic.

I swept my gaze around me, trying to understand what was happening. I was in a living room, with three doors leading from it, two led to bedrooms, while the last led into the hallway of the apartment building. A young woman with light brown hair who knew my daughter well based off the scents clinging to her was cowering in the corner, but she wasn't important as the placement of the furniture. They'd pushed it to the sides and stacked on it top of each other to make room for the demonic teleportation circle I'd damaged when I attacked Kathrine.

My focus moved from the room to myself.

I was wearing my Day Walker set, an enchanted outfit made from the blackened skin of an ancient vampire, and had my Kilij, Slaughter, beside me. The contents of my storage pouches littered the apartment floor, twisted and broken beyond recognition.

I put everything together and immediately understood what had happened.

Nearly a year ago, I'd sent Kathrine a letter with a lock of my hair. In that letter, I told her if she ever wanted to see me, she could use her blood and my hair to summon me through the demonic teleportation circle I'd attached to the letter. To anyone else, a teleportation spell would be a death sentence, as the individual always arrived inside out, but an ancient vampire could survive the experience.

She must have done as I told her, teleporting me across the world while I recovered in my sarcophagus, because it was the only explanation for everything I saw.

Summoning me was never supposed to be dangerous.

I could control my hunger.

I could control my impulses.

But seven months of torture had left me so beaten and exhausted I'd fallen into a catatonic state the moment I entered my grave. If she had summoned me a few months earlier or later everything would have gone to plan. Instead, she had summoned me when I was at my absolute weakest, when I wasn't in my right mind, when I couldn't control myself.

A wave of grief washed through me as Kathrine reached out to me with the last of her strength. I peeled off my glove and took her hand in mine, feeling the weakness in her grip as her soft hand touched mine. A moment later, she passed out with her eyes open.

I swept my gaze through the room again, searching for a solution. There was a bookcase, several couches, and the young woman cowering in the corner. I sniffed, running every scent through my nostrils. There were no healing potions to save Kathrine, and my storage pouches and their contents had been destroyed in transit. I couldn't risk making a run for it to search the building.

Kathrine didn't have that much time.

I didn't have that much time.

There was only one way to save my daughter's life and keep my soul. The choice was so horrible that—even as a vampire—I hesitated.

Her heartbeat slowed.

I squashed my parental instincts to save her.

I let go of Kathrine's hand and blurred to the cowering young woman, picked her up, and blurred back to my daughter's side. The young woman had light brown hair, pale skin, freckles, and was above average height. Her nose was a little too small for her face, but her cheekbones made up for that by giving her a striking and alluring appearance, rather than being traditionally pretty. Her expensive green dress with matching jewellery, along with her soft hands, suggested she came from money. None of that would help my daughter, so I pulled the athame from Kathrine's belt and shoved the handle into the young woman's hand.

"Stab my daughter through her eye and into the brain. Letting her turn into a vampire is the only way to save her life. If you don't do as I say, I will kill you slowly." My voice was calm and even, offering a level of sophistication as sharp as any sword.

I stared at my daughter and felt myself want to vomit as I took her hand in mine again.

"Sweetheart, Daddy is going to fix this. I promise."

"I can't do this," the young woman said, athame falling from her fingers, voice trembling with her body. "She's my best friend."

I caught the athame and shoved it back into her fingers. "You're not killing her. You're saving her life."

"I—"

My fangs descended as I turned to her, anger flaring. "Do. It."

The young woman shuddered as she gripped the handle in both hands and then shoved it through my daughter's eye with all her strength, killing her instantly. Kathrine's body bucked and twitched as nerve impulses made her flail about.

"Now, the heart," I growled.

She pulled the athame free and tried to stab Kathrine in the heart, but the blade bounced off her ribs.

I pointed to her diaphragm. "Through here, at this angle."

She repositioned the athame where I said and stabbed her again. This time, she got it right.

I pushed the young woman away with too much force, throwing her across the room and into a wall. Then I took Kathrine's hand between both of mine. The cold analytical part of my mind fell away, and grief overwhelmed me.

Tears began to run down my cheeks and into the corners of my mouth, making me taste salt. "Daddy's sorry, Sweetheart. Daddy didn't mean to hurt you. Daddy will make it better." Her lifeless hand offered no comfort as I kept repeating those three sentences over and over again, unable to escape the living nightmare.

I wept, for the first time truly feeling like the monster I was.

HOURS PASSED as I sat there holding my dead daughter's hand and apologising for what I had done to her. Every moment of it was a waking nightmare as I waited for her to come back to me. As I waited for everything to be right.

I sobbed harder when her injuries began to heal when the demonic parasite in my bite reached into Hell for the strength to infect her flesh and repair the damage I had done. I watched her flesh close with hyperfocus, unaware of the world around us.

Her hair was matted with dried blood. In death, her delicate features were contorted in an expression of pain. She had my grey eyes and height, but everything else reminded me of Sandra when we met. She was beautiful.

My little girl had spent half her life without me. She had grown into a woman all alone. And the first thing I'd done when we were reunited was kill her.

I was a monster.

Her lifeless, grey gaze stared at the ceiling as her body grew cold. The smell of her blood tantalized me for the first few hours, causing me to salivate and hate myself even more. As the infection spread, the inviting smell faded, but my self-disgust never went away.

Then she blinked.

I watched her head turn as everything came into focus. It was like watching her birth, but without all the nausea and body secretions. Anyone who tells you childbirth is a beautiful and moving experience is either lying or wasn't in the room during the event.

She blinked again, adjusting to her new, enhanced vision as quickly as I had. She turned and stared at me. One minute passed, and then another. Finally, she spoke. "Dad, did you just turn me into a fucking vampire?"

"Language, Sweetheart."

I wiped the last of my tears away, as happiness replaced my sorrow. My vampiric nature didn't allow me to dwell in the past or worry about the future. I existed purely in the present, and in the present, my daughter was safe and alive.

Indignation crossed her face as she stared at me from the floor. "You did, didn't you?"

"You were dying."

"Because you ate me!"

Her indignation was completely justifiable, but it was not the reaction a normal person would have had. She should have been overcome with fear and horror. She should have been terrified out of her mind. But she was a vampire.

She pulled her hand from mine.

That small action hurt more than any pain I'd experienced. "You teleported me away from my grave after I'd succumbed to exhaustion. I was dying and so weak I couldn't control the monster in me."

"Now I'm a fucking vampire."

"Language, Sweetheart."

"I don't fucking care about your stupid rules. You turned me into a fucking vampire. What the fuck am I supposed to do?"

"We will take you to a cleric and have them remove the curse. In a few hours, you will be back among the living."

Her head twitched too fast as she began sniffing the air. "Why is everything so loud?"

"You don't have a heartbeat."

She began to smile. "What is that delicious smell?"

"Try to ignore it."

"It's making me hungry."

"Try to ignore that, too. This will be over shortly. We just need to get you to a cleric."

I gently lifted her to her feet.

She swayed on the spot. "I feel woozy."

"The wooziness will pass."

I remembered what she was going through. It was a very disorientating experience.

Kathrine turned to the young woman cowering in the corner and frowned. "Riza, are you okay?"

Riza slowly raised her head from the ball she'd curled into. "Kat?" She stared at my daughter for several seconds. "You're alive."

Kathrine nodded. "Are you okay?"

Riza shook her head. "He broke my ribs after he made me kill you."

Kathrine turned and scowled at me. "You broke her ribs."

Vampires found it incredibly difficult to care about anyone they didn't already love. Kathrine must have really cared for the young woman to show this much interest.

"You were dying. I needed her to kill you, so I wasn't responsible for it. Time was limited."

"You made my best friend kill me, so you weren't responsible!"

"I would have lost my soul."

"Apologise now."

I'd hurt her friend, which meant I'd hurt her. I didn't want to do that. So, I turned to Riza. "I'm sorry that I broke your ribs and made you kill my daughter."

Riza cringed as I looked her way. "You threatened to kill me, slowly."

"I'm not apologising for that."

"Yes, you are!"

"Fine, I'm sorry for threatening to kill you slowly if you didn't kill my daughter and stop me from losing my soul, which would have resulted in me and then her becoming soulless vampires and given rise to a very dangerous family of vampires who would have terrorized this world and caused unimaginable amounts of death and destruction."

Kathrine tilted her head to the side, the way she always had when thinking, deciding if she wanted to make an issue of my apology.

There were more pressing matters. "We should find you a cleric before you get hungry." I distracted her by adding, "They will also be able to take care of your friend's broken ribs."

Kathrine nodded and started walking towards Riza.

I caught her shoulder before she had taken two steps. "Sweetheart, you're a newly turned vampire, and your friend is now food. You're going to feel all sorts of urges and impulses, and you might kill her before you can regain control."

Riza's blood had been calling to me ever since I'd stopped being overwhelmed by grief. Now that I knew what blood tasted like, controlling my impulses was more difficult, but I had the willpower to restrain myself.

"Help her to the infirmary for me, then."

I turned to Riza. "Is that all right with you?"

She shook her head and made a pained expression as she climbed to her feet. "I can walk."

I glanced at Kathrine. "How are we going to explain your condition?" She was a local, and I understood how logical her thinking would be, so I trusted her judgement.

Kathrine frowned. "I left the academy to have dinner at Antari's in town and was attacked by a vampire and dragged into an alley. You were wandering past when you heard the commotion and investigated. You killed the vampire, but it was too late to save me, so you waited beside me to see if I would come back. When I did, you decided to return me to the academy so the clerics in the infirmary could restore my soul. We ran into Riza on the way to the infirmary, and I attacked her, breaking her ribs."

It was simple, believable, and hard to disprove. It was also very cold and detached. Kathrine didn't seem to notice.

"We're at Darksmith Academy, I take it?"

I'd seen the crest on her robe and remembered it from a history book. It was a prestigious dungeon academy along the border of North and South Murdell.

Murdell was a caste-based nation where pureblood sorcerers sat at the top. Two decades ago, a darklord had risen to power by preaching magical purity. This caused a rift in the upper castes as more and more restrictions were placed on anyone whose families weren't as pure, which led to a war and the nation fracturing.

Now, there was North and South Murdell.

A little over a decade ago, the two nations had been about to go to war again, when the South successfully summoned a hero—my daughter. Not wanting to risk having to face a hero, the Darklord had backed down. A treaty was signed requiring the elites of both nations to send their children to Darksmith, leading to an uneasy peace, which had more or less continued ever since.

Murdell didn't use dungeon legions to contain their dungeons. They used academies. They didn't use adventurers, either. They used former academy students to deal with threats on the surface. It was a very power-based society, where the strong ruled, and the weak remained quiet or left.

Those without magic made up less than a thirtieth of the population, as the sorcerers had made it clear they didn't want or need them.

"Yes, we're at Darksmith," Kathrine replied. "Also, I ran away from the South, and no one knows I am here, so don't mention it."

Luke had told me the South Murdell government managed to convince the Darklord that the hero they had summoned was a powerful old sorcerer who saw their magic as a trivial plaything. They had built a massive palace for this fake hero and spared no expense, lavishing the palace with wine, women, and trinkets. The successful ruse was the only reason they hadn't been obliterated. Kathrine's way of fighting the Darklord was merely continuing to exist in obscurity.

"I won't say a word."

"Good."

Riza began walking to the door.

It was a mistake.

I was between Kathrine and her friend before Kathrine harmed her. Riza leapt back with a squawk of pain and surprise as my daughter mindlessly fought me with everything she had, tugging at my arms to get to her friend. She wasn't anywhere near as strong or fast as I was, so there was no real danger. However, she was stronger than I expected. Becoming a vampire had helped her as much as it helped me.

"Calm down, Sweetheart. Riza is your friend. You don't want to eat your friend, do you?"

Kathrine's struggling slowed as she regained control and realised what she'd tried to do. Tears began to run down her cheeks as the horror set in.

I rubbed her back as she cried. "It's okay. You didn't hurt her. That wasn't you. That was the monster inside you."

I motioned for Riza to go around us.

She shuffled to the door, hugging her sides. She hissed as she opened the door and stepped out into the hallway.

I motioned for her to keep going.

She frowned at Kathrine and then headed off to the infirmary. I listened, waiting for her to call for help, but she never did.

When Riza was far enough away, Kathrine whispered, "I tried to eat her."

"I know. It's something I live with every day."

Kathrine wiped away her tears as she stood up straight. "I hate this."

"I do, too."

2

BYE-BYE, VAMPIRE

The head of the infirmary was an elderly cleric named Dalin. Dalin had a beer gut, a long white ponytail, and a white robe covered in food stains. His appearance gave the impression he was a retired hippy, except for his gaze. It had a soft white glow, showing he was favoured by Heaven, and anyone favoured by Heaven usually had more important things to worry about than their appearance.

He fussed over my daughter with gentle care as she mindlessly tried to bite him, and I held her down.

Crossing the academy grounds had been too much for her. Despite it being the middle of the night, there were plenty of students in the open spaces taking advantage of the higher levels of ambient mana that existed here at the edge of the dungeon. They were studying or practicing magic, and their scents quickly drove my daughter insane with bloodlust.

The relief I'd felt upon seeing her return to the land of the living had quickly faded. I wasn't concerned about my daughter being a vampire, that was a simple fix, but I was concerned about the damage her soul had taken when I fed on her. I wasn't like other vampires anymore, and I didn't know what the ramifications would be once she became human again, but I knew they wouldn't be good.

Murdell didn't have many natural streams and rivers I couldn't cross, but the Bo Empire to the east had many. Getting through the Bo Empire to Arcadia, the kingdom where my grave lay, would be impossible to do alone. I was trapped here until help arrived.

On my way to the infirmary, I'd seen an aged flier on a message board with a job opening for the Occult Studies professorship. It made for a convincing cover story for why I was here and a good reason to stick around if I had to. I knew more than enough to teach the subject.

"She's lucky you found her," Dalin said, quickly pulling his hand away so he didn't lose a finger to Kathrine's teeth. His voice was calm and relaxed with a gentle tone, despite the close call. "Most don't know you need to leave a person where you find them for them to come back. And not many sorcerers have the strength to manhandle a new vampire."

Darksmith infirmary was state-of-the-art, filled with magical equipment to ensure that their wealthy clients received only the best care. Dalin wasn't using any of that equipment. He was an expert in his craft and didn't need a crutch.

I stifled a fake yawn. "I came to Darksmith to apply for the Occult Studies professorship. Leaving one of my future students in distress wasn't something I could do."

Dalin raised an eyebrow. "As far as good first impressions go, this is certainly one of the best I've seen."

Kathrine tried to lunge again. I felt her right collar bone fracture from the strain as I held her down. She didn't even notice, blinded by bloodlust.

"Can you lift the curse?"

Dalin waved away my concern. "I wouldn't be the head of the infirmary if I couldn't."

Dalin continued his physical examination, which wasn't part of the standard procedure for removing the curse. If he didn't have the glow of a righteous soul, I would have suspected he was being inappropriate.

"What are you looking for?"

He continued to prod her stomach and hips. "Vampires are extremely sturdy. They can survive having a knife embedded in their gut, while a human cannot. I don't want to complicate matters by lifting the curse and then discovering she has a nail in her lung. It will be easier on her if I remove it now."

I hadn't even considered that. "You've seen this happen?"

"No. I heard about it second-hand, which is why I'm checking."

The infirmary had enough beds to house several hundred people. It needed that many beds to deal with threats that could arise from the dungeon. At the moment, the beds were empty, and there were only a handful of clerics on duty. Dalin hadn't been one of them. Riza had warned the staff that Kathrine was coming, and they had woken him.

"She seems fine," he said, collecting a pair of small metal bowls and a knife from the side table. "I'm going to slit her wrists. Black ooze will trickle from the wounds shortly after I cast the spell to remove her curse. This ooze is toxic, and you don't want to get any on you, so hold her tight. When the black ooze is replaced by blood, she will die for a few moments, which is meant to happen. After, I'll heal her and restart her heart."

He made two quick cuts that didn't bleed and placed the bowls under her wrists. Then he cut his palm and sprinkled his blood at the bottom of the bowls.

The aroma of Dalin's blood was so much more inviting than in the past. I wasn't hungry, but the smell made me want to eat. I felt like I was missing out on a wonderful experience.

My mouth began to salivate as Kathrine thrashed harder, trying to reach the blood.

When I'd first awoken, I was little better than Kathrine's current state. It was only through prolonged suffering that I'd been able to get used to the urges and regain control. She wasn't weaker than me for being like this. She just hadn't had time to adapt.

Dalin healed his hand with a spell before placing it on Kathrine's forehead. The spell he was going to cast on her wasn't actually a curse-breaking spell, but a cleansing spell that removed infection and disease. The spell forcefully separated the demonic parasites from her blood and healed the damage this caused.

His palm glowed white as he cleansed her.

Freed from her blood and unable to re-enter, the vampiric parasites followed their instincts and searched for food. The only food they could find was Dalin's blood sitting in the metal bowls. Black ooze began to trickle down Kathrine's wrists as the parasites went for the easy meal.

A few minutes later, blood followed, and Kathrine died again. Watching her lying there lifeless hurt just as much as the first time. It made me dwell on how monstrous I'd become. It forced me to remember that my daughter was suffering because of what I'd become.

Dalin allowed her to bleed for a few more seconds and then cast a simple healing spell, closing the wounds on her wrists. He then cast another spell that restarted her heartbeat and forced her to inhale. Finally, he cast a holy spell on the vampiric parasites in the bowls. Without Kathrine's soul to protect them, they burned.

Dalin smiled as he took away the ash-filled bowls. "Thanks to you, she's back to her old self. Lay her down on the bed, and we'll go see the headmaster."

"Why do we need to see the headmaster?" I asked, grabbing a folded blanket and tossing it across her to keep her warm.

"You made a good impression. So, I'm going to vouch for you. Passing the tests will be something you have to do on your own, but I'll get you through the door."

I made sure I smiled and showed the right emotions. "Thank you."

"No, thank *you.* This institute is under incredible scrutiny, and the loss of any student outside of defending the dungeon can start a war." He waved over one of the other clerics to clean up the equipment he'd used and then walked me out.

Headmaster Wink's office reminded me of Dumbledore's office if Dumbledore had been a functioning alcoholic. There was all the magical paraphernalia you'd expect to see in a magical academy's headmaster's office, along with a larger-than-necessary bar. Behind the headmaster's desk was a door that led to a staircase that went to his study and living quarters. Dalin had gone up, leaving me alone in the office while he explained the situation. Then they had come back down together, and Dalin had patted me on the shoulder before heading out.

Headmaster Wink was a bald elderly man with a long sloping moustache. He wasn't an imposing man, despite having one of the strongest auras at the academy. "I'm Headmaster Wink," he said, as he placed a glass of gin and three files on the table. His words were crisp and smooth, despite his inebriated state. "I'm told you wished to apply for our Occult Studies professorship. Do you have any references?"

"Not on me, I'm afraid. My references are with my things at the inn."

He sighed and rubbed his tired eyes before taking a seat. "Of course they are. Why would it be otherwise, considering the circumstances of your arrival? It's fine. We'll do this without references." He picked up his glass of gin and took a drink to calm himself. I could smell the stress coming from him as he pointed to one of the files. "This is one of two written tests. If you pass this one, you can take the second. These tests are used to weed out the uneducated. You need a perfect score to pass this one. You can begin when you're ready."

I took the pen and test he offered, flipping it open. Wink sat drinking in silence as I worked my way through the test. It wasn't a difficult test, but it was extremely thorough, covering more aspects of the occult than I'd expect for a simple test. But then again, this was Darksmith, and it catered to the heirs of the elite.

I handed the test back five minutes later.

Headmaster Wink opened one of the other files, pulled out an answer key, and harrumphed, scowling at the page. "Bother. I gave you the wrong test. Might as well mark this one since you filled it in."

He quickly checked my work and started to frown before the end of the first page. The frown grew bigger the further he marked.

He finished marking the test, before lifting his gaze and scowling at me. "A perfect score."

His reaction confused me. "Why do you sound upset?"

"I was hoping you'd fail."

"Have I done something to offend you?"

"No. I just don't like to employ handsome or pretty professors. They bring all sorts of problems."

"I promise not to bring any problems?"

He took another sip. "That's what they always say. It's always proved false. However, you're overqualified for the position, and we need the position filled, so today is your lucky day."

"How overqualified?"

"Our secondary tests are designed to make academics weep. Correctly answering one in five questions is considered a passing grade. Only three of our teachers have aced their tests like you just did, and none did so as quickly."

"Would you like me to get my references?"

After my display, he wouldn't need them, but by bringing it up now it wouldn't become an issue in the future.

He shook his head. "I'm sure they're prestigious, judging by your test scores, but you don't need them." He took another sip of gin. "What branches of magic do you practice?"

"Only death and necrotic."

His upper lip began to turn with disgust before he controlled himself. "That's a pity. Can't practice necromancy myself. Otherwise, I'd do your magical aptitude test immediately. Come back in ten days to sit the test. If you pass, the position is yours. Now, if you'll excuse me, it's late, and I need to get some sleep before these buffoons claiming to be students wake up and begin coming up with new ways to make my hair fall out."

I chuckled.

He took another drink. "That wasn't a joke. I used to have a beard."

I STOOD outside Kathrine's dorm room door, listening to her sob into her pillow. Without the emotionless haze of vampirism, the horrors of my actions were all too real. I'd attacked her. I'd caused her pain. I'd made her best friend kill her. I'd behaved like an utter monster, and I wasn't sure if I could ever make this right.

I let myself into her dorm and noticed the changes to her scent. I'd witnessed enough traumatized individuals in this world to recognise the scents of PTSD, uncontrolled panic, and depression. Kathrine had all three. She was a turbulent ball of negative emotion.

The damage to her soul was worse than I'd imagined.

I walked through the debris from my storage pouches and gently knocked on her bedroom door. "Can I come in, Sweetheart?"

I heard her heartrate spike. "Go away."

She'd summoned me because she wanted to see me, but a moment in my company had been enough to destroy any goodwill I had with her. "Please let me in, Sweetheart. I'm sorry...I'm so sorry. I never wanted to hurt you."

"You're a monster."

Her words cut deeper than any sword ever had. "A very sorry monster."

"I don't care. I never want to see you again."

The last time she had seen me, she was eleven. That was an age where everything was kind of fuzzy by the time you were an adult. She didn't know me the way Luke did, and now she didn't want to. "Please let me come in and explain."

"Go away!"

Thrice asked and denied. The demonic part of me urged me to either open the door and do as I pleased or leave. For once, I listened to the demon.

I opened the door and entered her bedroom.

She trembled under the covers as I took a seat on the edge of her bed. "I know you're afraid, Sweetheart. But I need you to listen to me. What I did to you was horrible, but the way you're reacting isn't natural. Right now, you feel worse than you've ever felt in your life, and that's my fault. It's my fault because I'm not like other vampires.

When I feed on people, I take a bite out of their soul. That ache inside of you that makes you feel like you've lost everything that was dear to you is one of the side-effects. The deep depression, anxiety, and uncontrollable fear are others."

"Each second is worse than the last," she whispered with a shudder. "I feel like I'm going insane."

"That might happen, which is why you need to go to sleep."

Despite her fear, she managed to roll over and point her wand at my forehead. I flicked her stomach hard enough to wind her, caught her by the throat, and placed my thumb against the artery. She passed out before she could get her spell off.

I pulled out the vial of sleeping potion I'd stolen from the infirmary and poured it down her throat. It was the same potion I'd used on Luke. She would be unconscious until a cleric healed her.

I rolled her onto her back, wiped her face, and then tucked her in like I had when she was a child. Then I climbed to my feet and walked across the living room to Riza's bedroom.

I could hear her erratic heartbeat as I turned the doorknob and opened the door. She stood inside a barrier, held in place by a ritual circle, and she was pointing her wand at me.

I ignored the wand and looked her in the eye as she trembled.

Riza had had countless opportunities to expose me. She hadn't done that. She'd kept mine and my daughter's secrets. She cared for Kathrine. So, I decided to trust her.

"How much did you hear?"

She took a deep breath to calm herself. "All of it."

"Good. Look after Kathrine for me until I get back. I won't be long."

DALIN LIVED ALONE in a small apartment near the infirmary. Getting inside unnoticed was easy. I could hear every sound in the academy, so navigating my way around people wasn't an issue. I entered his apartment while he slept, making my way to his bedroom. The bedroom was large but sparsely decorated. He didn't seem to be a man who cared for wealth or luxury.

Katherine's condition was beyond my worst expectations. Her mental state had deteriorated to a point where she would be committed to an institution in less than an hour. She needed help, help I couldn't give.

But a cleric could.

Dalin slept on his back, without any covers. As I stood over him, I silently drew Slaughter and placed the blade against his throat. His eyes snapped open, and I showed him my fangs.

He trembled but didn't cry out. By the way he carried himself, I knew he hadn't always been a healer.

"I need your help, Dalin."

He took a slow breath in. "Doing what?"

"Taking care of my daughter."

"What's wrong with her?"

"I fed on her soul. I need you to examine the extent of the damage."

Comprehension entered his gaze. "That young woman you brought me was your daughter?"

"Yes. Now, I need to prove a point. Cast your most powerful holy bolt spell at my head."

He lifted his arm without any hesitation and cast the spell, forming a ball of bright yellow energy. I closed my eyes as the bolt flashed and slammed into my head. When I opened them, Dalin was staring at me with disbelief.

I smiled at him. "I am the Vampire Vincent, and I have never taken an innocent life."

"Your daughter—"

"Was an accident. She teleported me here while I was asleep, and I attacked her before I could regain control. I made her roommate kill her so I wouldn't be responsible and lose my soul."

Several thoughts seemed to pass through his head and then he paused. "You don't intend me any harm, do you?"

"No." I pulled the blade away from his throat. "I needed you to understand the situation, so you didn't complicate this by calling for help." I walked over to the armchair in the corner of the room and sat. "Let's have a polite conversation."

He rubbed his throat for a moment and then sat up and leaned against his headboard. "Why did you break in here?"

"I told you. I fed on my daughter's soul and need you to examine her."

"Why me?"

"You won't harm my daughter or use her against me."

He paused. "How do you know that?"

"I'm an ancient vampire, and I can see you're favoured by Heaven."

He sucked in a sharp breath. "Prove it?"

I drew Slaughter and lopped off my hand. It snapped back into place, healing in a fraction of a second. His frightened expression pleased me.

"I survive by feeding on Unseen. You and your academy are perfectly safe. The only thing that could change this would be for you to tell them what I am or for them to try to harm my daughter. The church in Arcadia will confirm this."

"You work with the church?"

"No. I passed the Trial of Purity, so they tolerate my existence. Now, get dressed. You need to check on my daughter."

RIZA WATCHED from the doorway as Dalin finished his examination. She'd done exactly as I'd told her to while I was gone. Watching over Kathrine while she slept to the best of her abilities.

Dalin pulled his hand from Kathrine's forehead and stepped back, frowning. "Her soul is mangled."

I was afraid of this. "How long does she need to be asleep?"

He scratched his chin. "I'm not sure. It could be a month, or it could be several years. I won't know until I see how quickly her soul heals. For now, don't wake her up. Don't let anyone else wake her up.

She's in an extremely delicate state and might go insane or kill herself if woken. She needs to be surrounded by friends and family when she wakes. But that can only be done after she's been given a chance to heal."

My daughter had told Riza everything she knew about me, and Riza had passed this on to Dalin. Her confirmation did a lot to settle him. He was willing to wait for an answer from the church before acting. The threat an ancient vampire posed was too great to ignore a potentially peaceful solution.

I turned to Riza. "I need to leave for a few days. Kathrine is your responsibility until I return."

She swallowed.

I turned to Dalin. "Help her while I'm gone. Make an excuse for why she doesn't need to attend classes."

I couldn't safely move my daughter across borders by myself. I needed to set things up so I could stay here without raising suspicion, protecting her until reinforcements arrived.

"Where are you going?" he asked.

"The Abyss."

I left Kathrine's dorm room, wandered through the hallways, and down the staircase to the entrance. I needed to send a message to my people and there was only one way to do that.

Right before I'd gone to sleep, I'd met a strange little girl named Amelia. She was daughter of Denton, the first person who had ever sworn my hero's oath. Her mother had been carrying her when her father swore the oath, and we had some sort of connection. She dreamed about me, seeing everything I did in a surprising amount of detail.

I stared at my reflection, using a mirror near the main entrance. "Amelia, I need you to pass along a message to Davina when you wake up. Tell her I'm awake and at the Darksmith Academy in Murdell. Tell her what I did to Kathrine. I need her to find Luke and bring him here to help me fix this. I don't think I can do it alone, and I'm not leaving until Kathrine is better. Make sure she brings my library. We might be here for a very long time."

Contessa's research had shown that blood had more restorative properties than straight life force. Familial blood had even stronger restorative properties, from what I'd learned from other sources. Hero familial blood seemed to have even more than that, because I felt perfectly fine, actually better than fine. I felt stronger than when Luke had woken me up. That meant I had time. Time to protect my daughter and make this right.

It meant the good impression I'd made on the headmaster mattered. Darksmith was one of the safest places in Murdell, and I wasn't going to risk moving her while I was alone, and she couldn't defend herself. But to stay here, I had to show my skills with magic.

Magical skills that I'd never developed.

I had ten days to change that, and all I had on me was Slaughter and the Day Walker set. I had no money, no other equipment. The academy likely had all the materials I needed to develop my core and mana network, but I didn't want to risk being caught stealing something so valuable and lose my chances at a teaching position.

I was left with only one choice.

I needed to descend into the Abyss.

3

THE GOR

Everyone believes they can spot the wolf among the sheep, the fox among the chickens, but I made my way unnoticed and unrecognised through hallways filled with the most powerful young men and women Murdell had to offer. As I stepped outside Kathrine's dorm and into the soft glow of the dungeon crystals, I continued to move unseen. The crystals left the campus without shadows, but that light provided no protection from a predator like me. I could hear every heartbeat, every whispered word, and I could easily navigate my way through the academy without being noticed if I wanted to. Riza and Dalin were the only ones who knew a vampire walked among them, and Dalin only knew because I wanted him to know.

I strolled to the main gate, through the orange crystal gardens, which decorated the edge of every footpath, listening as the two of them discussed my daughter's care. Coercing Dalin into looking after Kathrine was the right choice. He knew exactly what they needed to do to keep her stable, and he understood how dangerous I was, so he wouldn't speak out or do anything to endanger my daughter's safety. Not when I'd offered him a peaceful solution.

With that sorted, I began to plan my next move, so I could stay at Darksmith.

Vampires possess a strong affinity for death and necrotic magic due to our death aura. This aura improves our control and the subsequent power of our spells. Both branches of magic were highly destructive and not particularly helpful if you were a vampire trying to keep his soul, which was why I hadn't put any of my time into learning magic since I read the adventurer's guild library in Hellmouth.

My daughter's condition had changed that.

If I could master enough of those branches to pass my assessment, I could safely hide at Darksmith until Kathrine recovered. Truly mastering magic in so little time was beyond me, but mastering enough to fake competence should be doable.

The student sitting beside the gate, monitoring the academy's protective barrier and those who entered the school's grounds, didn't comment as I stepped into the tunnel which connected the dungeon to the surface. I turned left, heading downhill towards the dungeon fortress.

Darksmith and magical academies in general sat at the edge of the dungeon zone, where the bedrock didn't share the near indestructibility of the deeper dungeon walls. The high mana environment made it easy for the students to recover their mana to practice spells, so it offered the perfect place for sorcerers to train their skills.

When I reached the fortress, I climbed the tunnel walls to the ceiling, holding my bodyweight with my fingertips. The students guarding the outer fortress wall were half-asleep, safe in the knowledge that they were protected by the enchantments around them, so they didn't notice me pass overhead.

The dungeon surge, caused by the ants, hadn't spread to Murdell yet, so there wasn't a press of monsters waiting for me as I crossed the cavern ceiling. Groups of students dotted the landscape below, fighting dungeon monsters to gain levels and experience. Lightning bolts and waves of fire were met by monstrous roars, causing enough distraction for no one to notice me.

I silently dropped to the ground as I reached a tunnel on the far side of the chamber and started running, following my nose, searching for the entrance to the Abyss.

I needed to create my core and mana network to practice magic and secure my place at Darksmith. Outside a mana concentration circle, which would draw all sorts of attention, the Abyss was the best place to do that.

Humans had a very low magical affinity from what I'd read, even the ones who could use magic. This low magical affinity meant they didn't have the natural ability to store large amounts of mana within their flesh like most magical creatures. So, humanity had cheated, creating a spell that allowed them to form a core like a dungeon monster.

Creating your core correctly was important.

The larger and stronger your initial core, the faster and easier it was to make it grow. Most sorcerers established their core hundreds of times before they were happy with it, and some older sorcerers even broke their core to begin again because it was easier than trying to push through a bottleneck with an inferior core made during their youth.

I didn't have enough time to do that, so I needed to head deep into the Abyss, where the ambient mana was much higher and forming a core was easier. For anyone else, going alone would be suicide. However, I'd read enough accounts of high–level warriors to know that I wouldn't have any problems so long as I didn't go deeper than the second level of the Abyss.

Fifteen minutes after I set out, I found the Abyss entrance. I could tell it was the entrance because of the small pockets of orange crystals surrounded by yellow moss. There was also a clear slope that descended into the ground, and the ambient mana saturation was triple what it was in the central dungeon chamber. It would grow ten times stronger before I reached the bottom of the first level of the Abyss.

Where I stood was the point where humans began suffering from mana sickness. Prolonged exposure would cause mana crystals, like the ones on the wall, to form in their circulatory system, which eventually led to death. The creatures that lived down here had an immune system that protected them from this and many of the other threats that existed here.

I didn't have their protection. But I could out heal any damage the crystals caused. I began projecting my hunger through my aura to the local monster population and headed deeper. They immediately gave me a wide berth, fleeing before me in every direction.

They knew their place.

This satisfied the monster in me.

Halfway down the tunnel, I stopped running because a mild tickling sensation was coming from my skin. I pulled aside my coat to look at my abs and froze.

I was sparkling.

My body was expelling the crystals that were trying to form in my circulatory system. Pushing them through my flesh and skin. The result was a fine layer of millions of tiny, glowing crystals.

I stared at my skin for far too long, hoping that this was just a temporary issue. The fine glowing grains continued to appear in an endless glowing crystal dusting.

An unhappy frown began to crease my face as I accepted that it wouldn't stop. I decided then and there that after today, I was never going to come back to the Abyss. I was never going to mention that I had come down here. And if Luke asked me to bring him here to train and help him level, I would refuse.

No one respects a vampire who *sparkles*.

I would never live this down.

My mind made up, I headed deeper.

Twenty minutes later, I was running through the first floor of the Abyss, trying to find the entrance to the second floor, when a familiar scent caught my attention. It was deep and pungent, with a weight and power that was rare. I changed direction, following my nose, withdrawing my aura.

The monsters immediately reacted, coming out of hiding to hunt.

After another few minutes of blurring through the Abyss, the tunnel gave way to a cavern five miles wide. Monsters that made the ones in the dungeon look like puppies hunted through the expanse, searching for prey. They flew down from the ceiling and crawled out of cracks. They looked like insects and wolves and everything in between, warped in a way that showed they weren't natural.

In the centre of the cavern was a fifty-foot gorilla-like creature with porcupine spikes covering its back. It sat on a bench carved from orange crystal while a dozen equally large gorillas lay around it, curled over so only their spikes were exposed.

I dashed toward it, crossing the massive cavern and ignoring everything around me.

The floor boss watched me approach, giving a loud hoot that woke its companions. They clambered to their feet, surrounding the leader. I stopped just outside their circle, lifting my head to look at the giant monster's face. It was smaller than the last one I'd met.

It glowered in my direction. "I am Gorbaron, master of this cavern. Why do the demons of men walk in the monster realm?" His voice was a deep rumble that I felt in my bones.

I had a serious set of lungs on me, so I matched his volume. "I am the Vampire Vincent. I came down here to form my core and mana network and noticed your scent. Do you have news of the war with the ants?"

Kathrine could be asleep for a very long time, and I needed to be prepared to move her if the war reached Murdell.

Gorbaron seemed surprised by my question. "You know of the war?"

I nodded. "I came across one of your kind very far from here. Gorgath told me of the nature of the war, so I spared him."

He sniffed the air. "You wear the blackened skin of your kind and carry a curved blade. Gorgath has spoken of this."

It was my turn to be momentarily surprised. "Gorgath mentioned me?"

"Yes. It was a wonderous tale, shared with all Gor. You offered the least of us food and shelter in our time of need. A debt is owed."

Leaving all the loot behind after my familiars and I killed the acid centipedes had been painful, but there was too much to carry and not enough time to harvest, so I'd left it where it was.

I wasn't going to tell this creature that, though. "Will you repay this debt?"

"The method humans use for making their core is known to us. Is your method similar?"

"It's the same."

He nodded. "I will take you to our city, where one of our kind will offer you shelter and the materials you need to grow stronger, like for like, so the debt is repaid."

That sounded very familiar, almost Mandalorian in nature. "This is the way," I replied jokingly.

He tilted his head to the side and then nodded all too seriously. "This is the way."

TALKING to Gorbaron taught me a lot. His people, the Gor, lived on the ninth floor of the Abyss, but they controlled areas from the first floor all the way down to the fifteenth through a series of tunnels and chambers where they hunted to grow stronger. The higher floors were where they sent their young, making Gorgath and Gorbaron little more than children.

We travelled through the Abyss via a series of well-travelled tunnels. When we reached the edge of the first floor, my guide gave a loud, clear hoot that sounded like a bomb going off. Then we waited.

A short time later, a troop of larger, stronger members of his species came to us from the second floor, and they escorted us to the bottom of the second floor, where the process was repeated.

The Gor were a warlike society, from what I could see, but they weren't willing to spend lives unnecessarily. They happily played escort to their weaker members through their more dangerous territories. By the fourth floor, the common monsters we passed were as strong as Gorbaron, making them first-floor bosses.

At this point, my guide and his troop of mindless gorillas climbed onto their larger elders for safety, and we went deeper. By the seventh floor, the common monsters concerned me. They were so powerful that

I would have difficulty killing them, and if the bosses were as powerful as our escorts, then I stood no chance.

I briefly considered leaving at that stage, but since they couldn't kill me either, I decided to stay. I might find something that could help me protect my family down here and I was unlikely to ever get a chance to safely travel like this again.

The tunnel system we travelled through connected directly to their city, but without secure tunnels, there would have been no way for the weaker members of their species to reach it. Gorgath must have been cut off by the surge when I met him, which explained why he was so frightened and panicked.

It took eight hours to reach the edge of their city, and the last tunnel came out in the middle of a cavern wall. Massive vines as thick as thousand-year-old redwoods clung to the ceiling far above me. In places, they were woven together to create hanging nests. I spotted at least one of Gorgath's people standing guard at each nest, watching the skies for threats.

Titans roamed the floor of the cavern, hunting and being hunted in an endless ballet of death. Orange crystal forests stretched as far as I could see, growing at a speed that was visible to the naked eye. The crystals were being eaten just as quickly.

The cavern was larger than most countries back on Earth. It stretched for thousands of miles in every direction. It was the perfect hunting ground for a race like the Gor.

We followed a path along the cavern wall to a cave guarded by dozens of Gor. A creature that was a cross between a worm and a bat, which could have eaten a dragon in a single bite, waited at the mouth of the cave. We climbed onto its back, behind the rider, and over the next four hours, we flew to our destination.

It was a nest more than ten miles wide, hanging from the ceiling miles above the cavern floor. We had passed hundreds like it during our journey, some smaller, some much bigger. Nothing about it stuck out.

Gorbaron got off the wormbat behemoth long enough to explain to the guard why he was there. "The demon has come to collect his debt.

He wishes shelter and materials to help form his core, like for like. This is the way."

The guard, who was close to two hundred feet tall, tilted his head to the side, the way all the others had when they heard the phrase. "This is the way." He turned to me. "Climb onto my shoulder, demon."

I stared at him. My instincts were telling me that I couldn't kill him, no matter how hard I tried. Slaughter wouldn't pierce his hide, and his natural defences would make it hard for me to feed on his life force. Even if I could, he had so much life force that I would be like a mosquito. No matter how quickly I ate, I would never be able to take enough to harm him. While I couldn't kill him, he couldn't kill me either, so I clambered up his body onto his shoulder.

He carried me through the nest, past rooms formed from twisting vines, and deposited me in the middle of what was probably a dining room table. Dead dungeon monsters the size of warehouses littered the table, as six two-hundred-foot-tall creatures feasted. The flesh and blood of their dinner didn't hold any appeal to me, but the bodies held a staggering amount of life force, despite being dead.

The guard lowered his head until it was below the head of the largest one. "The demon has come to collect his debt, Troop Master. He wishes shelter and materials to help form his core, like for like. This is the way."

I'd spotted Gorgath sitting against the wall, by himself. He'd been drooling over the meal and smelled like he was hungry. The moment he heard the announcement, he ran up to the table and peered down at me, hooting happily. He then titled his head to the side and nodded. "This is the way."

The guard left.

I had a feeling I may have accidentally spread Mandalorian culture to the Gor, but I didn't care enough to fix it.

I lifted my head to meet the kid's gaze. "Hello, Gorgath. I am the Vampire Vincent, and I have come to claim my debt."

He bounced happily. "Gorgath greets the demon Vincent and offers his thanks for sparing his life and giving shelter and food in his time of need."

The other creatures at the table all gave the same loud hoot, forcefully punctuating his point. Then they continued eating, like nothing had happened.

"Gorgath looks forward to repaying his debt, so he may return to his training."

The others hooted again.

"Gorgath will take you to his uncle on the fifteen floor when he knows which cores you desire?"

"Death and necrotic magic."

Gorgath turned to the largest individual at the table, the Troop Master, and hooted. The other ones all had babies suckling, so I took it to mean he was the only male.

The male hooted back and forth with Gorgath for a few seconds before they both nodded.

"My sire recommends the cores of a sharn beast. Gorgath will trade for these cores. None shall harm you while you rest at my sire's table." Gorgath climbed to his feet, went over the corner, and collected a large sack, before leaving.

His father turned to me the moment he left. "I am Gormanth, Troop Master to this clan. Thank you for sparing my son, demon." The others hooted to punctuate his point. "And thank you for giving him a chance to repay his debt." They hooted again. "Without it, he would have remained ostracized by our people."

I frowned. "Why is he ostracized?"

"We cannot allow one of our people to grow in strength who is indebted to one who is destructive by nature. It will cause disharmony and weaken our people, and the monster realms are no place for weakness."

There was a very simple logic to his statement that made perfect sense, and it explained why I couldn't sense a hint of demonic activity around here. "How goes the war with the ants?"

Gorbaron hadn't told me anything.

"Poorly. Their queen resided on the seventeenth floor before her passing, controlling much territory. Without her leadership, they expand in all directions as their nature dictates. We are but a fraction of their number, formally protected from their appetites by treaty and trade. The threat of extermination kept our people in check, causing us to control our breeding and limit our strength. Now we breed and grow stronger to hold off annihilation."

That was concerning. "Will you be able to stop them?"

"We hope we will not have to. Civilisations much deeper than our own are dealing with the same issue. If one of them cannot end this war, then I would not bet on our chances of survival."

Gormanth went back to his meal, and I stayed silent. Every so often he would spit out a monster core the size of a couch, like it was a peach pit, and then continue eating.

An hour later, Gorgath rushed into the dining room. "I have returned from my trading for the cores of the sharn beast."

His family hooted supportively as they continued to eat.

The hooting was clearly a language, and a highly complex one that seemed to convey an entire conversation of meaning with a single sound. I was reminded of that one episode of Star Trek where Picard met an alien species who talked through shared stories. I got the impression that this was something similar.

Gorgath walked over to the table and looked down at me. "Demon, I will take you to my uncle on the fifteenth floor and repay my debt."

"This is the way," Gormanth stated.

GOR SOCIETY INTERESTED ME, because it was a society where the very weakest of them could safely travel from one side of their empire to the other without fear or concern for their safety. That was the exact sort of world I wanted to create for my family, so I was taking notes.

The deeper we went the more marvellous the world they'd created became. After the tenth floor, Gorgath's people lost the spikes on their backs and began using magic. It was an interesting development that confused me.

I sat on Gorgath's shoulder as he clung to the chest of our most recent guide. We were on the twelfth floor and moving faster than a fighter jet. Our guide had surrounded us in a sphere of magic, before levitating into the air and flying us through the tunnels like a hypersonic missile.

It was a frightening display of power and had made me curious. "Gorgath, why do your people only use magic on the deeper floors?"

Gorgath turned his massive head to his shoulder to look at me. "The higher floors lack mana. Performing magic is much more difficult there, so my people do not train to use magic until we reach the ninth."

I didn't see their logic. "That makes it the perfect place to train. If you can perform magic under those conditions, then you can perform magic anywhere."

Gorgath frowned and then looked up to the face of our guide he was clinging to. "Is what the demon says true, elder?"

The behemoth nodded. "The demon speaks the truth. This is the path to true power."

"Am I indebted to the demon again, elder?"

"No. The demon offered you nothing you could not have gained yourself with no cost to yourself or your troop, however unlikely. There is no debt."

I looked up at our guide, confused by their exchange. "You don't instruct your children on how to grow stronger?"

"Threats do not come from above, so we use those floors to discover the character of our children."

"How?"

"Returning with all their troop alive shows us they are good leaders and protective of their own. Returning with the ability to form spells shows that they are both patient and focused, willing to struggle through difficult tasks. Returning with unique evolutions for their troop shows they are lucky or a careful hunter. Gorgath is one we would consider lucky."

Gorgath hooted.

I frowned. "Why is he lucky?"

"The acid centipedes you left for him to eat had very rare peak bloodlines. He and his troop can now spit acid and are resistant to it.

They will be immune when he allows them to go through their first evolution."

"Gorgath is not ready to evolve anymore. Gorgath will hunt and eat a mana crab."

The elder frowned. "Are you saying, you're willing to give up your spikes?"

That was a good question. From what I had seen, Gor weren't flexible. They couldn't reach their backs, so if something latched on, they had no way to remove it. The spikes were their only defence. Without them, Gorgath wouldn't be able to run from his enemies and would have to face them down every time.

"Gorgath has run. Gorgath does not like the cost of doing so. Gorgath will give up this choice."

The elder continued to frown. "Yet, you chose to hunt a monster that will both help you develop magic and give you a soft exoskeleton."

"Gorgath is willing to lose his spikes. Gorgath is not willing to let anything that reaches his back kill him."

The elder stopped frowning. "You show wisdom. You honour your sires."

Gorgath grinned, showing teeth. "This is the way."

The elder turned his head to the side and then nodded. "This is the way."

THE GOR HAD ONLY MANAGED to descend a third of the way through their section of the fifteenth floor, but they had a camp near the edge where several thousand of them lived. It was a small fortress, relatively speaking, in the largest cavern they could control. They'd reinforced the tunnel entrances with magical barriers, so nothing could charge through, and built kill boxes beyond the barriers in case their magic failed. Unlike in the higher floors, here they wore powerful armour and carried weapons fashioned from the monsters they had killed.

Our new guide took us through the centre of the camp.

Everywhere I looked, the Gor sat in groups of four to six, either discussing tactics for their next hunt, trading for the materials they needed, training with new weapons and equipment, or just laying on their backs, sleeping. It was very well organised and kind of reminded me of the adventurer's guild. There was an area for craftsmen, another for enchanters, one for training, and another for butchering their kills—mostly ruby-shelled ants that were larger than the largest Gor.

Our guide dropped us off at the edge of the enchanter's section.

Gorgath sniffed the air and began walking towards his uncle, following his nose. The air down here was so thick with mana that we moved through a perpetual blue haze. I'd read a legend that said on the lowest floor it became a liquid, forming a great ocean of mana. Down there, new creatures would spring into existence only to be gobbled up by something else. Anything that escaped the primordial sea, tended to head as high as its biology would allow, as quickly as it could. I had nothing to verify whether this was true, but the Gors' interest in fighting their way deeper suggested that it wasn't.

Gorgath stopped before a truly massive specimen of his species. He would have been over three hundred feet tall when standing, but he was sitting on a stool bent over a knee-high table, etching an enchantment into a bone knife.

His uncle had the power to crush me like an insect. Anything down here did. And I wasn't entirely sure that I'd survive the experience. Something had fundamentally changed when we reached the fifteenth floor. Even Gorgath now felt like a threat to me.

"Uncle Gorak, the demon has entered the Abyss to forge and strengthen his core. I have offered him shelter and materials to repay my debt, like for like. This is the way."

Gorak put down his tools and turned his massive head towards Gorgath, tilting it to the side, before nodding. "This is the way." He turned his gaze on me, and I felt very much like a mouse standing before a tiger. His leg was twice the size of Gorgath. "Once a human named Tarmis lived among my ancestors. He was born of the surface world but was not of the surface world. He was born with a core and could not live outside the place you call dungeons. As he aged, the mana grew too thin, and he descended to the Abyss, where he met my ancestor. He was not the first to do so and he will not be the last, but he was kind and caring and offered my ancestors many tales of the surface world and the things you call sun, sky, and magic. He lived among us for the remainder of his days, much loved and cared for. For this he is remembered." Gorak gave a distinctive hoot unlike any I had heard.

If my guess was right, the appropriate response was to hoot it back, so I did.

Gorak flinched.

I did my best to hide my smirk. "This is the way."

Gorak got over his shock and nodded. "You learn quickly, demon." He leaned to the side of his table and opened a leather sack that could have fit a midsized apartment building in it. He removed a bone plate the size of a basketball court and placed it on the table. "This is a mana-condensing circle. I use it to temper my enchantments. At its centre, it will rain liquid mana. To do this for my own kind would be impossible, but it is a simple matter for one as small as you. You will sit at its centre and forge your core while I empower the circle."

I'd figured out I was able to create a perfect core with ease by the time we reached the third floor. The only reason I hadn't was I wanted to see what would happen if I did it further down. I hadn't expected to run into liquid mana, though.

Liquid mana was pure theory on the surface. To my knowledge, no one had ever seen it first-hand, and if they had, they hadn't been able to share their story. The legends about the substance were so old that no one remembered where they came from or whether they were true.

Gorgath held out the sack he'd been carrying. "Gorgath has brought sharn cores from the ninth so the demon Vincent may strengthen his core."

Gorak reached into the sack beside him and fished out a core that was the size of warehouse. "Trade this for an Ambrax core from the eighteenth. The demon will surpass the ninth with my help."

Gorgath placed me on the table beside his uncle, and took the core with both hands, grunting with the weight, before staggering off to trade. Down here, he truly did look like a child.

I stood on the oversize piece of stone furniture, watching Gorak work and weighing my options. Their people had treated me as a guest. Their family had shown me their best hospitality. They'd even been polite.

I needed to be polite in return. My memories told me that. Also, it didn't hurt to build good will. Being on good terms with monsters this powerful might be helpful at some point.

It was time for a little bureaucratic bull.

"Gorgath will assist you in powering the circle. Too many others have offered him assistance, and he will not repay debt like for like without offering aid himself."

Gorak turned to me and paused. I caught what looked like the briefest of smirks before he nodded. "This is the way."

4

MANA NETWORKS AND CORE FORMATION

I'd taught my son to never question bureaucratic bull that works in your favour. Gorak seemed to agree with this philosophy because he didn't argue or question my demands. When Gorgath returned with the core, his uncle informed him that he would have to participate in empowering the circle to repay his debt. For Gorgath to be able to do this, Gorak awoke some of his ancestral memories by placing his hand on Gorgath's head and manipulating his aura.

The Gor seemed like a very straight cut and traditional people, so I got the impression that Gorgath only received the ancestral memories that directly applied to what he needed to do. We were on the fifteenth floor of the Abyss, so that was likely a lot more information than he would receive having to do this anywhere else. The kid might not know any spells yet, but he knew how to manipulate mana as easily as any adult. It would give him a massive advantage as he descended through the floors. And it would build a lot of goodwill with his family.

When that was done, Gorgath sat down and held his aching head, groaning softly, and clearly in pain. Gorak went back to preparing his condensing circle, letting his nephew recover.

A few minutes into fiddling with it, he paused. "Demon, are you certain you require no special conditions beyond a mana-rich environment?"

To make my mana network, all I needed to do was flood my nervous, circulatory, and digestive systems with enough raw mana to refine my body's natural ability to circulate mana. I could do this over time, or all at once. Neither offered any benefits or drawbacks, because a mana network just allowed large amounts of mana to move freely through your body without causing harm.

"As far as I'm aware, my requirements for forming my core are identical to a normal human's."

Gorak nodded and finished what he was doing. He beckoned me over to the condensing circle, and I sat cross-legged in the middle of the basketball court-sized device.

Without any warning, he empowered it.

The moment it began to rain mana, I learned something important. Vampiric flesh could not withstand liquid mana. The raindrops tore through any exposed skin, cutting through my flesh like bullets, coming out the other side without ever slowing down.

The hundreds of thousands of minuscule runes etched along the Day Walker set and Slaughter began to glow as the first drop hit them. They drank in the liquid mana rain, filling the runic patterns, and reinforcing them in a way I'd never felt before. I could sense them growing stronger. And I immediately noticed that Day Walker set wasn't taking any damage from the liquid mana the way my flesh was, so lifted my hood and buttoned my coat.

I had absolutely no reference for what was happening, so I turned to Gorak. "Do you know what is happening to my equipment?"

He peered down at me and then picked up what looked like a massive, rune-etched magnifying glass to see me properly. "It's called mana tempering. Liquid mana is the true state of mana. Your equipment has never been exposed to it, so the enchantments have never reached their full potential." He put the magnifying glass down. "Nephew, you are needed."

Gorgath was still holding his head, but he lifted his hand, and a stream of mana flowed into the condensing circle. The rain fell faster and harder, becoming a deluge, like a tropical rainstorm.

Not wanting to miss the opportunity, I drew Slaughter from its sheath and placed it on the ground in front of me. The blade began to glow as it sucked in the liquid mana.

Gorak continued to feed mana into his condensing circle, increasing the density of the rain. "You may begin building your mana network."

I nodded.

Mana wasn't a hard thing to sense, if you had a magical aptitude and understood what you were looking for. I'd been able to sense it without any effort ever since I put my first points into mana regeneration. At the time, I'd been far too busy and exhausted to explore what I could do with it, so I'd done nothing, not even bonding with my equipment.

That was about to change.

Passive mana regeneration was only useful for powering magical equipment, because storing mana in your core wasn't a natural biological process, but a conscious action you had to undertake. New magical practitioners normally had to meditate to guide mana into their core, but those with the right skills could do so while they walked around.

I didn't have those skills, but I doubted I needed them.

Stilling my mind to a meditative state came naturally to me, and my predatory senses allowed me to focus on the mana around me the way I would prey. I guided my hunter instincts, capturing the mana around me with my will, and I slowly inhaled, tilting my head back to the storm above.

A whirlpool appeared above my mouth as the liquid mana was pulled off-course. It streamed down my throat, like I was funnelling beer at a frat party. The liquid mana entered my lungs and stomach, before burning a path through my circulatory system, digestive tract, and nervous system.

Did this hurt?

Yes.

Did I scream?

Also, yes.

Did it work?

Yes, because I eventually vomited the rest of it back up, instead of experiencing it burning a hole straight through me.

When I finished vomiting, I inhaled a small amount of mana, small being relative, and cycled it through my body, testing the full extent of my transformation. This was a simple exercise to work out if you had fully built your mana network.

I hadn't.

So, I repeated the process.

Eleven attempts later, I was successful. I did it again to see if it made a difference to how easy it was to move my mana around. Sadly, it did make it easier. A hundred and eighty-three repetitions later and I stopped seeing improvements. A hundred attempts after that and I was sure I wasn't going to see any more benefits.

For the final test, I filled my lungs and stomach with liquid mana, holding as much as I physically could. With another effort of will, I instantly expelled it through my mana network and out my hand, in a long, thin jet of liquid mana. The mana flew for several meters before splashing on the ground.

A satisfied smile sat on my face when I was done.

The mana I could channel through my mana network was now limited only by how much I could pressurise my mana. There wasn't even a twinge of discomfort. And I was one step closer to keeping Kathrine safe.

"I need to take a break," I said.

Gorak didn't ask why, he simply stopped empowering the circle. The mana storm immediately vanished, spreading out to take on the consistency of the mana around us.

Light spilled from the edge of my cuff as the liquid mana disappeared. I pulled it back to see my veins and capillaries glowing blue under my skin. This was not the way this usually happened. But, since there seemed to be no adverse effects, I ignored the change.

I held out my hand and willed the ambient mana around me into a small ball. Manipulating mana was the first step in learning how to cast a spell. As a vampire, I could learn extremely fast, but I still needed practice.

Gorak went back to etching the dagger, while Gorgath stood and watched what I was doing.

Eventually Gorgath's curiosity got the better of him. "What are you doing?"

"I'm learning how to cast spells. Manipulating mana outside your body is harder than manipulating it inside. Being able to condense mana into a ball like this and passing it from hand to hand is the amount of control you need to cast the most basic spell. Making two of them and swapping them is the amount of control you need to cast any basic spell. Once you get to three, you need to juggle."

Gorgath summoned two balls of mana, one in each hand, and swapped them over. Then he looked at me. "What is 'juggle'?"

I'd only just managed to summon and swap two mana balls, so I wasn't ready to do three. I glanced over at the knife Gorak was working on and saw bone chips lying on the table.

I blurred to his massive hand, with fingertips larger than my body, and pointed to the chips. They were the size of baseballs, but when you were three hundred feet tall, they were chips. "Can I borrow these to teach your nephew?"

"Yes, but you must return them."

Any other time, I would have protested, trying to claim his unused loot. These were bone chips from the fifteenth floor of the Abyss, after all. But Gorak was a nice guy, and more importantly, he could crush me like a bug and possibly kill me. "No problem. I'll bring them back in a moment."

I picked up an armful and blurred back to the other side of the table, where Gorgath waited.

I put down all but three and started juggling in a circle. "This is juggling."

Gorgath frowned and then summoned three balls of mana and copied.

I started juggling in a crisscross pattern. “This is a crisscross pattern that is slightly more difficult.”

Gorgath copied.

I added another chip.

Gorgath added another ball.

I added a fifth chip.

He copied, summoning another mana ball.

I changed the pattern. “This is called a crisscross circle. Two balls are moving in a circle and two are moving in a crisscross pattern. The fifth ball swaps between each pattern each time you finish it.”

Gorgath frowned but copied. “This is more difficult. What level of spell does this represent?”

“Intermediate spells.”

“So, I will find advanced spells challenging.”

“The high end of intermediate requires nine balls. Advanced spells require eleven.”

“Show me the advanced pattern.”

I picked up six more bone chips and added them to the five I was juggling. The pattern was extremely complex, but it was a simple thing to manage when I was moving so slowly. “If you can manage this pattern with each ball being a different density of mana, then you can cast advanced spells.”

Davina would have been able to do this with her eyes closed.

Gorgath let his mana balls fade and picked up his uncle’s magnifying glass to get a clearly understanding of what I was doing. “I would struggle to make such a pattern. My arms do not move as easily as yours.”

That was true.

My student had special needs, and as his teacher it was my responsibility to assist him. The prince said he had a bright future ahead of him. I needed to make sure that came to pass to keep the prince happy.

I tossed aside all the bone chips and effortlessly summoned six mana rings, one around each wrist, ankle, waist, and head. They moved like hula hoops as I summoned another five mana balls.

"Make six rings like I have while you juggle five balls and give them all different mana densities. If you want to make it more difficult and push to the upper edges of advanced magic, then you can vary the timing and rotation of the hoops and oscillate the density of the balls."

Showing my student how to do this simple exercise with such an unorthodox method took all of my considerable magical skill. But I wasn't an archsorcerer because I had a pretty face.

My student tried to copy, but the pattern was too complex for him. I let my demonstration fade and reached out with the ambient mana to reinforce his patterns for him, to help him understand what he was trying to achieve. It took a staggeringly massive amount of mana, but that was why we were working in this training facility.

Fifteen minutes passed as I continued to instruct my student. Then it all seemed to finally click for him. I stopped guiding his magic and watched as he took over the pattern all on his own.

A twinge of envy ran through me at how quickly he picked it up. He was brilliant. Too brilliant. *He needed to go, or I might lose the prince's favour.*

A nasty smile tugged at my lips. "You have done a wonderful job. You have progressed to the point where you can learn your first advanced spell." The backlash from this spell would kill him instantly and leave no body to resurrect. *The prince was mine.*

I reached for the mana in my core and froze.

Where was my core?

Panic set in as I searched through my body; everything I saw was wrong. It was all wrong. *It was like it wasn't even my body.*

A cascade of memories from several different lives hit me all at once, as I snapped back to reality. Magical knowledge from the elder vampires I'd eaten ran through my head as the world spun around me.

It had happened again, just like the first time I trained with Sir Brandon. I let the memories wash through me the way they had in the past as I flopped to the ground.

"Gorgath is ready to learn."

The giant gorilla child was looking at me with expectant eyes, but I needed a break. Also, giving him an advanced spell might not be the best idea, since he was about to return to the first floor of the Abyss, and that much power so close to civilisation might constitute a threat to my family. Gorgath had done everything I had, but ten thousand times bigger. An advanced spell would be like setting off a nuke.

I turned to Gorak, easily noticing the way he wove magic, because of my new memories. It was at an intermediate level of spell casting. His control was as good as any expert practitioner, but the magic he wove was only mid-intermediate.

He noticed me staring at him. "You have unlocked ancestral knowledge."

"Of a sort. Is that the most advanced spell work you can perform?"

"Yes."

"Are you one of the better enchanters of your people?"

"I stand among the best."

I turned back to Gorgath. "Your people do not practice advanced magic. You would owe me a debt if I taught it to you."

Gorgath turned to his uncle and opened his mouth.

Gorak leapt from his stool, sending it clattering across the ground, as he loomed over his nephew. He didn't say anything or raise his fists, but the message was clear from his body language, 'Boy, if you open your fool mouth, you are going to be in for a butt whooping'.

Gorgath maintained his posture, proving his statement that he would never back down again. Then he turned his head to me. "Gorgath does not wish another debt. Not one so great that it would upset his family."

Gorak flared his nostril, about to lay a beat-down.

I came to the kid's rescue. "This is the way."

Gorak tilted his head to the side and reconsidered his nephew's words. The offer of advanced magic would help their people. His nephew was willing to take on such a debt to help them, but not at the cost of upsetting his family. He was essentially saying he was willing to sacrifice himself for his people, but not in a way that would upset his family. It was a very brave and selfless thing to do.

Gorak finally nodded. "This is the way." He leaned down and

bumped his nephew's forehead with his own. Then he picked up his stool and went back to his work.

Gorgath continued to look at me. "Gorgath is ready to learn an intermediate spell."

IN THE END, I taught the kid three basic spells, because Gorgath didn't have access to death magic. The barrier and bolt spells were standard spells every sorcerer learned and would keep him safe when he lost his spikes. He immediately grasped how to perform the spells just by sensing how I channelled mana. If he were a human, he'd be considered a savant with that sort of ability. It was like learning to play the piano by watching someone play a song once.

Because it amused me, the third spell I taught him involved his acid spit ability. It allowed him to hawk an acid loogie as far as he could see, and he and I found it incredibly amusing to be able to spit across the entire camp. So did his uncle Gorak, who stopped working long enough to learn the spell.

Spells, like cores, were broken into tiers: basic, intermediate, advanced, expert, master, and divine. Each tier had three ranks to it, making a total of eighteen ranks. Very few people knew that the last tier and three ranks existed. I only knew because of Contessa's library and the secret, secret vault in Arcadia's Royal Northern Library.

A 1st-rank core had enough mana capacity to store exactly one 1st-rank spell's worth of mana, if the spell were cast by an unskilled sorcerer. This was around ten times the mana you needed if you had mastered casting the spell without wasting mana, but it was normally what a sorcerer needed in order to practice casting a new spell, so it wasn't an arbitrary measurement.

Strengthening a core beyond the basic tier required materials, special potions and pills that held magical properties that joined with your core's enchanted structure to make it stronger. If you weren't one of the wealthy, with access to potions and pills designed specifically for your mana types, then you used monster cores, which was what the core spell was originally designed to mimic.

Gorgath had already said he had me covered in that department. So, when I was finished teaching, I sat back and waited for the memory cascade to settle down.

It took several hours, but once it was over I was back in the concentration circle to make my core.

Mana rain poured over my coat as I sat cross-legged. This time, the runes covering Slaughter and the Day Walker set failed to glow. Gorak's statement, that my equipment was going through mana tempering because of the liquid mana, suggested that several theories I'd read about higher states of mana were true. One theory postulated that the spells sorcerers cast were not true spells, but something akin to a reflection.

This theory was used to explain why only advanced spells worked against demons, yet even the most basic demon spells could cut through anything but an advanced barrier. If that were true, then liquid mana was the true state of mana, and any spell cast with it became a true spell, not a reflection.

I slowly began to inhale as I tilted my head back. Liquid mana poured down my throat and through my mana network until I reached capacity. I tilted my head forward and then closed my mouth, feeling the liquid mana surge through my mana network.

I began to cast the core spell.

With my new knowledge, the spell came together easily, forming a perfect peak-3rd-rank core. However, the core didn't feel like any 3rd-rank core any of my memories had ever felt.

Usually, a core was just a ball of mana that resided within your body. It was denser at the centre and grew less dense the further out you went. The core spell was like a lodestone holding mana in place, so it didn't cause any issues or escape your body. Mana would still constantly trickle out, so you had to replace it to keep your core full. But this trickle was very slow, taking over a week for most people.

My core still felt like a ball, but instead of one dense point at the centre it had three layers. Each layer housed a different density of mana. It was like I had three cores inside each other, each one capable of casting a spell of each rank. Actually, it wasn't capable of casting a spell for each rank. The first layer held enough mana to cast three 1st-rank spells, and the second layer held enough to cast two 2nd-rank spells.

A notification appeared as I finished the spell.

You have mastered the Magic skill.

The notification definitely pointed to the theory of magic on the surface world being just a reflection. No one had ever mastered the magic skill by casting a core spell.

Out of curiosity, I flooded all three layers with liquid mana. The mana flowed into the outer layer without any trouble but began to condense as it reached the second layer and condense further as it reached the third. It worked similar to a regular core, except with liquid mana.

I put my curiosity aside. "I've formed my core. We can begin the next step."

The mana rain vanished, and the density in my core immediately dropped to match the mana saturation of the floor we were on. With the drop in density went my hopes that I had discovered a way to keep my family safe. Moving between the surface and the Abyss to refill my core would have been a pain, but the results would have allowed me to create unbreakable barriers.

Gorgath reached into his sack and pulled out a sharn beast core. It was the size of a minivan. He casually placed it on the circle beside me, like he hadn't just offered me a core the size of a freaking minivan.

"Gorgath gave the smallest one to start in case you make a mistake and waste it."

I stared at the absolutely massive thing. There was more core to work with than most sorcerers saw in their lifetime. I turned to Gorgath because the kid was looking at me expectantly. "This is a small one?"

Gorgath nodded and lifted his sack. "I have more."

I mean it made sense that something his size would consider this small, but it was still absurd enough to upset a vampire's sensibilities. I could fund my academy for a decade with one of these.

I climbed to my feet and leapt onto the black crystal surface. Usually, sorcerers held their monster cores in their mouth while they tried to strengthen their core. That wasn't an option with a core this big, so I sat on top. "Ready when you are."

The mana rain started up again.

Monster cores were mostly crystalised mana. Inside the crystalised mana were particles that helped stabilize a core and make it stronger. You had to break down the crystalised mana to free these particles and then ingest the mana and circulate it through your core while it was at capacity.

In this state, you then had to recast the core spell and force the particles to bind with your core. The particles the monster core gave off also had to match your own magical affinity, because you couldn't build a core beyond the 3rd-rank with just raw mana, not unless you were willing to forgo internal magic or having internal magic performed on you. Sorcerers who were willing to forgo this still occasionally exploded when hit by spells.

It was not an experience that interested me.

The core I was sitting on was a mix of death, necrotic, and raw mana, so it contained the perfect materials for me to strengthen my core.

I got to work, and before I was even a thousandth of the way through the monster core, more prompts appeared.

You have mastered the Death Magic skill.
You have mastered the Necrotic Magic skill.

MY NEW CORE was a hungry mistress. She liked expensive monster cores and lots of them. By the end of the sack Gorgath had brought, I'd reached the thirteenth layer. After I used Gorak's core, which was the size of a warehouse, I reached the eighteenth.

Gorak picked up his enchanted magnifying glass as he ended the mana rain and peered at me, muttering an incantation. "Eighteen layers. Good. Gorgath and I have done all that we can. Do you accept that the material part of your debt has been paid, demon?"

I stopped examining my core and looked up. "Yes, Gorgath has repaid the material part of the debt to me in full. When he returns me to the first floor of the Abyss, I will also consider his shelter part of his debt paid in full." I turned to Gorgath. "Thank you for protecting me from your elder and sparing my life." Core or no core, they could crush me like a bug.

Gorgath nodded. "This is the way."

"This is the way," Gorak repeated.

WE STOPPED by Gorgath's home as we made our ascent, and the kid informed his parents that he had repaid the material part of his debt and that he was taking me to the first floor, where he intended to remain until he was strong enough to return to their society. He was still a kid, so he couldn't help showing off his magic skills before he left, which caused his father to puff up his cheeks and beat his chest. Gorgath then collected the non-sapient members of his troop, which I learned were his brothers, and we continued our ascent.

The higher we travelled, the lower the saturation of mana in the air and the more my core leaked mana. By the time we reached the first floor, the mana density had become just a fraction of what it had been; less than a thousandth of the mana remained. Yet, it was still enough to make an archsorcerer foam at the mouth with envy.

Gorgath carried me into the chamber where I met Gorbaron. My original guide was sitting on his crystal bench, surrounded by his sleeping troop.

He roused them with a small hoot and then rose to his feet as we approached, staring at Gorgath. "You have entered my territory. Do you come seeking shelter?"

Gorgath raised his chin as his troop followed behind us. "I seek no shelter. Only to return the demon so I may finish repaying my debt."

"By the ways of our people, to enter an equal's territory in the wild and not seek shelter is a challenge for their territory. You must best me and claim my territory as your own or return the way you came."

I understood what was happening. Gorbaron knew his territory sucked and was looking for an excuse to leave and find a better territory. He knew he had Gorgath trapped, because Gorgath had to deliver me to the other side of the cavern. If he wanted to clear his debt, he would have to claim this terrible territory.

I turned to Gorgath's massive ear. "A nice quiet place is the best sort of place to practice magic."

Gorgath continued to look at the floor boss as he reached up to his shoulder and placed me on the ground. "This is the way."

He exploded towards his opponent, looking like he was going to tackle him, but he pulled up right before he reached him, and spat a glob of acid on Gorbaron's forehead.

Gorbaron hissed in pain as he wiped away the acid and lowered his head in defeat. "You could have blinded me but chose not to. I have been spared great injury."

"This is the way," Gorgath replied.

"My territory is yours. Take it with my respect."

Gorgath did not gloat. He was strictly business. "I am in need of mana crabs."

Gorbaron raised his hand and pointed down a side tunnel. "That way. They're small and weak, but they are what you seek."

"Gorgath will raise them to be strong, and then he will eat them and grow mighty."

"This is the way." The other youth hooted and began heading for the exit. His troop followed, keeping their heads low as they passed Gorgath's larger troop members.

Only when they were gone did Gorgath come back and pick me up, placing me on his shoulder. Then with great ceremony, he carried me across the cavern to the exit on the other side and placed me on my feet.

I looked up at him. "You have repaid your debt in its entirety, like for like."

He smiled down at me. "This is the way."

I smiled back. "This is the way." I turned to leave.

"Gorgath will be here for many generations. Will the demon Vincent be nearby?"

I could hear the loneliness in his voice, and I had a soft spot for children. Even sixty-foot giant gorilla children. "Would you like me to show you where I'm going to be living, so you can come and visit?"

"Gorgath would."

5

TESTS AND OTHER INTERESTING ENDEAVOURS

Dungeon bosses and Abyss bosses never run from a fight. Once they claimed a territory, the only thing that could make them leave was the need to find a better territory to continue growing stronger. The massive arachnid, which ruled the cavern where the dungeon fortress lay, trembled as Gorgath casually walked over to it. The students on the wall watched in terror as Gorgath ripped all but two legs off and then used the last two as straps, throwing the dungeon boss over his shoulders like a backpack, stabbing the spider into his spikes, before picking up the torn-off legs and heading towards the tunnel I was standing in.

Gorgath had caused a minor surge by entering the dungeon. Every dungeon monster had either run or hid. It was nothing like the surge taking place in Arcadia, but all the students who'd been hunting had fled for the safety of the fortress. The Gor normally didn't interact with humans outside the Abyss, but Gorgath could smell how useful the dungeon boss's bloodline was, so he had walked into the chamber to collect his prize.

The moment Gorgath released its remaining legs, the dungeon boss began trying to grab onto something to escape. Gorgath ignored it as he made his way to the tunnel where I was waiting. He stopped just inside and peered down at me as he grabbed one of the torn-off legs he'd tucked under his arm and took a bite, cracking the exoskeleton with his teeth.

"Gorgath is going now." He stepped around me and continued down the tunnel, heading for the entrance to the Abyss without looking back.

The activity and heightened alertness at the fortress meant nothing to me. I wasn't leaving the dungeon yet. I needed to find somewhere hidden and out of the way where I could practice magic in peace.

Half an hour later, I wriggled my way through a large crack in the dungeon wall, entering a narrow shaft, before dropping into somethings' nest, flipping mid-air to land on my feet. The chamber was only fifty feet wide, and the unnamed somethings that lived inside were pretending to be rocks, hiding among the bone and chitin, ready to leap onto anything that entered their nest. With my aura threatening anything near me, they continued to pretend to be rocks.

I brushed the dirt from my shoulders as I walked toward the largest creature, kicking aside bones. It remained perfectly still as I sat on top of it. The smell of the creature's fear amused the monster in me.

I had five days left before I needed to pass my magical aptitude test to secure the professorship. There were several lifetimes of magical knowledge bouncing around in my head, along with a lot of information from Contessa's library. None of the elder vampires I'd eaten were necromancers, and everything I'd read about magic said converting spells from one school of magic to another was only applicable to the advanced spell tier; anything beyond required a different approach.

I continued brushing the dirt from my coat.

Spells were broken into the six tiers, just like cores: basic, intermediate, advanced, expert, master, and divine. Each tier had three ranks to it, making a total of eighteen ranks. Students of these academies traditionally left when they had mastered advanced-tier magic or became an apprentice to one of the professors to progress to expert-tier magic.

I needed to display at least an expert-tier spell to secure the job. I also needed to show my basic aptitude across all elements, converting raw mana to elemental mana, the way any professional could.

I flicked away the last speck of dust, held out my hand, and cast the basic fire bolt spell, without using an incantation. A cantaloupe-sized ball of fire appeared at the end of my palm, illuminating the chamber, before I launched it against the nearest wall. A few seconds later, I cast the water bolt version, pulling the moisture from the air.

Fire, water, earth, wind, death, necrotic, and lightning bolts all struck the wall in quick succession. The knowledge in my head told me my spell work was sloppy. I'd work on refining my technique later. Right now, I needed to make sure I could perform the basics.

To make sure my understanding of basic magic was complete, I cast every basic spell the vampires I'd eaten knew. Each one came together without any trouble.

As my levitation spell faded, I floated down to the creature pretending to be a rock returning to my seat.

Beyond basic tier magic, I, like every other human practitioner, was restricted to practicing branches of magic for which I had the corresponding skill. This was because the human body was incredibly conductive to magic, but not very resistant, and despite being an ancient vampire, very little of those underlying mechanics had changed.

Between my mana network and my magic skill, I could convert raw mana to any form of elemental mana and then pressurize it up to a 3rd-rank spell. If I tried to pressurize elemental mana beyond the 3rd-rank, without the skill for that branch of magic, the pressure would overwhelm my mana network's resistance and allow the mana to pass through my flesh, effectively draining away all the mana and injuring me in the process.

There was no way around this limitation to my knowledge.

Even as an ancient vampire, my body's natural resistance to death and necrotic mana wasn't as high as what I received when I gained the death magic and necrotic magic skills. So, I was limited to just these two branches.

Of the two, death magic had far more utility. It could be used to weaken my enemies, create undead, kill, protect, consult with spiritual entities, see if someone was a murderer, and even heal to a limited degree. In many ways, it was a reflection of life magic. Necrotic magic, on the other hand, was just a concentrated form of death magic that broke the bonds between atoms, making it pure destruction, comparable to a disintegration ray.

Of the two, death magic would make a better impression, but everything I'd read told me that necrotic magic would be easier for me to reach expert in, because of its limited scope. With only five days to practice, I decided to take the easier path.

FIVE DAYS LATER, I walked into Darksmith's administration building and was sent for testing. Madrine, the death magic-practicing sorcerer whom Headmaster Wink had brought in to test me, met me at the door of the training hall and immediately began the test. Five minutes later, I stood in the middle of the room juggling fifteen mana balls, with fifteen different branches of magic that I'd created using ambient mana.

The basketball court-sized room had recently been cleansed and smelled strongly of cleaning products. There were no traces of other branches of magic in the air that could interfere with the test, showing they had gone to a lot of trouble to make this test as accurate as possible.

Madrine watched me juggle for nearly a minute, before making a note on his clipboard, chuckling. "I asked you to display your control over the various branches of magics. I didn't ask you to display your mana manipulation ability."

"It seems simpler to do both at the same time."

He smirked. "Show off."

Madrine was an undertaker by day.

He specialised in keeping the dead *dead*, and in their resting place. To keep his spirits high, he wore bright, multicoloured robes, and to have some semblance of professionalism, he kept his full head of silver hair slicked back. Those were his words, not mine.

He turned and pointed his pen at the training pole. "It's not really necessary after that display, but would you please demonstrate a basic fire, lightning, and wind bolt at the target?"

I shot off the three bolts in quick succession. They were basic spells, and anyone who could perform expert-tier magic would do it just as quickly. The three bolts slammed into the barrier around the training pole.

As the thunderclap faded, he made another note. "Nonverbal spell casting. I would have been shocked if you couldn't do it. Please levitate yourself."

I cast a basic levitation spell and hovered above the ground.

He made another note and asked me to perform another basic spell. Thirty spells later he made his final note on basic skills. "Perfect marks. It's a shame that you're a necromancer. You would have made one hell of an archsorcerer."

I shrugged, trying to appear indifferent, despite completely agreeing with him. "Life is rarely fair."

Madrine nodded, knowingly. "We've covered the basics, so I'll let you show me the extent of your capabilities. Your pay will be based on the upper limits of your skill."

From what I understood of Murdell society that was pretty normal. "This room isn't rated for master-tier combat spells."

Madrine chuckled. "Darksmith prefers academic curiosity over raw power. A lot of sorcerers learn how to cast master-tier combat spells without ever understanding the fundamentals of expert magic."

This worked in my favour, as I'd only been able to learn a single expert-tier spell. It had taken me three entire days to figure out how to cast it successfully, and I was still a long way off from being able to cast master-tier spells.

I made two finger guns while giving a simultaneous double thumbs up. I pointed them at the training pole while doing my best Fonzie impression. "Ayeee."

Two intense beams of black necrotic energy slammed into the

barrier around the pole, causing the barrier to buckle. Multicasting this spell was a rather lethal combination. A regular sorcerer would have disintegrated, even if they'd tried to block them.

I was the Fonzie of death.

Luke would find it funny.

Madrine scowled. "Multicasting the finger of destruction spell."

I smirked. "Which is technically classed as a master-tier spell, because of the difficulty of multicasting and the mana control requirement."

Madrine reached into his pocket and tossed me three small crystals. The moment I caught them, they glowed purple. "You failed to mention that you've mastered magic, death magic, and the necrotic magic skills."

"I assumed you would have realised I'd mastered them."

"I did, but when you didn't bring it up, I assumed you were embarrassed you hadn't."

"So, we both made reasonable assumptions and were both wrong."

He made another note. "I'm putting you down as a master-tier talent. Please perform the finger of destruction spell as many times as you can."

I raised my finger guns. "Pew, pew, pew, pew, pew, pew, pew, pew, pew, pew, pew, pew." The training pole lost its barrier and disintegrated on my twelfth shot. I turned to Madrine. "Do you want me to keep going?"

HEADMASTER WINK WAS all scowls when he met me outside my classroom the next day. He reeked of gin and smelled angry. "Let's get this over with." He shoved open the door, waving for me to follow. "Perfect marks on your theory, a master of death and necrotic magic, an exceptionally large core, and master-tier talent. You're almost too good to work here."

The finger of destruction spell was an 11th-rank spell. It wasn't that impressive, considering Davina could cast 9th-rank spells at will.

I gave him a genuine smile, which he didn't return. "I'm just happy to be here, Headmaster."

At the moment, Darksmith was the safest place for Kathrine to recover. There was nowhere else I would rather be.

Wink sighed as we walked into the classroom. It was like any university lecture hall from the 1900s. It had terraced seating and a blackboard up front. It could seat exactly one hundred and twenty people, which was how large my classes would be.

My desk had seen better days. There were scorch marks along the wood. And the oak seat didn't have a cushion. There were also a dozen cursed objects, placed around the room, which radiated black smoke to my gaze. That would normally concern me, but I'd spotted hundreds of students carrying cursed objects since I'd arrived.

Curses were far too common at Darksmith.

Wink glanced at me. "Did my assistant inform you of your duties?"

"He did."

Beyond teaching my class, I had to participate in extracurricular activities every second evening. I also had to tutor no less than three students privately. The workload was high, but the bad pay made up for that. Well, not the bad pay, but the other benefits. I had access to a private occult library, workshop, training hall, and apartment. Everything I needed to take care of Kathrine.

The terraced seating rose to my left as I followed Wink to the other door in the far-right corner of the room. We entered an enchanters' and crafters' workshop. The equipment was completely top-of-the-line and looked like it had barely been used. Based on what I could see, I'd be able to study any changes the mana tempering had done to my equipment.

Wink waved to everything around us. "This is your private workshop. Occult Studies doesn't typically involve crafting or enchanting, but every teacher has one, and you can give students permission to use it if you so choose."

"Am I allowed to craft undead here?"

Wink frowned as he headed for the staircase at the back of the workshop. "That's a point of contention here at Darksmith. We have too many students capable of practicing necromancy and not enough cadavers to supply them with. I've restricted everyone to using dungeon monsters or animals."

"Why?"

"Scarcity of cadavers pushed up the price the academy was willing to pay, and then the local murder rate."

That didn't appal me, even though I knew it should have. "I'll restrict myself to using dungeon monsters and animals, then."

"Please do."

Wink led me up the staircase, and, at the top, we entered a grand reception room with a set of double doors. Wink held up an amulet and then waved his hand, casting a basic dispel magic spell to unlock the doors.

He tossed me the amulet. "The doors are magically sealed. The barrier is only advanced, so it can be easily overcome, which is intentional. There are master-tier enchantments on the door that will warn you and all the members of the faculty if anyone tries to force their way in here."

That was a lot of security. "Why?"

Wink opened the door, and we entered a lavish hallway.

He pointed to the first door on the left. "That door leads to your private occult library. This is a restricted library. You may not lend books out to students, but you may invite them to read them here. A private terrace runs down that side of the building with a private garden, so don't leave the library door unlocked, or one of our more idiotic students will run off with something that could drive them insane."

I opened the library door to check whether what he said was true. I immediately felt the dark aura that saturated the room. Their concern seemed to be justified. The second I closed the door the aura was cut off.

"That's an impressive containment system."

"We try to do our best. Now, beyond the library on your left, you have your dining room and then your kitchen. You can prepare you own meals or eat in the dining hall with the students and faculty. The rooms on the right are your training hall and bedroom. The room at the end of the hallway is your study."

Wink led me to the study and opened the door. The study was similar to Wink's office, with bookshelves down either side and a large desk. The only thing it lacked was a private bar.

Wink went to one of the shelves and began reading the spines. "Your predecessor quit quite suddenly, which is why we weren't ready to replace her, and we have been scrambling to find someone qualified."

The news would concern a normal Occult Studies professor, so I spoke up. "Changes in behaviour usually points to corruption in our profession."

"It wasn't that. The Northern students just drove her over the edge with their antics. She walked into my office and told me that she was seriously considering cursing some of them, and that if she had to spend another day teaching them, she was going to start. She then quit. It was an entirely rational thing to do."

"Why?"

"The North serve their darklord. Many practices that are banned in other civilisations are common there. They consider Occult Studies a joke, so you're going to find yourself the target of a dozen minor curses each day."

"Is that allowed?"

"Technically, yes. If they outright attack you, you can kill them. But minor curses and inconveniences are something the staff at Darksmith are supposed to be capable of dealing with. Thankfully, Darksmith is neutral territory. Because of the treaty, the Northern students can't seriously harm the Southern students while here, so they attack us or their own people. Some of the Southern students do the same, but it's not nearly as common or as bad."

That was annoying. "Do you have a school rule book I can read?"

Wink waved his hand to the bookshelf he was searching. "It's somewhere among these, along with your curriculum. I'm sure you were informed that Occult Studies is a mandatory class for all students. We have a maximum of six thousand students at any one time, and they all have one class with you every ten days. Your class is outside of the school's main curriculum, so it isn't part of their final grades, but you're welcome to punish them for failing a test or not doing homework. Feel free to get creative."

I SAW Headmaster Wink to the door and then went to check the bedroom. I'd been listening to Riza taking care of Kathrine, ever since I'd returned to Darksmith. She talked to my daughter's sleeping form while she worked, sharing stories from when they were younger. From what I had overheard, they had been friends since Kathrine was summoned.

My daughter needed round-the-clock care, similar to an infant, so I needed to be prepared. As I entered the apartment's bedroom, I immediately noticed it didn't have any windows. That was good. It meant there was only one entrance. Illumination crystals sat in the chandelier and sconces along the wall, providing plenty of light. There was a small vent in the wall that provided good air circulation and a device near the door that you could feed mana into to provide heating. I directed a little mana to it to increase the room temperature.

A gigantic four-poster bed sat against the far wall, with two bedside tables. There was a wardrobe and a bureau on either side, and a couch and two armchairs near the entrance.

Normally, I didn't care about decorations, but this was going to be where Kathrine stayed while she was asleep. Her dorm room was neat and tidy, so I knew she'd put effort into making it prettier. I wanted her to wake up to the same experience, so I fussed over everything while I waited for the students to go to bed.

In the early hours of the morning, I entered Kathrine's dorm, triggering a magical alarm that woke Riza up. As I closed the door behind me, I heard her leap out of the armchair in Kathrine's bedroom and snatch something off the table. A second later, she opened the door with her wand pointed at me.

Exhaustion clung to her scent, but anyone could see how tired she was. The bags under her eyes showed she'd barely slept in days.

The tip of her wand glowed white as she glared at me. "You're back."

"I am. And I've secured a professorship here. I'm moving my daughter to my apartment."

Riza continued to block the doorway. "Is she safe with you?"

"You can't stop me from taking her, and you won't trust my word if I say she is, so answering is pointless. However, you may visit her if you like."

Riza didn't move.

I walked over and gently placed my hand on her wand and pushed it down. "I will not forget what you did here, Riza. My family means everything to me. If you ever need anything, you only need to ask."

Riza stepped out of the way.

They didn't have catheters or colostomy bags, so Kathrine was wearing an adult diaper under her dress. Judging by her scent, Riza had been giving her a sponge bath twice a day. Her hair had been brushed, but she was still lying on her back. Kathrine had more constitution, endurance, and recovery than the average person, but not by much. After eleven days of being asleep, she was beginning to show signs of muscle wasting and atrophy.

I'd have to correct that.

I picked her up as gently as I could and carried her out of the room. "I'll be back for her things shortly."

My only priority was taking care of Kathrine, but to do that safely required my presence at Darksmith to go unnoticed. If that failed to continue, I needed to be ready for extreme violence. No one would give me the benefit of the doubt, and a few of the faculty were powerful enough to concern me. That needed to change.

When I finished making my daughter comfortable, I went downstairs and locked the door to my workshop. Liquid mana tempering had changed the nature of the enchantments Lavire had laid upon my equipment, and I needed to understand what those changes were and whether they were dangerous. I also needed to bond with the pieces of my equipment, once I knew they were safe.

Slaughter and my Day Walker set were grossly underutilized.

The workshop was state-of-the-art, with equipment from a dozen different kingdoms. I went over to the bookshelf and read the instruction manuals, quickly making my way through the dense text. I knew what most of this equipment was and how it worked, but some of the designs were foreign to me. Once I was familiar with how everything functioned, I drew Slaughter from its sheath.

The blade immediately began drawing in the ambient mana from the dungeon environment.

I willed Slaughter to go dormant and placed it on the balancer, a device enchanters used to examine their finished work. An enlarged visual representation of the kilij appeared above the balancer in the form of an illusion as I fed it enough raw mana for a 1st-rank spell.

The balancer was supposed to scan the item and show a visual representation of the runes, their connections, materials, and the power flowing between. This was its most basic function, and it wasn't doing that, because the enchantments were too powerful. I fed the device more mana, slowly increasing the mana level, rank by rank.

Details didn't appear until I reached the 15th rank, which meant the kilij contained peak master-tier enchantments. The illusion transformed, losing the physical properties of the kilij to only display the enchantment's runes and their connections.

Error symbols floated over every rune and every connection. From the balancer's perspective, everything about Slaughter was broken. Including the structure of the runes. I focused on a single rune and fed more mana into the balancer, increasing the size of the magnification.

Runes, like spells, had tiers and ranks. It looked like Lavire had layered the rune with all fifteen rank variations of the exact same rune, using the weaker-rank versions to reinforce the stronger ones. Nothing I'd read had ever mentioned this technique, which explained why the balancer thought everything was broken, despite it functioning perfectly. Without the mana tempering, I doubted I would have been able to see this change. The adventurer's guild in Hellmouth had studied Slaughter with a similar device, so they could destroy it, and this sort of runic structure hadn't appeared in the investigation notes.

I ignored the oddity and went back to studying the rest of the kilij.

Slaughter didn't have a lot of the bells and whistles most weapons of its calibre possessed, for one simple reason. Ancient vampires didn't need them. Lavire had crafted Slaughter from an unknown magical metal that absorbed magic and broke it down into raw mana. He'd alloyed this unknown metal with alchemy reagents extracted from elder vampire blood to change its nature, so it could also absorb life force.

The enchantments were designed to enhance the weapon's ability to eat life force and magic and reinforce and repair the structure of the blade so it didn't break, while storing the excess mana and life force in the hilt to grow stronger over time. The growth property had long since reached its limits, and the mana tempering hadn't changed that.

From what I could see, the enchantments still did everything they were supposed to. Only now they did it far more efficiently, overcoming what the balancer said should have been possible, even for a master-tier weapon. Its existence was unlike anything I'd ever seen or read about. Perhaps the Darksmith's library would answer my questions, because I couldn't.

I didn't bother to investigate further.

I placed my hand on Slaughter and wove a strand of unbroken mana from my core, through the runes, following the power flow sequence I saw before me. As I reached the last rune, a bond snapped into place. The excess ambient mana Slaughter consumed from the environment began to trickle into my core.

Now that we were bonded, Slaughter wouldn't just feed me life force, but mana, too. It was a good improvement.

I returned Slaughter to its sheath and stripped naked, adding the Day Walker set to the balancer, before I poured more mana into it. Red error runes showed up everywhere.

Lavire had made the Day Walker set for his elder vampire brother.

He must have cared a lot for him, because every component of the enchantments used only the best materials. There was no weak link, so the Day Walker set was now so sturdy it could even block Slaughter.

As I continued to study the set, I realised that the material components might not have been selected by choice, but as a necessity. The Day Walker set wasn't just designed to protect the wearer; it was designed to give them the same capabilities as an ancient vampire. However, Lavire wouldn't have been the genius that he was, if the armour had become redundant once his brother achieved ancient vampire status. There was a series of runes that changed these properties when the wearer was an ancient vampire. It directed the enhancements into the wearer's constitution.

On my character sheet, my constitution had an infinity sign next to it. However, this was because my recovery essentially made me unkillable, so it was showing that my constitution was not currently relevant. Because of this, I'd never invested anything into my constitution, which meant I was nearly as squishy as a regular human. Luke, on the other hand, could walk away from a car crash unharmed and pull a roast out of the oven without mittens.

I created another thread of mana from my core and wove it through the enchantments. The bond clicked into place, and I felt magic surge through my flesh, reinforcing it and making it stronger, despite not wearing it. I pulled up my character sheet.

Race: Ancient Royal Vampire Variant
Class: Hero
Level: 35
Strength: 340
Agility: 520
Endurance: ∞
Constitution: ∞
Cunning: 240
Perception: 480
Recovery: ∞
Mana Regeneration: 400

Nothing had visibly changed on my character sheet, but I felt different.

I needed to investigate.

As I dressed, the magic reinforcing my flesh grew stronger, which immediately told me that while the set did work at range, it didn't work well. I put the balancer away, unlocked the door, and headed for my private training hall. It had a master-tier barrier system, capable of cutting me off from the outside world, so I could practice magic without giving my skills away. However, that wasn't what currently interested me.

I made my way to the back of the large, empty room and opened the storage chests. They were bigger on the inside than a storage pouch but didn't contain the massive storage space that a master storage chest would. They were still the size of a four-car garage.

I found a constitution-testing device in the third chest. The tube was small enough to fit inside the palm of my hand. It had a button at one end and a very sharp needle only a few millimetres long at the other. I placed the needle side against the forearm, until the tube around the needle sat flat against my skin. If my constitution was under one hundred, the needle would have penetrated my skin. It hadn't.

I began pressing the button.

The counter, along the side of the tube, began going up by one each time I pressed the button. When the number reached 600 without the needle stabbing through my skin, I pulled the testing device away from my arm. High-level sorcerers didn't typically have constitution this high, so I was unlikely to find a better testing device in Murdell. Even without it, my instincts told me the needle would have pierced my skin sometime within the next hundred presses of the button.

I released the tension from the tester and then placed it back in the storage chest. The increased durability was nice, but not enough, so I opened another storage chest and removed a shielded training pole, so I could spend the rest of the night practicing magic.

There wasn't a lot of time before I had to teach my first class, and I needed to do everything I could to keep Kathrine safe.

6

PROFESSOR VINCENT

Teaching Occult Studies was something I could do. Not only did I know more than most about the subject, but I also felt teaching the subject lined up nicely with my goals. This world shrouded the occult in far too much mysticism to be practical, overcomplicating the subject to the point that most people had no clue what was safe and what wasn't. The curriculum my predecessor had given me muddied the waters in such a way that it even implied many things that were safe weren't and many things that weren't safe were.

People needed to understand the occult better in order to stop making so many mistakes that caused them and others to end up corrupted, making the world less safe for my family, so I was happy to teach the academy's students how to do that. They would one day be some of the most influential people in Murdell, so stopping even one of them from being corrupted could prevent disaster.

Eight days into my new job, I was sitting with my feet on the desk, meditating to refill my core with mana, when my classroom door opened. It happened during the lunch break, which was a little odd.

A young blonde woman, wearing the plain black robe all students wore, tried to sneak into my class and head for the back of the room.

Unlike most of the students, she had chosen to have her family's coat of arms embroidered on her uniform.

It failed to distract me from the dark tendrils of black smoke wafting off her body.

I sighed as I took my feet off my desk. "Miss Winterton, my desk *now*." I was getting very good at doing a stern professor voice.

Heather froze and then dropped her head, walking to my desk under a cloud of anxiety and depression. "I didn't do anything," she said weakly, hiding her face with her hair.

This was an all-too-familiar sight. "You should meet a person's gaze when you're talking to them. It shows confidence." She forced herself to look up. Her eyes were gentle blue and her face... "Wow, that's a lot of acne." Her lips trembled as she blushed with embarrassment, on the verge of tears. "Empty your storage pouch onto my desk."

"I didn't do anything," she repeated.

I'd had this conversation a dozen times a day since starting this job. "Yes, you did. You walked into my class cursed. Now empty your storage pouch so I can find the cursed item."

As the Occult Studies professor no one found it strange that I could tell that people were cursed. They expected it, so I hadn't bothered to hide my abilities.

She blinked a little surprised. "I'm cursed?"

"Common problem around here. It's nothing to be embarrassed about." Darksmith had more curses than universities had STI's, and that was saying something.

She removed her storage pouch from her waist and began emptying it on the desk. I quickly ran out of desk space as she unloaded everything except a kitchen sink. In total she had twenty-three cursed items. Then I opened her purse and added all her platinum to the pile of curse items.

It was the largest haul yet. "Congratulations, you win the prize for being the most cursed student at Darksmith."

She frowned. "What?"

"It's a joke."

"It's not very funny."

"I'm your professor, so you have to laugh."

That got me a small smile.

"Good enough."

I started picking up the items. Ancient vampires were immune to all but the nastiest curses, and we could tell what those were, so there was no risk of us picking them up. I'd been exposed to hundreds of minor curses over the past eight days, so I could tell what each one did just by looking at them.

The curses before me weren't that powerful, but in combination they were mildly horrible. One made her feel self-conscious. Another made her forgetful. Another increased all negative emotions. Another made her scared. Then there were the others that made her sick.

I picked up bottle of perfumed oil and frowned. "This one is going to be a problem."

"Why?"

"It leaves you barren, and it's not a minor curse." I picked up the trash bin next to my desk and placed it on top, holding the bottle above.

With one spell, I disintegrated the bottle. With another, I captured the curse. As the bottle crumbled to dust, joining all the other cursed items I'd destroyed so far today, a sickly black shadow was left behind. It wriggled between my fingers, trying to force its way through my skin, but it was blocked by the layer of death magic that protected my hand.

Curses were thought to be a form of living magic, like a bacterial infection. They could grow stronger or weaker over time and even change from their intended purpose. I sensed no life force inside the curse, but that didn't mean that those theories were wrong. They certainly behaved like they were alive.

With a small effort of will and mana I made the curse stronger, before encapsulating it in another spell. A ball of dark violent energy formed in the palm of my hand, surrounding the curse. I made a throwing motion, sending the curse out into the world.

We watched as it faded from sight within a few feet.

Heather continued to frown. “What did you do?”

“Return to sender spell. Whoever created that curse is going to end up barren. Unlike with you, it’s not going to be easily fixed.”

“Are you allowed to do that?”

“Page thirty-eight, line seventeen of the school rule book. A professor may use excessive force in defence of themselves or students. A curse constitutes an attack, and sending it back stronger constitutes protecting you with excessive force.”

She leaned away from me. “Couldn’t you do it without making the curse stronger?”

“I could, but there is no rule that says I have to.” I opened the top drawer, pulled out a piece of blank paper, and wrote a quick note. “Take this note to the infirmary at the end of the day. They will correct the damage this and the other curses did to you.” I met her gaze. “This curse is not a free pass for you and your boyfriend to have a bit of fun. The sooner you go the better. I’ll be visiting the infirmary tomorrow morning to make sure you went.”

This wasn’t the first time I’d had to deal with this sort of curse. And the new rules were because of how some students had treated my instructions as suggestions rather than requirements.

I glanced at the other curse items. “Are any of these items important to you?”

She pointed to an expensive and tasteful broach. “That cost three months of my allowance, please don’t destroy it.”

I put the broach aside. “Anything else?”

She shook her head.

I picked up the items one by one and disintegrated them, capturing the curses, and returning them to the creators stronger than before. The spell didn’t form for eight of the cursed items, which meant they were naturally occurring curses from unstable enchantments or improper storage. I dispelled them and moved on.

When the last item was destroyed, I gave her a very pointed look. I’d noticed a trend with her items. “You like to shop at discount antique stores, don’t you?”

She nodded.

"Stop."

She scowled at me. "But they're so much cheaper than the high-end stores."

"The reason those places sell their items so cheap is because you can get cursed. Argument over."

I turned to her box of healing potions and lifted the lid. I pulled one from the box and broke the seal. I lifted it to my nose for show, already knowing it was clean.

She went back to frowning. "What are you doing?"

"You've got so many cursed items that it wouldn't surprise me if your healing potions were poisoned."

Her surprise was amusing. "You know the smell of poison?"

"I know the smell and colour of healing potions and when it comes to poison all of them alter the colour or smell of a healing potion. This is clean. Now would you like me to remove your acne?"

A smile exploded across her face. "Yes!"

I passed her the potion. "Put the liquid in your mouth and swallow it when the pain starts." She did as I instructed. "This is going to hurt a lot."

Her eyes widened as I tapped her forehead and used a basic spell to scan her body. Then I used death magic to kill all the bacteria causing the acne and necrotic magic to disintegrate the effected skin. They weren't spells, just a direct and controlled application of magic which made this much harder for most people.

I found it easier than casting spells.

My scan showed sixty percent of her body was covered in acne, so this would have felt like getting a second degree full-body sunburn.

She swallowed the potion as the pain hit her. The painkiller aspect immediately took effect as her recovery rate massively increased. Her hand reached for her mirror, then she hesitated.

"Your face is currently covered in ash and is going to be quite red for the next little while, but it should be back to normal by the time class starts. If you hurry, you have enough time to pack away your things and take a quick bath before my lecture."

Heather threw her things into her storage pouch as I wrote her a receipt for the items and money she wouldn't be getting back just yet. I made her wait long enough to read the receipt and sign my copy, then she dashed out of the room.

I got one of the many cloth bags from my bottom drawer and swept the broach and the platinum into it. Then I wrote her name on a piece of card and tied it to the bag. Finally, I went to the workshop and added hers to the other ten bags of items I'd confiscated today. Then I returned to my desk and wrote a report to her parents outlining what the items were and how the curses functioned.

I didn't embellish or withhold any details. The North and South had a shaky truce, and all the students were members of the elite, so this could have been the result of espionage or family infighting. Darksmith was neutral territory, so we didn't take sides, only report what we found. I did emphasise that I had cast a return to sender spell, like I had with all the others. Hopefully, the thought that those who had harmed their daughter were now suffering worse than she had would stop her parents from escalating the situation too much. I didn't want war to break out while my daughter was unconscious.

When I was finished writing my report, I went back to meditating and restoring my mana.

In the past eight days, I'd mastered the full range of intermediate-tier spells that death magic practitioners had access to, and I was now working my way through advanced magic.

Practicing advanced magic required one of two things: talent or high agility. The memories sitting in my head covered the talent portion, and my vampiric nature covered the agility. If these were the only advantages I had, I wouldn't be progressing so fast.

Being aware of everything around me meant I noticed any mistakes I made, and, more often than not, I was able to stop the spell from falling apart. My memory made it simple for me to correct any part I did incorrectly, so mistakes only happened once. Also, my body's ability to regenerate allowed me to be far more reckless than any sane person would be. I'd already blown myself apart several dozen times to train faster.

Practitioners traditionally worked through each tier of spell for that very reason, and while it was okay to occasionally skip ahead for a spell or two, a proper grounding in each tier of magic sped up the process of learning the tier above it. So now that I had the job and Kathrine was safe, I wanted to learn magic properly.

That didn't mean I hadn't skipped ahead a little.

I'd learned two more expert-tier spells, the deathlock and deadlands spells. The first was the most powerful stationary barrier spell a necromancer could create, which would be useful if I needed to protect Kathrine. The second opened a portal to the Deadlands.

The Deadlands was a slightly out-of-sync reality, invisible to the normal world. Ghosts and other spiritual entities resided there, watching the living world, looking for a chance to push through the barrier to join the living. Entering the Deadlands would allow me to move as quickly as I wanted in an environment where time moved three times faster. I'd even be able to cross running water, but every second I was there would cost me a small amount of life force.

Crossing through the Deadlands also came with risks. There was a creature that lived there that could kill me, so it wasn't something I planned to use very often.

The lunch break ended, and my students began to file into class. A few minutes before the second bell, I watched a bad romance movie playout in the front row, as Heather—the most cursed young woman at Darksmith—returned and took a seat next to an average-looking guy who didn't recognise her.

What followed was a very predictable plot where a now very attractive young woman excitedly asked out the only guy who had been kind and friendly to her when she was an ugly duckling. The young man was just as excited about her transformation as she was, and not just because of his attraction. He cared about her deeply and he was happy for her. They were going to live happily ever after and have a dozen kids, by the enthusiasm she showed.

I pulled cursed students aside as they entered and made them empty their storage pouches onto my desk, clearing my students of their curses, and showing the other students what I did with the curses I found. None of my students made a fuss, until a boy at the back of the room was hit with my return to sender spell. He started screaming as boils appeared over every inch of his body, causing everyone to turn and watch in horror.

I was building a reputation as a professor you did not want to cross; and whenever something like this happened, it reinforced that reputation. His friends floated him out of class with magic, rushing him to the infirmary.

I thought that he was going to be my most interesting example, until a girl walked through the door with a serious curse. Her curse involved a possession, and the entity controlling her tried to attack me the moment it was exposed.

I ended up having to carry her bruised, unconscious form to the infirmary, where I handed her over to Dalin to deal with, having to shout over my other screaming student.

I'd brought Dalin hundreds of cursed objects and several dozen students by this stage, so he didn't make a fuss as I explained the situation and tied the girl to the bed. I told him I had more cursed items to drop off at the end of the day and then headed back to class.

Yesterday, Dalin had received a letter from the church confirming what I'd told him and had finally begun to relax. Despite the lack of confirmation until now, he'd still visited Kathrine twice a day to check on her condition, bringing potions to stop muscle wastage and keep her healthy, along with clean feeding tubes. He didn't like that I was sending curses back to their creators rather than destroying them, but he did like how thorough I was when it came to my job.

Everyone was in their seats in the middle of a conversation as I walked through the door. There were a few empty spaces in the 120 seats, because this wasn't a full class, but that was normal. Darksmith rarely had a full roster of students.

The room immediately fell silent as I walked to the chalkboard, the class peering down at me, partly curious and partly nervous. "Good afternoon, students. I'm Professor Vincent, your new Defence Against the Dark Arts instructor."

They all frowned.

I was used to this reaction.

"Today is going to be an introductory lesson, and if you pay attention I don't really care if you sleep through my other lessons, because today's lesson contains everything that most of you will ever need to know to protect yourself from the occult."

A young man at the front of the class held up his hand and waited for me to nod in his direction. I'd noticed the classes where I cursed a student were all exceptionally well-behaved. "Sir, isn't this class Occult Studies?"

"Good first question." I waved my hand towards the chalkboard and took control of a piece of chalk with basic spell. "What is the occult?" The piece of chalk wrote my question on the board. "Does anyone know?"

A few hands went up.

I'd given this lecture more than forty times, and I was getting very good at it. I pointed to the class's youngest student in the front row. Her name was Celest, and she was the Darklord's daughter.

Celest had a full head of bushy red hair and was one of the few students to have her book open and ready to take notes. She looked to be only sixteen, which meant that she had to be some sort of magical genius or savant to be enrolled here. She gave me serious Hermione vibes. I liked students who gave that vibe because it didn't slow down my lecture.

Celest stood up, challenging my authority. "The occult is that which can only do harm." The chalk added her answer to the board.

"Which is also known as what?" I pointed to her again.

"The dark arts."

"What is the only safe question you can ask about anything to do with the occult?" I pointed to her again.

She rolled her eyes. "There are no safe questions about the occult."

"Wrong. The only safe question you can ask about anything to do with the occult is, 'What does this do?' It could be a curse, a spell, an item, a condition. It doesn't matter. The only safe question you can always ask yourself or others is, 'What does this do?' Now, why is that important? I'll give you a hint. It's related to combat magic."

A new hand shot up, and I pointed to the owner. He was in his early twenties but had a little more muscle than the average student, showing he actually exercised. He was the son of a baron and of little consequence.

"Um, ah, if you know what your opponent's spell will do, you might also know a way to counter their spell."

"Slightly off-topic, but perfectly on point. If you know that an instrument will possess anyone who picks it up and make them play until they die from exhaustion, then you know not to pick it up. Knowing what something related to the occult does is most of the battle, and this knowledge is perfectly safe. Does anyone know what's the most *unsafe* question you can ask about anything to do with the occult?"

Another young man spoke up as I pointed to him. "How will this give me power?"

"No, but good answer."

Heather Winterton tried her luck. "How can I use this?"

"No, but also a good answer. These are both bad questions to ask yourself about anything to do with the occult. But they are not the *most* dangerous." I pointed to Celest.

Celest blushed. "I don't know."

"Another good answer, and something you all need to remember. There is only one safe question that you can ask about the occult: 'What does this do?' And if your answer is 'I don't know,' your only response should be to turn around and walk the other way."

Celest raised her hand again. "What's the most dangerous question you can ask?"

No one was raising their hand anymore, which showed how poorly this subject was taught before I got here. "The safest question you can ask about anything to do with the occult is, 'What does this do?' The most dangerous question is, 'How does it do it?' This question is also the most *important* question to answer, and is why the vast majority of those who study the occult go insane. Why do they go insane?"

Celest raised her hand. "Because the occult can be described as that which only does harm, and sometimes even knowing how something works the way it does can involve knowledge that is harmful to you."

"But why is this class called the Defence Against the Dark Arts?" the first guy blurted out.

I grinned. "Because the occult is that which only does harm. It is also known as the dark arts. And this is a class that teaches you how not to be harmed by it. So, I renamed it to what it should have been called in the first place. So welcome to Defence Against the Dark Arts, I'll be your lecturer, and by the end of this class you will know everything you need to know to stop yourself from being needlessly harmed by the occult."

AN HOUR AFTER DINNER, I lifted Kathrine's arm and gently wiped it with a damp, soapy rag, before drying it. Sponge baths were the only way to keep Kathrine clean, and they needed to be done twice, sometimes three times a day. Keeping her asleep and fed was extremely messy, but I didn't mind. It reminded me of how Sandra and I had taken care of her as a baby.

To my disappointment, Kathrine had mostly invested her attributes into her agility and mana regeneration. She was more prone to bedsores and muscle wastage than a hero of her level should be. If she'd invested her attributes like her brother, it would have been much easier to take care of her.

As it was, I turned her every few hours, and once a day manipulated her arms and legs to help with circulation. Dalin was feeding her a diet of raw eggs, so she wouldn't choke to death if she vomited in her sleep. With my hearing, that would be close to impossible, but I liked the extra precaution.

I knew I couldn't keep her asleep forever; eventually she would have to wake up, but not yet. She was still suffering from what I had done to her soul, and waking her up might drive her insane. I would move Heaven and Earth to make sure that didn't happen.

When I was done cleaning her, I gently put her on her side and threw a clean blanket over her. I cast the deathlock spell, surrounding her in a protective barrier, and then left the room and headed for the training hall.

When my core was empty from casting spells, I checked on Kathrine and turned her again. I'd already read my entire private occult library, which contained several books on hollows that concerned me, and I'd visited the academy library this morning, so to help keep the Curse of Sloth at bay, I went to my study and began writing another book. Contessa's library had a lot of useful information that I needed to condense into textbooks for my academy.

These books would help me keep my family safe, so I remained aware of the world around me while I worked on them. I wasn't sure what would happen if I ran out of things to do, but I wasn't willing to find out. I was already taking other steps to keep me more active.

IT'S amazing how cursing a bunch of your students can motivate the others to take your class seriously. Despite my offer to let my students ignore my lectures, only a handful across the entire school had taken me up on it, and every one of them had apologised before doing so, explaining that they were behind in another class, and couldn't pass up an opportunity to catch up.

The bell rang right as I finished my lecture, like it did every lecture. "There is a signup sheet for extracurricular activities beside the door. I've created an undead enhancement club, and anyone who can perform death magic is welcome to attend."

One of the necromancers raised his hand. "Sir, there's already an undead club."

"Professor Fergus's club is about *summoning* undead. If you want to learn how to summon a death knight, his club is where you should go. If you want to learn how to *turn* an undead skeleton you've already created *into* a death knight, then my club is for you. While going through each enhancement stage takes longer, the undead this process creates are significantly stronger and easier to maintain."

As my class continued to file out, several necromancers stopped and added their names to the signup sheet.

7

THESE CURSED STREETS

The six storage pouches I normally carried on me came through my teleportation experience as twisted and as broken as I did, turning the gold and silver I kept on hand into nothing but warped lumps of metal. Everything except my Day Walker set and Slaughter were destroyed. Melting the lumps of gold and silver down and casting them into bars wasn't difficult with my private workshop, but it did take time, time I didn't want to waste on something so meaningless.

This stance only changed when one of my wealthiest students complained to Headmaster Wink that I was teaching my classes shirtless, without buttoning up my coat, causing the young woman he liked to ignore him. The headmaster politely informed the young man that my outfit was a powerful magical set, and that wearing a shirt would interfere with the enchantments, like I'd told him.

Under the school dress code, I had every right to wear my equipment the way I was.

The young man then donated enough money to give Darksmith's library another wing, and Headmaster Wink politely informed me that I would have to wear a shirt and over robe from now on. Which is how I found myself carrying newly minted gold bars in one of the free carriages that shuttled students and faculty between Darksmith and the town above the dungeon the following evening.

It was a short trip.

Murdell was a nation of sorcerers, making the average citizen significantly more dangerous than those in Arcadia. Because of this, they built their towns directly outside the dungeon entrance, unafraid of what would happen if it should surge. The free carriage stopped at the dungeon tunnel entrance and let me out among the noise and madness of Merchant Boulevard.

Merchant Boulevard was the Murdell equivalent to Rodeo Drive. The long, straight boulevard ran all the way from the dungeon entrance to the town's main gate. Magnificent, magical trees with a scent like sandalwood and leaves that gave off a florescent blue glow ran down the centre of the street, providing shade in the day and light after dark, when most of the students did their shopping. The cost of cultivating such exotic and expensive plants was paid for by the wealthy owners of the stores that ran along either side of the boulevard.

"Need to memorise a subject for a test," shouted the nearest unlicenced vendor as he walked past the dungeon entrance with his sales cart floating beside him. "Try Uncle Mork's Memory Potions. They're guaranteed to do the job. Not suitable for anyone with less than 50 points in recovery."

"Aunty Wing's Sleepless Potion," called a woman going the other way with her own floating sales cart. "Need to study for an exam, but don't have enough time? My potions will keep you wide awake for up to a week, without any negative side-effects, so long as you follow the instructions on the bottle."

I started walking, ignoring the unlicensed vendors shouting over each other to get the attention of the students who had more money than sense. Having so many members of Murdell's elite in one place made the town a hub for both nations' luxury goods market. Sorcerers came from far and wide in search of items that couldn't be found anywhere else.

Everywhere I looked, magical animals sat in cages on floating carts, ready for sale. Most were not pets, but fresh ingredients for specific types of potions.

As I left the tunnel behind and made my way through the free-for-all that was the dungeon entrance, the number of unlicenced vendors targeting students dramatically decreased, giving way to the luxury shops that Merchant Boulevard was known for. Every sign was covered with gold leaf, and every store front was immaculate.

The evening air was cool and pleasant as I quickly arrived at Solomon's Robes and Fashion and saw a sign on the door that said 'Closed for Renovations'. It listed a new location, a quarter of a mile further down the boulevard. I'd been told that Solomon was the only tailor on the boulevard who didn't produce magical clothing. That didn't make his wares cheap, but it did mean I needed to see him.

I followed the sign's directions, ignoring the shop assistants standing beside open doors inviting me in, but I took note of the many antique shops I saw with cursed objects displayed in their front windows. Too much of my time was spent dealing with cursed objects students had picked up. If I could lower the influx of these objects into the school, I would have more time to pursue other matters, and Darksmith would become a safer place for Kathrine to stay.

Five minutes later, I arrived at a nice, but less lavish version of Solomon's Robes and Fashion, and entered. The short man behind the counter matched the description Dalin had given me of Solomon. His skin held a deep tan, and his goatee and short hair had an unnatural silver sheen to them that highlighted and intensified the purple in his eyes.

A magical harp sat in the corner of the shop, playing soft, calming music, and mannequins displaying examples of his work dotted the walls. There were no racks with clothes on them. Everything here was made to order. Solomon put down the novel he was reading, measuring me with his gaze as I walked over.

He gave a friendly grin. "Judging by your outfit, you must be Professor Vincent."

I raised an eyebrow. "You've heard of me?"

He rose and walked around the counter. "You've caused quite the stir among your students and have single-handedly doubled my business with how many alterations I've been asked to make to robes and dresses that need to be tightened, raised, or lowered. How can I help you?"

"I need shirts."

I could have made them myself, but that would draw unnecessary attention. Sorcerers in Murdell didn't do that sort of thing.

Solomon chuckled as he pulled out a measuring tape. "I take it someone complained about your gossip-worthy physique."

"Something like that."

Solomon gave a fake sigh. "How unfortunate. I've been enjoying the extra business. This new location is simply dreadful for sales." He ran his gaze over my Day Walker set with a practiced eye. "I assume you don't own any shirts because they interfere with the enchantments that have been laid on your outfit."

"They do, which is why I prefer not to wear them."

"May I ask what sort of interference they cause?"

"There is a minor reduction in the constitution benefit."

The reduction was minor enough that I didn't mind wearing a shirt, but I still would have preferred not to. Also, the cursed properties of my coat didn't allow regular clothing to survive more than a week before they rotted away.

"Arms up, please."

I raised my arms.

Solomon began taking measurements. "Do you have any preferences?"

"I would prefer thinner material."

"Why not a material that will assist the enchantments?"

"I strongly doubt you have anything that can keep up with what I'm wearing. This outfit tends to destroy everything it encounters."

Solomon took a step back and grasped his chest dramatically. "Sir, you wound me. I have materials that can keep up with an archsorcerer's robes."

"I'd need something better than that."

He blinked. "How much better?"

"A lot better."

He tapped a pair of scissors on his toolbelt. "Do you mind if I see for myself?"

"Be my guest."

Solomon took his rune-etched scissors and tried to cut through my cuff, channelling mana into the scissors and squeezing them together with everything he had. He gave an extra loud grunt, before giving up and looking at my cuff. His enchanted scissor hadn't left a scratch.

He shook his head as he put the scissors away. "That resistance and the fact that I don't recognise what sort of leather it's made from certainly lends your claim credibility. A simple cotton with silk embroidery shirt it is, then. Is there anything else I can do for you?"

"I'd also like an open robe that I can wear over my equipment."

He took a step back and ran his gaze over me again. "I think black on red should do nicely. It will complement the leather. Do I need to be aware of any special conditions?"

"So long as it isn't enchanted or magically sensitive, there won't be an issue."

"How many shirts and over robes do you want?"

"Three to begin with. With another set sent to the academy every five days."

Solomon's eyebrows rose. "Why every five days?"

"That's how long they'll last, before the material will become too rotten to look professional."

Solomon winced. "I hope your equipment is worth the trouble, considering how much this is going to cost you."

"It is."

"Do you want a range of styles for the shirts and over robes?"

I didn't care.

"What would you suggest?"

"Considering how powerful your outfit seems to be, I must assume it's the only thing you wear. In that situation, I'm inclined to go with a single shirt and over robe design that makes your outfit pop. It shouldn't take me long to come up with a few interesting designs, but if you have other shopping to do, you can come back later."

Darksmith had an adequate supply network, so this morning I'd ordered my replacement storage pouches through them, along with the usual contents I'd kept inside. The new storage pouches were top of the line, better than what I'd had before. They wouldn't survive a teleportation, but they might survive the rough lifestyle I tended to subject my equipment to.

Because of that, I didn't have any shopping that I needed to do, but the antique shops I'd spotted selling cursed objects on my way here needed my attention.

I gave Solomon a polite smile. "I've got a few errands to run."

Solomon returned the smile. "I'll see you when you finish, then."

I left his shop and walked down the street to the corner antique store with the strongest cursed items I'd seen on my way to Solomon's. I was in a luxury shopping area, but the store was even more impressive than the rest.

The elderly doorman, who doubled as security for the place, gave me a slight sense of danger, as he raised his hand as I approached. "Do you have an appointment, sir?"

It was the politest, 'You can't afford to shop here,' I'd ever heard. "Would I be able to speak to the manager of this establishment?"

The doorman frowned. "Not unless you have an appointment, sir."

"That sounds like too much trouble."

The doorman relaxed. "I'm sorry I couldn't be of more help."

"Would you mind passing along a message to the manager for me instead?"

"Not at all, sir."

"Tell the manager that Darksmith's new Occult Studies professor was passing by their store and noticed that you had a few cursed items on sale. Most of them aren't anything to worry about, but that rook in the display case over there will slowly drive the wielder mad."

I turned and left, knowing that the doorman would chase after me. Behind me, the doorman stopped the first passing student and asked them if I was Darksmith's new Occult Studies professor. The student informed them I was the new Defence Against the Dark Arts teacher, but that they were practically the same thing.

I was two blocks away when the doorman caught up and tapped me on the shoulder.

I turned around. "Can I help you?"

He sighed. "Sir, I think the manager will want to see you."

"But I don't have an appointment."

"I believe she will make an exception this time."

"Wonderful."

I followed the doorman back to the store, where he lowered the barrier protecting the entrance, and led me inside. The store was much bigger than the ones around it, with a layout like an art gallery with large spaces between each item. It also seemed to operate via appointment like the doorman claimed, because there were only three saleswomen. Each of them were with a client and had an assistant who was bringing their clients canapes and drinks to keep them entertained as they discussed each antique item on display.

The Darklord's daughter Celest glanced in my direction as I followed the doorman to a door at the back of the store. "Is something the matter, Professor?"

"Nothing serious. I noticed a few of these items were cursed while I was passing by the window."

"That's preposterous," the saleswoman replied. "We've had this collection verified by three different assessors."

I chuckled. "You should ask for a refund, then."

The doorman opened the door at the back and stuck his head inside. "I'm sorry to bother you, ma'am, but Darksmith's Occult Studies professor is here. He believes some of our inventory is cursed."

"Send him in, Jorn."

Jorn the doorman stepped back and waved me through. "Don't touch anything. She hates it when people touch things in her workshop."

I nodded as I walked through the door.

The workshop contained hundreds of wooden crates, dozens of which oozed cursed smoke. They were stacked around a large worktable, which held numerous magical items used for assessing magical phenomena. In the middle of the table was a black sarcophagus, sealed with dozens of enchanted and cursed binding strips. None of that interested me, but on the table against the far wall was an unrolled scroll that gave detailed instructions for how to build a powerful undead-empowering ziggurat. I filed the design away for future consideration.

The small, elderly woman was examining the runes around the outside of the sarcophagus, making notes of everything she saw, as she slowly broke the protective enchantments and curses that kept it closed. Her hair was pale white and tied back in a bun. Her hands were covered in scar tissue, with a faint black smoke wafting from them, showing that the injuries were cursed.

She glanced in my direction. "You believe some of my inventory is cursed, Professor."

"Call me Vincent. And yes, four of the items you have in your gallery are cursed."

She scowled. "That's unfortunate. How much will this information cost me?"

"It's free."

She frowned. "That's usually the most expensive sort of advice."

"Normally I would agree with you, but Darksmith has a problem with cursed objects. As the Occult Studies professor, more often than not, I am the one who must deal with them. Since I have a little time while I'm waiting for a tailor, I decided to do a little pre-emptive work."

Her face softened. "In that case, I'm happy to help. Which items in my display room are cursed?"

"The only major curse is attached to the rook. It will drive the wielder mad over decades. Standard assessments wouldn't pick it up because it works too slowly."

"Can it be removed?"

"I would have to look at the runes to tell you. It's clearly a magical focus, so the curse may be part of its function."

"What else is cursed?"

"The dragonfly jewellery set makes the wearer miscarry. Each of the three pieces are cursed, but the curses are also accumulative, increasing the chances when more pieces are worn. The situational nature of the curse is easily missed by standard assessments."

Juna sighed. "It would appear that this collection is more troublesome than I assumed. I suppose that will teach me for buying from tomb raiders."

I picked up a stick of charcoal that was lying on the table and began marking the crates with cursed objects inside. "Each of these crates have something cursed inside."

Juna picked up a pen and followed behind me, writing the word cursed on each crate. "You should have just said you can sense curse aura."

"I don't have my papers on me."

"So, the only reason you're not charging me for your services is because you can't."

I gave a fake chuckle.

"I suppose you're going to visit my competition to provide them with similar services."

"That's my intent."

"I'll send my doorman Jorn with you to vouch for your abilities. It should save you time."

I tossed the charcoal back on the table as I finished. "You're very trusting."

"I'm not." She pointed to the stamp on the crate, beside the spot I'd just marked. "You see this stamp?"

I nodded.

"It means the object inside this crate is cursed. You've marked every one of them, *and* several I didn't know about. You likely aren't a charlatan, so let me get my doorman." Juna left her pen on the last crate and led me out of her workshop.

Celest was looking at the dragonfly set as I walked past.

"Those are cursed," I said.

"That will soon be corrected," Juna added.

Merchant's Boulevard had dozens of antique stores. Juna's store was one of the most expensive, so Jorn was on a first-name basis with her direct competition. Each of them were high-end, the sort of place where money didn't matter, so they were just as dedicated to not selling cursed items as Juna was. That meant I only found a few minor cursed items at each store.

That number drastically increased as we began visiting the lower end of the market. Juna's doorman helped me bypass any hesitancy or arguments the owners offered, getting me in and out with little fuss. The promise that I would inspect anything they sent to the academy for free also helped.

"This is Nor's Antiques," Jorn said as we walked up. "He deals with estate sales. Juna doesn't like him, because he doesn't have his purchases assessed before he sells them."

I could tell that just by how many cursed objects were sitting in his front window. Jorn opened the door for me, falling on old habits, and then followed me inside, before walking ahead of me to speak with the owner.

Heather Winterton, the most cursed girl at Darksmith, who was now a radiant beauty free from acne, stood ten feet away from me with a guilty look on her face while holding a cursed hairpin she'd just picked off the shelf. Her new boyfriend, Damien Black, stood beside her with a happy, dumb smile on his face while he held the four bags of items she'd already purchased, two of which held cursed objects.

Heather swallowed. "I can explain."

I sighed. "One would think that someone with your personal experience would have learned their lesson the first time, Miss Winterton."

"I did. This place is much nicer than the places I normally shop."

"You mean *used to* shop."

"Ah, that's what I meant."

Her lie was painfully obvious, even if her boyfriend hadn't winced.

I shook my head. "The hairpin you're holding is cursed. Along with three of the items you've already purchased. Hand them over?"

Damien's spine stiffened, and he stepped forward with the bags, clearly afraid of my reputation around cursed objects.

Heather's face fell. "But I just bought them."

Damien froze, glanced at his girlfriend, and then met my gaze. He instantly decided that upsetting his new girlfriend was preferable to upsetting me and continued walking over.

I looked through the bags and pulled out a cursed hairbrush, hand mirror, and ceramic duck. Each item was tastefully decorated and quite elegant. I could see why they interested her.

I held up the hairbrush. "Using this hairbrush will thin your hair until you go bald." I disintegrated it with a spell, caught the curse with another spell, and then returned the curse to the creator stronger. Next, I held up the hand mirror. "This will make you obsessed with yourself." I treated it like the first item and then picked up the ceramic duck. "This will slowly make you deaf if you sleep near it." It received the same treatment as the other two while I looked Heather Winterton in the eye. "This is exactly why you don't shop at discount antique stores in a nation with North Murdell's reputation."

Heather scowled. "This isn't a cheap place, Professor."

"The items might be more expensive, but the authentication and safety procedures aren't. You can tell that because it doesn't have any safety certification displayed on the walls."

Heather looked around but didn't lose her scowl. She clearly liked antique shopping far too much. I could see this was going to be an ongoing problem if I didn't set her straight.

"Your evening is cancelled, Miss Winterton. The two of you will be following me around while I deal with cursed items that are being sold from these antique stores. It should give you a good idea of how extensive this problem is."

EVERY ANTIQUE STORE I walked into had cursed items on display, and many of them were trying to sell those items to students from whom I'd already removed curses. The guilty looks they gave me matched

Heather Winterton's and told me that they weren't about to change, so I added them to my impromptu Defence Against the Dark Arts lesson and made them follow me from store to store with the growing crowd.

At the eighteenth store, I stopped before Barok's Antiques and turned to the dozens of students that were now following me and Jorn. Only a handful of them were with me as punishment; the rest were just bored and curious about what I was doing.

Every item inside the store behind me was cursed, which meant I was dealing with something more nefarious than greed and stupidity. "As you've all seen, cursed items come in all shapes and sizes. The effectiveness of using them as tools of assassination or destabilisation for a family should be clear to you all by now. Once a family's wealth is shattered, these items then get sold off to circulate among the population. However, that's *not* what is happening in the store behind me."

Jorn frowned and raised his hand. "How do you know there's a difference here, Professor?"

The doorman found my lessons quite interesting.

"The concentration of cursed objects is far too high to naturally occur, which indicates we're dealing with some form of Unseen class. I believe it's either a curse weaver or a corruptor. Both will react violently upon discovery, and both would prove fatal to any of you if you were to follow me into the store; so, please remain out here while I deal with the creature inside. Let me be clear: If you enter this store, you will die. I suggest you stay out of sight and cast listening spells to follow what's happening."

The small crowd began muttering spells as I walked a little further down the street and entered the shop. It wasn't a big store, but the *thousands* of objects on the shelves were *all* cursed, and the man behind the counter had the smoky gaze of an Unseen.

He gave me a charming smile as I walked in. "How can I help you this evening, sir?"

I returned his smile and ran my gaze over his cursed objects. "You have quite an impressive collection."

"You're too kind, sir."

I picked up a mother of pearl jewellery box with a bone-wasting curse and turned to the Unseen. "Do you have the curse weaver or corruptor class? I'm leaning toward the curse weaver class based on the layout of your shop. It enhances the power of your curses, doesn't it?"

The smile faded from his lips. "Who are you?"

"I'm Darksmith's new Occult Studies professor, though I prefer the term Defence Against the Dark Arts professor."

The smile returned to the Unseen's face, but without the charm. It was dark and twisted, very close to a sneer. "In that case, you should know it's not wise to walk into a curse weaver's domain. Not when I'm surrounded by my sweet children, who don't like you."

I gave a dry chuckle at his confidence. The Unseen hadn't lied about his class. I could tell if he had. And a curse weaver was someone I could easily deal with. If he'd been a corruptor, that would have made this difficult.

Corruptors had to corrupt the world around them to level their class, so all these cursed items would have come from another source. I would have had to track down his suppliers and worry about someone being killed by one of his spells when he attacked me. Instead, I could just kill him.

The Unseen didn't like the way I chuckled.

He gathered his will and pointed his index finger at me. The curses immediately tore themselves from the objects that contained them, trying to smother me under an avalanche of curse energy. They found themselves blocked by the death magic I'd surrounded my body with, leaving them completely incapable of burning their way into my flesh.

Black cursed smoke, now visible to the naked eye, wafted from me as I grinned at him. "Was that supposed to kill me?"

The Unseen swallowed. "Was *what* supposed to kill you? I didn't do anything!"

I released a necrotic wave, disintegrating the contents of the store, along with the shopfront. A cloud of dust spilled into the surrounding street as I remained in place watching him.

"Help!" the Unseen screamed. "A madman is trying to kill me!"

A spell filled the store, cast by Jorn, and the dust immediately settled.

The horde of curses trying to kill me were steadily chewing through my mana, so I needed to hurry this up.

"You can safely approach," I called out.

I glanced over my shoulder to see the crowd of students pouring into the street as the locals ran for cover. Whispers broke out as they spotted the black, cursed smoke that now visibly surrounded me. The more knowledgeable students explained what they were all seeing to those who didn't know.

Jorn was at the front of the group frowning, ready to unleash a barrier spell if it became necessary.

"Help me!" The Unseen cried out again.

I turned so I could see my students and the Unseen at the same time. "Welcome to my after-hours lectures on the importance of knowing what you are dealing with when confronting the occult. Beside me is a curse weaver. These creatures level up by cursing others, and a prerequisite of the class requires them to be Unseen."

The Southern students shuddered at my announcement.

"It is important to know that a curse weaver is at their most powerful when they are in their domain, surrounded by the cursed objects they have made. This curse weaver's domain was this shop. As you can see by the visible black smoke that is rising from me, he has already attempted to kill me with these curses, and I have countered this attempt with skilled application of death magic. Are there any questions?"

Heather Winterton's hand shot up from the front row, and I gave her permission to speak. "How are you so calm, Professor?"

"Curse weavers lose the ability to cast spells as they grow stronger. When this happens, they become reliant on their curses. As I've destroyed the objects that the curses trying to harm me came from, he can't pull back these curses and redirect them to another target. He's essentially powerless until his curses kill me."

Jorn's hand shot up. "So, because you knew what he could do, you took the appropriate steps to deal with him safely."

"Yes, it is also why I cannot send his curses back at him stronger like I usually would when dealing with curses. If I did, he would regain control of them."

"How will you deal with him, then?"

"Curse weaver's curses are tied to their maker. They disappear when they die. So, the only way to eliminate the threat of his curses is to kill him."

The Unseen laughed, giving up on playing the victim. "You still have to deal with my death curse."

I raised my hand and shot a finger of destruction at him. The beam of black energy struck him in the chest, and he exploded in a cloud of dust. The black smoke wafting from my body vanished.

"A curse weaver's death curse is not to be trifled with, but it requires a curse weaver to be close to death to create, so killing them instantly mitigates this issue. Are there any more questions?"

Several hands went up as other students vomited.

THEY SAY it's better to ask for forgiveness than permission, especially when you kill a man in the middle of a busy night market. Headmaster Wink glanced at me through the bars of the holding cell the local authorities had put me in and took a swig from his flask. The investigation had already confirmed that the man I killed was an Unseen curse weaver, so I was free to go once the headmaster confirmed my identity.

Investigator Iver waited until the headmaster had lowered his flask. "The students claimed that he is your Defence Against the Dark Arts professor, but we have no record of such a class being taught at Darksmith, Headmaster."

Headmaster Wink sighed. "Vincent changed the name of our Occult Studies class to something he felt was more accurate to what he taught. You can let him out."

Iver scowled. "I can't just let him out. He killed a man."

"You said your cleric investigated the death and confirmed the shopkeeper was an Unseen curse weaver."

"Your students all agree that he entered the shop fully intent on killing the shopkeeper. He even turned the whole event into a lesson for them. His actions were premeditated."

Headmaster Wink took another swig of his flask. "Did he break the law?"

I gave the investigator a lazy smile. "Of course not, it was self-defence."

Iver scowled. "You executed him."

"After he tried to kill me."

"You knew that he couldn't harm you when you walked in there."

"That doesn't negate him trying to kill me or stop my actions from being self-defence. It just means he was an idiot."

"Your own students say he couldn't attack you anymore."

"Only because he was already attacking me. It was costing me quite a lot of mana to hold off that attack, I might add. It wouldn't have been long before the curses burned through my mana, and then I would have died, leaving you to deal with a rampaging curse weaver."

Headmaster Wink turned to the investigator and scowled. "It is my understanding that Professor Vincent has dealt with a curse weaver who has been trying to harm Darksmith's students under your very nose. You are free to hold him if you like, but I will be protesting your actions and bring the full power of my academy's connections against you if you do."

The investigator went pale, quickly placed an amulet against the locking mechanism, and then threw the cell door open. "You don't need to do that." He turned to me. "You're free to go."

I gave Iver a friendly nod as I walked out of the cell and headed for the door. "Thank you for being so understanding."

I could have had the local authorities deal with the curse weaver, but I wanted to leave a lasting impression on everyone. The local antique shopkeepers were greedy rather than malicious. Killing the curse weaver in front of so many witnesses would make sure that they heard about my actions. I expected that would scare them into being a little more careful with what they sold. It would cut down on my workload and make Darksmith safer for Kathrine, so I was very happy with the outcome.

"I want to talk to you about your actions, Professor," Headmaster Wink called after me.

"Can we take a rain check? I still need to talk to a man about a shirt."

8

AN ARMY OF ONE

Ten days after I posted the notice for the Undead Enhancement Club, I hosted the first meeting. It took place in my classroom after dinner. There were plenty of dedicated club rooms I could have used, but I wanted to be closer to Kathrine in case something happened.

I watched as the last student entered my classroom, followed by a zombie wearing a stylish dark blue robe. The young man directed his zombie to the back of the room, where the others were waiting, and found his seat while waving to dozens of students he knew.

His display of control was appalling. A thought was all it usually took to control undead, but some of the students couldn't even do what he'd just done. They had to keep their undead next to them to remain in control, and I noticed several zombies staring at the students with an intense hunger. Almost all undead shared my hunger for life force, even though most of them couldn't draw it out of their victim.

I stood up and cleared my throat, causing instant silence. The monster in me liked how afraid they were.

Every necromancer at Darksmith was from Necropolis, a nearby border city in North Murdell. It was the only place in both nations where Necromancers weren't treated like second-class citizens and the more I learned about the city and its citizens the more I respected it.

Necropolis was run by a group of families called The Grave Diggers' Society. As far as I could tell, they were old necromancer families who shunned the actions most necromancers were known for. They had strict rules that curbed their people's darker tendencies. They enforced these rules to the extreme, leaving their people in constant fear of drawing their attention. The students' inability to control their undead was a byproduct of their mindset. The shunning of the traditional necromancer path left them without these basic skills.

It also led to the necromancers being some of the politest and well-behaved students at Darksmith. Of the two hundred that attended the academy, eighty-two had signed up for my club. That was more than I expected, even though the school didn't offer many extracurricular activities for necromancers.

"Welcome to the first meeting of the Undead Enhancement Club. I'm glad some of you read the signup form correctly and brought along your undead. However, for future reference, any undead that cannot maintain muscle coherence is not permitted. Necromancers have a bad-enough reputation as it is without us being constantly surrounded by the putrid smell of rotting flesh."

Lidia, the eldest daughter of one The Grave Diggers' Society's high council, blushed from the third row. "I brought Mr. Bitey because I wanted to learn how to get rid of that issue."

The red zombie snake sitting on her desk hissed at me, before snapping at the person below. Mr. Bitey's head struck a magical barrier the student had put up after the first attack.

"I'll cover muscle cohesion at our next meeting, and please raise your hand before speaking. Right now, I want a general understanding of everyone's capabilities. Does anyone here not have the create undead skill?"

I could see and feel what most of them were capable of based on the undead they had brought in, but I still needed to go through the motions.

Everyone looked at each other, but no one indicated that they didn't.

"You will not be asked to leave. The minimum requirement for this club is access to death magic. So, who doesn't have create undead?"

Several hands went up.

"Who here has access to create undead skeleton?"

Thirty-two hands went up.

"Who here has access to create undead zombie?"

Eighteen hands went up.

"Does anyone have access to anything more advanced?"

One hand rose.

I pointed to her, indicating for her to share it with the club. "I have access to the create undead zombie knight skill."

"Does anyone think this gives her an advantage?"

Everyone nodded.

Several of the poorly controlled zombies nodded, too.

"Good. You all have common sense. This club is not going to involve a lot of lectures, so bear with me as I run over the basics. There is a long list of undead creatures that a necromancer can create. However, for practical purposes, everything that isn't a skeleton or zombie should be created using another branch of magic. This is because those branches of magic can achieve the same results with a lot less fuss than what we have to go through to do the same. This is also why necromancers generally stick to these two forms of undead, despite having a wider array of options than any other branch of magic. Both forms of undead have practical combat applications, along with a host of other mundane uses. However, for combat purposes, skeletons are superior.

Lidia's hand shot up, and I nodded. "Professor, zombies are better."

I was expecting this. "Are you speaking in a summoning sense or in a crafting sense?

"Both."

"When you're on the battlefield and you need cannon fodder to protect you, summoning a zombie from a corpse makes perfect sense. Zombies have flesh, which makes them both stronger and more resistant to damage, but summoning a zombie is not the same as crafting one. For the same time and resources that it will cost you to craft a zombie, you can craft three skeletons. In a situation like that, the skeletons win."

"Only because it's three vs one. In a one-on-one fight, the zombie wins."

"No. This is where the art of undead enhancement and summoning undead differ. Because skeletons are easier to create, it also means they are easier to enhance. Everyone in this room has the talent to create a skeleton death knight, but only a few of you have what it takes to craft the zombie version. A skeleton death knight will defeat a zombie knight, even though the two share the same resource costs, difficulty to make, and time costs to craft. When it comes to crafting and enhancing undead, skeletons are king. Summoning undead and crafting undead are two entirely separate disciplines and need to be treated as such. Does anyone not understand?"

Half the hands went up.

"Let me put this another way. The difference between summoning undead and crafting undead is like the difference between casting a spell to fly and enchanting an item to make you fly. One is a temporary tool for a temporary solution, and the other one is a tool you intend to use long-term. Yes, as you grow more skilled at summoning undead, they gain more independence, power, and capabilities, but this is a mere shadow of what crafted undead are capable of, which is why these are separate disciplines."

Baris raised his hand, scowling. He was one of my better students and tried to engage me during my Defence Against the Dark Arts classes. "Is crafting undead similar to crafting in general?"

"Yes, and if anyone has a problem with that, they're welcome to leave."

Baris stayed, but a third of the room left. They were rich kids and unwilling to dirty their hands with what they viewed as labour.

I waited until they were all gone before continuing. "While skeletons are preferable for combat, zombies are more intelligent. This makes them preferable for leadership roles."

Baris raised his hand again. "I thought the leadership position is given to the necromancer."

"How many undead can a necromancer typically control at once?"

He frowned. "It depends on what tier of magic they practice, I think."

"Correct. Someone who practices advanced magic can typically control around thirty undead. If you craft thirty intelligent zombies that are capable of directing twenty undead skeletons each, you would effectively be able to control six hundred undead. This is the main benefit of crafting undead and why everyone who left is an idiot."

Baris blew out a breath. "Is that how necromancers raise armies that can topple towns and villages?"

"Yes. Some of them use items, or make dark pacts, but the rest crafted powerful undead minions and used those minions to control others. It's why everyone's afraid of us."

Baris glanced at the other students uncomfortably. "I'm not sure you're allowed to teach us this."

"Crafting an undead army takes time and dedication and usually ends with the creator being hunted down and executed. You're all at Darksmith to learn how to become dangerous individuals. There are a hundred ways you could become monsters from what you learn here, so I'm just giving you one more option."

"I suppose."

"Let's get back to my lecture. Zombies also have one other advantage over skeletons. Because they can be more intelligent and have all the flesh that's needed for fine motor control, they make good assistants. An intelligent zombie can be taught to perform practically any repetitive task. This is useful, because you all have to be concerned about spies or assassins in your households. So, if nothing else, this club will help you improve your own personal security. Does anyone here know the drawbacks from crafting undead out of dungeon monster parts?"

Every hand shot up.

I picked a random young woman because she seemed the most excited.

"Dungeon monsters need a magic-rich environment to survive. Outside of a dungeon, their bodies deteriorate. This deterioration also occurs when they're turned into undead, but not when they are turned into enchanting materials."

"A perfect textbook answer. With the exception of dungeon monsters that contain death magic cores, undead made from dungeon creatures cannot be enhanced to survive outside of dungeons. Those that can be, are usually inferior to undead made from materials from the surface, because they require far more mana to maintain them. However, while they remain in dungeons, they are significantly stronger. For those of you who have crafted a basic-tier undead skeleton before, please collect an instruction sheet from my desk and the monster bones I've provided in the storage bags. For those of you who haven't, please wait until everyone has collected what they need and join me at the front. I'll walk you through the process."

I was down to fifty-eight students. Fifty-seven of them came forward to collect the instructions and bones they needed before returning to their seats. Baris was the only one who didn't know how to create a basic undead skeleton and came down, looking slightly embarrassed to be the odd one out.

My Defence Against the Dark Arts class was a theoretical class, so I hadn't seen my occult educator or educator skills level. Neither skill would level from theoretical teaching until they reached level ten. To work through the lower levels, my students had to achieve tangible results, which was half the reason I'd chosen to create this club.

I gave Baris a friendly smile as he stopped before my desk. "Your family doesn't practice death magic, I take it?"

He sighed. "We do. It's just not the only thing we can practice, so we tend to ignore it."

"You don't sound like you want to be here?"

"I don't. Death magic is nothing but trouble. But my lack of skill is affecting my ability to strengthen my core."

"Why join my club then?"

Baris shrugged. "I like your Defence Against the Dark Arts class. You treat the occult more seriously than anyone I've ever met, and I figured this sort of sensibleness would crossover to your death magic lessons."

"Let's clear up a misunderstanding you have before we begin. The occult is inherently evil in nature. Death magic is not. However, the reason most people view death magic as evil is that it has very few applications that are practical in nature. Most of what you can do with it is destructive. Which means, the only time most people hear about or see death magic used is in a negative fashion. Death magic is no eviler than the other elemental magics."

"I strongly disagree."

"I look forward to changing your mind."

He smiled. "Where do we start?"

I passed him the instructions and pulled a rib bone that weighed close to a pound from one of the storage pouches. "It's a common misconception that human-shaped undead skeletons require human bones. They don't. However, *sapient* skeletons *do* require their bones be from sapient creatures. And certain creatures, like lich and dracolich, can only come from humans and dragons. Any questions so far?"

"No, professor."

"Good. The first step to crafting an undead skeleton properly is making and enriching bonemeal. This is done through the basic bonemeal spell. You will find the spell on the handout."

"Does using human bones make stronger undead?"

He asked good questions. "It's easier to strengthen undead crafted from human bones, especially bones of someone who had a magical talent, but it's not necessary to use them. Outside of making sapient undead, the skeletons made from human, animal, or monster bones have the same maximum limit to their strength."

"Is the same true for zombies?"

"No. Materials are incredibly important when it comes to creating zombies and explaining that topic would involve weeks of lectures. So, I won't be explaining any of that today."

I placed the rib bone on the desk in front of me and cast the 1st-rank bonemeal spell. It crumbled to a sand-like consistency. I pushed it into a pile with my hands and then cast the spell two more times at the 2nd and 3rd rank, and then three times at the intermediate-tier ranks. Then three more times at the advanced-tier ranks. The bone fragments changed with each spell, finally becoming a fine white powder.

Baris frowned. "Why did you cast the spell nine times?"

"The bonemeal spell, like the bolt spell, has fifteen different rank variations for the spell. These go all the way up to the peak of the master tier, though few know those master-rank spells anymore. Each spell builds on the previous one, and while it costs more mana, performing each variation of the spell makes the materials more refined and enriched."

I pulled out another rib and repeated the process.

"Why enrich it?"

"There is always magical leakage when you create undead. The material we use isn't suited to death magic. Enriching or enhancing the material before you make your creation requires more work, but the end results are a more powerful undead creation."

"Is that why some necromancers destroy their undead?"

"Yes. Each time you turn a corpse into a zombie, the materials become slightly more receptive to death magic. The same is true for skeletons."

"Why not do that then?"

"Why not do both?"

His eyebrows rose. "You can do both?"

"Yes. The skeleton everyone is crafting today is going to be used over and over. Each enhancement will make it slightly stronger, until it becomes something none of you ever thought possible."

Baris didn't seem to like my answer. "Why make it out of dungeon monster bones then?"

"This club is here to teach you how to craft undead. If you know your creation won't be leaving the academy with you, then you won't be concerned about pushing the boundaries."

"That seems like a lot of wasted work."

"It's called *practice*, and *good practice* occasionally results in failure. Would you consider the mana you expend practicing a spell wasted work, or would you consider it practice? Obviously, you would consider it practice. Just because there can be lasting results, doesn't mean they need to be kept, and sometimes, the fact that they can be kept slows the learning process."

Baris watched in silence while I finished making nine pounds of bonemeal. Eventually, a large pile sat in front of us. "Now what happens?"

"Now we put it back together in the shape we want. There are two ways to do this. There are the fifteen bone stitch spells that require you to make one bone at a time and can be performed through the ranks to enhance what you're doing. Then there is the form skeleton spell that allows you to do it all at once, which also has fifteen ranks. Knowing what you do now, which method do you think is better?"

Baris grinned. "Trick question. You use the form skeleton spell to get the proportions right, and then you break each bone down with the bonemeal spells and use the bone stitch spells to reform them."

"There are 206 bones in the human body. That is 1,854 basic, intermediate, and advanced spells to break down the bones with the bonemeal spell and the exact same number to recreated them with the bone stitch spell. Do you think this is an appropriate use of your time?"

He gave me an unhappy expression. "No."

"Wrong. This club is about learning undead enhancement, and the best way to learn that is to practice."

He ran his hand through his hair, exasperated by my comment. "Do you have any idea how long that will take?"

"Do you have any idea how much your spell efficiency will improve if you practice that much?"

He shook his head.

"Every bone in the human body has a unique shape. That is 206 unique shapes you have to create nine times using different spells. If you successfully reach the advanced stage, you will have the sort of control that literally halves the mana cost of any death spell you cast. If you reach the expert stage, spells will cost you a third. If you reach the peak of the master stage, you will have enough control to cast any spell with the minimum required mana."

"So, it's going to be tough?"

"No. It's going to be excruciating."

Baris began to smile again. "But the reward will be worth it. That sort of efficiency is something only an archsorcerer is capable of."

"Only if you practice." I brushed the bonemeal into one large pile in the middle of my desk, so we could move on. "The form skeleton spell creates a replica of your skeleton, or the skeleton of someone you are touching. It will interest you to know that this spell is one of the few death spells that has a practical medical application. If someone has a fracture or minor broken bone, you can use this spell to repair the damage."

His eyebrows rose again. "You can heal a broken bone with death magic?"

"Yes, but only if it's a fracture or a minor break. You can only use the 1st-rank spell to do so, and you have to draw the death magic out of the patient once the spell is complete, so they don't become sick."

"Why can't you heal a major break?"

"Because the bones will pull back together, even if muscle is in the way. This can cause a lot of damage if there are bones shards throughout the patient's muscles." I could see he didn't understand. "It's easier to understand if I show you."

I gathered my will and cast form skeleton nine times.

The bonemeal flowed like water, forming a replica of my skeleton on the desk. Despite teeth not being bones, the spell didn't differentiate, and my sharper-than-normal canines appeared in the skeleton's mouth. I hadn't expected that to happen.

I quickly picked up one of my leg bones and snapped it into pieces.

Baris raised an eyebrow. "You invested in strength?"

While he was distracted, I cast the bone stitch spell and changed the shape of my fangs to normal canines. "The necromancer class gives three more attributes than the sorcerer class, despite them both being a basic practitioner class. This is to balance out the limitations of our class. Investing those attributes into your physical capabilities is not something most will regret and isn't encouraged enough." I laid out the broken shards of leg bone on the desk, leaving a few inches between them. "This is why you don't use the form skeleton spell to repair major breaks."

I cast form skeleton again.

The bone shards pulled together with a violent snap.

I pointed to the repaired bone. "Imagine what that would look like with muscle in the way."

Baris winced. "I see your point. You would have to alter the spell to be gentler, in order to repair major breaks."

"Do that on your own time. This is an undead enhancement club, not a medical studies club. Normally, I would suggest you begin studying the spells in the handout, but I'm about to do something you likely won't see anywhere else. With enough practice and a larger core, you can replicate my feat."

"What are you going to do?"

"Just watch."

I stared at the skeleton as I accelerated my focus, drawing on my agility. The room slowed down as my thinking speed sped up. Everyone began to move in slow motion as I allowed my agility to push me to my limits.

I hadn't been exaggerating when I told Baris that creating a skeleton this way would improve his spell efficiency. Mine was currently atrocious, and I'd adapted this method for myself, not for the class. I would have done this alone, but I wanted to improve my educator skill.

As I began casting spells, I pulled in ambient mana to offset the mana cost. Switching between the bonemeal and bone stitch spell wasn't easy, even though I was casting each spell slowly to be as effective and efficient as I could. Between each spell, I assessed what I was doing and tried to make improvements based on everything my memories told me.

Everyone's body reacted slightly differently when they performed a spell. Longer or shorter arms and legs meant mana had to travel further or shorter distances, before escaping the body, and this resulted in different timings for each spell. In addition, your mana network and core affected everything, so just because I had memories of sorcerers who had been able to perform spells at only a third of the traditional mana cost, that didn't mean *I* could. But I could learn, and lifetimes of practice shrunk the learning curve.

One by one, each bone crumbled into bonemeal before reforming back in their original shape. Someone with the skill I claimed to have, could cast a 1st-ranked spell in under a second, so the bonemeal had barely fallen apart before it was forced back together.

It took me less than five minutes to go through the entire skeleton with the 1st-rank spells, and my efficiency had improved by the end of it. Moulding my magic to each shape was significantly more difficult than performing the exact same bolt spell over and over again, which was why I was seeing more improvement.

I began casting the 2nd-rank versions.

This method for enhancing skeletons was developed by Contessa. She hadn't created the original method, but she had expanded upon the original creators' theories and proven them to be true. Casting the bonemeal spell at each different rank before you created the skeleton made a layered structure in the bone that was sort of like rebar used in concrete. Breaking each bone down and then bone stitching them back together strengthened each subsequent layer, providing more reinforcement.

When I finished the 2nd-rank, I moved on to the 3rd; by the time I reached the 4th, most of the class had stopped what they were doing to sit and watch. By the time I reached the 5th, they were all watching. I reached the 7th-rank before the end of the first hour and 9th rank just after the end of the second.

As the last bone flowed back together, I stood up and looked at the class. "Are there any questions?"

Every hand shot up.

I pointed to Lidia.

"How much of a difference will what you just did make to your skeleton?"

"If I make no other alterations, the base attributes of this skeleton will double. However, this enhancement is just the primer to larger enhancements that wouldn't be possible otherwise. This skeleton has far more potential than most."

I pointed to another student.

"Professor, how big is your core? That was insane."

"I'm not going to answer that. Are there any questions about what I just showed you?"

"Sir, why did your spell efficiency improve while you worked?"

I was hoping they wouldn't notice that. "As you master each rank of these spells, you will become more efficient at casting death magic spells. I wanted to demonstrate what mastering this method would look like, so you would understand what sort of improvement you should expect."

My answer seemed to intimidate them, because they dropped their hands.

"I will now be using the create undead skeleton spell, using a spell variation of my own creation. Do *not* attempt to replicate this method, as the backlash will kill you."

I held my hand above the skeleton, multicasting all nine ranks of the create undead skeleton spell simultaneously, layering them into each other so they reinforced each other's structure. I'd learned this layered method from studying the enchantments Lavire had placed on my equipment.

This layered spell technique was why I went through the trouble of breaking down and rebuilding everything. Those steps would theoretically allow me to layer the same spells over each other more easily, enhancing my undead creation.

As my magic infused the bones, black orbs filled its bleached white eye sockets. A moment later, a notification appeared.

You have mastered your Create Undead skill.
You have mastered your Create Undead Skeleton skill.
Your Enhance Undead skill has increased to level 10.
You have mastered your Prodigy skill.

I'd been hoping my vampiric thirst skill wouldn't stretch into these skills and would finally allow my prodigy skill to level. The memories my vampiric thirst skill had given me had nothing to do with creating undead, but I wasn't sure how much that mattered.

It had managed to cross over into my regular spell work, because of the similarities across all schools of magic, but this was different enough that it didn't count. If this hadn't worked, then I would have been cut off from making any progress on the prodigy skill with magic. While my efforts weren't as impressive as Davina's, they were still impressive enough to master the prodigy skill.

I smiled, happy to see I was right, and dismissed the notification, only for another to notification to appear, which killed my fleeting happiness.

Congratulations, you have leveled your Hero class.
Your class has leveled.
You are now a level 36 hero.

Your class has leveled and unlocked a new skill.
Create Vampire

You have 20 attribute points to spend.

The sight of my first vampiric skill didn't please me. The reason I'd earned my new skill was currently in a medically induced coma in the apartment above me, missing weeks of her life because of what I'd done. There were also other concerns its appearance raised, but those could be dealt with later, if those concerns turned out to be a pattern rather than an anomaly.

I repressed a sigh, dismissed the notification, and returned my attention to the crowd of fascinated necromancers. I willed my new creation to climb off the table and stand behind me. Now that I had shown them what they were aiming for, it was time to motivate them.

Two weeks later, I looked around Darksmith's basement training hall and saw nothing but grinning faces. Some of them had been here for hours and were already drunk. The undead they'd crafted stood against the far wall, completely under their control, which was a good improvement.

I rolled my eyes at the crowd. "I see a lot of new faces today, which tells me we need to go over the rules again."

Several necromancers snickered.

"The first rule of Undead Fight Club is you do not talk about Undead Fight Club. The second rule of Undead Fight Club, is you do not talk about Undead Fight Club! The third rule is the fight doesn't stop until the complete destruction of one undead. Fourth rule is only two undead to a fight, unless it's a demonstration fight. Fifth rule, only one fight at a time. Sixth rule, the fight is between undead only; outside influence is strictly prohibited, including using enhancing techniques or spells that are beyond what I've taught you in Undead Enhancement Club. Seventh rule, beer and betting are not encouraged; they are required."

The last rule was just so Undead Fight Club could have seven rules like Fight Club. But it made the club a lot more fun. And made it easier for my instructor skill to level.

Enhancing undead without showing the students the differences in power was a great way to make everyone give up. Running a second club where the students could battle their undead while drinking and making bets was the perfect way to build their competitive spirit and validate their work. Suddenly, the painstaking hours they spent casting spells over and over had purpose and became entertaining as they dreamed of returning to the next Undead Fight Club and scoring that win. Hosting the club in the basement also meant I was on hand if anything happened to Kathrine.

All of the students who had left the Enhance Undead Club had returned, so they could gain access to the Undead Fight Club. And many students who hadn't attended the first meeting now did. The Enhance Undead Club now met three times a week, and every meeting was full. There wasn't a necromancer at Darksmith who didn't attend.

I had eight students I was working with personally, which was finally making my educator skill improve. And running these fights counted as combat practice, so I was improving my instructor skill. The three nights also covered the extracurricular activities I had to do, so everything, except Kathrine's condition, was going to plan.

I glared around me at the smiling faces, until someone was smart enough to run forward with a beer. This made everyone laugh as my false anger faded. "Who would like to make the first challenge?"

Professor Fergus, the head of the necromancy department, stepped forward. "I challenge you, professor."

Everyone cheered.

My advanced skeleton was the reigning champion, and more than a few were a little sour about this. Between each Undead Fight Club, I broke my skeleton down and repeated all of its enhancements. With two of these events each week, it was on its fifth generation.

Professor Fergus had showed up just before the third meeting, joining both clubs. Officially, he was my co-professor. In reality, he was a man-child who wanted to battle undead for the fun of it.

I mentally instructed my skeleton to enter the ring and fight the other undead to the best of its ability. It gracefully walked into the ring, moving with smooth, fluid motions. It was completely different to most of the skeletons in the room, which had slow, shambling steps and movements. Only the students who had reached the intermediate stage had skeletons that could move as naturally as a normal person, but none of them had the gracefulness that mine showed.

Professor Fergus grinned, sweeping back his dark fringe, before waving forward the massive crate he'd brought to the basement. The crate levitated off the ground and slowly hovered towards him. It stopped near the edge of the ring and the sides fell open, revealing a huge intermediate skeleton. It rose to its feet, standing twenty feet tall.

"Cheater," a drunk necromancer roared.

Professor Fergus continued to grin. "I haven't cheated. I've just been a little more creative with my spells than the rest of you."

"That thing is massive! How is that not cheating?"

I returned Professor Fergus's grin and then turned to the drunk necromancer. "Professor Fergus used the bone stitch spell to alter the size of his skeleton, which is a spell everyone has access to. He's followed the Undead Fight Club's rules to the letter. How large you make each bone, along with its shape, has always been up to you."

"We can do that. Fuck yeah!"

"Language."

The drunk necromancer immediately sobered. "Sorry, sir."

I turned back to Professor Fergus. "What are we betting?"

"A small keg of Cristoriazan Ale."

I hadn't tried it, but I'd heard it was good. "Deal." I was going to lose badly, but that didn't bother me. It would encourage the others to try harder and give me more levels.

Professor Fergus nodded to his creation, and it stepped into the ring. The runes on the floor lit up, blocking our control, and sealing the combatants inside the barrier. My skeleton didn't even come up to its waist.

What followed was a good old-fashioned beatdown, where my skeleton ran around in circles, trying to dodge the giant skeleton, while hacking at its knee with only its fists. The first time my skeleton failed to dodge, it was kicked into the barrier, and then it was all over. The next few minutes were filled with laughter as Fergus's skeleton crushed mine underfoot.

Everyone cheered as I stepped into the ring with a brush and shovel and began sweeping my skeleton up. There were a few catcalls and crude jokes as I put the pieces of crushed bone into a bag, but it was all in good fun.

Professor Fergus, being a good sport, held the bag for me. "Are you going to warn them that making a skeleton that large makes them harder to control?"

I snorted. "Only a few of them have the patience to spend that much time refining bonemeal, and they're all aware of the difficulties."

"You don't seem upset?"

I grinned. "I was waiting for someone to get creative. Now we get to see what they're really capable of." I put the last of my skeleton into the bag and turned to the crowd. "Who's next?"

9

BAD PLANS AND HIGH JINKS

Every morning, before classes started, the faculty got together for a risk assessment briefing. Teaching thousands of wealthy students how to harness advanced magic in a confined space came with many risks, so everyone needed to be aware of what disaster we should expect next. Without constant oversight, Darksmith could easily be pulled into a snowball event that led to everyone's death.

As I walked through the door into the massive staff room, Professor Fergus caught my shoulder and dragged me over to the bar.

Finding a fully stocked bar in the staff room had seemed odd to me my first morning, until I realised that most of the professors shared the headmaster's stress level. Students were always getting up to something, trying to use their wealth to shortcut a new skill level, forcing growth they hadn't earned. On top of that, there were the numerous magical accidents, so the professors were always waiting for the next crisis.

Fergus and I ended up in the drinks line behind Professor Burdin, the head of the exorcism department. He was someone I would have preferred to keep away from today. The muscular cleric had bags under his eyes and a grim expression as he talked to the other members of his department. They were all equally tired. I'd listened to them performing an exorcism most of the night, pitting their wills against the demon that had possessed one of the cleaners.

The demon they were exorcising had implied that it knew I was here, and I didn't want to get on the man's radar with that still fresh in his mind. A week from now there would be another crisis that would distract him and his department, but not today.

Fergus pulled me closer while we waited. "A mutual friend told me that you were sourcing materials for creating zombies. Since I know you don't intend to go that route with the club, I can only assume you're doing something interesting. *I want in.*"

I hadn't run out of tasks to do yet, but I was trying to find new jobs that would keep me from succumbing to the Curse of Sloth. Crafting more complex undead zombies was a lot more tedious and time-consuming than creating skeletons, and it would both fill up my time and work toward my goals.

I took Fergus's hand off my shoulder. "What makes you think I'm doing something interesting?"

He gave a single dead chuckle. "Because you can't help it, Vincent. You're an overachiever. The mundane will never interest you. Now, what are you up to?"

"I'm studying the living dead."

He frowned. "You need cadavers for that, and the headmaster has a ban on cadavers."

"Only if you want to craft something sapient, and I don't want to do that. They take too long to train, and I don't have that much spare time."

Fergus shrugged. "I still want in."

"Do you have the skill?"

"Do you?"

The line moved forward as he asked his question, and we stopped our conversation while we grabbed something to drink. Holding up the line for the bar was a taboo around here. Fergus went for a stein of barley beer, while I picked up a goblet of red wine.

My first morning, I hadn't drunk anything, which caused many of the professors to snicker. They told me that my drinking habits would soon change. I'd overheard enough conversations to know that everyone started out sober, but no one lasted long, requiring a little buzz to get through the day, so I started drinking in my second week to keep up appearances.

The stress level for this job was too high for a normal person. Untrained sorcerers got into all sorts of trouble while they were learning advanced magic, so you had to do something to cope.

For Darksmith, that meant day drinking.

We took our drinks to a pair of empty chairs at the back of the room. Darksmith had almost six hundred professors and twice as many cleaners. The cleaners didn't have to intervene if the students did something stupid or made a mistake, so their risk assessment meetings were only held every second day. They had their own meeting room, because they needed more space, and I'd been told they had a better bar selection. They'd negotiated for it in their contracts, which was a sore spot for most professors.

Fergus took a long drink and smacked his lips. "So, do you have the create living dead skill or not?"

"I don't."

"Then you'll be no better at creating them than I am. So let me help?"

Fergus was the only other necromancer on staff, and he was treated like a second-class citizen because of it. The other professors shunned him the way they shunned me. The man was looking for a friend, and I was the only person who fit the criteria. He was being painfully obvious about it, too.

The monster in me wanted to exploit his weakness and bend him to my will. The man I'd once been was conflicted. On the one hand, Fergus needed a friend, and since he seemed nice enough, I should give him a chance. On the other hand, I was here to protect Kathrine, and the longer he spent around me, the more likely he was to notice something was off about me.

Also, I couldn't give him the sort of friendship he needed. I wasn't capable of that. But I could spend some time with him and use him to further the projects I was working on. It might make him feel a little less lonely.

"I would prefer not working with a partner," I said, honestly.

Fergus's face fell.

"However, would you be interested in replicating my research and comparing notes? I'm curious to see how easily it can be replicated."

He began to smile again and took another drink. He wiped his mouth with the back of his sleeve and grinned. "How would this work?"

"I'll create my project. Then I'll create it a second time while you're present, and then you'll go off and use my techniques to replicate the work, making notes for any issues you face. I'm trying to simplify the process for creating the living dead."

Used properly, the undead would be able to make the world a lot safer for my family, but I needed to work at scale, and that required being able to teach others what they needed to know, or crafting living dead who could craft undead for me.

Fergus paused. "Is this similar to the way you're simplifying enhancing undead skeletons for the club?"

"I wouldn't call that simplifying, more like teaching necromancers how to do it correctly."

Fergus snorted at my reply. "You would think that."

I raised an eyebrow questioningly.

"Vincent, you've got a wider knowledge base than anyone I've ever met. I wouldn't be surprised if you told me a lich taught you everything you knew." He nudged my arm with his elbow as he chuckled. "No one has a teaching philosophy on this subject, except you. Everyone just gets by with using separate techniques and trying to force them to work together."

Which led to far too many abominations being created, in my opinion.

I drained my goblet and placed it under my seat. "Once you've studied enough techniques, you'll see a pattern that makes sense. Also, most of my knowledge on the subject comes from the Bo Empire.

Their necromancers have a lot more freedom and are more highly regarded than we are."

That was where Contessa came from, so it wasn't a lie.

"That would have been my second guess," he said. "I would love to know how you managed to get one of them to part with their knowledge."

"She had something I wanted. I had something she wanted. It's honestly not that interesting."

Fergus roared with laughter, thinking I was implying sexual favours. "Why am I not surprised. Now how old are we talking?" He leaned in closer. "Be honest. I'm not judging."

"Ancient."

By the time Fergus had stopped laughing, Headmaster Wink was heading for the podium. The last of the professors found their seats as he placed down his notes.

Wink had his customary glass of gin in hand as he opened his notes and sighed. "Another day, another idiot trying to kill us all." Magic projected his voice through the room, causing everyone to chuckle. "Professor Trip would like me to remind everyone that he's halfway through his demon summoning course with the second-year students, and that you should be on the lookout for students showing signs of succubus and incubus addiction, along with any student with rapid development in their magical abilities. Also, there has been a slightly higher than usual rate of demonic possession of late, due to a weakening of the barrier between Darksmith and Hell. Our running theory is that a student attempted a lesser demon summoning on their own time and accidently summoned a true demon, weakening the barrier."

There were lesser demons that came from tortured souls, and then demons that had always been demons. True demon was just the local naming convention for demons.

Professor Burdin stood up. "Last night my department dealt with a rider demon that was possessing a cleaner. The demon claimed that it came here because it sensed the presence of demonic royalty within Darksmith, which is concerning. For those of you who don't know, riders are lesser demons and not the smartest of lesser demons, but they are totally subservient to demonic royalty. So, if demonic royalty was here, even for a moment, we'll be dealing with them for a decade. I'm inclined to think that a student has brought something a royal demon may have touched, as the presence of such a powerful entity would not go unnoticed with Darksmith's defences."

Dalin glanced at him from across the room. "An ancient vampire could walk these halls, and we would be none the wiser."

Professor Burdin scoffed back at the head of the infirmary. "An ancient vampire wouldn't cause a rider to take notice. They might be pseudo true demons, but they sit low within demonic hierarchy."

Dalin sighed but nodded. "It was just a thought."

Headmaster Wink cleared his throat. "Would this object cause the weakness in the barrier, Professor Burdin?"

The cleric paused. "It's possible, if it was a summoning aid."

"Please put together a description of such an object, so the cleaners can be on the lookout for it. Now to the main news of the day. The potions department has begun teaching the fourth years advanced potion making. Incorrectly stored advanced potions can result in all sorts of unpleasant consequences, so be ready for explosions, blizzards, and anything else you can think of. In addition, the third years began studying mind illusions yesterday. Professor Brat forgot to inform us. We've already had eight instances of students either caught within their own illusions or someone else's."

Fergus created a small sound barrier, so his voice wouldn't carry. "Slow day, it seems."

I shrugged. "The mid-year exams are coming up soon, and most of the faculty don't want to distract their students with new subjects."

Darksmith was a five-year school, but even with five years there wasn't enough time for the students to learn everything. It took all that time just to cover every subject and push the majority of students to a mid-advanced understanding, which was 8th-ranked spells. To get to the 9th-rank, they had to teach themselves.

It was an intense curriculum, but the students left with a broad understanding of everything they could do, and the knowledge of where their strengths and weaknesses lay. They would push for expert understanding with private tutors, so that their competition didn't know where their true strength lay.

"You're being too modest, Vincent," Fergus replied. "You've been purging curses so quickly that our students aren't making half the poor decisions they were making before you got here."

"Yet, I'm still finding dozens of new curses every day."

"Well, that's to be expected. Evil always finds its way into the hands of the influential, and Darksmith has the highest concentration of influence in Murdell."

"It doesn't help that both sides are funnelling cursed objects into the town so that the students pick them up."

"That's never been proven."

"We'll know in a few months. Between killing that curse weaver and throwing so many curses back at their makers, the number of people willing to make them is going to start dropping very soon."

"You're going to make powerful enemies if you keep going."

I chuckled. "They can get in line."

TWO WEEKS LATER, Fergus looked around my workshop and shuddered. Progressing from crafting undead skeletons to crafting the living dead was too large a jump in skill for me to pull off, so I'd been playing around with zombies for a little bit. I'd crafted sixteen zombie versions of myself, using a tissue sample, a large vat of alchemy reagents, and a small herd of dead pigs. The sixteen clones lay on dissection tables or hung from meat hooks. They were all attached to monitoring equipment. Some had their entire bodies. Others didn't. They were all animated, so their eyes followed us wherever we went.

"I'm beginning to reconsider whether or not I should help you," Fergus said, looking rather pale. "This room is going to give me nightmares."

"Blame the headmaster."

"What?"

"Wink underplayed how many students were curious about my private occult library and failed to mention that there is a long-standing tradition at Darksmith where fifth-year students try to steal a book from it. I've had a break-in attempt twice a week since I arrived here. Those attempts stopped shortly after I began these experiments."

"I don't follow."

"Most of the students that try to break into my library come through my workshop, so the first one to enter after I began my experiments had a panic attack when she found that zombie version of me half-dissected on that table over there. She was so upset that she went to the headmaster and confessed what she'd done, demanding I be let go. The headmaster talked with me about what I was doing, and found the student's panic funny, so he asked me to increase the number of experiments and make this room as nightmarish as possible. The break-ins have stopped, for the most part."

Fergus looked around. "I'm not sure if I should be amused or disturbed."

"Why not both?"

He smirked, until he glanced at the one without skin, and quickly covered his mouth.

"You'll get used to it," I said.

"I don't think I will. I'm looking at you in a half-dissected state on one table, another version that has your organs stretched outside your body, and one that has been cut down the middle and pulled apart. I think I'm going to throw up."

I passed him a bucket and he emptied his stomach. It was loud, messy, and smelly until he broke down the vomit with a basic necrotic spell.

Fergus rose, wiped his mouth, and stared at me. "What are you trying to achieve, beyond scaring the students?"

I pointed to the one that was half-dissected. "Over there, I'm testing a method to improve muscle cohesion." I pointed to the one with the organs all outside its body. "That one is for studying regeneration properties. And that one is a technique for using a mana-integrated nervous system to make a zombie move while dismembered.

It's actually the most interesting. Despite being cut in half, it has complete control over both halves."

Curiosity replaced disgust as Fergus turned to look at the experiment. "It's still in control of both halves?"

"Yes."

He moved closer to investigate, touching the halves and casting a basic scanning spell. "This is fascinating. How does it work? No. No. How did you do it?"

"I grafted a mana thread network onto its nervous system with the enchanters' table, before animating it. The mana thread can stretch far enough that the brain remains in control of the body, even when pieces are separated. This is my second experiment."

"What was the first?"

"I dismembered it and spread the limbs. The number of pieces and the distance drastically increases the mana cost for keeping it animated. It ran out of mana within the day, when it should have been able to lay there for over a year."

"Fascinating. I mean, it's still ghastly, but it's fascinating."

"Thank you. I put a lot of effort into making this room terrifyingly educational."

Fergus didn't chuckle, but he nodded. "So, where is the experiment?"

"This way."

I led him to a sheet-covered table at the back of the workshop. The main difference between the living dead and the undead was the need for mana. The living dead didn't need it to survive. Their biological functions worked, which allowed them to be a lot more versatile. That versatility came at the cost of strength. An undead zombie was almost always more powerful than the living dead when first created, but the living dead could level their class, not just their skills, so with enough time and effort they would be stronger.

I pulled the old sheet off my research project, exposing the nine-foot-tall Anubis-looking creation. Its fur was entirely black with an elongated snout and thick layers of muscle. It was humanoid with ten fingers and ten toes, but all were tipped with claws. It would never carry a weapon, because it wouldn't be smart enough for that, but it would be able to open and close doors.

Fergus glanced at my creation and then at me. "Did you craft this from dogs?"

"Yes. Despite the change in appearance, it still thinks and behaves like a dog, so it's pack-oriented, which will make it easier to control. The enlarged brain makes it slightly smarter, but not by much."

Fergus nodded. "Does it need to be taught to stand on two legs?"

"Yes."

"What's the purpose of such a creature?"

"Home security. Its sense of smell is much stronger than ours, so it will know if someone is hiding under an invisibility spell. It can also be taught to track specific types of monsters, making it easier to hunt them."

Fergus ran his hand over its arms and legs. "It's got a lot of muscle, but its skin isn't much thicker than human skin. Was that intentional?"

"It was."

"Why?"

"Temporary lack of talent. I understand how to enhance skeletons, and these experiments helped me understand how to enhance muscles. Organs will be my next area of focus."

Fergus nodded. "Alright, let's get started."

10

TRANSFER STUDENTS

Six weeks had gone by since I had to put Kathrine to sleep and there was almost no change to her soul. The damage I'd done was too extensive. She wasn't getting better on her own. She needed Davina or Father to help her. The knowledge in my head told me they were her best hope. Contessa's library was unsurprisingly light on the sort of information that would help Kathrine, and the adventurer guild's library only brushed the surface, so I didn't know what else I could do. Dalin didn't know either.

Riza had stopped by several times to check on Kathrine, loudly stating where she was going so several people knew where she was if she disappeared. She offered to take Kathrine to the church to help speed up her recovery, but I wasn't willing to let her. The clerics there might not know what they were doing, and that could make her worse.

All I could do was wait.

Dalin noticed me as I walked into the infirmary, scowling at everything around me. A handful of beds were occupied today, so the staff were more active than usual. The patients were my fault. Learning Kathrine still wasn't recovering had left me in a foul mood, and for the past several days I hadn't bothered to restrain myself when I returned the curses to their creators.

I nodded to the box I was carrying. "I've got another batch of cursed items for you."

Dalin returned my scowl with his own. "Can't you see, I'm dealing with your latest cursed student? His genitals are shrinking as we speak."

The terrified young man began hyperventilating. "They're still shrinking!"

I chuckled.

"Don't you dare laugh! I don't know what you did to empower this curse, but I'm not entirely sure I can remove it."

"You can't remove it! No. No. No. This can't be happening." He began rocking back and forth.

I continued to chuckle, amused by his suffering. He'd gone so far across the line that it was socially acceptable for me to revel in his misery. Even some of the staff were smirking, and they were members of the church.

I drew Dalin's attention back to the reason I was here. "I've got six items that need their curses lifted, so I can safely return my students' property. And I need to make sure everyone came in to be cleansed." I held out the list of students to him.

Dalin waved over one of his assistants, who took the list and went to check it against the logbook.

As the assistant walked away, magic filled the academy and then Headmaster Wink's voice boomed through every building. "Would senior staff and the duelling club please make their way to the main auditorium."

Dalin sighed. "That's us."

He levitated off the ground and started flying to the door. Unlike a lot of clerics, Dalin had studied the other branches of magic he had access to and was quite proficient. I ran behind him, following him out of the infirmary.

"What about my penis!"

Neither of us stopped.

Dalin turned down several hallways and then flew out a window. I leapt after him, casting a basic levitate spell to slow my descent before

I hit the ground. Dalin had only cast the intermediate version of the fly spell, so he wasn't very fast. I kept up, without it being obvious how high my strength and agility were.

Darksmith was spread across more than a dozen buildings, with the auditorium near the gate. The open spaces were filled with tables, chairs, and crystal gardens so students could study outdoors. The alarm was a common enough occurrence that most hadn't looked up from their work.

Professors and students flew or ran towards the auditorium at full speed, descending on the building like bees at a picnic. I was far from the last one there, running into the building and taking a seat at the back like so many others. Dalin headed for the front.

Wink stood on the stage, discussing the situation with a group of professors from the scrying department. This was a minor call to arms, which meant something had gone wrong in the dungeon and some students needed to be rescued. The only thing that made this alarm different was that only senior staff and the duelling club were called.

Wink didn't wait for everyone to arrive, stepping away from his conversation when only a third were in attendance. "We've got a massive, time-sensitive problem. The floor boss you've all heard about has climbed up to the dungeon again and attacked a party that was training near the entrance to the Abyss. It has four of our students trapped."

Professor Stint threw up her arms. "They're dead. It's very sad, but fighting a floor boss from the Abyss will get more people killed, even if we make it in time."

Wink ignored her. "The party has several VIP students among it, and a scrying spell has confirmed they had a greater barrier scroll with them that the monster hasn't penetrated. The party is made up of the Darklord's daughter, Celest; Duke Kran's daughter, Lora; Baron Graynor's daughter, Erin; and Merchant Pim's daughter, Penelope."

Those were some of the most important students Darksmith had. There was no doubt in my mind that they were going to kill Gorgath to get them back.

The kid being in danger snapped me out of my mood.

Without stopping to consider the consequences, I cast the deadlands spell, entering the Deadlands in a room full of sorcerers who knew what that meant. The world was plunged into a black and white scene devoid of colour, as everything around me slowed to a crawl, moving at a third of their normal pace. The life force inside me began to leak out in a slow trickle.

I blurred, sprinting out of the building and academy. I didn't slow as I entered the tunnel, nor when I passed through the fortress and dungeon chamber, nor when I overtook the quick-reaction rescue team that was stationed in the fortress.

I passed through a series of tunnels before I reached the one that led to the Abyss and kept going. I was the first to arrive in the tunnel, and I immediately spotted the party standing behind Celest. The young genius was protecting them from Gorgath, and the greater barrier she'd raised was still intact.

A wave of relief washed through me as I examined the situation, ignoring the mangled black spirits that were crawling over the dead monsters like fleas, feeding on the corpses' fleeing life force.

Celest was out front holding the burning spell scroll that maintained their barrier. The pulverised remains of the creatures that had climbed out of the Abyss lay in puddles all around the magical sphere, as Gorgath towered above them, bringing his fists down as he attempted to break the barrier. By the way the barrier rippled, this wasn't the first time he had struck it.

He'd clearly killed most of the creatures that had attacked them. But I don't think he'd attacked the party immediately, because even a greater barrier wouldn't survive this sort of punishment for more than a few minutes. So, something had triggered him to attack.

I had a feeling it was him finding out about the existence of the academy or them being sorcerers. The grin on his face was far too excited.

I put myself between the barrier and Gorgath and then stepped out of the Deadlands. As I appeared in the real world, I triple cast the deathlock spell, creating three jet-black barriers above me. Gorgath's fists smashed through the first two, only just being stopped by the third. I cast the spell three more times to pin his arms and back, along with a silence spell to cut off the sound coming from his mouth.

I turned to Celest. “Fly, you fools!”

Her companions didn’t need to be told twice, unleashing the flying spell they’d prepared. Celest dropped the barrier and all four of them shot down the tunnel, as fast as their spells would carry them.

When they were out of sight, I turned to glare at Gorgath, dropping the silence spell. He’d frozen the moment he realised I was here. Before he said anything, I threw a massive death wave spell. The magic crashed through the tunnel, decaying any magic it touched, withering the corpses, and making it impossible for anyone to scry on us for the next fifteen minutes.

Then I folded my arms. “Explain yourself.”

Gorgath swallowed nervously as he shattered my barriers to free himself. “Gorgath was not going to hurt them. Gorgath noticed they were in distress when he was coming to visit, so protected them. Gorgath was only going to take them, so he could learn their magic, and then trade them with their academy for more spells.”

Five minutes arounds humans, and the kid was running a racketeering business. He knew about the academy, but I believed him when he said he wasn’t going to harm them. He was a smart kid, and his people didn’t seem to believe in needless bloodshed.

“I’m their guardian, Gorgath. Do you understand what that means?”

He nodded, even more nervously.

I held his gaze. “You protected them, but then you tried to take them. One action cancels the other. I owe you no debt or retribution. Nothing has changed between us.”

Gorgath grinned, losing his nervousness. “Vincent did not mention that he was staying at a place where Gorgath could learn spells.”

“This is the way.”

Gorgath paused, thinking over his statement, and then nodded. Among his people, children were supposed to learn on their own, so my not mentioning was expected. The real reason I hadn’t mentioned it was that, at the time, it would have complicated everything I was trying to do at Darksmith.

Now, things were different.

"I take it, you would like to learn at the academy?"

He grinned. "Gorgath would like this very much."

There was an opportunity for loot here, and a way to turn this situation to my advantage and give the faculty something else to worry about. "Academies require their students to pay tuition."

Gorgath frowned. "What is 'tuition'?"

"It's trade. You give them something they want, and then they teach you spells."

"Gorgath is not allowed to be in Vincent's debt."

"That's why I didn't mention the academy."

He grinned again. "Thank you."

I smiled at the oversized child. "Here's what I'll do for you. You know those monster cores you got for me to strengthen my core from the ninth floor?"

He nodded excitedly.

"For every monster core you give me of that size, I'll convince them to teach you a basic spell. For three, they will teach you an intermediate spell. For ten, they will teach you an advanced spell. You will pay upfront, so there's no debt."

By human standards, I was fleecing him. By the wealth standards of the ninth floor of the Abyss, I was offering him a reasonable deal. A week of work for his parents would pay his tuition for a year.

He rose to his feet. "I will go and request cores from my sire."

THREE DAYS LATER, Headmaster Wink stood in the middle of the fortress courtyard, scowling. The rest of the department heads were also scowling. I'd saved the party before they'd even left the auditorium, preventing a potential war, which was the only reason we were even having this conversation.

Wink heaved a sigh. "Let me get this straight, Vincent. A floor boss from the Abyss wants to join Darksmith and learn magic."

Hundreds of students stood on the wall above us, listening to the conversation. A floor boss from the Abyss entering a dungeon was a rare event, outside of a surge; and even though it had happened several times recently, it was still exciting news.

"Yes. He's intelligent, capable of learning and casting spells, and is willing to take his classes sitting outside the fortress wall."

Wink shook his head. "No. Absolutely not."

His answer was to be expected, but I was going to convince him. "He's very set on joining the academy."

"I don't care if he's willing to come up here and make a fight of it. He is not joining Darksmith."

"He's offered to pay tuition."

The head of the wind magic department frowned, curiosity getting the better of her. "With what?"

"Monster cores. He's offering one core for every ten basic spells we teach him. Another for every five intermediate spells. And one for every advanced spell."

Yes, I was taking most of his tuition.

Wink continued to scowl. "I don't care if these cores are as big as my head and from the Abyss. There is no way we're teaching magic to a dungeon monster."

I opened the lid of the storage chest I'd borrowed from the fortress.

The headmaster massaged his forehead. "Don't bother showing me. I don't care."

I ignored him and levitated the core out. The higher it went, the bigger it grew, until I placed a minivan-sized core beside me. "He's offering cores from the ninth floor of the Abyss, and they're all this size."

The silence that descended over the fortress as the sorcerers stared at the core with envy was amusing. So was the change in Wink. One of these cores was worth more than the annual tuition of the entire academy.

Wink's smile couldn't have been bigger. "Will Gorgath be requiring lunch when he attends his classes?"

TWO DAYS LATER, I was on the fortress wall having a conversation with Gorgath. He was a nice kid, so he'd managed to spark up conversations with several of the more curious students. His intimidating presence also kept anyone that wanted to take advantage of him from trying to manipulate him.

"So, how was your first day?"

Gorgath gave a cheerful hoot. "Gorgath has learned he can perform five types of magic: fire, water, earth, wind, and lightning. The professors have taught me the first of thirty basic spells and how to convert a spell from one magic to another. Gorgath used this to convert his basic bolt spell to each of the five elements, and now Gorgath is banned from using magic in the dungeon without permission."

The student standing guard on the wall near me muttered under his breath, "He incinerated the new dungeon boss with a single bolt of lightning. The thunderclap left everyone on duty deaf. What the heck did he expect?"

I pretended not to hear. "So, you had a good first day."

He hooted. "Gorgath is very happy."

"I'm glad to hear it."

"Gorgath is going to become the strongest sorcerer ever."

"That very well might be the case."

11

MESSAGE FROM THE APOCALYPSE

The Darklord's daughter, Celest, was his only surviving child, but based on the conversations I'd overheard, he viewed her as more of a tool than a daughter. The sons of her father's inner circle were all trying to court her while she was here at Darksmith, so she spent most of her time outside of class studying, shopping, or training to get away from them.

She'd been kidnapped twice over her young life, and neither time had her father offered to pay the ransom. Instead, he'd found the kidnappers' extended families and began hanging their heads outside his palace wall until they returned her. The kidnappers were then handed over to the surviving members of their families, who killed them rather brutally.

Celest was utterly useless as a bargaining chip, so I didn't care about her any more than my other students. But I wasn't surprised when at the end of our next class, she stopped by my desk instead of leaving.

I gave her a friendly smile as I leaned back and folded my arms. "How can I help you, Celest?"

She tucked a stray lock or red hair behind her ear as she took a deep breath. "My father would like to know if you came to my aid because you were hoping to make me your apprentice?"

That was a reasonable assumption. "I'm a necromancer. You are not. An apprenticeship is out of the question."

She paused. "You risked your life traveling through the Deadlands to get to me in time, and then faced down an Abyssal floor boss alone so I could escape. My father would like to reward you."

Her father was known to be as generous as he was cruel. I wasn't surprised he wanted to reward me.

My smile grew. "Dramyin's Skeletal Texts, Revised Editions. I wish to borrow them for a week."

"Excuse me?"

"From what I understand, your father has one of the three remaining collections. I would like to read them."

"You want to borrow books?"

"Very expensive and very rare books."

She frowned, flustered by my reply. "I'll pass along your request."

"Thank you. Now what do you really want? Based on your expression and body language, you didn't stop here just to pass along your father's message."

She nodded. "I would like to know if you think it's safe for me to study the occult?"

"Outside of clerics and death magic practitioners, only those who have made demonic pacts of some form can safely study the occult, and I use the term, 'safely' in the loosest possible sense. You fit none of these categories."

"What form of demonic pact would be required?"

There was too much curiosity in her tone.

I watched the last student exit the room and used a spell to close the door. "Put whatever you want to study on the table."

"I don't—"

I pointed a finger gun at her. The tip glowed with an ominous black necrotic energy. "I wasn't asking."

She stared at me, searching my gaze. She was trying to see if I was bluffing. "You aren't afraid of what my father will do to you if you kill me."

"Do I look afraid?"

"No. Your gaze has the same intensity as my father's. You're confident you can deal with the fallout of your actions."

She shivered, as she opened her storage pouch and placed an ornate box on the table. She flicked the clasps and lifted the lid. Inside was an engraved porcelain orb, covered in thousands of layers of enchantments. A small crack ran through half of it.

She took a step back the moment the box was open. "This thing has been giving me nightmares since I was a child."

"No, it hasn't."

She flinched as I picked up the orb, turning it over to examine the crack.

"I saw this orb in my nightmares before I ever saw it in real life."

That was interesting and explained a few things that I'd heard about her father.

"I'm sure you did, but that's not because the object is cursed. This is a Saints' Seal. It's a *holy* object."

"Then why does it appear in my nightmares?"

"Because you're a seer, and you're seeing *the end of the world*."

She frowned. "What?"

"The Saints' Seals are warning devices. About three thousand years ago, a fissure between this world and Hell opened up. There were a lot more saints in that time, and all but one of them sacrificed themselves to close the fissure. Without the last saint, they only managed to seal the fissure instead of permanently closing it. The surviving saint made these seals on his deathbed to warn everyone when the seal on the fissure was breaking."

The crack was slightly bigger than the accounts I'd read, but it wasn't concerning. There had always been a crack in the seals, and the crack had always been growing.

"In my nightmares, I see demons running through the streets, slaughtering everyone."

"Did the nightmares occur more frequently after you found the Saints' Seal?"

"Yes."

"That's typical of seers. Untrained, you tend to have the same premonitions over and over again, especially when you keep something related to the premonitions close. My advice is to join the Divination Club. Professor Zora has some minor ability to see the immediate future and will help you train your ability so you can unlock the premonition skill."

She held out her hand for the seal.

I didn't give it back.

"Seers have a way of twisting fate to what they see. If I give you this back, what you see is more likely to occur. Given that what you see is the end of the world, I'm not giving this back." I opened up my top drawer and placed the seal inside. "Enjoy the rest of your day."

12

A MEETING OF SOULS

It had been three months since Kathrine summoned me, which meant Davina and the others must have set out to find me almost immediately and pushed hard to get here so quickly. I sensed the intense life force of Carolyn's Old Monster guards as I approached their hotel in the town above Darksmith. The smell of their blood lingered in the air, as inviting as a delightful meal in a flower-filled meadow. It would have made me curious enough to stop by, even if they weren't my destination.

Old Monsters stood in front of every window and door eyeing the people walking by. Angelica's dracolich was stationed on the roof with several more guards, drastically lowering the amount of foot traffic in the area, but not removing it entirely. Clearly, the king hadn't stopped trying to rescue Carolyn once I'd gone to sleep. Her personal guard was now over a hundred strong, based on the life force I could feel coming from the building.

Sir Trent, a grizzled seven-foot giant of a man, who served Princess Carolyn as the head of her personal guard, scowled at me as I approached the entrance, carrying a stack of storage chests filled with ninth-floor cores. He was dressed for war, wearing thick grey plate armour that was covered in enchantments. A sword with a blade as wide as my hand was strapped to his back, radiating an intense death aura that concerned me. It was powerful enough to slow down how quickly I could heal.

He stepped in front of the entrance, blocking me from entering with his massive frame. Normally, this sort of posturing wouldn't concern me, but Sir Trent was Arcadia's strongest knight and in a contest of skill and attributes he had me beat.

He glared down at me. "Do you have any idea what we had to fight through to get here so quickly? How many borders we had to cross? How many threats we had to put down?"

I met his glare with an easy smile. "You don't have to thank me for making your life more fun."

He dropped the glare and chuckled. "How did you know I was trying to mess with you?"

"You don't smell upset. Now why are you here?"

I hadn't told Davina to bring Princess Carolyn, so I had no clue why she was here.

"I can't say."

"Can't or won't?"

"Both. Now, do you still want me to train your unarmed combat skill?" He seemed excited by the prospect.

"The moment I have some spare time."

"Good. Follow me." He turned and opened the door before leading me through the lobby.

They seemed to have rented the entire hotel, because Gregory's people and Davina's clerics and paladins were everywhere. Gregory's people saluted as I passed, taking the storage chests from me with instructions to transfer the contents to the master storage chest they'd brought. Davina's people didn't even acknowledge I was there, continuing with their work.

Unburdened, I followed Sir Trent up a staircase and down a hallway, passing more of his people, before entering a lavish suite, where I was led to a sitting room.

My second familiar, Davina, had tied her black hair into a ponytail and was sitting in an armchair, with her legs tucked under her while she read. Her complexion remained pale, despite the lack of death magic in the air, and she still looked like she was sixteen, even though almost a year had passed since we met.

She'd grown significantly stronger since I'd gone to sleep, likely as the result of having cleansed the death magic locked in her mother's city, which would have increased her mana regeneration. Judging by how strong her aura felt, she would now be able to cast expert-tier magic at will.

My son Luke, the hero of Arcadia, was sleeping on the couch, with one arm hanging over the side. Luke had allowed his facial hair to grow out, giving him a dense beard. He'd lengthened his light brown hair to his shoulders, making him look completely different. It seemed like he was going for a Captain America look.

The presence of a second hero in Murdell might have made the Darklord think the South was making a move and triggered a war, so I assumed he was moving incognito. His scent didn't hold any traces of his party members.

My first familiar, Angelica, was in another armchair, with her waist-length blonde hair over the back. She was wearing her dull, blood-red armour and reading a book on mana control. Over a year had passed since we had met, and unlike Davina, she had changed. Her features were slightly more adult, reflecting slightly more woman than child. She was closer to eighteen than seventeen now, and it showed. It made it harder for me to care about her.

Angelica was the first to notice I'd entered the room. She immediately threw down her book as she launched to her feet. "I'm free!" She blurred out of the room as quickly as she could, so I couldn't command her to stay.

Luke snorted himself awake, raising his hand and conjuring a ball of fire, which was new. "What the...Dad!" He leapt out of his chair and raced across the room, face red with rage. He threw a right hook the moment he reached me, still holding the ball of fire in his other hand.

I planted my feet and let the punch hit me.

My head snapped back as his fist collided with my cheek. My jaw broke and my skull fractured, as the tiles under my feet cracked from the force. I heard one of Luke's knuckles break as my higher constitution came into play, making my body much tougher than in the past.

He didn't throw a second punch.

My bones snapped back together as my flesh healed. "I deserved that."

He glared at me. "Damn right you do. Do you even feel bad about what you did?"

"Every second of every day since the moment it happened."

Luke seemed surprised by my reply. "You mean that literally, don't you?"

I nodded, dropping the façade that everything was alright. Holding it together until they got here had been hard. Every day I wanted to go out into the world and kidnap someone, anyone, who could help Kathrine get better. I wanted to pull the world apart until everything was alright, but I couldn't let myself do that. I had to be better than my impulses and instincts.

He engulfed me in a hug, cracking my back, forgetting the anger from a moment before. "How bad is she? Amelia isn't sure."

"She's asleep. Within a few hours of feeding on her, she was terrified, paranoid, and in a deep depression. She's hurt, and I haven't been able do anything about it."

Luke pulled back and gave me a sad smile. "Sit down and explain from the beginning."

When Luke stepped away, Davina was waiting for a hug. Her glowing white eyes showed she was favoured by Heaven, and her gaze held all the compassion in the world. It was the sort of gaze only a saint had. "Do you want me to make it stop hurting?"

I shook my head. "I don't deserve it."

She gave me a simple hug that made me want to protect her, and then made me sit next to her, so she could hold my hand. She didn't do anything to take the pain away. She just let me know that she was there for me. That the necrosaint didn't think I was the monster I saw myself as.

I wished it helped.

I told them what happened. They had heard Amelia's version, but this version was more intimate. Amelia didn't share my pain in her dreams or my thoughts. She only saw what I experienced, not how I experienced it.

Luke gave a heavy sigh as I finished. "This is a completely different problem to what I thought it was."

Davina gave my hand a squeeze. "I can repress emotions and hide memories for a short time, but I can't heal trauma or soul injuries with a wave of my hand. Amelia is only just coming to terms with what she saw happen to you, and it's taken me months. What do you want me to do?"

"Help her."

She squeezed my hand again. "I will. Are you hungry?"

I shook my head. "I'm still working my way through everything I ate after the demonic parasite mutated."

"Are you tired?"

"Not since I fed on her."

Luke raised an eyebrow. "Was her blood that good?"

"It worked better than anything I've ever heard of. It made me master my royal vampiric thirst skill while pushing my royal vampiric bloodline skill to level 15."

"Mine's probably better."

It was, and I hated myself for the way it made me salivate. "It's not a competition."

He grinned. "Still winning, though."

"We are *not* finding out if that's true."

His grin grew. "If I flicked a drop of blood at you, do you think you would behave like a dog and catch it in the air with your mouth?"

Davina giggled.

I scowled at him. "Your sister is suffering. This is not the time for jokes."

He continued to smile. "This is the exact time for jokes, Old Man. You need some humour in your life. There is far too much vampire teen angst."

That got me to chuckle. "How long have you been saving that?"

He smirked. "A few months. Have you found anymore teenage girls to follow you around yet?"

I groaned as he chuckled.

Davina came to my rescue. "Like father, like son."

Luke stopped chuckling and groaned too. "Please don't mention that in front of him."

"I wouldn't dream of mentioning that the princess ogles your butt every time you enter a room."

I saluted my son. "That's America's ass."

"I didn't steal Captain America's look," he said indignantly.

"Only his butt."

"Okay, that's enough humour," Luke said. "What are we going to do about Kathrine? Davina can't fix this with a wave of her hand, and Carolyn can't remain here long without causing a disturbance. We came through the South, but the Darklord will eventually learn she's here and try to kidnap her."

That was a good point. "Why did you bring her?"

"We needed Amelia to keep tabs on you in case you were discovered and had to move," Davina replied. "The princess and Amelia's parents weren't willing to let us take her alone, so we brought them with us."

There was more to that story, but I had other priorities.

"How skilled is Carolyn when it comes to magic?"

"She's at the low end of advanced. At her age, that makes her a savant. She's also already an archsorcerer."

"What about Angelica?"

"High end of intermediate."

"That was fast?"

"It took her ten days to realise that your compulsion wasn't a death sentence because your wording allowed her to train all of her deathlord skills. She switched to studying magic, because it required her to think clearly letting her sleep more. She's been studying magic nonstop for five months. With only two branches of magic, her set, and attributes, she can train much faster than a normal person."

"Why didn't she stop three months ago when I sent for you?"

Davina sighed. “She should have been able to stop studying when she saw that your sarcophagus was empty, but in her mind that didn’t mean you were awake. Only that your resting place was empty. I think it has something to do with her parent’s abuse.”

“Did she talk to you about it?”

Davina shook her head. “She doesn’t trust anyone that much. But I listen to what she says and what she doesn’t. It doesn’t take a genius to realise they were as monstrous as my mother. Did she cry when you killed them?”

“She smelled relieved.”

“I thought so.”

Davina leaned into my side. She was worried for her friend and had no one else she could be vulnerable with. Something inside me changed as she leaned into me, and I put my arm over her shoulder to comfort her. Normally, I couldn’t care about her even when we were this close. Whatever she was doing was making it possible for me to care the way I once had. She was growing stronger, and she was trying to use that strength to help me.

“So, what’s the plan?” Luke asked.

I turned to him. “That depends. Why do you suddenly have magic?”

He smirked and folded his arms. “There I was, minding my own business, being a talented and dashing young hero, devoid of magic, but still making the world a better place. When lo and behold, my father eats most of the royal family and gains the royal bloodline without telling me. So, I’m none the wiser when I mosey into the local adventurer’s guild to use their class hall, getting the shock of my life as I discover that not only do my new levels give me a bunch of magical skills, but I’ve also unlocked the royal family’s bloodline.”

“Happy Birthday and Merry Christmas.”

He chuckled. “Does this count as one year or all of the ones you missed?”

“It covers the decade I was asleep.”

“Damn it. Now I have to get you something.”

“You know what I want.”

"I'm not getting married and giving you grandchildren!"

I chuckled. "What branches of magic can you practice?"

"The four elements, plus death and necrotic magic."

"How good are you?"

"Low intermediate. I had a few skill upgrades that were collecting dust, so I upgraded the sorcerer sovereign skill to tier three. Between it and my prodigy skill, magic comes naturally."

That was too low. "Davina, Angelica, and Carolyn are all talented enough to gain immediate entry into Darksmith, if we lie about Davina's age. You'll have to become my assistant."

Davina frowned. "You're planning to stay here long-term."

"As long as it takes. I want Kathrine to wake up somewhere familiar."

Luke rolled his eyes. "And I have to be your assistant to do that?"

"More like an apprentice. I can't actually hire an assistant."

"Can't I just join the academy?"

"By your age, the students that haven't left are practicing expert-tier magic. You don't qualify."

"Can't you get me in some other way?"

"Not without people questioning it."

"Why are you including the princess?"

"Because you brought her with you, and you're right. Out here she's a target. Inside the academy, the Darklord would start a war if he touched her."

"What if she doesn't go for it?"

"This is Darksmith. The student body is made up of Murdell's elite. She will never get another opportunity to build alliances like the one she has here, nor a chance to show how much better she is than them."

"Her guards won't like it."

"The school rules allow her to have as many servants as she wants, on top of her guards. The only stipulation is that they cannot practice magic above the intermediate tier. There is nothing in the school rules that say those servants can't be Old Monsters."

Davina smirked. "Still sticking to the letter of the law while crushing its spirit, I see."

I grinned. "It's the best way to get things done."

LUKE SAT beside his sister on my fourposter bed, holding her hand, and watching as Davina, Father, and Mother completed their examination. He was worried, more worried than I'd ever seen him. His strength meant nothing here, and being powerless didn't sit well with him. It hurt me to see him like this. It hurt more to know that I was the cause.

Father walked over and took a seat next to me on the couch. He and Mother were in their eighties, but because of Davina's ability to consume death, they now looked like they were in their late thirties. Before devoting his life to Davina, Father had been an archbishop focused on healing. He was the same level as Carolyn's Old Monsters, but because of his focus and my immunity to holy magic, he wasn't a threat to me.

Father folded his arms and turned his white gaze to the ceiling. "Your ability to eat souls is significantly stronger than I anticipated. Without soul healing, she won't recover for at least a decade."

"Can you heal her?"

"That depends. Have you improved your soul regeneration and strengthening skills?"

I didn't trust him or Mother the way I did Davina. "Why do you want to know?"

"With a strong and healthy soul, you could learn techniques to heal your daughter's soul. Parents are better for this than strangers, and your nature would allow you to master the techniques in days instead of decades."

He was trying to help, so I decided to extend some trust to him. "They haven't leveled."

He scratched his chin. "Do you know why?"

"I don't know how to exploit my demonic parasites correctly."

"I'm not sure I understand."

"When I raised the level of my vampiric touch skill, the demonic parasite within me didn't get better at pulling life force from someone. *I* got better at using them to pull life force from someone."

"You tapped into what they were already capable of, rather than building a new skill."

"Yes."

"Then you need to learn how to exploit their soul regeneration and strengthening capabilities in order to level these skills."

"I believe so."

"May I examine your soul? If I can understand what they're doing, I might be able to help you develop these skills. If your soul recovers, I'll teach you the techniques you need to heal her."

"Do it."

He reached out and placed his hand on my forehead, casting a spell. Father was the foremost expert on souls in Arcadia, so if he didn't know what was going on, no one would.

He began to frown. "Your soul is in even worse shape than your daughter's."

"Do—"

"Give me a moment."

His moment lasted fifteen minutes. Davina and Mother worked on Kathrine while I waited, helping her to recover faster in any way they could.

He pulled his hand away. "The demonic parasites seem to be releasing soul energy for your soul to gather, so it can recover on its own. Strengthening seems to occur while they are feeding on your soul. They strengthen the sections around where they're eating, and when they run out of weaker sections to eat, they begin eating the sections they've strengthened. They always seem to eat the weakest point first, stopping your soul from being able to recover or strengthen evenly. I think I've got a book that might be helpful, but I can't remember which one it is."

"Give me them all. I can read them faster than you can sort through them."

He reached into his storage pouch and began passing me books to read. "Monks have created dozens of techniques for strengthening and healing their souls. Some of these techniques are practiced by clerics who perform exorcisms. If you can't improve your vampiric skills, you will need to practice one of these techniques, anyway. In a year or two, your soul will fade from existence without them."

Father had over one hundred books on the soul, with various techniques that could be used to strengthen and repair it. These books were entirely different to the ones I'd read in Contessa's library. Those dark arts were devoted to how you could use souls to empower spells or harness them to strengthen your own soul. They treated souls as a fuel source. The books Father gave me treated your soul like a muscle, showing you how to exercise it to make it stronger, so you could use techniques.

When I finished reading them, I handed him a book titled, The Root and Branch. "I think this is the one you were trying to remember."

I pointed to the section that explained the technique.

Despite clerics and monks being able to see souls, they only had a basic understanding of how they worked. They knew your soul copied memories as they formed, and that with the right spells, these memories could be reintroduced to the flesh, which was how you could resurrect someone whose brain had been crushed. They knew souls sometimes reintroduced memories on their own, but they didn't know why. And they knew that painful memories could injure souls as they were reintroduced.

They also knew that souls consumed life force to maintain themselves, regenerate, and strengthen themselves, and that magic could be used to strengthen them further, but that this effect was only temporary.

You could safely train your soul in a number of different ways without causing harm, like how different athletes trained different muscles for different sports. However, trying to change your soul's nature usually resulted in disaster. This was like giving yourself extra arms and legs. It caused all sorts of problems.

Father put down the book I'd handed him. "This wasn't the technique I was thinking of. What made you suggest this one?"

"The technique creates a three-braided soul root system: One root absorbs life force, another converts it to soul energy, and the last uses the soul energy to regenerate the sections of the soul around the roots. You said the demonic parasites eat the weakest parts of my soul, strengthening the sections around it. If I make the soul roots thin enough, then the demonic parasites will only feed on the regenerated sections of my soul, while strengthening the roots. If the roots become strong enough, the demonic parasites will never view them as a food source, unless they've eaten the rest of my soul, which with the increased efficiency from using this method should become impossible."

He folded his arms and leaned back. "From what I remember, the technique doesn't work that way."

"It doesn't, but if I combine practices from the other techniques, it *could*. Let me write it out so you can understand and give me your thoughts."

Father followed me to the study and began reading as I finished writing the first page.

Unlike the human body that had different cells for different purposes, every piece of your soul had the exact same capabilities. They could all absorb life force, store memories, regenerate, produce soul energy, and strengthen the soul, but they could be trained to be better at one task over the others.

The technique in the book required thick roots, but thick roots wouldn't work for me. My demonic parasites were everywhere, and they would eat the thicker soul roots when that was all they were surrounded by. The damage would stop the roots from maintaining an equilibrium and destroy the increased efficiency, leading to an even faster rate of decline.

To make this work, I needed to interweave unimaginably thin soul roots that absorb life force, with unimaginably thin soul roots that could convert the life force to soul energy, with unimaginably thin soul roots that could absorb and use the soul energy to repair my soul, and then use the demonic parasites to make the roots stronger, while they fed on the newly regenerated pieces of my soul the roots were creating.

I'd be working on a microscopic scale, which was something humans couldn't do. And my soul would only recover if I could make these unimaginably thin roots long enough to make a difference.

The roots I created would be a three-braided cord that would hopefully work *with* my demonic parasites rather than against them. It wouldn't be the strongest soul technique, but it would be the strongest technique that worked for me. None of the other techniques were this promising.

Father read the last page and put it down. "This technique will make your soul degrade faster."

"Only in the beginning. Once the demonic parasites start strengthening the roots, the roots will become more efficient at converting life force to soul energy and regenerating my soul. They should also become more efficient at collecting the soul energy the parasites excrete."

"True, but it's terribly inefficient, compared to other techniques."

"This technique will never be as efficient as the techniques the monks practice, but it has the best chance of working with my parasites and the skills they offer, and if I can level those skills, it won't require me to do much more than feed to maintain my soul."

"True. My oaths prohibit me from offering you aid with the power that Heaven granted me, but the necrosaint spent her time traveling here mastering any magic that could help your daughter. She can do what you need."

I pushed my chair out and we returned to the bedroom.

Luke was still sitting next to Kathrine, but Davina was on the couch, talking to Mother about my daughter's condition. Mother was an archbishop and Arcadia's greatest healer. Her lessons were the main reason Davina's healing skills had grown so quickly. Davina might have been magical genius, but Mother was an exceptional teacher, turning everything into a lesson, including my daughter's condition.

I interrupted their conversation and told Davina what I needed her to do, handing her the technique I'd created.

When she was finished reading, she turned to me. "If I reinforce your soul with a spell, the demonic parasites won't be able to eat your soul as quickly, which will be significantly more efficient than using this method alone."

"That's fine with me. How long do you need to prepare?"

Davina stifled a yawn. "I can do this now."

"You don't need to practice?" I asked, concerned by how casual she was being. The spells she had to cast were some of the most complicated magic I'd seen outside the vault under the Northern Royal Library in Arcadia.

"It's less complicated than when I reinforced your soul at the capitol. All I'm doing here is casting a spell that temporarily makes you *aware* of your soul, and casting another that will allow you to manipulate it."

"That's less complicated than reinforcing my soul?"

She nodded. "That was like filling my hands with water and trying not to spill a drop as I walked from one side of a city to the other. This is more like covering the crack in a cup with my thumb, so water doesn't spill out. Are you ready?"

I nodded that I was and sat on the floor in front of the couch, crossed my legs and began breathing, matching the cycles I'd read in the book. The monks who practiced the original soul-strengthening method used it to fight. It caused their strikes to have a spiritual weight to them, which allowed them to fight ghosts and demons, and to beat someone into a dark, depressive state.

I glanced at Kathrine, glad that I could finally do something to help her. "I'm ready."

Davina placed her hand on my forehead and cast the first spell.

Becoming aware of your soul is like becoming aware of your skeleton. You know it's inside of you, but you can't quite pinpoint where it is or how it works, only that it is there. With the help of the spell, I could feel how my soul interacted with my body, drawing life force into itself to convert to soul energy, similar to the way my lungs used to breathe in air. It also drew in my thoughts and memories, copying them away, like a data backup.

My soul felt like a mangy dog with patches of missing fur, two heads, and oozing, pus-filled wounds. The demonic parasites were attached to every inch of it like invisible maggots, gnawing on it everywhere they could.

No wonder Father had said my soul looked worse than Kathrine's. The books I'd just read told me I should have gone insane with my soul in this state.

Davina cast another spell, allowing her to see my soul.

She flinched at the sight and then took a deep breath. "Where do you want to start?"

I turned to Father. "Any recommendations?"

"I'd begin with the most-damaged section. If you make a mistake, it will be less costly."

"Heart it is, then."

Davina cast the second spell. "You should be able to feel what your soul is doing in that section and how it is doing it. You can add your will to the spell to train your soul the way you want."

I felt how the tattered wisps of soul behind my chest wall allowed life force to enter them, so they could convert it to soul energy, and use that soul energy to repair themselves, as they were eaten by the parasites. Occasionally a section of my soul would get ahead of the damage and try to help the neighbouring areas, but this was incredibly inefficient.

I began training a section smaller than the head of a pin, so that it was only absorbing life force. This temporarily weakened my soul in that area, causing the surrounding parasites to attack like I'd rung the dinner bell. Before I could finish doing what I needed to do, that part of my soul was *gone*.

I wasn't surprised by the results. It was exactly what I'd expected to happen. It proved my assumption were correct. "Davina, reinforce my soul."

She cast the same spell she'd used to reduce the rate at which my demonic parasites had eaten my soul in the past. With my perception, I could sense where the demonic parasites were, by where they were eating my soul. These were the weak points. I could also tell which stage each parasite was at based upon how quickly it was feeding.

I found the strongest stationary parasite, inside the muscle wall of my heart, and began training my soul next to it to become soul roots. The roots were halfway through their training when the parasite began to eat them. They were almost done, before they were consumed.

The problem was simple enough to overcome. I needed to distract the demonic parasite with another food source, while I trained my roots.

I found another candidate to work with and began forming the interwoven roots next to it. At the same time, I moved weaker pieces of my soul toward the demonic parasite and trained those pieces in a way that made them weaker and easier to eat. The parasite happily ate what I supplied as the root system finished training next to it, the way I wanted. After the roots were finished, I kept feeding it. The demonic parasite continued eating everything I supplied, unaware it was strengthening the roots I'd just made.

Slowly, the roots grew strong enough to start expanding. The life force root brought in life force more quickly, which was passed over to the soul energy root to convert into soul energy, which was then picked up by the regeneration root, which used the soul energy to grow and repair everything around it, which was predominantly the roots. The regeneration was the hardest part, as it needed to expand all three roots, while also regenerating pieces of my soul for the parasites to eat.

The roots system slowly grew to surround the demonic parasite, feeding off the soul energy the demonic parasite was giving off, creating a nest of roots that fed it pieces of my soul while the parasite strengthened them in return. Once that was done, the roots began to spread, sending out nano-thin roots in every direction. It was slow at first, but whenever they came in contact with a demonic parasite, the growth rate sped up. The roots, which were now too strong to eat, would circle the new parasite and build a nest, before sending out more roots.

As the more mobile demonic parasites moved, the root system followed them, feeding off the soul energy excretions the parasites left behind. After nearly an hour of slow progress, the roots reached the section of my heart wall connected to blood. The higher concentration of mobile demonic parasites made the roots spread more quickly, and over the next few hours they fully engulfed my heart.

"You need to expand the soul reinforcement," I said.

Davina frowned. "Why?"

"The root system has spread through my heart?"

"It has?"

"You can't see it?"

"Your soul looks slightly more stable there, but that's all I can see."

"Just do it."

Her spell spread to engulf my rib cage, and then later, my entire body.

The roots fed each other, so the longer they grew, the more efficient they were. It only took another hour for them to spread through my circulatory system, which gave them access to every part of my body.

Luke had fallen asleep next to his sister, and Mother and Father were dozing in the armchairs, when the root system finished spreading across my skin and began to connect to each other. These connections established shorter paths for the roots to share resources and entirely changed the way they worked.

One moment everything was perfectly normal, and the next the majority of my life force was gone, and my soul was healed.

"Help!" Davina shouted, as she threw a silence spell at my mouth and leapt away.

Luke exploded out of bed, drawing his sword, before getting between us. At the same moment, a notification appeared before me.

You have mastered your Ancient Vampiric Soul Regeneration skill.
You have mastered your Ancient Vampiric Soul Strengthening skill.

The soul reinforcement vanished, but I could still see what was happening to my soul. The demonic parasites were only feeding where they were supposed to. It was the root system that had consumed my excess life force, leaving me with what a normal hero with my attributes would contain. Somehow encapsulating my body and soul had made it easier for the roots to tap into my life force. It probably had a lot to do with the soul reinforcement spell, but I wasn't sure.

Davina hurled a holy bolt at me while I was considering whether or not I needed to be concerned by this change. "His soul is still intact," she said, purposefully *not* looking at me. "We need to contain him and get him to the dungeon to feed."

"I'm fine," I mouthed as Mother and Father trapped me inside a holy barrier.

Luke frowned. "He says he's fine."

"I just saw his life force vanish," Davina stated.

"Not all of it," I mouthed.

"He says not all of it."

Davina continued not to look at me, afraid I would compel her. "How much does he have left?"

I told Luke.

"He says about as much as a person with his attributes would normally have. He thinks the root technique he created somehow tapped into the life force and absorbed the excess. Souls apparently don't typically kill you unless you're extremely old or your soul is altered, and his soul is behaving by these rules despite what happened. He theorizes that the speed of the conversion was only possible because of your soul reinforcement spell."

She continued not to look at me. "Throw Slaughter out here and empty your core. If you don't go crazy in a reasonable amount of time, I'll tell Mother and Father to release you."

I tossed Slaughter through a hole in the barrier and emptied my core. I trusted Davina's instinct in these sorts of matters. It was better to be overly cautious than to take unnecessary risks.

While I waited, I talked to Father through Luke.

"Dad wants to know if you know why the root system encapsulating his soul would cause it to absorb his excess life force?"

Father frowned. "It might be because the changes to your soul could correctly measure the life force once it had encapsulated it. Once it could confirm that the life force was, in fact, excess and not some strange concentration, it consumed the excess to repair itself, because that was what you designed it to do."

It was the same assumption I'd come to.

"He asks if you think he will be able to store excess life force in the future?"

"I'd need to examine your soul, but I wouldn't think so. On the positive side, your soul will now grow stronger as you feed."

Luke scowled as I gave him my next message. "You're seriously worried about your ability to make armour right now?"

I nodded.

Luke sighed. "He wants to know if there is a way around this. He can't donate blood easily with this condition."

I wanted to replicate what we had done for Angelica's armour for Gregory's men. Without the more powerful reagents, the armour would be weaker, but it would still be powerful enough to make them stronger.

"There might be. I would have to study your soul before I can give a definite answer."

"He says, he wants Davina to end the spell that allows him to see his soul."

"I ended that spell when I silenced him," Davina replied.

"He's asking if you're sure. He can still sense and manipulate his soul."

Father frowned. "He would be able to sense and manipulate his soul unaided if it was strong enough, but this would be too soon."

"Seriously, you mastered more skills," Luke said indignantly. "This is anime protagonist cheating, Dad. No, I do not want to hear about the skills you've mastered before I got here."

I chuckled.

"He says he mastered his soul regeneration and strengthening skills. And that these skills only seem to be related to him fully utilizing the capabilities of the demonic parasites. They're not eating the roots, which he says might account for why he could sense his soul."

Father folded his arms. "It's possible, but they would have to be significantly better at strengthening your soul than what I saw them doing."

"He says he'll wait for your assessment."

A couple of hours passed before Davina decided I wasn't a threat. I used the time to talk to my son. Apparently, he hadn't left his party behind to come here. Kidnapping the king's daughter had given him the excuse he needed to part ways with them. Since reuniting with me, he'd out-leveled them so significantly that they were becoming a liability.

He wasn't exactly happy with the change, but he wasn't bitter either. He was able to do more alone than he had been able to do with them, even if he couldn't take on such a wide range of threats. In a year or two, when they had trained some more, he'd power level them, so they could adventure together again. But for now, he was a lone wolf.

When the barriers dropped, Father walked over to me and place his hand on my head to examine my soul. "Can you manipulate soul energy?"

I moved a little soul energy around.

"Strange. Based on what I can sense, you shouldn't be able to do that. It would appear whatever you've done to your soul is too small for me to detect. It might be possible that only these roots have been strengthened and you're using them to see and manipulate the rest of your soul."

That was a reasonable assumption. "I'm in all-new territory then?"

"It would appear so. I strongly suggest you practice soul healing techniques on someone else before you use it on your daughter. I can supervise if you like."

"I'd appreciate that."

"WHY AM I being used as a test subject?" Angelica complained the following night. She was sitting in one of the armchairs in my bedroom, glaring at me. "I didn't do anything. Make Luke do it."

Luke sat beside his sister, rolling his eyes. “I’m a hero. If he practices on me, I might gain a skill that I don’t want.”

“What about Davina?”

“We’re not sure how his technique will interfere with my unique constitution,” she replied. “And Father and Mother both practice soul-strengthening techniques already.”

“Kidnap an Unseen, then.”

“We considered that,” I said. “But it might be counted as helping them, and I don’t need that sort of attention from Heaven.”

“Why does it have to be me?”

“You’re tougher than everyone else, which means your life force is stronger, so any complication will be easier for you to recover from.”

I didn’t add that her soul was damaged from going through the reaping and the lifetime of abuse her parents had subjected her to.

“Can’t I just kidnap one of the students for you? I’m sure there’s an asshole that has it coming to them.”

“Language.”

“Pleeease.”

“No.” I picked up the other armchair and placed it beside hers. “Give me your hand.”

She immediately held out her hand.

I took off my glove and grabbed it.

Father came over and placed his hand on ours, casting a spell so he could see our souls. “You can begin using the healing palm technique when you’re ready.”

I manipulated the excess soul energy the demonic parasites produced to move to my palm, and then I passed the soul energy from my hand into hers. I’d spent all day playing with my soul, trying to figure out my limits. Two-thirds of the soul energy the demonic parasites produced needed to be fed back to the demonic parasites to stop my soul from being eaten. The rest could be taken away from strengthening my soul to heal someone else.

Father smiled. “Everything appears to be normal.”

“Why don’t I feel anything? Angelica asked.

"You can't feel your soul, so you can't feel what's changing," I said.

"Can you?"

"Not yet."

"So, the three of us are going to just stay here, awkwardly holding hands like this."

I nodded.

"How long do we have to do this?"

"Most of the night. We need to be sure there are no complications. You can sleep if you want to."

Angelica reached out with her boot and pulled the footstool towards her. Then she slumped in the chair and put her feet up.

I turned to Father. "How quickly will Kathrine recover, using this technique?"

"At this speed, you're looking at six weeks, uninterrupted."

I'd already tested what reinforcing my soul would do, so I knew that it didn't improve anything like I'd assumed. My soul sensed that my body couldn't regenerate life force now that it didn't have excess, so it refused to convert more life force than was required to maintain itself. The excess soul energy I was feeding Angelica was only coming from the demonic parasites. They had no problem feeding on my life force and the ambient mana that my mana regeneration drew in but didn't place in my core for me.

I'd gone into the dungeon and killed a few monsters to see what would happen. Their life force had been absorbed by my soul so quickly I couldn't gather the excess soul energy before it was used to create more soul roots.

This was the best I could do.

13

NEGOTIATIONS

Amelia stood behind Carolyn's chair as I entered the princess's hotel sitting room. The kid smelled happy and content with life, which I took to mean she enjoyed her new role as the princess's handmaiden. She waved enthusiastically as I sat down, instead of running over to say hello, which I could tell took a lot of self-restraint on her part.

Rupert, Keeper of the Eastern Gate, gently grabbed Amelia's wrist for breaking etiquette and lowered her hand. She stuck her tongue out at him, breaking it again, which made me chuckle.

Our bond was much stronger than when I'd gone to sleep, but it no longer seemed to be growing stronger. Amelia's presence had been the first I'd detected, and I'd felt it over a week before they arrived. It had taken all my self-control not to pick Kathrine up and run towards her when she appeared at the edge of my awareness in a way that I could tell exactly how close she was. I knew if she was here, then Davina would be too.

The bond we shared was not like my other bonds, and I didn't know what to make of it. I felt no attachment to her or need to use her. She seemed exempt from my influence and darker tendencies, despite how useful she could be to me. She was an oddity which I wasn't interested in understanding.

Princess Carolyn's scent held none of the anger that it had when we last saw each other. It had been five months, and with Davina's help, she seemed to have come to terms with what happened to her family. She didn't like me, but the unrestrained hatred was no longer there.

Her expression remained guarded as she took me in, weighing what she saw. "I'm told you're enrolling me at Darksmith."

"I am."

"I want something in return for my silence."

Rupert, Keeper of the Eastern Gate and Carolyn's spymaster, cousin, and advisor, smirked at me, enjoying finally having power over me. Carolyn knew what I was, and things would become awkward for me if this became public knowledge. While killing her was an option, it still wasn't an effective one, nor a good one. For now, I had to play nice, even though she was working against me.

It was obvious that the reason Carolyn had chosen to come here was because it would allow her father to lay a trap for when I returned to my resting place. This plan didn't interfere with her guards' oaths, as no one was helping her try to escape. The trap the king set might even be able to free her, considering how much time he had to work with.

"What do you want?" I asked, willing to make some concessions.

"I want you to sign a betrothal contract between your son and I."

Rupert's smile vanished, clearly not hearing the request he thought he would. Carolyn had just turned sixteen and Luke was twenty-seven, which made her request very amusing to me.

"I'm not sure you are allowed to negotiate your own marriage contract, Princess."

"I've been informed you gained a royal bloodline, making you vampire royalty and your son a prince."

Angelica.

I'd read Arcadia's laws, and I got where Carolyn was going with this. "Because he's technically royalty, you can negotiate your own marriage with him or with his father."

She nodded.

"Why do you want to marry my son?"

"She likes his butt," Amelia blurted out, before erupting into a giggle fit.

Carolyn blushed as she turned and glared at her handmaiden.

"What! You do."

I smirked. "I've been informed she ogles it every chance she gets."

Carolyn's embarrassment became mortification as Amelia giggled while nodding her head enthusiastically. This was not going the way Carolyn planned. When she looked to Rupert for help, she saw no sympathy or help waiting.

She was on her own.

"Why do you want to marry my son?"

A lifetime of etiquette training let her meet my gaze, despite her being beet red. "He has my family's bloodline constitution, which assures it will be passed on to our children. He also doesn't covet the throne or seek power, so I won't have to worry about strife within our household."

Those were good reasons for a political marriage, but not good reasons to let her marry my son. "I want my son's wife to like him for more than just his political goals and bloodline. Now, why do you honestly want to marry Luke?"

She paused as if choosing her words carefully. "Luke has nothing but love for you and his sister. I've never seen anyone care about their family as much as he does. I want to be cared for that way, and I know he's capable of doing so."

"And she likes his butt."

I chuckled. "Good answer."

Carolyn's face lit up. "You'll sign the betrothal contract?"

"The contract won't give you what you want. Love doesn't work that way. You have to show someone you're worthy of their love and then hope that they want to love you. You can't force it."

Rupert cleared his throat.

Carolyn frowned at my statement, but indicated he could speak.

"Political marriages can involve the sharing of love potions."

I was aware of that. Love potions didn't make someone a slave or have romantic attachment. It just made them love the other person as much as the person they loved the most. Kings occasionally shared them when they signed treaties so that they would treat each other like the person they cared for the most.

I met Rupert's gaze. "I will make sure the princess dies within the day if she manages to make my son unknowingly share a love potion with her."

Killing her would void the love they shared. Rupert wanted me to make my position clear so that the oath her guards took to protect her would force them to make sure she didn't have access. He wasn't helping her marry my son. He was stopping a teenage girl, who's orders he had to follow, from doing something foolish.

He gave me the briefest of smiles. "If you indirectly threaten Her Highness again, I will remove you from her presence, vampire."

I turned back to the princess, unconcerned by his threat. "I won't sign a betrothal contract. However, my son is about to become my apprentice. As he's not even at the advanced tier of magic yet and I don't have the time to teach him, he's in need of a private magical tutor. One who is aware of how his bloodline will help him. Anyone who is willing to teach him would have the perfect opportunity to get to know him and build a closer relationship."

Carolyn began to smile again. "Lessons every night after classes, no exceptions."

"Three nights a week and I'll make sure your guards can't attend."

Rupert glared at me.

"Five nights a week, no guards, and no handmaiden."

"Four nights a week, no guards, no handmaiden, and I'll arrange things so you can train with him with his shirt off for an entire lesson."

"Deal."

Your Negotiate skill has reached level 10

HEADMASTER WINK GREETED me at the door to his office, smiling and holding a glass of wine. "How's my favourite Occult Studies professor doing? I mean Defence Against the Dark Arts professor." He waved for me to follow, and we both took a seat at his desk.

He'd been referring to me this way ever since I'd handed over Gorgath's first tuition payment. Darksmith wasn't strapped for cash, but the immediate doubling of the tuition the academy received for teaching one more student, who had been a model student, kept Wink in a perpetual good mood. Each additional core he received improved this mood further. Pretty soon he might even begin drinking water.

"Better," I said. I meant it, too. Kathrine was on the road to recovery.

"What can I do for you today?"

"I need a favour."

He groaned. "What's her name and how far along is she."

"It's not that sort of favour."

He groaned again. "Please don't tell me you eloped with a noble. There is only so much I can protect you from, Vincent. This isn't a minor matter, like killing an Unseen curse weaver in a busy street."

"I'm not sleeping with one of my students."

His face fell. "Oh, no. How many? And how many of them know about each other?"

"This has nothing to do with any of the students."

"Thank goodness. Please continue being discreet. I understand everyone involved are adults and that you're a very attractive man, but the school has a reputation to protect. If people knew a professor had a harem it would look bad for us."

I decided to ignore his comments. "Look, I came here because I have three underage sorcerers who would like to apply to join Darksmith."

He frowned. "Three."

"Yes."

"How old?"

"Between sixteen and eighteen."

"Do they meet our requirements?"

"Yes."

"I'm not sure why you brought this to me. My assistant could have dealt with this."

"One of them is Carolyn Ironheart, heir to the throne of Arcadia. She's demanding we perform her and her friends' assessments tomorrow morning."

He groaned, put down his glass of wine, and reached for his bottle of gin. "I'll begin the paperwork."

14

THE ART OF MANIPULATION

Sir Trent's fist collided with my cheek, shattering my skull and jawbone. His blow redirected my line of sight to the ceiling of my private training hall, so I didn't see him sweep my legs. My body spun and I ended up on the ground, facing the ceiling.

Again.

Like my first training session with Sir Brandon, the fight didn't stop. I rolled to the side to dodge a heel strike and threw myself to my feet, barely dodging the massive fist going for my head. My injuries had already healed, and I was back in fighting form.

Sir Trent grinned at me as he threw a dozen quick punches in a mystifying combo. "This is as fun as I imagined."

We were training my unarmed combat skill, and he was enjoying his chance to beat me around my training hall. Considering that I was responsible for his death for a short period, that was fair. "What level am I at?"

He threw a series of high and low kicks. "Somewhere around eighteen. You need to focus on your footwork and dodging to reach nineteen."

"It would be easier to do that if you didn't keep kicking me in the face."

He laughed. "Where's the fun in that?"

Sir Trent was a master brawler and a better swordsman. With items, his agility was slightly above mine, which made him the perfect training partner. He wasn't even out of breath.

"It would be faster," I pointed out.

"I want to get my money's worth after training your men to kill me."

"If you're that upset with how quickly I'm progressing, I'll let you help me train my parry skill. I won't even wear armour."

"You're not my type."

"I'll wear pants."

His foot connected with my chest, breaking every rib. "Tempting." He followed it up with a dozen vicious blows that all broke bones before I managed to headbutt his nose.

I followed the headbutt with several punches to his ribs, which he barely noticed. Sir Trent had his own bloodline, and it made him stupidly tough when it came to blunt force trauma. I put some distance between us.

He closed that distance. "Will it hurt if I cut you?"

"It might itch a little."

"So, you won't object to me using my sword, then?"

His sword was almost as dangerous as he was and would hurt a lot more than a regular one. "Why do you want to use it?"

"I've got a few skills I haven't been able to master."

"Active skills?"

I only had two active skills: impale and heavy blow. But that was still one more than Luke had when I met him. Warriors with enough attributes became more than just the sum of their parts. They developed an aura and were able to use it to direct mana. It wasn't like the way sorcerers manipulated mana. It was blunter, less refined. Impale was like a command that all the mana nearby get out of the way and take everything with it. It made whatever you were thrusting against weaker and was how Luke could thrust through solid stone.

"I wouldn't need your help if they weren't."

I ducked under another kick, while delivering a punch to his thigh that he barely felt. "I'll let you train yours, if you help me train mine."

Sir Trent didn't slow his attack. "Which skills?"

"Impale and heavy blow?"

"Amateur."

"Is that a yes?"

"Answer one question for me and I'll consider saying yes."

"What question?"

"Did you know who they were?"

He was asking about the royal family. "I was half-mad from hunger, and all I knew was I was meant to eat any Unseen inside the palace, and they were in the palace, so no, not at first."

"Would you have held back if you knew?"

"I would have been less obvious about it, but I would have gone out of my way to kill them. They had too much power and influence to let them live."

He tried to kick me in the face. "I pledge my life and my soul to the Hero. Let his path be my path and his fate be my fate."

Sir Trent glowed with a holy light as he finished the pledge and continued to try to beat the stuffing out of me. I felt a bond form between us and then snap into place, urging me to protect him and make him stronger. He didn't stop fighting.

A foot flew past my chin.

"You heard my call," I said, honestly surprised.

"A lot of us Old Monsters do. It's hard to turn down a call that wants you to make the world safe for your children."

"Why answer?"

"Because if I'm in trouble, you will come for me, and I will always be with the princess."

"So, if you're in trouble, she will be, too."

"And here I was thinking you were slow. Now stop rotating your foot so far; your footwork is appalling. It looks like you're trying to swing a sword."

For the rest of our training session, Sir Trent taught me how to fight, rather than let me figure it out while he whaled on me. He adapted the memories I had from other fighting disciplines, showing me how they could be incorporated into what we were doing. By the end of it, I'd seen a lot of progress.

You have mastered your Footwork skill.
You have mastered your Block skill.
You have mastered your Dodge skill.
You have mastered your Unarmed Combat skill.

"Did you seriously have to destroy my shirt?" Luke complained.

"You were fighting sloppily," I replied, swiping his towel and storage pouch from the table in my training hall as I walked to the door.

"Where the hell are you going? You promised me you'd help me train all night."

"Don't swear, Son. And I'm going to let your magic tutor in, so I expect you to be on your best behaviour. I went through a lot of trouble to arrange this tutor for you, and you won't find a better one in Murdell."

I unlocked the door and pulled it open.

Princess Carolyn was standing in the hallway all alone, wearing a new dress. Based on the scents I could smell, Solomon had made it. Her eyes widened as she looked past me and saw my shirtless son. A big smile spread across her face as she blushed.

"One shirtless hero, as promised." I handed her Luke's towel. "He's a little sweaty. Do you mind giving this to him for me?"

She took the towel without taking her eyes off him. I stepped out of the way, and she walked past me in a daze.

"Have fun." I gave Luke my biggest grin, holding up his storage pouch filled with clothes. The look he was giving me promised retribution. He'd get over it when he figured out that I'd managed to find him a teacher who understood his new bloodline. His chest would keep her so mesmerized that she'd spill all her family secrets to him.

I closed the door and sealed it by triple casting the deathlock spell, before heading for my classroom. Personal guards and servants weren't allowed into classrooms or clubrooms while lessons or activities were taking place, so separating Carolyn from them was as simple as signing her up for my Undead Enhancement Club.

I left Luke's storage pouch in the workshop, next to my latest experiment. It was significantly less grotesque than my previous ones. I no longer needed entire zombies to study the aspects I wanted. I could get by with a single limb or organ, which allowed me to develop my skills a lot quicker. My living dead project remained under a pair of sheets, waiting for Professor Fergus to finish replicating my results, but now that my books were here, I didn't need them to keep me occupied. Working my way through the Royal Northern Library and the last of Contessa's library was a time-consuming process.

I was the last person to enter the classroom, so I saw a room filled with students. They all had a skeleton standing patiently at the back of the room and there was a nervous energy in the air as I passed the three inanimate skeletons lying on the tables and took a seat at my desk. I'd prepared the skeletons for today's club meeting, and they were different from anything we'd created before. Davina was seated front and centre, with a notebook in front of her.

"Sorry I'm late, everyone. I hope you used my brief absence to familiarise yourself with the handout for today's activity."

Baris raised his hand. "Sir, are we really moving on to creating undead skeleton warriors?"

"Yes. Does anyone know why?"

A dozen hands went up.

I pointed to Lidia.

Mr. Bitey hissed at me, looking far healthier than he had several months ago. "We've exhausted all nonfinancial enhancement techniques that can be performed on an undead skeleton."

"Correct. There are many financial avenues that can be explored to craft stronger undead skeletons. Barring a handful of these techniques, they don't teach you anything you can't learn from expending time and mana to craft undead skeleton warriors. That doesn't mean an undead created from butchers' scraps can outperform undead created with financial investment. It only means that the techniques can be learned at little expense."

It also meant that students couldn't buy their way into winning Undead Fight Club, only win it with hard work and skill. Only the uber-wealthy hated this rule. Everyone else accepted I was making an even playing field.

"Baris, can you tell me the three basic forms of skeleton warriors?"

He grinned. "Spearman, knight, and mage."

"Can you also tell me what's special about an undead spearman?"

"They have much higher mobility and the strongest ability to regenerate."

"Correct on both accounts. Which of these three is the strongest?"

Davina's hand was the only one to shoot up.

"This isn't a hard question, people."

Davina waved her hand more vigorously.

I'd never ignored a student, so my students found it amusing that I was ignoring one now, especially one so young. Envy was prevalent among sorcerers, and they thought that might be something I suffered from.

"The answer is related to common combat."

I saw several faces light up with understanding, but they didn't raise their hands.

I sighed, rolled my eyes, and then glared at Davina.

She lowered her hand.

Baris raised his. "Sir, why aren't you letting her answer?" He was a good young man.

"Davina isn't here to participate in club activities. She's here to assess my skill at creating undead." This caused a stir of interest, which derailed my lesson. "Davina, please stand up and introduce yourself."

She gave me her biggest smile as she stood and turned to the class. "Hello everyone, I'm Davina. I'm a master practitioner of death and necrotic magic, and an expert practitioner of life and holy magic. I'm attending Darksmith to further my understanding of the other branches of magic, so if you have any questions about death or necrotic magic, feel free to introduce yourself." She sat back down.

Baris raised his hand again, as everyone sat dumbfounded. "Sir, will Davina be joining *the club*?" The way he said *the club*, told me he was referring to Undead Fight Club.

"That's up to her. Now, the answer to my question was that it depends on the circumstances."

"No, it doesn't," Davina blurted out. "The mage is significantly stronger."

"Please ignore Davina's outburst. When undead warriors are created by a master, mages are significantly stronger than the others. This is still a circumstantial situation, the circumstance being you have mastered death magic and making undead warriors. You may correct me if I'm wrong, Davina?"

Several people chuckled.

Davina, however, tried to correct me. "At any stage of skill, skeleton mages are the strongest of the three. Their destructive power is superior in all ways."

"So, you would put one in a child's nursery to protect them from assassins?"

Davina blushed and shook her head.

"Strength is circumstantial. What can be a benefit in one situation can be a hindrance in another. You need to always think about what purpose your creations serve and how they will act. If you need them to fight in groups, spearmen are the best. If you need them to fight inside a building, knights win. If you need them to fight at range or on a battlefield, mages are clearly going to get the job done. Davina, would you please step forward and assess the skeletons I've created for today's demonstration?"

Davina gathered mana as she walked to each skeleton and touched each skull, casting an expert-tier holy spell that caused several students' jaws to drop, despite her earlier announcement. "These are what I would describe as working failures. Every enhancement is expert tier and functions correctly, but they've been created with the minimum amount of mana with which you could personally perform the spell. One of the greatest benefits of using enhancement techniques that only require mana is that you can overcharge the spells you use, strengthening the enhancement effect. However, these skeletons are made with dungeon monster bones, so they are not something you're looking to invest in long-term. Having said that, you need to practice these techniques. You've only mastered the basic tier, and the number of inefficiencies and inadequacies that I see increase with each tier. However, you meet the minimum requirements for what is necessary to master each of their related skills."

I turned to the other student. "Mastery of low advanced magic is all that is required to master the create undead skill; mastery of high advanced magic will allow you to master the create undead skeleton skill. Mastery of expert tier magic and investing in your agility is required for mastering the create undead warrior skills. Mastering anything above this requires financial investment, as the attribute costs become too high. I will now demonstrate how to multicast twelve spells at once. Do not attempt to replicate this, because the backlash will kill you."

Davina's mouth dropped open. "What!"

I smirked at my familiar. "Is there a problem?"

"That shouldn't be possible. *Six* is the theoretical limit."

"I've seen him do nine," Baris said.

Everyone in the class nodded.

Davina stared, mouth open, for several seconds, before coming to her senses. "Show me." She cast another spell, and her eyes began to glow with a gentle blue light.

I walked over to the nearest skeleton and held my hand above it. I accelerated my perception and then multicast the first twelve ranks of the create undead skeleton spell, weaving them together to form a single complex spell. Black flames filled the eye sockets as it took effect. I went to the next two and repeated the process.

When I was done, Davina raised her hand, holding her palm up, and began gathering mana. The class stared in awe at the speed with which she gathered mana and the way she stored it in her body to use. When she had enough, she replicated what I had done, except with a death bolt spell, creating twelve complete layers. She then looked around and realised she didn't have anywhere to send it, so she ate it. Her skin took on a slight mummified quality for a second, before returning to normal.

The entire club lost it, not understanding what had just happened. Several people jumped out of their chairs and ran down to investigate, while others raised their hands.

I ignored them, focusing on the notification that had appeared.

You have mastered your Educator skill.
You have mastered your Instructor skill.

Those skills had been sitting below level 10 for weeks, waiting for someone to display a higher technique that I'd taught them. To jump to mastered was absurd. What kind of technique was I using?

Davina walked over to me, and the room fell silent. "That was surprisingly easy. Where did you learn how to do that?"

"It's obvious if you understand multicasting, layering, anchoring, and spatial theories."

"Do you mean that you created this technique?"

I shook my head. "The Vampire Lavire did. He used it in his enchantments. I just adapted it for creating and enhancing undead."

Baris injected himself into the conversation. "What's so interesting about this technique?"

Davina turned. "That depends on what you're using it for. With spells, it makes it more difficult for someone to counter spell you. It also increases the power output, but this is negligible for the mana cost. For creating undead, it drastically increases the amount of mana that is available to the undead. These expert tier undead skeletons have twelve ranks of mana crammed into them. They will continue fighting long after a normal undead would collapse from mana expenditure. This is not normally how you are taught to create undead. However, it will become the standard practice from now on. This is completely revolutionary."

"We're getting off-topic," I said, to regain the club's attention. "Can anyone tell me the greatest limitation of a skeleton mage?"

Lidia's hand shot up. "They aren't intelligent."

"Correct. While undead skeleton warriors are more skilled than their undead skeleton counterparts, they aren't truly intelligent, making them unable to learn and grow. This means that skeleton mages are essentially only mobile weapons capable of throwing out a handful of spells. Why is this important?"

Baris was the only one to hold up his hand. "It's important because you always need to remember that no matter how skilled they appear, they aren't capable of thought. This limits how they can be used."

"Correct. Undead skeleton warriors are just a more powerful version of the basic undead skeleton. While this is useful, direct oversight is still required. This changes when you move onto advanced skeleton warriors. Advanced skeleton warriors can be summoned directly but are more powerful when crafted from two regular skeleton warriors. Death knights are crafted from a knight and a mage. Sorcerers are crafted from a spearman and a mage. Lancers are crafted from a spearman and a knight. These can be modified further by sacrificing more than one of each type, but that is another entire lecture, so I won't go into it today. Instead, I'll demonstrate what's required to master the three create undead skeleton warrior skills."

I held my hand above the spearman I'd crafted and multicast the required spells, layering the new spell over the old. The bone spear and armour I'd created, moulded into the undead skeleton spearman's form, as the black flames in its eyes became a deeper black that drank in the light around it. I moved onto the knight and repeated the process, before finishing with the mage.

A notification appeared as I finished.

You have mastered Create Undead Skeleton Spearman skill.
You have mastered Create Undead Skeleton Knight skill.
You have mastered Create Undead Skeleton Mage skill.
You have increased your Enhance Undead skill to level 15.

I turned to the club. "Now that you understand what is required to master these skills, are there any questions?"

Davina's was the first hand to go up.

THE CLUB MEETING WAS OVER, and everyone, except Davina, had gone to bed. She walked around my creations, examining them with various spells, before taking a seat beside me.

"What do I need to practice?" I asked.

"Your spell work is your biggest problem. It's sloppy. I'm assuming you're leaning on what you learned from the other practitioners' memories to grow faster, rather than learning the techniques yourself."

"Is that a problem?"

"Yes. Master-tier magic doesn't allow for errors in technique. The peak of expert is the furthest you can go, cheating the way you are."

"Are there any drawbacks to continuing things my way?"

"Normally, I would say yes, because you're creating bad habits, but you aren't normal. Finish mastering expert magic your way, and then I'll teach you how to do it properly."

"Anything else I need to be aware of?"

"Nothing that will help you now."

"Good."

Davina took a seat on my desk and turned to look at the classroom. "I liked your club. Everyone was attentive and friendly, and you're a better teacher than I expected. Have you done it before?"

"A long time ago."

She smiled because I rarely talked about myself. "Why did you stop?"

"I was given the opportunity to practice what I was teaching in a way that did a lot more good."

"What did you teach?"

"Law and ethics."

Davina giggled. "You were a lawyer."

"Yes. Why is that funny?"

"Angelica always talks about how evil is in her blood because her father was a lawyer. I'm willing to bet that she'll think she is twice as evil when I tell her this."

I chuckled. "She'll probably use it to justify her bad behaviour."

"I probably shouldn't tell her, then."

"Are you going to join the club?"

She shook her head. "You're not teaching anything I don't already know or can't learn in a fraction of the time alone. And I've seen enough undead destroy themselves for necromancers' amusement for one lifetime. I think Angelica would benefit from it, though."

"Why?"

"These people aren't evil. Angelica hasn't spent any time around necromancers like them. It warps her views of what necromancers are like. Also, she's competitive, she has the necessary skills, and they are only slightly more skilled than she is, so she'll enjoy it."

Angelica and Davina had leveled drastically, before I went to sleep, and there hadn't been time for me to assess these changes. "Speaking of enjoying it, I need to go give my son a shirt. Get me a list of both your skills by tomorrow morning, so I can assess your progress."

She reached into her storage pouch. "I've got the list on me."

I took the list and read it. I then pulled a pen from my storage pouch and began placing numbers next to their skills, before handing it back. "I suggest you and Angelica prioritise training your skills in this order."

Davina frowned as she read. "Mine are all holy skills."

"All my people have access to death and necrotic magic. You are by far the most talented, but that isn't what makes you special. You're the necrosaint. You need to work on your holy skills."

"Is that a suggestion?"

I nodded.

She smiled. "And if I were to ignore that suggestion?"

"You've both made more progress than I expected, so I'm not going to tell you to stop what you're doing. If that should change, my suggestions will become orders, but for now you're both doing well enough that I won't interfere."

"Then I'll continue what I'm doing."

The smile on her face sat at odds with the turmoil coming from her scent. She didn't want to practice holy magic and was happy I'd let her off the hook. I knew why she didn't want to practice it, and I felt that she needed know that I knew.

"Davina, you can only put off becoming powerful enough to kill me for so long. I won't hate you for putting me to rest if you need to. I trust that if you have to do it, you'll have a good reason."

She dropped her gaze to her feet. "You're a good man, your Dark Eminence. I'm not sure if I can live with your death on my conscience."

"I won't have a soul. I won't be me."

"You and I both know how monstrous your impulses are and how closely you tread the line between hero and villain. I can see you crossing that line while still having a soul, and if I have the strength to end you, then I'll be the one who has to bring you down. I'll be the one who has to watch your soul be dragged down to hell."

"I'll do my best to make sure that doesn't occur, but I can't promise it won't happen."

"That's what I'm afraid of."

"Which is why I want you there to stop me."

Davina didn't promise anything before heading out. She was too conflicted. That was fine. She knew that I knew why she was shirking her duties, and she was mature enough to come to terms with what she needed to do if I gave her enough time.

She also wasn't the only person I was relying on to take me out if it became necessary. I had plans for a lot of people.

The moment she left, Sir Trent and Carolyn's other guards walked in. They followed me to the training hall, where I removed the barriers sealing the door. Sir Trent used the doorknocker but didn't force his way in. Opening the door on a sorcerer in training was a great way to cause accidents, and the sound from the knocker would enter once the wards didn't sense magic being actively used.

He folded his arms and leaned against the wall. "You know, Rupert is furious about this."

"What did I do?"

"You went along with it?"

I chuckled. "Yeah, that was pretty funny." I reached into Luke's storage pouch and found a shirt. I began to alter it with magic, causing it to shrink just enough to be tight against his skin. It would expand in an hour when the spell wore off, but it would be funny while it lasted.

Sir Trent chuckled as he watched it shrink. "That's mean. How did you get him out of his shirt to begin with?"

"Told him we were going to do some light training and then cut it off just before she arrived."

The guards laughed.

A minute later, my son opened the door brandishing a sword. When he saw it was me, he glared.

"I found you a new shirt. Sorry that it took so long."

He yanked the shirt out of my hand and pulled it on. Behind him, Princess Carolyn was staring at his butt. He immediately noticed how tight it was. He didn't say a word as he stalked back into the training hall and said goodbye to the princess. He escorted her to the door like a proper gentleman, then he tried to yank me into the room.

I ducked around his hand and stepped inside, kicking the door closed. "How was your first lesson?"

He pointed to his nipples poking against his shirt. "Cold, very cold."

I laughed. "How do you like your new instructor?"

Luke rolled his eyes. "When she's not staring at my butt, she's a very good teacher. She understands her bloodline in a way that no one else does. I made more progress with her in one lesson than with any of my other instructors. How did you convince her to teach me? And please don't tell me I have to be shirtless for every lesson."

"She wanted me to sign a betrothal contract. I negotiated her down to private lessons four nights a week and the first one being shirtless."

"She what?"

"She wanted to see you without a shirt on."

"No, the betrothal part."

"Yes, that probably would have required you to be shirtless at some point too."

"Dad, will you be serious?"

"Not while your shirt's that tight."

Luke groaned.

"I believe you said I need more humour in my life."

"I'm beginning to regret what I said."

"That's very big of you, unlike that shirt."

"Dad, I'm over this. Can you please be serious?"

"Hi, Over This, I'm Serious. So, you can trust me when I tell you, that princess wants to marry you."

Luke finally chuckled. "So, you used that to convince her to teach me magic."

"Which is something no one else in her family would have done if I had asked. You're welcome."

"I'm not saying thank you for treating me like a party favour and handing me out to a hormone-addled teenage girl."

"I mean I didn't betroth you to a teenage girl, as well, so you could be a little grateful...unless you're upset I didn't go through with the engagement." I turned and started walking to the door. "Don't worry, I can fix this. And I'll make sure you get to wear a shirt for a few hours every day."

Luke grabbed my collar, stopping me cold, forcing me to walk in place.

"How many children are you capable of fathering? Should I say twenty or twenty-five?"

"Thank you for not betrothing me to a teenage girl. I understand that this must have been difficult for you to comprehend how this is socially unacceptable, with how you seem to collect them like Pokémon, so I do appreciate the gesture."

"I would say that's rich coming from someone who spends their evenings alone in a room with one, but Davina says she needs to teach me how to perform magic properly, so I can't really talk."

Luke chuckled. "You still owe me a training session?"

I activated the training hall's barrier, completely cutting me off from the noise of the outside world and drew Slaughter as I followed Luke to the middle of the training floor. "How does the sorcerer sovereign skill work?"

Luke drew his longsword and made a two-handed slash. "It allows us to bond with people the way we would bond with magical equipment, so we can draw on their mana without needing to be in contact."

I knocked aside his blade and tried to kick his knee.

He dodged the kick, while striking my raised ankle with his palm, trying to throw me off balance. "The further away you are from the people you're bonded with, the less efficient the mana transfer is, and you can only bond with people who practice the same schools of magic you do. When they're not training, the royal family predominantly uses the skill to strengthen their cores and the cores of the people who bond with them."

I blocked several quick slashes. "How do you level the skill?"

"By becoming more efficient at drawing mana from the people you're bonded with. The royal family uses the skill to practice magic as much as they want without having to refill their cores. It's why they're so much more talented than everyone else. They don't have to stop training to meditate."

"I imagine it also helps that upgrading the skill, upgrades all their magical skills."

"That helps, but additional practice is more important. It allows them to reach archsorcerer by level 20. You should bond with Gregory and his men. If you can draw enough mana from them, you will be able to form a perfect core."

"I've already got a perfect core."

"How?"

"I went into the Abyss. Higher ambient mana makes it easier to form a perfect core."

"Well, you can still help *them* form perfect cores."

I WAS HOLDING Kathrine's hand and using the healing palm technique, while reading the books from the Northern Royal Library, when the head of my personal guard, Gregory walked through the door. He nodded to Davina who was reading on the couch as he picked up an armchair, and he carried it over to the bed, taking a seat beside me.

Gregory was in his early forties, with dark brown hair, and an impressive physique. He'd grown substantially stronger since I'd saved his life and the lives of his men, but he still didn't pose a threat to me. His level may not have impressed me when we first met, but his leadership, organisation, and diligence for those under his command did.

I had no regrets over putting him in charge.

Gregory folded his arms and sighed dramatically. "My wife told me to tell you, that if you get me killed, you have to march down to Hell and bring me back."

I chuckled. "If I have to come and get you, then its counting as your holiday."

"Seems reasonable. What do you need, sir?"

"Why did you bring two hundred deathlords with you?"

Davina told me that, the moment I'd gone to sleep, Gregory and his men had thrown themselves into training, with an intense ferocity. Their skills had exploded, and being stuck at level 80, they were able to advance from death knights to deathlords.

"I got the impression we were going to walk into a mess."

"What gave you that impression?"

"We always walk into a mess."

That did seem to happen a lot.

"I need your help to train one of my skills. It will involve bonding our cores, so I can draw and send mana to you."

Gregory sighed. "I have a very weak talent for magic, sir. It makes it harder for me to cast spells. You should get someone else."

I frowned because what he said made no sense. "There's no such thing as a weak talent for magic. There's only a weaker magical talent, which is the ability to gather mana."

"Isn't that what I said?"

"No. They're completely different things."

"Does it matter?"

"You said it was affecting your ability to cast spells, so yes, it does."

"Davina said it's perfectly normal."

"It's not. If you and your wife had the same number of points in your strength attribute, which of you could lift more?"

"Me."

"Exactly. A weak magical talent just means that your mana regeneration attribute is less effective than other people's, which is more common for men. This has no direct effect on your ability to cast spells, but it can make it incredibly difficult for you to build a proper mana network, which would definitely make it harder for you to cast spells. Give me your hand."

Gregory held out his hand. I grabbed it and cast a basic scanning spell. There were holes throughout his mana network, and it barely spread through a third of his body.

"Davina, get over here."

She put down the book she was reading and walked over. "Why do you sound upset?"

I scowled at her. "You failed my men."

She raised an eyebrow, not at all flustered by my scowl. Considering the creatures she'd spent the majority of her life around that wasn't surprising. "How?"

"Have a look at his mana network."

Davina took his other hand and cast the same spell I had. "I don't see the problem. Gregory has a weak magical talent."

"That just means he's bad at gathering mana."

"Which is what a mana network is built from."

"Which can be overcome with a high ambient mana environment."

"Which is why I made one."

I frowned. "This is with a high ambient magic environment?"

She nodded. "The environment I created was as concentrated as the first floor of the Abyss. Gregory's talent is just that weak." She turned and walked back to her chair.

Gregory shrugged. “Like I said. You should find someone else. My core can barely hold anything.”

“Let me try with you. You should be able to draw the mana I give you from your core to refine your mana network.”

“Will it hurt?”

“It shouldn’t.”

“Go ahead.”

I drew an unbroken cord of mana from my core, through my mana network, and out of my mouth. The cord wriggled through the air, before entering his mouth, moving down his poorly established mana network to enter his core. Then I cast the spell that Luke had taught me. The mana cord became a permanent connection, creating a magical cord between our cores. The small amount of mana inside his core was yanked from his core through the cord and into mine. Wherever the mana touched the edges of the cord, it broke free, spilling into the air.

I let go of his hand, no longer needing to see his mana network.

Gregory frown. “Did you just take my mana?”

“Not intentionally. My core’s different to most people’s, and it emptied yours on its own.”

Davina blurred across the room and appeared beside me. “Can I see?”

I nodded.

She placed her hand on my stomach and scanned me. “Your core is completely stable. You’re not leaking any mana.”

While Davina continued to scan me, I pushed mana from my core, through the cord, and into Gregory’s core, being careful not to touch the side of the cord I sensed. Even though I was learning, it only took a few seconds to refill his core.

Gregory immediately noticed the change. “Do you want me to draw the mana from my core and circulate it through my mana network?”

“Draw as much as you can. I’ll keep supplying you.”

“Tell me when you’re running low.”

Davina giggled. “That’s not going to be an issue. His Dark

Eminence has the biggest core I've ever seen. How did you make this?"

"Fifteenth floor of the Abyss, using liquid mana, and enough monster cores to fund a kingdom for a century. Creating my core caused me to master the magic skill. Improving my core made me master death and necrotic magic. It's strong evidence that the magic we practice is just a reflection of true magic."

Davina pulled out paper and a pen and began drawing the structure of my core. When she was done, she began adding notes and calculations.

The calculations grew more and more complex until she looked at me and smiled. "My calculations say you can create your core without liquid mana. It would require a master-tier spell that aligns with the type of magic a person practices, which is probably why you mastered the different magic skills when you created and grew your core."

If that were true, then perhaps the magic we practiced wasn't a reflection of true magic.

"Can you create the spell?"

"I'm not sure, but I'm going to try once I've mastered life and holy magic. This type of core shouldn't interfere with my constitution."

She picked up her notes and returned to the couch.

A few hours later, Gregory opened his eyes. "I think I'm done, sir."

I grabbed his hand and scanned him. His mana network had spread through his entire body. "Circulate your mana."

He did as I said.

There were hundreds of spots where his mana didn't move smoothly. "You're not done. Keep going."

Gregory went back to work.

When it came time for the morning risk assessment meeting, I left him guarding Kathrine, continuing to feed him mana. It was significantly more difficult to maintain my efficiency over distance, but by the time lunch had rolled around, I had the hang of it. The walls between us were a major problem, but the mana I sent him didn't leak through anywhere else.

I returned to the bedroom at lunch to check his progress, and then again after the school day was finished, before finally returning after the Undead Enhancement Club meeting.

I let go of his hand as I finished scanning. "You've refined your mana network well enough to move on. Do you know how to actively channel ambient mana into a spell?"

Gregory grinned. "I've more experience channelling ambient mana than anything else. It's an important part of doing a proper death or necrotic strike."

"Practice channelling mana into the core spell. Once you get the hang of it, we'll reform your core."

He held out his hand and muttered the incantation, forming a core spell above his palm. He held the spell in place as he continued to channel mana into it. The more mana he channelled, the more the structure of the spell improved until it was flawless.

He grinned the entire time. "It's so much easier now."

"That's still impressive."

He shrugged as he dismissed the spell. "The core spell is the only spell I know, and I've had a lot of practice."

"You ready to reform your core?"

He nodded.

"Hold as much mana outside your core as you can, and I'll break your core for you."

"Done."

I placed my hand on his stomach, scanned his body, and cast the core-breaking spell. He hadn't strengthened his core, so it was a simple matter. He released a small grunt of pain and leaked a little mana but held on to most of it.

It took a few minutes for the mana structure of his core to completely dissipate, because he didn't know how to force the magic from his body. "You can cast the spell now."

He took a slow breath and then muttered the incantation.

I watched the structure of the spell come together as he slowly fed it more and more mana. When it was stable, I reached out with a cord of mana and connected my core to his, forming the link to his core through the same point where he was feeding mana into the spell. Then I cast the spell that made the connection permanent.

The moment the connection formed I took over the spell, becoming the sole source of mana. I flooded the connection, giving the spell all the mana it could possibly need. Unlike when I'd formed my core, the process wasn't instantaneous. The spell slowly strengthened over the next few minutes, until it couldn't strengthen anymore. Mana began to leak from places, changing to death mana which damaged his body. As the leaks spread, Gregory began to groan.

I waited until the strength of his core had been evenly distributed throughout, ignoring the mounting injuries, and then cut of the flow of mana after his core was ready.

The spell snapped together.

"Congratulations, you're now the proud owner of a perfect 3rd-rank core."

Gregory didn't smile as he swayed in his chair. "I think I'm going to pass out."

A moment later he was proven right.

A notification appeared as he slumped into his chair.

Your Sorcerer Sovereign skill has reached level 3.

15

PEOPLE IN PLACES THEY SHOULDN'T BE

In Murdell, most dungeons belonged to the local academy, and there wasn't a dungeon in the nation that didn't house an academy for higher magical learning. Darksmith, like many of the better academies, didn't allow outsiders into its dungeon. But unlike most of those academies, Darksmith preferred to use their students to guard the fortress, regularly putting them in a small amount of danger to keep them sharp.

Getting the Undead Fight Club in control of the academy's fortress and tunnel security for two separate shifts, three days apart, took me two weeks to organise and required numerous bribes, blackmail, and everyone to forgo the start of the Lunar Festival. Other than this brief window, I had no easy way to sneak Gregory and my men into the Abyss.

Helen, Gregory's wife, glanced at the necromancers on the walls distrustfully as we entered the fortress and made our way through the central courtyard to the gate. "What did you have to promise these instruments of darkness for their aid?"

"The worthy among them will be allowed to die for my amusement," I said, dryly.

Helen stumbled, shocked by my reply.

Gregory's hand snapped out and he caught his wife before she fell. "He's joking, dear."

I sniffed the air, smelling Amelia. Her scent shouldn't have been anywhere near the fortress. She was supposed to be with the princess or in town. Amelia's scent wasn't fresh, which meant she wasn't currently here, so I put it out of my head and turned to Helen. "Your husband and his men are going to teach my students how to fight with weapons."

She scowled at me. "You could have just said you intimidated them into helping."

"If I'd intimidated them, I would tell you. They're helping us in return for training."

"Why would they do that? Murdell's citizens are well known for their prejudice against what they consider to be mundane arts."

"That prejudice is exactly why they need your husband's help. There aren't many people in Murdell who know how to fight without magic, and those who do won't teach their skills to necromancers. Without a greater understanding of how to fight, they can't program their undead warriors to do anything more than a basic hack and slash."

"Why are they trembling, then?"

"They're from Necropolis. The city uses deathlords to hunt down wayward necromancers and execute them. We look like an army of executioners to them."

We passed through the fortress's gate and my students began to relax. Gregory called for a quick march, and they broke into a run, crossing the cavern quickly, before entering the tunnels. I threw a necrotic bolt at anything that crossed our path, until we reached the tunnel, and then I used my aura to keep everything at bay, so nothing would bother us while we travelled.

Gregory had gained a perfect core and mana network thanks to me eating the royal family. Now that he wasn't restricted by his poor mana network, he was learning how to wield death and necrotic magic as fast as he'd picked up using a kilij. His oath to me was letting him draw on my skill to improve his own; in a year or two he'd be as good with magic as he was with a sword.

The deathlords Gregory brought with him were predominately made up of those who had a weak magical talent. Most of those with a regular magical talent had split their time between practicing their martial skills and magic and hadn't unlocked the deathlord class before everyone left to come here. That meant almost all of those here struggled with magic in the exact same way Gregory had.

Helping them one at a time would take almost half a year, so I'd decided to take them into the Abyss, where the ambient mana was more concentrated. I would use them to raise the level of my sorcerer sovereign skill while I helped them form a perfect mana network and core.

Davina, Angelica, and Delilah Morgana Frostwing the 3rd were waiting for us at the entrance to the Abyss when we arrived. Getting the dracolich down here was a simple matter. Headmaster Wink had no problem with Angelica bringing her dracolich into the dungeon so long as she didn't bring it into his school.

I stopped before my familiars and turned to my right, where I could hear a heartbeat without a visible source. "What are you doing here, Amelia?"

"Can I please come, Vincent?" she replied, invisible to my sight.

Angelica and Davina both jumped with surprise.

I continued to stare at the spot where she stood. "Do your guards know where you are?"

"I left a note."

"Does the princess know you're borrowing her invisibility cloak?"

"It's in the note."

"Are you going to try to follow us if I say no?"

Silence.

"I can't see you nodding your head, Amelia."

She pulled back the hood of her cloak and became visible. She nodded once and then lifted the hood and vanished.

"Fine, you can come."

Gregory gave me an uncomfortable glance after his wife elbowed his side. "Is that wise, sir?"

"We can't stop her. The medallion around her neck is a phase medallion. If we try to grab her, our hands will pass through her. Nobility use those medallions to protect their children from being kidnapped."

"Vincent can remove it with Slaughter," Amelia added. "But he has to be able to see it."

Helen elbowed her husband a second time.

"I would still rather she not come, sir."

"Everything on the first floor of the Abyss is scared of Vincent," Amelia grumbled. "I'll be fine."

She was correct, which was why I didn't care if she came. "You can ride on the dracolich with Angelica."

She lowered her hood, becoming visible, and ran over to the dracolich, scrambling up her body to reach the designer saddle. Once she was in place, she kicked her heels against the dracolich's ribs. "Onward, noble steed."

The dracolich turn her head to glare at Amelia. "My name is Delilah Morgana Frostwing the 3rd. Make her use my name, Angie."

Angelica walked over and leapt on the dracolich's back, before sitting on the saddle behind Amelia. "Don't be rude, Amelia."

Amelia sighed. "Fine. Onward, Delilah Morgana Frostwing the 3rd the noblest of steeds."

The dracolich leapt into the air and beat its wings. "Try to keep up."

We passed through Gorgath's chamber on our way to the entrance of the second floor of the Abyss. The kid was off hunting for food for the mana crabs he was raising, so we reached our destination without having to stop. The mana concentration at the entrance was fifty times higher than what it was at the academy, which would drastically reduce the timeframe for helping everyone create a perfect mana network and form a perfect core.

The walls of the tunnel were coated in glowing orange crystals, providing plenty light to see, and my aura was keeping every threat at bay, as I slowed before the ground began to dip.

I turned to Gregory. "We're stopping here."

Gregory turned to his troops and began shouting orders. They fell into line, forming rows, as they pulled meditation mats from their storage pouches and took a seat on the cold stone floor. Once they were seated, they pulled out canteens and rations, replacing the lost fluids and calories from their run.

While they ate, I walked from person to person, bonding with their cores. I scanned each deathlord before bonding with them, so I could get a good idea of where they were at, but I stopped once I realised Gregory had already sorted his people for me. The thirty with the most progress were all in the front row.

Angelica took a seat in front of Gregory's people and Amelia joined her.

Angelica turned to Amelia. "I'm sitting up here, because my mana network is nearly flawless. You should go to the back row."

Amelia stuck her tongue out and shuffled further forward without replying.

As I finished bonding with Angelica's core, I walked over to Amelia and crouched down, placing my hand on her head. My scan showed she had a flawless mana network and a near-flawless core, proving she did deserve the front spot. "How did you manage to build a perfect mana network without a class?"

Amelia grinned up at me as I took my hand away. "I borrowed Princess Carolyn's meditation mat."

That was incredibly dangerous, but the kid seemed to have survived the experience, so I bonded with her core, knowing she could only practice death and necrotic magic, like everyone else here.

The moment our cores were bonded, her grin grew. "Can you help me form a perfect core now, Vincent?"

"No."

Her grin faded. "Why not?"

"Because you haven't earned my help yet. If you want a perfect core, you have to help everyone else form their perfect core first."

She groaned, the way children do. "But that will take ages."

"So will making a perfect core without my help."

"Please, Vincent."

"Those are my terms, Amelia."

She stuck her tongue out at me.

"I'll take that as a yes."

I walked to the front of the group, where everyone could see me. Behind me was the entrance to the second floor of the Abyss; if anything came up, I would deal with it. Behind the everyone were the clerics and dracolich, so nothing could sneak up on them from the other direction.

They were as safe as you could hope to be in the Abyss, so I moved on to why I'd brought them here and looked at the sea of faces. "As Commander Gregory has explained to you, the sorcerer sovereign skill allows me to draw mana from your cores or give mana to them. It's going to take a horrendous amount of mana for all of you to complete your mana networks, so I'll be focusing on leveling my skill first to make this easier on everyone. After that, I'll work on those who are closest to completing their mana network. Once their mana networks are complete, I will help them form a perfect core, so they can provide mana for everyone else to do the same. We can safely stay on the first floor of the Abyss for up to three days before mana sickness begins to affect anyone, so if everyone manages to complete their core early enough, we will work on strengthening your cores. If we manage to do that successfully, we'll go hunting. Any questions?"

Gregory raised his hand. "Why would we go hunting when we're all at the dungeon limit?"

"The dungeon limit raises by 80 levels each time you descend a floor."

Angelica frowned. "How did I level to 87 during the dungeon surge, then?"

"You killed a floor boss from the Abyss on the dungeon level. The dungeon limit doesn't always apply when something like that happens."

"Why?"

"The release of enough experience can temporarily lift the dungeon limit, but it massively reduces how much experience you receive. You would have got twice as many levels if you had killed the acid centipede down here." I turned to the rest of the crowd. "If there are no other questions, we'll begin."

No one had any questions.

I nodded to Davina, indicating she should get ready to heal Angelica, as I took a seat on the ground. Mana began pouring into my core, as I focused on the cords linking me with my people. Sending mana to this many people at once was beyond me.

I needed to level the skill, before I tried.

Luke had been asking Carolyn all sorts of questions about the sorcerer sovereign skill and how to level it. It was relatively straightforward. Quickly transferring an 18th-rank spell's worth of raw mana to or from someone without any mana leakage would level the skill to level 17.

I sent enough mana for a 5th-rank spell to Angelica. Angelica closed her eyes and began pushing the mana through her mana network as a notification appeared before me.

Your Sorcerer Sovereign skill has increased to level 4.

I did it again with a 6th-rank spell but didn't notice any assistance from the skill from the new level. Another notification appeared.

Your Sorcerer Sovereign skill has increased to level 5.

I went level by level, but only noticed a reduction in the difficulty after I reached level 15. I took note of the changes and continued.

Your Sorcerer Sovereign skill has increased to level 17.

Angelica was trembling, with sweat dripping from her forehead, as she tried to move the massive amount of mana I'd just channelled into her core through her mana network. Davina stood behind her, watching closely in case Angelica accidentally converted the raw mana to elemental mana and needed her to intervene.

Based on Carolyn's family's historical accounts, the original owner of the sorcerer sovereign bloodline never mastered the skill. She reached level 14 and never worked out how to go further. It wasn't until several generations and a lot of experimentation later that her descendants discovered another way to level the skill once it reached level 14.

Instead of transferring the mana for higher-ranked spells to or from a sorcerer, you transferred a 15th-rank spell to or from twice as many sorcerers, doubling the number for each additional level. To master the skill, all you had to do was work with 64 sorcerers with master-tier core capacity that matched your own. If you had mastered the prodigy skill, like I had, you only needed 48. Carolyn's family kept hundreds of sorcerers with a core that could hold a master-tier spell's worth of mana on hand for this very reason, but even then, they couldn't grow their skill as fast as I could.

I had a truly absurd amount of mana at my disposal. Far more than any sorcerer would usually contain, but it still wasn't enough with using my current method. The best I could do was transfer an 18th-rank spell's worth of mana to two people and reach level 18. But judging by how much trouble Angelica was having, that would be a mistake.

If *she* could barely cope with that much mana, no one else would be able to handle it. That meant I had to switch to Carolyn's family's method, but even with my full mana capacity, that would only bring the skill to level 19.

"I'm going to replenish my mana now," I instructed. "Those in the front row, prepare to receive enough mana for a 15th-rank spell. Clerics, please come forward to assist anyone who is injured."

I pulled the mana from everyone to refill my core and waited until everyone one was in position.

"I will begin in three, two, one."

While I counted down, I accelerated my mind and focused on my bonds with my twenty most-skilled deathlords. My new skill levels helped to stabilise the mana flow as I forced a torrent of raw mana into each of their cores in a few short seconds.

Three people cried out and one man's stomach exploded as they tried to pull the mana from their cores too quickly and accidently converted the raw mana to elemental mana. Davina blurred to the man's side, ignoring his injuries to syphon the mana away. A second later, she cast another spell, and his flesh flew back to his stomach cavity, making a wet, slapping sound. His organs pulled themselves back together, the pieces regenerating to form perfect organs, before his skin covered them up.

Your Sorcerer Sovereign skill has increased to level 18

Those who had cried out and the man who was injured had all failed to absorb the raw mana that I sent them, which would have stopped me from leveling my skill if I'd only transferred mana to the twelve I needed.

While Davina stabilized the injured man, I refilled my core. After a few minutes, she moved him to the side of the group and left him in Helen's care.

Everyone patiently waited for me to refill my core, and then I repeated my actions with the next twenty most-skilled deathlords. This time three people's stomachs exploded and five people cried out.

I moved the twenty-four with the most skill to the front row, refilled my mana, and then tried transferring a 15th-rank spell's worth of raw mana to all of them. No one exploded or cried out, but I failed to transfer the mana fast enough. After three hours of trial and error, I finally saw the notification I was waiting for.

Your Sorcerer Sovereign skill has increased to level 19.

I stood up, so everyone could see me. "Thank you for helping me level my skill. We will now begin refining the mana networks of those in the front row. When Davina taps you on the shoulder, your mana network will be complete. At that time, I will help you form a perfect core. Once you've formed a perfect mana network and core, please move to the back row and supply mana for everyone else."

As I took a seat, I closed my eyes and began sending mana to those in the front row, steadily increasing the amount rank by rank until they began to struggle. At the same time, I pulled mana from everyone else. My higher skill level helped to stabilize my actions, but I still only managed to draw from so many with a fifty percent efficiency. That was good enough for what I needed.

Fifteen minutes later, Davina walked over and tapped me on the shoulder. "Angelica is ready."

I opened my eyes and climbed to my feet. I walked over to Angelica, placed my hand on her head, and scanned her. "Cycle mana around your body."

She did as I said.

Her mana network was flawless. I wasn't surprised. She had absurdly high attributes, and her mana network had been basically complete even before she started.

"You can break your core and reform it when you're ready."

She closed her eyes and muttered an incantation. She didn't wait for the magic inside her to dissipate naturally, the way Gregory had. She took hold of it and expelled it from her body. Then she muttered another incantation.

I threaded a new mana cord into her forming core and took over the channelling for her, feeding it the way I had fed Gregory's. When it had been strengthened everywhere, I cut the connection. Davina healed her.

Angelica moved to the back of the group and began to supply mana. As I walked back to the front, Amelia turned and poked her tongue at me again without stopping gathering mana.

I chuckled as I took a seat and went back to helping my people grow stronger.

A DAY LATER, I helped the last member of our expedition form a perfect core. Amelia wasn't happy that I'd made her wait until last, but I didn't want to encourage her to run off to join me in the Abyss every time I came down here. Everyone stopped for a short break, pulling food from their storage pouches, or taking a quick nap. An hour later, I gathered them all together.

I looked at all the smiling faces. Many had been testing their new abilities to see what they could do. "I'm not exactly sure how effective this next step will be, but we will give it a go. Remember: If you reach a bottleneck, I want you to stop trying to strengthen your core." I opened one of the small storage chests I'd borrowed from the academy and levitated one of the sharn beast cores out.

Gorgath's people didn't use them, so they were worth far less than the other cores he usually provided. The going rate was four to one. I'd told him I'd allow him to pay for half of his tuition with them at a three to one ratio. He'd been very grateful for the discount. And I was very grateful for his loot.

The moment it was out, the stupid dracolich leapt over everyone's head, spread her wings, and snatched the minivan-sized core from the air, before beating her wings furiously to try to fly off with it. The core weighed more than she did, so she barely stayed in the air as she turned and headed for the surface.

I leapt after her, casting a levitation spell and landing on her saddle.

I drew Slaughter. "What do you think you're doing?"

Her tail whipped around and knocked me from the saddle, making a small sonic boom with its speed. I slammed into the tunnel wall with a dull cracking thud, surprised that she'd gone through with the attack. I'd wrongfully assumed she was too afraid of me to strike. She crashed into the ground a moment later and clambered on top of the core and began roaring at everyone.

I held onto the tunnel wall as I finished healing, watching her roar and beat her wing to push everyone back. She'd turned primal. I'd never seen her like this.

She even roared at Angelica when she began to approach and commanded her. "Give it back."

I kicked off the wall and landed in front of the dracolich, throwing up a deathlock barrier in front of me. A torrent of death fire engulfed the shield, spreading around the sides of the barrier. I threw up two more spells to stop her from killing my people in her deranged state, as I closed the distance and punch her jaw closed, cutting off the fire.

"Be nice or I will take it back."

The punch seemed to knock her out of whatever state she had been in. She ducked her head and folded her wing over the core protectively.

"But it's mine." She gently brushed her claw across the surface. "My precious."

She was fixated on it, the way dragons fixated on gold and other shiny objects.

Nothing in my vast collection of knowledge told me why she would fixate on the core. "Why is it precious to you?"

"I need it."

"For what?"

"It will make me stronger."

"How?"

Her entire body trembled for a moment, and she finally looked away from it. "I don't have veins or a digestive system like you meat bags. I need special materials to strengthen my mana network, like necromancers. This is the most wonderous material I've ever seen for that purpose. Every bone in my body tells me this is precious."

Angelica approached slowly and stopped beside me. "I'll buy it from you."

I turned to her. "Why?"

"I can sense her feelings through our bond. You'll have to kill her to get it back. And I like her more than I like gold."

I felt her assessment was true. "Fine."

The dracolich squealed with delight. "This is almost as good as a princess. Thank you, Angie." She scraped her claw along the surface again. "My precious."

The core vaporized in a flash, flowing up and over the dracolich's body as a black cloud, pouring into her bones, creating thin black lines through their ivory finish. Black death flames sprang from her claws, and her aura grew more intense.

"Fear me, mortals, for I am the dracolich Delilah Morgana Frost Wing the 3rd."

"I'm not mortal."

"Of course, you're not included, your Dark Eminence. That's why I said mortals. Now stop ruining my moment. I am darkness. I am the long silence. I am the moonless night that makes you tremble in your beds."

She continued on like that until I went back to the storage chests and pulled out another sharn core. This one also got plucked from the air, just as quickly. Thankfully, this time she didn't lose herself to instincts and try to attack anyone.

Angelica chased after her dracolich. "I'll pay for that, too." She came back a few minutes later. "She says she needs more."

"How many more?"

"How many do you have?"

"Sixty-three."

Angelica ran off and came back with the dracolich.

Delilah towered over me as she stared at the chests. "My precious."

I levitated the cores out of the storage chests one by one, allowing her to absorb them. It took twenty of the cores to satisfy her, and by then, magic radiated from her in waves. She wasn't physically stronger than she used to be, but she was firmly on the road to becoming a greater dracolich. There was a magical weight to her that everyone could feel.

I pulled out a piece of paper and wrote out an invoice, before handing it to Angelica. "Your bill."

Angelica read the amount and dropped the invoice. "That *can't* be what they're worth."

"The smallest of those cores is worth more than the annual tuition for the entire student body of Darksmith, which is sixty million gold. The total value of what she absorbed was a little over two billion."

She looked ill. "Can I have a bulk discount?"

"Sure, I'll drop the bill down to a billion."

"Thank you." She walked off in a daze.

I levitated another core out of the chest and placed it on the ground. I turned to Gregory's men. "Now, where were we?"

STRENGTHENING your core required three components. Skill. Patience. And materials. Any of these components could be traded for the others, which was good because Gregory's people lacked skill, and I lacked patience. Most of them had to stop strengthening their core once it could hold enough mana for an advanced spell, but a third ended up being able to store enough mana to cast an expert-tier spell.

I watched as the last seven reached the master stage. Angelica and Amelia were among the seven, including Commander Erin, Commander Taylor, and three male lieutenants with whom I rarely spoke.

The sharn beast cores they were using to strengthen their cores had barely lost a tenth of their size. Normal cores might have been smaller than mine, but they were significantly more efficient, because they could be held in your mouth. Davina had groaned when I told her how many cores it had taken to strengthen my core.

The others dropped out between the 13th and 14th rank, leaving Amelia and Angelica to battle it out. Everyone was making bets on who would win, laughing and joking or catching up on sleep.

Having a core that held enough mana to cast a master spell wasn't common, but it wasn't rare, either. Most of the students at the academy had cores that big. Being able to cast a master-tier spell was much rarer, so most sorcerers settled for casting multiple expert-tier spells, or dozens of advanced spells. Growing your core beyond being able to cast a single master-tier spell was much harder, but both Angelica and Amelia pushed through the 15th rank and continued on.

Davina eventually walked over. "Angelica's armour is helping her strengthen her core, and Amelia's technique is flawless. They could keep going like this for another day or longer."

"I'll give them a few more hours, then. The others have enough mana for me to master the sorcerer sovereign skill."

I got Gregory's people together and finished leveling the skill.

You have mastered your Sorcerer Sovereign skill.

At level 19, moving mana back and forth had been relatively simple. Mastering the skill boosted my functional level to 23.5 because of my upgraded and mastered prodigy skill, which made moving mana back and forth effortless. I could transfer mana to and from everyone without leakage when we were this close. On a battlefield, a mile would be my limit, and I'd lose half of the mana in transit, but this was still a massive boost.

This skill didn't have many practical applications, beyond being a training aid and battle enhancer. It would help with enchanting and crafting undead, but it would never be a source of unlimited mana, unless I was close to my people. That might change if I worked out how to use it with undead, but that would require skills I didn't have yet.

I walked over to Angelica and Amelia when we finished. They were sitting on the core in the lotus position. "You two can strengthen your cores on your own time. We're going hunting."

Amelia opened her eyes and grinned. "Finally!" She shuffled to the side and jumped down, pulling out a wand.

It was like seeing a child with a gun. "Do you know how to use that?"

She pointed her wand at the wall and unleashed a necrotic bolt without needing an incantation. It was just a 3rd-rank spell, but her use of mana was extremely efficient.

"Impressive. How did you learn how to cast spells without words?"

"I remember everything you read."

I turned to Gregory, quietly projecting my voice. "Gregory, I need you for a moment."

He blurred to my side, heart pounding. "What's the emergency? You're never this calm unless something horrible is about to happen."

"Amelia remembers everything I read. Sir Trent needs to increase her security."

He frowned. "I'm not sure I understand."

"Amelia knows more about magic than any archsorcerer could learn in a dozen lifetimes." I turned to Amelia. "Do you remember what I read in the vault under the Northern Royal Library?"

"Only the first secret vault. Everything in the *secret* secret vault is weird. I remember you opening the books and closing the books, but I don't remember anything that was inside them."

"Do you remember how Davina got her class?"

Amelia's bottom lip began to tremble as grief washed through her scent.

Our bond didn't allow her to see divine knowledge, but she could see divine events. Either the knowledge was too powerful to transfer to her, or it had damaged me in a way that didn't allow it to transfer. I'd have to work out which one it was, before I went digging for more divine magic. Otherwise, Amelia's brain might melt.

Amelia stumbled over to me as she burst into tears. She hugged my side as she bawled her eyes out, remembering how the angel died. It was easily a hundred times more traumatic than watching Mufasa die, which was even traumatic for adults, but I'd needed to know for her own safety.

I picked her up and put her head on my shoulder, cradled her in my arms the way I had my children when they were younger. I rubbed her back and rocked her from side to side, and I told her what I thought she needed to hear.

"Sometimes good people will sacrifice themselves to save bad people. They don't do this because the bad person deserves it. They do it because that's what good people do."

"It's not fair."

"It's not about being fair. It's about being good. If everyone got what they deserved, it would be very hard to make the world a better place. We should treat people better than they deserve, and hope they become someone deserving of the way we treat them."

"Is that why he did it?"

"I think so."

She continued to cry until Davina came over and soothed her soul. Amelia had been awake for almost two days, only stopping for a short nap. She was more resilient than any kid her age should be, because of our bond, but she was still a kid. She quickly fell asleep in my arms, and I surrounded her in a silence spell.

Gregory sighed. "Are we cancelling the hunt?"

"No. I retracted my aura a while ago. We're at the entrance to the second floor of the Abyss. The monsters are on their way."

Gregory swore and began shouting orders.

I levitated the cores back into the storage chests and closed the lids. I levitated the chests to the tunnel wall, putting them in a line, and then I took a seat on top. Letting Amelia rest was more important than killing a few dungeon monsters.

Defensive lines were formed as everyone checked their equipment. Fighting a floor boss was unlikely here, but they would fight numerous monsters as strong as dungeon bosses.

Amelia continued to sleep peacefully as the first monsters arrived. We were on the main tunnel between floors, so there would be a lot of activity. The dracolich circled above, wary of getting too far from support, remembering what had happened the last time she did that in a dungeon. Angelica provided support where it was needed, and Davina, Helen, and the other clerics provided healing.

With each passing hour, the number of monsters steadily grew, as more and more monsters tried to return to their territory now that they thought I wasn't here.

Casting spells without gestures was significantly harder than with, so I limited myself to basic necrotic bolt spells. But when you could fire six of those a second, it hardly mattered. I dissolved the wings of flying monsters and anything climbing along the tunnel wall.

We weren't supposed to be down here, so carrying the monster corpses out of the dungeon wasn't an option. Even with magic, they would rot long before we could transport them to a black market where we could sell them. As each monster fell, I used my vampiric aura to draw the life force from their body, turning them to dust. Monster cores littered the ground, occasionally gathered by a deathlord, who added them to the chests.

The life force reserve inside me never increased. Each time I went over my limit, my soul immediately absorbed the excess life force and grew a little stronger and more efficient. The time I lost down here would hopefully be offset by my increased efficiency. If it wasn't, then coming down here to hunt wasn't going to help speed up Kathrine's recovery.

Five hours after falling asleep, Amelia woke up. She smiled as she snuggled into my chest.

"Do you feel better?"

She nodded as she raised her hand. A necrotic bolt exploded from her wand, disintegrating a giant moth flying overhead. She giggled sleepily.

"When you're awake, we'll go kill a floor boss."

Amelia didn't seem to hear me as she opened her storage pouch and pulled out some dried peaches. She nibbled on them, while I held her, slowly waking up. It was almost half an hour before she was awake enough to want to stand up and an hour before she really got going. She reminded me of Luke when he was her age. He'd always had to be dragged through the first hour of the day, but when he finally got going, he was a little ball of boundless energy.

Monsters fell from the sky as she threw basic-tier necrotic bolts as quickly as she could. I kept topping up her mana, so she didn't run out. Most sorcerers would have collapsed from mana exhaustion, but she healed too quickly for it to affect her.

Her face lit up as she killed an oversize dragonfly with a well-placed spell. "Did you see that?"

I chuckled. "It was a good shot. You ready to go hunt something bigger?"

She grinned.

I STOOD on the back of the gargantuan spider. After cutting all fourteen of its legs off, I'd stabbed Slaughter into its skull and begun sucking the life out of it. Gorgath knew all the local floor bosses and was happy to show us where the ones that were stronger than him lived if he could feed their corpses to his mana crabs.

The cavern was filled with the sounds of battle, as he stood nearby cracking the spider's legs and throwing the flesh to the thousands of fist-sized, glowing crabs inside his sack. The mana crabs were the eighteenth generation of the original crabs that he'd found. The food would muddy their bloodline but would make them grow incredibly fast, which would make them more territorial and violent. They'd soon begin killing and feeding on each other, which would correct their bloodline, until only one male and one female were left. At which point, they would breed and create a new generation.

Gorgath would then kill them, feed them to their young and repeat the process. Each generation would refine their bloodline further until Gorgath had a pure bloodline that could do what he wanted.

Gorgath finished feeding the crabs the spider meat and closed the top of the sack. He gave it a violent shake to stir them up, and then left the sack on the ground, so they could fight to the death. Monsters could grow incredibly quickly under the right conditions, so Gorgath immediately began cracking more legs for the next generation.

I stopped draining the life from the floor boss beneath me right before it died so it didn't turn to dust. I yanked Slaughter from its head as it breathed its last breath and jumped off. Gorgath walked over and began tearing the corpse apart, throwing chunks of meat he didn't need to his troop, who hooted happily, as they received their new meal.

"How much more do you need?" I asked.

He placed several organs on the ground and shrugged. "Breeding bloodline beasts isn't simple. It could be one more generation or one hundred."

"Couldn't you just pick the two with the purest bloodlines and breed those?"

Gorgath nodded. "This is one possibility, but this eliminates the chances of them developing a unique bloodline." He pointed to his troop. "My unique bloodline is what makes me sapient. Without it, I would be little more than a beast, like my brothers."

"How many bloodlines can you incorporate into your evolution?"

"As many as I wish, if I do not care about becoming an abomination."

I didn't understand what he meant. "Do you mind explaining how this works?"

Gorgath sat down, crushing several smaller spiders. "When I eat a beast with a pure bloodline, I know what effects each of its bloodline traits will have on my body when I incorporate them. The less pure the bloodline, the less certainty I have about the effects. If I take the wrong trait, I could lose my sapience, which is why my people do not take risks and incorporate any creature without a pure bloodline."

"Is this why some monsters can suddenly become sapient?"

He nodded. "Much can be gained and lost from bloodlines. And the traits I gather will not be passed along to my spawn. Only one in ten Gor is born sapient, and the traits I gather to grow stronger will lower this chance. If I take too many bloodlines before the ninth, I might be unable to sire the next generation, and have to continue my descent without adding to our people."

"What if you gain a trait that increases this chance?"

"Such a trait is extremely rare and is the reason my people hunt deeper. We have exhausted our options on the higher floors. Unless something unique evolves, our only chance lies below us."

"What are you hoping to achieve?"

"We wish to be like humans."

"Why?"

Gorgath turned and glanced at his troop, and then he looked at his sack. "The ninth floor is the deepest my people can survive without sapience. When I reach the ninth floor, my brothers' only purpose will be to hunt to feed our people. It is a limited existence, and it pains my people to watch our family hunt and die without ever understanding that there is more to existence than base instinct."

Gregory ran over. "Sir, the remaining spiders are pulling back. We'll be ready to move on to the next chamber shortly."

Gorgath opened his sack and looked inside. He nodded to himself and reached in. I heard two loud cracks as he killed the breeding pair. He shredded their bodies to make it easier for the hatchlings to eat them and then closed the top and licked his hand clean, checking their bloodline.

He turned to me. "I will be ready to move on shortly."

AT THE END of our three-day excursion, we headed back to the dungeon and stopped outside the entrance to the Abyss. There Davina walked from person to person, casting healing spells, forcefully removing the larger mana crystals from their bloodstream. Her healing spell couldn't remove the ultrafine crystals; only time away from the Abyss would do that. Right now, none of my people could safely re-enter the Abyss for another month. They had to wait for the crystals to leave their system.

Gregory sat beside me, going over the report. "Everyone has leveled twenty-two to twenty-five times. Our lowest level is now 102. We've seen minor improvement in skills. But the equipment situation is messy. Everyone has out-leveled what they're using and needs their equipment replaced."

"Can I afford the refit?"

"Yes, but it will wipe out most of the money we brought with us."

"Do it."

"Can you get more money? We don't work for free."

"I think so."

When everyone was taken care of, we headed for the fortress. I scouted ahead to ensure that only the necromancers were on guard and then ushered everyone through the fortress to the surface.

Amelia was sitting on my shoulders when I walked into the hotel lobby where they were staying. The timing of our return was well known, so her parents were waiting for her. The look her mother, Sanna was giving her said she was going to be grounded until she was thirty.

I lifted her off my shoulders and placed her on the ground. Then I caught her collar as she tried to run. She looked at me like I'd betrayed her as her mother grabbed her ear and began dragging her to the staircase. Her stepfather, Juro remained behind with me, trying not to laugh.

The moment she was out of sight, Juro let out his chuckle. "Did she have fun?"

"I had to drag her away."

He smiled. "She's a good kid. Takes after her father a little too much for my wife's liking. She's afraid of losing her, the way she lost Denton. She wants her to be safe and happy, but for Amelia to be happy she can't be safe."

"She's a natural adventurer."

Juro nodded. "I see it. Her guards see it. The princess sees it. Sanna refuses to."

"Amelia needs training."

"Why do you say that?"

"She's got too much energy. She needs a way to burn it off, or she'll go stir-crazy again. And stir-crazy Amelia thinks it's a good idea to join an expedition to the Abyss."

"I'll talk to my wife about it. Thank you for keeping her safe."

Having said his peace, Juro walked off after his wife.

Amelia's stepfather was much more comfortable with me than his wife was. Down in the Abyss, Amelia had told me that he'd asked her all sorts of questions about me, after we met. She'd told him all her best stories and he'd listened. His lack of concern told me he didn't consider me a danger to his kid, which surprised me because I could smell how much he feared me.

I turned to the guard holding my master storage chest, ready to take back the cores that we'd taken with us and opened it.

Among Gorgath's people, the value of cores was based upon how useful they were to their people. Sharn beast cores were exceptionally large, but his people didn't practice necromancy, so they were almost worthless. A single elemental core of the same size was worth four. A twin elemental core was worth nine times what a single elemental core was worth, and the prices got more ridiculous the more elements a core had.

I collected a core the size of my head, which had the same value as a minivan-sized sharn beast core, and I placed it in my storage pouch. The first time Gorgath paid his tuition, there had been dozens of these smaller cores in the bag with the others. Gorgath's father had sent them as a token of his appreciation, because unlike the larger cores I asked for, they were valued by their people.

I left the hotel and made my way back to Darksmith. The Lunar Festival would continue for another two days, so there weren't many students around as I made my way through the academy grounds.

Carolyn was living in a VIP dorm that was separate from the other students' dorm. It was the only building with its own enchanted defences, and it was filled with Old Monsters who acted as guards. The entire student body was made from Murdell's elite families, but some families were more elite than others.

Until Carolyn and Davina arrived, only Celest and Marin, the son of the current empress, had been in the building. Now four out of the five floors were taken.

A barrier shielded the entrance as I approached. Sir Trent stood behind the barrier, having sensed me walking towards the building. He opened the barrier for me and let me inside. We didn't talk until we reached the fifth floor and were inside the front entrance of Carolyn's opulent suite, where the magical safeguards would stop us from being overheard.

Sir Trent closed the door behind me. "Why are you here?"

"I've got something to sell to the royal family."

That made him curious. "What are you trying to sell?"

"A core from the ninth floor of the Abyss that matches the royal family's magic."

He immediately lost interest. "When will you be free for another training session?"

"Give me a week."

Sir Trent nodded and left me at the entrance.

Rupert came to find me a few minutes later and led me to a sitting room. We both sat down, and I pulled the core from my storage pouch and placed it on the table.

He pulled out several magical instruments and examined the core. He muttered to himself while he worked. When he was done with his examination, he folded his arms and leaned back.

"I'll give you half a million gold and deed Angelica Count Bodo's land for it."

Count Bodo's land was next to Angelica's.

I folded my arms and waited.

He eventually sighed. "The princess doesn't have access to her family's wealth here in Murdell. A million gold is all she has until we return to Arcadia. It's the best I can do, and I wouldn't be making this offer if this core was something she could turn down."

His offer was far less than the core's worth, but I understood their predicament. "Give me a one-time tax waiver for the goods my people and I bring back to Arcadia as well, and you have a deal."

"Why?"

"I don't want to bother with sneaking my loot across the border and then pretend like I don't have it."

"Fine. Do we have a deal?"

I offered him my hand. "We do."

16

THE SLOW GRIND OF THE INEVITABLE

Ancient vampires are accustomed to solving their problems with ease, the way birds are accustomed to flying away from danger. We are remorseless. We are cunning. And we possess a physique that makes us an apex predator in any environment. Few problems cannot be solved with such advantages.

I had grown accustomed to being able to solve my problems with ease, but there were no more shortcuts for healing Kathrine. My healing palm technique was slightly more efficient from visiting the Abyss, but the days I spent strengthening my soul with the life force of monsters weren't worth the minor gains I received. I'd wrongfully assumed hunting in the Abyss would help Kathrine's recovery, but based on the results, hunting would do the opposite.

Eleven days after returning, Sir Trent sat on my training hall floor, checking the slab of metal he called a sword for any damage cutting me apart might have caused it. The smile he wore as he caught his breath and ran his fingers over the blade suggested he'd leveled one of his skills. When he was sure I hadn't damaged his precious slab of metal, he placed the palm-wide blade beside him and leaned back to relax, looking at the ceiling.

A moment later, he turned to me. "The simplicity of your oath is insidious."

Everyone who had taken my oath considered it to be a boon. There were drawbacks to the oath, but I'd never heard anyone describe it as insidious.

"In what way is my oath insidious?"

He returned to staring at the ceiling. "I turn sixty-eight this winter. I'm a knight of the first order, level 163, and I have mastered more skills than any other knight in Arcadia. I don't feel my age, but until I took your oath, I was content. Now every day, I remember the men and women who trained me. Knights who had leveled past 200 and become Dragons, instead of Old Monsters. Knights who could defeat me as easily as you could. Your oath pushes me to become like them, so I can make the world safe for my children. I don't even have children."

This seemed like a problem that was unique to Sir Trent, and the reason was obvious to me. "You're fighting my oath, aren't you?"

"I don't like being told what to do."

I chuckled, amused by his problem and discomfort.

"Why's that funny?"

"The oath you gave isn't pushing you to become stronger, you are. You're a brilliant teacher, but you know deep down that you're a better fighter."

"You would say that."

"Humans are goal-oriented beings. When our goal is big and important enough, our entire life and focus revolves around achieving this goal. The things that don't help us achieve our goal get left behind or ignored, and anything that helps us achieve it is noticed faster. Its obvious to me that those who take my oath accept my goal and make it their own. How they go about achieving my goal is based upon how they believe they are most effective. My oath isn't doing anything to you that is insidious. You're just recognising how you can best accomplish the new goal you've committed your life to."

My comment seemed to annoy him because he changed the subject. "Which combat skills do you have left to train?"

I had done what was right and helped him with his problem, but I didn't care if he continued to suffer, so I let him change the subject. "I only have active skills which you can help me with. Impale, heavy blow, and cleave. I've mastered the rest of my nonmagical combat skills."

He turned to me and frowned. "Cleave isn't normally an active skill."

He was right.

Cleave was an advanced skill that made you use the correct technique to cut through your enemy, so your weapon didn't get stuck in their body. It tended to make warriors more lethal and was one of the easier advanced skills to master. The fact that I hadn't leveled the skill at all while I was in the Abyss pointed to it being the active version of the skill.

Active versions of normal skills were rare. They had the same name as their underlying skill, but they could do what the original version of the skill could do and more. You could also only level the skill through using the active technique.

"Cleave should have leveled when I went to the Abyss, but it didn't. The only reasonable answer is that it's the active version of the skill."

"If it didn't level, you're probably right."

Sir Trent's breathing had returned to normal.

"Are you ready to spar again?"

He shook his head. "I don't adapt as quickly to level changes as you. I need to meditate on how leveling my skill has changed me before sparring again. We'll work on developing your aura for now."

He held out his hand and one of the wooden training swords on the nearby crate flew toward him. He jumped to his feet while it was in flight, caught the weapon, and waved for me to follow him.

We walked over to the wooden training pole that I'd set up earlier. It was a regular wooden pole rather than one of the enchanted ones, so it wouldn't produce a barrier.

Sir Trent placed the tip of the wooden sword against the pole and gently pushed. Without any pressure, the wood parted around the tip of the blade, and the training sword went halfway through before stopping. He let go of the training weapon, leaving it lodged in the pole, and turned to me.

"When our attributes go beyond what our physical body can achieve, the nature of our existence changes. We become more than a being with just a body and soul. We become beings that possess an aura. Aura is a force that reinforces our existence and takes us beyond our physical limits. The strength of our aura is a manifestation of our excess attributes. Like our attributes, we cannot push beyond this limit, only harness its full potential."

"I know all this."

Sir Trent ignored me. "When we harness and use our aura, the effect our aura has on our attributes weakens. This makes active skills dangerous, as they lower your attributes to your physical limit, which leaves you vulnerable. So, learning *how* to use active skills is not half as important as learning *when* to use them. Any questions?"

"You forgot to mention that a portion of our aura isn't used to enhance our attributes, and that mastering active skills allows us to use this portion without affecting our strength and is what makes mastering active skills so important."

"That wasn't a question, and I was going to mention that in lesson two."

"I won't need a lesson two."

He sighed and pointed to the wooden blade in the training pole. "Grab the handle and I'll use my aura to show you how to harness your own."

I took a step closer and grabbed the handle. Sir Trent placed his massive hand over mine and I felt his aura invade my body. I made sure not to resist, so he could work more effectively. Over the next few minutes, I slowly grew weaker as my aura was forcefully drawn from my body and directed into the sword. While this happened, Sir Trent held my hand in place so the blade wouldn't move forward and complete the skill.

I paid attention to the way everything felt. How my aura moved through my body and how it changed as it passed through my skin into the sword. The only reason I couldn't do this alone was that my vampiric aura blended so seamlessly with my aura that I couldn't differentiate between the two. Sir Trent couldn't sense my vampiric aura, so he didn't have this problem. My aura was as clear to him as his own, and it let him manipulate it when I couldn't.

When my aura had been entirely moved into the blade, Sir Trent allowed my hand to slowly move forward. The wooden blade drilled through the pole like it was soft butter, having almost no resistance. He let go when the hilt reached the pole.

"How much of that could you feel?"

"All of it."

Sir Trent raised an eyebrow. "All of it?"

"All of it," I repeated.

He stepped back and summoned another wooden sword to his hand and passed me the blade. "Show me."

I placed the tip of the blade against the pole and pushed my aura through the handle, willing my aura to impale the pole. I felt myself grow weaker as I held tight, stopping the sword from moving forward. As my attributes dropped, so did my ability to perceive what I was doing. When I reached the point where my perception had dropped so much that I couldn't sense my aura clearly and direct it into the blade the way I wanted, I stopped holding the sword back.

The blade slammed through the pole. My aura shot across the room and struck the barrier protecting the wall. There was a loud crack as it drilled through the barrier and damaged the wall behind. Active skills were the sort of attacks you would see in Chinese martial arts movies. They were also the reason high-level warriors could keep up with high-level sorcerers.

A notification appeared.

Your Impale skill has increased to level 16.

Sir Trent turned to the small hole in the wall and scowled. "Did you just master an active skill with a single thrust?"

"No. I got to level 16. *This* one will let me master it."

I pulled the blade free and impaled the pole a second time, much faster and more easily than before. The barrier cracked louder this time as a notification appeared.

You have mastered your Impale skill.

I dismissed the notification.

Another notification appeared.

Congratulations, you have leveled your Hero class.
Your class has leveled.
You are now a level 37 Hero.

Your class has leveled and unlocked a new skill.
Vampiric Soul Bite

You have 40 attribute points to spend.

The sight of my new skill upset me even more than receiving the create vampire skill had. I needed skills that would help Kathrine get better. Instead, it confirmed what I'd suspected. Drinking her blood and creating a vampire had changed me, bring my vampiric nature to the forefront. I'd only be gaining vampiric skills until the list of basic skills was exhausted.

That wasn't entirely unexpected.

Once the right conditions were triggered, classes always prioritized the skills that an individual needed to thrive before anything else. It was most commonly seen among those with unique bloodlines. They often gained a dozen or more related skills before their class offered them anything else.

A vampire seemed to be the same.

If claiming my good deeds and levels would gain me the skills that I needed to heal Kathrine, I'd claim them in a second. But there were a lot of vampiric skills waiting for me; and after I was done with them, I'd have to deal with Carolyn's bloodline.

My foray into magic had triggered it.

That was over forty skills, before I was back to gaining skills related to my actions. And I didn't even want to level.

I didn't want to level, because killing monsters far above my level amplified the experience I earned from killing them. Experience that went to Luke, ultimately making him stronger and safer. I'd be risking his and potentially Kathrine's progress for a roll of the dice that might not come up in my favour.

The skills I gained from my hero class were too arbitrary to take that risk, so I was left with only myself to blame.

I dismissed the notification, ignored my new attributes, and pulled back my fist to punch the training pole with my aura. The pole exploded as the weight of a logging truck collided with it. Another notification appeared.

You have mastered your Heavy Blow skill.

Sir Trent continued to scowl, unaware of what had just happened to me. "Why did you bother getting my help if it was this simple for you?"

"You've mastered the instructor, weapons instructor, aura manipulation, and impale skills, so you're able to manipulate someone else's aura much more effectively than most and guide them through the process. With my perception, cunning, prodigy skill, and instinctive knowledge of how to use my vampiric aura, I can master these skills in moments instead of months, but only with your help."

I turned, drew Slaughter, and swung, directing my aura into my weapon. A blade of aura exploded from the edge and struck the barrier. The barrier barely stopped it from going through. Another notification appeared.

You have mastered the Cleave skill.

Sir Trent held out his hand, summoning his sword to him. "I suddenly feel like cutting you again."

LUKE WALKED around my classroom handing out instructions for the Undead Enhancement Club. People had been commenting on his absence, so I was making sure he was seen more often, so Headmaster Wink didn't complain about me having an apprentice who did nothing of value for the academy.

Angelica sat in the front row, chatting with Lidia and reading the instructions that everyone was being given. The undead Angelica created were weaker than the undead everyone else created, but she knew a lot more about fighting than anyone else and could program that knowledge into her creations. She'd shown everyone why they needed to expand their skillset, as her undead regularly won fights against stronger opponents.

Luke finished handing out the instructions and placed the rest of the handouts on my desk. Then he left the classroom, heading upstairs for his lesson with Carolyn.

I climbed to my feet and immediately had the entire room's attention. It was part fear and part respect that made them all react so quickly. The monster in me found both appealing.

"Can anyone tell me why you don't find undead outside of places with high concentrations of death magic?"

Baris raised his hand. "Mindless undead can't convert raw mana into death mana, which means they can't gather mana from an environment that's not corrupted by death magic. Outside of these environments, they're constantly consuming the mana that holds them together, and they fall apart before most people come across them."

"Correct." I opened the top drawer of my desk and pulled out the bone orb I'd prepared for this lecture. "This is called a false core. It allows undead warriors to gather mana in any environment. Why was crafting it a waste of my time?"

A young woman named Horu in the back row raised her hand. "They're not very efficient."

"That's not entirely true. False cores will allow an undead warrior to walk around indefinitely. If they stay still, they can even recover their mana."

Baris raised his hand. "They're difficult to make in large quantities."

"That's only true if you are planning to make thousands of them. The reason this false core was a waste of my time is that recharging the mana of undead warriors is more easily done with a mana concentration circle. A mana concentration circle is faster to make, cheaper, and more effective than false cores. False cores are a novelty unskilled necromancers created to amuse their egos."

Horu raised her hand again. "But what if you were sending them away from you?"

"Then I'd send them with an undead sorcerer. A sorcerer would construct a mana concentration circle when necessary, allowing them to continue indefinitely."

"What if your sorcerer was destroyed?"

"Then the undead I sent away would be destroyed."

"Isn't that wasteful?"

"No. The materials used to make a false core cost practically as much as the undead warrior you place it in. This makes it more cost effective to make advanced undead warriors, because they can gather mana from any environment, and are significantly stronger than an undead warrior." I put the false core on my desk. "Unskilled necromancers have created hundreds of enhancement techniques to overcome their inability to create advanced undead warriors, like sorcerers and death knights. Most of these techniques aren't worth learning because they're designed to mimic what advanced undead warriors are naturally capable of. I know you've been complaining that I'm not teaching you any of these techniques, but teaching you these techniques is a waste of your time and mine."

Baris raised his hand. “Will you teach us these techniques eventually?”

“No. Once you can create advanced undead warriors properly, you’ll be able to learn these techniques yourself. However, today I will teach you which techniques are useful, and which will be a waste of your time, once you reach this point.”

I took control of a piece of chalk with a spell and began my lecture proper. Too many people had been complaining about the lack of diversity in my lessons, so I’d decided to explain why I wasn’t bothering with teaching them more techniques. I was planning to use the Undead Enhancement Club as a template for teaching Gregory and his people how to build an undead army, and they were likely to raise this same question, so I needed to come up with an effective answer now to save me the trouble later.

A few hours later, the necromancers filed out of the room, unhappy but well informed. A few minutes after that, Carolyn left with her guards.

Luke came down as I was cleaning the chalkboard. He smelled annoyed as he looked around the empty classroom and sighed. He was unhappy about something.

“What’s bothering you?” I asked.

He stared at me for several seconds. “Do you notice when women are flirting with you?”

“I notice. I just don’t care.”

“You don’t care?”

“I don’t care.”

His shoulders relaxed. “That makes sense.”

“Why was that bothering you?”

“I left you with a room full of college girls that all wanted to be the teacher’s pet, and you had zero interest. It’s weird. I know you’ve said you’re not a sexual being, but Data has more of a libido than you do. Be honest with me, Old Man, does the plumbing in your house still work?”

“Vampires don’t use their plumbing for procreation, so a libido isn’t necessary.”

He cringed. "I didn't actually want you to answer that."

"Everything below the belt might as well be a Ken doll."

"Please stop."

"Except when I think of your mother."

Luke shoved his fingers into his ears. "Lalalalalala."

I chuckled.

DALIN, the head of the infirmary, sat in an armchair beside me while I healed Kathrine's soul and worked my way through Arcadia's Royal Northern Library. He hadn't visited nearly as often since help had arrived, but he still stopped by once a week. He was genuinely worried for my daughter's health and my familiars' safety, which was why he kept coming.

Unlike him, Riza now visited more often. Having the necrosaint around made her feel safer when she was around me. She'd even gone to Mother on multiple occasions for moral guidance.

Dalin watched Davina, as she sat on the couch in the corner of the bedroom. He was deep in thought. "Why did you make the necrosaint your familiar?"

"She was my familiar before she became the necrosaint. I offered to release her, but she chose to stay."

"May I ask why?"

"She said Heaven had no problem making her a saint while she was my familiar, so she had no problem remaining one."

He frowned and raised his voice. "Davina, do you have the evil eye skill?"

She looked up from her book and shook her head. "I know a good man when I see one, and his Dark Eminence is a good man. But if you need reassuring, someone who does have that skill has told me he is favoured by Heaven."

Learning that I was favoured by Heaven meant absolutely nothing to me, but the monster within me shuddered with disgust.

Dalin frowned. "Do you know why he's favoured?"

"His capacity to do good is limited. Yet his Dark Eminence exceeds this capacity at every opportunity."

"In what way?"

"He sits beside you, healing his daughter, while every instinct tells him to tear into her with his teeth. He's suffering in silence, without complaint, so he can help and do good, and very few understand what this truly means to fight that sort of temptation."

Dalin folded his arms and considered her words. "Why are you trying to help him?"

Davina turned back to her book. "Because the people who should be, aren't."

Davina sat in an armchair beside the bed, ready to teach me death magic. Yesterday, she'd made me perform every death magic spell I knew to get a feel for what I was doing wrong. She'd then gone away to meditate on what she had seen. It had clearly confused her.

She finished straightening her dress and leaned back. "Do you understand the emotional influence principle, your Dark Eminence?"

"I would have said yes, but since you're bringing it up, I must not understand it as well as I think I do."

"Magic is influenced by emotions. Without emotions, magic produces consistent results. With emotions, magic produces inconsistent results. Magic with emotional enhancement is stronger than magic without, but it's also unpredictable."

That was the standard explanation for the principle. "I'm aware of everything you've said so far."

"Are you aware of anything I've missed?"

"Nothing I would consider relevant."

"Good, then my theory is most likely correct. As far as I can tell, you're doing exactly what any professional sorcerer would do when casting a spell. You're purging yourself of emotion, maintaining a calm mind, and weaving the spell correctly. The problem is your emotional control is so strong that it's letting your demonic parasites' emotions influence your spells. Death and life magic are more sensitive to emotion than elemental magic, and you're more attuned to death magic than any normal person would be, because of your death aura. I was wrong with my earlier assessment. You're doing everything correctly. The problem is the correct method doesn't work for you."

"There shouldn't be any emotional interference from my demonic parasites. Even my natural affinity wouldn't be powerful enough to make me that sensitive to death magic."

"I don't think this issue stems from just your nature, your Dark Eminence. I think this is related to how you formed your core and mana network. You used liquid mana. You mastered skills you shouldn't have mastered. This instability and emotional sensitivity might be the results."

"If you're correct, I'll have to learn to wield all magic with emotion."

Davina nodded and reached for my hand.

I pulled it away before she could take it.

She sighed and went back to what she was saying. "It's almost impossible for a human to learn how to safely wield death or necrotic magic influenced by emotions, but the good news is you're not human. And I don't believe there is a death or necrotic magic spell powerful enough to kill you if you lose control."

"Physical danger is not the only issue. We also have to consider the time involved. Your mother's transformation into a lich caused her to have obsessive tendencies which ruined her emotional control, and with it went her ability to wield death magic properly. It took her two centuries to regain her old capabilities. The only reason I'm even considering this is because once she regained her abilities, she was much more powerful."

"My mother was exceptionally talented with death magic. It would take a normal person much longer, but once again you're not a normal person. I expect you could master this ability much faster than she did."

I turned to Davina, surprised by her assessment of her mother. "You think your mother was talented?"

She nodded. "She was powerful enough to make armies tremble and rulers turn a blind eye to her existence."

"Your mother was an average necromancer who became exceptionally powerful due to a very long life. Her earlier diaries speak of her mediocre abilities. She had none of your talent."

Davina paused. "I didn't know that. In all my memories, she was always a master necromancer, capable of feats none of her minions could replicate."

"Your mother was once just an angry young woman obsessed and in love with a man who didn't love her back. That obsession led to her becoming a creature that could threaten nations. People overlook how much hard work and drive play a part in other people's success. They see the results and call it talent, unwilling to accept that the other person worked harder than they did and took risks they weren't willing to take. Don't make that mistake."

"Yes, your Dark Eminence."

"Was that sarcasm?"

She smirked. "No, your Dark Eminence."

"Is this because I didn't let you hold my hand?"

Her smirk grew. "No, your Dark Eminence."

I held out my hand.

She quickly took it and smiled, content with a comforting touch.

Her mother had never held her hand, and I had a suspicion that I was the first person she had ever hugged for comfort. Even before she became the necrosaint, Davina seemed to have the ability to sense people's nature, and I was sure she had hugged Angelica to comfort her, not to receive comfort.

I didn't want to encourage her attachment to me, because she might one day hesitate to kill me, but she seemed to get her way more often than I liked. She was far too skilled at passive resistance, and her nature influenced mine in a way that no one else could.

"Do you know how my mother mastered wielding her emotions?"

"She studied how her emotions influenced her spells and would adjust the mana flow to her spells to suit her emotional state when she cast the spell. She also changed the timing of the spell sequence and almost every other variable that comes with casting a spell correctly."

"That sounds complicated. Can you recreate those sections of her diaries so I can read them?"

"Do you want me to include the calculations?"

"Only if you want me to help you."

"You're being sarcastic again."

"Yes, your Dark Eminence."

CUNNING WAS without a doubt my most useful attribute. It allowed my brain to process unimaginable amounts of data and correct my mistakes even as I made them. It was what made it possible for me to master skills in a night and unravel the actions of my opponents before they made them. Experiments and insights that took Contessa decades to achieve were completed in days as I fundamentally changed the way I cast spells.

What had taken Contessa 158 years took me nineteen days, because a motivated ancient vampire was a walking calamity. Contessa's meticulous notes might have also helped.

Davina watched me from the side of the training hall as I performed the new version of the death bolt spell.

Hunger and an unrestrained need for destruction filled me as black energy exploded from my palm in a howling orb of darkness. It slammed into the barrier around the training pole, turning the barrier a brighter shade of blue as it buckled under the pressure.

Death magic, when used in offensive spells, was a decaying and draining energy. It weakened everything it touched, drawing away its strength to make it rot.

Some of the magic in the barrier was pulled into the orb, which destabilised the spell formation, allowing the orb's other destructive energies to accelerate the barrier's decay. The barrier quickly crumbled, and the shadowy orb burst across the wooden pole, ageing it centuries in an instant.

The wood rotted away, becoming crumbled powder, as the spell's uncontrolled energies washed over the second barrier that protected the training hall.

I took control of my emotions and restrained the monstrous impulses I'd released. Over the past few weeks, I'd become intimately familiar with the emotions the monster in me could stir up. They were dark and dangerous and would see the world burned down to its foundation if I ever lost control. Releasing them and then restraining them again and again had helped me gain a little more control over my hunger. I still salivated over the smell of blood, but I no longer unconsciously turned my head to follow high-level people while they were walking by.

Half a second after I'd released the spell, I was back to my old self and in full control of my emotions.

I turned to Davina as the blue glow faded from her eyes. "I'm in complete control of my magic while in an emotional state."

Davina walked over to what was left of the training pole, crouched, and passed her fingers through the powder, absorbing the traces of death magic that were left behind. She closed her eyes, feeling the magic as her body digested it.

"This doesn't feel like you're in control, your Dark Eminence. I know what my mother's death magic felt like. It was a smooth, constant pull that sucked the life from everything it touched and replaced it with decay. This is jittery and jarring, like someone tugging on a rope."

"Could it be because I'm a vampire and she was a lich?"

"I don't think so. My mother isn't the only abomination I've met whose death magic was laced with emotion. She had dozens of guests over the centuries and would bring me out to try to trade me for something she wanted. You're magic reminds me more of theirs than hers. You're getting closer, but you're not there yet."

SEVERAL WEEKS LATER, Davina ran her fingers through another pile of decayed wood and finally smiled. She rose to her feet and turned to me. "Your death magic reminds me of my mother's now."

That was good news. I was getting questions about why I was destroying a dozen training poles each day. There wasn't a limit on how many you could requisition, but the headmaster was beginning to rethink this rule.

"You may begin teaching me when you're ready."

Davina shook her head. "I want you to craft a shade to the best of your abilities before I teach you anything."

A shade was a ghost crafted from death magic and an imprint of your soul. Creating one properly required you to damage your soul, but it left you with an autonomous minion with your intelligence and knowledge. The shade wanted what you wanted, knew what you knew, and only existed to fulfil these wants. It wasn't you, though. It didn't have your emotions. It was a cold and sterile creature, which could make it incredibly dangerous, especially if I used all of my skills to craft it.

Shades were mostly used to spy on others.

They weren't particularly good at it, though. Any of the teachers would be able to see it, along with the more skilled students. However, if I made it to the best of my abilities, it would be able to do much more than just spy on people. It would be able to interact with the world around it. It would also feed on more of my life force to sustain itself.

I folded my arms and frowned. "Why do you want me to craft a shade?"

"Shades are imprinted with your intelligence and knowledge, but not your emotions. If you're in complete control of how emotions affect your death magic, then your shade will behave normally. If you're not, it will exhibit odd behaviours. These past few weeks, I've been thinking about how to test whether you've mastered harnessing your emotions for practicing magic, and I believe this is the most effective way to do so. It's not the safest way, but it is the most effective way, and you need the most effective way more than you need the safest, since you want to practice master-tier magic."

Master-tier magic was on an entirely different level to expert magic. If I hadn't harnessed my emotions as well as I thought I had, I could destroy Darksmith, and my son and daughter with it. Testing to see if I was as good as I thought I was before moving on was something I could accept.

"In that case, I'm going to need to read the rest of your mother's library."

17

THE REPERCUSSIONS OF ACTIONS

Four months after she arrived, Davina lifted her hand from Kathrine's forehead and said the words I'd been waiting to hear. "Your daughter's soul has recovered, your Dark Eminence. Give me a moment to heal the last of the physical deterioration from being bedridden, and then I can wake her up when you're ready."

I snapped my fingers.

Shadow slid from his favourite hiding place inside my coat, as a vaguely humanoid black blur, crossed the bed in a rush, and then hid inside the shadow cast by an armchair.

Davina and I hadn't noticed any problems with my shade Shadow so far, except his proclivity to hide in shadows. Neither of us could figure out whether this was a stealth habit he preferred or influence from uncontrolled emotions leaking into my magic, and I hadn't been willing to make a second shade to find out until after Kathrine was healed. It had taken me four nights of hunting floor bosses in the Abyss to recover from the soul damage creating him caused and I had more important uses for my time.

"Find Luke and Riza and tell them we're ready to wake Kathrine," I instructed Shadow.

Shadow slid under the door and disappeared.

Davina grumbled from the other side of the bed as she finished casting her spells on Katherine. “There are less terrifying ways to deliver messages than using a shade.”

“I’m recovering the time I wasted making him.”

“There are safer ways to get your time back.”

I rolled my eyes. “Shades are only dangerous when you lack the skill to control them, they grow too powerful, or you aren’t aware of what your greatest desires are. Otherwise, they’re as predictable as any other undead creation.”

“Only when they’re made correctly, and we still don’t know if you have the emotional control you need to do that.”

“Fine. I’ll stop sending him to deliver messages until you’re certain I’m in control of my emotions.”

Davina smiled. “Thank you, your Dark Eminence.”

Davina still wasn’t teaching me master-tier magic, but she was helping me improve my technique and mana efficiency. My technique was now as flawless as hers, up to the high advanced stage, and my efficiency was getting close. Expert-tier magic was still a work in progress, but Davina rarely pushed her body. With her placing all the attributes she received from leveling into her physical attributes, she got by on less than an hour of sleep. It meant that we had been able to get a lot done by working through the night.

While I liked using magic, outside of crafting undead, only a handful of expert-tier spells made me more dangerous. The changes made to how I cast spells had provided me with a death bolt that was more effective against barriers than my finger of destruction, and the grim reaper’s eyes spell let me see murderers, magic, and someone’s killer if I saw their corpse, but that was more of a useful trick than something I could add to my arsenal to keep my family safe.

An ancient vampire was simply too powerful for expert-tier magic to make a difference. Master-tier magic was a different story. It would turn me into an army of one.

Fifteen minutes later, Riza opened the door and entered the bedroom, taking a seat on the couch. She was still wary of me, and that was unlikely to ever change, but she was less afraid now. Seven months with no missing persons and no more attacks on my daughter had shown her I really was in control of my thirst.

Most people wouldn't have stuck around after what had happened to her, but Riza was one of the most loyal people I'd ever met. She'd helped my daughter run away from South Murdell and wouldn't run away from me until she knew Kathrine was safe.

Luke showed up a few minutes later, wearing his armour. His scent was layered with excitement and trepidation. He'd been in town, judging by the scents coming off him.

We shared a smile, and then I turned to Davina. "You can wake her when I leave."

I wasn't going to subject Kathrine to my presence. I'd already hurt her enough and I wanted this to go as smoothly as possible.

I climbed off the bed, walked out of the bedroom, and closed the door behind me. Davina had been telling me that Kathrine's soul was close to restored for the past week, so I'd stocked the kitchen with all of Kathrine's favourite foods.

Shadow hid in my coat as I walked into the kitchen, waiting for his next command. Inside the kitchen were two pantries, each covered in enchantments. The one that stored dry goods would vacuum seal to extend the life of everything it held. The other was for frozen goods. Anything placed inside would instantly freeze and then instantly unfreeze when removed. I injected mana into this world's equivalent to a stove and oven, filled pots and pans with water from the tap, and then blurred around the room as quickly as I could, throwing together dozens of dishes all at once.

I was trying to distract myself, and cooking seemed to be the best use of my time. All I wanted to do was run back to the bedroom. I wanted to be there when Kathrine's eyes opened, when she returned to the waking world. I needed the reassurance that everything was all right. That I wasn't the monster I felt I was.

But that wasn't what Kathrine needed.

While I worked, I listened to a hundred thousand objects in motion, each one distinct and unique. I could hear every voice in the academy, every conversation, and every heartbeat.

Kathrine's voice cut through them all.

"Luke," she mumbled. There was a groggy pause as she tried to get her bearings. "What are you doing here?" There was another pause and then happy tears and excitement as she snapped awake and leapt on her big brother, engulfing him in a hug. "Luke!" she shrieked.

"Hey, Sis," he replied catching her in his arms and holding her tight.

My boy sounded a little choked up.

The two of them hugged for nearly a minute, overjoyed at being reunited. It was a very human reaction.

Kathrine broke the hug first. "What the hell am I wearing under this dress?"

Luke laughed. "A diaper."

"Do I want to know why? Forget that. Why are you here? *How* are you here?"

"I heard you were in trouble, so I came to help."

"I was in trouble?"

"You've been asleep for seven months?"

There was a long pause. "What?"

"You were asleep for seven months. Do you remember what happened to you?"

She shuddered as her heartbeat turned erratic and fearful. "I don't want to…" There was another pause. "Did you kill him?"

"Not yet. Do you want me to?"

"He's a monster."

This might have been me hoping, but I thought I heard a question in her statement.

"How did you get me away from him?"

"We didn't get you away from him," Riza replied. "He's been protecting you for the last seven months, taking care of you while you slept. He's also the one who healed the damage he did to your soul. He didn't want to scare you, so he went to the other room."

"Where are we?"

"The occult professor's apartment," Luke replied. "Dad got a job at Darksmith so he could keep you safe. And you didn't answer my question. Do you want me to kill him?"

"Will you hate me if I say yes?"

Luke chuckled, trying to pretend like everything was alright. He wasn't well equipped to deal with emotions.

"I've tried to kill him on two occasions, so I won't hate you for wanting me to kill him. I've been where you are. I've been afraid of what he might do. I even let him roam near innocent people so he would kill one and lose his immunity to holy magic."

Luke had set me up.

No wonder he was there to kill me the moment I killed my first Unseen. He hadn't trusted me at all, and he'd been willing to sacrifice an innocent person to put me down. It explained why his eyes didn't have a white glow, showing he was favoured by Heaven. My instincts told me he had made the right choice, but my memories told me he hadn't. His choice disappointed me as his father.

I wasn't used to being disappointed in him. It made me sad to know how much I'd failed him. The son I raised wasn't the type of person to sacrifice others.

Kathrine had the same reaction. "You were going to let him kill someone?"

"It was one life against the lives of thousands. And I did let him kill someone. It just turned out the someone he killed was Unseen."

She dropped her voice to a whisper. "You're supposed to be a hero."

"I'm not perfect, Sis. No one is. My training taught me ancient vampires were one of the biggest threats I could face. That thousands of people's lives were at risk. Sacrifices had to be made."

"They're supposed to be made by you. Not by others."

"I didn't come here to talk about me."

"Doesn't matter. You brought it up, and now we're going to talk about it. Good people don't sacrifice innocent people for the greater good, Luke."

"No, they don't." I heard Luke sit on her bed. "I never claimed to be a good person, Sis. I don't actually think I am anymore. But I save people, and I make the world safer. It's the best I can do."

"Well, I want you to be better than that."

"I can't be better. You might want me to kill Dad."

Kathrine froze, as her heartrate accelerated even more.

"He's the one who told me what happened," Luke continued when she didn't reply.

"You talked to him?"

"After I broke his jaw."

"You broke his jaw?"

"He had it coming. He had promised me he could control himself."

"What are you talking about?"

"Dad promised me he could control his thirst. That he could limit his feeding to only Unseen. He sent his familiars to find me right after he attacked you."

"Why?"

"Because he's more worried about you than he's worried about himself. He broke his agreement with the guild. I'm here as his judge, jury, and executioner. Now do you want me to kill him?"

"An innocent person has to die for you to do that."

Luke sighed. "It doesn't matter."

"It *does* matter."

"I can't kill him without him losing his soul. Someone has to die."

"Then let it be me."

Luke's anger matched my own. "What the fuck, Kathrine!"

"I'm not letting you kill some innocent person just so you can kill him."

"That doesn't mean you have to volunteer."

"Yes, it does."

"No, it doesn't. You're a hero. Do you have any idea how much of a difference you can make?"

"Yes, I can help you kill an ancient vampire."

"Do you really want him dead that badly?"

"Do I have a choice?"

There was a pause.

Luke seemed to be in disbelief. “You have no idea what he’s done, do you?”

“I’m aware he helped you kill a lich.”

“He didn’t just help me kill the lich. He saved the church of Arcadia, the only surviving daughter of the king, and millions of people by warning the army about a nation-wide dungeon surge that was about to take place. He’s done more good than I have!”

Kathrine burst into tears, unable to keep it together with her brother yelling at her on top of everything else. “Why did he attack me, then?”

I heard Luke get up and walk to her, hugging her tight again. “He’d been in an unawakenable slumber for two months when you summoned him with that spell. He was so beaten up and exhausted, only the demon woke up, and it woke up inside out. He didn’t attack you. The demon did. But he heard your voice, even though he was asleep, and he tried to stop the demon from killing you. But it was already too late. You were dying and there were no healing potions nearby to save you, only your best friend. So, he made her kill you and let you become a vampire, because without his soul to keep the demon in check, it was unlikely it would let you return to being human.”

“Do you actually believe that?”

“Killing the lich was a suicide mission. Dad let himself be tortured for nine straight days to make sure I came out alive. He let the church torture him for seven months to prove he could control his thirst and that he was still a good man. Yes, I believe he’d do anything to keep us safe. Even kill us if he had to.”

“I just wanted to see him. I missed him so much.”

“I know. I missed him too.”

“He scares me.”

“He used to scare me too.”

“He’s not our dad, is he?”

“I don’t think he’s anything else except our dad. From what I’ve seen and read about demons, he can’t change. He’s read tens of thousands of books. He’s got other peoples’ memories in his head. But his personality hasn’t changed at all. A normal person would grow and develop, changing who they are. He stays the same. He’s the exact same man we knew before we were all summoned here, and he's never going to change."

"You really believe he's still in there."

"I do."

"He hurt me."

"The demon hurt you. Dad just wasn't able to stop it."

"You aren't going to kill him, are you?"

"No."

"Even after what he did?"

"He hasn't stopped beating himself up over what happened, and he's more awake than I've ever seen him. The memory of what he did to you causes him constant pain. It wasn't something that he wanted. So, he's not a monster, and I can't make myself kill him until he is."

"Does he expect me to forgive him?"

"No. He hasn't forgiven himself, so he doesn't think he deserves your forgiveness."

"Where is he?"

"He's making dinner. You can see him if you want to."

She changed the subject, which told me she didn't want to see me or that she was too afraid. I kept making dinner.

"How long are you going to be here?"

I could hear the fear in her voice.

"For as long as he's worried about you. You, me, and Mom, are the only people in the world he cares about. And he's not always reasonable when it comes to keeping us safe. He's currently holding King Linus's daughter hostage, so the king doesn't kill me."

"I thought you said he saved her?"

"He did. The queen had been taken over by a body snatcher and replaced all but one of the king's children with Unseen. He ate the heir and his brothers before he realised who they were. He knew the king would kill him for that, and that if he couldn't kill him, he would likely kill me instead. The king's kind of a dick that way. So, after he ate the rest of the king's Unseen children, he kidnapped his only remaining child to keep me safe."

"Couldn't he have just found you and run off?"

Luke laughed. “That’s where the unreasonable part comes in. He knows I like what I do, and he wanted me to be happy. Kidnapping the king’s daughter let me continue with my life unaffected. He didn’t care that it affected the king or his daughter, so long as it didn’t affect me.”

“You’re afraid of what he will do to keep me happy and safe?”

“What part of him literally getting into a standoff with an entire kingdom makes you think I’m afraid of what he will do to keep you happy and safe?”

“He sounds like a monster.”

“He also sounds like our dad.”

KATHRINE TALKED to Luke and Riza for over an hour, trying to piece together what had happened since I attacked her. Luke eventually convinced her to let Davina help, and the two of them sat down together. Kathrine went through her experiences, playing them over in her mind and talking aloud, while Davina smothered her negative emotions.

Traumatic unprocessed experiences continue to affect us until they’re processed, but sometimes processing them is nearly impossible, so we can’t move on. What Davina did allowed Kathrine to gain a detached perspective, to overwrite her emotional response. She had done the same for Amelia, to help her get over all the violent torture she’s seen me subjected to, and she was now helping her with the angel’s death.

While they did that, I kept myself busy.

My wife had done the majority of the cooking at home, but I had watched her work, washing dishes as she prepared meals. I’d copied what she had done from memory, creating dishes I knew Kathrine liked as a kid. There was potato salad, roast chicken, burgers, mashed potatoes, hashbrowns, macaroni and cheese, and everything else I’d been able to find the ingredients for.

Kathrine had been through a lot, and I would do anything to make this easier for her. Luke came to find me as I was setting the table.

He scowled when he saw the food and smelled upset. "This is youngest child favouritism. I've spent months with you, and you didn't cook dinner for me once. Kathrine wakes up and you whip up twenty different dishes and get out cushions for your chairs, so her butt doesn't go to sleep."

He grabbed a plate and began piling food on top while he stuffed mashed potatoes in his mouth.

"I don't have a favourite."

He spoke with his mouth full. "The evidence would suggest otherwise. These are good mashed potatoes."

"They're the smoothest I've ever made."

"You don't look happy about it."

"They're a reminder that I'm not the man I was."

"None of us are."

"Some of us have changed more than others."

"I thought you said you were okay with Mum remarrying."

I threw a cushion at him.

He knocked it aside with magic and continued eating.

"You should go tell your sister the food is ready."

"Are you staying?"

"That's for her to decide."

Luke finished his first helping and went to talk to Kathrine. She wasn't ready to see me, so I left the dining room and went to the study to deal with one of the other problems that had arisen tonight, mainly Luke thinking it was okay to sacrifice people for the greater good.

Kathrine had a lot of questions, and the others answered them as well as they could. Eventually, she ran out of questions and left with Riza.

Luke walked into my study after escorting her to her dorm. "What are you writing?"

"It's a guide to show you how to build a utopian society."

Luke raised an eyebrow. "What?"

"I heard what you said to your sister. How you set me up to lose my soul. How you thought your actions were for the greater good."

Luke scowled. "It was one life against thousands, Dad. You can't honestly say that you would do something different."

This was the trolley problem, one life not against three or five but against thousands. But the trolley problem became far more complicated in a world where you could sacrifice a child to a demon to end a village plague. The morality of the question wasn't as simple as throwing a switch, and it highlighted the biggest weakness of the trolley problem.

It wasn't really a question of who you were going to save, but of who you were willing to sacrifice for the outcome you wanted. It told you nothing of value that would help you build a better world. It was just a thought experiment, in a sterile environment, detached from the realities of life.

The world got better when people did the right thing and accepted the cost. It was as simple as that.

I could turn this world into a sacrificial utopia if I was allowed to sacrifice one in ten children. It was a world that would be safe for my family. It was a world that would be a sickly-sweet Hell on Earth, cuddling everyone in the safety of others.

Luke needed to see that world, because that was the type of world his actions would lead to.

I dried the ink on the page with a spell and pushed the book to him. "Did you know half the people in this world don't die from old age, despite them not having medical issues?"

He picked up the book. "I didn't realise it was that high."

"It is, and one in twenty of those are children who don't make it to their first birthday. If I were to sacrifice those children for the greater good, I could eliminate the others' death rate."

"What the fuck, Dad!"

"If I doubled the number of children I sacrificed to demons and other entities, I could create a utopian society where threats from monsters and demons were non-existent. People would live happy lives, where they wouldn't need to be concerned about their safety. It would only require me to sacrifice every tenth child they have. Isn't their sacrifice for the greater good worth it, Luke?"

"Dad, what you're saying is really fucked up."

"Yes, it is. But the monster in me agrees with your philosophy, so I need to make my point. Read the book."

He scowled but took a seat and began reading. The colour drained from his face as he read. I could smell his mounting disgust with every page he flipped through. The most horrible part of the book he was reading was that it really would create a utopian society. It would be a safe world for my family. Weirdly, both the monster and I found this world repugnant. But for different reasons.

The moment Luke finished reading, he burned the book with a spell and glared at me. "That was the most fucked up thing I've ever read. Why the hell would you think I'd consider this?"

"What's the problem, Luke? The total number of people who die or receive harm goes down and everyone's standard of living goes up."

"This is fucking evil."

"So is sacrificing an innocent man to kill an ancient vampire."

"I agree it's messed up, but it's not *this* evil."

"Son, what you tried to do was one small part of the plan you just read. If everyone was willing to make the same choice as you, they'd be able to create the utopian society in that book."

"It's not the same."

"It *is* the same, but on a smaller scale. You made a choice, Son. The choice was who you were willing to sacrifice to achieve the outcome you desired. If I were willing to make the same choice as you, the world in that book would be the result."

"I can't do what you can."

"No, you can't. But with enough likeminded people you could."

His shoulders slumped. "Why did you show this to me?"

"I don't agree with the choice you made, Son, but I don't love you any less for making it. It's a choice many in your situation would have made. And I believe at some point, someone told you that it was the right choice to make. Based on your reaction to the book, they failed to show you what that choice truly meant. Which is why, I wanted to give you another perspective."

"Can we talk about something else?"

Challenging your own beliefs is difficult. But I'd left him with no other choice. What I'd written was too horrific for him to ignore. Even if he ran away now, it would haunt him until he either accepted a different perspective or rejected it completely and held on to what he thought was true.

"Would you mind crashing on your sister's couch for a while? She'll feel safer with you around."

"Do you really think she needs it? She seemed okay when I left."

"She's tough, but everyone needs to feel loved. She'll kick you out when you're more annoying than helpful."

"Do you want me to pass along a message?"

"Tell her, I'm willing to speak with her when she's ready."

18

LIFE GOES ON

Luke was right. Making Kathrine dinner when I hadn't cooked anything for him was unfair of me. He'd been at Darksmith for months. We'd trained together. We'd talked about his sister. But we hadn't hung out. Everything I did with him revolved around survival. None of it was about enjoying life.

So, to make it up to him, I'd been cooking dinner every night for the last week, trying to improve my abilities with each new meal I made. Like everything I put my mind to, there was clear and quick progress.

Luke pushed his empty plate aside and leaned back in his chair to undo his belt. He released a loud groan. The noise echoed off the dining room walls, making the large empty room seem even larger and emptier.

"You're definitely getting better," he said. "That mushroom sauce was something I'd only expect from a high-level chef."

Seeing my son happy and with a full belly made me feel content. "The secret ingredient is love."

Luke snorted at my cheesy joke. "You know, it's terrifying how quickly you pick up everything. A week ago, you were able to replicate Mum's old recipes and now you're imitating high-level chefs without any skills." His mood sobered. "It makes me think everything we know about ancient vampires is wrong."

"What you know isn't wrong."

"It feels that way?"

"It feels that way because there are gaps in your knowledge, not because what you know is wrong."

He raised an eyebrow. "Can you fill those gaps for me?"

I folded my arms and sighed. "Not safely. I don't know if what I've experienced is universally true for ancient vampires or if these experiences are unique to me. And filling gaps about ancient vampires with assumptions or false information is extremely dangerous, which is why the little you know about ancient vampires doesn't contain any speculation."

He frowned. "There must be something you can tell me?"

There were many things, but all of them came with life-threatening risks if my assumptions were wrong. However, telling him nothing could be equally as dangerous. Luke liked to get himself into trouble.

I picked up my last slice of steak, dipped it into the mushroom sauce, and popped it into my mouth. A world of flavour exploded across my tongue as the meat fell apart. I savoured the last bite and then pushed my plate aside.

I looked at Luke. "I'll give you an example of something I believe to be true, if you promise to disregard it once we finish this conversation."

His frown deepened. "You're *that* worried about it?"

"Yes, and I'm not the only one. Otherwise, those gaps in your knowledge would be filled with commentary and speculation instead of being left blank."

He smirked. "Fine, I'll ignore your life lessons this once, but you owe me."

I didn't laugh at his bad attempt at humour. What I had to say next wasn't something to joke about.

I waited until he accepted how serious this conversation was. "I believe ancient vampires are at their most dangerous when they know they're being hunted by something or someone that can kill them. In this scenario, their survival instincts will overpower the Curse of Sloth and allow them to tap into their ability to quickly grow their skills. Because of this, if you fail to kill an ancient vampire, you should take obvious steps to make sure that it's aware you're not chasing it. This will allow the Curse of Sloth to take hold of the ancient vampire, so you can grow your skills to kill it in a future encounter."

Luke whistled as he leaned back. "That seems dangerous."

"That's because what I'm saying is counter-intuitive. Most threats become more dangerous when left alone. Ancient vampires become less dangerous."

He nodded. "I can see how you would make that assumption, but would your strategy work if you found its resting place?"

"No. You would be a constant threat until you were eliminated."

"That makes sense."

"It makes sense, but I could still be wrong about what I just said. And if I'm wrong—"

"People will suffer for your assumptions."

"A lot of people. Which is why I don't want to share my speculations with you, until I've confirmed them to be true."

"I see why you're concerned. I'll forget everything you just said."

"Thank you."

He smirked again. "That's alright. I'm getting better at forgetting things I shouldn't know. Hopefully, I'll be able to forget the fact that you're a furry someday."

I chuckled. "The living dead in my workshop are called dog warriors, and they would likely eat a furry on sight."

Luke chuckled with me as the second dinner bell chimed, signalling the start of after-dinner clubs. I lifted my hand and lazily snapped my fingers.

Shadow Two leapt out from his favourite hiding place under my coat and began to clear the dishes from the table, zipping out of the room.

Luke raised an eyebrow. "Did you just use Shadow as a waiter?"

"That's not Shadow. That's Shadow Two. And I'm not using him as a waiter, I'm field testing him."

"Why?"

"I need to prove that he's identical to Shadow, so Davina will teach me master-tier magic."

"I thought that was why you made Shadow?"

"It was, but Davina is being overly cautious."

"Wait…if you had to make a second shade, you had to damage your soul again." He looked to the door Shadow had passed through and then glared at me. "You promised to take me to the Abyss to hunt. Why am I just hearing about this now?"

Dread filled me as images of me sparkling and Luke laughing played through my mind. I'd been staying away from this conversation for the past week, but Luke had managed to steer me towards it without me noticing.

I tried to look concerned rather than panicked. "Your sister needed you."

His glared vanished. "That's fair, but you're going to make it up to me, right?"

"Are you sure you want to risk gaining skills related to hunting dungeon monsters?"

I'd come up with a long list of excuses for why he shouldn't come with me to the Abyss, so if this one didn't work, I'd move onto another.

He scoffed. "I've been practicing magic for months, so the chances of me gaining those sorts of skills are low now."

"Unless we're hunting floor bosses, which is exactly what I intend to do."

He paused. "You're hunting floor bosses?"

"Yes."

"Alone."

"They help me recover and strengthen my soul a lot faster than regular monsters."

"I'm out, then. Hunting floor bosses will definitely give me skills I don't want."

I decided to change the subject. "How are your lessons with Carolyn going?"

"They're going okay. They would be going better if someone would convince their students to help me refine my mana network."

I rolled my eyes. "I'm not going to owe my students favours because you can't be bothered refining your mana network yourself."

"You used to be cool."

I chuckled. "That didn't work when you were twelve and it doesn't work now."

Luke smiled as he stood up. "I better get going. Kathrine wants to visit the night market in town, and I said I'd go with her."

"Keep her safe."

"Always."

"Keep yourself safe, too."

He grinned. "Where's the fun in that?"

THE FOLLOWING EVENING, I knocked on the door to Headmaster Wink's office. I'd spent the past few nights hunting in the Abyss to repair my soul after making Shadow Two, so I wasn't sure why I'd been called there. He hadn't mentioned it once today.

The doorhandle turned, and the door swung open. Headmaster Wink sat behind his desk, rubbing his scalp and smelling more stressed than usual. There was a half-drunk bottle of gin beside him, but no glass.

Wink only drank straight from the bottle when he was exceptionally stressed. It wasn't a good sign.

I walked in and took a seat. "What can I do for you, Headmaster?"

He sighed. "Is your assistant, by any chance, your son?"

I'd clearly missed several important conversations over the past few nights. "Yes, he is."

Honesty seemed to be my best option.

Wink groaned and rubbed his scalp harder. "Vincent, did you intentionally come to Darksmith to facilitate your son's affair with Princess Carolyn, or are the two events unrelated? Don't try to deny the affair. I know she turns up early for your club meetings and goes upstairs with him while you teach. You're clearly using the school rules around guards to get them alone."

This conversation might have taken a dangerous turn. I needed to see how much he knew.

"Headmaster Wink, facilitating an affair between my son and the only heir of Arcadia could be viewed as treason in Arcadia. And if I were doing anything like that, I would never admit to it."

Headmaster Wink frowned and finally looked at me. "What do you mean the *only* heir?"

If he didn't know Carolyn was the only heir, then it was highly unlikely that he knew Luke was a hero. I didn't need to be concerned about this talk. This was just the headmaster being his usual stressed self.

"Carolyn's siblings were massacred shortly before the dungeon surge began in Arcadia. She was the only one to make it out alive."

His eyes widened. "You brought her here to protect her."

"I did. Darksmith is one of the safest places outside Arcadia's border, and until they catch the killer, it's safer than anywhere inside the border."

"And the affair?"

"What affair?"

He scowled. "Don't pretend this is just about her safety. You and your son are making a play for the throne."

"Headmaster Wink, there are easier places to facilitate an affair than Darksmith, and Arcadia's laws around succession and children born out of wedlock are quite clear."

Wink leaned down and reached into his drawer for a glass. He placed it on the table and half-filled it. He took a long drink, emptying it.

He sighed as his shoulders relaxed. "I apologise for my assumptions, Vincent. In the future, I would appreciate it if your son would be a little more discrete. Try to teach him some of your tricks. You're much better at hiding your trysts than he is."

"I'll do my best, Headmaster."

Headmaster Wink didn't seem to hear me as he picked up the bottle of gin and refilled his glass. "I can't believe I have to deal with two of you."

DAVINA COULDN'T DECIDE if my shades were identical or just extremely similar, so I created Shadow Three to speed up her decision. Davina had watched all three perform various tasks side by side. To my eyes, their actions and reactions were identical, so either the emotions influencing my magic were completely the same all three times, which I knew for a fact wasn't true from the way I made my last shade, or I had mastered applying emotion to magic. After three more days of observation, Davina finally agreed my shades were identical and that I was ready to practice master-tier magic.

Before that could happen, I had to combine Shadow with Shadow Two and Shadow Three. Maintaining three shades cost me far too much life force. Souls weren't meant to have a ghost wandering around, and that included if they were trapped inside a vampire.

However, combining my shades created a new issue.

Davina's eyes glowed blue as she circled Shadow in my workshop, evaluating the unexpected changes that occurred when I combined him with the other shades. "I don't think this has anything to do with you using the layering technique, your Dark Eminence."

My workshop contained several dozen active undead projects split between skeletons, zombies, and the living dead. They'd been moved to the side while I combined Shadow, so there wasn't any room for me to sit.

"Then why do you think the power transfer was so high?"

Shades, like ghosts, grew stronger when they consumed other ghosts and shades. When I'd combined Shadow with the other shades, the strength transfer had been a two-to-one exchange, which should have been impossible.

Shadow was now twice as strong as he used to be, and when he stood in the open like this, he reminded me of Peter Pan's shadow. He was a silhouette of darkness in the exact shape of my body and powerful enough to strangle a man to death.

Davina let the spell fade from her gaze, and her eyes returned to a soft white glow. “Demons don’t change, and you’ve proven you share this characteristic many times, your Dark Eminence. I think the power transfer was higher because both the imprint of your soul and the magic you used to create your shades remained identical all three times. There was no incompatibility to weaken the transfer.”

I had come to the same conclusion but wanted to be sure Davina agreed with it. Now that she had, I was ready to move onto more important matters.

I snapped my fingers and Shadow leapt into his favourite hiding spot inside my coat. “Since you’re here, we might as well begin my new lessons.”

Davina turned around, looking for a chair among the clutter. “Have you decided where you would like to begin?”

“I’d like to learn the master-tier version of the create undead skeleton spell.”

“I can’t help you with that. The knowledge is lost.”

Several months ago, Celest had come to me after class and handed me the reward for saving her life. Dramyin’s Skeletal Texts was a collection of fifteen books filled with everything the lich king Dramyin knew about creating undead. The collection carried a curse that killed anyone who tried to copy it.

The curse had tickled.

I reached into my storage pouch and began placing my spare copies of Dramyin’s Skeletal Texts on the table beside me. “I think these will be able to help us.”

Davina walked over and picked up the first book, read the cover, and squealed with excitement. She stopped paying attention to everything around her, and it was several hours before she noticed I’d left the workshop and came to find me.

19

THE UGLY TRUTH

Kathrine met with Davina every other day to help process what I'd done to her. After the first week of sessions, Kathrine returned to her daily life at Darksmith and began catching up with old friends. After the second week, she'd gone to town with Luke. During the third week, she'd kicked Luke out of her dorm, because she needed her space. During the fourth week, Riza told me Kathrine had started acting like her old self.

My daughter wasn't ready to see me, though.

Kathrine skipped my classes the first five times she was supposed to come, but she attended the sixth. At the end of the lesson, she stopped in front of my desk as the other students hurried out for their next class.

Someone had trimmed her hair, leaving her wavy dark blonde locks just long enough to rest on shoulders that were slightly wider than her mother's. The bags under her eyes from restless nights were finally gone and the faint smile lines were back. Most people wouldn't notice them, but I could see them as clearly as the nose on her face and the dimples that so reminded me of my wife.

She took a deep breath and glanced around, making sure other people were nearby. "When are you free to talk?"

It had taken two months of patiently waiting, and keeping myself occupied, but she was finally willing to speak to me.

I swallowed my excitement. “Would tonight work for you?”

She paused and then nodded. “I can do tonight.”

“Then I’ll see you when the dinner bell rings.”

I watched her leave, feeling quite excited.

I sent Luke to town for supplies and started cooking the moment the school day ended. In my excitement, I went a little overboard, filling the dining room with everything Kathrine might be interested in, along with the best of the new dishes I’d learned how to cook.

As the dinner bell rang, I stood at my front door waiting for her to arrive.

For the next two hours, I listened to her in her dorm, on the other side of the school, as she tried to psych herself up to come here and see me. She was still scared of me. I frightened her. But she wanted to see me, so I waited at the door, keeping the food warm, hoping she would come, and hating myself for being the cause of her fear.

Time means little to vampires, especially when they have nothing to do but wait, and I was still standing at my door when she cried herself to sleep. I waited there all night, unable to move, unable to think about anything other than wanting to set this right, but then the need to maintain my cover as a teacher forced me to start my day.

Kathrine didn’t come to her seventh lesson, but she kept talking with Davina and making progress. She came to her eighth lesson, and we arranged to have dinner again.

That night, I listened as Kathrine walked through my workshop and climbed the staircase. This time she froze when she reached the doors to my apartment, heart racing. I could tell that she was about to run, so I reached for the handle and opened the door.

She stood there, staring at me, frozen in place. I could smell her fear. It was heavy and present. It was instinctual. I’d hurt her so badly that it was a reaction, not a choice.

I smiled at her. “Would you like me to show you that you’re safe?”

She gave a small nod, unable to speak.

The healing palm technique wasn’t the only soul technique I could perform. Ever since Kathrine woke, I'd been practicing the open-heart technique. It let me share my feelings with others, and it wasn't something you could lie with. You could only use it to show others how you truly felt.

I gathered a small amount of soul energy and projected my intent to protect her and not cause her harm. Showing her that all I wanted to do was make a place that was safe for her.

She relaxed but didn't return my smile. "Can I come in?"

"Always."

She took a tentative step inside and then sniffed. "Did you cook dinner for me?"

"I've cooked dinner for your brother quite a lot over the last few months and felt that it's only fair that I do the same for you."

I turned around and walked to the dining room. The table was just as overloaded as the last time Kathrine said she was coming over to talk. I waved my hand and used a little magic to pull her seat out as I sat in mine.

She stood in the doorway for several seconds, before walking inside to sit across from me. She stared at the buffet and frowned. "Do you even eat food anymore?"

"When I want to. It's not a necessity."

"So, you only drink blood."

"No. I don't need to drink blood to survive. I just need life force, and all that requires is a touch."

Kathrine paused. "Why did you go for my blood, then?"

I didn't want to lie to her. She didn't trust me, and I wanted her to trust me. To know she could depend on me. That meant, I had to tell her the truth, unfiltered and whole.

"Blood has restorative properties for vampires that life force doesn't. I can live without it, but doing so makes it harder for me to recover. Familial blood is better for healing and strengthening vampires than the blood of strangers. It's similar to the blood of extremely high-level people. Heroes' blood is better than both. You are both my child and a hero. So, yours and Luke's blood is the greatest healing elixir that exists for me. When you summoned me, I was asleep. When I arrived, only the vampire was awake, and it awoke to the knowledge it was dying. Your blood was an oasis in the desert when it was dying from thirst."

"If blood is so helpful, why don't you drink it?"

"I was trying not to tempt myself. Controlling my hunger was hard enough without knowing the taste of blood matched the most exquisite smell I have ever experienced."

"Then I'm the only person you've ever fed on?"

"No. I've eaten other vampires."

"Why?"

"I wanted to survive. Vampires contain life force they take from others, so we can share or steal that life force through blood."

"Vampires aren't people."

"Is that how you feel about me?"

She briefly looked at my face and then dropped her gaze back to the table. "I'm not sure. I know I'm scared of you. I know I don't trust you. But I also know you spent months helping me recover from what you did to me, proving that my fear isn't rational."

"I'm still your dad...but I'm also a demon. Trusting me completely isn't something you should do."

"Luke said the same thing. I just wish I knew where you ended, and the demon began."

"You've got it wrong, Sweetheart. It's where the demon and I end, and I carry on."

"What do you mean?"

"There are lines I won't cross. When I don't cross those lines, you're dealing with me and only me. There are lines the demon won't cross. When I cross those lines, you are also dealing with me and only me. The rest of the time there are the things me and the demon do together."

"What sort of lines will you cross that the demon won't?"

"Helping people. Giving money to the poor. Protecting people. Saving people. Encouraging people."

"Those are good things, though."

"And the demon in me wants no part of that. Are you hungry?"

Kathrine glanced at the food and her stomach gurgled. "I could eat."

"Help yourself. There is plenty of everything."

She finally smiled. "I can see that."

She didn't load anything onto her plate. Instead, she took her fork and started tasting each dish. When she found something she liked, she added it to her plate. She'd done the same thing as a child, and watching her do it here brought back fond memories.

I took note of the things she liked as I loaded my plate.

She finished making her choices and then took a single bite and put down her fork. "What did my blood taste like?"

I finished chewing on a piece of fried chicken, before wiping my mouth with a napkin. "It tasted like joy. Like the happiest moment of my life."

"That's not a flavour."

"Then blood doesn't have a flavour. It has an emotional profile."

"Drinking my blood brought you joy."

"It's more like a reaction to a drug. The moment I drank your blood, the demonic parasites within me probably flooded the part of my brain that feels joy with happy chemicals."

"Why?"

"Because that's how you turn a man into a monster. You reward him every time he does something horrible, and you punish him every time he does something good. Eventually, he's so twisted up he doesn't know what he is. He just knows how to react to what makes him feel good."

She picked up her fork and continued eating. "Was attacking me the worst thing you've done, since coming here?"

"I feel worse about it than anything else I've done, but it's not the worst thing I've done. It's the second worst."

"Will you tell me about what you did?"

"Do you need to know?"

She paused. "I think I do…The person I thought you were and the person that you are, aren't the same. You're almost a stranger to me. I need to learn who you are, so I can decide if you are worth getting to know."

"Do you know who Angelica is?"

"Davina told me about her, and I've seen her around the academy. She's your other familiar, right?"

"She is. The worst thing I've done since I arrived was make Angelica worthy of being my familiar."

"Why is that the worst thing you've done?"

"Because the night I met her, I forgot one of the fundamental parts of being human."

"And that is?"

"The worst human behaviours are often learned."

This was not a good story to start rebuilding our relationship with. But Kathrine wanted to hear it. And I wanted to be honest with her.

"When I first came across Angelica, all I saw was a young lady participating in a sacrificial ritual in a room filled with Unseen cultists. I let the demon slide her into the mental box conveniently marked *bad guys*, because it was easier than taking the time needed to get to know her. After sliding her into that box, the demon showed me a way to use her, and I saw value in its idea. She was a *bad guy*. She didn't deserve mercy or self-restraint, so doing what it suggested was acceptable."

Kathrine frowned. "What did you do to her?"

"I turned her into a weapon. Her cult had a ritual that was triggered by runic blood magic. It allowed them to steal the attributes from the people they sacrificed. I knew the part of the ritual, called the reaping, that would allow me to sacrifice them and give their attributes to Angelica. So, I sacrificed the Unseen, including her parents, to make her stronger and then forced her to sacrifice the rest."

Kathrine's expression turned grim. "You made her murder people she knew."

"I actually don't regret making her do that, and I know for a fact that it didn't and doesn't bother her."

"You're not painting a pretty picture."

"This isn't a pretty story, Sweetheart, and it gets much more grotesque. The reaping ritual comes with side-effects. These side-effects turn those who undergo the ritual into a homicidal maniac and a magnet for evil. This isn't a problem if you're Unseen, but it is if you're a normal young lady. When I dragged Angelica into the adventurer's guild in Tobil the following morning to make her my familiar, I knew I'd made a mistake. We had spent the night clearing her cult from the town, so I had a chance to watch her and learn who she really was, and she was not the person I had assumed she was. I was completely wrong about her."

"She wasn't a bad guy."

"No. When I walked through the guild's doors, all I saw was a scared little girl who had been taught to be a monster. To be selfish and self-centred because it was the only way to survive her parents."

"I'm not sure I understand what you mean."

"Angelica has experienced every form of abuse you can imagine. And I mean every form of abuse. Everything that is bad about her, was beaten or tormented into her. And because of my short-sightedness, she is too dangerous to be left alone. She is a living weapon of my own creation. A danger to everyone around her."

"She was a victim of circumstance."

"Yes. And I discovered this too late. If I hadn't turned her into a weapon, I could have left her with people who might have been able to help her. But I had already made her too dangerous to be around normal people. I had already cut her off from having a chance at a normal life."

"You didn't want to make her your familiar, did you?"

I shook my head. "Following me around would only lead to a harsh life. And a harsh life is all she has experienced since we met. But I had to take her. Making her my familiar meant I could compel her not to harm people. It meant I could keep the worst of what I did to her at bay. And for the most part, I've been successful. Angelica isn't even aware of how monstrous she truly is."

If I could go back to the basement and kill her parents all over again, I would. It would not be swift this time. It would not be merciful. The things they had done to that girl were beyond forgivable.

She was kind and sweet-natured, but they had twisted that nature into a monster.

So, I had taken their monster and made her my own.

My monster.

My sad little monster who can't think for herself because her parents beat it out of her. Who only acts in her own self-interest because life has taught her that it's the only way you can survive this horrible world she was born into.

The only justification I had for the life I'd forced upon her was that it was not a cruel life. It was not a limited life. She could grow into whoever she wanted to be, and I would make sure she did, so long as it wasn't the monster her parents wanted her to be.

She was *my monster*.

And *my monster* would be better than them.

Even if the only way I could show interest in her was to think of her and treat her as a tool.

"Do you feel bad about what you did to her?"

"I only feel bad about the harm I cause if it affects the people I love. But I know what I did was wrong. I know what I did was terrible. I know that I screwed up and that she has to pay the cost. I know that's not right."

Kathrine placed her knife and fork on her empty plate. "What you did to her was worse than what you did to me. But it also sounds like a mistake. A mistake that you've learned from and are trying to make right. That is someone I might want to know. Would you like to have dinner together tomorrow night?"

"I would like that."

20

UNEXPECTED RESULTS

After months of effort and dozens of working failures, Professor Fergus had finally created an exact replica of my living dead dog warrior. It turned out switching from creating undead to creating living dead was not as easy for Fergus to do as I'd assumed it would be. The mental gymnastics he needed to perform to change from one discipline to the other, without having the create living dead skill, were too much for him. He was a professional necromancer, but he relied too heavily on his skills to easily adapt without them. It was almost like he had to learn everything from scratch.

Which is why it wasn't until a few days after Kathrine started talking to me that Fergus succeeded. We didn't even realise he had, until we ran his latest creation through the battery of tests I'd developed, comparing my project against his, like we had all the others. We were both surprised when there was only a 3% variation between our creations, which was a perfectly acceptable replica for this kind of work. In some ways his was slightly better than mine, and in other ways it was slightly worse.

After so many working failures, everything was finally exactly as I expected it to be. This, of course, changed when we made our dog warriors fight inside my training hall.

My creation was programmed with a greater understanding of martial arts and combat than his and had quickly dominated his dog warrior, which triggered his project to react submissively, something he hadn't programmed it to do. Mine had immediately stopped attacking when this happened, which wasn't something I had programmed it to do. Verbal instructions to continue fighting hadn't worked for either of us. The only way to make them attack each other was for us to compel them with magic, overriding their thought processes. However, the moment we stopped forcing them to fight, they stopped fighting.

Neither of us understood what we were seeing, but it happened every time we made them fight, so we decided to take our creations to the Undead Fight Club to gather more data.

Bones rattled as Fergus's dog warrior slapped aside a skeleton knight with its clawed hand, towering over the sea of undead that was trying to tear it apart like an Egyptian God. An undead spearman darted forward, to stab his distracted dog warrior in the back. My dog warrior leapt over several other undead warriors, dodging several poorly aimed death bolts, and landed on the undead spearman's shoulders.

The bolts fizzled across the barrier as my dog warrior's weight crushed the undead spearman into the ground, pinning it in place. Several drunk necromancers cheered the destruction of their creations while others booed.

Fergus made a note in his book. "I think we can safely conclude that they don't have a problem destroying undead."

I nodded. "The issue is probably related to using dogs to make them."

"But how?"

Angelica's undead knight ducked under a claw swipe and delivered a cut to my dog warrior's forearm, exposing muscle and bone. Her knight then stepped back and allowed the other undead to distract the dog warrior, before darting back in for another strike.

"Perhaps it's the brain," I suggested, hoping he would say something to make me come up with a better idea. "I made it larger, hoping to increase their intelligence, but maybe I increased some other instinct which prevents them from killing each other."

Fergus considered my suggestion. "It can't be empathy. They're too aggressive against other undead. It could be a pack-oriented survival instinct. They might recognise that they're the same and that they have a greater chance of surviving together. They could equate killing each other with killing themselves."

"It's possible."

I honestly didn't know why our creations were reacting the way they were. Nothing I'd read gave me any hints. Contessa's work with the living dead mostly revolved around humans, and she was by far my largest source of information on the subject.

Fergus scratched his chin. "You have to admit, they're incredibly robust killing machines, for a basic living dead. They're doing much better than I expected."

Fergus was right about that. They had a massive size and weight advantage over their opponents, but that wasn't why they were winning. They were fighting together in a way that supported each other, covering each other to increase their chances of survival. The two of them were fighting the entire Undead Fight Club, so they should have been torn apart by now, but they kept protecting each other from being crippled, which allowed them a chance to regenerate. This sort of behaviour usually required programming and years of focused training, but it seemed instinctual to them.

"They have potential," I admitted. "But we need to run more tests."

"I can have another specimen ready in a few weeks."

"That won't be necessary."

Fergus smirked. "Rule three of Undead Fight Club: Fights don't end until one side loses."

I chuckled. "I'm aware of the rules, and I don't need to break them for us to win."

I put my fingers in my mouth and gave a shrill, sharp whistle. The students took control of their undead and made them freeze in place, before turning to me.

"I apologise for cutting everyone's fun short, but Professor Fergus and I just decided we need to study our creations further before you destroy them. This is your only opportunity to withdraw from this demonstration fight."

Angelica rolled her eyes. "This is Undead Fight Club, and fights only ends when one side is destroyed."

Her undead knight took a swing at my dog warrior, which triggered the rest of the club to attack. The laughter immediately started back up. I wasn't upset by her comments. Everyone knew the rules to Undead Fight Club. But I needed to give the students a way out before I thoroughly destroyed their creations. Otherwise, they'd complain.

I took control of my dog warrior with a basic control undead spell and released the restrictions I'd placed on its programming. It was time for my students to understand exactly how important growing their own combat knowledge was.

In the space of a second, the fight went from being reasonably fair to a one-sided slaughter. Bones went flying as my dog warrior struck down undead, while side-stepping blows that would have hit only a few seconds before. It began using its jaw, biting off skulls and crushing the bones between its teeth. It was a vicious and violent battle that was much faster than any of them were prepared for.

Angelica's knight managed to survive to the end by ducking and weaving around attacks, until a lucky backhanded blow scattered its bones. It wasn't the most powerful undead, but it did have the best programming.

I lowered the barrier and walked into the middle of the ring as the bones bounced across the floor. There were a lot of unhappy faces as I looked around and levitated into the air.

"What you just saw is the difference between an undead that has been programmed to utilize its power and fight effectively and an undead that only has a basic understanding of how to do so. You can make the most powerful undead imaginable, but if you can't program it to utilize the power you've given it, then it's no better than a lesser creation. I'm glad to see that many of you have taken steps to correct this weakness by training with Commander Gregory's people. I know how difficult it is for all of you to be around deathlords, let alone train with them, which is why I feel it's time I share some good news with everyone. Would the following people please step into the ring."

I began listing names.

Seventy-three students passed their drink to a friend and came forward, confused by what was going on. I hadn't mentioned anything about this, and this wasn't a normal part of Undead Fight Club. But my students had made a lot of progress, and it was time to show them the results of their hard work.

I remained floating in the air as I looked around the room. "You've all been working exceptionally hard, but some of you have been working harder than others. The necromancers standing in the ring have unlocked the boneweaver subclass. Does anyone here know what a subclass is?"

It was a basic question, but they were rich kids, so some of them might not know.

Baris raised his hand from the front of the group. "Subclasses are mainly connected to lower-tier crafting classes and require enough understanding of a specialisation to unlock. Subclasses are not considered a class or a class upgrade because the amount of attributes a person receives and skill choices from their original class remain the same. When someone unlocks a subclass, they gain three skills that are related to the specialisation the subclass offers but receive no other benefit or penalty. There is no known downside to taking a subclass."

"That's a textbook answer and entirely correct."

I pulled one of Darksmith's mobile class stones from my coat pocket, making sure no part of it touched my skin. It wasn't a universal class stone like the adventurer's guilds used, but it could level every magic-based class, including hero. I tossed it to Baris and watched it tumble through the air. The mobile class stones were for students who wanted to keep their class changes secret, so they worked anywhere in the dungeon. Baris fumbled as he caught it and then immediately went into shock.

The necromancers of Necropolis either didn't know how to unlock the boneweaver subclass or they didn't know how to do so safely. Judging by Baris's reaction, he hadn't expected to have unlocked a subclass.

I cleared my throat. "A little faster, please, Baris. There are a lot of people who need to use that class stone."

He blinked and looked up at me. "I've gained access to the boneweaver subclass."

"I believe I said that. Now please take the subclass and pass the class stone on to the next person. If everyone acts this surprised, we'll be here all night."

Baris handed the stone to the next person and turned to me. "Why didn't you tell us you were helping us unlock a subclass?"

Because I didn't expect to be here this long, I thought to myself.

"I prefer to teach students who wish to study for their own personal interest rather than students who study for a reward." I rotated in the air to look at the rest of the necromancers. "You've all reached the point where gaining this subclass won't change your reason for being here, only encourage you to study harder. Starting next week, we will spend a month studying zombies and how the undead enhancement techniques you've learned for skeletons can be integrated into their creation. If you're diligent, you'll unlock the boneweaver subclass. If you're hyper diligent, you might unlock the corpseweaver subclass as well. These will give you an advantage over your competition, so this next month will separate the amateurs from the professionals. I wish you all the best of luck."

I used the levitation spell to return to the ground and then walked over to Fergus. He was feeding his dog warrior mana to help it recover faster.

He smirked as I stopped beside him and started feeding mana into my dog warrior. "Why am I not surprised to learn that you know how to safely unlock the boneweaver subclass?"

I watched as the cut to my dog warrior's thighs pulled back together. "Considering how much I've taught them already, it would be stranger if I didn't know how to do it."

He chuckled. "That's true. What do you want me to do with my working failures?"

"Do whatever you like."

"What I'd like to do is upgrade them into living dead warriors, but I have no idea how to do that?"

"I'll give you a guide I wrote tomorrow morning. It will let you take your experiments as far as you like."

Fergus grinned. "Why not show me how to do it?"

"I would, but figuring out why our creations are acting strangely is taking all of my spare time."

"Anything I can do to help?"

"Do you know how to make the day longer?"

"Stop drinking."

I chuckled. "It was a serious question."

"And that was a serious answer."

"And if I've already stopped drinking?"

"Then I suggest you restart, because anyone who tells you to stop drinking at Darksmith clearly isn't trying to help you. What's got you so busy, anyway?"

"I'm crafting master-rank undead skeletons."

Fergus chuckled, assuming I was joking. "Fine, you keep your secrets."

IT WAS A WELL-KNOWN fact that casting a master-tier spell changed your relationship to magic. It was also a well-known fact that these changes to control and power took place over decades, which was why practitioners with equal levels, attributes, and skills were not the same if one of them cast a master-tier spell a decade before the other. It was also why practitioners were willing to risk their lives to learn master-tier magic, even if they only managed to cast a spell once.

What wasn't a well-known fact was why these changes occurred. I only knew why they occurred because I'd almost turned myself into soup when I read several books which were stored in a secret vault within a secret vault.

Master-tier magic required soul energy.

It was an insignificant amount, something most practitioners would never notice. However, the changes which eventually occurred from casting a master-tier spell occurred because that insignificant amount of soul energy was enough to link your soul with your magic. This link allowed your soul to feed off your mana regeneration the way my demonic parasites did. Unlike my parasites, once your soul understood the link wasn't dangerous, your soul tried to help, which eventually resulted in more power and control for spell casting.

My soul's reaction to casting a master-tier spell was no different to anyone else's, even with all the changes I'd made to it. My demonic parasites' reaction to casting a master-tier spell was a different matter.

The moment I finished casting my first master-tier spell, a death bolt, my vampiric instincts told me the next one I cast would be stronger. I immediately cast a second master-tier death bolt, which was in fact slightly stronger than the first. Again, my instincts told me the next one would be stronger, so I threw another death bolt.

Davina had noticed the increase in power, between the first and second death bolts, and watched in silence as each bolt grew stronger until I ran out of mana. The necrosaint had been in full research mode ever since, trying to understand the phenomenon.

It had taken a week of her working with Father and Mother to confirm it was the demonic parasites strengthening my magic. After confirming that the changes were because of the demonic parasites, she wanted to know if these changes only effected death magic or necrotic magic too.

To find this out, she'd taught me the death spell and the destruction spell. They were the most powerful single-target death and necrotic spells, but also two of the easiest master-rank spells to learn.

The death spell grew stronger.

The destruction spell did not.

From there, Davina taught me how to create a death void, call the dead, claim the dead, raise the dead, dominate the dead, rule the dead, wake the dead, and many other equally creatively named master-tier death spells. When it came to death magic, there was very little she didn't know, and she wanted to confirm that all of these spells grew stronger when I cast them repeatedly, and that they grew stronger in measurably consistent ways.

They did.

When it came to necrotic magic, Davina only knew six master-tier spells: destruction, necrotic bolt, void barrier, wall of destruction, barrier of destruction, land of destruction.

None of these spells grew stronger.

Davina and Father concluded that my demonic parasites were only capable of strengthening death magic. Their working theory for why this was the case was that the demonic parasites' ability to strengthen death magic was somehow related to how they could reanimate and strengthened their host. This was plausible because becoming an ancient vampire had given me extremely high attributes. These attributes were in no way related to a class, because at the time I hadn't unlocked one, which meant that they were purely a byproduct of how I'd been reanimated.

While that was all plausible, I didn't think it was the reason my necrotic spells couldn't get stronger. Necrotic magic was just a concentrated form of death magic, after all. Anything that could strengthen death magic should in theory be able to strengthen necrotic magic. My instincts told me that the reason my demonic parasites didn't strengthen my necrotic magic was because they were afraid. If my necrotic magic became too powerful, it would be able to destroy them, and survival was at the forefront of their existence.

Wanting to know if there was a limit to how powerful my death spells could grow, Davina turned to Dramyin's Skeletal Texts. It contained the master-rank versions of the bonemeal, bone stitch, form skeleton, and create undead skeleton spells. The bonemeal and bone stitch spells were spells that I could perform over and over again without feeling like I was wasting time.

That only lasted until I completed my first master-tier undead skeleton. Then Davina told me she wanted me to create a second one.

And I insisted I needed help if I was going to do something so tedious.

It was after midnight when I walked into the closest meditation chamber to town, carrying a storage chest filled with equipment for making undead. Murdell was a nation of sorcerers, and many of their professions required mana, so almost every dungeon had a meditation chamber at the edge of the dungeon zone where sorcerers could go to quickly replace their mana. The one near Darksmith was a massive chamber filled with a thousand small mana concentration circles, which increased the ambient mana everyone could absorb.

Gregory was waiting for me and meditating in the concentration circle closest to the entrance. His people were meditating in the concentration circles beside and behind him. All three hundred of them wore identical crimson robes, so it looked like I'd walked into a chamber full of cultists.

Gregory opened his eyes as I approached and pulled back his hood. "Helen already said we look like cultists, so I don't need to hear the same from you. Let me make it clear, we're not giving up a threefold increase to mana regeneration just because the colour of our robe makes people uncomfortable."

"You know that's exactly what a cultist would say."

Several people broke their meditation to chuckle.

"Our robes have never been used in a cult ritual."

"Only because you killed the cultists that were supposed to deliver them."

Gregory and Sir Trent had several interesting adventures on their way here, mostly because without me around, Angelica kept attracting evil. They'd put down several cults and even banished a few lesser demons.

Gregory rolled his eyes. "We're ready when you are, sir."

The entrance had the largest open area in the meditation chamber, which seemed to be why everyone was sitting so close. I put down the storage chest I was holding and removed the undead crafting table I'd taken from Contessa, placing it in the entrance.

"What the hell is that thing?" Gregory hissed.

I rarely saw Gregory flustered anymore, so I decided to pretend like I didn't know why he was bothered. "It's an undead crafting table."

"It's made out of human skulls."

"The best ones are."

"Why do you have an undead crafting table made out of human skulls?"

"Contessa didn't need it anymore."

"Are you joking? Does the adventurer's guild know you have that?"

"I hope not."

"Please be serious, sir? That thing looks evil enough for my wife to leave me if I take part in something that requires its use."

I glanced at him and realised he wasn't joking. Helen was a cleric, so her leaving him might have something to do with an oath she'd made to Heaven to gain her powers.

I patted a skull near the edge of the table like a used car salesman. "This undead crafting table is made out of necromancers who died peacefully in their sleep without a grudge in their heart. Their skulls have been partially reanimated and programmed to assist in stabilising the enrichment and enhancement of undead materials and the creation of undead creatures. Contessa made sure that this was not an evil or unholy crafting table, because if it was it would have messed with her results. The adventurer's guild is not happy that I have this, but it's not evil, so they don't have a say."

"Necromancers who died peacefully in their sleep without a grudge in their heart," Gregory said sceptically.

"That's Contessa's way of saying they were murdered in their sleep after they'd killed all their enemies."

"So, just to be clear, your 'not evil' undead crafting table was made by an evil lich, out of the skulls of murdered necromancers, who had killed their enemies. I'm not sure if my wife is going to believe that we're doing good work here, sir."

"I used the table to craft Shadow, so Davina will vouch for it."

"That won't help."

"She's a saint."

"Half a saint. My wife believes she's under your influence, which is why she allows you to perform questionable acts."

"It's just a crafting table."

"Made from human skulls."

"They were terrible people."

"That's a fine reason to kill them, but not a fine reason to turn them into furniture."

"Fine, I won't use the crafting table, but if you all die it's on you."

Several dozen people turned to glare at Gregory.

He sensed their gazes. "Um, why could we die without the crafting table made out of necromancer skulls, sir?"

"I'm going to be using nine master-rank spells to form toe bones and other bones just as small. That much death magic concentrated into such a small space can be highly unstable. The undead crafting table you don't want me to use can detect when these instabilities are occurring and also stop these instabilities from occurring. Without the crafting table, I won't notice that the magic in a bone is becoming unstable until there is nothing that I can do to stop the bone from releasing a death wave. Whether or not I can open a portal to the Deadlands fast enough to throw it through will come down to luck."

The glares intensified.

Gregory sighed. "Just to be clear, you're not using the crafting table to make this undead skeleton?"

"No, it will slow me down."

"Fine, I withdraw my objection."

Gregory seemed honestly conflicted. "You can sit to the side if you want?" I made the offer because it was the right thing to do. Not because I wanted to increase my influence over Gregory, thereby increasing my influence over his men.

"I'm good, sir."

I turned to the others. "If this makes any of you uncomfortable, you can move to the side."

No one moved.

A few smelled uncomfortable, but they stayed where they were.

They didn't want to look weak or unwilling to help in front of the men and women they had fought and died beside.

I finished setting up the undead crafting table and then pulled a massive dungeon monster bone out of the storage chest and placed it on top. A few basic spells converted the bone to bonemeal, and another basic spell transformed the bonemeal into a replica of my skeleton. I then swept the excess bonemeal into a bag and threw the bag into the chest.

I turned to everyone and began gently drawing the mana from their cores to replace the mana I'd just used. "You can go back to gathering mana."

They closed their eyes and went back to meditating.

I swept the skeleton into a pile, before casting an overcharged 1st-rank bonemeal spell. Months of enriching bonemeal had taught me exactly how much enrichment I could achieve with a single spell. I cast the spell nine times until the bonemeal all shared a consistent quality and texture. Then I moved on to the 2nd-rank version of the spell.

What I was doing here was the same as what I'd done to teach the Undead Enhancement Club how to create an undead skeleton. The only difference was that I was using fifteen ranks of spells instead of nine ranks, and I was doing more material enhancement before I cast the form skeleton spells. Unlike the expert and lower tiers, the master-tier versions of the form skeleton spell caused instability. They were too powerful for unenhanced material and would cause the bones to melt.

This was a common issue necromancers had to deal with when making powerful undead. The more powerful you made an undead, the harder it was to keep the magic that reanimated them stable. Without Dramyin's Skeletal Texts, there was no way I would be able to do this. It would have taken me decades to recreate these spells and then decades more to figure out how to use them without my undead exploding.

Even Contessa's work with the living dead wasn't on this level, and hers could breed.

By the time I cast the 15th-rank form skeleton spell, most of the cores I was drawing from were empty. Forming the skeleton was the only time outside of casting the create undead skeleton spell where I could overcharge the spells. When creating master-tier undead skeletons, Dramyin advocated for using the least mana possible when casting the bonemeal and bone stitch spells, because it provided more stability. If you wanted to create a more powerful undead, then repeating the enhancement process was advised.

I picked up the left pinkie bone and waited for my core to refill. This bone was the one that had given me the most trouble the first time I created a master-rank undead skeleton. It had become unstable more than a dozen times; and if Davina hadn't eaten them, the death waves would have killed everyone at Darksmith.

We'd since worked out why the instability occurred. It was because of Davina. Her constitution consumed some of the death magic that was used to stabilise the spell. This wasn't an issue for weaker undead, but it was an issue for master-tier undead. However, if I could make a master-tier undead skeleton with her around, I could make one anywhere.

There was almost no chance of this pinkie bone exploding and killing everyone.

Almost.

…

I turned as I heard feet dropping to the ground. I recognised it as the sound of sorcerers' landing near the tunnel entrance to the meditation chamber. They'd be here in less than a minute.

I tossed the pinkie bone onto the table and glanced at Gregory. "You said no one used this place this late at night."

Gregory opened his eyed and frowned. "They don't."

"You can tell that to our guests."

I carried the undead crafting table to the side of the entrance to make room and turned to see twenty alchemists stepping around the corner, grumbling to each other.

The middle-aged man at the front scowled at the ground in front of him, looking like he wanted to go to bed. "I say we stop complaining and strike. The size of these orders is getting completely out of hand. What does that blasted academy need thirty barrels of basic enchanting solution for? They don't even teach basic enchanting."

"At least they gave in to our demands for double overtime, Cid," the woman next to him said, before yawning.

Cid continued to scowl. "I haven't seen our new baby awake in nearly a week. Money doesn't give me back the time I'm missing out on."

Most of the others were all having similar conversations and not paying attention to their surroundings, but I was still surprised when the man and woman passed me with only a brief, "Evening."

Two of the younger alchemists at the back of the group who were more awake than the others had stopped and were staring at the undead crafting table beside me. An older man had also stopped, but he was staring at Gregory's people.

I watched as Cid and the woman at the front finally spotted Gregory and his people. Their feet froze as their gaze lifted, taking in the three hundred silent figures in crimson robes. This caused the others to notice. They all looked around them, not sure what to do.

I smirked at Gregory. "These nice people seem to be concerned by the rather incriminating robes that you're wearing?"

Gregory turned to Cid. "We're guards, but tonight we're supplying mana to that necromancer over there. As for the robes, a few months back we killed a group of cultists who were supplying equipment to their cult. The robes triple our mana regeneration, which is why we're wearing them."

All of the alchemists remained frozen.

Cid was the first one to move. He turned and glanced at my undead crafting table. He did a double-take and then swallowed. "We don't want any trouble. Just let us go and we won't tell anyone what we saw here."

I turned to the three in the tunnel and motioned for them to pass me. They all swallowed, and the younger two meekly walked into the meditation chamber.

The older man stopped beside me and looked at the table. "Is that what I think it is?"

I shook my head. "Probably not."

He sighed. "Good. For a moment, I thought it was a Corpse Gate."

"Oh, it is. Sorry, I didn't expect anyone around here to know what it was."

Gregory had stood up and was glaring at me again. "You said it was an undead crafting table."

"It is. It just happens to be a fancy enough crafting table to be called a Corpse Gate."

Cid turned to the old man next to me. "Are we dead?"

The old man reached into his storage pouch and pulled out a small glass bottle with clear liquid inside. It was filled with holy water, based on the smell and feeling it gave off. He opened the top and flicked it at the leg of the table. The holy water dripped down the skulls without any effect.

"The Corpse Gate's not corrupted, so they're not performing some evil ritual. We'll live as long as no one knows it's here."

"Why only if no one knows it's here?" Cid asked.

"That table is worth as much as a Phoenix Furnace. Despite the cultist robes, I think those guards are here to make sure no one kills him and steals it while they supply him with mana."

Cid swallowed. "Why would he need that much mana?"

"I'm repeatedly casting master-tier spells," I said. "Gregory can explain the rest. I need to work."

The old man next to me smiled and then walked down the side of the room to an empty mana concentration circle. Several of the older alchemists took this to mean everything was safe and joined him. The less-trusting alchemists hounded Gregory with questions while I picked up the pinkie bone that would kill everyone if I failed to enhance the material properly.

It was time to get back to work.

21

DINNER DATES & MOBSTERS

Kathrine originally didn't have a problem with me exploiting Gorgath for ninth-floor monster cores, but then she met the kid. His polite and respectful attitude to everyone at Darksmith changed her feelings on the matter. He was no longer a callous monster devoid of sympathy, but an intelligent being worthy of fair treatment. So, for the first time ever, I had to choose between my daughter's feelings and loot.

It was a hard choice for me to make.

Mainly because I didn't see anything morally wrong with what I was doing. Yes, to humanity the cores were worth more than some kingdoms' GDP, but to Gorgath's people it was pocket change. The same was true for the spells he was learning. To humanity, basic and intermediate spells were common knowledge, the kind you could find at your local bookstore. To Gorgath's people, it was cutting-edge magic.

So, to clear the air and set Kathrine straight, I took her with me the next time I went to collect Gorgath's tuition. Which was how we found ourselves standing against the tunnel wall, outside the entrance to the Abyss, as monsters rushed past us on the other side of the tunnel.

The local monster population had become used to Gorgath moving between the Abyss and the dungeon, and very few monsters made their homes along his path anymore. The monsters rushing past us were all wandering predators, creatures that bred quickly and died just as quickly.

Under the influence of my open-heart technique, Kathrine wasn't concerned by any of the monsters. Then a horse-sized cockroach flew out of the tunnel. Without thinking, her hand shot up and she unleashed her most powerful combat spell, a howling fire lance.

The beam of fire cut through the monster's exoskeleton, igniting it from within, while she shuddered in place. As the cockroach began to burn, the second stage of the spell initiated, and pure oxygen was pulled towards the flames, tripling their size and causing them to release a deafening howl.

When Kathrine was four, my wife and I had to put up with numerous presents left on our pillows. These presents took the form of pretty spiders, cute grasshoppers, lovely ladybugs, and funny worms, but never cockroaches. Cockroaches always died around Kathrine, and that hadn't changed as an adult.

The howling cockroach fell from the air like a flaming comet crashing into the stampede below. The racing monsters didn't stop, rushing around the flaming corpse as they tried to get away.

Kathrine's heartrate suddenly spiked even higher. I smelled shock and confusion, and I turned to look at her face. Her eyes were focused on an empty space right in front of her, as she read a notification.

I tried not to smile. "Was that the first monster you've killed since waking up?"

"I think so," she replied absently.

"Did you reach level 80?"

She nodded without thinking.

Davina appeared to be right. Consuming Luke's life force was how I'd formed the bond that gave him my excess experience. Drinking Kathrine's blood and life force had either created a similar bond or a stronger bond. Either way, she received the same benefits now.

"Your sudden growth is why Luke's been trying to get you to go hunting with him."

She frowned and turned to me. "What?"

"This is rather complicated to explain, but I'm the reason you leveled."

She stepped back, looked around, and then took a seat on my master storage chest. "Why are you the reason I just leveled?"

"The short answer is that because of my hero class, I gain experience from killing monsters, but because of my ancient vampire race, I can't absorb that experience, but because of my hero class, that experience is passed on to those I'm bonded with. Now that I've drunk your blood and consumed your life force, you're one of the people I'm bonded with. Your brother, my familiars, and my guards also receive experience from me."

She folded her arms. "Why didn't you tell me this before now?"

"Until you leveled, I wasn't sure if I shared a bond with you, and your brother and I didn't want you to think we were trying to coerce you into forming a bond with me if you went hunting and it turned out we didn't already share a bond."

She paused and then unfolded her arms. "That makes sense, but I'll be asking Luke to confirm your story."

Kathrine understood better than Luke that I didn't have the same emotional reactions as when I was a human. She was a lot blunter with me about her feelings and her level of trust. She knew knowing exactly where our relationship sat wouldn't upset me but help me to regulate my behaviour toward her.

She threw another howling fire lance past my head and a second flying cockroach died. "I still don't really understand why I gained experience from you."

"It's hard for me to explain something I don't fully understand myself."

"You don't understand why I leveled?"

"Not completely."

"Why not?"

"There is too much guess work involved. For example, it's well known that good and evil classes exist, and that these classes gain a lot more experience than neutral classes when they perform actions related to their alignment. This means a hero will gain more experience for killing a troll that is attacking a village than they will for killing a similar-level troll that is wandering alone in the middle of nowhere. However, that same hero won't gain any experience for murdering a high-level elderly couple to steal their money."

"That's just because classes gain experience from actions that are related to their class. A baker isn't going to level their class by working in a blacksmith's forge, so a hero isn't going to gain experience from murdering nice elderly couples."

"But a baker will gain experience from killing a monster."

"What does that have to do with why you can give me experience?"

"Let me ask you a question instead of answering. Does a class generate experience when someone kills a monster, or does it take experience from the monster they kill?"

"Depends on the class. Some take experience that the monster collected. Some generate experience from killing the monster. Some do both."

"And where does your class reside?"

"What do you mean?"

"Is your class a part of your body or soul?"

"I don't know."

"I don't know either. The literature is conflicted on this subject. The church has managed to resurrect people with just their soul, which has resulted in them returning with their class and levels, which suggests a class is bound to the soul. However, vampires inherit the class, skills, and levels of the person they were before they became a vampire; and even when the soul is gone, the class, skills, and level remain."

She paused for several seconds and then shook her head. "You're starting to confuse me."

"This will start to make sense in a second. Let's say I kill a monster. As a hero, my class draws the experience from the monster, and because I've done a good deed, it adds extra good guy experience on top, mixing the two together. However, as an ancient vampire, my flesh has an evil alignment, which means the monster good guy blended experience can't pass through my flesh. My class is pulling the experience to me, but my flesh won't allow it to pass through and merge with my class to level me, so it just sits there outside my body, until it's drained by those I share a bond with."

"Why would it transfer to those you share a bond with?"

"Because the hero class can't differentiate between a strong bond and someone who took my hero's oath."

For a second it looked like she understood, but then she shook her head. "Your class treating everyone you're bonded with like they're your sworn brothers and sisters might explain why everyone gets some experience but not all of your unused experience."

"Unless…"

Her eyes lit up. "Unless your class never stops trying to absorb the cloud of experience around you, even though it can't reach it, so it keeps sending small amounts of experience to everyone else until it's all gone."

"That's what we think is happening, but there are a lot of holes in our theory."

"Like the fact that a hero having sworn brothers and sisters who grow more powerful with them is extremely rare."

"Yes."

Kathrine shoulders relaxed slightly as she turned away from me. She seemed to have accepted why she'd suddenly leveled. A smile spread across her face. "I can't believe I'm level 80."

Her eyes flicked through notifications, and she started biting her lip as she weighed the pros and cons of what she saw. This was the first time she'd let her guard down around me. Even with the open-heart technique projecting my intentions to protect her, she was always on edge. Seeing her looking at her new skills rather than watching me like a hawk was nice.

And it made me realise part of why she was so afraid of me was because she felt defenceless when she was around me. The sudden influx of levels was like a security blanket. They made her feel safe for the first time since she'd woken. I could see that. I could smell that. But I knew it was an illusion. She wasn't safe from me. Not yet.

Monsters continued to rush past us, on the other side of the tunnel, terrified by my reduced aura, but more terrified by the aura that was following them.

Kathrine finished reading her new skills. "Do you mind if we do something different for dinner tonight?"

I smiled. "What were you thinking?"

"I'd like you to invite the people you share a bond with."

"The dining room isn't big enough to fit all my guards."

She frowned. "How many do you have?"

"Gregory brought three hundred with him, but I have nearly six hundred in total."

"And you share a bond with *all* of them?"

"All except the clerics."

"Gregory or one of his subordinates should be enough representation for your guards."

The ground began to shake as the flow of monsters disappeared.

"I can manage that."

Gorgath came lumbering out of the tunnel with a sack in one hand and eight blank bone staffs in the other. He gave me a big toothy grin. "Professor Vincent, Gorgath's sire has sent him many bone staffs so that he may practice his enchanting. Uncle Gorak said he will owe Gorgath a great debt, if Gorgath can produce a functional intermediate-tier rune his people have not seen."

Kathrine stood up and nudged my elbow, as if she needed to remind me why she was here.

"Gorgath, this is my daughter Kathrine, who you met the other day. She has some questions she would like to ask, if that's okay with you."

Gorgath placed his staffs on the ground and then took a seat. He peered at Kathrine for several seconds, inhaled her scent, and then folded his arms. "Gorgath has some time before his classes to do Professor Vincent a favour."

I felt my eyebrow raise. The kid was becoming a regular mobster with the way he acted. "What would you like in return for this favour?"

He gave me another big toothy grin. "Gorgath would like Professor Vincent's endorsement for the head of the student council."

Several questions flashed through my head. I chose the simplest one. "Why do you want to be the head of the student council?"

He slapped his chest. "Gorgath would like to change where the duelling club meets so he can join. Gorgath would also like to lift the restriction on him not casting spells in the dungeon. Gorgath is more experienced than he was before, but the restriction remains."

His reply answered several of my other questions. "How exactly am I supposed to endorse you?"

"Gorgath's friend Arro is putting up fliers and telling people to vote for Gorgath. Professor Vincent can help."

"You have friends?"

"Gorgath has one friend."

Good for him.

"Sure, I'll help your friend."

"Professor Vincent must remember not to harm the students to make them vote for Gorgath. Gorgath is a student of Darksmith, and students cannot take actions that will harm each other. Gorgath wants only the help he has described."

I chuckled. "I'll do my best to restrain myself."

Gorgath nodded and turned to Kathrine. "What questions do you have for Gorgath?"

Kathrine muttered a spell to amplify her voice. "Do your people use money?"

He shook his head. "My people prefer to be independent and produce what we need ourselves. We only barter when there are restrictions on our time, we are young, or we have reached the deeper floors and must work with others for survival."

"But you have debts?"

"Yes. Gorgath owes many debts for the food and cores his sire provided him as he grew and many more for his tuition. He also owes debts to his uncle and several others."

Kathrine frowned. "Your parents make you pay for the cost of raising you?"

"No. Gorgath wishes to repay these debts. Gorgath wishes to be independent, and Gorgath feels he cannot do so until he owes nothing to others."

"You mentioned that if you can make a functional intermediate rune your people haven't seen that your uncle Gorak will owe you. Why will he owe you?"

He paused for a few seconds. "Gorgath has learned that the high ambient mana in the Abyss makes it extremely difficult to study the subtleties of spells and enchantments. This difficultly, combined with the backlash of intermediate spells being able to kill Gorgath's people, is why Gorgath's people have only been able to develop new basic spells and enchantments. To gain the knowledge of an intermediate rune without hundreds of unnecessary deaths is of great value to Gorgath's people. Uncle Gorak will owe Gorgath because Uncle Gorak will be the only one Gorgath teaches."

"How much will he owe you?"

"Uncle Gorak will pay Gorgath's tuition for a hundred advanced spells for a new basic enchantment rune, but he will also clear Gorgath's debt from repaying Professor Vincent if it is an intermediate rune."

"One new rune is that valuable to your people?"

Gorgath nodded vigorously. "A new intermediate rune is much more valuable than what Uncle Gorak can offer, but Uncle Gorak helped Gorgath, so Gorgath will help him."

"Does your sire think your tuition is expensive?"

Gorgath began to chuckle. He then stifled the chuckle and dropped his gaze to the tunnel floor, where he began drawing on the stone with his finger, like he'd been caught with his hand in the cookie jar.

In a very quiet voice he said, "Your people find cores that my people throw away useful. My sire has been collecting what others toss from their nest to pay my tuition."

Her eyes widened. "You're paying your tuition with trash?"

Gorgath glanced up and made a so-so motion with his hand. "Gorgath and his sire did not realise this at the beginning, so Gorgath has only been able to pay most of his tuition with what others discard."

The kid was fleecing me, like the way I was fleecing him. He was definitely becoming more of a mobster.

I respected that.

I turned to Kathrine, hoping she had enough information to let Gorgath and I continue extorting each other. "Do you have any more questions, Sweetheart?"

She ignored me. "Why do your people consider these cores trash?"

Gorgath scratched his jaw. "They contain magic that is incompatible with our cores and make us sick if we eat them. Some of them are so incompatible they can kill us."

"Why don't you filter those magics out?"

"This is harder to do in a high ambient magic environment like a dungeon. It is impossible to do in the Abyss."

"How do you know that?"

"Gorgath's friend has been teaching Gorgath to read, and Gorgath has learned many things his people did not know."

"Have your people ever tried to separate the contaminants out?"

"My people have tried many times. We have never succeeded, so we have never been able to gather data on what does and does not work."

Kathrine smiled. "Thank you for answering my questions."

"Gorgath is happy to help, which is why a vote for Gorgath is a vote for progress."

He gave Kathrine two thumbs up and a rather fearsome grin.

FOR THE PAST TWO WEEKS, dinners with Kathrine usually involved her asking unflattering questions and me giving unflattering answers. Kathrine didn't have Luke's carefree attitude. She needed to understand everything about me, from the way I acted to how I mentally justified those actions. By the end of the first week, she knew me better than Luke did.

Inviting Luke, Davina, Angelica, Gregory, and Amelia to join us for dinner that night was an entirely different experience to our usual meals, which were like police interrogations. By comparison, this was almost a family dinner with friends.

Kathrine's mouth dropped open as she looked at everyone around the dining room table. "You're all over level 100."

Luke kept his fork stabbed into the last steak and continued his staring contest with Amelia. "It's less impressive than it sounds. Skill levels play a larger role after level 100."

Davina nodded as she added more mushroom sauce to her baked potatoes. "And they play less of a role after level 200."

Kathrine snapped her head to Davina. "Some of you are over level 200?"

"No, but Angelica and I have attributes that are like someone level 200 with a first-tier class. If you're looking for advice on skills and attributes, you won't find anyone better than his Dark Eminence."

"Davina says that," Angelica said, with a grin, "but she hasn't listened to any of his advice recently."

Davina poked her tongue at Angelica. "I'm working my way through my necromancy skills because they're easier for me to master."

"Which is purely for your ego," I replied.

Davina didn't have a response to that, so she folded her arms and sulked. "I wanted to be a necromancer."

Luke groaned. "Can we *please* not have this argument again?"

Gregory wiped his mouth and pushed his plate aside. "I don't see what the problem is. The standard attribute alignment for magic users is three points into agility and mana regeneration, and one into everything else."

"And that's exactly why you're not qualified to give class advice," I replied.

Kathrine frowned. "Why's that bad advice?"

I pushed my empty plate away. "It's bad advice because everyone's different. Someone who is extremely talented at magic like Davina doesn't need extra agility for complex spell casting. Angelica and Luke's armour makes the recovery attribute obsolete after a certain point, because anything that is powerful enough to breach their armour will instantly kill them. My infinite recovery makes endurance pointless, and constitution a poor investment. The standard attribute distributions are designed for people who don't have access to someone who knows what they're talking about."

"What would you suggest for me then?"

"The Kingmaker distribution. 183 Strength, 227 dexterity, 237 agility, 196 endurance, 214 constitution, 237 recovery, and 147 mana regeneration. It's what the majority of people need to master any skill and is a good place for you to start."

Kathrine frowned. "But I'm not a fighter."

"Your point?"

"I don't need that much strength, endurance, constitution, or recovery."

"Do you get tired when you train?"

"Everyone gets tired when they train."

"You won't if you invest your attributes this way. You'll be able to train in peak condition all day, which will greatly enhance how quickly you improve."

"But then I'll be left with useless attributes when I'm competent."

I rolled my eyes. "That's a falsehood that keeps getting repeated by the ignorant. You won't be left with useless attributes. You'll be left with a better quality of life and the capacity to master any skill, which is far more valuable than you think it is."

"Oh."

"Murdell likes to preach magical superiority, even in the South. They forget that attributes make everything easier. If you use my suggestion as your starting point, you'll be able to discover where you have trouble and invest the rest of your attributes where you need them. Having a wide foundation is more important for a hero because we gain skills based on what we do. Only after we've made sure we're capable of doing everything, should we begin to specialise."

"My instructors would disagree," Luke said.

Amelia hadn't given up on the staring contest, but she'd half-climbed onto the table and was trying to pull Luke's fork out of the steak they were fighting over.

"No, they wouldn't," Amelia replied. "Your dad is giving advice based on your sister's current circumstances."

Luke continued to hold his fork in place. "What circumstances?"

"Your sister gained more than fifty levels at once, which is over a thousand attribute points. Before now, most of her existing attributes were used to increase her mana regeneration and agility to get into Darksmith. She's about to have a threefold increase in power, even if she only distributes her attributes like a sorcerer would. She could be ten times stronger if she invested into physical attributes, which would make her a danger to herself and others because she wouldn't know how to control her strength. Your dad is trying to prevent that from happening."

Luke removed his fork from the steak.

Amelia picked up her prize with her hand and returned to her seat. Princess Carolyn was making Amelia take etiquette lessons, and her poor manners here tonight were her way of rebelling. Amelia deliberately wiped her hand on the tablecloth after adding the steak to the plate of fried chicken she'd won from Gregory.

Kathrine threw a napkin at her. "Don't wipe your hands on the tablecloth, Amelia."

Amelia stuck out her tongue. "Your dad said I could."

"No, he didn't."

"I did."

Kathrine frowned, remembering how strict I'd been with them when she was Amelia's age. "Why are you letting her get away with being rude?"

I turned to Luke. "I don't have any grandchildren to spoil."

He threw a bread roll at me.

I caught the roll, broke it in half, and reached for the butter. "Carolyn is trying to turn Amelia into a refined young lady, so Amelia doesn't have a lot of personal freedom at the moment. She only agreed to come to dinner if I let her do whatever she wanted."

Amelia took a bite of chicken leg while staring at Luke and daring him to take the untouched steak she'd fought him for. "I had to walk around with a book on my head all day. It was stupid."

Angelica sat with a puzzled look on her face. "What was the book for?"

"It's supposed to correct my posture."

I watched Angelica have flashbacks of whatever horrible experience she'd gone through to correct her posture. Her scent changed as her mood dropped.

I turned back to Kathrine. "My advice is to invest the minimum attributes for the Kingmaker distribution for now and let yourself get used to the changes. It shouldn't take you more than a month to get a good idea of where you need to invest the rest of your attributes, and you won't suffer any adverse effects when you increase them."

"You didn't mention what I should do with my new charisma attribute," Kathrine said with a slightly accusatory tone.

"He probably didn't think it was necessary to mention something so basic," Luke replied. "Everyone knows charisma changes your personality while it improves your looks and charismatic presence, and that the only way to offset that change is to increase charisma by a single point each year."

I swallowed the mouthful of bread roll I was eating. "What Luke said."

Gregory wiped a piece of bread along the inside of the gravy boat and then ate it. "Are we taking her into the Abyss during our next training session, sir? You killed a lot of monsters down there last time, so her level should be a lot higher than 80."

Luke turned to me. "Why is this the first time I'm hearing about a trip to the Abyss?"

Amelia giggled. "I know why."

I turned to Amelia. "Don't you dare, Amelia."

Her mischievous giggling grew louder.

Luke raised an eyebrow. "Why didn't he invite me?"

"You don't need to know," I said, trying not to panic.

Kathrine turned to me. "What are you trying to hide?"

"It's nothing important or dangerous. Can we please leave it at that?"

She frowned. "You've answered every question I've asked you. What's so bad about this one to make you not want to share?"

Amelia giggled. "He hates it."

Gregory wiped his mouth with his napkin. "I don't remember seeing anything in the Abyss the boss would hate."

"The way he sparkled was a little weird," Angelica muttered.

Luke's turned his head slowly, until he was staring at Angelica with far too much hope in his gaze. "What did you say?"

"I said, the way he sparkled was a little weird."

"Dad sparkles?"

Davina nodded. "His Dark Eminence's body expels mana crystals before they can cause him harm, which results in them exiting his skin as a fine crystal powder."

"And this fine crystal powder makes him sparkle?"

The last time I saw such a big smile on Luke's face, he was seven and it was Christmas morning.

Davina nodded. "It's quite noticeable."

Luke howled with laughter. It was loud, obnoxious, and unrestrained. He slapped the table so hard it cracked.

Kathrine giggled.

I put my elbows on the table, placed my face in my hands, and groaned.

"You sparkle!"

I groaned again. "I'm never going to live this down?"

Luke laughed harder. "Never! You're a walking cliché."

"Why is this funny?" Davina asked.

I sighed and looked over. "It's only funny if you're from our world."

"Is this another anime protagonist quality?"

Luke held his sides as he continued to laugh. "It's *so* much worse."

"Can I come to the Abyss, too?" Amelia asked.

"If your parents say you can."

Gregory gave me a very pointed look.

I ignored him. I had bigger problems. I needed to distract my children from what they had just learned.

I turned to my daughter. "You shouldn't understand this reference enough to find it funny, Kathrine. You weren't allowed to watch those movies or read the books, before we came here."

Kathrine's giggling died off at my tone of voice. "Luke let me watch the movies when he babysat me."

I turned to Luke. He continued to laugh, as I tried to talk to him, ruining my attempt to change the subject.

"I can't breathe," he said through too much laughter.

I turned back to Kathrine. "That was naughty of him for letting you do that and naughty of you for not telling me. You can make it up to me and your mother by taking my advice now."

Kathrine rolled her eyes. "Why's it so important I do what you say?"

"Because it will make you stronger. And the stronger you are, the less I have to worry about you."

"What if I get strong enough to kill you?"

"Nothing would make me happier."

"You mean that, don't you?"

"Yes."

She sighed. "Fine."

"Thank you. Also, please upgrade your willpower, sorcerer sovereign, and prodigy skills."

"I wanted to see if you were influencing my mind, so I upgraded all three of those the minute I leveled."

I frowned. "Is that why you've been more relaxed around me since you leveled?"

"It's part of the reason."

"And the other part?"

"I'm now strong enough to get away from you if I don't want to know you anymore."

If only that were true.

22

FINALS WEEK

Darksmith wasn't like other magical academies. It didn't give out degrees or fail you for poor performance. The students enrolled in one-year courses and then used their end of year results to decide if they should take a new course, the next course, or repeat the same course again the following year. Headmaster Wink insisted they use this method because Darksmith was an academy of learning, an institute where you could expand your mind. It was not an academy where you were trained to perform a task, which was why Darksmith refused to offer credentials.

The real reason Headmaster Wink refused to offer credentials was that he was terrified by the idea of hosting a graduation ceremony. Filling Darksmith with the leaders of the North and South would only invite assassination attempts, honour duels, and dark pacts potentially restarting the war. Headmaster Wink couldn't cope with that level of stress, so Darksmith didn't offer credentials.

However, Wink had learned the hard way that you couldn't give students nothing to work for and expect them to put in effort, which was why Darksmith now published the exam results of the top three students in each class. These results went to all corners of Murdell, and with each passing year, these top three positions grew more and more lucrative. The prestige of families would now rise and fall based off these results.

With the final exams only two days away, desperate students were willing to do anything to improve their chances of getting into the top three spots, even help Gorgath's campaign for private tutoring.

I watched my eight most promising Defence Against the Dark Arts students hurry out of the Dungeonology Club's cramped club room, carrying stacks of campaign posters I drew. They were a Gorgath version of the old Uncle Sam posters, with the words 'I want you to vote for Gorgath' on them. I'd laid several minor enchantments over each poster to produce illusions that would draw people's attention to them, which was why I needed students to distribute them. Minor enchantments didn't supply their own mana, and it was too much hassle to do so myself.

As the door closed, Gorgath's friend Arro tucked a wayward strand of blonde hair behind her ear and turned to look out the window. She reminded me of a cheerleader with her blonde hair, blue eyes, and large dimples, but that's where the comparison ended. She was tougher than the typical students at Darksmith. She had a 1st-tier class and had invested evenly between her physical and magical attributes. She was one of the few students who could train in the dungeon alone.

"Is there anything else you can do to help Gorgath's campaign, Professor?"

Despite her question, Arro didn't move from her seat by the window, nor turn to look at me, and the smile on her face as she watched the spot outside the fortress wall where Gorgath took his lessons never went away.

I cleared my throat to draw her attention. "I've made posters. I've convinced the Undead Enhancement Club to vote for Gorgath, and I'm ending my lessons by telling my class to vote for him. I've done more than enough to fulfil my end of the agreement."

Arro continued to stare out the window. "Have you asked Princess Carolyn for her endorsement?"

"She'll want something in return."

"What about Celest? Everyone knows you rescued her."

"I rescued her from Gorgath."

Arro paused. "Would you be willing to lift the curses you've placed on students if they vote for Gorgath?"

"Not particularly. Anyone who is still cursed deserves it."

She finally turned to me. "Is there anything you can do?"

"That depends. Do you wish to get political?"

She frowned. "In what way?"

"The South students won't vote for the North candidates, and the North won't vote for the South candidates. Some of the North students won't vote for the North candidates, because of family rivalries, but they won't vote for the South candidates, either. The same is true for the South. If you could convince these students that it would be funny to see their nation's candidates beaten by a dungeon monster, they would vote for Gorgath."

She scowled, insulted by my suggestion. "If I do that, people will continue to treat Gorgath like an animal. That will make it even harder for me to convince them that he deserves our respect."

Arro was the head of and the only human member of Darksmith's Dungeonology Club. Dungeonology was the study of dungeon ecosystems, and her family was famous for being able to raise or lower the average level of a dungeon's monsters in less than a year.

The appearance of a dungeon monster who could speak was the opportunity of lifetime for Arro, and she was the very first person to introduce herself to Gorgath. The two of them had traded questions twice a day for several weeks, before Gorgath had asked if he was allowed to join the Dungeonology Club. She'd agreed, which was how Gorgath ended up being a member of his first club and how the Dungeonology Club meeting room ended up in the dungeon fortress.

I understood why my suggestion upset her.

I leaned back in my chair and folded my arms. "Do you know how to change the thinking of a nation?"

"What does that have to do with anything?"

"Just answer the question."

"No."

"To change the thinking of a nation, you give one person enough information for them to choose to change their mind and then move onto the next person. If you want people to change how they treat Gorgath and show him respect, find a person and show them why he deserves this treatment. Let them work it out for themselves, because if they do, you won't have to ask them to help you convince others he deserves respect; they will do so of their own volition."

She turned back to the window. "What does that have to do with encouraging people to make fun of him for votes?"

"If you approach people as individuals in the future, encouraging people to make fun of him for votes now won't make it harder for you to eventually convince them that he deserves their respect."

"It's still wrong."

"Only if you did it behind his back, but if you talk to him about it and he agrees, then it's a sound campaign decision."

She turned back to me as her mouth dropped open. "You want me to tell him?"

"That shouldn't be shocking to someone who claims that they want people to respect him. Gorgath's not an animal. He's an intelligent being. Yes, there are cultural differences, but he can make his own decisions if he's provided with information. Refusing to give him that information because you think you know better or because of some condescending need to shelter him is not respect. It's a superiority complex."

"I don't think I'm superior to him."

"Then why are you surprised when I suggest you should talk over a campaign decision with him?"

She didn't have a response.

"I think I've made my point."

She dropped her gaze. "I'll talk it over with Gorgath."

"Do it quickly. You've only got two days until everyone votes."

THAT NIGHT, Rupert, Keeper of the Eastern Gate, wasn't happy with me. His expression was neutral, but his scent revealed his displeasure as he stared at me in the meditation chamber entrance.

I was making another master-rank undead skeleton. This was my fifth. The repeated casting of the master-tier bonemeal and bone stitch spells had begun to make a significant difference to my creations. My fourth skeleton had attributes that were 25% higher than the first one I made, and the spells were still growing stronger with each casting.

"Why can't we come to the Abyss with you?" Rupert asked calmly. "You're taking the necrosaint's people."

"Davina's people are grossly under leveled and receive special consideration because she's my familiar. Despite your oaths, you still serve the royal family. Taking you into the Abyss to level under the protection of the necrosaint offers me nothing and makes you more dangerous."

Rupert scowled. "What do you want?"

"I don't want or need anything from you."

"The princess is willing to give Angelica a third countess title."

No matter how many countess titles Angelica acquired, she wouldn't be able to increase the size of the personal guard she could travel with, which meant I wouldn't be able to increase the size of my personal guard. However, each territory allowed her to raise a small army for regional protection, so it wasn't entirely useless.

"It would have to be a neighbouring title."

"That shouldn't be a problem. The princess intends to speak with several minor barons on the matter."

I turned away from Rupert and waved to Cid and the other alchemists as they came through the side tunnel for their nightly mana refill. They were wearing crimson robes, like my people. They'd convinced their boss to buy them from Gregory because it lowered their downtime.

"Do you people ever sleep?" Cid asked, as he walked past me. "I swear, I see you more than my wife."

"Cultists never sleep, Cid."

The alchemists all chuckled as they continued on their way.

I turned to Rupert. "Your people can come, but you have to follow orders."

THE FOLLOWING DAY, during lunch, Headmaster Wink knocked on my classroom door. I looked up from the practice exams I was critiquing and motioned that I was free to talk. Wink wore a worried expression as he hurried inside and stopped beside my desk.

I immediately noticed that something was off. It had been months since I'd struggled to read someone's emotional state from their scent alone. Wink's emotional state was so far outside the norm that I didn't know what to make of it.

I pushed the practice exams aside. "What can I do for you, Headmaster?"

His hands trembled as he leaned down and gripped the edge of my desk. "How's the curse situation looking, Vincent? I hope they won't interfere with exams tomorrow."

I opened my top drawer and placed a sheet of paper with students' names and the curses they'd received on the desk in front of him. "I'm seeing twice as many curses this week as I saw last week, but it's significantly fewer than when I arrived. The students and those who supply them with cursed objects seem to have gotten the message that I won't show mercy to anyone. I expect the students will be trying to poison each other instead."

He gave me a slightly unhinged grin. "Poison we can deal with."

"Then you've got nothing to worry about."

"If only that were true." Wink pulled a flask from his robe and took a swig, dribbling a little down his chin, which he didn't wipe away. "I'm told you added your Occult Studies class to the exam."

Headmaster Wink had been referring to my class by its new name for months, so something was off. "Is that a problem?"

"I'm not sure. Maybe. Maybe not. We've never included Occult Studies in the final exams."

"That's because you've never had anyone qualified to teach this class before. I've told my students that if they can achieve 80% or higher on the exam, then they know enough to voice their opinion on any occult subject where they feel confident doing so."

Wink frowned. "How many do you expect to achieve that score?"

"A tenth of them. My students have been quite diligent."

"You expect a tenth of them to be competent enough to speak on the occult."

I nodded. "I've taught them how dangerous the occult is, and those who have paid attention understand that if they don't feel entirely confident offering their advice on a subject, they shouldn't. Do my students know everything about the subject? No. But what they do understand, they understand well enough to inform others and stop them from making dangerous mistakes."

"That's good to hear, but it makes what I say next more difficult." Wink cleared his throat. "I'm afraid I'm going to have to let you go, Vincent. You've done a wonderful job, but you're only here because of Princess Carolyn, and I can't have such an important position empty if Arcadia becomes safe and you suddenly decide to leave. I hope you understand the position I'm in."

"I do. When will my replacement be here?"

Wink turned to the door. "You may come in, Vesh."

I was on guard the moment Headmaster Wink turned to the door. As far as I could tell, there was no one waiting outside in the hallway. And I hadn't heard Headmaster Wink speak with anyone before coming here. That, mixed with my inability to understand his scent and his bizarre behaviour, was cause for concern.

I pushed my chair back and rose, brushing my coat aside so I could access Slaughter. I wasn't quick enough.

A hollow walked into my classroom, and every demonic instinct I possessed told me to unleash my most devastating spells to destroy it.

My vision blurred as the hollow psychically projected the image of a healthy middle-aged man into my brain while my evil eye skill showed me a lumpy, misshapen corpse with a pair of small tentacles protruding from the eye sockets. The two images fought each other for a second, until the evil eye skill won, and the mental projection vanished.

A notification appeared.

Your Evil Eye skill has increased to level 3.

I dismissed the notification.

All that was left of the man was skin and hair. A misshapen body suit out of sync with reality that the hollow wore to anchor itself to reality and remember what it was pretending to be.

Researching and studying the occult came with many dangers. Hollows were one of the worst, and I was well aware that I wasn't equipped to remove one.

Its psychic attack slammed into my mind and collided with my willpower before I could take a step forward.

"Submit," the eldritch horror wannabe instructed.

The command smashed through several of my mental barriers and locked my legs.

I released Slaughter and raised my right hand in one smooth blurred motion, not bothering to hide my agility. I snapped my fingers, weaving together a 15th-rank master destruction spell.

Necrotic magic that was supposed to consume and disintegrate collided with a telekinetic shield of raw willpower in a cloud of black death, creating a howling vortex around the hollow. The shield stopped my destruction spell from making contact with its flesh but locked the creature in place and redirected its focus away from the mental attack to its defence.

Hollows were creatures of destruction from beyond our reality, from beyond Heaven and Hell. They didn't understand our reality and couldn't fully enter, but that never stopped them from causing utter carnage as they moved through the world for reasons only they understood.

The hollow's tentacle gaze snapped towards me, peering through the destructive energies. Its will was so strong that I could physically feel its gaze probing my body.

"*Reveal,*" it whispered in my head.

The psychic command slammed through other mental barriers and my fangs descended. My fingernails transformed into claws, and my skin took on a corpse-like quality.

Headmaster Wink leapt away from me. "Vampire!"

I ignored both the headmaster and the mental attack as I made a snatching motion with my hand and cast a 15th-rank inverted void barrier around the hollow. A bubble of pure necrotic energy surrounded the hollow, cutting it off from the world around it. The master-tier spell created a no-go zone. Nothing could pass through, not even an ancient vampire. You needed magic to break it.

The psychic attack on my mind ended as every alarm at Darksmith sounded.

Headmaster Wink shook his head, as he was released from the psychic controls he'd been under. "How did I get here?" He glanced at me. "Why do you look like a corpse, Vincent?"

I took a moment to forcefully retract my fangs and reverse the other changes as I held the barrier in place. "You're under a psychic attack, Headmaster."

"I am?"

My claws began transforming back to fingernails and the black faded from my veins. "Yes. This is a level 4 situation and you've been compromised. Would you be so kind as to contact the head of the banishment department and inform her that there is a hollow in my classroom. I'm afraid I don't have the skills to remove the creature, only to contain it."

Headmaster Wink blinked several times, still coming out of a daze, and then rubbed his forehead. "What did you say, Vincent?"

"I've trapped a hollow inside a void barrier and need the head of the banishment department to remove it for me. This is a level 4 security threat."

Wink finally got his thoughts together and tapped the medallion hanging from his neck.

His voice filled the academy. "Would the banishment department and anyone familiar with combating a hollow please make their way to the Defence Against the Dark Arts classroom. Professor Vincent has contained a hollow but is unable to destroy it. This is a level 5 security threat as I am currently compromised."

The headmaster dropped his hand and leaned against my desk, closing his eyes. After a few seconds, he opened them again and looked at me. He gave a relieved sigh when he saw that I looked human.

"I was never very good at dealing with psychic attacks," he said, rubbing his forehead. "Do I need to call Professor Burdin?"

Professor Lint, the head of the banishment department, flew through the door like a bullet. "Only if you want this abomination to possess a hundred bodies instead of one," she shouted at him, while looking down at the void barrier. After getting a decent look, she turned to me. "How long can you hold the void barrier?"

"Long enough."

Professor Lint turned to Wink. "Headmaster, please vacate the classroom and head to the infirmary. I have everything in hand."

THREE DAYS LATER, Dalin guided Headmaster Wink into my classroom while I was marking the final exams. The headmaster was dressed in a casual robe and wore a set of bracelets that weakened his ability to cast spells. The hollow had been in his head for several hours before he'd come to my classroom, and both the head of the infirmary and Professor Lint were concerned that it had used that time to reprogram the headmaster into a sleeper agent. He had months of recovery ahead of him and would most likely have to leave for additional medical care.

The two of them stopped in front of my desk.

I forced down the impulse to disintegrate Wink. My instincts were telling me to use a scorched earth policy for anything related to the hollow. "What can I do for you, gentlemen?"

Dalin gave me a grim smile. "The headmaster believes that you're a vampire, Vincent. This delusion is related to several other delusions that I can't break, so I would like to prove to headmaster that you're not a vampire."

Wink scowled. "I'm not crazy."

Dalin patted Wink's shoulder. "I know, old friend. Vincent, with your permission, I would like to use a holy spell on you."

I nodded.

The cleric raised his hand and hit me with a master-tier holy bolt spell. The light was so bright that it momentarily blinded me. There was no pain. I just couldn't see.

As the spell faded, Headmaster Wink splashed holy water in my face and held up a holy symbol. "Back, demon."

Neither the holy water nor the symbol reacted to me, but that didn't put Wink at ease. He began weaving a spell but was slowed by the bracelets. Dalin sensed the attack and cast his own spell first.

The headmaster's eyes rolled back as he passed out.

Dalin caught him and lowered him to the ground, before turning to me. "Professor Lint said the hollow came here to gain access to your private occult library. Do you know why?"

"With it, it could gain access to another of its kind."

As I'd lowered my void barrier, Professor Lint had severed the hollow's connection to the rest of its body outside our reality. She'd bound what remained here, questioned it, and then banished it back to its reality. She did everything strictly by the book, but she'd uncovered something about hollows that was previously unknown.

Hollows were prisoners and they were kept separate from each other.

The moment the hollow had taken over its host, it had sensed traces of another hollow coming from my private occult library. With those traces, it would have pulled the other hollow into this world. It had been excited for the two of them to slaughter this world together.

Dalin frowned. "Is Darksmith in danger?"

I shrugged. "Professor Lint is tracking down the host's home and business. She's bringing back everything that was being studied so I can determine whether there is a risk."

"And if there is?"

"I'll remove it."

"Because your children are here?"

"No. Because hollows are a threat to everyone. Both Heaven and Hell will ignore each other to destroy hollows if they're near."

"I thought hollows were demons."

"They're not. But don't feel bad for thinking that. I thought they were demons, too, but a few seconds in its presence disabused me of that notion."

"Why?"

"Every demonic instinct I have told me the creature was an enemy. For context, I've stood in the presence of an angel and my demonic instincts considered it to be less of an enemy than that creature."

Dalin scowled. "That's blasphemy."

"That's fact."

"When are you leaving Darksmith?"

"When my daughter wants me to."

"When do you think that will be?"

"Not for a while, hopefully."

23

AN EVENING OUT

College life is the same in any world. Once the final exams are over, students party, faculty drink, and everyone tries to ignore the fact they have to do it all again far too soon. Darksmith's administration was rearranging schedules, clearing out and cleaning the dorms of fifth-year students, and welcoming in the new wave of first-year students. Enchanters from all over both nations were repairing and replacing equipment and double-checking that the security system was working.

Usually, this was a minor concern, but a hollow had been walking around Darksmith for several hours without triggering a single alarm, so it had far more scrutiny this year. There was even talk of adding additional security measures, but that was easier said than done. Darksmith offered a vast array of classes which would constantly trigger a more complicated alarm system. And an alarm system that triggered eighty times a day wasn't an improvement.

The academy had to walk the fine line between too little security which offered no protection and too much security which was triggered by all the dangerous things that happened every day. Based on the conversations I'd overheard, nothing about the alarm system was going to change, while they lied that they had beefed up security.

They were going to make sure that the current system was working the way it should, though. All the double and triple-checking had turned the academy into a worksite, and everyone was finding an excuse to get away.

Everyone except Kathrine.

Convincing my daughter to put aside her studies for the evening to celebrate passing her exam at Antari's in town had taken me far too long, but she'd finally given in to my pestering.

As our free carriage came to a stop, I flicked opened the door with a little will and magic and stepped outside, offering Kathrine my hand to help her step down into the chaos of unlicensed vendors who plagued the dungeon entrance.

Kathrine ignored my hand, but she didn't shudder like she had in the past, which was an improvement. She climbed out and looked down the busy boulevard filled with glowing blue trees that provided easy light. Students were still celebrating their success during their exams or using retail therapy to deal with their failures. The result was a small fortune flowing into every shop we saw.

While Kathrine had barely passed her exams, considering how many classes she'd missed, that wasn't a bad result. She didn't agree with this assessment, which was why it had taken me days to convince her to let me take her out to celebrate.

"Let's get this over with," she said, far from impressed, as she began walking down the street. "I still don't understand why you insist on going out to eat. You're a better chef than anyone in this town."

"You need to get out more."

Kathrine groaned. "I get out plenty."

"A night out every two weeks isn't the definition of plenty."

"It is when you're so far behind."

I began to smile as we entered the glowing canopy, folding my hands behind my back, enjoying a stroll with my daughter, and ignoring the yells coming from the staff in the nearby shops saying things like, "He's here. Get the owner."

I turned to Kathrine. "The kingmaker distribution will more than make up for the time you lost. By the end of your second year, you'll be competing with the most talented sorcerers of your year. By the end of your third year, even the geniuses will struggle to keep up with you. So, what you need is a better work/life balance."

"What I need is to study more."

"You're going to burn yourself out if you keep going like this."

"I'm fine."

Kathrine was not fine, and she refused to see that. She was as stubborn as her brother, but in her own way.

Behind us, a door flew open. "Vincent, wait!"

Kathrine and I turned to see Solomon running out of his shop carrying a thick black over-robe that had fur trim around the collar that looked like a lion's mane. It was elegant, stylish, and clearly expensive.

I nodded to his store as he skidded to a stop before me. "I see they finished with the renovations."

Solomon nodded, looking up to meet my gaze. "Months ago. I've been waiting for you to visit since before I moved back. Put this on."

I frowned at the power I sensed radiating from the robe. "I didn't order any additional attire."

He grinned. "I know, but I was inspired by your outfit. The design for this piece came to me in a dream. It's the most complex piece of clothing I've ever created, and I'm hoping I'll level several skills if you wear it."

There were no signs he was lying. "What's so interesting about it?"

"If I'm correct, it will remove the debuff that wearing shirts causes your equipment."

That was interesting if it were true.

I turned my back to Solomon, and he helped me put on the over-robe. The thick fabric was surprisingly heavy, but also surprisingly flexible. It moved over my body like water, pulling tight against the over-robe I was already wearing. I felt a slight change go through my body as it settled onto my shoulders, signalling that the robe had the effect as Solomon hoped it would.

I turned to Kathrine. "How does it look?"

She ran her gaze over my new robe. "It suits you, but it also makes you look more intimidating, like you could dismantle an empire because it annoyed you."

I turned to Solomon to see an even wider grin on his face. "How much for the robe? And congratulations on leveling your skills."

Solomon chuckled, clearly happy with his success. "What gave it away?"

"The lack of disappointment."

Solomon continued to chuckle. "I suppose that's quite obvious."

"How much for the robe?" I asked again.

"It's not for sale. Call me sentimental, but I like to keep the garments that increase my level. They remind me of how far I've come when I feel like a fraud."

I could respect that, so I didn't argue. I took the robe off and handed it back to him.

Solomon grinned. "Thanks for understanding."

"You won't be thanking me when I ask for a discount on my next purchase."

He laughed. "What do you need?"

"Solomon, this is my daughter Kathrine. She's desperately in need of new robes. Would you be able to help her for me?"

Kathrine rolled her eyes. "I don't need new robes."

"You've grown four inches since you increased your constitution; none of your clothes fit you as well as they should."

"They're fine."

Solomon shook his head. "Actually, your father is correct. When it comes to learning advanced magic, clothes that don't fit quite right interfere with any gesture or action you take while casting a spell. This slows down the learning process."

"A tailor with the right skills can even make you clothes and robes that assist you in learning magic and leveling skills faster," I added.

"For a modest fee," Solomon added.

Kathrine glanced at me. "I don't—"

Kathrine didn't have any money, because she'd run away. She'd borrowed money from Riza to cover her tuition and had been making ends meet by hunting monsters in the dungeon. "Consider it a present for passing your finals."

Kathrine frowned, clearly not sure what she wanted to do.

I turned to Solomon before she had a chance to say something that might embarrass her and gave her a way out. "We've got a reservation at Antari's we need to get to, but send me the bill when she turns up. Make sure she has your best work."

Solomon smiled. "Anything for my best customer."

"You know I'm not happy about that."

Solomon chuckled as I turned and started walking down the boulevard, filled with the gentle aroma of sandalwood.

Kathrine caught up a few steps later. "I'll pay you back."

"It's a gift."

"I'm not comfortable taking gifts from you."

That bothered me, but I didn't let her see that. "If that's the case, you can join Luke and I when we go to train in the Abyss in two days? The cores we collect down there are much larger than the ones you find in the dungeon, and you should be able to pay for the robes yourself."

"I'd be a liability."

"You won't be the only one."

"I mean, I'm not sure I'm ready."

"If you want to grow your skills quickly, the Abyss is the best place to do it. A day down there among the chaos is equivalent to a few months of training at Darksmith."

Kathrine sighed. "I'll think about."

"We'll be leaving with or without you, so don't feel pressured." That got me a small smile. "Any thoughts on what you want to do in four years when you finish studying?"

"I know I want to leave Murdell, but I'm not sure about where I'd go or what I'll do beyond that."

"We could leave tomorrow if you like. I can take you anywhere you want?"

Kathrine shook her head. "I can't leave yet. The only time I've left Murdell was six years ago, when I went to the Bo Empire to visit Luke. Within days of leaving, the Darklord broke the treaty. There were skirmishes all along the border while he moved his armies south to invade. I had to race back when I heard the news. The day after I got back, the skirmishes stopped, and the Darklord withdrew his armies. My presence in Murdell is the only thing keeping the South safe."

My daughter was doing a poor job of hiding her intentions. She obviously felt she needed to kill the Darklord. It explained why she was so devoted to studying. She thought studying would give her the advantage she needed. She was a bit too naive in her thinking, but her heart was in the right place. I respected her for wanting to help people.

She needed to learn patience, though. She was a few decades too young to confront a threat like a darklord. Especially one as powerful as the one in North Murdell. Even with Luke and my familiars backing her up, they didn't stand a chance against him right now.

I decided to change the subject. "Any thoughts on what classes you'll be taking this year?"

Kathrine's shoulder relaxed ever so slightly. "I'm thinking of taking the full array of combat magic classes."

"I imagine your advisor strongly suggested against this route."

I'd listened to the entire conversation, so I knew she had.

"She did. But I need those classes."

"Because you believe they will make you more dangerous."

"No, because I need to know where my strengths lie. I missed too many classes for my advisor to assess me properly."

That wasn't the answer I expected, and it wasn't the one she'd told to her advisor. "If you're only taking those classes for a clear assessment, I can tell you what you want to know."

Kathrine turned to me, showing surprise. "You can?"

"Measuring someone else's talent comes naturally to me."

"How accurate are you?"

"You've got a decent talent for all branches of magic, which is why magic came naturally to you until you reached advanced magic. You have a strong talent for fire, air, death, and necrotic magic, which is why you excel in those areas. Those branches should only become difficult once you reach the middle of expert-tier magic. However, your strongest talent lies in potion making."

“My potions exam was only my second-best result.”

“Yes, but you didn’t study for the exam and skipped half of your classes since you woke up to study your other subjects.”

Kathrine stopped walking and frowned. “Why did that doorman just run inside when he spotted you?”

“Juna must need me to look at a cursed object that’s too big to transport to Darksmith.”

“Why would someone want you to look at a cursed object for them?”

“I authenticate cursed objects for most of the antique stores in town. Doing so has massively reduced the number of curses that affect the students.”

Kathrine looked over her shoulder. “There’s a crowd of merchants heading for us. Actually, there are two crowds of merchants heading for us. What did you do?”

I turned and looked over my shoulder.

Everyone in the two groups was lavishly dressed and walking behind a single individual carrying an item. The leader of the first group was a middle-aged woman in an emerald-green gown. She had tan skin and gave me a deep bow when she stopped before us. The moment she rose, she held out a beautifully enchanted case. She snapped it open without a word to display the contents.

Inside was a potion with the colour and consistency of blood with a syringe next to it.

She gave me a beaming smile. “My name is Mora, and I represent the Southern Merchant’s Association for the boulevard. Please accept this token of our appreciation.”

Kathrine frowned at Mora as I picked up the unknown potion. “Why are you giving my father a gift?”

Mora smiled at Kathrine. “Your father killed a curse weaver who had been operating here for many years, at great risk to himself. Like many merchants who own shops along the boulevard, I make it a habit to purchase something from a merchant’s store when they move in to show support. It was a pen for my grandson. Shortly after I brought this pen, my grandson began falling behind his peers at school and becoming forgetful. His mother and I thought it was just a phase, but he never grew out of it. The day after your father killed the curse weaver, my grandson was back to his old self. Because of that curse weaver, my grandson has struggled needlessly for years. Your father ended that struggle, so I and many of the other merchants who share my habit wish to show our appreciation."

I held up the potion. "What is this?"

Kathrine grinned. "You don't know what it is?"

I rolled my eyes. "Despite my best efforts, I don't know everything."

Kathrine's grin grew. "Well, I know what it is."

Mora chuckled. "It's a blood refinement potion. Injecting it into your bloodstream will increase all your attributes to beyond their natural limits."

Blood refinement potions were extremely expensive and hard to acquire without the right connections. From what I'd read, they were also green, but that might have only applied to the version made in Arcadia. I knew King Linus had given Luke one when he was younger to help with his training. Carolyn had also been given one. Judging by the fact that Kathrine knew what it was, she had also been given one.

"I thought they were green."

Mora nodded. "That is the standard variation of the potion. Murdell has developed a version which focuses the attribute growth beyond your natural limits into mana regeneration. There is also another version in the Corrant Empire which focuses the growth into agility. It's a bright orange colour, I believe." Mora took the syringe from the box and held out her hand for the potion. "If you have no objections, I'll administer the potion now. If not, you can come by my store anytime you like. The potion takes up to ten days to achieve the full effect, so don't expect an immediate change."

She clearly didn't want me to sell their gift, which was what I'd intended to do, because it likely wouldn't affect me. Since that wasn't going to be an option, I handed her the potion. "Now's fine."

I began unbuttoning my shirt as I withdrew my mana from the bond with my equipment. With how high my Day Walker set made my constitution, her needle wouldn't penetrate my skin. I pulled my shirt open, giving her a direct shot at my heart.

Mora filled the syringe with the potion, gave it a moment for the enchantments to remove the air, and then placed her hand on my chest. "Don't flinch."

"I think I'll be fine."

Mora pushed the needle through my skin and into my heart, before pressing down on the injector. To my surprise, my heart began to beat. The thump, thump, thump, thundered through my ears, drowning out the world around me, making me feel very small. I found the experience unsettling.

Mora finished injecting the potion and removed the needle. "You might feel a little funny, but that will quickly pass."

My skin flushed with the sudden introduction of blood flow.

Kathrine noticed the change. "Are you alright? You look a little strange."

"My heart's beating a little fast. It shouldn't be a problem."

Her mouth dropped open.

"That's perfectly normal," Mora said, not understanding the context. "The potion does that to disperse itself through your body. It will be over soon."

About twenty seconds after it started beating, my heart suddenly stopped again.

A notification appeared.

+64 Strength
+57 Agility
+61 Endurance
+59 Constitution
+58 Recovery
+78 Mana Regeneration

The fact that the potion had worked both shocked me and dispelled many of my beliefs about how my demonic parasites worked. Everything I'd read, along with many assumptions I'd made, all pointed to my demonic parasites having long since pushed my attributes well beyond their natural limits. Only my mana regeneration should have been affected. Instead, *all* my attributes had been affected, like they'd never been enhanced before.

It didn't upset me in the slightest that I'd been proven wrong, but it did mean I needed to do more research into my condition when I got the chance, because it opened up all sorts of possibilities.

Mora put the syringe away. "I hope our gift helps you as much as you have helped us."

I gave her a genuine smile. "I think it will work better than you imagine."

Kathrine raised an eyebrow at my statement.

Mora turned to the leader of the other group. "May I introduce my associate, Tarmin, who represents the Northern Merchant's Association for the boulevard."

Tarmin was an average-looking man, with tears in his eyes and a smile on his face. He stepped forward with a small jewellery box that billowed cursed smoke to a degree that I'd never seen before. He opened the box, unveiling an enchanted glass case, which was covered in containment ruins that were doing a poor job of containing the cursed energy.

Inside the glass case was a Ring of Power.

The ring was blood-red in colour and appeared to be identical to the one the anti-saint Lilith had worn, except it was cursed. Cursed with a death curse that was so powerful it would instantly kill anyone I tried to put it on, *including me*.

"As Mora said, my name is Tarmin, and I represent the Northern Merchant's Association for the boulevard. My wife and I have been trying to have another child for eight years. We owned a vase we brought from that curse weaver when he first moved in. She feel pregnant shortly after you killed him. Please accept this token of our appreciation."

The reason for his happiness spoke to a part of me I hadn't thought about in a long time, and I returned his smile, despite his attempt to kill me. “Congratulations, I know how painful it is to want more children and not be able to have them.”

Kathrine blinked and turned to me. “You and Mum wanted more kids?”

I nodded, remembering sad times. “We were trying for years.”

“You never said anything.”

“Parents don’t share their problems with their children, Sweetheart.”

Tarmin motioned for me to take the cursed Ring of Power.

Mora sighed. “Tarmin, he knows the ring is cursed. He’s not taking it because he’s waiting for you to explain why you’re trying to give him a cursed ring. You forgot to tell him.”

Tarmin blushed with embarrassment. “I did.”

“You did,” I said.

“This is a Ring of Power.”

“A *cursed* Ring of Power.”

“We wouldn’t be able to afford it otherwise.”

“Where did you get it?”

Tarmin pointed down the street. “Juna found it among the burial collection she purchased. She tried everything to remove the curse. She even had the Southern pope and her archbishops try to cleanse it, on the condition that they could purchase it if they succeeded.”

“Obviously, they failed.”

“Two archbishops died, I’m told.”

“What’s a Ring of Power?” Kathrine asked.

“It’s very powerful ring,” I replied. “It increases all the wearer’s attributes by 100 and has the same effect as the prodigy skill and can be stacked on top of the prodigy skill’s effects. While wearing the ring, any skill you have mastered becomes level 23. If you’ve also mastered and upgraded the prodigy skill, then it becomes level 26. That brings the five-level canyon into effect, which essentially doubles your attributes.”

“Making you more powerful.”

“Hence the name.”

“Where do they come from?”

"Dead angels and demon lords. Based on the colour, this one came from a demon lord. However, it shouldn't be cursed."

Everything I'd read about these rings said cursing them was impossible.

Tarmin nodded. "We were hoping that your ability to hold off the curse weaver's curses would allow you to be able to use it for short periods of time."

He clearly didn't understand how powerful the curse on this ring was if he thought my display with the curse weaver would allow me to use the ring. Despite that, I accepted the jewellery box, playing the part of the cautious Defence Against the Dark Arts professor as I examined the ring through the glass case.

I didn't want to touch it. This wasn't the sort of curse that I could mess around it. I didn't know how the curse worked, nor how the curse weaver had managed to attach their death curse to it. Rings of Power were supposed to be immune, even the ones from demon lords.

Tarmin leaned forward. "Do you think you can wear it?"

I'd learned a lot about curses since I'd come to Darksmith, but this was in an entirely different league. If this had killed two archbishops who were backed by a pope and everything their cathedral offered, I wasn't willing to let Davina look at it. But I was willing to study it when I had some time to spare. A Ring of Power would be a very useful tool to have.

I gave Tarmin a friendly smile and snapped the box closed. "It might take me a few years to learn how to do it safely, but I believe I can."

Tarmin returned my smile. "Good. I'd hate to think we'd given you an expensive paperweight after everything you did for us. Now, I won't take up anymore of your time. There are a lot of other people who want to thank you, as well."

Tarmin stepped out of the way, letting the next person come speak with me.

Well after midnight, Kathrine and I wandered through the empty boulevard under the glowing canopy. Kathrine was carrying bags filled with dozens of gifts. When the merchants had found out we were in town to celebrate her passing her exams and that they were holding her up, they had run into their shops to get her something. She'd received beauty products, jewellery, textbooks, cushions, blankets, and a large assortment of fudge, laughing with them as they gave her another bag to carry.

When Kathrine began to smell stressed, I turned to her. "What are thinking about, Sweetheart?"

"The merchants."

"What about them?"

"The fact that they weren't afraid of you."

"Why does that surprise you?"

"It doesn't surprise me, but it's made me realise I can't see you the way they see you. They look at you and see a good man. Someone who did something very dangerous to keep them safe. No matter how hard I try, I can't see that when I look at you."

"That's hardly a fair comparison. For starters, you know what I am."

"So does Luke, but he's not afraid of you."

I turned to her. "What gave you that impression?"

Kathrine sighed. "You two are always together."

"Part of the reason he spends so much time with me is because he's watching to see if I'll break character. He's afraid that everything I show him is a façade. A sick little game I'm playing to torment him. He might not be as afraid of me in the way you are, but he only trusts me slightly more than you do."

"He's never mentioned that to me."

"That's because he doesn't know he's doing it, which is what happens when you don't confront your emotions."

Kathrine frowned. "Do *I* do that?"

"No. You have a healthy level of self-reflection. You'll eventually work through your problems."

"But Luke won't."

"Not without a little prompting, which I'm happy to give him. It's what dads are for, after all."

Kathrine sighed.

"Is something else bothering you?"

"It's nothing."

"It's not nothing if it's bothering you."

"It's selfish."

"Then it's probably better to get it off your chest."

"Luke said the moment you learned I was here, you wanted to set out to find me. Is that true?"

I smiled. "Hearing that you and your mother were here was one of the most exciting moments of my life."

Her lips began to quiver, her heartrate sped up, and her voice turned shaky, as a wave of negative emotion crashed over her. "Why didn't Mum feel that way?"

I could hear the rejection in her voice, the pain and the grief. I very much wanted to put my arm around my little girl's shoulder and comfort her, but that would have the opposite effect on her.

"Luke told her where I was when he found her, but she's never written to me. She's never tried to find me. She's never shown a hint of interest." Tears began to flow. "Why doesn't she want me?"

There weren't many secrets I was willing to keep for my children, but this was one I had kept from them. Though it wasn't one I was willing to keep if it made Kathrine think her mother didn't love *her* or want her.

"Your mother loves you more than you can possibly imagine, Sweetheart, and she's in more trouble than you know."

I handed her a handkerchief.

Kathrine wiped her eyes. "What?"

"Contessa, the lich I killed, had dealings with high-ranking members of the church your mother is fighting for. They supplied Contessa with a steady stream of clerics and paladin for her experiments."

"What?"

The church was both a unified and a fragmented entity. They

operated independently in each nation, with their own pope and goals, but they worked to support each other.

"The church your mother is fighting for is corrupt to its core, and the lich king she's fighting against is their former pope. Your mother knows this, too, I believe. She's had numerous confrontations with him, and they've both gotten away every time."

"Does Luke know?"

"No."

"Why not?"

"Your mother told him a very convincing lie."

"Why haven't you told him the truth?"

"If I told your brother, he would march off to save her, without considering the consequences."

"What consequences?"

"I'm honestly not sure. Your brother did everything he was taught to test for mind control, slave oaths, and the like when she refused to leave with him, and she passed with flying colours. He was left with the impression that she really believed she needed to stay and defeat the lich king, and he respects her decision."

"But you don't believe that."

"Not since I read Contessa's diaries."

Kathrine paused. "These are all assumptions."

"Yes, which is part of the reason I don't feel the need to race off and attempt to rescue her."

"What's the other part?"

"She may not need me to rescue her. She survived eleven years without me and seems to have a long-term plan. By all accounts, she's already an Old Monster and pushing towards being a Dragon. Her growth is astonishing, even for a hero. In a few more years, no one in Altar will be able to stand against her."

"You're worried about interfering with her plan?"

"Mildly."

"If you knew she was in trouble, would you go?"

"In a second."

"So, you're not staying because of me?"

"No. There are some extremely powerful paladins in the Altar, and if they decide to strike me down, I won't be able to stop them. I need to level my people substantially before I'll be able to safely attempt a rescue, which is why I'm taking them into the Abyss tomorrow."

"I thought that was in two days."

"It's after midnight."

"Oh."

I looked at her bags. "It's going to be a long walk back. The carriages don't run after midnight."

"I can carry my own bags," Kathrine snapped.

"I know you can, Sweetheart, but I still want to help."

Kathrine sighed. "I know you do, but I'm not ready to accept your help yet."

I gave her an understanding smile, finally comprehending the depth of the heartbreak she carried with her. For years she'd believed that her mother didn't love her, that she'd rejected her, so she'd jumped on the chance to get me back, hoping I would save her from her misery, only to discover she'd brought a monster into her life. She was so lonely. So sad. And my action had forced her to close off her heart. All my little girl wanted was to have her daddy back so he could make things right.

And I wasn't sure if I could do that.

24

LONG-TERM PLANS

I've overheard more than one cleric give a sermon on Hell's instruments. Clerics like to emphasise that these instruments are made from kidnapped souls, and that the tortured screams of these kidnapped souls are Hell's version of music. Unlike on Earth, these sermons are less about living a life of purity to stop eternal damnation and more about killing yourself and your family as quickly as possible, if you should ever find yourself about to be captured by the forces of Hell.

It was very practical advice.

The screams Davina's clerics and paladins made as they were torn limb from limb by the monsters of the Abyss were a sweet symphony to my demonic ears, more so than the screams of regular people. Each cry sent a pleasurable shiver down my spine, suggesting that the sermons I'd overheard were true. Hell's music was the tortured screams of the innocent. The smell of blood and pain added to the music, leaving me enchanted and distracted in a way that had never occurred before.

As I sat on a boulder in the Abyss, I was vaguely aware of Luke decapitating a pair of monsters strong enough to be dungeon bosses. He then leapt away from the frontline like a metal comet, sheathing his longsword mid-flight. With his free hand, he cast a simple levitation spell to remain airborne and sail through the air to land beside me. He quickly turned and scanned the battlefield for other threats.

This cavern wasn't like the other caverns Gorgath had taken us to in the Abyss. The ambient mana was denser, which led to faster crystal growth, which when combined meant more monsters. The higher monster population density created a different type of monster to the usual dungeon monster. It was one that only cared about eating, breeding, and fighting. It resulted in a zone that was constant carnage.

The immense cavern held more than a dozen floor bosses. Each one birthing tens of thousands of its kin each day, trying to overwhelm the other bosses with numbers. Whenever one of their spawn grew as strong as a dungeon boss, they regained their individual senses and created a pack, subjugating their weaker brethren into their service. They behaved exactly like their parents, using their pack like cannon fodder, pushing them to make suicidal charges to kill prey and fuel their growth. This instinctive behaviour had led to a very active battlefield between hunting floor bosses.

Luke swept his gaze over the frontline, checking how the battle was progressing. Gregory's people were fighting side by side with Carolyn's Old Monsters, holding the line in front of Davina's people, who provided support. Davina's clerics and paladins were the weakest warriors on the field, and the dungeon bosses sensed this. So, more often than not, they found themselves the targets of a dungeon boss, who was more than willing to send their cannon fodder pack after them. These weaker monsters didn't care about survival, which resulted in them throwing themselves into blades to break through lines and reach their targets. And reach their targets they did.

Luke moved his gaze behind the battlefield to where Gorgath was busy dissecting the latest floor boss, choosing portions to feed to his mana crabs and tossing others to his brothers. I could smell the purity of the mana crabs' bloodline now. They were almost ready. A few more generations and the kid would have what he needed. Maybe then he would stop sulking about losing the election.

Luke finally took a seat beside me and turned to face me. He took one look at my sparkling skin and burst into laughter. *Again.* The sound filled the air around me, but didn't distract me from the music of the clerics' screams.

You would think after more than a day of seeing me in this state, Luke would get over his amusement, but it hadn't happened. Based on his amused scent, it wasn't likely to happen any time soon either.

Luke raised his hand and tried to mutter a basic spell through his glee. It didn't work. I felt his mana transition to wind mana before it slipped from his control and ran rampant through his body. His muscles locked and the air shot out of his lungs, winding him without killing his amusement.

Luke continued grinned as he took a slow, deep breath to calm himself and recast the spell, sealing us in a soundproof bubble.

Without the screams of the injured to captivate my attention, the world came back into focus. This wasn't the first time I'd seen and heard Davina's people being ripped apart, but it was the first time I'd had such an experience without the threat of something dangerous to keep me focused. Without an external motivator, their suffering was a much stronger distraction, and I was far more susceptible to it than I imagined.

I could have sat there forever.

I hadn't expected their blood and screams to overwhelm me so thoroughly, so I hadn't mentally prepared myself to deal with them, like I did with regular blood and hunger. But despite how distracted I was, I never came close to feeding on anyone. I was in complete control.

Luke's gaze moved from my sparkly physique to his sister, who was throwing spells at a dungeon boss, to the princess and her guards. He was trying to regain his self-control by not looking at me. After several seconds it seemed to work.

Luke sighed. "You shouldn't have let Carolyn's people come down here to train with your people. They're seasoned veterans. They can achieve as much with each additional level as your people can do with three."

"Your sister wants to leave Murdell at some point in the future, so that takes precedence."

Luke paused. "What does Kathrine wanting to leave have to do with making Carolyn's people stronger?"

"Your sister believes that the Darklord will invade the South if she leaves."

"I still don't see what that has to do with them."

"It means I have to evaluate how useful they can be."

"For what?"

"Killing the Darklord."

Luke turned his head, until I could see his eyes through the gap in his visor. "I can't tell if you're joking. Or if it just sounds like a joke because you're sparkling."

"I never joke about killing."

He paused and then looked away. "That's true. So, you want to kill the Darklord. A man who is supposed to be over level 300. A true Demigod, if the rumours are true."

"The rumours *aren't* true. He's nothing but a Dragon. His unmatched reactions come from the ability to see the immediate future, not from being over level 300."

Luke turned to watch the frontline. "What makes you think he can see the future?"

"His daughter Celest is a seer, and foresight is a hereditary trait. Her father having the ability to see the immediate future and some of the distant future would explain his meteoric rise to power, his combat ability, her ability to see the future, and why he hasn't taken over Murdell."

"Maybe to you," Luke muttered as he watched another dozen monster packs leap into the frontline with wild abandon. "Some of us can't read a history book in a few seconds."

That was true, but also an exaggeration. My son could still read a history book in half an hour. His ignorance was a choice at this point.

"As a professor, I could give you a history lesson?"

Luke chuckled. "Only if it helps me understand why you want to do something as stupid as try to kill the Darklord."

"I can manage that.... Murdell has always been what you would call a social-status-based society. Those with magic have a higher social status than those without magic. And those with access to more branches of magic, have a higher status than those with access to less. On top of this, skill also applies, so someone with more skill has a higher status than someone with less skill. The Darklord changed Murdell's society when he began preaching bloodline purity. He told everyone that what mattered most wasn't how many branches of magic you had access to, or how skilled you were with them. It was how far back you could trace your direct ancestry before finding someone without magic."

"So, he's Voldemort."

"No. Voldemort believed what he was preaching. The Darklord simply used his rhetoric to divide and conquer Murdell's population."

"How?"

"The people of Murdell have always been willing to do anything to boost their social status, so when the Darklord's rhetoric artificially boosted a portion of the population's social status, those who were affected in a positive way were more than willing to accept what he said. These people were also typically more prejudiced than your average citizen, because of their long, pure bloodlines, which made them more willing to pay more than lip service to these beliefs."

"Who started the war?"

"A better question is who started the *killing*. The younger generation of the Darklord's followers were duelling anyone who looked at them sideways three years before the war officially started, and those duels successfully destroyed the up-and-coming generation of their opponents. That was important, because the Darklord had only convinced half of the military to follow him by the time the fighting broke out. During the war, the two sides lost people at relatively the same rate; and if the war had continued, the Darklord would have ended up being the only Dragon of the old generation to survive. He also would have been the only one with a new generation of Old Monsters to serve him. A generation that had grown up loyal to him."

Luke shrugged off my speculation. "All of that could have been coincidence. It doesn't mean he can see the future."

"I would agree with you, but when the war turned in the Darklord's favour, the South tried to summon a hero and ended up summoning your sister."

"What does that have to do with anything?"

"No one in their right mind would believe the South's claim that they summoned an unbelievably powerful sorcerer hero to protect them."

"The Darklord believed them."

"The fact he believed them is why I know he can see the future."

"That's not evidence."

"Yes, it is. Would you believe them?"

Luke paused. "No. The timing's too convenient, and there's no proof."

"Exactly. A man who killed seven Dragons, archsorcerers who were over level 200 with more than 3000 attributes, believed one of the most juvenile lies I've ever heard. He believed these lies so much that he agreed to a truce and recalled his army. Doesn't that seem strange to you?"

"He's supposed to be insane."

"Ruthlessness looks like insanity when you're on the receiving end. Besides, his daughter is too emotionally stable for him to be insane."

"Why do you think he believed them, then?"

"He believed them because he has some ability to see the future, and every time he saw a future where he killed South Murdell's hero, he also saw his death. He didn't know *why* he saw his death, but he always saw his death."

"You think he saw his death because you would have hunted him down."

I nodded. "Without mercy."

"There's a flaw in your logic."

"I'm listening?"

"If he was able to see you killing him over a decade before it happened, how come he can't see you coming to kill him this time?"

"Different people view the future in different ways. If his ability to divine the future is weak, like I suspect, he'll only be able to ask a question and receive an answer. The question would be something like, *'Will I die if I try to kill the hero?'* When that comes back with a yes, he can ask his next question: *'Will I die if I kidnap the hero?'* That might come back with a no. Reading the future this way can be incredibly helpful for navigating politics and life, but it has its limitations. The further away something is, both physically and timewise, the harder it will be for him to get a clear answer."

"How did he see his death over killing Kathrine then? His death would have been more than a decade away."

"Unless someone is a true seer, seeing the future is mostly about probability. That means if there is a 100% chance of something happening, it's able to be seen from decades, even centuries away."

Luke turned back to me. "What about the butterfly effect?"

"What about it?"

"Don't our actions change the future?"

"They do, but the meteor that killed the dinosaurs was going to kill them whether or not you stepped on a butterfly a million years before it crashed into Earth. Events outside our control can become absolutes, and I can say with absolute certainty that he would have died if he killed Kathrine."

"That implies you would always have beaten Contessa."

"No. When I first asked you about your mother and sister, you would have told me someone killed Kathrine. I then would have tracked him down before doing anything else, changing the course of history."

"I suppose that makes what you say possible. But why won't he see us coming after him this time?"

"I never said he won't see us coming. He will. He just won't see us coming with any accuracy to begin with. The first time he sees us coming, he'll divine the future and ask questions. The closest these questions will get him to us will be Darksmith. Darksmith which has the largest concentration of future magical talent and threats in

Murdell. He'll either send someone to watch the academy or wait until something changes; either way, we'll have more time."

"What if he runs away instead?"

"I don't care if he runs or stays and fights. I'm only doing this so your sister can leave Murdell with a clear conscience."

"What if you're wrong and he can't see the future and is over level 300?"

I pointed to the reforming frontline, where the paladins were dragging the injured to the clerics. "That's why Carolyn's people are here."

"You think you can make them strong enough to kill a level 300 archsorcerer?"

"No, but they might be able to provide enough support for my people to kill him."

Luke shook his head. "Your people are good, but there's a big difference between an Old Monster and a Dragon, and just as big a difference between a Dragon and a Demigod. Gregory and his men are children next to the Darklord, even if he is only a Dragon."

"Is that you volunteering to help?"

"That's depends on if you can keep leveling me this quickly."

"I can, but I'm not planning to kill him next week. Your sister has another four years of studying at Darksmith. That's four years of training, with dozens of hunting trips into the Abyss. If Carolyn's Old Monsters are as good at magic as I think they are, I'm willing to hunt deeper and push their levels higher. They're the deciding factor. Without sorcerers to counter the Darklord's magic, fighting him is suicide, and I won't send you to your death."

"And if they're not good enough?"

"Then I'll come up with another plan."

"Why don't *you* kill him?"

"I can't. He's a Darklord, and I'm a creature of darkness. He'll have a dozen skills that he can use to manipulate and compel me into his service. I'll end up as his puppet."

"So, *I* have to kill him."

"If you don't mind."

Instead of answering, he changed the subject. "Do you know where Kathrine's going to go when she leaves?"

"No, but that's because she doesn't know where she wants to go yet. She just knows she doesn't have many good memories of Murdell."

"That's because the South has used her as a pawn ever since they summoned her."

"I know. The only reason she doesn't abandon them to their fate is the South is where Riza's family and her adoptive parents live."

"So now I have to defeat a darklord."

"And I have to topple his private army."

"Can you stay awake that long?"

I nodded. "Barring serious injuries, I can hold on for another five years without needing to sleep."

The frontline was getting slowed down by corpses, so I waved my hand and released my hunger. Across the battlefield, every monster corpse withered and crumbled to dust as the last traces of life force were pulled from their bodies by my vampiric aura.

The life force rushed into my body, only to immediately be syphoned away by my soul, which grew a little stronger.

Luke looked at me again. "That's longer than I thought you could stay awake for."

"Unlike visiting you, visiting your sister doesn't get me tortured every other week."

Luke reached out and patted my shoulder as his eyes crinkled with amusement. "Yes, but visiting Kathrine led to you sparkling. So, I think I can safely say you prefer visiting me and torture, over visiting her and sparkling."

That was true.

25

UNPLANNED EVENTS

Our recent excursion to the Abyss taught me that my bond with Kathrine was stronger than my bond to Luke. Hunting and killing the floor bosses gave her forty-one levels, while he only gained twenty-six. Considering Luke killed eight times as many monsters as Kathrine had, saving countless people from experiencing resurrection in the process, the difference in how many levels each one gained had very little to do with Luke's starting level being twenty levels higher than Kathrine's and everything to do with her bond being stronger.

Angelica and Davina both gained twenty-one levels, and my deathlords had gained at least fifteen. Carolyn and Davina's people both saw positive gains, but they were natural gains in line with what people expected. I still wasn't sure if Carolyn's people had enough skill to face the Darklord. Their levels were too low for me to be certain, but it looked promising. Promising enough for Luke to start training and consolidate his gains.

Every day for the past three weeks, Luke had been adding a few points to his attributes while we sparred. The gradual increase didn't throw off his timing or mess with the strength behind his strikes, so he never lost his edge. It meant that each day he grew a little more lethal than the one before.

I blocked Luke's blade half an inch from my throat, locked my arm in place, and let his strength push me away from him. My feet skidded across my training hall floor as I used a palm strike to knock aside the dagger that he'd thrown. The dagger flew off to the side and hit the magical barrier protecting the walls, before clattering across the floor.

Fights between warriors with low and high attributes were entirely different affairs and required different training. Warriors with high attributes could climb a rock wall with two fingers and jump over small buildings. Those with low attributes could not. This meant if you had high attributes and executed an underhand slash, and your opponent blocked your blade with theirs, they could end up thirty feet away from you because your sword swing contained enough force to easily throw anyone's body weight that far.

Throwing them away from you might be exactly what you wanted to happen if you were planning to make a run for it. Or it could be something you didn't want to happen because they might then run off instead. It meant fights at Luke's level looked more like something from *Crouching Tiger, Hidden Dragon* than like a medieval war movie. There was a lot of knocking your opponent across the room and trying to land a blow while they were in the air.

Luke's right eyebrow twitched as he spotted what he thought was an opening. It was one of his tells and wasn't a big issue, because outside of sparring, he'd be wearing his helmet. He went for a thrust.

I placed one finger on the flat of his blade and pushed myself out of the way, using his strength against him. This opened up his left side, and I tapped Slaughter's tip against his armour-covered kidney.

"That's my win," I said.

Luke stepped back, indignant. "Stop cheating, Old Man. In a real fight, the enchantments on my blade would shred your fingers before you could push yourself away."

That was almost true.

"In a real fight, your opponent would be wearing gauntlets similar to yours. Do you have a plan for fighting someone who can safely hold your sword blade?"

"I'll slam them into the ground so hard they get stuck."

That was an actual technique high-level knights occasionally used.

Luke carried on. "Then I'd stab them in the eye with a dagger."

"You threw your dagger at me already."

Luke glanced down at his empty sheath. "Shit."

"Language. Also, that's my win."

He scowled. "Fine."

I slid Slaughter into its sheath.

Luke had taken my advice when we first parted ways. Trainers had been following him and his party wherever they went. With their help, he'd made a lot of progress in a short amount of time, and there wasn't a lot that I could teach him anymore, but I could be a training dummy for him to beat up. It let him push himself to his limits without needing to worry about hurting anyone.

He'd still improved over the last three weeks. He wasn't entirely sure about fighting the Darklord, but he was willing to train like it was going to happen. He understood Kathrine wanted out of Murdell, but not if it meant war, so this was the only way for her to gain her freedom.

Luke sheathed his longsword and began stretching, allowing his body to recover for our next spar. Now that the new school year had begun, I had less free time to train with him at night, so he made sure that we got the most out of our time together.

Through my bonds, I sensed one of my deathlords go from being fine to standing at death's door. He was bleeding out and too far away from me to help. A fraction of a second later, a dozen deathlords were fighting for their lives.

My head blurred until I was staring up and towards town. I focused on my bonds, my connections to those who had taken my oath. Many of them weren't where they were supposed to be. It was nearly midnight. They should have been in bed or inside the hotel, studying and practicing magic. Instead, they were all moving through the hotel or in the streets around it.

Another group of deathlords began fighting for their lives. They'd been moving through the streets far from the first group. A third group ended up in the same situation, and then a fourth. Their actions finally made sense. They were establishing a perimeter.

Something was going down in town.

Something big.

I cast a spell, flicking the switch on the wall to disable the training hall barrier. I needed to get up there.

Thousands of objects in motion filled my ears as the barrier disappeared. I heard heartbeats pounding erratically, doors being broken, people fighting for their lives, screaming, yelling, begging, and the sound of spurting blood being lapped up and guzzled with abandon.

Magic filled the school, and Dalin's voice announced what I could hear before I could warn Luke. "The infirmary is under attack by vampires. Requesting immediate assistance. This is a level 5 security threat."

I couldn't sense the auras of any vampires, but I could hear people fighting for their lives and losing. I knew the sound that was made when something drank blood from the living, and I could hear it taking place all over Darksmith. If they really were vampires, not some other creatures, then we were dealing with elder vampires and stronger. They were the only ones who could hide their auras.

If my guess about elder vampires was correct, we had a very big problem. I could hear close to a thousand of them moving through Darksmith. They were everywhere. By itself, that was bad, but my people were also fighting in town. And a few elder vampires weren't a threat to them. They would have to be facing a similar situation to what we were facing here for me to sense so much danger. And if there were that many elder vampires here and there, there had to be an ancient vampire somewhere.

We were in trouble.

I turned to Luke and chose my words carefully, because we were being listened to. "Your mission, should you choose to accept it, is to make your way to the infirmary and convince Dalin to give the command to evacuate Darksmith. Once he's given the command, help him and his staff fall back and hold the gate."

Luke blurred to the corner of the room where his helmet sat. "Why the hell are vampires attacking the school?"

My son understood I could piece together a situation much faster than he could and let me take the lead. "Most of the students live in warded homes. Once turned, they can bypass those wards and turn their parents."

"That implies a wider plan."

"There is no reason for vampires to be at Darksmith unless there is a wider plan. The scale of this attack is absurd."

He slammed his helmet on and buckled the chin strap tight. "Let's do this, then." He blurred toward the door.

I pulled aside my coat as I blurred through my apartment to my private occult library. There were several books in the library that were too dangerous to fall into vampire hands and too valuable to destroy. "Shadow. Summon Gorgath. We might need his help."

Shadow slid from my coat and disappeared under the door as I shoved the last valuable tome into my storage pouch and released a necrotic wave. Every book in the library dissolved under a whirlwind of black necrotic energy. They crumbled to dust, utterly destroyed.

I went to find Kathrine.

I blurred my way down to my classroom and through the door to the main hallway. One of the few weaknesses of entering the Deadlands was you couldn't easily interact with the physical world or pass through solid objects or barriers, so doors remained shut. That meant I needed a path free from obstructions when I entered.

Once outside my classroom and through the department doors, I wove the deadlands spell together and entered. Everything took on a black and white quality as I blurred through the hallway in the opposite direction Luke had taken.

The infirmary wasn't the only place under attack; hundreds of vampire elders had descended on my building to intercept the professors while they were alone. I passed shattered classroom doors and signs of battle. Faculty had been ambushed from behind as they tried to make their way to the infirmary to give support. Their lifeless bodies lay on the ground, drained of blood. There were magical battles taking place in other sections of the hallway and classrooms, each one between a group of vampires and a lone professor.

The vampires knew that if enough of the faculty could get together, they would be a serious threat. They were making sure that didn't happen.

I moved around anyone or anything that got in my way, ignoring everything I saw. These people didn't matter. Only my children mattered, and I had to get them out of Darksmith. I might be powerful compared to humans, but I was on the weaker end of the bell curve compared to my own kind, and only an extremely powerful ancient vampire would be able to gather and control so many elder vampires.

The scale of the fighting grew as I exited the building and blurred through the crystal gardens and walkways. Battles were taking place everywhere as students tried to escape or form large enough groups to protect themselves from the hundreds of elder vampires that had descended upon the academy. Fire rained from the dungeon's ceiling as a group of students attempted to surround themselves with enough violence to keep themselves safe.

I spotted Professor Fergus as I approached the dorm entrance. He was leading a small horde of dog warriors and two dozen members of the Undead Fight Club into battle against the elder vampires blocking their path.

The Undead Fight Club all followed the rules when it came to the club events, but they also experimented in their free time. Each of them had half a dozen undead under their command to back up Fergus's dog warriors.

The students were exchanging spells with a pair of elder vampires, using their undead as shields, while Fergus directed his dog warriors and their undead to tear several elder vampires limb from limb.

He must have managed to impart a class on his dog warriors and level them, because they were almost able to keep up with the elder vampires. Alternatively, he could have been using control undead spells to weaken his opponents.

His battle became unimportant as I ran through the entrance and made my way down the hallway to the staircase. I went up three flights, until I was on Kathrine's floor, and then made my way into her hallway.

It was a mess.

Half the doorways were broken in. The other half were in the process of being broken into. Kathrine's room was one of the ones missing a door.

I stopped in the entrance to her dorm room.

The cold, calculating part of me that had said to put my house in order and improve our chances of escape before trying to help my daughter vanished as I spotted a vampire with Kathrine's throat in her mouth. She had my daughter pinned against the wall, feet a few inches off the ground, twitching. Riza lay dead on the floor behind her, the right side of her face caved in by a single strike.

The vampire wore a long, flowing white gown with a belt. A holstered wand sat on her right hip, and a sheathed athame sat on her left, next to a storage pouch. Blonde hair tumbled over her shoulders, enhancing her beauty in the most predatorial way.

The vampire was in a blissful trance, fully engaged in feeding. Luke's blood and life force had an intensity to it that Kathrine's didn't have when I arrived. That had changed when Kathrine leveled.

Rage filled me at the sight, the kind that would end empires. It was cold and focused with a deep need to be satiated.

I drew Slaughter and exited the Deadlands behind Kathrine's assailant. The vampire's scent reached me as I slammed my blade through her side, directly into her core. Her scent said I was dealing with an ancient vampire, not an elder.

My rage didn't blind me to the need to get it away from Kathrine or the fact that I was in over my head.

Raw mana rushed from the vampire's core, through Slaughter, and into mine. Kathrine was too close for me to use combat spells, so I wove a control undead spell using Slaughter as my focus and commanded the vampire to focus on the pleasure Kathrine's blood was giving her.

I extended my fangs and lunged.

My teeth tore through the muscle in the vampire's neck to reach the artery in her throat. At the same time, I unleashed my vampiric soul touch and vampiric soul bite upon her, trying to suck the life force from her in every way I could, nearly blind with rage.

As her disgusting blood met my tongue, a feral growl escaped my lips, and I saw flashes of memory, random events in different places and times, all jumbled and out of order. The flashes were too short to make sense of, but I caught one detail. A name. Her name. Aroneska.

Raw mana raced down my sword arm and into my core, as I wrapped my other arm around Aroneska's stomach and kicked off from the wall, tearing her off my daughter. I couldn't be gentle. I had to move fast. Aroneska's teeth ripped through Kathrine's throat, but I put that out of my head, as I flicked the contents of a healing potion over her wound with a spell.

Without holy magic, I only knew one way to put down an ancient vampire. Starve it to death. I drank mouthfuls of disgusting cold blood and consumed her life force faster than I'd ever been able to do it before. Aroneska's body replaced the blood as quickly as I drank it, but my vampiric soul touch and vampiric soul bite caused an unexpected reaction as I used it.

Aroneska grew weaker.

For the most part, vampires didn't have souls, but they did have demonic parasites, and demons were mostly made from the same energy that souls were. Demonic parasites were made from very small, concentrated amounts of soul energy, so the nibble I took when I fed destroyed and consumed the weakest of them.

Flashes of memories continued to flicker through my head as my back collided with the far wall. I kicked off again and threw us out of the room and into the hallway, casting minor spells to remove the powerful wand and athame from her belt and slide them into my storage pouches. Next, I stole her storage pouch and added it to my collection. The blissful trance Kathrine's blood induced and my spell to enjoy the experience faded as Aroneska's massive reserve of life force poured into me.

As she came to, I felt her instinctively use her vampiric touch to slow the drain on her life force. She then calmly reached for the arm circling her waist. I wrapped both my legs around her legs, clenching the muscles tight, right as she ripped off my arm, with as little effort as a child's doll.

I ignored my missing limb as the last of Aroneska's mana rushed into me. Now that I was the only one with mana and we were far enough away from Kathrine for me to use combat magic, I had the upper hand. With Slaughter still inside her and my rage begging me to hurt her, I used my blade as my focus and cast the destruction spell. It was my most powerful single-target spell, and with this much anger it would be so much stronger.

I felt her try to weave the ambient mana around her to counter the spell, but it was too little too late.

She threw her head back and screamed an ear-piercing, inhuman sound as her demonic parasites were forced to turn their attention to containing the necrotic energy that was trying to disintegrate her from the inside out. This spell caused too much damage even for our kind.

Elder vampires poured out of the surrounding rooms in slow motion as I triple cast the Deathlock spell, cutting off the hallway on both sides, and the door to Kathrine's room. At the same time, my arm tore itself from her grasp and reattached itself to its socket.

Despite the crippling pain, Aroneska's skill levels prevented her from losing control of her vampiric touch, and she continued to slow her death. However, the pain did stop her from being able to hide her aura, and I was immediately aware that I was in over my head.

Her aura was several orders of magnitude stronger than mine—and that was *with* her growing weaker.

Across the academy, I felt three even stronger ancient vampire auras appear and disappear like sparks in the night. If I was them, I would have used that display to determine who was the closest, so they could come to assist.

I had seconds at most.

Based on how quickly I could feed, I needed thirty seconds to finish her off. My children's safety came before revenge. One ancient vampire this strong was hard enough to defeat. Four were an impossible enemy to overcome. We had to escape.

A dozen scenarios played through my head with each passing millisecond as I tried to come up with a plan that would ensure my children's survival. I had planned for two ancient vampires at the most. Three working together was unheard of. Four wasn't something I'd even considered.

I needed a new plan and a better escape route for Kathrine.

The infirmary was one option; Luke was there. Davina and Angelica were another. They were with the princess, who had dozens of Old Monsters guarding her, which I could use as meat shields to protect my children. The VIP dorm was the safest building at Darksmith, even if there was currently an ancient vampire inside it.

My bond with Sir Trent suddenly flared, warning me that his life was in danger. Gregory's flared a moment later.

Gregory was fighting at the town's dungeon entrance. His people were fighting all over town, but based off their locations, they were trying to evacuate people toward him. With each passing second, more and more of my people were entering life-and-death situations.

I had the strong impression that the town was lost, and my people were running here for safety.

With a spell, I levitated Aroneska and I to a standing position, while listening for the sound of footsteps coming from where I'd sensed the nearest aura. I waited until the footsteps reached the building, and then dropped the Deathlock spell covering Kathrine's door and pulled my mouth from Aroneska's throat.

A notification appeared.

Your Ancient Royal Vampiric Bloodline skill has increased to level 17.
You have mastered your Vampiric Soul Bite skill.

I snapped my fingers and cast a second destruction spell as the knowledge from mastering my vampiric soul bite skill showed me how to feed with the same intensity whenever I wanted. Instead of turning to dust, Aroneska dissolved into a pile of bloody mush that landed at my feet. I stepped back and snapped my fingers again, weaving an inverted void barrier around the mush. It would prevent her from healing and eventually kill her if her ally didn't break her out.

I blurred through the doorway into Kathrine's dorm, recasting the deathlock spell behind me. Kathrine's kingmaker distribution had her on her feet and chugging a healing potion despite the wound to her throat. I disintegrated her window and wall with the wave of the destruction spell as I ran to Riza's corpse. Kathrine would be upset if I left her friend behind, and I owed the girl for keeping my daughter safe.

"I'm getting you out of here," I said as I bent down and threw Riza over my shoulder.

"I can—"

I threw Kathrine over my other shoulder before she could finish her sentence and leapt through the hole I'd made, heading for Davina. Kathrine's scent transformed as I fled. It went from pure terror to relief. I didn't slow to enjoy the fact that my daughter was relieved to see me.

I had to move.

It would only take a few seconds for the ancient vampire who was coming to help Aroneska to break my void barrier and free her. Aroneska would then have to convey what had happened, which would take longer. If their minds worked the way mine did, they wouldn't act until they understood the situation. And I'd want to know everything I could before engaging an unknown, ancient vampire. Especially one I thought was weak enough to casually invade their territory, only for it nearly kill one of us.

The reason I'd waited until the last second to run was meeting another ancient vampire in the open would've resulted in Kathrine's death. I needed the helper distracted, so we could safely leave the dorm.

I ignored the fighting and the dying going on around us and ran as fast as I could. The number of elder vampires increased as we approached the VIP dormitory. Someone had stationed them on the balconies around the building, cutting off every exit.

Positioning them there also made it possible for them to compel those inside. They had a second, larger group waiting below for someone to succeed so they could invade the building.

That wasn't their only plan. A dozen true elder vampires stood in front of the entrance, trying to perform a ritual casting that would bring down the building's barrier. These ones were a lot stronger than the others I'd passed. They weren't newly turned elders raised on the blood of ancient vampires. They were the real thing. I could smell the centuries in their blood.

All of them were dressed in armour similar to Luke's, except theirs had centuries to grow stronger. They would not be easy opponents.

I could hear a battle taking place inside the VIP dorm as guards tried to deal with the ancient vampire that had walked through the building's defences. The threat to Sir Trent's life had diminished, which suggested he'd been running reconnaissance. He was now back on the fourth floor in Davina's suite. I could hear the scratching of pens near him, which told me they were making a plan.

I circled around the building to catch the ancient vampire's scent and learn what I was up against. He was male and old, very old. Judging by the lack of secondary scents, he was also naked and unarmed.

Curiosity sated, I leapt from balcony to balcony, heading for the one where I sensed Angelica was waiting. She'd moved to it as she sensed my approach.

The vampires guarding the balconies ignored me, making the logical assumption that I was an ally. I did nothing to interfere with this assumption.

When I arrived, Angelica was standing inside the balcony door, staring through the glass into the eyes of the elder vampire. She was wearing her Crypt Keeper set. and I could see she was trying not to laugh at the elder vampire's attempts to compel her.

She continued playing the distraction as I placed Kathrine on her feet and passed her Riza's body.

Faster than the elder vampire could react, I caught him by the throat, cutting off his voice. I then drew Slaughter and impaled his core.

Angelica opened the door, dropping the barrier covering it. She pulled Kathrine and Riza inside, then she stepped aside so I could enter with the struggling vampire.

I turned to Angelica as I kicked the door closed to reinstate the barrier. "Compel this vampire for me."

Angelica turned her gaze on the elder vampire and harnessed the power of her set. "Stop resisting."

It went slack in my arms.

I let go, placing it on its feet. Unlike the true elders outside, this one only wore a set of sorcerer robes. He'd been turned so recently that I could still smell traces of his living scent.

"Compel it to answer my questions," I said.

Angelica rolled her eyes. "Answer his questions honestly and try to be helpful."

I turned to the elder vampire. "How many ancient vampires are here?"

It stared blankly at the wall in front of it. "There are twelve. Four at the academy. Four in the town. Four protecting the perimeter."

"Why are they here?"

"To turn the students?"

"Can you be more specific?"

"No. My position in my scourge is low."

I was dealing with a useless pawn. "Apart from the ancient vampires, who would know why you're here?"

"Members of the Outer Court. They are elder vampires who have the vampire queen's respect. You can tell them by the smell of their blood. It is old."

He was talking about the vampires who'd been performing the ritual to get inside.

"Is the vampire queen here?"

"I don't know."

This was getting me nowhere and taking up too much time. An ancient vampire could do a lot in a few seconds if they felt threatened.

I swung Slaughter and removed his head. I caught his body as it fell and sucked the life from him, leaving nothing but dust.

I tossed his robe and wand into a storage pouch as I turned to Angelica. "At some point, I might say 'that one' and point to an elder vampire. You will compel that vampire to follow us."

Angelica nodded. "What's the plan?"

"Vampires are attacking Darksmith, so we're leaving."

I turned to Kathrine. She was holding Riza's corpse, without a hint of tears. Kathrine had seen Davina's healing ability while we were in the Abyss, and her panic had fled the moment I appeared in her dorm room.

"Sweetheart, it's important that you don't say a word to anyone. There are plans in motion that you're not aware of. We'll take care of your friend shortly, so please follow me."

Kathrine and Angelica followed me as I made my way through Davina's private suite to her training hall. Like all the other VIPs, she had a dozen personal guards. There were six paladins and six clerics standing outside the training hall, guarding the door against Carolyn's people.

Davina was nowhere in sight.

Instead, there was an hourglass on the table beside the training hall entrance. It looked like there was a minute left until Davina unleashed her spell.

I flicked my gaze to Sir Trent and gave him a series of hand signals that I'd learned from watching his people.

One ancient vampire in building.

Three ancient vampires outside.

Area fully compromised.

Retreat necessary.

Local threat impeding retreat.

Engage local threat.

Sir Trent nodded and turned to his people. Of the forty-eight Old Monsters guarding Carolyn, thirty-six followed me out of the hallway into the sitting room. Six of them were archsorcerers. The rest were nonmagical knights.

Even with them, our chances of killing this ancient vampire were low. He was the strongest of the four, but he would likely run the moment he realised we could kill him. Ancient vampires preferred to run when they didn't know what they were getting into, and a saint and a hostile ancient vampire would have that effect.

I walked over to Angelica and checked the straps on her armour. They weren't in the right place or tight enough. That wasn't her fault. She needed help getting her armour on. If Davina hadn't had time to help her put it on, she would have done it herself rather than asking for someone else.

I began correcting the mistakes.

Everyone checked their equipment while they waited for my signal. I heard the ancient vampire below us finish killing everyone on the first floor and listened to him make his way to the second floor.

Luke completed his mission while we prepared.

Dalin's voice filled Darksmith. "Students and faculty, this is a level 5 security breach. Please flee the academy with all possible haste. We cannot contain the vampire threat, nor provide protection while you are in transit. The rally point is the entrance to Darksmith. We will hold it for as long as we can. The vampires are numerous and well-coordinated, so anyone who does not make it to the rally point before we retreat will be dead before help can arrive. Running is your only option. Good luck, and may Heaven favour you."

His voice cut off.

Sir Trent and his people had put away their dress armour, the stuff they wore around the academy when they were playing guard. Today they wore their *real* equipment, and it was the best Arcadia had to offer. It was good that they had it. They were going to need it.

A pair of Davina's clerics had followed us into the room and were silently casting buffing spells over everyone. Sir Trent and the others nodded their thanks.

I listened to the fighting down below and heard when Celest abandoned her guards and surrounded herself in a greater barrier. The act probably saved her life. It bought her the time she needed for Davina's spell to be ready.

I signalled Sir Trent with a few seconds to spare and then I blurred down the stairs, listening to the screams of the dying as I followed our target's movements. I reached the second floor ahead of the others, and charged through the broken front door, down the hallway littered with bodies, and into the large dining room.

Celest stood at the back of the room, holding a greater barrier in place, through the spell scroll in her hand. Her guards lay in a broken mess around the room, dead and drained of blood.

I didn't see our target as I blurred into the room. It turned out to be because he didn't want me to see him.

He landed on my back without me sensing anything. His body was much larger and taller than mine and his agility far greater than I'd imagined. He lifted me from the ground and pulled my head back before I was fully aware of what had happened to me.

His fangs sank into my throat, tearing through my flesh despite my constitution.

I couldn't fight his strength or compete with his speed, so I drew Slaughter and reversed the blade, impaling both of us. The blade went through my kidney and into his core. Magic rushed from his core into mine as I used my ancient vampiric soul touch to slow the life force draining from me to buy time.

Due to what I'd done to my soul, I could no longer store excess life force within my body. That meant he could drain me to a starving state a lot faster than I liked. Thankfully my ancient vampiric soul touch was stronger than his, but he was drinking my blood, so he came out on top.

I pointed my finger at his head and cast finger of destruction. The skin around his forehead blackened, regenerating too quickly for the spell to do serious harm. He was a lot tougher than I was.

Seeing how ineffective my spell was, I immediately gave up and began casting deathlock barriers around us to pin us together and slow his escape. His brute strength was likely enough to break the spells, but it would take a moment.

Sir Trent led the charge, blurring into the room, with his massive sword. Angelica was close behind him. They both stabbed their weapons into the massive vampire's back, which was impressive considering Angelica was using a staff. I smelled necrotic fire, and sizzling flesh, but my attacker didn't react. Another three Old Monsters quickly joined them, as they all tried to pin the creature. Sir Trent's fastest archsorcerer entered the room and unleashed a pillar of fire upon the two of us.

Then the last second ticked by.

An explosion of holy magic blew through the building, passing through walls, before spreading through Darksmith. The holy magic slammed into the ancient vampire behind me, with the intensity of the church's cathedral defences, setting his skin aflame and increasing the damage from the spells that were bombarding us. To my surprise, he didn't die.

He just panicked.

He released my throat and tore his body through the weapons impaling him, before leaping over me in the direction of the nearest exterior wall.

I caught one leg and Sir Trent caught the other, as we both brought our blades down and through his thighs. His legs separated from his body, and I continued to feed on the life force inside the leg with my vampiric soul touch to replace what I'd lost.

Neither of us let go, expecting him to return for his limbs. He didn't. Instead, mid-air, his naked body shifted form to something like a bobcat. The leg in Sir Trent's hand dissolved into a liquid, shooting forward and flowing into the creature he'd become. I was feeding on the leg I was holding, which seemed to prevent it from doing the same.

He didn't turn around for his missing leg. Instead, he remained in the bobcat form, covered in holy flames, and smashed headfirst through the dining room wall into another hallway. Debris went everywhere as I hurled a destruction spell after him.

His skin slagged off, holy flames continuing to burn, as he turned the corner and fled. With another loud crash, he escaped the building.

Sir Trent gave a shaky breath. "That was a very old, very powerful vampire. Was it the only one?"

I shook my head. "There is another that is nearly as strong and two that are weaker."

"We need to leave."

I couldn't agree more.

I was still holding the vampire's leg. The demonic parasites inside the leg were still trying to repair the damage. Blood was spurting from the end, being regenerated as quickly as it vanished.

I drastically reduced how much life force I was drawing from the leg, until I felt it begin to change into a less solid form. The moment that happened I slightly increased my feeding rate. It stabilized in my hand. Drinking Aroneska's blood had given me flashes of memories. Hopefully, this would do the same.

I lifted the bloody flesh to my mouth and drank.

There were more flashes of memory. They came disjointed and incomplete like they had with Aroneska. A name came to mind.

Lusor.

Sir Trent ignored me and turned to his people. "Find the survivors and collect the bodies. You have until she's ready to move."

They blurred out of the room, taking the bodies with them.

I walked over to Celest and watched her face grow pale. I didn't stop drinking from the leg as I paused before the barrier and drew Slaughter.

I shouldn't have bothered.

Celest dropped the barrier and stepped forward, grabbing my hand with hers. She pulled back my cuff and bit down on my wrist as hard as she could. My constitution should have stopped her, but it didn't. The moment her teeth pierced my flesh, and her tongue tasted blood, her jaw clenched.

Her teeth struck bone, locking her in place.

The girl was a seer. She'd come first in the divination exams. There was no doubt in my mind that her actions were meant to save herself. This was somehow tied to a future she'd seen. The question I had to ask myself was, *'Is this a future that would help me escape with my children?'*

Her only benefit from becoming my familiar was that it would be impossible for another vampire to turn her. If she saw that her death was inevitable, this might be her way of stopping herself from coming back. That could tie me to a future where my children died with her. Or it might be a future where they survived. Or it could be a false future, and she was too inexperienced to know that.

I didn't have time for her to explain.

She smelled hopeful instead of defeated, so this likely wasn't a future where she died painfully but didn't turn into a vampire. It was likely a future where she survived.

I could use that.

I lifted my mouth from the bloody leg and slammed my fist into my chest, stimulating my heart to beat, once for her, once for me, and once for the bond we forged.

As the third beat faded, her jaw unclenched, and I felt the bond slide into place.

I pulled my hand from her grasp and lifted her chin until she met my gaze. "You will follow and protect my daughter to the best of your abilities, taking any risk that is necessary to ensure her safety. You will take no action that endangers her, and you will do your best to act as an ally. Angelica will introduce you."

Angelica walked over, shaking her head. "You'd think someone who grew up with a darklord for a father would know not to make deals with hellspawn." She grabbed Celest by the scruff of the neck and blurred out of the room.

I went back to drinking the blood oozing from the leg. The flashes of memory continued as I blurred my way downstairs to the hallway nearest the entrance. Sir Trent's people came out of the first-floor suite with bodies and dropped them on the ground next to me, before moving higher.

There were only four VIPs currently at Darksmith. Celest, Davina, Carolyn, and Marin. Marin was the son of the empress of Bo, but 83rd in line for the throne and trying to improve his standing by becoming an emissary to Murdell. The Bo Empire didn't believe in selecting their next ruler just from the emperor's children. Three quarters of the time, the next emperor was chosen from relatives. This had made them one of the most stable empires in the region, because succession wasn't a popularity contest. It was a competence and character test.

Davina and Angelica appeared beside me as I looked down at Marin's dead body. He was a dark-haired, handsome young man. He'd paid attention during my lessons, and he hadn't cursed anyone, so I had nothing bad to say about him.

Davina dropped to a knee and began resurrecting him. "Angelica said you fought an ancient vampire. Is the threat as serious as I fear?"

"It's worse. We need to run for it. How long will your spell incapacitate the elder vampires?"

"The strongest ones will have already recovered."

That seemed wrong. "Was that by design?"

"Yes. I saw them feeding on everyone they encounter through a window, so I chose a spell that would stop those that had been fed on from turning."

Marin opened his eyes and gasped for breath.

He spotted Davina and smiled. "Is this the afterlife?"

Angelica took Davina's place as Davina moved on to the next person and slapped the smile off Marin's face. "You're not dead, idiot. You've just been resurrected. Now, which of these dead bodies belong to your strongest guards? We need them back in the fight."

Marin blinked and then sat up. He looked around him, noticing the hallway filled with dead. His hand flew to his mouth, and he turned pale like he was about to vomit.

Angelica slapped him in the back of the head this time. "Which are the strongest?"

His eyes darted among the bodies, and he began to point. He froze as he turned to me and spotted the large, human-looking leg I was feeding on.

Angelica hit him in the back of the head again. "Ignore him. He's on our side."

Marin's gaze moved past me, and he finished showing them the order in which they should resurrect his people. He took a deep breath and stood up. "Where do you need me to fight?"

"We don't need you until we make a run for the gate." Angelica replied as she moved bodies around for Davina.

"You're fleeing?"

"That's what I just said."

"I've got something that will help."

Marin turned and sprinted back into his rooms, using his agility to move five times faster than a normal person would. He appeared a few seconds later, carrying a master storage chest. He placed it on the ground, flung it open, and then used a spell to retrieve a large, deep-blue carpet.

He turned to Davina and grinned. "This is a royal carpet, crafted by legendary enchanter Zortin during his final decade. It is one of a kind." He picked it up and held it out to Davina. "It will help you escape."

Davina didn't look up from her work.

Angelica laughed at him. "This is the wrong time to flirt."

I stopped drinking. "He's not flirting. That's a flying carpet equipped with an expert-tier flying spell, master-tier defensive spells, and a carrying capacity of up to twenty people."

Marin nodded. "It is the finest war carpet in my collection."

I stuck the bleeding leg back into my mouth and blurred to his side. He froze in place. I looked down.

His master storage chest had clothing, furniture, and all the trappings most wealthy people carried, but it also had a truly massive collection of flying carpets. If Marin was from Earth, he would have been a car guy, a very rich car guy.

There were nearly *a thousand* carpets in his collection. Half of them looked so badly damaged from age that they wouldn't work. Then there were the ones that would work but would work poorly. Based on appearance, only about a tenth of his collection had been crafted in the last century, and only half of that collection was worth the reagents used to craft them.

I lowered the leg again as I spotted something interesting. "Is that a mobile palace?"

Marin swallowed. "Yes."

"Does it work?"

"If you have enough archsorcerers to power it."

Far above me, I heard Carolyn's argument with Rupert finally get to an explanation of why she didn't want to leave yet. "Luke's coming for me. We just have to wait a little longer."

Stupid teen hormones.

I blurred through the building until I was standing beside her and then lied through my teeth. "Stop wasting time, Princess. Luke is out there risking his life to make a safe path for you to escape through. We need to get to him and help before something finds him that he can't deal with."

Carolyn's demeanour immediately changed, and she turned to Rupert. "We're moving now."

I blurred my way back downstairs and stopped beside Davina as she resurrected the last of Marin's guards. "Carolyn's on her way."

I turned to Marin's guards. Half of them were already on their feet. They seemed to have taken their deaths in stride, but their equipment was destroyed. They were pulling replacement battle robes and staffs out of their storage pouches.

"Marin will move with Princess Carolyn," I said. "Half of you will provide barrier support, and the other half will provide ranged support to those clearing the path. Do not hold back and I won't have to undo your resurrections."

Their gazes moved to the leg I was holding and then back to my bloody mouth.

"Act now, think later. If I meant you harm, I wouldn't have had you or your boss resurrected."

That was enough to convince them.

I used a necrotic spell to disintegrate the blood on my face. The last thing everyone outside needed to see was me sucking blood from a leg. It was not a good impression when vampires were trying to kill you.

Without drinking the blood, the flashes of memories were no longer coming. That was a problem, because they were finally beginning to give me some insights which made sense. I needed to see more, but we had to move first.

Sir Trent came racing down the hallway behind me. He stopped beside me and began using hand signals.

Threat assessment.

I replied in the same manner.

Twelve dangerous hostiles.

Large number of secondary threats.

Remove primary threat.

Running battle to rally point.

Sir Trent nodded and relayed the message.

I turned to Davina. “You’re with me.” I looked at Angelica. “You’re guarding her.”

They both nodded.

I blurred to the end of the hallway and ran into the building’s entrance, looking through the glass doors. The dozen elder vampires that had been performing a ritual to bring the barrier down were covered in holy burns. Despite that, they were holding their position. I threw open the door and charged towards the nearest one.

Each of them raised a hand. Twelve fingers of destruction flew towards me. I triple-cast the Deathlock spell, blocking six. I caught two on Slaughter’s blade while taking four directly on my coat as I closed the distance.

My coat wouldn’t last long under such a violent attack, but it could block them.

A holy wave flew past me as Davina entered the field. The wall of light forced three of the elder vampires to cut off their attack and unleash an unholy wave of their own. The spells collided with each other. They didn’t cancel each other out. Instead, they bounced off one another and flew in random directions.

I finished closing the distance and swung Slaughter at the nearest threat. Her gauntlet blurred and she conjured a barrier to intercept the blade. Slaughter cut through the barrier so quickly she didn’t have time to look surprised. Slaughter passed through her armour’s barrier with the same ease, before loudly tearing through the metal protecting her throat. Her head disconnected from her body, flying away.

“He carries Lavire’s kilij,” one of the more well-informed males shouted. “He can cut through magical barriers. Switch to swords.”

I raised my sword and pointed. “Angelica, him.”

Angelica raised her voice. “Stop resisting.”

I turned and charged the next-closest. He drew his sword and met my blade with his.

"Attack the strongest among you," Angelica commanded. There was a fraction of a second pause. "Stop resisting." That order was Angelica's first mistake. It was quickly followed by several others. "No, stop attacking him. We need him. Stupid fucking vampire, you ripped his head off. Attack the one who knows the most, but don't rip off his head. Stop hitting yourself and attack another vampire. Not the one you decapitated, another one."

Angelica managed to say all that while engaging one of the other elder vampires in single combat. The one I was dealing with had found a friend, and it was taking everything I had just to keep ahead of their blades. They were strong, fast, and skilled; and if I had been alone, they probably would've been able to incapacitate me.

I fired off several fingers of destruction, but unlike their ancient vampire masters, they knew the value of quality gear. Their armours' magical barriers blocked my spells.

With the elder vampires safely engaged, Sir Trent and his people rushed from the building. The elder vampires noticed the speed of those rushing towards them and realised the odds were steeply against them. Those that could disengage did. In less than a second, nine became one.

The unfortunate one was my opponent.

He stepped back and raised his hands in surrender.

I took off his head and turned to Sir Trent as he removed the head of the elder vampire Angelica was controlling. "Don't destroy them. We need to interrogate them."

Sir Trent bent down and threw the body and head to the people behind him. "Take the prisoners and keep them under control. We're moving now."

Marin dashed out of the building with his rolled-up carpet and tossed it on the ground. It unrolled itself and lifted into the air a few inches above the ground. Marin leapt onto it as his guard formed a circle around the carpet.

"Ready," he shouted.

Carolyn exited the building and joined him on the carpet. Kathrine and Riza followed a few paces behind with Celest and stepped on. Barriers sprang up around them as archsorcerers gave them the best protection possible, and Marin engaged the flying carpet's defences.

Kathrine was as safe as I could make her.

Davina and Angelica appeared beside me as I turned to take in Darksmith. Everywhere I looked there were elder vampires writhing on the ground. Davina unleashed holy bolts whenever she spotted one, causing them to explode into flames. In other places, the stronger elder vampires were on their feet fighting, exchanging spells with students and faculty that were trying to make their way to the entrance.

Students spotted our group and jumped from windows to rush towards us. Other groups of survivors running through the open areas saw us and changed direction to join up. There was safety in numbers.

Elder vampires began to throw spells from windows, but only at people who looked too old to be a student. I got the strong impression that the weaker vampires had been compelled into service, because they made less than logical decisions, fighting in the open instead of sniping from cover.

I heard hundreds of frightened heartbeats throughout Darksmith. Students who were too afraid to move. Even the old me agreed that there was nothing I could do for them. The vampires were already regrouping.

I slid Slaughter into its sheath and raised my hand, creating a finger gun. I cast finger of destruction spells in quick succession as I led the charge through Darksmith to the gates. I had a lot of mana to work with, but I had far more enemies. Each shot distracted an elder vampire or disintegrated one writhing on the ground, but there were always two more to take their place.

Nearly a hundred students had joined us by the time the entrance was in sight, which was where our next problem lay. The vampires had triggered Darksmith's defences. The entrance barrier was working at full power, and there was no way to shut it off to pass through.

Against the barrier were lines of students and faculty with their own overlapping barriers. They were watching the windows for any sign of threat, with spells ready to unleash. Clerics from the infirmary stood in their ranks, spread out so they weren't easy targets. I counted close to fifteen hundred. It was less than a quarter of those at Darksmith.

In front of them all was an undead horde controlled by the Undead Fight Club and Professor Fergus. They were ready to engage ground assault. Luke was standing with them, shouting orders. He didn't look over as I rushed past, but he ordered Sir Trent to reinforce him.

Students leapt out of my way as I rushed to where Professor Jirt was trying to bring down the barrier. Their fear-thickened sweat and frightened, panicked heartbeats intensified when they realised they were in my way.

It was good to have a reputation.

As I got close to the barrier, I shoved aside several professors who had their backs to me and stopped behind Professor Jirt, the head of the enchanting department.

"What's the problem?" I asked.

She didn't look up from her work. "For the last time, the failsafe has been activated. The barrier's working at full power, and it won't power down for another day. We can't access the academy's mana generator because its barrier activates when this happens."

Good, I wasn't missing any details. "Was the barrier created using the direct line or socket method?"

"The cheap bastards used a direct line, not even a multi-line. It's right through the barrier here. I'm—"

I heard four different voices issue the same order as they overheard our conversation and came to the same conclusion as me. "Attack now!"

I pushed Jirt aside and slammed Slaughter through the barrier and into the main mana line.

A flood of mana shot through my blade, down my mana network and into my core. The mana I'd expended was replaced in fraction of a second. My flawless mana network had no limit to how much mana it could move at once, so I redirected the mana through my sorcerer sovereign links, allowing it to pour out of my core as fast as it entered.

The barrier vanished as I pushed all the mana through my links to Gregory and his people. Letting the mana spill out around me would only allow it to keep powering the barrier enchantment on the gate, though less effectively. I needed to get the mana away from here without shattering my people's cores, which would happen all too quickly.

I didn't have to tell anyone around me what to do.

The moment the barrier vanished, everyone moved. Everyone yelled, "Retreat. The barrier is down." And everyone pulled people with them.

If all of them had to move along the ground, it would have taken ten seconds to get them all through. But they didn't. A lot of them could fly. The faculty turned and shot into the air, passing above everyone's heads. The older students followed a second later as others ran into the tunnel. Marin zipped into the tunnel, weaving through the fliers, taking Kathrine to safety.

Professor Jirt saw that the barrier was down and leapt through without a second thought.

The Undead Fight Club were the last ones through, having held the frontline, and they left most of their undead behind, to move quicker. Luke and Sir Trent didn't wait for them, knowing my temperament.

Start to finish, the evacuation took four seconds. In that time, the windows filled with elder vampires and spells flew across the distance and began colliding with the barriers.

I was the last to step through the gate into the tunnel, and by that time I saw a powerful, naked figure blurring towards me.

I withdrew Slaughter from the main mana line. The flood of mana racing through me cut off as the barrier reappeared in place. I sheathed Slaughter and shoved the bleeding leg back into my mouth. The flashes of memories began again.

When the gate was at full power like this, I couldn't pass through it. Based on their reaction and how quickly they had given the order to attack, they couldn't either.

We'd gained a head start.

But we needed to escape.

26

ESCAPE VELOCITY

Retaking the dungeon fortress from the vampires took my familiars and I less than a minute. Only their commander, Talon, was a true elder vampire. The other eighty-five were all recently turned and compelled to follow his orders. I had Angelica take control of him with her armour and then used him to make the rest surrender. After that, a few old chairs turned into wooden stakes were as effective at keeping them under control as an army of guards.

We were so quick that I had time to spare before the others caught up. I decided to use that time to answer a few questions I had, so I dragged him into the fortress cafeteria.

Angelica finished repeating my instructions to Talon, bringing him entirely under her control. The quick and sloppy commands she gave during battle weren't what I needed right now. What I needed was an informant who would try to help us to the best of their ability.

"Remove your equipment," I instructed.

Talon pulled off his gauntlets and dropped them on the cafeteria's stone floor. His belt and weapons followed next, before he removed his helmet, and began on his breast plate.

Talon had short, light-brown hair and a dense beard, which hid a strong jaw. He looked to be in his late twenties, but the scent of his blood told me he was old. Not as old as the owner of the leg I was holding, but old enough to make the other true elders look young.

I needed answers and I didn't have much time, so I accelerated my perception. "Are you a member of the vampire queen's Outer Court?" My words came out in a fast, sharp string that would make a speed rapper jealous.

He tossed his breast plate aside and accelerated his mind to match. "Yes."

"What does that entitle?"

"It means the queen respects my abilities enough to compel me into her service."

"You act autonomously?"

"Only in small matters like this fortress. Usually, I am under the command of a member of the Inner Court."

Those had to be the ancient vampires.

"Why did her court attack Darksmith?"

He stopped undressing and reached into his storage pouch to pass me a newspaper cut-out. It was Murdell's end-of-year exam announcements. He'd circled the divination results and the name of the student who had achieved 100%.

Celest.

The moment he handed over the paper, he went back to removing his equipment. "Two weeks ago, the queen informed the Inner Court she wished the seer to join her kingdom. Members of the Outer Court were sent to investigate the seer, and we discovered her familial connection to the Darklord. We established that her ability to see the future was inherited from her darklord father, not her mother, and that taking her would risk a confrontation with him. The Outer Court could not contain such a threat, so we brought the matter to the Inner Court, and the Inner Court decided to go to war with the Darklord to fulfil the queen's wishes. We are here to collect the seer and turn the students at the academy so the next phase of the plan can begin."

The door banged open behind me, and Luke rushed into the cafeteria, carrying the bodies of four headless vampire elders we'd captured at Darksmith. He had two bodies on each shoulder and a sack filled with heads in one hand. He dumped them beside me. "Learn anything helpful yet?"

"They're after Celest and are willing to start a war with the Darklord over her."

Luke paused and then his hand went to his sword. "Will it stop a war if she's dead?"

I didn't like how quickly Luke's mind had turned to murder, but it was a valid question. I turned to our informant as he began removing his boots. "Will it?"

"No. The Inner Court is currently spread across Murdell, executing the Darklord's generals and allies. Killing the seer will only result in the queen's displeasure and the killer being *turned into an example* for the new generation of cattle."

The way he said, 'turned into an example,' sent an excited shiver down my spine. It spoke to the monster in me, carrying far more meaning than it would if spoken by anyone else. The sentence represented a horror beyond horrors, a living nightmare that would remind humanity why they feared us.

Luke needed to be reminded that I was the exception, not the rule, when I came to vampires.

"What form would this example take?"

"The killer will be captured alive. For the rest of their life, they would be compelled to spend each day torturing a friend, family member, or ally. At the end of each day, we would restore their mind so they could understand the horror of what they have done. This would continue until all of those they cared for are tortured beyond madness and broken enough to become Unseen. Finally, these Unseen will be released from their bondage and allowed to drag their soul into Hell, where they will torture them for all eternity."

Luke swallowed.

He'd learned his lesson, so I moved on to my next question. "How many ancient vampires serve the queen?"

"The Inner Court is made up of sixty-six ancient vampires, and the Outer Court is made up of six hundred elder vampires. Each member of the court has their own scourge at their command, along with allied scourges they can call upon."

"Fuck," Luke whispered.

"Language."

"Did we hear different numbers? 'Fuck' seems appropriate."

I didn't have enough time to argue the point. "Is the number of members in her courts fixed, or does it fluctuate?"

Talon shrugged. "I can't say. And I imagine no one else can, either. She's been asleep for longer than any of her court have walked this world. Even the most ancient of us don't have memories of any myth or legend that mentions her. And no being as powerful as her falls into obscurity without ten thousand years of silence to let mortals forget."

"Do you know why she's awake?"

"She sensed the rise of The Broken King."

"Is that a name, title, or description?"

"It is the name, title, *and* description of a vampire king who should not exist. A being of contradictions, who brought about a new age of curiosity within our queen, awakening dormant intrigue to once again drag her attention into the land of the living."

"If she's looking for The Broken King, why is she after Celest?"

"The rise of The Broken King ignited her curiosity and pulled her from her grave. Satiating that curiosity is not high on her list of priorities."

"What's her goal, then?"

"To leave an *impression* on this age."

Another shiver ran through me at his words. She intended to do to the world what her court would do to Celest's killer. It was a tide of terror that would leave everything broken.

I pushed killing her to the top of my priorities list.

Thankfully, I wasn't at the top of hers.

I took the sack of heads from Luke and turned back to Talon. I needed to keep this conversation moving. "Why haven't you become an ancient vampire? You're more than old enough."

He paused for the slightest fraction of a second, showing the first signs that his servitude wasn't all-encompassing, and that he was still in there, fighting to be free. "I prefer to exist in the world rather than watch the centuries stroll past from my grave."

He was talking about the Curse of Sloth. The curse was stronger for ancient vampires than elder vampires.

"Are you saying, elder vampires can choose *not* to become ancient vampires?"

"Yes."

"Can an ancient vampire choose not to become a primordial vampire?"

Talon tossed the last of his armour down and stood before me naked. "Yes. Becoming a demon is not a choice any vampire will take unless they have to."

"Why?"

He smiled. "We sit at the top of this world, but we stand near the bottom in Hell. Transforming to a primordial vampire is an act of desperation. It is only to be taken when certain death awaits you and descent into Hell is your only escape."

I pulled a notebook and pen from my storage pouch and quickly wrote out something I couldn't say aloud, and risk being overheard.

"Don't speak about anything you read in this note," I said, before showing it to Talon.

The note said I knew nothing about using my innate vampire powers, and that I needed to know how I could feed on the elder vampires at my feet to learn what I needed.

He finished reading the note and met my gaze. "During a spontaneous feeding, our kind is only capable of gaining miscellaneous knowledge. This knowledge is always related to performing actions or skills." He pointed to the strongest of the four elder vampires we'd defeated. "Sod has mastered the arts of giving and taking knowledge from our kind. It's how he grew so powerful. Restore his head to his body and then compel him to transfer this understanding to you. Due to his advanced skill, there will be a complete transfer upon his death." He pointed to the female vampire I'd first defeated as we left the VIP dorm. "Tarla has mastered how to mesmerize, charm, and compel, despite not being able to perform the third action. Use the skill you gain from Sod to take that ability from her." He pointed to one who'd surrendered. "Prog has a passable ability for controlling animals." Finally, he pointed to the one who had recognised my sword. "Olont is the Outer Court's most-skilled telepath." He then pointed at the leg I was holding. "Once your understanding is sufficient, you can extract the knowledge of shapeshifting from Lusor's leg."

"What about telekinesis?"

"It is the least valuable of our powers. I could offer it to you, but you would lose me as a source of information, which I believe is more valuable to you."

That was true.

I didn't have time to consider if my next action was the right decision or not. I'd already been talking too long, and I needed to understand my enemy better. This would allow me to do so. I gave Luke and Angelica orders as I bent down and stripped the elder vampires of equipment.

Davina was moving through the fortress resurrecting the students who were here when the vampires attacked, and the princess and the other VIPs had just arrived outside. Carolyn's guards were following my lead for once. The fact that all I wanted to do was take my children and run frightened them into submission.

If it wasn't for Kathrine, I'd already be on my way to the Abyss. The monster in me knew I could save her and Luke if I took them and ran. It also knew that I could probably save her and Luke along with everyone else if I tried hard enough. However, getting my children to safety would eventually result in Kathrine asking me if I could have saved everyone else. Answering truthfully would end any relationship we had.

I wasn't willing to lose her.

And I wasn't willing to lie to her either.

That left me with only one choice.

I had to save the survivors.

Luke dashed out of the room as I tossed the last piece of equipment away and upended the sack of heads. The severed heads didn't roll across the ground like soccer balls like they did in the movies, they just rocked back and forth.

I scooped up Sod's head and shoved it back onto his neck as Luke ran in with a staked elder vampire. He placed it on ground next to Sod and then shoved its wrist inside Sod's mouth. Sod's decapitated head instinctively bit down, and the wound at his neck began to heal as he drained the blood and life force from the staked vampire.

The recently turned elder vampires had all sorts of mundane skills that would have been helpful for me to learn, but I could also learn most of what they knew with time and effort, so I didn't mind sacrificing them for the life force they carried.

A few seconds after Sod began to feed, his eyes opened, and Angelica began to compel him into submission. Her instructions were much shorter than with Talon. Sod only needed to do one thing: pass on his knowledge and die.

When she'd finished explaining what he needed to do, Sod turned to me and glared.

He was *barely* under Angelica's control. "To do this properly, I need more life force to replace the blood I've expended."

He was trying to buy himself time, but he couldn't lie, so what he said had to be true. Luke ran out of the room for more vampires.

I turned to Talon. "What's the correct method for feeding on him?"

Talon turned to Sod and smirked.

He was fighting against Angelica's control and enjoying the other vampire's predicament. "First drain him of blood, then use your vampiric touch to feed on his life force. The knowledge will transfer as he crumbles to dust."

Sod grimaced as he took hold of the elder vampire Luke gave him and began to feed. Three meals later, he bent his head back, exposing his throat. He stepped forward so I could feed on him, while still glaring daggers at Talon.

As gently as I could, I bit through his flesh and began to drink, being careful not to consume his life force through my recently mastered vampiric soul bite skill. I didn't want to trigger any instincts that would overwhelm the commands Angelica had given him, which was why I was taking this slow. He had far too much freedom. He was close to breaking loose from Angelica's control.

I swallowed mouthful after mouthful of unappealing but nourishing cold blood until it stopped flowing, at which point I used my ancient vampiric soul touch and vampiric soul bite on him. As his life force fled, he regained some control and tried to run. I didn't let him, holding him in place with my vice-like grip.

It took eight seconds for him to crumble to dust.

Before the dust reached the ground, a lifetime of knowledge and experiences rushed into my head. It was every time Sod had ever fed on a vampire to gain knowledge, and every time he fed his blood to another vampire to impart knowledge. This wasn't like when I'd triggered a memory cascade. This was fast, complete, and whole.

I immediately understood what the knowledge transference ability was, how I could use it, and the extent of its capabilities. It was all there, like it had always been a part of me.

I could now organise my mind and allow a weaker vampire to experience one of my memories by projecting it into their consciousness while they drank my blood. This was a powerful form of telepathy and was mainly used to show a vampire how to use their innate abilities for the first time.

I could also now steal another vampire's memories by feeding on them. This would allow me to experience their memories the way they had experienced the events. It reminded me a lot of how Amelia saw my life in her dreams, but the two weren't exactly the same. She saw my memories without me expending any energy.

The only problem I saw with this method for stealing memories was that it was much slower than what I'd just done to Sod. However, the benefit of this method was it didn't require anyone to die or to have an entire body.

Because of Sod, I now had close to a thousand experiences of stealing memories from other vampires as I killed them. He'd used this skill to great effect, opening his mind to absorb more information as his telepathic ability tore what knowledge he wanted from them.

"You okay, Dad?"

Luke was looking at me with his hand on his pommel, but his heartbeat was accelerating from worry, not fear. He'd seen and heard about what happened when I experienced vampires' memories.

I waved away his concern. "The personality changes I experienced in the past were a side-effect of incorrect knowledge transference and extreme circumstances. Eating Sir Denton and the others in such a starved state caused their knowledge and personalities to overlap and merge into a single, insane, hyper-competent personality, which made it difficult for me to draw upon the knowledge I gained. The temporary changes to my personality were caused by my cunning being too low for my consciousness to remain dominant when I unpacked the insane consciousness and absorbed its experiences. I've sectioned off the rest of the unincorporated memories so that they won't inadvertently be triggered again."

"I didn't understand most of what you just said."

"It means that I'm okay, Son. We need to move on to the next one."

While Luke reached for the next elder vampire, I opened my character sheet and increased my cunning with the attributes I'd accumulated from leveling.

+40 Cunning

The extra cunning would help me gain more knowledge while I fed, which was something I desperately needed right now. As I started at my character page and attributes, I considered claiming my past heroic deeds and the levels they would give me.

Race: Ancient Royal Vampire Variant
Class: Hero
Level: 37
Strength: 404
Agility: 575
Endurance: ∞
Constitution: ∞
Cunning: 280

Perception: 480
Recovery: ∞
Mana Regeneration: 478

I decided against claiming my deeds. I'd need over 100 levels to close the gap between my attributes and the other ancient vampires' attributes; and based on how many levels my deeds had given me in the past, that wasn't going to happen. I was better off remaining at my current level and syphoning as much experience to my children and familiars while we fled as I possibly could. They had a stronger chance of closing the power gap than I did.

I dismissed my character sheet.

Luke passed me the next elder vampire Tarla and I repeated the same process, only this time I opened my mind to absorb more knowledge and attacked her consciousness. Everything she knew about mesmerizing, charming, and compelling people rushed into my mind as she crumbled to dust, which was when I discovered they were three parts of the same psychic ability, and a notification appeared.

Your Ancient Royal Vampiric Physique skill has increased to level 5.

I dismissed the notification, focusing on the knowledge I'd just gained.

Mesmerizing was a surgical strike where you captivated your victim through manipulating their nervous system and hormones. We could psychically make our victims' bodies release the chemicals we needed for them to lower their guard. It was the first step for charming a person, which involved flooding the victim's brain with other hormones that made them like and trust us. The final form was compelling our victim, which was where we used the first two steps and telepathic commands to overwhelm their free will, until they did what you wanted.

These abilities existed because, when we became vampires, the structure of our brains changed, unlocking psychic abilities. As we evolved forms, our brains would change again and again, giving us a larger range of psychic capabilities.

That meant, vampires could mesmerize.

Elder vampires could charm.

And ancient vampires could compel.

These abilities were not separate abilities, but a single, complex psychic ability used in multiple ways. They could be compared to how your body was capable of playing piano, dancing, painting, fighting, or performing gymnastics. All of these actions were just your body in motion, but being skilled at one didn't mean you could perform the others.

And like a body, you needed to learn to crawl, stand, walk, and then run with your psychic abilities. Just because vampires had an innate psychic ability, it didn't mean it didn't require effort to learn.

Tarla's knowledge had expanded on Sod's in a way that made me understand why I was supposed to consume the other two elder vampires before I consumed Lusor's leg. Each set of memories would give me insights into the other memories that came before them and would expand what I could do with the earlier abilities those memories had given me.

Consuming Prog gave me the ability to control animals. This was similar to what Tarla did, only it was applied to simpler but more varied lifeforms. There wasn't a huge improvement to my psychic control, but my understanding of animal anatomy exploded, and I had a feeling that would be important for shapeshifting.

Eating Olont and gaining his knowledge of telepathy resulted in significant improvements to all my psychic abilities. He had a level of control that put the others to shame.

As Olont crumbled to dust at my feet, I slid into Talon's mind and experienced his racing thoughts as he tried to overcome the compulsion he was under and find a loophole in the instructions. If I wanted to, I could start a conversation with him. He was a vampire, so two-way communication was possible. Human brains were limited to receiving messages, but if I had their psychic signature, those messages could be sent over large distances with enough magical enhancement.

Telepathy was both a big asset and a big liability.

I turned to Angelica. "I can now send messages to you telepathically. Until I say otherwise, you're to ignore any command I give you telepathically and use your best judgement for any suggestion I send you telepathically."

Angelica raised an eyebrow. "Why do you want me to ignore commands?"

"I want you to ignore *telepathic commands*, because telepathic commands can be made to sound like they come from anyone, which risks another vampire *pretending* to be me and ordering you to do something I don't want."

"Like freeing me?"

"Like murdering Davina."

"Oh."

I turned to the bleeding leg I was still carrying.

Without the rest of Lusor's body, I couldn't kill him to steal his memories of shapeshifting. What I could do was *relive* his shapeshifting memories through drinking his blood. Demonic parasites were like a soul in that they recorded every experience their host had. I was certain that it was them, not the blood, that allowed vampires to experience another vampire's memories when they fed on them.

The memories I'd gained from Sod told me that even if I didn't feed on my victims' life force, they would still lose it very quickly. He didn't know why, but I assumed it was because the psychic attack we directed at their blood destroyed the demonic parasites in it, which forced the other demonic parasites to replace them.

It meant I had a limited amount of time strolling down Memory Lane. I had to focus on what was important.

I put the leg back in my mouth, focused my mind on the memories I wanted, and then forced the demonic parasites inside the leg to give me that knowledge. The flashes of memories transformed into a single memory of Lusor feeding on me as Angelica and Sir Trent stabbed him in the back.

The world fell away as I experienced Lusor's arrogance and amusement at our pitiful actions. I felt his intrigue over my vampiric soul touch, which was far stronger than his own. He wanted to understand how I was doing what I was doing, and he was planning to consume me to find out.

He didn't notice as more weapons struck him, nor when the spells began. From his perspective, they were insignificant.

Then Davina's spell struck him.

It wasn't the holy magic that scared him, but the familiar feel of an angel's grace mixed through it.

Lusor was five thousand years old, and he knew the burn of a saint's holy gift. His arrogance vanished as he recognised that he'd taken the bait and let himself be surrounded, while a saint was nearby. Every survival instinct kicked in as he tore himself through the weapons, shattered the barriers, and leapt over me.

I experienced what it felt like as his legs were cut off and then experienced him instinctively change his shape to gather himself back together. It was an overriding thought, a command of mind over flesh, a complete restructuring of all that he was.

I sensed his horror as he realised a part of him was trapped by me and felt him decide to shapeshift to a smaller form that would allow him to concentrate his strength and defence as he escaped.

I lived through every thought, every process that he had to undergo to achieve the transformation. I felt what he felt as he became the bobcat and crashed through the wall, and then I felt what he felt as I hit him with a destruction spell. He blurred down the hallway, through a side room, and then exploded through a balcony door, before shifting his form back to his original human form, only this one was slightly smaller than the last.

Once again, he tried to pull his leg to him during the transformation, and once again he failed. Concern for the saint and what they would do with his leg replaced his frustration, and though he was loathe to give up some on his strength, even temporarily, it was preferable to death. I felt him reach out with his vampiric aura to his missing limb and relinquish the connection to the power trapped within it.

The memory stopped there.

Once again, I was standing in the fortress's cafeteria; only now, I knew why he was so strong. Lusor didn't have an attribute aura. Somehow, he'd used his shapeshifting ability to transform his physical body so that every attribute could be physically incorporated. His attributes represented his physical capabilities, as opposed to the limits his aura could push him to. It had turned his peak performance into his general operating level.

I needed to figure out how he'd done that.

I dove back into his memories, searching for how he started the process.

A very old memory of him walking to his sarcophagus began to play out. In the memory, the sarcophagus was half-filled with dirt. I felt the grave calling him as he approached, but he ignored the call, even as he climbed inside and lay down. Once there, he let the grave call him just a little and sank below the surface of the dirt.

I felt his annoyance over his grave dirt no longer being capable of letting him fully sleep away from his grave, now that he was an ancient vampire. It was a fleeting thought, but one that taught me something I didn't know.

As the thought faded, he reached out with his vampiric aura in a way I'd never even considered, reopening gaps near his grave which led to Hell. The gaps were so small that only soul energy could pass through. I instinctively knew they were the gaps that had opened the night he was turned.

Using his vampiric aura, he bathed his body in the soul energy that came through the gaps; and because of his connection to his grave, this accelerated his recovery. A day of doing this would restore him as much as a month of unassisted sleeping in his grave.

In his mind, this improvement in recovery did not make up for being tied to his grave. It also wasn't easy. Without a conscious effort, this speedy recovery wasn't possible. But natural rest only opened a few of the gaps, not all of them, so he had to endure.

While he lay there bathing in soul energy, he began to practice the technique he'd stolen from a monastery. The technique used soul energy to strengthen the body, and he was intrigued to see if it would work on him.

I pulled myself out of the memory with more questions and some answers. Apparently, elder vampires could sleep outside their grave, which was something I needed to investigate, but only after I understood what I'd seen.

Lusor clearly didn't know about demonic parasites, but I was almost entirely certain that those gaps to Hell that he opened were made when his demonic parasites had first crossed over to turn him. The only reason I could see for those gaps opening when he slept was that our third-stage demonic parasites needed soul energy to recover. And if they needed soul energy to recover, it made sense that they would be programmed to recover while we were in our grave, because that was where they could open these gaps to draw soul energy through.

These days, my demonic parasites were almost always surrounded by soul energy. Would that accelerate my recovery time when I returned to my grave? Based on what Lusor knew, it probably would. But I was certain he was wrong. Unlike his, my demonic parasites produced soul energy, and that soul energy hadn't helped me recover quicker at all. There was something different about the soul energy from Hell, but I could investigate that later.

Curiosity sated, I turned to Talon. "Can elder vampires sleep outside their grave?"

He sneered. "We can, through the use of grave dirt. Grave dirt is created by filling your grave with dirt and sleeping in it. Should you need to rest outside of your grave, surrounding yourself with this dirt will allow you to rest. The more often and longer you sleep in the grave dirt before you remove it for use, the longer the effects will last away from your grave. Two years in your grave for one year away is what you should expect, unless you sleep more or less often."

"What's the limit?"

"I once slept for three centuries outside of my grave, as I waited for a church order to die out."

The limit was the effort you were willing to put in.

“Could I use grave dirt?”

“Grave dirt will allow you to rest away from your grave, but it won’t allow you to recover. It would be like catching your breath after running, as opposed to sleeping.”

He'd answered my immediate questions, which meant I didn’t need to use the leg for those answers. I lifted the leg to my mouth and slid into the memory of Lusor reading the soul technique that strengthened his body.

This time, Lusor was in a library filled with scrolls surrounded by dead monks and scholars. There was a burning sensation coming from a cursed brand on his chest, and he was searching the shelves for the information he needed to remove it.

He snatched up the next scroll on the shelf and read it through. It was the body-strengthening technique he’d used in the last memory. He tossed it aside when he finished.

He picked up the next scroll and read it front to back before I could pull myself from his memory. The scroll contained a soul-strengthening technique and one that wasn’t like any I had read. It was so interesting I let the memory continue. The next technique was just as interesting, and so was the one after that.

Lusor’s gaze skimmed over a gold plaque as he worked. Etched onto the surface was the image of a crane standing on a lake under a crescent moon. The plaque explained why every technique was so interesting. He wasn’t at a monastery, like he thought. He was at the Dancing Crane sect.

There were references to the sect in one of the books Father had given me to read. If it was accurate, then this memory was nearly four thousand years old. The Dancing Crane sect had been a place of research. Their members travelled to every corner of this world, searching for those who practiced soul arts to convince them to entrust them with their techniques. They then sought to improve these techniques, before returning them.

The sect existed for three hundred years, and the century before its disappearance was considered the golden age of all soul arts. Two centuries of accumulated knowledge and insights let them push the arts to heights not seen before or since.

The sect's disappearance was a mystery.

A mystery that had now been solved.

I experienced Lusor reading the rest of the techniques in the library, before pulling myself from the memory and going back to the beginning to read the techniques I'd missed.

Lusor had thoughts referencing the head of the sect's teachings which caused me to shift to his memories of going through her private library. It was an odd memory. Her dead body lay in the middle of the room, with her disembodied soul standing over it. She spoke, but no sound came out of her lips. She tried to step away from her corpse but couldn't move from the place she stood.

Her situation began to make sense to me as Lusor read through her library. She'd strengthened her soul to the point where it could survive outside her body, but she hadn't reached the point where she could travel. She'd tried to use astral projection to save her life but hadn't mastered the skill. The result was that she was trapped exactly where she'd exited her body.

He finished reading her library and moved on to the head disciple's private library to see if it had the answers to his problem. From there he went through the various branch heads' private libraries. He was almost done reading the head of the soul healing branch's library when the memory faded.

I returned to the cafeteria clutching a handful of dust.

Only a few minutes had passed while I was observing the memories, but half of Darksmith's survivors were now inside the fortress. I put that out of my head as I focused on what I'd learned.

The Dancing Crane sect's knowledge was vastly superior to my own and showed me how badly I'd failed to grasp the basics of soul enhancement. The technique I'd created for strengthening and restoring my soul worked, but its structure was ineffective, inefficient, and fundamentally flawed in a very dangerous way.

I walked over to the pile of staked elder vampires that Luke had brought in and picked up the nearest one to begin making changes to my soul. With the techniques I'd just learned, I could now make my soul consume my life force even when it didn't want to.

I made my soul guzzle my life force, depleting my reserve. When it got low enough, I used my vampiric soul touch on the elder vampire I was holding. The influx of life force did *not* overflow my reserve, stopping my soul from automatically trying to strengthen itself.

As the elder vampire crumbled to dust, I picked up the next.

The changes I needed to make to my soul were drastic and would normally have been enacted over a lifetime of slow meditation. That was how long you needed to gather that much life force to create the soul energy I'd need. I didn't have a lifetime to get this done, and I preferred to steal the life force I needed, anyway.

The vampires in the pile had all killed and eaten the students guarding the fortress, so they were full to the brim. That was good, because I needed all they had. Luke and Angelica ran to get more elder vampires as the pile grew low, pulling others in to help them.

My soul currently looked like a network of braided vines woven into a vaguely human shape. The soul vines had done a wonderful job of keeping my demonic parasites under control. They were constantly fed and evenly distributed throughout my body, so they didn't need to move to do their work. This immobility stopped them from eating something I didn't want them to eat, which meant they were more efficient.

The Dancing Crane's teachings told me that efficiency would last exactly up until the point where I gained a serious injury. The moment I did, they would move out of their local habitat to regenerate the injury, causing immense soul damage in the process.

What I hadn't known when I created the technique was that souls liked to keep their structure once they had them, and that my soul would consider my demonic parasites part of its structure after them being in the same places for so long. Once they started moving to heal a serious injury, my soul would try to push them back to where they had come from, resulting in a lot of unnecessary damage to my soul.

It would take something like a limb being disintegrated for them to move in this way, but right now that was a serious possibility. After all, I'd just been holding an ancient vampire's leg.

Removing the soul vines wasn't an option. They were designed to survive demonic parasites feeding on them nonstop, so resilient didn't begin to describe how invasive they were. They would always come back. So instead of removing them, I brought order to the chaos.

I made it so they grew in the shape of my bones, muscles, and organs. I gave the clusters of soul vines different densities and structures depending on where they lay within me and what they were supposed to mimic.

Anywhere blood moved was now flooded with soul energy. It moved in and out of the structures as it flowed around me, freeing my demonic parasites to move where they wanted with as little damage as possible.

I finished the changes by the time I was three-quarters of the way through our elder vampire prisoners, but I decided to keep feeding on them to strengthen my soul and cement the changes I had made. Time was short, so I couldn't feed on them for their memories, and I didn't want to take them with us and risk something going wrong.

Prisoners dealt with, I flicked the last of the dust from my hands and began tossing their equipment into my storage pouches.

Luke raised an eyebrow. "What just happened, and do I need to be concerned?"

"I fixed a mistake made from ignorance."

"Did it make you stronger?"

"Not against what we're running from." I turned to Angelica. "Bring Talon with us. I have more questions for him, but we need to move."

I left the cafeteria as Angelica ran over to get our informant. Outside, I walked through the crowded courtyard to where Kathrine was waiting with Princess Carolyn and her guards.

Luke followed a few steps behind, until we got closer, and Carolyn rushed past me. She threw her arms around Luke's middle and stared up into his eyes, giving him the biggest smile. "I can't believe you went off on your own to secure a safe path for me to escape."

Luke blinked several times trying to understand what he'd heard in the context of what was currently taking place.

Kathrine grinned at her brother. "Dad told her what you did."

Luke sighed as he realised, I'd set him up again. "You're welcome, Princess."

I grinned at him and then stepped in front of Rupert.

Rupert didn't wait for me to start the conversation. "What's your plan?"

"We wait for reinforcements and then we run?"

"Did you send your shade to retrieve our people?"

"No. What's happening down here is happening up there. They're coming to us."

Rupert swallowed and then gripped his staff tighter. "Running from ancient vampires at night in open country is suicide."

"I know. That's why we're not running that way."

Rupert swallowed again. "I was really hoping we were here for a different reason."

Rupert needed to laugh. He was about to crack. "For a prisoner of war, you're far too optimistic."

He chuckled softly. "What do you need me to do?"

"Based on their speed, Gregory is bringing civilians. We need to move fast, but not everyone can fly. Marin has a mobile palace in his storage chest, but the archsorcerers he needs to power it will all be fighting, so we can't use it until we're on the second floor of the Abyss and the ambient mana is high enough to let the townsfolk power it. However, he's going to have to lend us his collection of flying carpets to get the civilians that deep. It's your job to convince him."

"That shouldn't be hard."

"He's a collector."

Rupert winced. "I'll see what I can do."

He hurried off.

Sir Trent took his place. "Is there anything we can do to slow them down?"

The ancient vampires attacking the town would be waiting for news of the success of the ones attacking Darksmith. When they didn't receive it, they would continue to wait. They would only come down here once they had finished their task and their underlings had proven that it was safe.

I might be able to slow them down by scaring their underlings, but I needed Gorgath for that.

I shook my head. "You can't do anything to slow them down, but your people can clear the monsters around the fortress so we can have a safe staging ground. Anyone not helping with that can help me organise everyone to escape through the Abyss. That means getting those who can't fly to go to Marin to board his flying carpets."

Sir Trent sighed. "We'd travel faster alone."

Gregory blurred through the crowd and appeared beside me, catching Sir Trent's comment. "I wish you the best of luck with that, my friend. My advice is don't go that way." He pointed the way he'd come.

I turned to Gregory. "Make it quick."

"We spotted them coming over the wall, and because of their arrogance, we were mobilized before they reached the entrance to the dungeon. We were moving to reinforce you when we got word of a second group moving towards the families responsible for the town's defence and pulled back for more information. That was when the people upstairs sent Mother a message. The message was 'run to the necrosaint and save as many townsfolk as you can'. I figured since they'd taken the trouble to send the message, it would be rude to ignore them."

"I can't fault that logic," Sir Trent said.

"We mobilised and pushed outward until we made contact with the vampires. The moment the first group was engaged, they sent the signal, and Delilah roared so loud she shattered every unenchanted window in town. She went a little off-script while informing everyone that the town was under attack, but she eventually got the point across. Everyone outside our perimeter ran towards us, and everyone inside followed our directions. That's when the vampires stopped playing nice. They hit somewhere before they came here and created a ghoul army. There must be twenty thousand up there to go along with the thousands of elder vampires."

This was too much unnecessary information. "Did you get everyone out or not?"

"Everyone we could, but we only managed to reach a few thousand of the nearby townsfolk before we ran into an ancient vampire. Lucky for us, it wasn't expecting to deal with a pair of archbishops or the hundred clerics they had backing them up. Mother and Father drove it off, which terrified them because they'd expected to kill it."

I'd actually meant, did *our* people get out. I didn't care that much about the townsfolk, not when my children's lives were at stake. "Did you recover *our* injured?"

He nodded. "The vampires preferred to use their necrotic magic against Davina's people, so we managed to recover all the bodies. Davina lost a few dozen people though."

That was because the backlash of using a powerful necrotic spell could kill an elder vampire, and killing a random warrior wasn't worth that risk. Killing a cleric or paladin was.

"Good. Make sure the injured are rushed ahead to be healed. There are magic carpets outside the fortress wall waiting for you to load children onto them, and then those who can't fly. We're moving the moment the last of our people reach here, and I expect you to hurry them up."

"That's not a lot of time."

"There are twelve ancient vampires coming after us, and I'm the weakest one I've seen, by a significant margin."

Gregory's optimism and cheerful attitude ended. "We're leaving the moment the last of our people arrive. You don't need to tell me twice, sir." He blurred back the way he'd come.

Sir Trent had run off while Gregory was talking, and his people were shouting orders at the students, breaking them into groups, and getting them to move outside the fortress walls. The first time a student protested, Sir Trent loudly told his people to leave the girl behind for the vampires. That statement was repeated just as loudly for any other student protest. The first student that tried to force them to listen with magic lost his head.

That made the message sink in.

I decided it was time to save my son from Carolyn. "Luke, I need you to find Dalin for me. He's the temporary headmaster and will convince the faculty to work with us, but only if we ask him to."

Luke disengaged himself from the princess's tearful embrace and ran off as fast as he could to find Dalin. Carolyn had managed to hold it together, but she'd fallen apart when she saw him. Luke made her feel safe, and that let the horrors of what had happened come loose from their emotional restraints.

I turned to Kathrine. "Are you okay?"

She shook her head, and her lips began to tremble. "She killed Riza, and she was going to kill me, too. I wasn't strong enough to fight back. I couldn't even hurt her."

"I'll fix that shortly."

"How?"

"With a lot of dead monsters."

She took a deep breath and dropped her gaze. "Why didn't you tell me I was still weak?" She asked in a small voice.

"I didn't want you to keep living in fear."

The sound of heavy footsteps finally reached me. Gorgath was on his way, and we needed to talk.

I reached out and squeezed her shoulder, using the open-heart technique to share how much I loved her. "Stay close to Carolyn, Sweetheart. If this goes poorly, she'll survive where others won't. I need to get back to organising our escape."

I turned to Talon. "Can the Outer Court travel through the third floor of the Abyss?"

That deep, my aura would act like a dinner bell rather than a roar to stay out of my way. The auras of the floor bosses would overshadow mine, and common monsters were as strong as dungeon bosses, so every step would be a battle for survival.

"The Outer Court have the skill and strength to survive moving that deep. However, while we might be able to survive, we would slow the

Inner Court down. If you are willing to flee that way, they will leave us behind."

That was valuable information, and it might change our plans, depending on what Gorgath said.

I HADN'T SEEN Gorgath since our last hunting trip to the Abyss, so I hadn't seen what he looked like without his spikes. I'd heard several students comment on his new appearance and the fact that he'd chosen not to take the mana crabs' exoskeleton bloodline, despite months of talking about it at length with anyone who would listen.

Gorgath now stood much straighter. Not having bone barbs spread across your back really improved your posture. Their absence freed up his movements and made the enchanted staff he carried much easier to wield. He looked a lot less ferocious than he had before, but he possessed a magical density that was unmatched with anything I'd felt on the first floor.

I stood in the middle of the tunnel where I'd come out of the Deadlands as the kid peered down at me and sniffed. "You smell of blood and battle, Professor."

I raised a soundproof barrier across the tunnel behind me, hoping that there were no ancient vampires in the tunnel to town to overhear us.

"My kind attacked Darksmith. I need to evacuate everyone through the Abyss to the nearest dungeon. Speed is the most important factor."

Gorgath frowned. "How deep will you go?"

"Third floor."

"Dangerous going that deep."

"What's coming after us is worse."

"Worse than ant territory?"

"Worse than me. You need to get your people to retreat to the sixth floor. What's coming after us will kill them."

Gorgath nodded. "Gorgath will call for the retreat while he leads his academy through the Abyss."

Until this moment, I wasn't entirely sure that Gorgath understood that being part of the academy meant protecting it, but then again, nothing close to the strength of a dungeon boss had been seen in the dungeon since he'd joined. So, I'd hoped he did. "This is the way."

Gorgath hooted his agreement.

A FEW MINUTES LATER, Gorgath was standing beside the fortress wall, directing human traffic. People were running through the fortress gate or flying over the walls with their mouths open. They had all heard about the monster who attended Darksmith, but no one outside the academy had met him. Both groups of escapees were being directed to where they needed to go, entirely unwilling to disagree with the towering gorilla.

It wouldn't be long until the last of the stragglers arrived. We needed to get moving.

Dalin floated above me in the middle of giving a speech, explaining what was going to happen. He didn't have all the details, but he understood that we were going to make a run through the Abyss. He understood that it was the only way we might survive.

Sir Trent finished giving instructions to his men and then blurred to my side. "Did you get directions?"

"I got something even better. Gorgath agreed to live up to the standards of the academy and help guide his fellow students to safety. The downside is that the path we need to take involves heading into ant territory."

"We'll deal with that when we get there. You probably overhead, but we're going to be moving in a snake formation. My people will take the lead, with Davina's support. Gregory and Davina's people are holding the rear with Luke. The faculty are holding the centre with Angelica and her dracolich and the townsfolk who can fight. Our pace will be set by the slowest of the flying carpets, which I'm told is capable of an advanced flying spell's speed."

"With this many people, the rear will be too far from my aura. I want a third of your people back there."

Sir Trent shook his head. "That's not going to happen."

"Then I'll send Davina back there and move her archbishops to the front. The back needs to either be strong enough not to take heavy casualties or capable of recovering from heavy casualties."

"Move her back, then."

His answer surprised me. I thought he would send his people back. "You're that concerned about what we will face?"

"I've hunted on the first floor of the Abyss enough times to know it's relatively safe for people like us. I've been to the second floor a few dozen times, even fought a floor boss. A running engagement down there is going to negate a lot of the effects of your aura. We'll reach monsters before they have time to run. It's going to be a mess. I'd pull more people to the front if I could."

I left him standing there, blurring through the lines to Davina. She was casting buffing spells. "Davina, you're swapping places with Mother and Father to help cover Luke."

She gave me a relieved smile. "Finally, someone can see reason." She blurred through the crowd, heading for the back.

I heard Dalin finish his speech and turned to see him lowering himself to the ground.

I was standing in front of him by the time he landed.

Moving this fast and this often was starting to make people comment, but I couldn't stop. There was too much to do, and Dalin and I still hadn't talked.

And I needed him to trust me.

He looked me in the eye, his gaze shining white. He took a deep breath, and then he dropped to one knee. "I pledge my life and my soul to the Hero." His words carried to everyone, amplified by the spell he'd used so all of them could hear his speech. "Let his path be my path and his fate be my fate."

Holy light surrounded him as he once again rose into the air with a flight spell, and then those who'd heard the call copied him.

"I pledge my life and my soul to the Hero. Let his path be my path and his fate be my fate."

I felt a bond with each one snap into place. Most of them were from the Undead Fight Club, but some of them were merchants from town and others I had never met, but I'd helped when I killed the curse weaver. I had to save someone's life for them to hear the call, so there were a lot of people who'd received the invite. Until now, they didn't know who the invitation belonged to.

The number who made the oath would have surprised me once upon a time, but Sir Trent had told me the call I gave was the call of a father who wanted to make the world a safe place for his family. It was a call that was easy to get behind, because it was not a call that required them to serve or protect anyone. It was a bond that helped you do what you knew was right.

I didn't want to be responsible for more people, but to get Kathrine through this alive, I needed every advantage. The ones who made the oath all moved to the outside of the group, suddenly having the courage to protect the others.

Dalin looked down at me. "Hero, would you like to say a few words?" There was unmistakable trust in his gaze, which was something I'd never seen before.

They say actions speak louder than words, but that didn't always apply to vampires.

I levitated into the air beside him and looked down. The sea of thousands of faces showed fear and terror. They had come face to face with why grown men feared the dark, and they didn't know what to do, now that they had. They were one loud noise away from screaming. The sight and sound of so much fear in one place was exquisite.

But I couldn't let that fear grow.

Not if I wanted my daughter to love me.

I reached out to the most fearful in the crowd and mesmerized them, one by one. It was just a little push to catch their attention, and if they pushed back, I stopped. Next, I pushed a little harder to those that were receptive, telling their bodies to release the happy chemicals they needed to calm down.

Your Ancient Royal Vampiric Physique skill has increased to level 10.

A long sigh spread across through crowd as the most afraid grew calmer. Those who weren't as close to hysteria interpreted this as a sign that they were temporarily safe. It made them relax, which relaxed others, leading to most falling into a heightened alert state.

"Let me make one thing clear," I said gently. "I don't expect all of you to make it through this night alive. You need to accept that you'll have to fight for your life if you're going to have any chance of making it through this. Accept that the people standing next to you will be torn apart. Accept that you will see them die. Accept that you might die, as well. If you can do that for me, you might have a chance of survival."

I pushed their bodies to remain calm.

"We're going to escape through the Abyss. It's a place I've been many times, and it is a place that holds no terror for me. As we travel, we will fight and die. Mark the bodies of those who fall with an orb of light and leave them where they lay. You're not professional killers or healers, and we're going to a place that scares both, so don't be a hero. The professionals will recover anyone they can. Your job is just to remain alive. To do that, don't save mana. Throw the biggest and most dangerous spells you can. We are going to a place where the ambient mana will allow you to weave spells endlessly, so I expect you to do so."

A little girl standing on one of the flying carpets shouted. "Momma says we can't escape."

She was loud enough for many to hear her.

"There are three heroes, a saint, and some of the most dangerous killers two kingdoms have to offer protecting you tonight. You and your momma came from the town, so you have my people to thank for getting you here. Those of you who came from the academy have me to thank, as I'm the one who lowered the barrier. We got you this far and we'll get you further until this night is just a bad memory."

Gregory ran through the outer gate and raised his hand to signal that he was the last one out. His people rushed to the flying carpets carrying crying children and placed them anywhere there was a space.

I turned and signalled Gorgath.

Gorgath lifted his staff over the wall and shoved it through the inner gate that connected the main tunnel to town. A moment later, there was a pull like gravity as he drew on his mana and gathered the ambient mana in the dungeon. It was like he was down, and all mana should fall towards him.

I could see why he was so adamant that he needed to raise a mana crab. That bloodline ability was intense. Blue sparks rose from his fur as he wove the mana into the spell we needed.

"Inferno," he roared, casting his largest 6th-rank fire spell.

A wave of magical fire exploded from the end of his staff. There was so much mana involved that everyone could feel the spell burning its way through the tunnel with the speed of a missile. We all felt the second that the spell erupted from the confines of the tunnel and expanded through town above us, because it disappeared from our senses.

I realised I may have underestimated at which point Gorgath would become a Nuclear Threat. I'd asked him to cast the spell to remove our scent from the tunnel and hide information about us. The only reason I'd told him to give it everything he had was that the spell needed to reach the academy.

He might have just destroyed the town and everything in it. Gorgath had been hiding his strength from me. After that display, even I would be extremely cautious about coming down here, and I knew the kid.

Gorgath retracted his staff and then stepped back, pointing the at the fortress. "Inferno," he said, casting the same spell with much less mana.

Fire poured from his staff, engulfing the fortress, removing every trace of our presence.

I turned and looked at those waiting below. "Move out."

27

CHANGE OF PLANS

A mentor I had in college once told me that the thing we call life is just everyone standing in line waiting to step up to the executioner's block. Our actions in the here and now can move us up and down that line, but nothing we do will ever let us leave it. He said the key to living a long, happy life under these circumstances was finding actions that made you happy, while moving you further down the line away from the executioner. Once you'd found what those actions were, you let them take over your life and then eventually die as a happy old man.

I'd told him that sounded like a simple way to view life. He said that was the point. With something as complex as life, you need a simple answer. Otherwise, the complexity overwhelms you when you're too tired or stressed to make good decisions. Envisioning a line to the executioner's block cuts through all that noise and clutter, putting everything into perspective for even the most-distracted mind.

Smoke a cigarette, and you move three spaces closer to the front. Go for a half-hour walk after lunch, and move a few spaces back. Decide to do 120 on the freeway because you're late for a meeting, and you get to roll the special dice. If anything other than a natural one comes up, you arrive at your meeting on time. Hit that natural one, and you move to the front of the line where the meeting no longer matters.

The simplicity of his method had always made it easier to understand the abstract repercussions of my day-to-day actions. This way of thinking wasn't something I lived by, but it was something I thought about every so often when I needed to simplify a choice.

Yesterday, I counted my children's lifespan in decades. Today, I counted it in hours. With each passing minute, they moved closer and closer to the front of the line. They were so close now that if they raised their heads, they'd see the executioner waiting for them.

That needed to change.

But before I could accomplish that, I needed to protect the thousands of survivors from the first-floor boss monsters that inhabited this second-floor chamber.

I leapt, hurling myself through the air, towards the mouth of a giant serpent that could camouflage itself to look like the terrain. As I flew through the air, I wove together a master-tier destruction spell.

I couldn't hold back. I couldn't keep my existence hidden. Every second counted, making it more likely that my children were going to die.

I snapped my fingers, unleashing my destruction spell on the head of the giant, purple wolf that was leaping for a family on a flying carpet. Electricity zapped across the wolf's body, striking anything that came near. My tendrils of necrotic magic wrapped themselves around its skin as the spell struck, dissolving the flesh and bone in a black flash.

What was left of its body passed through the cloud of dust that had been its head, as I flew between the serpent's teeth. I drew Slaughter, sliding it into the roof of the monster's mouth to slow my momentum. While I did that, I channelled mana through my sword, using it as my focus to cast the finger of destruction spell. The necrotic beam I released cut through the snake's flesh, dissolving its brain and killing it instantly.

I kicked off the spongy wetness at the back of its mouth and shot out the same way I'd entered. Kathrine wouldn't forgive me if I saved her and Luke and let everyone else die. I was willing to make that choice if it was necessary, but I was hoping Talon's answers would stop that from being the case. I just needed to free up a few minutes to figure out if my assumptions were correct.

I somersaulted through the air, firing a few more fingers of destruction to kill monsters harassing the flying carpets before landing on the largest boulder. Gorgath was at the front of Sir Trent's formation, holding his staff like a firehose and using it as the world's largest flamethrower to clear the lesser threats rushing towards those on the ground.

I raised my voice so he could hear me. "Gorgath, I've cleared the way!"

His ears twitched, indicating he'd heard. He gave a loud hoot, and his troop rushed towards him, forcing Sir Trent's people to leap to the side as Gorgath began dashing for the leader of this chamber.

Gorgath's people, the Gor, were extremely articulate, far more so than humans. This proclivity for articulation led to their native language possessing no polysemous words. You didn't need them when your species had no trouble memorising one hundred words for the variations of fire, ice, and every other aspect of life, which was how his people's hooting language came into being.

Think about it. Once you have memorised the words for everything you would ever see, the natural progression is to memorise words for the experiences you might eventually go through. That's where the hooting came in. These hoots summed up almost any experience a Gor could experience.

Almost being the key word.

The Gor had never had to deal with an invasion of ancient vampires, so Gorgath had no quick way to communicate our circumstances to the local leader of the second floor. Gorgath had warned me that he needed at least ten minutes to explain what was happening and that we, meaning the survivors, were going to be treated as invaders until he had done so.

This was why I was standing between the leader of the second floor and everyone else, with my aura completely unveiled. It was a little bit of overkill, and the local leader's troop was cowering behind him, but it saved me from having to do anything else and freed me up to interrogate Talon.

"Angelica, I need to speak with Talon," I telepathically projected to my familiar.

In the distance, I watched her receive my telepathic message and turn her dracolich, flying towards me as the two of them cleared the last of the major aerial threats in the second-floor chamber. The ten-mile-wide cavern held a more diverse ecosystem than the ones on the first floor, with dozens of monsters as strong as Gorgath.

Angelica and her dracolich were now a match for any of them. The extra levels from training, a larger mana pool, and her growing control over her armour all added up to a pair who were literally the stuff of nightmares.

Talon clung to her waist as they headed for me. The compulsions Angelica placed him under didn't include answering telepathic questions, and it was too risky to add those conditions, which was why I had to speak with him in person.

I changed my focus to the nearby threats and snapped my fingers six times, unleashing six destruction spells, killing the six strongest threats within a mile of our convoy. They weren't the only threats, but they were the biggest. The ones that could break through our formation if they reached our unorganised line.

Several members of the faculty saw my actions and stared in disbelief. Casting spells stressed and damaged your body. The more powerful the spell, the greater the damage. What I was doing defied everything they knew about magic, unless I was a Demigod.

I put them out of my head as I spotted Rupert and projected a telepathic message to him. "We're taking a short break. Transfer the civilians to the mobile palace. Raise your staff if you heard me."

Rupert raised his staff as he passed along the message.

Carolyn's guards welcomed the short break. The reprieve from the fighting gave them a chance to plan and change their formations to something more effective. My aura scared everything except floor bosses on the second floor, but our convoy moved too fast for all the monsters to get out of our way.

The fighting had been particularly intense once we reached this floor and was made far more complicated by the terrified civilians. Some were so overwhelmed by fear that they threatened everyone's safety.

The short trip here had shown us who were fighters and who weren't. Anyone who couldn't rise to the occasion only had one job from now on: Help power the secondary enchantments of the mobile palace. The ambient mana on the second floor was concentrated enough for the townsfolk to power the main enchantments on the massive flying carpet, so any student who couldn't cut it would be travelling with them.

The dracolich swooped down as she approached me. I watched Angelica clench her thighs as her mount spun upside down. Angelica held herself in place as she tossed Talon from the saddle. The elder vampire somersaulted mid-air and landed on his feet beside me as they continued on their way, keeping the sky safe.

I turned my gaze on him as he adjusted the shirt and pants Angelica had given him to wear.

During our all-too-slow trip here, I'd decided Talon was too great of a threat to keep alive. He was an incredibly useful source of information, as any thousands-of-years-old being would be, but our opponents couldn't find out how ignorant I was. If they did, they would take far more risks to recover Celest, killing my children in the process. I held no illusions about my abilities. I couldn't go toe to toe with them if they were prepared. The short-term risks of him escaping outweighed any long-term rewards.

But I needed more questions answered before I killed him, so I accelerated my mind and body like I had with our first conversation. "How do I increase my ancient vampiric regeneration?" The words came so quickly that a normal person wouldn't understand them.

Talon replied just as quickly. "Ancient vampiric regeneration is improved by recovering from injuries caused by holy and unholy magic. Those are the only injuries an ancient vampire will struggle to recover from, which is why the skill exists."

His answer explained why I'd never leveled that particular skill before it was upgraded to ancient royal vampiric soul regeneration by my demonic parasites. The new version of the skill would do what the old version did and more, so I wouldn't have to worry about hellfire injuries in the future. It also answered whether or not he was still under Angelica's control. It seemed like her compulsion was still dominating him.

"What does the royal vampiric authority skill do?"

Talon scowled, comprehending how our conversation would end from my question. He then gritted his teeth and began fighting the compulsion. If he were human, sweat would have beaded down his forehead. Instead, he froze, becoming so still that he no longer looked lifelike.

Eventually, he lost the fight.

His next words came out in a rush. "All vampires naturally project their authority to the world around them as part of their aura. This authority is what compels the weak to bow to the strong. To be subservient. The royal vampiric authority skill changes your authority from a passive effect to an active one. This allows you to strengthen your authority beyond the normal limits and make ancient vampires subservient to you."

"And how do you level this skill?"

He clenched his fists, digging his nails into the flesh, trying to use pain to fight the compulsion. It didn't work. "I'm unaware of how to level the skill, but I assume it involves strengthening your authority." His grip relaxed, and he stopped trying to fight the compulsion. "However, I would advise against this. Authority is like a muscle: Once strengthened, you cannot hide the changes that have taken place. Your royal status will become obvious to every vampire you meet, which is something I was completely unaware of until a few moments ago."

Talon was practically pleading for his life. His advice was him trying to show me how useful he was. How he could provide me with information I didn't know. On another day, I might be swayed, but not today.

I charged ahead with my questions. "Of the eight ancient vampires who might follow us, which will be the most useful for me to feed on?"

"Where do you wish to improve?"

He knew fighting me wouldn't work, so he was trying to be helpful. It was almost amusing.

"Which will make me the deadliest?"

He scoffed. "No member of the Inner Court would consider you a threat, no matter who you ate. How you ended up with Lusor's leg is a mystery to me, but I can assure you that you will not get so lucky a second time. The difference in power and experience between you and them is vast."

That was not what I wanted to hear, but it was important to know. Another time and place, that comment would have saved his life. But not today.

I threw out my next question. "Are any of them particularly gifted at crafting undead?"

"None that I'm aware of."

I raised my hand and fired off a finger of destruction, killing a large bat-like monster that was trying to fly off with a child. "What about crafting?"

Talon shook his head. "No, but Nomis was an architect enchanter of some renown while he was human. He designed the Crypt of the Immortal King."

The Immortal King was the name of a lich king from nearly four thousand years ago. Not a lot of history had survived about him. All I knew was that he destroyed six empires before he was stopped, and there weren't any references to his crypt.

I wasn't interested in an architect enchanter whom history didn't remember. I fired off more fingers of destruction. "What about combat magic?"

"None display skills beyond that of a typical talented archnecromancer."

"Telekinesis?"

He shrugged. "I'm just as skilled as any of them."

"Does one of them have a particularly lethal fighting style?"

He shook his head again. "The queen's combat specialists are confronting the Darklord and his minions. Lusor was our only warrior, and even then, I use the term warrior loosely. His unique physique and shapeshifting ability made him more dangerous than the others, but he didn't possess a fighting style or magic skills to make him truly dangerous."

I was missing something, because this didn't make sense. These ancient vampires had the most important job, so why weren't they the queen's most-skilled servants?

It was a good thing Talon was trying to be helpful. Otherwise, he probably wouldn't answer my next question properly. "Why are they here, if they lack talent?"

"Unlike other royals who use their authority to attract weak-willed creatures willing to serve, our queen only accepts the oldest vampires into her courts. Her authority was strong enough to draw the Inner Court to her side, but not strong enough to make them subservient like the Outer Court, so she compelled them to serve her. They all resisted and ultimately lost, but some lost worse than others. The ones who came to collect the seer are the most weak-minded. Unlike other members of her Inner Court, they can't fight our queen's compulsion, which lowers the chances of the seer having an accident while we transport her to our queen."

If they were all being forced to serve her, it made sense that they wouldn't want her to get hold of a seer. It would negate any chance of them breaking free from her compulsion and escaping.

"If they're not warriors, what are they?"

"Old."

I glared at him. "That's all?"

"Enough time will kill even the most talented fool. By the end of your third millennium, you are either cunning and in control of your appetites or dead."

When Talon said *old,* what he really meant was *dangerous*. Her Inner Court wasn't only comprised of the oldest ancient vampires but the most dangerous. The ones who didn't make mistakes. The ones who were cautious and careful.

I was afraid that that might be the case.

It meant I couldn't frighten off the next group like I had with those at the academy. They would come at us prepared, knowing exactly what they would face. They would have a plan for dealing with a saint, an ancient vampire, two heroes, and everything else we could throw at them.

If I were them and I knew what they knew, I would leave the elder vampires behind. I'd catch us while we were moving through the Abyss. I'd use the monsters against us, harassing our defence, creating openings that would wear us down. With eight of them, that wouldn't be difficult, and it wouldn't risk their lives or Celest's.

My next question was my most important. "Are the students a secondary target? By that I mean, are they disposable if you need to secure the seer?"

Talon nodded. "Turning the students was only a means to an end. It was designed to help us fight the Darklord. They are expendable. The seer is not."

There was no longer a scenario where I slowed down or distracted them enough for us to get away. The moment they felt secure, they would come after us as fast as possible.

I grabbed Talon's shoulder and yanked him towards me. I felt his body lock as he tried to fight the compulsion and run.

"Now would be the time to confess any secret knowledge that might make me keep you alive."

In a rush, Talon listed things that might be valuable to me while I surrounded us with a bubble of necrotic energy that no one could see through. Nothing he said would make me change my mind. I just wanted to enjoy his struggle while I killed him. He was part of an attack that targeted my children and would receive no mercy from me, so I let the monster out to play.

As my necrotic bubble faded, five loud thumps cracked through the noisy chamber like a battering ram striking a castle gate. Gorgath was beating his chest to emphasise his point. I glanced over my shoulder to see the local leader of the second floor still looming over him, like an older brother with a bratty younger sibling. His posture said, 'You better have a good reason to be in my space'.

It had taken nearly a minute for Talon to give up his secrets. His knowledge of telekinesis flowed through me, building on the knowledge I'd received from the other members of the Outer Court. I was now in control of my full range of vampiric abilities. There were no gaps in my knowledge. I had everything I needed to eventually master them.

I turned back to the convoy of survivors.

Rupert had pulled out the mobile palace while I was busy. The flying carpet covered nearly three acres and would hold several thousand people. Kathrine and Celest were helping direct everyone to their station as the survivors landed their borrowed flying carpets on its landing area. Davina walked through the crowd as the survivors headed where they were told to, putting terrified children to sleep.

Their constant screaming and frantic attempts to run and hide while on flying carpets distracted everyone around them and led to several deaths. Putting them to sleep was the only mercy we could show them. They were too small and weak to protect themselves and too much of a liability to let them stay conscious. If everything went wrong, they would never wake up, but they would also never suffer.

I swept my gaze over the chamber floor around me and then pulled a chunk of bone that was sitting on the ground towards me with my mind. It lifted from the ground and flew toward me. I snatched it out of the air with ease and then tossed it aside.

Your Ancient Royal Vampiric Physique skill has increased to level 15.

Telekinesis was a parlour trick.

Moving objects around with my mind was difficult and exhausting compared to doing so with a spell. The only time it might be of any value was if I was held inside an anti-magic field. Otherwise, by itself, it was utterly useless.

I put those thoughts aside for when I could safely indulge them. It was time to change my children's fate.

I searched the crowd and telepathically spoke to Gregory, my children, my familiars, Sir Trent, and Rupert. "Our plans have changed. We need to speak. Now."

Everyone dropped what they were doing. Sir Trent rushed to Rupert's side. Luke found his sister and Celest. Gregory, Angelica, and Davina didn't need to help anyone reach me safely, so they rushed toward me in a blur, ignoring the monsters and letting everyone catch up.

Davina arrived first but waited until everyone was there. "What changed?"

I looked at the grim faces. "We have less time to get through the Abyss than I thought we did. The Abyss is still our only chance of survival, but I wrongfully assumed our pursuers were going to take their survival into the equation when they came after us."

Gregory raised an eyebrow. "What's the plan, then?"

"I'm taking my children and familiars through the shortest route possible. You will all be leading the survivors in the opposite direction."

His eyebrow managed to rise even further. "A lesser man would accuse you of using us as bait, sir."

I shook my head. "Celest is their main target, so *we're* the bait. The plan is to reach the nearest city as fast as possible, throw Celest on the back of the dracolich with my children, and then send the three of them south to the Fortress Cathedral of Urk. If we're lucky, the ancient vampires hunting her will follow their path for the next week."

Gregory frowned. "And if we're not?"

"Then we're going to have four ancient vampires chasing after us when we come to reinforce you. The good news is that if we do this, they won't attack us until we reach the dungeon. They'll want to turn the students, since they can't capture Celest, and it's too much effort to do that in the Abyss. The other good news is that Davina and Angelica will be a lot stronger by the time we catch up with you. Between the three of us, we might be able to kill one of them and make the rest cautious enough to back off."

What I'd just said was a lie. Davina would be marginally stronger. Angelica, on the other hand, would be strong enough to command them to serve her. She'd gained a lot of levels since she'd arrived at Darksmith, and she was becoming more and more of a threat to me. The plan was to make her strong enough to threaten the ancient vampires chasing us. That also meant she would be strong enough to threaten me, but I would deal with that when my children were safe.

Rupert cleared his throat. "Why not stay as one group and kill one together to scare them off?"

"Numbers," Sir Trent replied. "If he doesn't bait them away, we will be fighting against eight, not four. That's an entirely different battle."

I nodded. "Also, they're willing to die to retrieve Celest. They aren't willing to die to turn the students. So, as long as she is with us, we won't be able to scare them off."

"You scared them off at Darksmith," Rupert pointed out. "Why won't it work now?"

"They were regrouping at Darksmith. They weren't scared off. They thought they had us trapped in the academy and assumed they had time to organise. They won't make that mistake again."

Rupert scratched his jaw but nodded.

Kathrine bit her bottom lip and then blurted out her question. "Why does it have to be *us*?"

I'd been expecting this question. "You and your brother are heroes. Of everyone here, your blood is the most intoxicating to them. And it's only going to become more intoxicating as you level. Sending you two away with Celest raises the chances of the eight ancient vampires following you. This would raise everyone else's chances of survival while ensuring you both live."

Luke snorted. "You'll drug me to save my life, but you won't drug her. There is a name for that. Younger child favouritism."

I chuckled. "That trick won't work on you twice, and I'm saving my better tricks for when I don't have a perfectly rational reason to get you two to safety."

Kathrine looked at Luke. "Do you believe him?"

"Yeah, he's totally got something up his sleeve for another time."

"Don't joke. You know what I mean."

Luke sighed. "As far as I know, the Darklord's daughter is the reason the vampires are here. With our blood enticing them to follow us, Dad's right. We have the greatest chance of drawing them away from the survivors."

"What about staying to fight?"

Luke shook his head. "Killing his problems is how Dad normally operates, so if that's off the table, it's off the table."

"I don't *always* deal with my problems by killing something," I replied.

"Yes, sometimes you steal. But mostly, you kill things."

I didn't have anything to say to that. Since becoming a vampire, most of my problems had been fixed by lying, stealing, or killing the problem. And I didn't plan to change how I operated just because my son had noticed.

Sir Trent folded his arms. "How many ancient vampires are there in total?"

"Twelve here, but there are sixty-six in total. They're the oldest of the old, and they serve a vampire queen even vampire history has forgotten."

Rupert huffed out a breath. "This is worse than the hellmouth. It could swallow nations."

Sir Trent glanced at Luke.

Luke gave him a grim nod. "I know my duty."

He was saying that he would kill Celest if the vampires caught up to them. I didn't judge him harshly this time. If they caught up to him, there would be no stopping them. A quick, painless death was a mercy. It was also going to be necessary, in order to save other people's lives.

I turned to Rupert. "If, for some reason, we can't re-join you, the moment you get above ground, have all the students head in every direction, scattering in the wind. It's everyone's best chance of surviving."

Rupert nodded back as Gorgath finished explaining the situation, and the other Gor relaxed its posture.

I turned to Angelica. "Get your dracolich. Kathrine and Celest, go with her. Luke and Davina, you're both on foot with me. If you don't have travel rations, find some. You're going to need the energy." I turned to Gregory and tossed him my spare storage pouches containing my loot to ease his concerns, and to let him understand that I intended to return. "Sir Trent sets the pace, but you're in charge of our people. Move quickly, but not so quickly that you get yourselves killed. Everyone who is coming with me, get moving. You have until I get directions from Gorgath to prepare. And Gregory, make sure you keep my loot safe."

28

FOURTH FLOOR OF THE ABYSS

Gorgath knew a shortcut through the fourth floor of the Abyss that would have my children at a foreign dungeon in two hours. It was the shortest possible route to safety, but only if you were crazy and tough enough to survive. I assumed we fit that description.

We did not.

Far above my head, the dracolich flared her wings, dodging the swarm of swordflies rushing towards her. The insects didn't have wings, but they did have bodies shaped like swords and a magical flying ability that made them a nightmare for me to kill. Every time I tried to put a necrotic cloud in their way, they pivoted around it, making turns that were close to right angles, so killing more than a handful at a time was extremely difficult.

If they were our biggest threat, I wouldn't be worried, but the fourth floor of the Abyss was fundamentally different to the floors above it. The ambient mana was so concentrated that every monster had magical abilities. Monsters that could be ignored on higher floors had to be taken seriously down here, and first and second-floor bosses were all too common.

A creature the size of a wolf blurred towards me from my right, unleashing a guttural snarl, only to charge head-first into my deathlock barrier. Its skull shattered, and its brains turned to goop as I continued sprinting through the tunnel ahead of Luke and Davina.

This deep in the Abyss, size and power were the best survival strategies. Flightless monsters that focused on speed were rare, and those that fit that description were never strong. They excelled at stealing food rather than hunting for it themselves, which meant that the safest way to travel was on foot.

Above my head, the swarms of swordflies closed their net around the dracolich, cutting off all avenues of escape. Angelica recognised the danger before her mount and swung her staff at the approaching swarm, releasing a wave of necrotic fire to drive them off and protect Kathrine and Celest.

A wall of black flames burst from the end of her staff, roasting the monsters alive, weakening their exoskeleton, and redirecting their trajectory. Dozens of swordflies missed her passengers because of her swift actions, but it wasn't enough.

Seeing the incoming threat, Kathrine let go of Celest's waist and threw herself over the side of the blood-red saddle, gripping it in one hand so she wouldn't fly off. She tucked her body in behind the dracolich, using its body as a shield.

The surviving insects began colliding with Celest's barrier like cannonballs, causing green bursts of light as they exploded against the intense wall of magical energy she'd summoned. The violent impacts quickly overwhelmed her defensive spell, causing it to fizzle out. As her spell dissolved, a secondary barrier conjured by her robe replaced it.

With a darklord father, Celest's equipment was top-of-the-line, but top-of-the-line wasn't built for the fourth floor of the Abyss. The swordflies' strikes came hard and fast, quickly triggering a failsafe. The barrier shrunk to save her life, only protecting her body and head.

The swordflies flew through Celest's arms, turning those sections into a pink mist of flesh and bone. What was left of the limbs began to fall. Without a connection to her mana, the flesh lost its appeal to the monsters, and they veered off after tastier targets.

Kathrine pulled herself back onto the saddle and tried to wrap an arm around Celest's waist to keep her from falling off. The barrier protecting Celest didn't like that. It released a concussive wave, snapping Kathrine's head back and almost knocking her from the saddle.

This was a dangerous problem.

I telepathically messaged Angelica as I changed directions to collect Celest's missing limbs. "Celest is injured, and her robe is attacking Kathrine. Get her to Davina."

Angelica heard my orders and turned the dracolich, immediately colliding with a dragon-sized, invisible, flying squirrel. The squirrel shimmered in and out of sight as the dracolich began raking her claws across its soft underbelly.

This wasn't the first time this had happened.

Angelica leapt from her saddle, landing on the attacking creature's arm. She was becoming more dangerous with each passing minute as her armour feasted on the ambient mana and life force from the monsters she killed. The fur around the squirrel's arm became visible as Angelica's armour fed upon its life force, and she attacked it with her staff.

We had the bad luck of trying to pass through this section of the Abyss while the local floor bosses marched towards each other. Every monster was on the move, hoping to get a taste of their purer bloodlines. If Gregory was here, he would make a comment about the world above matching the world below.

I blurred to where the pieces of Celest's arms would land and raised my hand. Since we'd entered this floor, I'd saved everyone's life a dozen times over, throwing out master-tier spell after master-tier spell to keep them safe. That wasn't going to change anytime soon, even though my spells were getting stronger.

Mana rushed from my core, weaving a path through my mana network to explode from my fingertips in the form of a destruction spell. The spell disintegrated the head of the second invisible flying squirrel heading for Angelica, killing a monster stronger than a first-floor boss. Too many monsters around here fit that description.

From the tunnel behind us, I heard another deep roar. It belonged to a creature that was a Godzilla-sized plesiosaur with four spider legs rather than flippers. The roar was answered by an even louder hiss from the direction we were heading.

Davina rushed by me, spotting the falling arms. Luke followed to protect her, striking down monster-shaped blurs, leaping at them from every direction. This was a dangerous place to rest and recover, but I had no choice. Celest's robe was an even more dangerous distraction.

I watched Angelica remove the flying squirrel's head by surrounding her staff with necrotic magic and passing it through its neck. She then kicked herself away from the squirrel's limp body, backflipping onto her dracolich's head. She easily clambered down its neck to her saddle as the dracolich released the squirrel and descended.

Another flying monster snatched the dead squirrel out of the air before it reached the tunnel floor, and I threw out more spells to cover their descent.

"You owe me a manicure," the dracolich complained loudly as she flared her wings and crashed into the ground behind me.

My spells exploded above her in black clouds, disintegrating the ravenous swarm of swordflies that had tried to follow her. Angelica turned and tried to grab Celest's blood-soaked, limp body. Her Crypt Keeper armour immediately went to war with Celest's magical robe as the robe tried to protect its wearer. Angelica recognised the danger and shoved Celest from the saddle.

Celest's armless and unconscious body tumbled to the ground with a dull thump, her red hair obscuring her face.

"We need cover," Luke shouted.

We were in a tunnel close to three hundred feet wide and almost one hundred feet from the edge. The only direction we couldn't be attacked from was below.

"I'm on it," I shouted back.

I raised my hand, drawing in a flood of ambient mana from the air around me. I cycled it through my core before weaving it into the seed of a spell. I snapped my fingers, bringing the ocean of death magic together and unleashing it on the world.

A death void appeared to our left, filling the tunnel with a swirling black mass and making an impassable barrier for the weaker monsters. The swirling vortex of darkness would consume all the life force and death magic that entered, growing stronger the longer I kept it in place.

It crackled, floating in the air, growing with each passing second, as I fed it mana. A swarm of diving swordflies turned away from what was now a suicide mission.

Luke grabbed his sister from the saddle, as the death magic washed over them, and pulled her to Davina's side. Davina's ability to absorb death magic made her a natural safe zone. The moment Kathrine was safe, he went back to killing monsters.

Davina didn't look up as she gathered the last of Celest's missing flesh to reform her arms.

I snapped my fingers again.

A second death void appeared to our right, blocking off the other side of the tunnel and consuming most of the turning swarm.

I snapped my fingers a third time, placing another death void behind us. This left us a thirty-meter gap between the three orbs of death where we could hide. I channelled mana into the death voids, growing their destructive power to maintain the temporary safe zone.

The dracolich raised her head and filled the tunnel around us with a massive breath of death fire, injuring or killing the remaining nearby threats.

She then closed her mouth and lifted her front right foot, showing it to Angelica. "Look at my claws. They're a mess." Blood and chunks of flesh fell to the ground as she wiggled them to show the problem.

Angelica leaned forward and stroked the side of the dracolich's neck bones. "They're not that bad, Dee. I'll get them cleaned up when we get to the surface."

"Angie, they're chipped! This is unacceptable. I simply must have a manicure this instant."

I glanced at Davina, checking how much time I had, then blurred to the dracolich. I'd planned to do this somewhere safer, but that didn't seem possible on this floor. "Give me your claws."

The dracolich backed up a step. “Angie, the evil vampire wants to give me a manicure. What do I do?”

Angelica leaned away from me, too. “Do what he says. The last time I tried to compel him, I spent months without free will.”

The dracolich offered me her foot. “You may file, soak, and buff, but only in that order. Right, Angie?”

Luke chuckled.

I took hold of one of her fifteen-inch-long bone claws and cast the first rank bonemeal spell on it, feeding the spell a horrendous amount of mana to overcome her body’s natural resistance. The claw crumbled into bone chips, falling from her skeletal body.

“My claw! Angie, he destroyed my claw. Stop him!”

I didn’t have time for their drama. “Both of you, watch.”

“Angie, he’s making me watch as he defaces my beautiful body.”

Angelica leaned to the side and looked at what I was doing. She raised her visor to see better. “I think he’s trying to help you.”

“By destroying my claw!”

“All of his help involves some sort of trauma.”

“I’m a delicate flower. I won’t survive his help.”

I met the dracolich’s gaze. “Stop being dramatic and pay attention to what I’m about to do to you.”

The dracolich managed to somehow make a gulping sound despite having no throat to swallow. “What are you about to do to me?”

“Watch.”

I broke down the bone powder from the claw using the fifteen ranks of the bonemeal spell and began reforming it with the bone stitch spell, before adding most of the undead enhancements I had taught the Undead Enhancement Club. The ambient mana in the air made it easy to overcharge the spells, and I was finished with my core still full in only a few seconds.

Resting on the ground was an eighteen-inch-long ivory-white claw that radiated undead power and a more intense death aura. I picked up her new claw and placed it against her foot. “Claim it.”

The dracolich reached out to the claw with her aura and claimed it for her body. There was a loud crack as bones slammed together, and the claw began to radiate death magic, projecting a black haze around itself. She turned her head to peer at her foot. When she realised how much I'd improved it, she began dancing from foot to foot excitedly.

"Angie, his manicures are amazing." She shoved her foot at me again. "Do the others."

Angelica frowned. "What did you do?"

I started on the next claw.

It crumbled like the first.

"I'm using undead enhancement spells to strengthen your dracolich. If you want to keep her as your mount, you'll need to start helping her grow stronger to keep up with you."

Angelica's frown became a scowl. "Dee isn't my mount. She's my friend."

"You tell him, Angie!"

"Well, your friend is being left behind. If you don't put in effort, you're going to end up taking her somewhere she'll be killed. Somewhere like where we happen to be right now."

Angelica stiffened, looked around, quickly climbed from her saddle, and walked to my side. "Show me what I need to do."

I hadn't mentioned enhancing the dracolich to Angelica before now because I'd been waiting for her to stumble upon it herself. Enhancing a dracolich was a mana-intensive process that would take years for someone with Angelica's skill. My plan was for Angelica to happily spend her spare time trying to strengthen her dracolich in the hopes of one day escaping from my service. It would have kept her busy while improving her casting skills and mental health.

Now that I was guiding her through the process, she wouldn't be excited or hopeful about any of this. If I was willing to show or teach her something, Angelica took that to mean it wasn't something she could use to escape.

She wasn't wrong about that.

I glanced at Davina again, double-checking how much time I had. She was still repairing Celest's arms. The area the pieces were spread across was slowing her down.

The dracolich needed to grow as strong as I could make her in the limited time I had. That time turned out to be less limited than I originally imagined.

I got to work enhancing the other claws. You couldn't do everything to a naturally sapient dracolich that you could to an undead skeleton, but there were still enough improvements to make a serious difference. Starting with her claws let me know if the dracolich was capable of quickly adapting to these changes without risking her ability to fly if she wasn't.

Getting through the fourth floor with everyone alive was no longer assured, so I wasn't willing to take unnecessary risks.

As the dracolich successfully reclaimed her last claw, I moved on to the wings. Unlike regular dragons, a dracolich didn't need to use magic to fly. They were skin and bone and could stay in the air without magic. That being said, with magic, they could fly faster.

Usually, increasing a dracolich's magical potential was a lengthy process. However, Angelica's dracolich had consumed so many sharn beast cores that she was on her way to becoming a greater dracolich. I wasn't infusing her with magic. I was allowing her to tap into the magical potential she already had.

The changes I was making would allow her to fly faster, further, and more easily. They would also make all her bones significantly stronger, helping her deal with the weight of extra people. These changes were changes a dracolich typically made to themselves.

The only reason she wasn't a greater dracolich already was that she seemed to have Angelica's work ethic. If someone didn't force her to learn to cast spells, it was unlikely she would ever learn how to do so herself, leaving her horrendously large supply of mana unused.

Even as I explained what I was doing to Angelica, I could tell the dracolich hadn't put that together. She was still preening over her claws when I finished working on her wings and started on her vertebrae.

I was almost to the tip of her tail when I sensed a change in Celest's condition through our bond. I finished the last few bones to stabilise the enhancements and then blurred to Davina's side. She was kneeling beside Celest, contending with her robe, as she reattached Celest's arms.

Davina didn't look up. "Do you want me to wake her, your Dark Eminence?"

The tunnel began to shake with the fast, even rhythm of heavy footsteps. We needed to hurry up.

"Yes."

Davina placed her hand above Celest's forehead, and the girl's eyes shot open. Pain flashed across her face as injuries made themselves known.

Celest was manipulating me into keeping her alive, endangering my children. It was hard for me to find reasons to be merciful to her. Right now, her weakness was slowing us down.

"Celest, immediately increase your attributes, using the kingmaker distribution." I shared the correct distribution in case she didn't know or couldn't remember them.

Pain turned to horror as my compulsion took over her body and forced her to do as I said. "No. No. No. Please take that back. No. No. No."

"Tell me when you've done as I commanded."

"It's done," she said a few seconds later, looking ill.

"From now until we leave the Abyss, you will spend your attributes the moment you gain more with this ratio: Four to agility, two to endurance, constitution, and mana regeneration, and one to strength, dexterity, and recovery. Spend the rest of your attributes using this ratio."

This time, Celest was so horrified she couldn't speak.

"I've never heard of that ratio," Davina said.

"It's a survivalist build. Nothing will be able to hit her, but she'll never be more than a mediocre warrior for her level, no matter how hard she trains."

I felt Celest's aura grow stronger as she increased her attributes. She was an archsorcerer, and like Carolyn, she'd been one since she was level 20, so when her aura finished growing stronger, I put her level at somewhere around 150. The fourth floor was as good for leveling as I thought it would be.

"Turn off your robe's defences so Davina can heal you."

Celest spoke a command word, and the barrier around her vanished.

Davina placed her hand on Celest's forehead, and her flesh finished flowing together, reforming without scars. The pain in her eye vanished as Davina began casting buffing spells. Gaining this many physical attributes at once would leave her bedridden for a week, but we couldn't let her pass out until we reached the surface. It would lengthen her recovery time, but that was fine.

The shaking in the tunnel grew stronger.

Davina nodded to Angelica while she continued to buff Celest. "You're worried about her."

"No. I'm worried about her armour. It's growing faster than armour typically should."

Davina frowned. "How much faster?"

"It's like she's had it for decades. It's developed a vampiric aura and is feeding off the ambient mana and life force of the monsters she's killing."

"Isn't that a good thing?"

"No. Fast growth is almost always unstable."

"I don't sense any instability."

"That's the part that worries me. I don't sense it either." Dozens of third-floor boss auras suddenly flared to my right, appearing out of the fourth-floor boss's aura. "Everyone get on the dracolich and to the ceiling!"

29

KILL STEALING TO GREATNESS

Davina didn't wait for clarification. She snatched Celest off the ground so fast that the whiplash would've killed her if she hadn't taken the kingmaker distribution and raised her attributes. Luke did the same for his sister as Angelica leapt onto her dracolich's saddle, shouting instructions. The five of them were ready to fly before I finished my sentence, reacting to the panic in my words rather than the words themselves.

The aura of the approaching monster made Gorgath's feel small. No spell was designed to confront that much mass or momentum, so I threw out deathlock barriers, bunching them together to make a wall. The appearance of the first barrier showed Angelica and Davina that the threat was coming from directly behind them, and they reacted appropriately.

Angelica continued to shout commands, turning the dracolich's head towards me before making her crouch in preparation for springing into the air. Davina kept her gaze locked over her shoulder with her hand raised, conjuring additional barriers beside the ones I'd created. The dracolich then leapt towards me, rising fifteen feet high and crossing the gap between us.

Wind from their passage ruffled my hair as the tip of her nose passed above my head, and a sixty-foot-wide python with scales resembling cracked rock exploded through the death void behind them. The behemoth ignored my master-tier spell like it wasn't even there before crashing through all our expert-tier barriers. The barriers barely slowed the creature as its size and momentum easily overwhelmed our spells.

Above my head, the dracolich was beating her wings twice as fast as she previously could, throwing her passengers skyward with impressive speed. But it wasn't fast enough, and we all knew it. The python was gaining on them.

As the others threw out spells to slow it down, Celest's hand darted into her storage pouch and emerged, holding a greater barrier scroll case.

Celest locked her gaze onto me, and her hand shot in my direction. "Catch!"

Due to her new strength and agility, the wooden tub cracked as it left her fingers and shattered as I caught it. Shards of wood bounced off my coat as I unrolled the scroll and lifted it towards the dracolich, feeding mana through the activation sequence. The power trapped inside the scroll exploded from the parchment, forming an expanding magical bubble above me and below the fleeing dracolich.

Celest probably thought I could use the greater barrier to stop the python, but, after seeing it blow through my barriers, I wasn't sure that even a greater barrier could stop it. I also wasn't willing to risk it not working when I knew the barrier could be used to throw the dracolich and her passengers out of harm's way.

The expanding barrier caught the dracolich's feet, violently throwing them skyward with explosive force right before the other side of the barrier collided with the top of my head. The barrier had gone from the size of my fist to eighty feet across in the blink of an eye, so I didn't have time to get out of the way before it crushed me like an empty beer can.

BETWEEN THE BARRIER pulverising me into the tunnel floor, the sixty-foot-wide python then smearing me across that exact same floor, and whatever else squashed me while I was mush, I was out of the fight for over a minute. A minute is a long time when you're on the fourth floor of the Abyss.

I came back to myself only after the mind-numbing pain of being pulverised was replaced by the simple agony of having every muscle and bone in my body broken. But I wasn't concerned about anything until my ability to sense my familiars returned. They were over a mile away from me. That told me two things: My children were safe, but only as long as the dracolich kept ahead of whatever was chasing her. There was no other reason for her to have gone so far back the way we came, which meant they needed help, and they needed help *fast*.

The massive python slithering over me had squeezed me out of my equipment like human toothpaste, so I was naked, unarmed, and lying on the ground in the middle of a monster stampede. It was not the best place to be, but Slaughter and my Day Walker set were scattered around me, waiting to be picked up.

The changes I'd recently made to my soul stopped my discovery of what it felt like to be transformed into hamburger meat from being a much bigger problem. My body had also somehow healed my mana network and core. Now wasn't the time to work out how that had happened. I'd do that when my children were safe.

Before I could finish healing, another gigantic monster stepped on my legs, returning them to a meaty goo. I ignored the pain as I drew in the ambient mana and pushed it into my empty core. The raw mana then passed through my mana network and exploded from my hand as a sphere of destruction. I placed the spell below my feet, in the path of the stampede, giving my body the few seconds it needed to reform.

On the surface, against humans, magic was a liability that could cost me my soul. Down here, it was the greatest asset I had. I needed to use it.

My extensive injuries had drained me of life force, and for the first time in months, hunger clawed at the back of my throat. I leapt to my feet, drawing in more mana, before blurring through the mass of bodies towards Slaughter. I scooped up my kilij, drew it from its sheath, and decapitated the nearest monster, feeding on its life force. The creature crumbled to dust as life force rushed into me, satiating the worst of my hunger. It wasn't the same as human life force, but it would feed me if I had enough.

I threw out spells and decapitated other monsters as I retrieved the rest of my equipment. In only a few moments, I was armed, equipped, and ready to save my children.

I took off, racing through the tunnel, sidestepping monsters or cutting them down with magic, whichever was faster. After ten seconds, I approached a bend in the tunnel where I could sense the fourth-floor bosses.

They'd reached each other.

The only reason they caught my attention was that I'd have to bring my children back through their fight. Depending on their abilities, that could be impossible. I dashed around the corner and leapt onto the back of a large nearby monster that looked like a warthog to get a better view.

Dead and injured pythons, like the one that had crushed me, filled the tunnel as dozens of others fought the spider-legged plesiosaur. The beast filled the three-hundred-foot-tall tunnel, towering over its opponents as it slammed its pointed feet through their stone scales with impressive precision.

A magical barrier surrounded the plesiosaur, protecting it from the crushing strength of the pythons wrapped around its body, neck, and legs. Both sides seemed to rely on defence, which was all the information I could gather in the time it took me to pass them.

It took me another minute to catch up with my children, and by then, the dracolich had travelled a few more miles in the wrong direction. The reason for fleeing was immediately obvious.

The dracolich was being chased by a murder of gigantic three-eyed crows. Hundreds of these dragon-sized crows flew in a tight formation, blocking the tunnel, and stopped the dracolich from being able to return the way it had come. They weren't faster or stronger than the dracolich, but there were enough of them that being mobbed was the only outcome if they tried to fight their way back through them.

If the crows were the only threat they had to deal with, they would have overcome it, but the need to flee kept pushing them towards other monsters, forcing Davina and Angelica to focus on the threat in front of them. Luke was standing on the dracolich's back with his sword drawn, cutting down swordflies while Kathrine and Celest threw out barriers and dodged.

My familiars sensed my approach and were ready when I caught up. The dracolich finished her dive and beat her wings, beginning a loop-de-loop. When she was upside down, she flipped her body right way up. This left her facing the opposite direction and the murder of crows.

I snapped my fingers, disintegrating the nearest crow's head with a destruction spell. Davina unleashed her own destruction spell on the next closest. I took out the third, fourth, fifth, and sixth.

The human body wasn't built to harness magic the way I could. Davina's spells were stronger than mine, but she wasn't as fast at casting, and she never would be. When one mistake meant certain death, you weren't willing to make mistakes.

Davina took out the seventh crow as I opened a path for their escape. Headless crows fell from the air, drawing attention. Crows began descending on their dead allies, ignoring the dracolich. By the time they were through the murder, we'd left enough fresh meat behind them that they weren't being followed.

The easy part was done.

Now, I had to get them past the fourth-floor bosses.

DAVINA WATCHED the ongoing battle between the fourth-floor bosses from atop a dead monster. We were a quarter mile from the main battle, and I couldn't find anything stronger than a first-floor boss nearby. Those were the sort of threats Angelica, Davina, Luke and the dracolich could deal with, and the four of them were easily holding the line.

All the python corpses had drawn the stronger monsters away from us like moths to a flame. They were tearing each other apart for a chance to feed on the third-floor bosses.

"You could try repeatedly casting the weaken spell on it," Davina suggested as she disintegrated a monster that had come too close. "It should shorten the battle."

I shot a finger of destruction through another nearby monster. "Without significant injuries, I doubt my spells will affect a fourth-floor boss."

Third-floor bosses could resist my magic. I was almost certain fourth-floor bosses could shrug it off. In the distance, the number of dead and injured pythons continued to increase without the battle slowing. There were now more pythons wrapped around the gigantic plesiosaur, restricting its range of movement and stopping it from being able to bite.

It was throwing its body against the tunnel walls to break them off. Its speed and strength made trying to pass it too dangerous. If the dracolich got caught between them and a wall, she would be turned to powder, and my children would become flesh smears.

"So, we're stuck here until they stop fighting," Luke said.

"Or until the way they fight changes," I said.

"How long will that take?" Angelica asked.

"Too long to stand here doing nothing," I said, looking towards the fight.

The first time I ran through, a python caught my attention. It had been impaled near the top of its spine, leaving the creature completely helpless. Its current state offered a unique opportunity.

"Stay here," I said before blurring through the battlefield.

As I passed a dead python, I fired a finger of destruction. The beam burned through the corpse with surprising ease, telling me they were only resistant to my spells when they were alive and healthy.

I kept going.

When I reached the dying one that had caught my attention, I fired a second finger of destruction to test its defences. The beam fizzled along its stone-like scales, burning away the material, but much slower than when I used it on the corpse.

It was the same as the bosses I'd encountered on the third floor. Offensive magic worked, but it would take time. Time was something I didn't have, but the severity of its injuries meant I had one more option to try.

I blurred to the beast's gigantic exposed spinal cord and jammed my hand into the spinal fluids, casting a powerful death spell.

Weaken was a debuff spell developed for fighting large monsters resistant to magic or armies. It corrupted flesh instead of destroying it, slowing down healthy opponents and speeding up the death of injured ones. The only reason it wasn't lethal was that necromancers rarely had the mana necessary to cast it enough times to kill something.

Green and black magic flowed from my fingers into the spinal cord, causing the fluids to take on a sickly pale tone as the spell spread through its body. With each additional casting, the python's flesh withered, weakening its body further. It took more than a dozen casts to make a noticeable difference, but once it did, the effects became obvious.

Despite being impaled and subjected to dozens of master-tier spells, the python still took half a minute to die. Third-floor bosses weren't something humans and vampires were supposed to be able to fight.

The moment it died, I leapt out of its wound and sent a telepathic message to Kathrine as I blurred to my next target. "Kill something and signal me with fire when you level. Flash once for each level you gain."

I found another torn-in-half python and blurred to its wound through the cacophony of monsters tearing each other apart. It was almost dead when there was a huge burst of fire from the back of the dracolich. I wasn't sure how effective finishing off these bosses would be. The floor boss had done most of the damage to them, and I didn't know how the experience would be shared. It turned out I didn't have to worry.

Kathrine released eleven flashes.

She'd gained eleven levels.

I'd found a way to improve my children's survival odds.

As the second python died, there were ten more flashes. I blurred to my next target and the next, finishing six more off as I worked my way down the list of the most-injured. There was a fundamental shift in how effective my weaken spell was when I reached my eighth target, and after casting the spell a dozen times, I knew it would take me ten minutes to kill the creature.

There were better uses of my time.

I headed back to my children, blurring through the fighting monsters. This time, when I got close, my instincts warned me I was approaching dire threats. Based on what I felt, my familiars were over level 200, and my children were well beyond that.

My instincts said that in a real fight, I only stood a chance at overpowering Celest and Kathrine. They didn't feel like a threat, but they also didn't feel like prey. My instincts told me that I could still kill them all, but I'd never be able catch them if they ran.

I ignored my instincts as I blurred past Luke and stopped beside the dracolich. Her head whipped towards me, and she held out her front foot, offering her claws for more work. I pushed her foot away as I cast a finger of destruction on the monster she was fighting.

The dracolich glanced at the dead monster before backing away from the frontline and turning to Angelica. "Angie, make the vampire give me another manicure."

Angelica glanced in my direction as she fought. I saw the calculations going on behind her eyes. She knew she was stronger and was trying to figure out if she could take me. Fear ultimately won. "You just had a manicure."

"And it was amazing. It changed my life. I need another one."

"Let him finish enhancing you first."

The dracolich turned to me. "You didn't finish?"

Luke snickered.

"I've still got your legs and ribs to do."

"But I'm so much faster."

"Imagine how fast you will be when I'm done."

She pouted. "Fine. Enhancement first. Manicure second."

I got to work.

"Any chance we'll see more levels?" Luke shouted.

I continued enhancing the dracolich's rib as I replied. "Not unless it leaves another python at death's door."

"If that's the case, we should hang around when we get to the other side."

It was easy to see how he came to that conclusion. "We can't. Each additional minute we take increases Angelica and Davina's chances of succumbing to mana sickness before we get the survivors to safety. They can safely survive three hours on the fourth floor and twelve hours on the third floor before getting sick, but this shortcut requires us to be on the fourth floor for over an hour to get you to the dungeon."

"So, what you're saying is that if you see a few injured ones when we pass, you'll double back and kill them, but if you don't see anything, we're moving on as fast as we can."

I finished enhancing the dracolich's ribs and moved on to her legs. "Precisely. Now, pay a little more attention to what you're doing. I can tell that your timing is off, and I shouldn't be able to do that."

Luke and Kathrine were past being Old Monsters and well into Dragon territory. If they had earned their levels, they would have been incredibly dangerous, but they hadn't. I put Luke's capabilities somewhere in the middle of the two titles, despite him having significantly more attributes than a typical Dragon. Kathrine was only slightly more dangerous than an Old Monster.

Luke gave another ill-timed slash. "I'm sorry, but some of us can't adapt to gaining fifty levels in a few minutes."

"And yet you still want more levels."

Luke laughed.

Our conversation ended as hundreds of lightning-fast scavengers rushed through the chaos. Luke and Angelica peeled off to engage them before they threatened Celest or Kathrine.

In the distance, past the sea of fighting monsters, the plesiosaur thrashed its body from side to side, stopping any chance of getting by. I kept working. The changes I was making to the dracolich were less important than the ones I'd already made but would give her more strength and endurance.

While I was working, Kathrine approached me from behind and I absently evaluated what she'd done with her attributes.

Today's events had frightened her into action.

She'd doubled down on speed and precision and now had more agility than her brother. She didn't have his strength or constitution, but she was more dexterous with higher mana regeneration and endurance.

She was reacting out of fear, but her choices weren't wrong. If you were afraid of being caught, it was wise to invest in agility and dexterity. Confidence was key in combat. Fear would cripple you, leaving you useless. You needed advantages that made you feel safe, and for Kathrine, that was being untouchable.

She stopped behind me. "Can we talk?"

"Always."

"You sure you're not busy?"

I glanced over my shoulder and smiled. "Not with anything important."

The dracolich turned and glared at me while I enhanced her leg. "Rude."

I ignored her. "What did you want to talk about?"

Kathrine didn't reply at first. Then, in a small voice, she whispered, "I saw the barrier crush you."

"I'm sorry if that upset you."

I could smell her shock. It had been a traumatic experience for her.

"You're what?"

"I'm sorry that upset you, but it was the best way to ensure that you and Luke survived."

This was the first time she'd ever seen me seriously injured, if you didn't count the day that she summoned me. Understanding that I was nearly indestructible and seeing it for yourself were different.

Luke coped with it by making jokes.

"Did it hurt?"

"Do you know a painless way of becoming minced meat?"

My joke fell flat, but she pushed forward with her thoughts. “Why didn’t you hesitate?”

“Why would I hesitate?”

“Everyone would hesitate. You experienced what it’s like to die.”

“No, they wouldn’t.”

“I’d hesitate.”

“You think you would, but you wouldn’t.”

“I froze when that vampire kicked in my door. I could hear the screams, and I thought I was ready to stop it, but the moment it came through my door, I froze.”

“I’m sure you did, but it's not the same. You think it is, but it isn’t.”

“How’s it different?”

“I can’t explain it to you, but one day, when you have kids, you’ll understand that pain isn’t something that makes you hesitate when your children’s safety is involved. You’ll happily march through fire for them without ever requiring a word of thanks. It’s what being a parent means, and the last time I checked, you were still my daughter. So, there was no reason for me to hesitate.”

She dropped her gaze. “Most days, I don’t know how I feel about you, but seeing you crushed to a pulp hurt me. It wasn’t the pain of losing you. I knew you were coming back. It was the sort of pain you feel when someone you care about is in pain.” She lifted her gaze and smiled at me. “Apparently, you’re someone I care about.”

She turned and walked back to Celest.

A single happy tear rolled down my cheek.

30

GOODBYE FOR NOW

Gorgath's people resided in the Abyss, so his directions ended at the base of the tunnel leading to our dungeon exit. His people didn't know what lay above the Abyss, and because of the thin ambient mana, they weren't particularly interested in finding out. But Gorgath promised there was a path to the surface. His people could smell that much.

After reaching the top of the tunnel, the lack of directions and human scent led me down several dead ends before we crossed paths with an old human trail. Those detours cost us ten minutes, but once I had a scent, I easily followed it back to the dungeon fortress.

Fortress alarms bleared as I stepped out of the Deadlands on the gatehouse wall. The teacher in charge of defending the fortress jumped in surprise. Dungeon academies had similar layouts and regulations, so it was easy to find him. The old man was in his nineties, but his second in command was barely twenty. The pair took three steps back as they raised their hands before them, conjuring balls of fire.

"Stand down," I snapped in my best teaching voice.

"Who are you?" the teacher snapped back before glancing over the wall.

It was understandable that he considered me his second biggest problem. A dracolich flying towards your fortresses is a terrifying experience. A dracolich flying towards your fortress from inside your dungeon is much worse.

"I'm Professor Vincent of Darksmith Academy, and I'm escorting a VIP student to safety."

Again, he glanced at the dracolich hurtling towards his fortress. "How did you get here?"

"Through the Abyss. Now, order your people to stand down."

He glanced at the dracolich again, noticed the two people keeping up with it on foot, and then did the math on what level they had to be to do that.

He wisely decided to do as he was told and turned to his second in command. "Tell everyone to stand down."

"Yes, sir," his second in command replied before they both ran off in opposite directions, shouting instructions.

A few seconds later, the alarm stopped.

I smiled as I turned and watched my children.

The chaos from the fourth-floor territorial dispute had slowed us down more than anything else on the fourth floor, but it wasn't the most dangerous part of our journey. Those territories were so stirred up that ambush and stealth predators had hunkered down, waiting for the chaos to settle. After we got beyond the python's chamber, we began running into hidden threats.

I'd quickly learned my agility couldn't keep up. One second, I would be racing ahead of Luke and Davina, clearing the way, and the next, I'd be in someone's mouth. They'd chew on me a few times before swallowing, and then I'd regenerate inside their stomach and have to cut my way out. This cost us more time, and the dracolich went from being our biggest liability to the safest option. At least, we saw most threats coming when they went after her.

Surviving the fourth floor was a serious accomplishment. On any other day I would celebrate, taking my children somewhere nice to congratulate them on their success. But not today. Today we had to run. All I could do was be proud of my children for making it through alive and hope I got a chance to show them that on another occasion.

Luke leapt as he approached the fortress wall, casting a basic levitation spell to get more lift. He sailed through the air before landing on the wall beside me. He was never going to be a sorcerer, but he'd found numerous ways to use magic to make him stronger.

At the same time, the dracolich flared her wings to slow her speed. She collided with the wall, ignoring the startled students, knocking several over as she leapt into the courtyard before galloping for the gate.

"We're going to lose time," Luke said, noticing her inability to fly as she folded her wings to squeeze into the gate tunnel.

"It can't be helped," I replied, stepping off the wall.

I dropped to the ground and dashed through the courtyard after the dracolich. Luke landed a second later and caught up.

"Do you know where we are?" Luke asked.

I pointed to the crest above the gate. "That crest belongs to South Murdell's Soon Academy. We're about sixty miles from the border and twice that from Darksmith."

Luke glanced back as we entered the tunnel. "Did you tell them what's coming?"

I shook my head. "Abandoning the fortress and clearing the tunnel isn't an order anyone here can give. But a dracolich racing through your tunnel isn't something an academy can ignore, either. There'll be someone to warn on our way back."

Up ahead, the dracolich ran over a student, taking my instructions not to slow for any reason to heart. Kathrine leapt off the dracolich's back and raced ahead to pull people out of the way to save them from being trampled. The poor student Luke and I jumped over had several broken bones, but Davina would have the girl back on her feet when she finished treating those knocked off the wall.

Luke pulled some jerky from his storage pouch and lifted his visor to shove it into his mouth. Despite eating on the go, he'd lost several pounds during our journey. I could smell his fatigue. The moment he stopped running, he would crash.

He offered me a piece of jerky, and I took it, chewing on it as I jogged behind the dracolich. Luke swallowed his mouthful and washed it down with water gathered from a spell.

Luke turned to me. "What's the plan?"

"When we reach the surface, you and your sister will climb on the dracolich and fly Celest to the Fortress Cathedral of Urk. Once you get there, you will convince them to give you sanctuary."

"That's the same plan as before."

"The plan hasn't changed."

"We're stronger."

"And if you knew how to wield that strength, the plan might be different. But you don't, so the three of you need sanctuary."

"I don't need protection?"

He did, but I wasn't going to point that out. "Without a divine warning, the church won't take the threat coming after you seriously unless the fortress is attacked. You need to train your sister and babysit Celest until that happens."

"And if they're warned?"

"Nothing changes. You and your sister still have to learn to harness your new abilities and skills. You've both got targets on your back, and it won't be safe to leave the fortress until you can stare down an ancient vampire without flinching."

"You overestimate our abilities."

Without warning, I turned, drew Slaughter, and swung at Luke's head, doing my best to kill him. He dodged my blade so fast I could barely follow, stepping back to put the wall behind him. I slid Slaughter back into its sheath as we both came to a stop and stared at each other.

He gripped his pommel. "What the fuck was that?"

I looked him in the eye as the dracolich raced off. "That was my best sucker punch, and you just dodged it like I was an angry toddler."

Luke stopped glaring, but his hand didn't leave his pommel. "That was your best shot?"

I nodded.

"Your swing looked telegraphed."

"Only because you're not used to your agility."

He huffed out a breath and pulled his hand from his pommel. “You’re right. I *do* need to train.”

“Seeing is believing.”

“Why do you want me to train Kathrine? She’s a practitioner, not a fighter.”

“She *was* a practitioner. That changed when she reacted out of fear and distributed her attributes like a duellist.”

Luke winced. “That was a mistake. Every leader she meets will think she’s an assassin.”

I snorted. “There isn’t a ruler alive who would let either of you inside their capital, let alone their palace walls, so I don’t think you need to be concerned about anyone thinking she’s an assassin.”

Old Monsters were a dime a dozen outside Arcadia, but Dragons, those with attributes above 3000, were much rarer. They were one-man armies. Luke and Kathrine lacked the lifetime of training to be true Dragons, but their attributes were now so much higher than the minimum that no one would view them as anything less.

“I didn’t even consider that.”

“That’s because you need time to get used to the changes.”

“I heard you the first time. Are you going to collect us when it's safe?”

I shook my head. “Ancient Vampires are most dangerous when they feel threatened, remember. I don’t want to give them that impression. You need to leave when you’re ready, because I’ll be doing everything I can to distance myself from what happened at Darksmith.”

“Will they still want Celest? I thought someone with an aura couldn’t be turned.”

“There are ways of syphoning off experience and reducing someone’s level. Vampires don’t usually bother with those methods, but they’ll go through the trouble for her.”

“Then they’ll still come after you for making Celest your familiar.”

“They’ll prioritise capturing her. Once they have her, they can use her to find me.”

“Doesn’t that make you a threat?”

“No. They’ll only consider me a threat if I’m actively hunting them. I'll do everything I can to show them I'm not interested in doing that."

We exited the fortress and entered the main tunnel to the surface. The tunnel was much narrower than other tunnels I'd seen, so there wasn't enough room for the dracolich to fly, forcing us all to move at a much slower pace.

"I don't think they'll buy it," Luke said. "You're running off with their prize."

"That's not how vampires think. To them, my prize is back with the other survivors, so it makes perfect sense for me to send them on a wild goose chase after their prize. As far as they're concerned, making Celest my familiar is just me being spiteful."

"Are you sure?"

"You have to look at it from their perspective. When they arrived, I'd been at Darksmith for months. The people I had the most contact with were a group of talented young necromancers. These are the kind of people ancient vampires typically use as minions. These are also the sons and daughters of some of the most influential necromancer families in Murdell. From their perspective, I was attempting to influence the next generation of Necropolis and bring the city under my control."

"And then they barged in."

"And almost killed me, so now I'm running away and trying to salvage as much of my efforts as I can."

"Those are surface-level assumptions."

"The Curse of Sloth will make it hard for them to do more than surface-level examinations, and they're in a hurry, so they'll interpret my actions as defensive."

"What if you're wrong?"

Luke didn't sound happy.

"If it looks like a duck, quacks like a duck, and waddles like a duck, it's safe to assume it's a duck. They won't treat me as anything other than an ancient vampire until I prove otherwise. And an ancient vampire isn't a threat to them. It's not a threat because it will always be willing to negotiate for something as trivial as a familiar's life. If I escape, they'll approach me politely, like I approached Contessa."

"You approached Contessa politely so you could backstab her."

"And I'll allow them to approach me just as politely so I can backstab them, too."

Luke laughed. "So, get to the fortress, train Kathrine, and come find you when we're tough enough to protect ourselves. How do we do that last one?"

"Use the dracolich to find Angelica. I won't be far away."

"How am I supposed to convince the church to give sanctuary to a dracolich?"

"Claim she's your noble steed or an emotional support dracolich."

"I'll think of something better than that."

"Suit yourself."

Luke glanced at me. "Are you going to make it out of this one?"

I was hoping he wouldn't ask this. "I'm going to try."

"You don't sound confident."

"We have a better chance against four than eight, but it's still not a good chance."

"You said there was a chance that they would all follow us."

"The odds were never in favour of that."

"Why go back, then?"

"Because your sister needs me to, because it's the right thing to do, and because the survivors have a chance if I do. It's not a pointless endeavour."

"You'll abandon them if it becomes hopeless, right?"

"I'm not going down with the ship."

"Good. Because we need you. We can't face this threat alone."

One day, my children would make a very good team. Kathrine was too idealistic, and Luke was too pragmatic. They were going to butt heads a lot until they found a balance, but once they did, they would be a force of good. They needed time for that to happen. Time they didn't have.

An army of vampires was a threat that could end the world.

Multiple cataclysms were working together, and my children weren't mentally or physically ready to face that.

"I can't promise you I'll get out of this," I told him honestly. "But I promise you I'll try my best."

"You better. But if you don't make it, can you leave me instructions for what you think I should do?"

That was a very practical suggestion.

"I can do that if you have a blank book I can borrow."

"Why do you need to borrow a book?"

"My remaining storage pouches need to be repaired."

"You have two of them."

"And they both got crushed under the weight of multiple third-floor bosses. If I try to open them before they're repaired, they'll exploded and destroy what's inside."

"Fine." He reached into his storage pouch and retrieved his journal and a pen. "I need you to promise you're not going to fill my journal with love hearts, the princess's name, or other weird shit. Only instructions."

I chuckled because that was exactly what I'd been planning to do from the moment I saw it. "I promise I'll only write instructions."

Luke reluctantly passed me his journal.

"I'll catch up in a few minutes."

Luke nodded that he'd heard, before turning to run after the others.

A smile tugged at my lips as I opened his diary and began writing a step-by-step guide for producing grandchildren.

CELEST WAS the last problem I had to solve before I sent my children to safety. Being able to trust her was paramount but compelling my familiars to serve me faithfully while letting them maintain their free will and independence was a delicate balance that required days of focused effort. I didn't have enough time to do that, so I stripped her of many of her freedoms, locking her up as tightly as Angelica when we visited Contessa.

When I finished my string of commands, Kathrine made her displeasure known. "Was that—"

I didn't have enough time to allow her to finish her question as I jogged beside them. "It's necessary, Sweetheart. She's a seer and the Darklord's daughter. She might not be her father's daughter, but I don't know that, and I can't take the risk that she is."

"You could—"

"I don't have enough time to learn the difference. Letting her live puts hundreds of millions of people at risk, so this is the compromise. Her freedom for her life. I'll return and fix this later, but nothing you say will change what's happening."

"What if you can't?"

"Then she'll have to wait. In ten years, my ability to compel her will fade, and she'll have her freedom back."

Kathrine pressed her lips together as we exited the tunnel into an open square. She didn't like my answer but knew we had run out of time to discuss the matter.

Luke had several dozen bruised and unconscious guards lying in rows, so they didn't interfere. They were students, so they hadn't put up much of a fight, but there were more than you would usually see.

The people in the surrounding buildings were all awake and talking about a bright light, loud noise, and the magical pressure they'd felt. People were checking their equipment and discussing what they would do if this were the first strike of a new war. I counted the heartbeats and positions of everyone nearby. No one knew we were here, though everyone knew about the spell Gorgath had unleashed.

The city was on high alert.

Angelica stroked her dracolich's neck one last time and then jumped from her saddle to take over from Luke. He nodded his thanks before blurring to my side and engulfing me in a hug.

"I love you," he said.

"I love you, too," I replied, knowing we didn't have time for this, while hugging him back. "Look after your sister for me, and teach her how to look after herself."

"I will. Try to let this not be the last time we see each other."

"I will."

I gently pushed him away. We were wasting time. He got the message without me needing to say anything and took his place up front. The dracolich would only let her friends hold the reins, and that was a short list that included Angelica, Luke, and a deathlord named Burt.

I turned to Kathrine as Luke picked up the reigns. "I love you, Sweetheart."

Kathrine smiled but didn't say it back. I might have been someone she cared about, but I wasn't someone she loved yet. She was still on guard, but saving her from a monster who would have killed her had done a lot to repair our relationship.

Luke turned and gave me a cheesy grin as he shouted. "Fly, Delilah. Show me the meaning of haste."

I snorted at his stolen line as the dracolich did a thirty-foot vertical jump and then beat her wings, launching the four of them into the air. Each stroke took them higher and higher as the sorcerers guarding rooftops began throwing orbs of light at the dark blur passing by. The dracolich turned south as the lights approached and accelerated, racing ahead of the spells to remain in the shadow.

I waved goodbye as my children fled to safety, watching them grow smaller as the distance grew larger. Before they were out of sight, they had reached speeds that ensured nothing would catch up to them. The dracolich was much stronger and faster than when we set off, and I was no longer concerned the vampires would catch them. I'd given them enough of a lead.

I watched as they faded into the distance, giving Davina the time she needed to heal the injured guards and put them to sleep.

Angelica walked over, smelling of fear, and squinted in the direction I was looking. "I won't be able to keep Davina alive like Luke. You better have a different route for the return journey."

"The fourth floor was a shortcut to buy them extra time to get away. We're going back through the first and second floors."

Angelica's fear was replaced by panic. The thought of returning to the Abyss, even a safer part of the Abyss, was too much for her. "I'm used to you taking me to insane places, but that was insane even for you. Those invisible flying squirrels were the size of Dee and were not the serious threats."

I continued to watch my children fade into the distance. "Davina, cast calm on Angelica. She's panicking."

A white glow enveloped Angelica.

Her panic was replaced by a wave of deep calm, which immediately began to fade. The spell was essentially an emotional reset, which helped prevent people from spiralling.

I turned to Angelica. "You good?"

She shook her head. "I don't think I'll ever be good again. That was horrible. And you made me go through it to escape something worse. And now you want us to go back and face that, too."

"The survivors won't make it through the third floor without us."

She scoffed. "They might not make it through *with* us. Give me one good reason to go."

"I'll clear your debt."

Angelica lifted her visor and grinned. "All of it?"

"All of it."

She turned to Davina. "How's he tricking me?"

Davina placed her hand against an unconscious guard's forehead and cast her spell. "Delilah is taking his Dark Eminence's children to safety. He's now happy that he let you feed her those cores, and he's morally obligated to release you from the debt."

I scowled at Davina.

She smiled in return.

"I want another one of those cores Dee consumed to help save the survivors," Angelica replied. "And another one for any ancient vampire I help kill, along with the first choice of loot."

"Over my dead body." She was being ridiculous. "You won't be getting the first choice of loot—or any loot. I'll give you a core to help save the survivors, but you must use it to improve your core. However, any core you receive for helping to kill an ancient vampire can be sold."

Angelica scowled and gave her counteroffer.

We went back and forth several times and were still negotiating terms when the archsorcerers from the Soon Academy came flying up the tunnel toward us.

Angelica took a defensive stance behind me as I turned to greet our guests. "A thirty-day holiday, the gold equivalent of my share of the loot, and a core for every ancient vampire I help you kill," she muttered.

"Twenty-five days, and if you help kill more than one, you can't take the holidays back-to-back, and the gold for your share of the loot," I countered as Davina joined us.

"Deal."

I reached behind me, and we shook on it.

My instincts warned me that the elderly woman flying at the front of the formation was a serious threat. The rest were minor annoyances. Their formation broke apart as they approached before flying past to surround us.

No one threw any spells, but I could smell their fear. They knew how we'd reached them.

A younger man with a wispy beard landed beside the guards and checked them over. "They're asleep," he yelled. "There are no signs of physical harm. They've been healed like the others."

He rose and walked towards me.

"You're not the one in charge," I said.

"But I am the negotiator," he replied. "Now, why did you come here, and where is the dracolich?"

Talking with him was pointless, so I held out my arms. "Show them what they're dealing with."

Angelica smelled happy as she wrapped her staff with death fire and brought it down on the wrist, delivering a necrotic strike and cutting my hand off. The hand reattached itself as Davina engulfed me with a powerful holy spell.

The young man took several quick steps back, throwing out a barrier to protect himself from an attack that didn't come.

I raised my voice, turned to the only threat in the group, and showed the elderly woman my fangs. "I am the Vampire Vincent."

She knew better than to meet my gaze, choosing to look over my head. "We have no quarrel with you, vampire."

"And I have none with you. But as many as eight ancient vampires are chasing the individuals who fled on the dracolich. You, your students, and your city are not their targets, but anyone in their way will die, so I suggest you get out of their way."

I started walking towards the tunnel.

Davina and Angelica followed me.

"What are you doing?"

"My familiars and I are returning to the Abyss. It is the only safe way to travel tonight. Your country is crawling with vampires. I suggest you sound the alarm."

31

A CHILD NO MORE

I'm a better man with my children around. The demonic part of me has no time for kindness or compassion, but my love for my children and my wish to see them happy allows me to exhibit my more-human characteristics. They make it easier for me to do what's right. They make it easier for me not to use people as tools. They make it easier for me to be the man I was.

Without my children around, I'm a little more monster and a little less man. It's rarely an advantage, except on days like today, when everything is on the line and the threat of death and destruction looms.

The first and last leg of our return journey to the chamber where we separated from the survivors required my familiars and I to pass down tunnels we'd originally travelled through. These were the same tunnels we'd baited the ancient vampires to hunt us through. Encountering them there was a death sentence for us, so my demonic instincts pushed me to send Angelica and Davina through the tunnels alone while I travelled through the Deadlands.

Speed was our only ally.

Speed to get off the path and into hiding before the predators began their chase. Without me there to slow my familiars down, their chances of survival improved. It was cold, calculating logic that made me send them off alone, and it was the same cold, calculating logic that would have seen me abandon them if they ran into the threat that I risked my children's lives to save them from.

Thankfully for them, that never came to pass.

I stood in a Deadlands intersection, staring down tunnels devoid of colour, looking past ghostly spectres crawling over living monsters, searching for life force that would be released in death, to where my familiars would soon appear, and stepped out of the Deadlands. The sounds of predator and prey filled the air as scents rushed through my nostrils. The smell of monsters and death permeated the tunnel as the local second-floor monsters noticed my presence. This was the tunnel the survivors had fled through when we left them behind. This was where we had to go to find them.

I categorised every scent, searching for any trace of vampires, but only found frightened people and the aroma of the Abyss. It was safe to continue, safe to try to save the survivors, safe to live up to my daughter's expectations.

So, I waited.

It was several minutes before Angelica and Davina came sprinting down the tunnel. Speed was still their only protection. The only way they might survive my kind. So, I'd left them with no alternative but to run as fast as they could. They both skidded to a stop before me, fighting for breath and reeking of hunger and exhaustion.

Angelica yanked open her storage pouch and pulled out a canteen, before prying open her visor. Her face and armour were covered in vomit, but she ignored both, fighting to drink between gasped breaths. The shortness of breath was an early sign of mana sickness. Angelica's attributes were distributed to prevent her from reaching this state.

Beside her, Davina heaved for breath as she gathered a ball of dense death magic in her palm and swallowed it. The colour drained from her face, but her breathing slowed as the undead aspects of her unique constitution reduced her need for air. Then she went for her canteen, guzzling water as fast as Angelica.

I threw out a few spells to keep the local monsters in check. After being on the fourth floor, the second was almost a joke. Each spell caused a death, and each death cause a distraction, detouring predators so that nothing bothered us.

Angelica lowered her canteen. "Your fucking command made me sprint so hard I vomited."

"Language."

"Fuck you! I was wearing my helmet!" Angelica's fist tightened on her bone staff as she stepped forward and glared up at me. "You slowed me down."

Her aggression and willingness to get in my face were new. On an unconscious level, Angelica probably now understood that she was stronger than me. The monster in me told me to leash her. To bind her so tight she wouldn't be a threat.

Davina placed her hand on Angelica's shoulder to gently calming her emotions. "She has a point, your Dark Eminence. We can't run blind."

I glanced at the soiled gap in her visor, picturing her vomiting while running, and her inability to slow to clear it because of the command I'd given.

She had a right to be angry. "Angelica, this next command supersedes all future commands. If you are ever about to vomit and you think it is tactically necessary for you to lift your visor or un-obstruct your face to do so, do so."

The monster wanted me to continue giving her commands, to strip her of her freedom, and to leave a tool in her place. The monster wanted Angelica under its control, but it couldn't have her.

She was *my monster*.

Angelica scowled as she undid her strap and pulled her helmet free. She dropped her helmet as she pulled out a bar of soap while conjuring water. The spell gathered water from the air to create an effect similar to a cold shower.

She began scrubbing her face and hair with soap. "Do you have any idea how bad it smelled in there?"

"Yes. I can smell it from here."

"But can you taste it?"

"I can when you're this close."

She smirked through the soapsuds. “Good.”

When she was done with her face and hair, she scrubbed out her helmet. She was tired, agitated, and upset. The self-care was having a soothing effect on her, so I let her continue. She stepped away from the shower she’d created and poured the water from her helmet, before burning away the remaining water from her armour with pure fire.

The flames didn’t come from a spell, but from her armour. Our time spent on the fourth floor and the death of so many powerful monsters nearby had greatly increased the power of her equipment, allowing her to tap into its individual element magics. She was no longer limited to necrotic fire, but could access fire, death, and necrotic magic or any combination she chose.

Angelica shoved the helmet back onto her head, while it was still hot, causing her wet hair to release steam through the gap in her visor.

“I may have not thought this through,” she said, as she tied her strap.

Davina giggled. “You look like a teapot.”

I placed my hand on her helmet, releasing death magic through it to accelerate the loss of heat. It was not an attack, but a manipulation of the nature of death magic. The steam vanished as the heat was expelled. Even archsorcerers who could cast master-tier spells would struggle with what I’d just done.

Angelica stared at me through the steamless gap in her visor. “Did you just kill heat?”

“Yes.”

She glanced at Davina. “Did you know he could do that?”

Davina was staring at me with an open mouth, entirely unaware I could do something she couldn’t.

“I’ll take that as a no.”

I raised my hand and shot a finger of destruction toward a monster that was getting too close, dissolving its head and leaving a meal for the other monsters. “Do either of you need to eat or recover?”

They both nodded.

“Then eat.”

They began grabbing rations, while I dealt with the monsters rushing towards us.

"Gorgath's spell seems to have spooked the vampires as much as I hoped it would. There's no trace of them here, nor along the path you just took. Once you've recovered, we're pushing forward until we catch up to the survivors. Do you need anything else while we wait?"

"Mana," Angelica said with her mouth full.

I transferred mana to her core. "Anything else?"

They shook their heads as they continued to eat.

"When we catch up to the survivors, they're either going to be traveling or in a defensive formation. If they're traveling, we're going to join the rear guard and assess their situation. If they've had to stop and form a defensive formation, Davina will join the healers, and Angelica will reinforce the frontline."

"Why would they stop?" Angelica asked, spitting out crumbs.

"We're heading toward ant territory, and Gorgath says they can't pass through it without me."

SENDING my children to safety didn't come without a cost. Without us to shepherd the survivors through the Abyss, each mile they crossed cost more lives than it otherwise would have. I kept track of deaths by whose scent was missing from the convoy each time I exited the Deadlands to point Angelica and Davina in the right direction. The deceased were faculty, students, Carolyn's guards, Davina's people, and strangers from town, but no one I knew.

I've read that heroes have a protective effect. Where they have vanquished evil, it doesn't return. I'd never been certain whether that applied to me, but every cursed student had made it out of Darksmith. Every one of Gregory's people was still alive. Most of the merchants from the boulevard were still alive. It was evidence that despite everything that had happened to me, I was still a hero, and I was still able to do lasting good.

It didn't mean they would survive this experience. It just meant they would be the last to fall.

By the time we caught up with them, the survivors had blocked a tunnel entrance to a second-floor chamber with a hundred-foot-high wall of giant ant corpses. The ants' vibrant red, Gorgath-sized exoskeletons looked like polished rubies as they caught the light of magical flashes from the ongoing battle.

Gorgath stood in the middle of the wall, striking ants with his staff, releasing electrical discharges each time he did. Exhausted sorcerers were spread along the wall on either side, unleashing their most powerful spells against the giant ants that were trying to kill Gorgath.

Gregory and my men remained out front, engaging the smaller ants. They were the size of pickup trucks, and dangerous in their own right, because their numbers seemed endless. The mobile palace and flying carpets sat above the wall, providing air support, and killing the ants that tried to enter the tunnel by crawling across the ceiling.

From the top of the wall inside the Deadlands, I surveyed the battlefield. The fighting didn't look desperate. It didn't look hopeless. Everything I saw suggested a tactical action to wear down the giant ants, before they made a push through the chamber to the next tunnel.

The problem was the giant ants. There were *hundreds* of them, and they were a serious threat to Gorgath.

I exited the Deadland near Gregory and snapped my fingers in the direction of the giant ant Gorgath was fighting. It was as strong as a first-floor boss. The destruction spell that I released disintegrated its narrower, unprotected neck, causing its head to fall from its thorax. I turned to the next-closest threat and wove the same spell before snapping my fingers. Another head fell off.

Snap.

Snap.

Snap.

The frontline of giant ants collapsed as I began on the second line.

Gregory sensed my presence and disengaged from the frontline, where he was fighting the smaller ants, and then he blurred to my side. "I didn't expect to see you again."

"You have my loot."

"I know your priorities, sir. Loot sits just below survival."

"Then you're lucky I think we can survive this mess. Now, what have I missed?"

He sheathed his kilij and turned, pointing to the centre of the chamber. "The ants are trying to establish a new nest. The small ones we're fighting are worker ants. The big ones you're killing are hunter ants. The workers take what the hunters kill and drag it back to the feeder ants over there in the middle of the chamber, beside the big one. The big one's the queen. You can ignore them for now. Our problem is the hunters."

"You can't push through this chamber without them killing Gorgath and suffering significant casualties."

"Exactly. Softening the enemy up is the only way to ensure that Gorgath and the townsfolk survive."

The ants didn't seem to be intelligent, nor to have a sense of self-preservation. Every time I killed a hunter, another moved forward to take its place. During our brief conversation, I killed more than twenty, and they hadn't even flinched.

Gregory glanced at me as I kept killing, before turning away and gazing off into the distance to access his interface. "You might want to slow down there, sir. I know your children are safe, so you don't care who knows you're a vampire, but these people are scared. They'll turn on us if they find out what you are."

"They die anyway, if we move too slowly."

Gregory's aura swelled as he spent his attributes from leveling and grew stronger. "Will we get a chance to catch our breath before pushing forward? My men have attributes to distribute and skill levels to acquire."

I swept my gaze across the chamber. The hunters were as strong as first-floor bosses, and there were hundreds of them. The feeder ants were just as strong. And the queen was a second-floor boss. These ants were the easiest source of experience I'd seen outside the fourth floor and leaving them alive would be a waste.

"You have until I've killed the nest."

GORGATH TORE through the queen's corpse, searching for his prize, as the worker ants ran away from his aura. Without the queen's or the hunters' auras to keep them calm, they were overwhelmed by fear. Gorgath grinned as he pried an organ from her thorax and shoved it in his mouth, chewing furiously.

The organ was prized by the Gor because it gave control over which bloodlines were passed onto offspring. Eating it would allow him to reproduce the organ within himself, so he could gain the same control over the bloodlines that he passed onto his offspring. It eliminated the need for him to limit the bloodlines he took before the ninth floor.

Gorgath swallowed his mouthful, wiped his bloody hand on the carcass, and turned to head back to the survivors. They were recovering from the battle while keeping the workers in check. He took a step towards them.

Giving him the organ meant nothing to me, and it got us alone so I could ask him an important question. "Wait a moment, please."

Gorgath paused and turned to look down at me. I was standing by his ankles, so he loomed over me.

"When did you become an elemental sorcerer?"

The kid suddenly found that everything except me required his attention, turning his head to search for imaginary threats that I'd failed to miss. "Gorgath must hurry back to protect Darksmith."

The amount of blood and death around us said that wasn't necessary. "They're perfectly safe. Now answer my question."

He still didn't look at me. "Gorgath hoped you wouldn't notice."

"I noticed. Now, how did this happen?"

"Gorgath asked Arro to borrow a mobile class stone for him to see if he could gain the sorcerer class. Gorgath is a student, and students are allowed to borrow the mobile class stones. Gorgath did nothing wrong."

The kid having a class explained the display of power I'd seen when he unleashed his spell at the dungeon fortress and why he was progressing so quickly. "Your teachers might have cared if they found out you have a class. I don't. I just want to know what happened. This could make it easier to pass through the ants' territory."

Gorgath lowered his gaze and grinned, excited to share, now that he knew he wasn't in trouble. "Arro gave Gorgath the mobile class stone, and Gorgath became an elemental sorcerer, like a human would."

"When?"

"Before Gorgath joined the Dungeonology Club."

That was months ago. He'd been sitting on this secret for a while. "Does everything work correctly?"

He nodded. "Gorgath can see the class interface, along with his skills and attributes. Arro has been tracking Gorgath's progress in developing his skills. It is similar to ancestral memories, but not the same. Gorgath finds it very helpful."

I wasn't surprised that he'd tried to become a sorcerer. I was just surprised that it worked. I was also surprised that I couldn't sense any changes in him, but then I might not be able to. He was already extremely powerful, and any additional power might have gotten lost among it.

"Have you distributed your attributes?"

Gorgath shook his head. "Arro says my attributes do not make sense, so I should not spend them yet."

"Why don't they make sense?"

"They are too high, and they change."

That was too vague for me to get an accurate understanding of what I was dealing with. With us going into ant territory this early, we were going to need every advantage we had to get the survivors through.

"Let's find Arro before we continue this discussion."

Arro had been sleeping in the Dungeonology Club room when the attack happened, so she was one of the people who Davina had to resurrect. She was tougher than most of the students at Darksmith, so she was on one of the smaller flying carpets aiding in the defence, rather than hiding in the mobile palace.

She had the pilot drop her off beside me on Gorgath's shoulder after Gorgath approached the convoy that was getting ready to leave and called her name. Like me, she was perfectly comfortable with the large gorilla child, grabbing his fur to keep herself steady beside me.

Gorgath signalled the convoy and then turned and broke into a run, expecting them to follow. Sir Trent and his people rushed away from the wall to catch up as Gregory and his people waited for the convoy to pass, so they could defend the rear.

As Arro held onto his fur to remain steady, she gave me a pensive look, like a kid caught with her hand in the cookie jar. "I take it you've found out."

"Yes."

She turned to Gorgath's ear. "I told you not to use your elemental strikes where people could see them."

"Too many hunter ants," Gorgath muttered back.

"Why did you do it?" I asked.

She turned back. "This is the way."

I raised an eyebrow.

She blushed. "Gorgath told me it's how his people show support when someone does the right thing in front of an outsider. It's rather poetic, don't you think?"

I chuckled and nodded my agreement. "What have you learned?"

Arro turned to Gorgath again as he crossed the chamber, crushing worker ants under foot.

Gorgath glanced at his shoulder, before returning his attention to watching our path. "Tell him."

Arro nodded and turned back. "Gorgath has a larger variety of attributes than humans do, but his attributes are absurdly high and growing each day."

"What do you mean by absurdly high?"

She reached into her storage pouch and handed me a notebook with his attributes and skills. I flicked through. She'd recorded his attributes every day since she'd helped him gain his class, and every day, his attributes had grown. I finished on her most recent entry for him.

Race: Gor
Class: Elemental Sorcerer
Level: 160
Strength: 11,842
Dexterity: 4,372
Agility: 2,139
Endurance: 9,352
Constitution: 19,832
Perception: 7,342
Recovery: 6,826
Mana Regeneration: 1,854

Some of the attributes had five digits. It was easy to see that they didn't correspond to human numbers, which meant that they couldn't be treated the same way as human attributes. If a human had over 9,000 strength, they would be Goku, capable of shattering a mountain with their fist. Gorgath was strong, but he wasn't *that* strong.

I turned to Arro. "I see you tested increasing his attributes. Why didn't you record the result?"

She took a step back. "How did you read that so quicky?"

I showed her my fangs. "I'm an ancient vampire, Now, kindly answer my question."

Gorgath didn't bother turning his head. "Professor Vincent will not harm you."

She swallowed her fear. "We only increased each attribute by five. There was no discernible difference."

With these numbers, there wouldn't be. I flipped back several dozen pages. "What causes this sudden jump in his mana regeneration?"

Arro glanced at her notes. "That was when he absorbed the mana crab bloodline. His growth rate has been different since he absorbed it."

She clearly couldn't see the pattern I could. I needed to test a theory. "Gorgath. Look at your mana regeneration attribute, and then spend two of your attribute points increasing it. Tell me how much it increases by."

"Don't waste his attributes," Arrow snap, taking a step forward as she scowled. "We can study this further without wasting them."

Gorgath glanced at his shoulder. "Gorgath's mana regeneration increases by five when he invests two."

Arro turned to him. "What?"

It was as I suspected. "Gorgath, do your people grow stronger from eating other creatures in the Abyss, even if you don't absorb their bloodline?"

Gorgath nodded.

"You've been growing stronger faster since eating the acid centipedes, right? It does something to your digestion which allows you to grow stronger quicker, along with letting you spit acid?"

Gorgath nodded again. "It is a very good first bloodline, even in a poor territory like Gorgath's."

Arro turned to me. "You understand what's happening to him."

I nodded. "His mana regeneration growth rate hasn't changed. The mana crab bloodline acts as a modifier. He's multiplied the underlying mana regeneration and the growth rate by 273%. The reason you couldn't understand his attribute growth rate is that his acid centipede bloodline has made his attribute growth erratic, giving him a little bit extra, here and there, depending on what he eats. A Gor without that bloodline would have more consistent growth."

She took a step forward to look at the notebook, academic curiosity overcoming fear. "How did you figure that out?"

I flipped through her notes, showing her different pages. "The dates for these slightly bigger increases all coincide with when I brought my guards to the Abyss to hunt first-floor bosses."

Arro turned to Gorgath. "You said you ate well. You didn't tell me you were eating first-floor bosses."

"Gorgath fed the most valuable pieces to his mana crabs and brothers, only taking small bites for himself. Gorgath did not want to confuse your data by informing you he ate them."

Arro sighed. "Is there anything else you haven't told me? I can't figure this out without knowing everything."

"You don't need to," I said. "Gorgath, did you level today?"

He nodded. "Gorgath reached level 240 when he descended to the second floor."

"Okay. Put all your attribute points into mana regeneration. Fully upgrade the magic, meditation, mana manipulation, multicasting, quick casting, and concentration skills, in that order. If you continue to level, upgrade the reinforcement, overcharge, and then each of your elemental magic skills."

Gorgath raised his staff, but didn't slow his run. "Gorgath likes it when his staff hits with fire and lightning."

"I'm sure you do, but you're a sorcerer not a warrior. Stop scowling. Increasing your mana regeneration and upgrading all these skills will increase your elemental strikes without you needing to upgrade them."

"Gorgath does not get tired or lose mana when he uses his elemental strikes. It is most useful."

"I understand that, but you don't have the same restrictions humans have. You'll level up enough to upgrade them before you reach the ninth floor."

"That is not what Arro said."

"Your friend did her best to help you, but she doesn't know anywhere near as much about classes and levels as I do. Now, do you want to become the most powerful sorcerer ever, or not?"

Gorgath immediately stopped arguing, and his eyes went unfocused as he accessed his character sheet.

Arro frowned. "Why are you having him put everything into mana regeneration instead of agility?"

"His people aren't natural magic users, yet it's one of their main weapons as they descend. The fact that his mana regeneration is still lower than his agility after he absorbed the mana crab's bloodline should tell you that *that* is where he needs to focus his attention."

"But he could double his agility."

I motioned to the chamber we were in. "Do you honestly want him to double his agility while travelling through the Abyss? Do you know how dangerous that is?"

"Then he should wait instead of wasting this opportunity."

I held up her notes. "This is his agility when he started, and this is his agility now. It's increased by 23%, and yet he's still a first-floor boss and no faster than he was before. That should tell you something."

Her frown grew. "His agility doesn't work the way ours does."

"Wrong. His *constitution* doesn't work like yours does."

"What?"

"The human body primarily grows tougher as constitution increases. Gorgath's body also grows *bigger* when his constitution increases. His people's strength doesn't keep up with their weight, so the effects of his agility are greatly reduced, along with any benefits for increasing it."

"Attributes don't work that way."

She wasn't wrong. "Not for us, but they do for him."

"How can you be sure you're right?"

I showed her my fangs again. "I have an infinity symbol next to my endurance, constitution, and recovery; because of my ancient vampiric nature, those attributes cannot be accurately measured by my class. Gorgath is similar. His class, like mine, is trying to provide the benefits that it's supposed to give, even though it's interacting with something that it wasn't designed to interact with."

"Then giving him a class isn't going to help him survive down here?"

She was concerned for his safety.

I felt Gorgath's aura begin to grow as his body absorbed more mana. He stopped running, dropped his staff, and beat his chest, hooting at the top of his lungs, as he sensed the changes taking place.

"You should know by now that *skills* make a much bigger difference than attributes do. Gorgath has nothing to fear as he descends, thanks to you."

Arro held onto his fur as she was thrown about. "What's he doing?"

"He's warning the Abyss that he's coming."

32

PREPARATION

Unlike members of the animal kingdom, the monsters of the Abyss were either herbivores or carnivores. One only ate crystalised mana, and the other only ate monsters. None ate both. This made the Abyss a place of chaos, violence, and fear, unless you were in ant territory. Unlike the other carnivores, ants could survive without prey, happily consuming the unfertilised eggs the feeder ants laid as they consumed the crystalised mana the workers brought them. This unique quirk made them completely different from every other monster in the Abyss and allowed them to strip their territory of every other species, leaving their crystal gardens to grow.

Sir Trent was barking orders as I stepped out of the Deadlands and scanned the mana-crystal-filled tunnel for threats. A dozen dead hunter ants, all now as strong as second-floor bosses, lay near the tunnel mouth where we'd entered to the third floor of the Abyss.

Davina and the Undead Enhancement Club were performing ritual spells to raise six of them as zombies, to provide additional security for when we pushed forward, while Gorgath was stuffing his face with the meat from the ones they didn't need, taking the choicest pieces to recover and grow his strength.

I found no threats, obvious or hidden, so I turned to Sir Trent. He was dressed head to toe in grimy plate armour, crusted over with entrails and blood. Our progress through the ants' territory on the second floor and my travels through the fourth floor had substantially raised his level, causing him to be someone I had to take seriously.

Sir Trent finished shouting and turned and spat. "What did you see?"

Like every other monster, ants changed as they descended lower. Just because we'd faced them on the second floor, didn't mean we knew what we were getting into on the third. Scouting ahead through the Deadlands was entirely necessary.

I pointed to the pile of ant corpses. "There are groups like this one at every intersection between here and the first chamber. They seem to be leaving the crystals in these tunnels to grow, so we won't have to deal with workers until we reach their nest."

"That's good news. Now what's the bad news?"

"There are now two varieties of workers. The regular ones from the floor above have grown bigger and significantly tougher, while a second variety has developed the ability to fly. The fliers are as tough as dungeon bosses, though substantially smaller."

"Are they rare?"

"One in twenty."

Sir Trent gritted his teeth and growled, immediately comprehending the threat they posed. I couldn't spare the time necessary for him to come to his own conclusions, so I pushed ahead with my plan.

"Do you have a good second in command who can take over leading Carolyn's guards?"

"Several. Why?"

"There are just as many hunters in these nests as there were in the ones on the second floor. The difference being, I can't kill these ones as easily as I killed the others. I need anyone who can survive moving among the ants to push forward and cripple the hunters' legs, so they don't overwhelm Davina's zombies and reach the convoy while I'm trying to kill them."

Getting through the third floor with the survivors would take everything we had, and it still might not be enough. The threats I'd seen were not easily overcome.

"What about Gorgath?" Sir Trent asked, trying to change the subject to buy him time to think. "He took down that hunter he was wrestling with. He could help."

Sir Trent seemed to believe his statement, which was a problem, because he was wrong.

"What you witnessed was an act of arrogance and desperation. The kid thought he was tougher than he is and was about to get himself cut in half by the hunter's mandibles. The lightning bolt he spat in its face cost him most of his mana while injuring him in the process. He still hasn't recovered."

Seeing the kid change his acid spitting spell into an acid lightning spitting spell on the fly had been rather impressive. A human wouldn't have been able to do it, mainly because they wouldn't have been able to survive the backlash. He'd half-cooked himself to pull it off, but it had worked, and sometimes that was all that mattered, when you were fighting for your life.

"What's he going to do, then?"

"You mean, besides guiding the way?"

Sir Trent snorted. "Yes, besides that."

"He'll be helping with the worker ants, covering for those we send after the hunters."

"They're going to be that big of a problem?"

"*Everything* is going to be that big of a problem. The workers are nearly as strong as dungeon bosses, the fliers are stronger, the hunters' chitin prevents anything less than an expert-tier spell from causing any damage, and the vast majority of our highest-level warriors fight with swords. On top of that, our sorcerers are going to have their hands full with keeping the fliers away from the convoy, so those on the ground aren't going to have any support, and this is all after having *already* lost one in five of our sorcerers to mana exhaustion. And once we get through this chamber, we have to do it *six more* times."

Sir Trent smirked. "It's almost enough to make me want to turn around and try to fight our way out."

"The keyword there being *almost*."

Sir Trent gave a weary grin. "I'll go out into the chaos to help slow down the hunters, but I'm not sending my people out to be slaughtered."

I raised an eyebrow. "Just you?"

"I know we're good, but we're not that good."

His reply made me realise he didn't know.

I chuckled.

"What's so amusing?" He asked.

"Seventeen of Carolyn's guards have taken my oath since we entered the Abyss."

His face lost all emotion. "When?"

"During my visit to the field hospital on the second floor. Nothing like dying to make you re-evaluate whether you're willing to accept a dark pact that might save your life. They're on the cusp of reaching level 200. Not as strong as you, but still strong enough to survive out there."

My visit to the field hospital only lasted a few seconds as I confirmed whether Davina would be ready to move on after I killed the first queen, but it had been enough time for them to spot me and give their oaths. My ability to help those who took my oath to level was an open secret, and the fresh memories of death or dismemberment had made the decision for them.

Sir Trent disappeared in a blur. He knew whom I was talking about because he was a good-enough leader to keep track of his peoples' injuries. They were undoubtedly about to receive a demotion and reprimand. Sir Trent had been asked to take my oath by Rupert and Carolyn for security reasons. The others had not. And any guard who would accept any power that was offered by a vampire couldn't be trusted with the princess's safety.

I left Sir Trent to deal with his people and went to find my own. On the other side of the stationary convoy, Gregory was watching over his wife Helen as she examined their people for injuries. Other members of my guard were handing over their sweaty and dirty clothes and armour to sorcerers for cleaning. Everyone else worked on repairing equipment.

Once again, they were working with equipment far below their level, and the wear and tear from all the fighting was leaving it all in a sorry state. There was no way to fix this issue in the short term, but if the problem grew too great, Davina would summon bone armour for them.

I stopped beside Gregory and gave him the same update I'd given Sir Trent while we followed his wife around the temporary camp.

Gregory listened with folded arms, nodding when I got to the end. "I'm seeing more variation in levels from all this fighting, so there's maybe a dozen of us who are fast and skilled enough to survive alone in this environment. I'll get them prepped for dealing with the hunters, but I need to stay back."

The entire time I'd been updating him, Gregory smelled worried. The way he was throwing glances at his wife didn't make it hard to understand why. She wasn't a warrior. She was a healer, so despite all the fighting, she had barely leveled since we'd met. This place was a death trap for someone like her, and his concern for her was distracting him.

Gregory was the head of my personal guards, and his role was too important for me to let this distraction continue. Until now, I had no interest in whether or not his wife took my oath. She wasn't necessary to any of my plan. Now, she was.

In the middle of our conversation, I turned to his wife. She was crouched beside a deathlord named Philipo, dealing with a broken finger. She noticed me looking and removed her hand from her patient's forehead. "What do you want?"

"Take my oath."

"No."

"Why not?"

"I don't want to."

"That's not a reason. That's a stance you take because you have a reason. So, what's the reason?"

Helen scowled. "My reasons are my own."

"Not when it's causing me problems."

"Why is this suddenly important to you?"

I pointed at Gregory, who had chosen to stay quiet. "Your husband is terrified for your safety, and it's interfering with his ability to do his job. If I don't do anything, he will begin making mistakes. And if he makes mistakes here, a lot of people will die. Right now, I can't stop him from making those mistakes without stripping him of his free will or compelling him to love and care for you less than he currently does; so, I'm starting with the least invasive option, which is making you stronger through my oath."

Disbelief turned to horror as Helen went through a range of emotions while I stated my position. She didn't trust me or my judgement, but she accepted everything I'd just said as the truth. The real truth was, even though I'd be willing to compel Gregory to love and care for her less if he allowed it, I hadn't practiced compelling people enough to make good on my claims.

Helen threw a holy bolt at my head, only to sigh as it did nothing. She then turned to her husband. "Are you just going to stand there?"

Gregory gave his wife a sad smile. "I don't want to take his side against you, so I'm staying quiet."

"You're taking his side!"

Gregory nodded. "I've listened to your arguments against him and his methods and raised every complaint you've asked me to, but none of your concerns have come to pass. Whether it is taking a child into the Abyss or teaching young necromancers how to fight, everything you're worried about has resulted in harmless consequences or a positive situation. I no longer believe you're objective in these matters, my love."

Helen opened her mouth to retort, when Dalin dropped out of the sky and landed in front of her.

The head of the infirmary whipped his head back and forth with his glowing white gaze and a frown on his face. "I'm sorry for my intrusion, but I just had a feeling that I was supposed to be here."

Helen blinked at the other cleric. "Heaven speaks to you?"

Dalin shook his head as he continued to search. "I'm not so

blessed. I just get feelings and impressions when they need me. I've had quite a few of them recently, but this is the first one that isn't obvious to me. No one seems to be injured."

He closed his eyes, muttering a silent prayer. Nothing happened. He opened his eyes and shrugged. "I guess I was wrong. Sorry for the intrusion."

Helen raised her hand and threw a holy bolt at Dalin's back, for reasons only she knew. The bright orb of light slammed into his body with a dull thud.

Horror once again transformed Helen's features as a rope of holy light extended from her hand to Dalin's back, draining her of her holy power. The power flowed into Dalin like water into a full cup, overflowing his limits, and causing his eyes to widen as his power surged. The golden energy swirled around his body, saturating his clothing, changing his food-stained robe to one made from the purest cottons and silks, infused with magic, and layered with enchantments.

Dalin turned to Helen as her power continued to surround him and light engulfed him, causing the power within him to settle into its new home. "What have you done, child?" he whispered, voice filled with sorrow.

Helen's connection to the power above was a mere shadow of its former self, no stronger than a newly appointed acolyte. "You...you walk in the light."

His face fell, realising her doubt. "Always."

"I could not see the truth."

"That is no reason for you to offer Heaven your past, present, and future to beg summary judgement, instead of beseeching Heaven on Heaven's terms."

A tear rolled down her cheek. "I had to know."

Dalin stepped closer, placed his hand on her head, and closed his eyes. "Do you accept Heaven's answer, child?"

The tears began to flow faster. "Yes, archbishop."

"Then rise, paladin, and return with me to the light."

Power and holy light flashed through his body and into her eyes. They glowed for several second as new power flowed into her, before returning to their normal brown. Shock replaced tears as Dalin placed a new path before her.

Gregory leaned over. "Did I just see what I think I saw?"

"If you think you just saw the birth of an archbishop and a new order of the church, along with your wife losing her cleric class and becoming a paladin, then yes. You saw what you think you saw."

Helen turned to me while I spoke to her husband, dropped to one knee, and took my oath. "I pledge my life and my soul to the Hero. Let his path be my path and his fate be my fate."

She spoke the words to me, but anyone could tell they were not for me or for her. They were simply part of her new path. Holy light enveloped her from above, as the bond between us formed, cementing our connection.

Dalin removed his hand from her head. "Welcome to the Soul Guardian's Order, Sister. Our only tenet is to protect righteous souls from the thieves of Hell."

I knew heroes weren't the only one with a class that could produce a call, but it was rare for an archbishop to have one. Normally, you needed to be someone like Mother and Father and follow a saint. Unless I'd missed something, Dalin walked his own path now.

The other clerics who worked under Helen seemed to have heard the archbishop's call, because they were all rushing towards him. Gregory and I took a few steps back as they fell to their knees before Dalin and kissed the hem of his robe, accepting the only tenet they needed to follow him, before taking my oath. Why they took my oath only after accepting his tenet, I had no idea.

Gregory leaned over again, but chuckled this time. "I see the weirdest things while working for you, sir."

"I had nothing to do with this."

"You sure? To me it kind of seems like the clerics you saved from soul reapers have now founded a religious order whose purpose is devoted to combating people like that, essentially copying what you've already done and giving their hero's oath a direction that they believe in."

When phrased that way, one could assume I had something to do with it. "I'm sure I had nothing to do with this."

"I notice none of the people who worked with Dalin are racing over here to take the oath. You would think one of them would hear his call, having known him for so long."

"Maybe I had something to do with it."

Gregory's chuckle turned into a laugh. "I'll go get our people ready to face the hunters."

"Make it quick. I plan to let you all use the ones guarding the intersections for practice."

"Good idea."

Gregory turned and raced off as Dalin turned his Heaven's blessed gaze on me and dismissed the clerics who had just joined his order. Dalin had been over level 100 before he took my oath. Now, his level was significantly higher. Very soon, people would be calling him an Old Monster.

He closed the distance. "You must be wondering why I took your oath back at the fortress."

"Not particularly."

"You're not curious?"

"No. But you're going to tell me anyway, so make it quick."

Dalin smiled. "The necrosaint once told me that she stays by your side because those who should help you, do not. I didn't understand what she meant until I floated before that crowd of survivors who were only alive because of you and those who follow you. You're a man who is forced to walk in darkness without letting it consume him, and yet you bring light to those who find themselves lost and surrounded by the same darkness you face. You're a man trying desperately not to fall from grace, and no one but those who accept your oath can help lift the burden you carry and reduce the risk that you will stray from the light."

He wasn't wrong. The more people that were trying to make the world safe for their children, the less likely it was that I would need to cross lines to protect them.

His explanation raised my curiosity. "How did that lead to you becoming an archbishop?"

"When I took your oath, I promised Heaven that I would devote myself to keeping your soul in the light and protecting the innocent from your nature." Dalin turned and nodded to Helen. "Heaven intended this to be *her* responsibility, but she denied your call for help, time and time again. When she offered Heaven all she was to learn if I still walked in the light after taking your oath, she offered Heaven the responsibility she should have borne, and Heaven chose to hand it to me, instead."

"So, now you're an archbishop."

"Yes, and I'm Heaven-mandated to walk beside you and keep you in the light." He patted my shoulder with a small smile on his lips. "Do you happen to need any moral guidance at the moment, your Dark Eminence?"

I chuckled. "No."

"Then my work here is done. Please continue with whatever insanity you were planning to drag us through next."

DAVINA and the Undead Enhancement Club had successfully raised five of the hunters as zombies through ritual raise zombie spells. Angelica had used the control undead ability her Crypt Keeper set gave her to control the first four, leaving Professor Fergus to contend with the fifth.

He was currently alone in another ritual circle, wrestling with the will of a gargantuan undead ant, and he was seriously struggling to keep it under control. It was shuddering and swaying, trying to get to its feet to tear everything around it apart. If no one intervened soon, it would cause serious problems.

"Need any help?" I asked as I stopped at the edge of the ritual circle.

Fergus gave me bloodshot side-eye in response.

I glanced at the runes on the ground that were designed to boost his control over undead and wove the appropriate spell form, before stepping in. The zombie's undead will slammed into my mind, trying to crush my consciousness, entirely unaware that its efforts were like a toddler trying to fight an adult's knee.

I patted Fergus on the shoulder as I began tearing the zombie's will apart, dissecting its consciousness to strip away its aggression. "The key to breaking the willpower of powerful undead is violence. Weaker undead you overpower. Powerful undead, you tear apart, removing any part of their consciousness that tries to fight you. Once you finish tearing them apart, you build them back up."

The undead hunter ant froze as the last of the pressure in my mind disappeared. It was big and it was powerful, but an ancient vampire's control over the undead was second only to a lich. It stood no chance.

Fergus suddenly gasped, sucking in his first breath in several minutes. "How did you do that?"

"Violence."

I raised my hand and cast a complex program undead spell to restore the damaged areas of its consciousness with something that was easier to control. The size of the hunter ant required me to pour in all my mana while pulling more from the air around me.

Fergus gritted his teeth as he fought for breath. "I took your hero's oath, Vincent, so no more lies. Who are you really?"

I took a step back to the edge of the circle and gave an elegant bow, flicking the edge of my coat. "I'm the Vampire Vincent. Hero. Father. And the only ancient vampire with a soul."

He glanced at Davina, where she was preparing to raise the sixth undead hunter ant, before turning his gaze to Angelica. Angelica was off to the side with the other four undead hunter ants, practicing directing them together.

Fergus returned his attention to me and straightened his back, before returning my bow. "It's a pleasure to formally meet you, Vincent."

I saw where this was going. "I'm not making you my familiar."

Fergus winced. "Don't be so hasty, my friend. If you think about it, you'll realise I'd make a great familiar. I mean, I did take several months to replicate your living dead project, but I'm a lot higher level now, and I have a lot of new relevant skills, so I'm sure I could do it in half the time. Also, if I stay in Murdell, the parents of the kids who didn't survive will have me assassinated. They'll have *all* the faculty assassinated."

I rolled my eyes at his truly terrible reasons for why I should make him my familiar. "We're leaving Murdell the moment we reach the surface. You're welcome to come."

Fergus perked up. "What about the rest of the faculty?"

"They can come, too, but you have to tell them what I am. Now stop talking and cast a control undead on this zombie so I can move onto my next problem."

Fergus nodded and turned back to the zombie, raising his hand and muttering the incantation for an expert-tier control undead spell.

The slight pressure that remained, vanished as Fergus took full control. I wove another spell form to exit the ritual circle and stepped outside, making my way to the other ritual circle that held all the students who were helping Davina power the spell to raise such massive undead. It wasn't more than twenty feet.

There were a lot of nervous faces as I stopped at the edge of ritual circle, but almost as many looked pleased to see me, pushing forward to speak.

I'd overheard that the Undead Enhancement Club had all been fast asleep when the attack went down, which meant they were all surrounded by at least four undead experiments, which exceeded Undead Fight Club's guidelines. Many had a lot more than four, focusing on training the skills their subclasses offered. With their bodyguards ready to protect them, they were able to escape with their lives intact, before returning to try and save others.

A few even still had some of their smaller undead with them.

Lidia held up her hand as she pushed her way to the front of the circle, having overheard my conversation with Fergus, and now even more terrified of speaking out of turn. Mr. Bitey sat on her shoulders, snapping at everyone nearby, giving her more room.

Lidia was one of the students who had taken my hero's oath. She had probably leveled drastically during the time, but she hadn't spent any of her attributes.

I nodded to her to let her know she could speak.

"Sir, are you really an ancient vampire?"

"Yes."

She pressed her lips together. "Does that make me your familiar?"

I chuckled. "No. That is an entirely different bond. I have no power over you, only the hero's oath you took does."

"Do you know why I'm leveling so fast?"

"I don't gain experience from fighting evil or killing monsters. The experience I gain seems to transfer to those who share a bond with me."

Several dozen of the students who shared a bond with me grinned, elbowing those next to them who hadn't made the oath. Dozens of students who had heard the call and done nothing decided to take my oath, despite having learned what I was. They were bathed in holy light from above as our connection formed.

Lidia cleared her throat. "On behalf of the entire Undead Enhancement Club, I would like to thank you for teaching us the skills we needed to save ourselves. Most of us wouldn't have made it out of the academy alive without you."

Their gratitude meant nothing to me. But it was best to be polite, given what I was about to ask them to do. "You're welcome."

Baris stepped forward, smelling angry. It showed through when he didn't raise his hand. "You've been manipulating us for months. What were you planning to do with us?"

He was a good young man.

"Nothing. My daughter was attending Darksmith, and teaching Defence Against the Dark Arts and the Undead Enhancement Club was my method for staying without drawing attention."

"Why should we believe you?"

I laughed in his face, partly because I knew it would weaken his argument, and partly because his concern was ridiculous. "Baris, you've seen what I'm capable of. Do you honestly think I need *any* of you to do anything?" I pointed to Davina. "That's the level of talent and skill I need. You've all come far, but none of you are at a level of skill or power where I need you for anything."

Baris opened his mouth to object, but then glanced at Davina and closed it again. He nodded a second later, agreeing with my point. His anger quickly faded as reason took over.

I cast a basic levitation spell and rose into the air so everyone could see me. "Many of you have taken my hero's oath. Many of you have leveled. None of you have spent more than a few attribute points. That is a mistake. Where we are going, you're going to need every advantage you can get."

Baris looked up and raised his voice. "We'll go into attribute shock."

"Clerics can postpone attribute shock."

"That just makes it worse."

"Only if you live long enough to experience it."

Lidia raised her hand. "Is it going to be that bad?"

I nodded. "Some of you might have seen how much longer it took me to kill these hunters compared to the ones of the floor above. That extra time means they will have a chance to swarm the convoy and overwhelm the undead guards you're raising. There is also a new threat from worker ants that can fly. You're going to have to engage significantly more aerial attacks than we have before this point."

Lidia raised her hand again. "Sir, do you know why we're not succumbing to mana exhaustion?"

"That's another benefit of my oath. You get some of my regenerative ability when you're desperate enough."

Gregory's sorcerers had never dropped from mana exhaustion during a battle, but they had many times during training. If they were here, it would be much easier to move forward.

Lidia raised her hand again. "Are there any other benefits of your oath?"

"Yes, but none of them will help you today. Now, those of you who have attributes to spend, I want you to invest them using the kingmaker distribution, starting with recovery. Those who know what the kingmaker distribution is, please confirm what I say to those who don't."

Baris raised his hand this time. "Sir, the archsorcerer distribution is more appropriate for necromancers. We should focus on what we know how to do."

"If any of you were capable of throwing expert-tier spells, I'd agree with you, but your current skills won't save you where we're going. Being able to leap out of the way and bounce back to your feet could. Also considering what we're facing, you're likely going to move past the kingmaker distribution by the time we leave the third floor, so you can take the archsorcerer distribution when that occurs."

Those who knew what the distribution required were openly shocked. To go beyond the kingmaker distribution would require a necromancer to pass level 120. That meant some of them would be tripling their level in a single day. For those who had already taken my oath, the news was less shocking. Many of them were likely already at that level, considering my weakest guards were all over level 150, with many being significantly higher than that. The number of powerful and boss-tier monsters I'd killed on our way here would take those sections of the Abyss generations to recover from.

Baris sighed as he raised his hand. "Sir, could you please remind me what the exact distribution is?"

I did as he asked, projecting my voice to everyone as I shared the numbers for kingmaker distribution.

Once I was done here, I needed to track down the rest of the people who had taken my oath and convince them to do the same. We were going to need every advantage to get through this without the majority of the survivors dying, so I wasn't going to let anyone slip through the cracks.

WALKING across a flying carpet is not like walking across a solid floor, I discovered. Each step causes your foot to sink as the carpet deforms under your weight. It was like walking across a trampoline, only without the bounce.

Cid, the alchemist who I regularly ran into while making master-tier skeletons, continued to stare off into space as I paced back and forth, bouncing his new baby on my shoulder. His wife was sitting nearby and stroked their sleeping children's hair with trembling hands, crying softly over the horrors she had seen, and her fear for what was to come.

Cid and the others had still been working all hours of the day and night, to provide enchanting material for Gorgath, so Gregory had known where to send his people to save them when the vampires attacked. My guards had helped them round up their families in the middle of the night, ushering them through the town, ahead of everyone else.

Cid's aura swelled as his attributes came into effect, pushing his capabilities to new heights. I motioned for Davina's cleric to come forward and stop him from passing out. His alchemist class might have not made him particularly skilled at combat, but he was still a sorcerer and could throw spells with enough skill to help.

Cid turned to me as the cleric began buffing him. "I never suspected you were a hero."

I shrugged as his fussy baby played with my hair as I continued to pace. "I'm not sure why a room full of deathlords wearing cultist robes would fail to give you the impression that I'm a hero."

Cid smiled, too stressed to laugh. "It might have been the lighting. Anyway, I'll tell the other alchemist who took your oath how to invest their attributes."

I lifted his baby from my shoulder and passed him back. "Thank you."

"I think I'm the one who should be saying that?"

"Your contribution matters."

"Not as much as yours."

"That doesn't mean you should go without thanks."

Cid gave a single nod in reply.

I turned and made my way to the front of the mobile palace. Finding everyone who had taken my oath was a simple matter; convincing some of them to listen to my advice was much harder. Anyone who was too disagreeable, like many of the merchants, I left to their own devices. I couldn't spare the time to convince them, so I'd been sending those who were more agreeable, like Juna, to talk them into it. Hopefully, they would listen, because we needed them.

When I reached the front of the mobile palace, the wall of archsorcerers parted, letting me through to speak with Princess Carolyn. Amelia stood nearby, guarding her mother and stepfather. She had a wand in one hand and a powerfully enchanted medallion in the other. She also wore an enchanted robe that was much too big for her but provided numerous buffs.

She gave me a grin as she waved, tossing about her too-big sleeve. “Hi, Vincent.” She didn’t smell stressed or afraid, only extremely excited by everything that was going on.

I smiled and returned the wave, as I stopped before Carolyn’s back. “We need to talk.”

She didn’t turn, playing the part of the heir to Arcadia receiving a petition. “I don’t agree. I’ve already prepared my people to abandon the mobile palace if the worst should happen. They will rendezvous with your guards before pushing on. I trust you and my guards will make sure this contingency does not come to pass.”

She still had a long way to go before she would make a good queen. “Preparing for the worst while hoping for the best is always wise, Princess. But cutting off an advisor as knowledgeable as myself when they come to you during a crisis may prevent you from learning something you need to know. Yes, it gives you an air of authority, but authority is useless if your ignorance leads to you marching your people to their deaths.”

Carolyn glanced over her shoulder and blushed. “I’ll remember. Now what did you wish to speak to me about?”

I nodded to Gorgath. He was sitting in the middle of the remaining dead ants, tossing aside the too-hard-to-eat chitin that he’d emptied of meat. The valuable third-floor material sat in massive piles, ready for the taking. And it would be the first of many such piles.

“Only the most important of subjects, Princess.”

Carolyn raised an eyebrow intrigued. “And that would be?”

“Loot distribution.”

33

THE COLONY

Mobile palaces were not designed for war, or for traveling underground. They existed purely so wealthy aristocrats and merchant princes could host dinner parties in the skies above their cities on clear, windless days, surrounded by powerful archsorcerers who would keep them aloft and free from assassins and thieves. Using one to carry the survivors through the Abyss was an act of desperation, like loading a billionaire's super-yacht with TNT and sailing it into an enemy port.

If the mobile palace flew too high, the worker ants crawling along the ceiling would instinctively recognise that they could survive the fall and happily release their grip, plummeting directly onto the mobile palace's barrier. One or two wouldn't be a problem, but worker ants were followers. They would drop one after the other until their combined weight broke the barrier or grounded the immense flying carpet.

On the other hand, fly too low and you would soon discover that worker ants could climb, as you watched them clamber over each other until they formed a living ant tower tall enough to reach anything they wanted. These were just the threats the workers posed to our mobile palace. The fliers and hunters were much worse, which was why I'd bullied everyone into raising their levels and taken steps to improve our chances. With everything I'd done and the short break we'd taken, we should have been able to waltz through this nest.

However, between the time I scouted this third-floor nest and the time we arrived, the number of hunter ants guarding our tunnel entrance quadrupled, drawn to the entrance by the acrid pheromones the hunters in the tunnel released upon death. With more than fifty gargantuan hunters crammed into the tunnel mouth, they had the ability to climb over each other and reach the ceiling, completely blocking the entrance if we didn't kill or cripple them first. That meant removing the hunters was essential for us to travel through the colony.

Wind howled in my ears, tearing at my coat, as I stood on the back of a racing carpet, anchored to the fabric by powerful enchantments. My pilot, Marin, was exceptionally skilled at controlling and manoeuvring any of his vast collection of flying carpets, but his skill truly came through when he piloted his personal racing carpet, the pride and joy of his collection.

With expert precision, he increased our elevation, hurling us towards the nearest uninjured hunter ant at three hundred miles an hour. His trajectory put us just above the hunter's fifty-foot-high shoulders as it bumped into its neighbours while trying to crush Sir Trent and Gregory's teams, which were rushing around its ankles.

The hunter saw us coming with its enormous compound eyes and instinctively threw back its head, swinging its mandibles to try to bash us from the sky. At the last moment, Marin dropped the carpet into a steep dive that took us directly beneath its throat, successfully tricking it into exposing the gap between the plates of ruby red chitin which protected its throat, allowing my spells to bypass its thick armour.

As the wind raged in my ears, I snapped my fingers, releasing the destruction spell I'd spent the last second empowering. A large section of the gargantuan ant's throat was engulfed by dark, destructive energy that consumed the light. The red flesh between the protective plates disintegrated, becoming a cloud of dust, as the air filled with more acrid, pain-induced pheromones.

I immediately began weaving a second spell.

Marin pulled up hard as we finished passing under the hunter's throat, performing an aerial loop that took us around its jaw and above its head. As we flew upside down, I snapped my fingers again, damaging a large section of armour on the back of its neck to keep its head raised.

I began weaving the spell again.

Marin finishing completing the loop-de-loop, taking us back under its throat. The third snap of my fingers decapitated the hunter, costing me only three spells instead of the dozen that it would take to get through its tough exoskeleton.

Marin cackled like a madman as we shot out from under the falling head, swerving through the air to dodge any flier ants that tried to pluck us from their domain. I shot a stream of basic firebolts towards our next target, and Marin cornered sharply, heading for the marked hunter.

Marin used the same tactic as he had with the last hunter, tricking it into raising its head, giving me another clear shot at its unprotected throat. Three spells later, its head fell to the ground, and we were after our new target.

We'd found something that worked.

Below us on the ground, Sir Trent and Gregory led their teams through the chaos, blurring around worker ants to hack at the hunters' knees and ankles. The injuries crippled their mobility and prevented the ants from being able to climb over each other and block the tunnel. The goal wasn't to kill them, but to cripple them effectively enough to push past them and race through the nest.

Our attack on the hunters was already gathering attention from the colony, and every ant in the immediate vicinity was converging on our entrance.

Over the deafening roar of rushing wind and clattering mandibles, I heard the synchronized chanting of Carolyn's archsorcerers coming from the approaching mobile palace. They were working together to raise a barrier across the front of the massive carpet, to barrel through the fliers like an ice breaker in the North Sea. They had no intention of slowing down and letting the fliers swarm them. The plan was to be in and out of the nest as fast as possible.

Marin's laughter grew louder, filled with pure, adrenaline-fueled excitement, as he began taking more risks and flying closer and closer to the hunters we killed. As we approached the twentieth hunter, he finally got us within arm's reach. I drew Slaughter and slammed the blade through the gap in the ant's unprotected throat, pushing pure necrotic energy through the blade as I used my vampiric soul touch, testing whether I could kill it faster.

The monster's mana and life force rushed into me as the destructive energies ran through its muscles, destroying large areas of flesh. We finished our loop-de-loop, but its head remained attached. It would die in a minute, but that was too long. I sheathed Slaughter and snapped my fingers, releasing a destruction spell to finish it off. The mobile palace rounded the far corner as the head fell to the ground.

I swept my gaze across the tunnel entrance, taking in every detail, and then I raised my left hand, releasing a stream of green firebolts to signal that it was safe to approach. The hunters weren't *all* dead or crippled, but they would be, by the time they reached us.

Marin never stopped his flight, continuing to manoeuvre through the hunters at breakneck speeds, relying on me to focus on casting spells. Marin's grin only receded when he spotted the mobile palace and the end of his freedom. The young man had volunteered to be my pilot against the wishes of his personal guards, partly because he hadn't contributed as much as he would have liked to our escape, but mostly because he knew he was the right man for the job.

A horn sounded as the mobile palace rushed in, signalling Sir Trent and Gregory to lead their teams into the nest. Marin heard the horn and turned his racing carpet to return to his mobile palace. His part in our attack was over for now.

I leapt from the carpet toward a hunter's corpse, throwing a destruction spell at the leg of an injured hunter that was trying to climb over the corpses and block the entrance from the approaching threat. Like lions, the ants didn't see thousands of people crammed onto a flying carpet; they saw one big predator moving towards their nest and prioritized it above everything else.

A now-familiar rhythm of clacking mandibles took over, and I felt the ants' behaviour change as all the fliers took to the air, filling the nest with the sounds of humming wings. Across the nest, every ant turned and charged toward us.

I threw several spells to make sure Marin made it to the mobile palace intact, while I directed Carolyn's guards and my deathlords through the corridor of corpses we created to usher them safely into the nest. A second later, the mobile palace shot through the tunnel above my head, quickly followed by Gorgath, who was running at full speed and acting as the rearguard with the zombie hunters.

I leapt onto the kid's furry shoulder, as he slammed his staff into the face of the first hunter that had lifted its body with broken legs and tried to grab him with its mandibles. I threw a destruction spell into the mouth of the second hunter that tried to grab him, momentarily stunning it as he used a basic barrier spell to stop a third from getting hold of his arm. Gorgath's fear filled my nostrils, exciting the monster in me and causing a demonic grin to spread across my lips. In a handful of seconds, he was over the blockade of blood and death and into the nest.

Millions of worker ants stood before us, clinging to every surface, while the fliers raced through the gaps. Hunters approached individually, from every direction, as Carolyn's guards and my deathlords battled their way through the workers to form a fighting wedge in front of the mobile palace, while others protected the sides. Gorgath raced ahead to take the lead position, while the mobile palace maintained its slower pace for the zombie hunters to catch up.

As Gorgath passed the mobile palace, I leapt off his shoulder and onto the barrier, blurring along the magical shield to a position near the back where Davina was hurling master-tier death bolts with mixed results.

Our zombie hunters were busy clambering over the dead and injured hunters blocking their way, as I began throwing out destruction spells to back up Davina and prevent the injured hunters from stopping our decoy from getting through. Leaving zombie hunters in the middle of the nest to run wild would pull most of the colony's attention away from us, so we couldn't lose them here. However, that might happen if Davina kept missing like she was.

"Throwing twice as many spells doesn't matter if you only hit half the time!" I had to shout to be heard over the humming of wings and clacking of mandibles.

Davina unleashed another master-tier death bolt, accidently hitting a flier and causing an explosion of death magic which killed the three closest to it. "I know that."

"Then why aren't you giving yourself the time you need to focus before you release your spells?"

"This is the perfect environment for leveling skills related to chain casting master-tier spells."

She wasn't wrong. "Good idea. Wrong time to implement it. If you don't stop missing, we're going to lose two of our zombies before we even get them into the nest."

"Oh."

Davina unleashed another master-tier death bolt. This time, the spell manoeuvred through the air around the fliers, striking an injured hunter's mandible, weakening its armour. The hunter was trying to grab one of our zombie hunters. I cast a destruction spell where Davina's death bolt had hit, and watched the mandible fall off, as I moved onto the next obstacle.

We needed every advantage to make this work, not just to get through this nest, but also through all the others. That meant I couldn't let Davina run around playing healer, or lose the zombie hunters at the entrance tunnel.

Below us, voices rose, as survivors and students began throwing their most powerful advanced spells through the palace barrier to kill and cripple the fliers. Throwing master-tier spells from within an advanced barrier, like the one we stood on, would have damaged it, which was why we were out here, and the other sorcerers were safely within.

Flying carpets began to rise from the mobile palace landing pad, bearing archsorcerers who could cast expert- and master-tier spells, forming a close secondary defence line outside the barrier. Everything was in motion as everyone did their part to see us safely through the chaos.

The top speed of the zombie hunters was sixty miles an hour, less than the mobile palace, but they would make up for that by providing the perfect distraction.

I watched the last zombie hunter escape the blockaded entrance. "Second position!" I shouted.

Davina and I turned and ran, stepping around lightning and fire bolts, to get to our position above the Undead Enhancement Club at the centre of the palace.

"Back-to-back," I shouted, as we came to a stop inside a storm of necromancy.

Davina shoved her back into mine, almost knocking me over with her strength. "Sorry."

I caught my balance before she'd apologised and had already thrown a destruction spell at the nearest hunter, trying to remove the threat as quickly as I could. Everyone who had taken my oath had leveled substantially, making them stronger, faster, and out of touch with their physical abilities. Mistakes like Davina's were common, but that didn't stop me from killing every hunter I could, to raise everyone's level further.

Being out of touch with their abilities might cause them to miscast a spell, trigging a magical backlash that might accidently kill them. However, not being strong enough to make up for all the sorcerers who were going to pass out from mana exhaustion would get everyone killed, so I didn't have a choice.

This was still the third floor of the Abyss, and despite the higher levels, we were transporting people who didn't belong here. If anyone failed to do their part, this could end in disaster. However, I didn't foresee any problems getting through this nest, now that we were through the blockade.

From the front of the convoy, Gorgath spotted our zombie hunters moving into position around the mobile palace and raised his bone staff. "Forward, Darksmith!"

ON THE FAR side of the chamber, I stepped out of the Deadlands beside a hunter that was blocking our exit, and snapped my fingers, hitting it with a destruction spell. Then I began slaughtering a path for everyone to safely escape through. I had to stop and throw out fingers of destruction to deal with the fliers that noticed me, slowing my progress, but this tunnel hadn't received reinforcements like where we entered, meaning there were only a dozen hunters in place. Killing four was enough to clear the way, but I continued killing until all but one was dead.

Sir Trent and Gregory's people were using their brief moment of freedom to chase experience, attacking the last crippled hunter with everything they had. They managed to kill it as the lower-level Old Monsters and deathlords raced past and the mobile palace flew overhead; and judging by their smiles, they'd all leveled. Gorgath passed through last, leaping onto the first corpse and using the others like stepping stones as he raced away from the nest.

I gave the nest one last look, considering what I'd learned and what we could do better in the future. A couple of dozen hunters were still chasing the mobile palace, but most were preoccupied fighting the zombie hunters we'd left near the queen. They were tearing everything around them apart and providing a good distraction.

Leaving the zombie hunters near the queen hadn't provided as good a distraction for the fliers and workers as I'd hoped. Most were still prioritizing us over the threat to the queen, likely because the threat was too big for them to engage effectively. That was a problem. As more and more of our sorcerers succumbed to mana exhaustion, the fliers would become a real threat.

They'd overwhelm our defences.

There wasn't anything I could do differently, based on what I had to work with, and no one was desperate enough to allow me to cross lines that would get us through this safely yet. For now, it was a waiting game.

I turned and blurred two hundred yards inside the tunnel and then stopped to face the horde of workers and fliers that were chasing after us. Angelica and Davina appeared beside me as the last of our people ran past.

I raised my hand, and snapped my fingers, weaving together a death void. A giant, swirling sphere of darkness appeared near the tunnel ceiling.

Angelica noticed Davina's slightly zombified state and wrinkled her nose. "You smell like a dried-up corpse."

Davina made a face. "Ewww."

"You also *look* like one. Are you okay?"

"I've been worse."

"So that's a no."

"I don't think anyone could be fine under these circumstances."

"Speak for yourself. I feel amazing."

Angelica slapped her breastplate for emphasis, slightly high off all the life force she'd consumed.

I wove two more death voids while they bantered, creating a triangle of death which would kill anything except the hunters if they approached.

"Davina, anchor these death voids for me. Angelica, cripple the hunters' legs after they enter the tunnel. We need to stop them here, or they're going to chase us all the way to the next nest."

Angelica blurred forward, while Davina pulled her ritual equipment from her storage pouches and began carving runes into the floor with her staff. Out of sight around the corner, the convoy had slowed to a stop. I could hear clerics and paladins racing around treating injuries, while officers checked equipment, and everyone caught their breath.

We'd survived passing through the first nest, proving we could do it. I didn't know if we could pull this off six more times, not while losing more people to mana exhaustion, but I was making plans as though we could. The only other option was to abandon everyone who couldn't keep up, and Kathrine would never forgive me if I did.

34

THE WINDS OF DEATH

Our foray through the fourth ant colony almost ended in ruin when more than half of our air defence passed out multiple times across two minutes. Most of the survivors, students, and faculty were now suffering from extreme mana exhaustion. The most functional kept forgetting the words they were trying to say, while the least functional were unable to do more than stare into space while drooling. None of them were fit to cast spells, as every time they tried to rely on their skills to force their bodies to comply, they passed out. This was a serious problem. Our current method for passing through the ant nests wouldn't work without enough air defence.

However, my only solution for finishing our journey through the third floor involved committing war crimes, acts which were universally condemned by every nation on the planet. That didn't bother me, but everyone else would disagree, which is why I'd had to wait until they were desperate enough to be more morally flexible.

Mandible clacks echoed through the tunnel entrance as Davina finished anchoring my latest death voids with runic circles, holding the spells in place to stop the workers and fliers from getting through. With the circles, the spells could self-sustain for a few hours before deteriorating and breaking apart.

Davina turned to me, leaning on her staff for support, as her zombifying body sapped her strength. Casting so many master-tier death bolts and being close to so many death voids was catching up with her, despite how much her unique constitution had improved.

"I'm done," she said. "Where do you want me to begin making the next layer of death voids?"

"At the next intersection. Use the hunter corpses to enhance the spells."

Davina nodded, turned, and dashed off, moving like a blur through the glowing crystal forest. Her speed was still impressive, but slower, due to her zombifying constitution and growing mana sickness. I turned to the entrance and leapt between the dark vortexes of death energy, unaffected by the vacuum pressure that tried to drain my life force and leave me a withered husk.

A hundred yards in front of me, Angelica was crippling hunters while dodging workers and fliers as she slowly blocked the tunnel with bodies.

Helping me kill so many hunters had pushed Angelica and Davina's levels beyond the mid-200s, firmly cementing them in Dragon territory. My instincts were still screaming at me to wrap Angelica up with compulsions so tight she couldn't think for herself, but I still refused to do so. Not only did the man I once was think it was wrong, but it was also short-sighted.

My ability to compel Angelica would always fade, given enough time. *My monster* was always going to gain her freedom. Reconciling her anger and bitterness, pushing her to have more self-control, and pulling her from the self-centred shell she'd created to survive her parents had been my long-term plan for her. Without those changes, nothing protected me from her wrath or her lack of comprehension over the horrors of what I'd done to her.

Angelica was my greatest mistake, and I wouldn't subject her to any more mistakes, even if that cost me my life. Luke understood that. It was why he was so concerned when he left. He could see how quickly Angelica was growing stronger, and *he* knew she could break free from my control, even if she didn't know that herself.

I'd once promised him that I would treat Angelica better, that I would be better so that he didn't have to be the hero who slayed the monster she became. I was no longer certain I could keep that promise, but I couldn't be anything other than the man I was. And the man I was, wanted what was best for *my monster,* even if I couldn't always give it to her.

I climbed the hill of hunter bodies and stopped beside Angelica, raising my hand and snapping my fingers to begin slaughtering the hunters she'd already crippled. Angelica raised the end of her staff, filling the air with enough death fire to impress a dracolich, before leaping towards another hunter that was trying to scale her wall of writhing victims. Death fire surrounded her staff as she released a powerful necrotic strike on a hunter's knee, dissolving a couch-sized section of chitin and destroying the muscle underneath.

She moved to the next leg and repeated the process until the gargantuan ant couldn't hold its own weight. Then, she left it to drag itself to the ideal position before breaking its remaining knees.

With only the two of us killing the hunters, Angelica's level continued to grow, though the growth was beginning to slow as she was getting close to reaching the same level as the hunters.

Her current skill was a mere shadow of the raw power her armour and attributes offered her, leaving her significantly less deadly than she could be. Right now, she'd be able to hold her own against an ancient vampire if they caught up, but she wouldn't be able to kill it, even though her vampiric touch and aura were now much stronger than before.

The growth and changes to her equipment no longer concerned me. There were no signs of corruption from the base materials. The craftsmen's precautions to curb the darker nature of the materials I'd asked them to use seemed to have worked. If anything, the stronger vampiric influence appeared to be calming her down, making her more analytical and focused.

For the next ten minutes, we killed hunters, clogging the tunnel with their corpses until there wasn't enough room for any of them to push through.

Angelica turned to me after knocking a worker from the ceiling with her staff. "Is this enough?"

I could sense that there weren't any hunters left nearby. The workers would take a long time to clear these bodies without them, so the chance of them breaking through and destroying the death voids, allowing the fliers to chase us before we moved on, was low. But it was still possible. That was why I had Davina producing other death voids to slow them down.

"It's enough."

Angelica turned and leapt from the pile of corpses to the crystal-packed tunnel floor three hundred feet below, hitting the ground and exploding forward at speeds I couldn't hope to follow.

I entered the Deadlands to catch up.

I stepped out of the Deadlands at the second intersection, next to the hunters' corpses and the runic circles Davina had created.

Two hours of fighting our way through ant territory had filled every storage item we had with chitin, growing my hoard of loot. The only thing we were taking now were cores, so each corpse had a gaping hole where Gorgath had torn the core free while he collected several of their more magically dense organs to eat.

I raised my hand and snapped my fingers three times in quick succession, creating three death voids. Davina finished empowering her circles, linking them to the spells above and anchoring them in place.

"Done," she said half a minute later before racing off.

Several intersections later, each warded with death voids, we caught up with the rearguard. Gorgath was busy tearing into a corpse for its core and organs, while Gregory and sixty deathlords, who could now fight the hunters alone inside the nest, stood guard.

I exited the Deadlands next to Gregory in a giant crystal forest that lit the tunnel as bright as day. The smell of ant blood and offal filled the air, lost among the pheromone the hunter ants released upon their death.

The ongoing fighting had finally destroyed Gregory's equipment. He was wrapped from head to toe in bone armour Davina had summoned. His aura radiated power to a degree that told me I couldn't harm him without magic. He was too tough and fast. However, he wouldn't survive more than ten seconds against the strongest of my kind without the necessary equipment to back him up.

Gregory gave me a stiff nod as he scanned the area for threats. "Did you get the tunnel blocked this time?"

"As well as we can under the circumstances."

"That's what you said last time, before we almost got the survivors killed trying to push through before we were ready."

He was stressed, subconsciously or consciously, knowing we couldn't survive another nest.

"That wasn't because we pushed forward too soon," I replied.

"I saw the barrier around the mobile palace flickering."

"The barrier issue is because we don't have enough air defence to keep the fliers at bay, not because we weren't prepared."

He gritted his teeth. "We need to change our tactics, I take it?"

I nodded.

"How much am I going to hate your new plan?"

"A lot. I'm going to summon a death wind."

Gregory whipped his head toward me. "Fucking hell, sir."

"Language."

Gregory ignored me. "Are you trying to lose your soul and get the rest of us executed?"

"It's the only way to ground the fliers."

"There has to be a better way."

"There isn't."

Gregroy froze. "You mean that literally, don't you, sir?"

"I do. We don't have the people, levels, or skills to go any further with brute force. Our only viable options involve crossing lines no one wants to cross."

"Then, at the very least, get Davina to make it."

Summoning a death wind would create a more toxic version of the environment that surrounded Contessa's city. It would be like standing inside a basic death bolt spell, and the more we killed inside it, the stronger the effect would become.

For those without the death magic resistance skill, entering it would be fatal. It wouldn't be fatal for the ants, not in a timeframe that mattered, but the fast-beating wings of the fliers would quickly burn off, corroding away in seconds, removing their ability to fly.

"Davina can't tap into your mana," I replied. "Her death wind won't be big enough to flood the nest. I'm the only one who can do it."

"Fuck."

"Language."

SUMMONING a death wind had more in common with crafting undead than with casting a spell, because of one detail: A death wind required large quantities of life's bane to be summoned. Life's bane was an undead material universally banned in every nation, even North Murdell. Its corruptive and destructive properties made radioactive fallout preferable to it appearing within your borders, because radioactive fallout couldn't self-propagate.

The first step of creating life's bane involved turning the hunters closest to the nest into zombies. The second step involved mutating those zombies' flesh into a cancerous, death-corrupted powder. The cancerous-powdered flesh was then infused with different corrupting forms of death magic, and the core of a sharn beast to enhance the effects. These forms of death magic weakened everything the cancerous powder encountered, allowing the powder to feed on life force and magic to transform living flesh into more life's bane.

Fire, life, holy, necrotic, or alternative forms of death magic were the only way to destroy the substance, though enough time away from life force would also do it. Creating a handful of the material was enough to get you banned from most nations, but only after a bounty had been placed on your head with every adventurers' guild in the country.

However, despite all that, it was still my *least*-destructive option for getting everyone safely through the third floor, and everyone only agreed to my plan after I brought up the other options.

While I performed the necessary spells, Gregory had my deathlords sit behind me in rows, gathering mana. The mana they gathered flowed from their cores into mine before I channelled it into the shrinking pile of life's bane. A thick, grey cloud of swirling decay billowed from the mutated zombie flesh and sharn beast core, racing down the tunnel towards the mobile palace.

Using the life force of those inside the mobile palace as a magnet allowed me to move the death wind through the Abyss without a trail of bodies. However, doing it this way wasn't without its risks.

Everyone who didn't have the death magic resistance skill was locked inside the mobile palace's barrier, protected by clerics and paladins who were cleansing the life's bane leaking through. I'd lose my soul if they failed to do their part, but our choices were between this, something worse, or leaving the survivors to die.

I wasn't going to leave them to die.

Kathrine finally cared about me.

As the last of the life's bane lifted from the floor and flew away, I wove an empowered expert-tier spell to slow the deterioration and control it. As the spell encompassed the swirling cloud, I lowered my hand and turned to Gregory. "We're ready."

Gregory grunted as he opened his eyes. "On your feet and to your positions!"

We'd spent half an hour summoning this death wind, but if I successfully maintained it, we wouldn't need to create another before we left the third floor. With enough corpses, I could use the life's bane's self-propagating properties to drag the death wind to the next nest.

Deathlords in bone armour blurred through the tunnel, forming a fighting wedge in front of the mobile palace, while Gregory and his team ran ahead to invade the nest.

Seeing everyone finally moving, Gorgath pushed himself to his feet and lumbered past me, heading to the mobile palace to join the frontline. The kid was already breathing heavy as his stronger life force attracted the life's bane, even as I tried my best to push it away from him.

Davina stood on his shoulder, absorbing the death magic in the air around him and nullifying the life's bane that clung to him with holy spells. The life's bane wasn't likely to kill him in the next few hours, but left untreated, he would be dead before the end of the day.

Gorgath glanced back as he approached the edge of the concentrated death wind. "Gorgath better understands why Professor Vincent is so feared by his people now." He turned and plunged headfirst through the cloud, making his way to the front.

I raised my hand and cast the death void spell as far behind the convoy as possible while maintaining the death wind. Death voids fed on all forms of death magic, including life's bane. The spell self-stabilised in the death-rich environment, feeding off the taint I'd created. It would purify the tunnel, destroying the horror I'd unleashed before burning itself out.

My last job done, I blurred towards the mobile palace and leapt, casting a basic levitation spell to lighten my weight. I landed on the barrier within the swirling, grey cloud of life's bane and sent a telepathic message to Carolyn to move forward, as I ran to the centre of the mobile palace.

As the mobile palace accelerated, I drew mana from the Undead Enhancement Club's cores. Most were true necromancers, so I'd been able to bond with their cores using my sorcerer sovereign skill. Moving the death wind with the mobile palace required more mana than just holding it in place, which was why the students had to step in.

With each nest we passed through, Gregory's team had grown. Almost one hundred deathlords could now survive in the colony. That was enough that I was no longer concerned about the hunters or the workers. If this worked, the fliers also wouldn't be a problem.

As the mobile palace approached the end of the tunnel, I sensed Gregory and his team leaving, having finished crippling the hunters blocking the entrance. A few seconds later, we reached the end of the tunnel and the entrance to the nest, and the amount of life force around me grew.

I sensed the crippled hunters lying across the tunnel floor, unable to lift themselves from the ground as the mobile palace passed overhead.

I then sensed the dead and dying workers on the ground below us, along with the fliers in the air around us.

Unleashing the death wind was as easy as releasing my hold over it. Freed from my restraints, it blew in all directions, a raging tempest drawn by the stronger life force of the ants, filling the nest with a thick, grey fog that poisoned everything it touched.

As my vision cleared, I watched the first ruby-coloured fliers enter their new environment. Their fast-beating wings immediately began to corrode from the quick, repeated contact with the caustic material. Within seconds, they began to fall, dropping to the ground with frayed wings, unable to fly without them, like monsters on the lower floors.

The death wind moved like a shockwave, spreading through the nest and corrupting everything it encountered. It spread faster because of the fliers' dissolving wings and the worker ants' corpses, which were breaking down beneath us.

I raised my hand and cast the death void spell at the entrance to the tunnel behind us. The spell shuddered for a second and then stabilised, not needing my input to maintain itself as it fed on the death wind, like the other death void I'd created. My new priority was destroying the death wind once it had served its purpose. Letting this spread through the Abyss was not something I wanted.

I was almost certain that the Abyss had some mechanism to protect itself from the material, but being *almost* certain and being *certain* were two entirely different situations.

I spent the six-mile journey through the colony creating a death void every quarter of a mile to cleanse the corruption I'd brought to the Abyss.

Ten minutes later, we entered the tunnel we sought without trouble. The threats from the fliers, hunters, and workers were all accounted for.

A hundred yards in, the mobile palace stopped.

As ordered, Davina leapt from Gorgath's shoulder and ran back to the tunnel entrance to join Gregory and his team. They then raced off to raise death voids at the other tunnel entrances to prevent the life's bane from spreading through the Abyss.

I leapt from the back of the mobile palace to a barren tunnel floor near the entrance and was immediately surrounded by Commander Taylor's people.

"Your Dark Eminence, we are ready to serve," she announced.

"You know what to do."

She turned to her people. The one hundred deathlords under her command dropped to the ground and began gathering mana before she gave the order, proving my statement true.

I turned to the nest, drawing on their mana, and wove the spell needed to summon the death wind swirling through it. As I released the spell, the grey cloud began to pour into our tunnel, over the heads of the other deathlords still holding the entrance against the workers. It blew past us to surround the mobile palace.

With each passing second, the cloud grew thicker and more destructive. I heard shouting coming from within as clerics and paladins did their best to control the leaks.

As I finished summoning the death wind from the nest, Sir Trent appeared beside me. With him standing so close, my instincts put me on edge, and my mouth began to salivate at the richness of his blood. Not only was he stronger than Gregory, but he also had the equipment and skill to back up his strength.

Sir Trent stared at the swirling, grey cloud around the mobile palace for a few seconds. It was even thicker than the previous one. The dead ants and high ambient mana made it easy for the life's bane to replicate itself.

Sir Trent grimaced. "Can you truly control this curse?"

"It's not a curse."

"So you claim."

"Have you ever heard of a curse that was this destructive?"

"No."

"So, not a curse. What do you want?"

"The princess wants to know if you foresee any further problems with our escape?"

I could sense exactly where Davina was, so I waited a few seconds to give my reply. "So long as they maintain the barrier and keep the life's bane that is leaking inside contained, we should escape the Abyss without any further problems."

To punctuate my point, a death void appeared in the centre of the nest. Every ant froze in place for a second. Then as one, they all turned and ran away, rushing to defend their queen.

Sir Trent glanced at the fleeing ants, before glancing back at me, smelling slightly intimidated by the timing of my pronouncement and everything he saw. He stared at me for another few seconds, before leaving in a blur to inform the princess of the good news.

35

REST AND RECOVERY

You can only push the body so far before it gives out. Fear and adrenaline will take you past the breaking point, with magic taking you further than that, but everything will catch up with you in the first moment free from danger. That's when you collapse. When you succumb to your body's weakness.

Just beyond the entrance to the Abyss, flying carpets littered the dungeon floor. The sorcerers who had flown them through the Abyss lay passed out on top, beside their equally exhausted passengers, filling the tunnel with harmonious snoring. The threat of death had faded with each floor we ascended, with each mile we travelled away from ant territory, but the survivors only felt safe enough to collapse after we reached the dungeon.

Nothing would rouse them now.

So, I stood near the top of the tunnel, planning our next move. Sir Trent was there with all twenty-six of Carolyn's guards who had taken my oath. Gregory was next to him with dozens of his strongest deathlords, the ones with death and necrotic resistance. Mother and Father each supported one of their groups, while Dalin and his small order stood to the side, guarding the most dangerous members of the faculty.

Our escape through the Abyss had strengthened everyone, giving us a real chance of driving off the ancient vampires if they showed up. However, our odds were still fifty-fifty, and I preferred we never meet them.

As I laid out my plan, Carolyn interrupted. "You can't just tell the students to pick a direction and fly once we reach the surface."

Too many nodded their heads in agreement.

"I can and I will," I replied. "It's their best chance of survival. Tracking someone through the air over a significant distance takes time, even for my kind. Depending on how much of a head start they have, the vampires can only capture and turn between ten and three hundred each. Worse case, half of the students die because of this plan. Best case, less than one hundred."

She glared at me. "Those are unacceptable losses."

"That doesn't stop them from being necessary, Princess."

"It does when we're significantly stronger than we were."

More heads nodded.

"I don't deny we're stronger. But when we left Darksmith, we couldn't survive a confrontation with two ancient vampires, let alone four. Now, our odds of winning against four are fifty-fifty. Those odds go down outside a confined space, where we can be targeted by hit-and-run tactics."

Carolyn took a step forward and glared up at me. "So, you'll let them die?"

"No, Princess. I'm giving them a chance to live. Sometimes that's the best you can do."

I watched her ball her fists as anger and frustration overwhelmed her. The time she'd spent alone with Luke over the past few months was beginning to show through. Like my conversations with my son, their discussions outside her lessons mostly revolved around morals and ethics. The thought of leaving people she thought we could save didn't sit well with her. It was a good change to see, even if her feelings were misplaced.

A good person did their best in life. Sometimes, their best wasn't enough to solve the problem. Knowing you couldn't fix everything was an important part of growing up. Knowing that just because you couldn't fix everything didn't mean you shouldn't try was an even more important part.

I was trying to save these people. I was going to fail some of them, and that was okay. The world would be a better place because I tried.

Everyone politely closed their lips and looked away as they waited for Princess Carolyn to regain control of herself. She was in a situation no one her age should have to face. She would also one day be their ruler, so none of them wanted her to remember a situation where she felt they embarrassed her.

I didn't care if she felt embarrassed.

Luckily for them, a distraction appeared.

Everyone turned as Marin's racing carpet shot down the tunnel towards us, carrying a handful of students who had reconned the dungeon. Marin slowed at the last second, bringing the carpet down smoothly beside our group. We could have come out in only a handful of dungeons based on the distance we had travelled, and the students he'd been ferrying around on his racing carpet all knew what those dungeons looked like and had maps in their storage pouches. Hopefully, one of them had figured out where we were.

Baris leapt off the carpet, leaving the other students behind. "We're in Necropolis's dungeon," he shouted excitedly. "I'm completely sure of it."

Everyone gave him their full attention.

"What can you tell us about it?" I asked.

"It's the second-biggest dungeon in North and South Murdell, with the most convoluted tunnel system for several kingdoms. We're about half a day from the fortress, even if we use the flying carpets."

A lot of people swore.

Half a day was too long.

I turned to Gorgath.

He was sitting against the tunnel wall, receiving overdue medical treatment. The kid had been exposed to so much life's bane that it had seeped into his flesh. I could smell him breathing it out with every breath. Davina was standing on his knee, trying to remedy the situation with holy magic.

"Gorgath, how far to the nearest dungeon?"

Gorgath turned his head towards us. "Not far. But we must pass through the third floor to reach it. If we travel higher, the nearest dungeon is half a day's travel."

Before anyone could protest, I ended that line of thinking. "Everyone is too exhausted for that."

Everyone closed their mouths.

I turned to Baris. "Give me your map and a pen."

Baris handed over the map and fished a pen from his storage pouch. "Do you need to know anything, sir?"

I scanned the map, memorising it and making note of how big the dungeon fortress was. It filled the entire first chamber. I'd known it was big, based on several books I'd read, but I hadn't realised it was that big.

"Does Necropolis have any powerful holy relics, clerics, paladins, or warriors who could help us fight ancient vampires?"

Baris glanced at Gregory before looking back. "As far as I'm aware, we don't have any powerful holy relics, and the church's presence is small. The Head Inquisitor is an Old Monster with a lot of skill, but I don't believe he could keep up with your people anymore. The Grave Diggers' society discourages everyone from leveling too high, and the Darklord's assassins take care of anyone who ignores their advice."

"See if anyone in the Undead Enhancement Club knows anything you don't."

"Yes, sir."

I turned back to the group as Baris raced off, nearly blurring with his speed. "I'm extending our rest period. Our new plan is to dig in and hold this position until the survivors reach the fortress and escape."

Carolyn frowned at the news. "Why are you changing your plan?"

"Half a day to reach the dungeon fortress drastically increases our chances of a confrontation. If we're going to have to fight, I'd rather fight from a reinforced position."

"And the students?"

"They'll get a chance to recover. The healthiest townsfolk will pilot the flying carpets to the dungeon fortress. That will give the students half a day to rest and recuperate before they attempt to make their escape."

Carolyn pressed her lips together but nodded.

I turned to Dalin. "I need multiple stationary barriers across this tunnel. Once you've set up the barriers, I need this place filled with every alarm spell the faculty knows. If they're travelling through the Deadlands, the barriers will force them to exit, triggering the alarms."

"Why not traps?" Dalin asked.

"We don't have the time to make a trap powerful enough to kill an ancient vampire, and their regeneration makes anything that doesn't kill them almost pointless. Knowing they've reached the dungeon is the only thing that can give us an advantage. Get the faculty working on it."

Dalin stepped away and began rounding people up.

I turned to Carolyn, marking three locations on the map. "After we've finished reinforcing this location, I need you to move ahead and manage the placement of barriers and alarms here, here, and here."

Carolyn took the map and glanced at my marks. "Why those locations?"

"There are multiple ways to reach those points, but every path eventually leads to them. There is no point in alarming places they could bypass."

Carolyn handed the map to Rupert. "If I'm going to build an early warning system, my people will need the help of all the faculty not participating in the fight."

I would've suggested that eventually, but I wanted to see if she would think of it herself. She had the makings of a good leader. She just needed a chance to practice and to continue listening to and learning from her advisors.

"Good idea. Dalin, make sure your people help her."

There was the briefest shadow of a smile before Carolyn turned to her people and started giving instructions. Gregory figured out what I would order him to do and blurred away to order everyone to rest before I could tell him to.

I turned to Mother and Father. "I need your people to make this tunnel hallowed ground before filling it with as many holy wards as you can manage."

Mother nodded. "We have no objections to your request but will ask the necrosaint to confirm your request."

I dismissed them with a wave of my hand.

Seeing I was temporarily unoccupied, Marin walked over and tilted his head slightly. It wasn't quite a bow, but as close to a bow as someone in line for the throne was allowed to give in the Bo Empire.

"Thank you for saving my life," he said.

"I don't need your thanks. I need you to warn your empress of the threat sitting on your border."

"That will be difficult. I have no intention of staying and learning the full extent of this threat. When Baris returns with my map, I will be leaving with my guards. If you survive, you may write to me, and I will pass your warning to my mother."

Marin and Carolyn had shared several conversations about me over our journey through the Abyss. Marin understood why she was my prisoner and the nature of my existence. He didn't understand how I fit into his worldview, but he was pragmatic enough to be temporary allies until a better option appeared. Now that he could escape, he was going to.

"No need. Shadow, travel with Marin to the fortress and answer his questions."

Shadow slid out of my coat, forming a black silhouette next to me. He'd grown stronger during our journey, drawing upon the life force I absorbed through my vampiric aura. His shape was more defined than when we left the academy, no longer just matching my body's outline, but also my features. You could count the fingers on each hand and clearly see his nose.

Marin leaned closer to Shadow with obvious interest. "Your shade can speak."

"Shadow is a true shade, not a poor imitation."

A look of wonder transformed his expression. "You really *have* kept your soul, haven't you? I thought it was a lie to placate everyone, but you couldn't make a true shade without one. I'll do my best to ensure your soul shard returns to you unharmed. And I will pass along what it shares to my mother." Marin glanced at his flying carpet collection, which was currently being used as bedding, and he sighed. "You may return my collection to me in the future or keep it as a token of my gratitude."

"I don't have any storage space for your collection. You would have to leave your master storage chest behind if you wanted me to collect them."

Marin looked like he was trying to pass a kidney stone as he decided between leaving his entire collection to gain a chance of the collection being returned or immediately losing the better half of his collection with no chance of getting it back. His shoulders slumped. "You may borrow my master storage chest. I'll travel faster without it."

"That's wise a decision. I strongly suggest you don't stop until you reach your empire."

"I don't plan to. Now if you will excuse me, I need to find where my map is."

Marin turned and walked back to his racing carpet to find Baris. I could hear the conversations Baris was having with the other necromancers. None of them had more insight into the city's capabilities, beyond mentioning wards and stationary defences that could help if we fought in the city.

It looked like reinforcements weren't coming.

Angelica was front and centre with Sir Trent and his toughest fighter, ready for a surprise attack if it should appear from the tunnel to the Abyss, so I had a moment to address my next problem.

I walked over to Gorgath.

Davina jumped down from where she had been scaling his chest, landing beside me. She still looked like a walking corpse but was much faster than when we left the third floor. A few more hours and she would be back to her old self.

She leaned against her staff as she turned and looked at her patient.

"More life's bane appears whenever I think I'm finished cleansing his skin. I don't know what I'm doing wrong?"

"I told you, it's in his lungs. It's coming out when he breathes."

"How am I supposed to cure that? He's resistant to all forms of magic. My spells won't go deep enough. Believe me, I've tried."

"You're overthinking this. Tie a rope to one of his teeth and climb down his throat."

Davina made a face, repelled by the idea of being surrounded by so much monster slobber. "There has to be another way?"

"You said it yourself. He's resistant to all forms of magic. You need to get closer to the source."

She sighed, accepting that my method was necessary, and pulled her enchanted rope from her storage pouch. She'd made it during her enchanting classes because I kidnapped people and took prisoners often enough to need one. She threw the rope over her shoulder. "Gorgath, can you open your mouth for me?"

The kid opened his mouth as wide as possible.

Davina jumped and landed on his tongue. She secured the rope around a tooth before diving down the back of his throat. An expression I'd only seen on those experiencing heartburn appeared on the kid's face.

"Don't swallow her," I said.

"Gorgath will do his best."

"After we get everyone out of the dungeon, I'll get you back to your people."

So long as my people weren't travelling with the students, I wasn't concerned about their safety. They had nothing the vampires wanted. It made no sense for them to be attacked.

"This is the way," he said as his mouth and nostrils filled with holy light.

The smell of life's bane coming from Gorgath's breath vanished. The holy glow radiating from his mouth continued as I smelled more stomach acid enter his breath. Davina had taken it upon herself to cleanse his stomach. It wasn't necessary. The stomach acid he'd gained from the acid centipede's bloodline broke down the life's bane that reached it.

A few seconds later, Davina climbed out of the back of his throat covered in saliva, untied her rope, surrounded Gorgath's body with holy magic to cleanse the last traces of life's bane, and jumped down.

She landed near me, looking like a shiny, drowned rat. She ran her palm across her face and flicked the saliva on the ground. "Yuck. That better have worked."

"It worked. We'll have to wait and see if it sticks."

"Call me if his condition changes."

A grin appeared on her face before she blurred towards me too fast for me to follow and then stepped to the side. Her manoeuvre flicked most of Gorgath's warm slimy saliva over me, soaking my front. I wiped the kid's drool from my face.

Gorgath laughed at Davina's antics as he pushed himself to his feet. "Gorgath no longer feels strained in the dungeon due to increasing his mana regeneration and wishes to know if he can visit the surface to tell his people stories of the sky."

Gorgath now had more than twenty times the mana regeneration he'd had when he first started attending Darksmith. It made sense that he felt comfortable in the dungeon. It would also make sense that he could survive on the surface, and his request could save me from having to walk him home.

"If you can survive on the surface, would you be willing to travel across it to reach a safer dungeon to enter?"

Gorgath nodded vigorously. "Gorgath would like that." He excitedly turned to the survivors. "Gorgath will ask Arro if he can visit her home with her."

I let him walk off. He was now someone else's problem to deal with, because I had ancient vampires to prepare for.

36

THE THREE-PROFESSOR PROBLEM

Luke would have loved our setup for the battle. Layered blue barriers that gave off a gentle hum sat in front and behind those of us who had stayed behind to fight, giving the tunnel a similar feel to the power-generating facility at the end of *The Phantom Menace*. The fact that we intended to confront pure evil here gave it a touch of authenticity, as if this was the final showdown between good and evil.

I was happy my children weren't here, though.

Their blood was too intoxicating. Ancient vampires would go out of their way to capture them alive, turning them into never-ending blood bags that could be thrown in a corner and nibble on for decades. My children would be left without limbs, without eyes, without ears, without access to any of their senses, cut off from everything except pain, so they weren't a threat. It was a fate worse than death.

And I would do everything in my power to ensure that never happened to them.

I watched the last non-combatants followed Gorgath away from the Abyss entrance tunnel and stepped from the frontline to deal with my last three problems. Everyone who had stayed behind could keep up with an ancient vampire's magic or attributes, but the list of people with the levels and equipment necessary to face both was short. Only Angelica, Davina, Sir Trent, and three of his people could engage the ancient vampires while they were at their peak. Everyone else had to settle for helping where they could.

That meant there were seven of us in the front row, thirty-five in the second, and one hundred and fifty-eight in the third. Each row was more vulnerable than the last. All that most of the third row could do was exchange their lives to slow the enemy down and give the heavy hitters a chance to do what they needed. The exceptions were the three I needed to speak with.

Helen and Gregory offered me a small nod as I approached the second row. Mother and Father stood nearby, holding a powerful holy barrier to protect the six meditating clerics maintaining the hallowed ground spell.

Entering hallowed ground wouldn't kill an ancient vampire, but it would reduce their regeneration. That was enough of a threat to turn the eight clerics into high-priority targets, drawing magical attacks away from everyone else in the second row.

I made my way through the second row to the exorcists in the third row, who served the similar purpose as the clerics in the second row. The unit of deathlords guarding them stepped to the side as I approached.

Professor Burdin, the muscular head of the exorcism department, saw me coming and approached the edge of his team's barrier. "We've locked down the tunnel like you asked. They won't be able to summon demons anywhere close to here."

I knew that already. There was a pressure in the air that felt stifling to me. Like it rejected my existence. Being here was unpleasant, but his anti-demon summoning field wasn't why I needed to talk to him.

"I need to know if you can banish a vampire?"

Professor Burdin scratched his chin. "Vampires are only half demon."

"That makes it harder, but not impossible," I pointed out.

"True, but you would need someone to hold them in place, and I don't think anyone here is willing to condemn themselves to Hell voluntarily."

"You'd have to banish them *with* the vampire?"

"I would."

"How long would it take you if I could find someone?"

"Too long. You've got a dozen faster ways to kill them."

There was nothing more I could say without warning Angelica of her new abilities. But I'd planted the seed in Professor Burdin's head. He would be ready if I needed him. "Keep it in mind, in case I find someone."

I turned to leave.

"Wait a moment."

I turned back. "Is this important?"

"It could be. Are you the reason so many lesser demons have been plaguing Darksmith, or is it something you brought with you?"

There was no accusation in his tone, just curiosity. "It's me."

"The lesser demons have been claiming you're a prince of Hell."

"Ancient royal vampire, so I'm not a prince of Hell yet."

"You're wrong about that. You're a prince. You just haven't returned to Hell to claim your kingdom."

"That's a matter of debate."

"Only among scholars. Those of us who do this professionally know it's a fact."

"Does this conversation have a point?"

"If we should fall and they summon lesser demons, the demons will follow *your* commands, not theirs."

His announcement ran against what I knew of his profession but aligned with my instincts. "You're sure about that?"

He motioned toward those he knew. "I'm willing to bet my colleagues' lives on it."

That was good enough for me to believe him.

"I'll do my best to take command of them, should they appear."

"That's all I'm asking."

I turned and headed for Professor Lan, the head of the planar studies department. She was hiding near the back of the third row. The woman was barely five feet tall, yet she was one of the few professors I considered a threat to my existence, because she could shift objects to other dimensions at range. She was also the only person we'd had to *force* to be here.

The group of thirty deathlords guarding her parted as I approached. Professor Lan noticed me and began nervously fiddling with the cuff of her robe.

"What do you want from me, now?" she asked, without looking at me.

"I want to know if you're ready."

She was an academic, not a warrior, and she began to tremble after my question. "No one could be ready for this madness."

"Yet, we need to be."

"Please go away."

She was truly terrified, and that would make it impossible for her to do what she needed to do. "I want to, but I could smell your fear from the first row. I came here to ask you if you would like me to compel you to calm down?"

Her eyes darted to her guards before looking at the other faculty members. "Is that how you got everyone to work with you?"

"No. Most don't consider me a threat because they've accepted that I've been living safely among you for months without causing harm, and it is in my own self-interest to do my best to fight with you and keep you alive."

She kept he gaze anchored to the ground. "You took us into the Abyss."

"And yet you survived."

"You said you were taking us there because we couldn't survive a confrontation with these vampires."

"And now we can."

She gritted her teeth, trying and failing to lift her gaze from my feet. "I'm not a brave person."

Her fear stopped her from seeing the truth. "You travelled through the Abyss without giving in to terror. You're braver than you think."

"Then why am I terrified now?"

"Because you have common sense." In a much softer tone, I added, "Let me help you."

Her trembling grew worse. "What do you need me to do?"

"Look into my eyes and try not to resist."

She slowly lifted her head and met my gaze.

With a gentle push, I invaded her mind. It didn't take any effort. It was like reaching out to take her hand.

I started by trying to overpower her aura and make her brain release happy chemicals to let her relax. Then, I tried to reduce the activity in the fear centres. After that, I moved on to more complex changes. Her aura fought me the entire time, so the changes I achieved were significantly less than I desired.

Twenty seconds after starting, I broke eye contact.

Your Ancient Royal Vampiric Physique has increased skill to level 16.

"That's the best I can do," I admitted.

She glanced at her hand, noticing it was no longer trembling. "I'm less afraid, but I'm still afraid."

"That's because you resisted me."

"How?"

"Your aura."

"Does that mean I'm immune to your control?"

She sounded hopeful.

I had to take away that hope, because it could get her killed.

"You're immune to mine, but *not* theirs. I also wasn't trying to harm you. That prevented me from exerting my full abilities."

She accepted my statement with an unhappy sigh.

It was time to give her more hope. I reached into my pocket for the item I'd borrowed from Princess Carolyn.

"This is for you."

Her eyes widened as she snatched the medallion from my hand. "Is this a phase medallion?"

"It is. Do you know how they work?"

She pulled the athame from her belt and pricked her finger,

covering the medallion in blood, before placing it around her neck and bonding with it. The moment she bonded with it, the blood sank into the medallion.

She immediately reached for the arm of my coat, and I felt her fingers touch my shoulder. "It doesn't work."

Carolyn had promised me it was working.

I peeled off my glove and reached for her wrist, testing whether the medallion was broken, or my Day Walker set had abilities I didn't know about. My hand passed through her wrist.

"It would appear my equipment is immune to objects moving out of phase with reality."

Professor Lan's face lit up as her academic curiosity overwhelmed her fear. "I know a dozen magical theories which claim that shouldn't be possible. But then, I saw it for myself, so either those theories are wrong, or there is some way to circumvent them. Can I study your coat? Not now, but when we get out of here."

"It's a cursed object."

She wasn't deterred. "What sort of curse? I can take precautions. Also, do you think the ability to interact with objects out of phase is because of an enchantment or a property inherent to the material? Or is it the curse doing it?"

Before I could answer, she had other questions.

"How much mana does it take to sustain the effect? You know being out of phase is linked to serious illnesses, right? This could kill you. Except, you're a vampire, which raises new and more interesting questions, now that I think about it. If you ignore the detrimental effects a multi-phase material would pose, is it possible to create one? Well, obviously, it is. It's right in front of me. Did you make the coat?"

"No, it was made by the Vampire Lavire."

"Never heard of him."

"He's one of the most skilled dark enchanters of the last three thousand years."

"I'll need to borrow any academic material you have on him while I study your coat. This could revolutionise my field."

We were getting off-topic.

"Professor Lan, take a breath and try to focus on the upcoming battle."

"I will in a moment. I need to test a theory."

She cast a basic fire bolt spell at my coat. It hit my shoulder and fizzled out.

"That's interesting. It can also interact with magic that is out of phase. I wonder if I could—"

"Goodbye, Professor Lan."

I blurred to the last person I needed to talk to.

Professor Firebrand was five-six and in her nineties. She'd tied her ash-grey hair into a bun with a defensive charm, replaced her academy robes with battle robes, and pulled out every offensive and defensive item she owned, making her jingle with every movement. None of that interested me, though. What interested me was the black, cursed smoke that oozed from her pale, wrinkled skin.

Professor Firebrand saw me coming and raised her staff. She had been the highest-level professor at Darksmith before we entered the Abyss, and even after that had changed, she was still the most dangerous—and not because she was the head of the combat magic department.

Professor Firebrand's family had a cursed constitution that allowed them not to experience mana exhaustion. But it also gave them access to something much more dangerous. Something we needed.

I could smell the hellfire in her veins, the unholy taint of the deal her ancestors struck. It made her dangerous to everyone, including ancient vampires.

I didn't have time to play nice, so I stopped before her and raised my voice so everyone could hear me. "Professor Firebrand, I hope to see your hellfire during the coming battle."

Professor Firebrand froze at my announcement.

Everyone else turned to stare at her with open hostility. Unholy magic was the most corruptive magic there was. There was no safe way to use it. Even those who dabbled in the occult refrained from using it before they were thoroughly corrupted.

Across the tunnel, Professor Burdin raised his hand and gathered mana from the environment, conjuring a ball of holy light.

I turned to him. "She's not Unseen."

Professor Burdin scowled. "I need to be sure."

"Vincent possesses the evil eye," Mother called out. "She would already be dead if she was Unseen. You have my word on that."

Professor Burdin dismissed his spell before turning to Mother and bowing. The fact that he hadn't drawn on the mana in his core showed everyone that he had never intended to harm Professor Firebrand with so little evidence.

I turned to Professor Firebrand as her shock gave way to anger.

She gritted her teeth, fighting the urge to attack me. "Why?" was all she could say through her anger.

"I need your hellfire."

"For that, you've condemned my family to death."

She wasn't wrong. There were a dozen different holy orders who would hunt them down if they learned the truth, and Mother and Father would undoubtedly pass along this information to them.

"I'm not that cruel. I know how to break your curse."

She sneered. "You think a half-saint can fix this. It's been tried with a *real* saint. My family has spent three centuries trying. It's impossible."

"It's impossible for a saint, but not for me."

Because Professor Firebrand was one of the few faculty members who threatened my existence, I'd taken steps to protect myself from her. I couldn't kill her or confine someone with access to hellfire, so I figured out how to remove her family's curse without killing her.

Professor Firebrand continued to glare.

"I understand your doubt," I said. "Your family has likely tried to remove the curse, died painfully in the process, and been resurrected only to discover you're still cursed. It must seem like removal is impossible. But it's not. A *demon* can remove it permanently without too much trouble, so long as they cleanse *everyone* in your family together."

She tightened her grip on her staff.

"Let me put it another way. If you choose not to use hellfire, you will lower your chances of survival. If we succeed and you die, your family won't have anyone to warn them that their secret is out. That could end badly for them."

"The necrosaint will resurrect me."

"That assumes there is a body left to resurrect. You're also assuming she would resurrect someone who wields hellfire."

"I would," Davina called out from the front row. "Professor Firebrand was one of my favourite professors, and she's a good person."

I turned and glared across the tunnel.

Davina gave me a big smile in return.

I turned back to Professor Firebrand. "My first point remains true."

Professor Firebrand growled through gritted teeth. "Do you know what you're asking me to do?"

"I'm asking you to injure your mind, body, and soul to save people's lives. I'm asking you to risk becoming a monster to destroy a greater monster."

"You're not asking me to risk becoming a monster. You're asking me to become a monster."

"The addictive properties of unholy magic are immediate, but the corruptive properties are not. Cleansing the unholy magic's corruptive influence from you will be the most painful experience of your life, but if you allow Davina to act immediately, you will come through this without becoming a monster."

"You're sure?"

"I wouldn't ask you to do this if I wasn't."

"If you're lying about being able to remove my family's curse, I'll do everything in my power to kill you."

"That's fair."

"I'll give you hellfire."

With her support, all that was left to do was wait for our enemy to arrive.

37

MISCALCULATIONS

Vampires do not guess. They do not assume. They take everything they know and filter all their problems through the sum of their knowledge until they have a plan with the highest chance of success. Based on everything I knew, there was a 94% chance of a fight occurring before we escaped Necropolis's dungeon. The dungeon was too big. Which meant it would take too long to travel through. In a race against time, everything was stacked against us. Escaping without having to fight for our lives was almost impossible.

Or so I thought.

Four hours after the survivors would have reached the surface and begun their escape, I looked around the entrance tunnel to the Abyss at the stressed defenders, weighing our options. Being attacked while moving would drastically reduce our chances of winning the fight, but staying and waiting for the vampires to arrive was still a worse option.

The attack should have happened by now. They should have caught up to us. Either they had all gone after Luke and Kathrine, or I was missing something important—a detail that could be the difference between life and death.

Unsure about what I was missing, I ordered our retreat and began the slow, coordinated journey to the surface. With my aura unrestrained, nothing crossed our path.

However, halfway there, Commander Erin, the fastest deathlord to leave with the survivors, blurred down the tunnel toward us. She passed through our ranks, ignoring those out front, before stopping her momentum in just three steps. She then pivoted and chased after Gregory, who hadn't slowed.

"Commander Erin reporting in," she said too quickly for anyone who hadn't heavily invested in agility to follow. "We reached the edge of Necropolis's dungeon industrial complex on time without casualties. Once there, we encountered a barrier equal to the one protecting Darksmith that prevented us from continuing. Additional barriers are believed to be blocking every tunnel into the complex. A student named Baris pointed out that the guards on the other side of the barrier were not his family's defence force, who manage the facility, but members of the Grave Diggers' Society. When I left to deliver this report, the guards were unwilling to lower the barrier without approval from the high council. Further reports will soon follow."

"Return to your post," Gregory instructed.

Commander Erin quickly disappeared down the tunnel in a blur. Most of us could have easily kept up with her, but we were moving in formation, which caused our slowest members to slow us down. Mother and Father and most of the exorcists couldn't fly and hadn't invested heavily in their physical attributes. Leaving them behind wasn't an option. Carrying them would hamstring our strongest fighters, which left us retreating slower than any of us would like.

Gregory glanced over his shoulder.

I nodded that I'd heard her report but didn't offer any change to our plans. I needed more information.

Over the next three hours, messengers arrived with extra details. Harvester cultists and vampires had attacked Necropolis when Darksmith was attacked. The cultists arrived during the day and let the vampires through the city's defences at night. The Grave Diggers' Society and Inquisitors had held off the cultists long enough to evacuate their families to the dungeon, seizing control of the industrial complex from Baris's family before falling back and leaving the city to its fate.

Now, they were trapped, caught between vampires and the Abyss, destined to survive only as long as their barriers held. They were afraid. That fear left them unwilling to help us or take any risks, so they wouldn't let us through their barriers.

Their situation might explain why we weren't being chased and didn't have to fight. If the ancient vampires who attacked Darksmith knew we were running *towards* danger, not away from it, they wouldn't bother following. This implied they knew the layout of the Abyss to the same degree as Gorgath's people. It seemed unlikely, but it was the only explanation for why we hadn't had to fight them yet.

We'd been herded like sheep to the slaughter, and I hadn't realised.

By the time I arrived at the dungeon industrial complex barrier, I knew what was going on, the reception I should expect, and how I planned to deal with that reception.

The glowing blue barrier that even master-tier spells wouldn't break sat across the eighty-foot tunnel entrance. The parents of the Undead Enhancement Club stood on the other side of the barrier, inside a square kill box, surrounded by a wall that housed Grave Diggers' Society's guards. The kill box allowed the guards to safely hunt dungeon monsters when the barrier wasn't in place, but it was more like a deer blind than a meat grinder.

I spotted parents writing messages of hope to their children, despite looking defeated. They wanted to let their children in, but the high council of the Grave Diggers' Society wouldn't let them. They feared they were vampires, which wasn't unreasonable considering their situation, and the directions of our arrival. No sane person would travel through the Abyss.

Negotiations had failed, and the council's position wouldn't change now that I was here. That left me with one option. Violence.

I blurred to the side of the barrier, weaving my way through upset students, and slammed Slaughter through the barrier into the main mana line it was shielding. Raw mana surged up Slaughter and into my core before I redirected the mana into my peoples' cores with my sorcerer sovereign skill.

Just like at Darksmith, the barrier vanished.

Gregory and his weakest deathlords blurred forward. The fastest were past the parents and halfway up the wall towards the small gaps before the guards realised the barrier was down. The high-level parents inside the kill box reacted the same way the guards did, by drawing on mana to defend themselves, forcing Gregory's people to incapacitate them. With Davina present, incapacitation meant decapitation.

The students stood there stunned as their parents' heads went flying.

"Don't just stand there," I shouted. "Get through the barrier."

Like the breaking of a dam, first one and then one hundred charged through the breach. They moved like a black tide, grabbing their parents and throwing them over their shoulders as they raced for the thirty-foot-wide open gate tunnel at the back of the kill box. Those whose parents had been decapitated grabbed heads and bodies, dragging them to the edge of the kill box to create a field hospital.

As the students rushed through the barrier, I stepped inside. "Barrier closing in three, two, one!"

The front line halted as I reached one and I withdrew Slaughter from the main mana line. The barrier popped back into place. Everyone was so used to following orders to survive the Abyss that they did exactly what they were told.

"Empty your cores," Gregory shouted from the wall. "Those with the smallest cores, push forward and establish a perimeter. We need to get everyone inside before we take control of the complex. Students who have entered and parents who haven't been incapacitated, please vacate the area so we can continue the evacuation. If you don't do so willingly, you will be forced."

Baris ran over while Gregory continued to shout orders. "Did you kill the vampires following us?"

Baris's family owned this complex, so I needed him to work with me. Ignoring him now would be a mistake. So, I answered his question while I emptied my core.

"The vampires never showed. I'm working under the assumption that they know the layout of the Abyss, like Gorgath's people. If it's true, they recognised the direction we were travelling and knew we would run into their people no matter which dungeon we reached. The dungeons we could reach are all in North Murdell, near the border, and if your city is a common example of what is happening here, it means they're trying to control the southern border. However, I could be wrong, and they're just slower than I think. It's why I need to get everyone inside and why the vanguard is still guarding the tunnel."

Baris glanced at the barrier before turning back. "The Grave Diggers' Society has taken my family prisoner. Are you going to kill them?"

"No, but I will free your family while I take control of your family's industrial complex. I need to understand what's happening so I can plan our next step."

"I don't think your people got the no-killing message."

I chuckled. "If you look over there, you'll see Davina is already resurrecting the people that have been decapitated. When she's around, we don't consider decapitation killing. It's more like an extra-strong knockout."

Baris turned to where I was pointing and relaxed. "What can I do to help?"

"Get anyone connected to my sorcerer sovereign skill to empty their cores so I can hold the barrier open longer. This one is a lot bigger than the one at Darksmith."

Baris turned and raced for the gate, yelling instructions to the Undead Enhancement Club to empty their cores. On the other side of the barrier, Davina's people ushered everyone forward to replace those who had gotten inside. Flying carpets rose into the air, carrying anyone still unconscious from mana exhaustion.

The courtyard began to clear as the last parents and children raced through the open gate into the industrial complex beyond the kill box. Those who had lost parents stood to the sides in numb stupors, conflicted over how they should feel after seeing Davina in action. After all, decapitation was a papercut to her. So long as you still had the body, she could bring you back, even if it was in pieces. The only thing she couldn't resurrect was dust.

When everyone had emptied their cores, I drew Slaughter and stabbed the main mana line, placing the blade into the previous cut. The barrier vanished, and survivors surged inside before I closed it again.

Most dungeons only had two of three central chambers where monsters bred, which meant the most you could build without affecting the ecosystem was a fortress across the entrance tunnel to the surface. This dungeon had nine, which was why Baris's ancestors had turned the entire first chamber into an industrial complex.

They had built this complex to process the industrial quantities of dungeon materials the dungeon produced, bringing in an outside workforce when they figured out that they needed more people. One of those people had been an alchemist necromancer. Alchemist necromancers had more control over preserving and manipulating the dead than regular sorcerers, so they produced far better materials when processing dungeon monsters.

That difference in quality had seen Baris's ancestors slowly invite more and more necromancers, until they were the majority of the population. Necropolis wasn't just a place where necromancers lived, but one where their talents let them thrive.

Over time, Baris's family had grown their facilities into a place that could ignore dungeon surges and be a safe haven during wars. However, they hadn't built it as a military base, so I could hear my people overrunning defences as they expanded the perimeter.

I needed control of this place to know what we were working with, so that I could plan the next step. Too much had changed. And I needed to adapt.

Five minutes later, Gorgath and a rearguard made up of our strongest fighters passed through the barrier without a scratch on them. They were tired and stressed. I couldn't offer them anything more than a short nap. If we were going to get out of here alive, we needed to keep moving.

Guarded by Angelica, Mother and Father followed the rearguard, walking backwards with glowing eyes, watching the tunnel through multiple dimensions for any sign of pursuit. As they stepped through the entrance, I withdrew Slaughter from the main mana line for the last time, allowing the barrier to reassert itself.

Mother and Father dismissed their spells and gave weary sighs before running to the wall to help Davina resurrect the defenders. She had finished with the parents and moved on to the guards. Each time a necromancer breathed a new breath, they were taken into custody by Gregory's deathlord, who took them to join the other prisoners in a nearby warehouse.

With the rearguard finally inside, I could finish taking control of the complex.

By the time I'd sheathed Slaughter, most of the rearguard had already abandoned the kill box. Gorgath waited for traffic to pass through the gate tunnel before he leaned over and looked inside. He could fit, but it was going to be tight.

I walked over and looked up. "It's big enough to squeeze through."

The kid looked at me sceptically.

"You don't have your spikes anymore," I pointed out.

Gorgath smacked the wall with the back of his fist, creating several cracks and a loud meaty thump. "This is not dungeon stone. Gorgath can break through."

"You can't break someone else's property just because you're afraid of small spaces."

The kid scowled. "It's dangerous."

Considering the threats that hid in tight spaces in the Abyss, claustrophobia made sense.

"No, it's not," I said more gently. "It just feels that way. You can do it."

Gorgath sighed as he lay down and began to shimmy forward unhappily. I walked behind the kid, shouting encouragement and smelling his fear. It took him almost a minute and a small panic attack, but he reached the other side.

We stepped out of the tunnel into an underground town.

Warehouses, workshops, and storefronts lined wide streets lit with glowing crystals. On the sidewalk, a handful of deathlords oversaw the recently resurrected necromancers, waiting to move them to a nearby warehouse. Worried civilians looked out of the surrounding windows, unsure what to do.

Gorgath stood up and scowled at the tunnel before turning to take in the town. A handful of death bolts flew his way from the surrounding buildings. I cast a few deathlock barriers to block them as I clambered up his body to his shoulder to take in the complex.

What I saw matched Baris's map.

The chamber was filled with wide streets, warehouses surrounded by dozens of processing and crafting workshops, and apartments. The local academy took up half the chamber, preferring to sprawl instead of building higher. On the chamber's ceiling were massive, crystalised mana farms that gave the town a bright orange glow.

I blocked more incoming death bolts. "Gorgath, you're scaring people. Lie down and meditate until we have control of this complex."

"Let them through. Gorgath has the magic resistance skill now."

"That skill doesn't resist magical damage. It resists magical effects. It won't protect you if someone throws a necrotic attack your way."

The kid looked at me and began to frown. "It won't?"

"I don't have time to explain, but it doesn't work like the death and necrotic resistance or any elemental resistances."

"Oh."

As he lowered himself, I jumped off his shoulder toward Angelica. She was leaning against a building, trying not to look as sick as she smelled.

I could hear people planning a counterattack in a building down the street and other locations across the complex. I needed to deal with the resistance, but first, I had to take care of my familiar.

I landed on the sidewalk next to her. "Go take a nap, Angelica."

Angelica gave a weary grin and immediately started walking in a random direction. "Where?"

"Helen is setting up a safe house in a warehouse two streets that way. Go there."

Happy to comply with my order, Angelica blurred away before I could give her something else to do. That wasn't going to happen. Her mana sickness was worse than everyone else's. If her attributes weren't so insanely high, she'd be dead.

With that problem taken care of, I blurred towards the nearest group of resistance fighters, wondering what I would have to do to free my people from this doomed nation's destiny.

38

RECALCULATIONS

I enjoy violence. I never used to, but it's hard not to smile at your enemy's fear or the scent of defeat when they realise fighting is hopeless. The screams as you break their bones are so very enticing. And now that I knew the taste of blood, the sweet ecstasy that filled their veins, with a smell that enticed me to drool, it was hard to hold back. It was hard to let them live. It was hard to be more man than monster.

Thirty minutes after passing through the barrier, I finished breaking the resistance. The soft groans of pain of the necromancers waiting to be healed filled my ears as I made my way to the negotiations.

Gregory's commanders were taking care of the prisoners. The only threat left was the civilian population. If they attacked, it would be mayhem. They outnumbered us twenty to one. Part of me wanted to see what it would be like.

That part didn't get a say in my actions.

Baris's great-grandfather Salic and Head Inquisitor Titus marched behind me as I entered the warehouse where Carolyn was trying to negotiate with the high council of the Grave Diggers' Society. Titus was unhappy that he had been taken prisoner and even more unhappy that I'd managed to round up all his people. But his appearance behind me as I walked in took any remaining shred of defiance from the high council. The current speaker fell into his chair as they all went silent.

Baris's great-grandfather glared at the twenty members of the high council. He was furious. His town was supposed to be a refuge for the entire city, but they had turned it into a refuge for themselves.

While I understood his anger, they'd made the right choice. Yes, it was a selfish choice, but they would likely all be dead if they hadn't made it. Trying to save everyone would have doomed them all.

I glanced around the warehouse, ignoring the stacks of materials and products waiting to be shipped. Everyone sat in a circle on chairs taken from nearby buildings, surrounded by my deathlords, so the discussion stayed civilised. Carolyn was with her guards, doing her best to vouch for me so we could move forward, but she wasn't getting anywhere.

Gregory nodded to the seat next to him, having arrived while I was collecting Baris's great-grandfather. "You need me to fill you in?"

"I'm good," I said, motioning for the head inquisitor to take my seat.

Lidia shuffled away from Titus while Baris ran to get a chair for his great-grandfather. In their minds, the head inquisitor was the bogeyman. An executioner the Grave Diggers' Society sent after naughty boys and girls.

I walked into the circle of chairs and turned to face the high council. They were the heads of the largest necromancer families. They spent their days managing their households and ensuring no one succumbed to their darker impulses. None of them had made dark packs or dabbled in any aspects of the occult I could sense. They were exactly what they claimed to be. Law-abiding citizens.

They looked at me with open repulsion and fear, forcing me to repress a smile.

I offered them an elaborate bow. "I am the Vampire Vincent. I know you've been trying to buy time for your people to enact a counterattack, but help isn't coming. The presence of your head inquisitor should tell you that you've failed, but if it hasn't, let me make it clear to you. I am in control of this complex."

Baris ran through the door with another chair and placed it behind his great-grandfather. The old man patted him on the shoulder before gently lowering himself into it. Salic was 133 years old and approaching the limits of how long attributes would let an Old Monster live. His strength and health were fading with the onset of rapid ageing. He'd be dead within another year, but until that happened, he was still the head of the wealthiest family in Necropolis.

I waited until he'd sat before gathering everyone's attention. "Let me also make this clear to you. I have no interest in harming your people, nor taking anything from you. My goals are to get the surviving students to the surface so they can escape, get my people out of Murdell, and not die while achieving these goals."

The necromancers fidgeted in their seats.

"Now, let me share what I know about this attack. An ancient vampire queen, forgotten by time and even the oldest ancient vampires, has awoken and established her court. She commands the sixty-six most powerful ancient vampires on the planet and the six hundred most powerful elder vampires. Her court has been tasked with capturing the Darklord's daughter, Celest. The court believes they need to destroy the Darklord's power base to do so without repercussions. That means they are going to raze North Murdell to the ground. I don't have the power to stop them. I barely have the power to escape them. All I want to do is run away from here as fast as possible. Now, carefully consider what possible reasons you could have for stopping me and keeping me trapped inside here with you."

The most vocal of the objectors rose to her feet. She was a woman named Cadence. Her blonde hair was streaked with grey, but she held herself with grace and resolve. Yet, for all outward appearances, she was suppressing a murderous rage, and it was not directed at me. "The Grave Diggers' Society stand in the light, even if it should cost us our lives."

Lidia groaned. "I told you that he has his soul."

Cadence scoffed. "You also said you've never verified that claim, child. We will not negotiate until we have proof."

"You didn't save any clerics when you evacuated," I pointed out. "I doubt you will trust ours, so do any of you have a holy symbol on you?"

One of the men took off his amulet and tossed it to me. I caught it out of the air. Cadence raised her hand in a blur and cast an expert-tier necrotic bolt at Titus's head.

The head inquisitor was behind me, so it looked like she was throwing the bolt at me, but her aim was too perfect for this to be anything less than a murder attempt.

She expected me to get out of the way.

That was what an ancient vampire would do.

I caught the bolt of dark energy with my empty hand to save his life. The dark energies crashed against my glove but were unable to penetrate the enhanced material. None of my people moved, unconcerned by the attack, but most looked at the head inquisitor with interest.

They had seen what I had.

I showed the undamaged amulet to the stunned faces as proof that I still had my soul.

Cadence lowered her hand, rage finally showing through. "The amulet proves nothing," she spat.

I turned to the head inquisitor, ignoring her. "Why did she just try to kill you?"

Titus sighed. "Her brother was a harvester cultist, Hero. I killed him last night."

"He's not a hero," Cadence hissed.

Titus pushed himself from his chair and dropped to one knee. "I pledge my life and my soul to the Hero. Let his path be my path and his fate be my fate."

Holy light filled the warehouse, surrounding him as it forged our bond. His presence became more tangible as he was added to the long list of people who I felt the urge to protect.

Cadence stepped back. It wasn't fear or pain that made her retreat, but shock. She was as stunned as everyone else on the high council.

Titus looked her in the eye. "Is that enough proof? Or will you deny what you see and feel?"

I had no time for their games. "What's the punishment for attempted murder in this city?"

Gwen, Lidia's mother, stood up from her seat beside Cadence. "Execution, if it's directed at an inquisitor."

Cadence snarled and lifted her hand in a blur, only to explode into a cloud of dust as Gwen calmly tapped her on the shoulder and released the destructive touch spell she'd been holding. The expert-tier spell was a short-range version of the destruction spell. It required precise control, or the backlash killed you.

Lidia's mouth dropped open. "You're the Judge."

Gwen pulled a medallion from her storage pouch and held it up for the other council members to see. "I was. Now that my status is known, I will need to appoint another."

This was some internal political structure that meant nothing to me. I pointed to eight members of the council. "Remove them. They have no intention of helping us."

Two of my people blurred towards each one, lifting them from their seats, and dragging them from the warehouse before they could fight back.

I waited until the initial shock had gone before continuing. "Now that the troublemakers are gone and I've proven I still have my soul, I need to know what you know."

Gwen glanced at Titus. "Make your lapdog tell you?"

"I would if I could. But I have no power over him."

She paused. "Is that true, Titus?"

Titus returned to his seat. "I took his oath to confirm it wasn't a dark pact masquerading as a holy one. It isn't, but I don't know how you will confirm that without believing me or taking the oath yourself. Not that it matters. I'm beginning to trust his word. He's caring for our injured, he's resurrecting our dead, and he has saved my life. He appears to be what he claims to be."

"He claims to be an ancient vampire."

Titus nodded. "He also claims to be a hero. And only a hero could maintain their morals as such an abomination."

"So, you think we should trust him?"

"No. But we should tell him what he wants to know so he leaves. He's dismantled any resistance we could raise, removed our strongest fighters, and circumvented our barriers. If he were working with the vampires or harvester cultists who attacked us, we would be in their tender care rather than in the middle of polite negotiations."

Gwen turned to the remaining council members. "I propose we tell the vampire what he wishes to know."

An elderly woman who hadn't said anything nodded. "Seconded. The council will vote. A majority of eleven is still required. All opposed." No one raised their hand. "All for." The eleven remaining members all raised their hands. "Motion passed. You may tell the vampire what he wishes to know, Judge."

Gwen turned to me. "What do you want to know?"

Finally!

"Are there ancient vampires in the city?"

"We're tracking five. There were four during the initial attack. The fifth arrived shortly before you did. It attempted to break through our barrier before retreating. Two of them patrol outside the wall, while the others are inside. Harlin, show him what they look like."

An older man closed his eyes and raised his hand, drawing on the tiniest bit of mana, not even enough for a basic spell. "Come to me."

The temperature in the room plummeted as the warehouse filled with the ghosts of the recently deceased. One second, we were the only ones here, and the next, we were in a crowd. Ice began to form over every surface as the dead walked among the living. My deathlords and Sir Trent took a step back, seeing what I was seeing.

I glanced at Gwen. "You keep a spirit caller on your council."

Gwen stared back. "He's useful."

"Show me your killers," Harlin muttered.

Five figures appeared as ghostly illusions. There were three females and two males. Lusor, the naked vampire, was among them. I didn't recognise the other four.

"Did they bring an army?" I asked.

"A small one, but it's strong," Gwen replied. "We believe there were nearly three thousand elder vampires controlling twenty thousand harvester cultists when they arrived. They spent the night pacifying the city, turning every skilled necromancer they could find before forcing those they turned to feed on those that weren't suitable. Our estimates suggest one hundred thousand vampires now serve them."

Necropolis was the right city to invade to build a vampire army. The vampire army wouldn't need to learn necromancy. They already knew it.

Gwen's answer raised another question. "What happened to their children?"

"The surviving cultists took them. They've been performing minor harvest rituals to strengthen their ranks before they enact a true harvest ritual for the demon king's chosen."

Harvest rituals were a demonic practice which reduced your age, strengthened your soul, and increased your constitution and recovery. It wasn't as corruptive as the reaping ritual, but you had to make a pact with a demon king to be able to perform it. If you were successful, it turned you into a paranoid megalomaniac. However, whether you performed the minor or true ritual, the drawbacks were the same.

If these chosen succeeded in performing the true harvest ritual, they would become immortal. The only way to take them out would be to throw them through a portal to Hell or banish them to another dimension. Left unchecked, they would become a threat worse than the ancient vampires, because the Curse of Sloth wouldn't slow them down.

However, the fact that the vampires were allowing them to perform these rituals told me that the chosen had been charmed. Charming them after the ritual would be impossible, but charming them before would be easy. I wasn't sure which ancient vampires they served, but it wouldn't matter if I could get to them before they finished the ritual.

Anyone sacrificing kids needed to die.

I had a new objective.

"How many harvester cultists are there now?"

"We're not sure. We believe somewhere between eight and twelve thousand. Our wards can't easily track them. We could only follow a few dozen, such as Cadence's brother, who wormed their way into our city. Most of them are outside the city now."

Titus sighed and ran his hand through his salt and pepper hair. "He put up a fight and was wearing a mask. I didn't realise who he was until he was dead."

"No one blames you for what happened, Titus."

"Cadence would disagree."

"Her actions are her own. Her death isn't on my shoulders or yours. She let her emotions rule her and paid the price."

"Back to the matter at hand," I said. "There are five ancient vampires, three thousand elder vampires, over one hundred thousand vampires, and between eight and twelve thousand cultists blocking our escape." I turned to Titus. "Do you have spare equipment for deathlords over level 200?"

Titus glanced at Gwen before nodding. "I've got six Deathbringer sets in a storage chest which haven't been used in a century. I also have a few dozen spare Deathwalker sets you can strip down for parts. They will slow your people if they wear the whole thing, but they will provide more protection than what they wear even if they only use half."

"Gregory, go with Titus. Get your best people equipped."

Gregory ignored my order. "If we can kill or chase off the ancient vampires, we'll have a real chance of ending this evil. I know you want to run, sir, but my oath won't let me walk away from this."

His deathlords nodded their heads.

I turned and released my anger, giving the man a demonic growl. "They're harvesting kids, Gregory. If you think for a second that I'm letting them leave this city alive, you don't know me as well as you think you do."

Gregory returned my growl with a feral grin. "Just checking your priorities, sir."

39

LUSOR

High Councillor Harlin's family were spirit callers, which was a class only available to necromancers with unique bloodlines. This class allowed them to speak with ghosts and bend them to their will. With how many ghosts were currently occupying Necropolis, they could track the vampires' and harvester cultists' movements throughout the city. It was an unconventional way to use their skills, but to everyone else's surprise, it worked nearly as well as other magical methods for tracking your enemies which necromancers couldn't perform.

Ghosts filled the warehouse as dozens of spirit callers summoned them to gather information. Every few seconds, someone would run forward and point to a building on Salic's massive map, giving a quick update of how many vampires and cultists were currently there and what had happened in the past day.

I stood at the side of the table, listening and taking in the flow of information. The map showed that the fall of Necropolis was an ongoing event. A work in progress, not a foregone conclusion.

The high council had failed to mention that to us or their people, choosing to keep them in the dark rather than argue against trying to mount a rescue for the survivors. Until we arrived, it would have been suicide. Now, they were looking at a fair fight. I hated fair fights, which was why I was trying to come up with a better plan.

The survivors in the city were typically the most skilled and wealthy. Anyone who couldn't protect themselves was already dead. The vampires seemed to value the survivors' knowledge and expertise more than they valued numbers. They had their army and could leave anytime, but they weren't. They were chasing down the survivors with the help of the two ancient vampires inside the city's walls.

"These attacks make no sense," Sir Trent muttered, scanning the latest reports. "They attacked this compound over here, crossed half the city to attack this one over here, only to return to attack the neighbouring compound here."

"They're being careful," I replied. "There aren't many weapons that can kill an ancient vampire, but in a city of necromancers, there might be one or two."

"An ambush won't work if we can't prepare a location."

"You underestimate my kind's perception if you think any ambush will work."

Sir Trent stared at me for several long seconds, before accepting my statement as true. "We could attempt a charge. With everyone, we would make it through the city."

"Only if the sun's up, and we don't have that much time."

Sir Trent frowned. "You think the harvester cultists will be ready before dawn?"

I pointed to farmland outside the city wall where the ritual circle was being prepared by the cultists. The children were currently unconscious in the middle of the ritual circle, incapable of fleeing. They were represented on the map by chips of glowing crystal.

"They've got a quarter of a million children they can sacrifice and thirteen chosen. With that many sacrifices, the ritual doesn't need to be precise."

"You're sure about that?"

I nodded. "I considered trying to perform the ritual with Unseen before I realised there was no way around having a demon king patron."

Sir Trent shook his head at my admission before pausing to listen to an update on Lusor's position that we'd been waiting for. "How do we deal with five ancient vampires?"

I smiled. "That's easy. Divide and conquer."

Thirty minutes later, my familiars and I reached the surface and exited the dungeon into an ornamental graveyard.

There were no bodies in the graves, just gravestones for those who had fallen in the dungeon. It was a memorial, a reminder of the dangers below. The deceased's age, class, level, and skills were included, to encourage anyone who entered the dungeon to take the risks that lay below seriously.

The thousands of weathered gravestones lined the worn path to the streets of Necropolis. Storefronts and restaurants sat at the edge of the memorial behind an iron gate, providing the students from their academy with easy entertainment that was cheaper than what could be found below. The shops remained untouched, because few vampires were interested in loot, but every home showed signs of invasion. Broken windows, shattered doors, and bodies were all common.

There was a heaviness in the air as I slowed my run and released my aura, inviting Lusor and the other ancient vampires in the city to speak with me. Harlin and his family were still tracking the ancient vampires outside the city, so I'd get a warning if they came our way. Davina, Angelica, and I couldn't win 3v5, but we could win 3v3 if Lusor were there.

Lusor had been the strongest ancient vampire to attack Darksmith, but my desire for his presence had nothing to do with his strength and everything to do with his weak will. Angelica might not be able to control the others, but she would be able to control him for a time. After he was under her control, we only had to kill one of them to put the odds firmly in our favour.

I wasn't sure if we could pull it off.

And I couldn't tell Davina or Angelica the plan without risking them giving it away with their scent, so they were going in blind. It was a calculated risk, but, as of late, my calculations had been repeatedly wrong.

I stopped walking fifty feet from the entrance and inhaled, sifting through the scents carried on the night air.

The city was soaked in blood and murder, loss and regret, anger and a thirst for retaliation. The dead walked the streets in many forms, seething for vengeance over the injustices they had faced. The wall between the living and the dead was crumbling. So much death magic had been released that the environment was warping, allowing the Deadlands to soak into the city. If it got much worse, Death would walk among us, and the sun wouldn't rise.

Nobody wanted that.

"What the hell is that thing?" Angelica asked, pointing at a stingray-shaped spiritual entity clinging to a storefront in the distance.

Angelica's surprise was justified, and so was her fear and anxiety. Wraith wisps normally only existed in the Deadlands. It didn't belong here.

"Be quiet," Davina whispered. "We're being watched."

"Of course, we're being watched," Angelica replied without lowering her voice. "Vampires overran the city. And stop whispering. I can't hear you."

"It's called a wraith wisp," I said. "Now, both of you pay attention to your surroundings."

Angelica turned and glared at me. "It would be easier to pay attention if someone wasn't whispering. It's distracting. I can barely hear her with my helmet on."

Angelica had been in a mood since I woke her from her nap, and I didn't have time to argue with her. "Davina, don't bother whispering. The elder vampires hiding in that building can hear everything we say."

"Is it dangerous?" Angelica asked, still pointing at the wraith wisp.

"Yes."

"Should I kill it?"

"Wraith wisps feed on vampires."

"So that's a no."

"That's a no."

"Why are we standing in a graveyard?"

"We're waiting for our guests to arrive."

Angelica turned to Davina and lifted her visor. "Do you have any more of those pastries?"

"You can have one," Davina replied, scanning the area for threats.

Angelica leaned closer, pouting and giving her fake puppy dog eyes. "I might die here. Do you want only giving me one to be our last moment together?"

"You can have two."

"Half."

"You're getting two." Davina pulled a small wooden box from her storage pouch and handed it to Angelica.

Angelica looked inside the box. "There are only two in here. Are these your only ones?"

"Mother didn't have any more."

Angelica pulled a jam-filled pastry from the box before offering the other one back to Davina. "You should have just said you only have two."

"You wouldn't have believed me."

"Take it. I don't want my last action to be bullying a saint."

"Half-saint," Davina replied, taking the box with a small smile at Angelica's rare display of kindness. She turned and held out the box to me. "Do you want it?"

I ignored her, listening to the sound of rapidly approaching footsteps. There were hundreds of them, but three were moving faster than the rest.

Davina started eating the pastry when she didn't get a reply. She didn't play around like Angelica, finishing her snack in only a few seconds before wiping her hands clean on a cloth and offering it to Angelica.

Angelica sniffed and screwed up her face. "Is that scented with garlic?"

"Garlic oil and holy water," Davina replied. "Mother gave it to me to make us smell less appealing to them."

"I'm not touching that. It smells revolting."

"You add garlic to everything you eat."

"That's because someone keeps looking at me like I'm food."

I chuckled.

"Stop looking at me like I'm food! It's not funny."

"It is when garlic is almost as appealing to ancient vampires as it is to humans."

They both stared at me, shocked. "What!"

"It's toxic to vampires and a deterrent for elder vampires, but we find the smell quite pleasant."

"I've been adding raw garlic to my salads! Do you know how disgusting that is?"

"We have bigger problems," I said, looking up.

The three sets of footsteps moving faster than the others were not the ancient vampires I was waiting for, but three elite elders sent as a distraction. The three we were waiting for had shapeshifted into clouds of bats, using the new forms as cover to approach unnoticed.

It almost worked, too.

The three clouds of tightly grouped bats slowed their flight as they noticed I'd spotted them, and the approaching footsteps stopped. The bats flew in at a more sedate pace, flying above the graveyard before diving toward the ground and morphing together to reform their human bodies. The transformations finished as their feet touched the graveyard path, stepping toward us together in human forms.

I had no idea how they could shapeshift into multiple entities or maintain their clothes, but I was interested in finding out. It seemed like a useful skill to have. Luke would also find the cliché funny.

Lusor walked out front with supernatural grace. He towered above us with his naked, inhuman size, holding his aura tight.

The pair behind him had scents so mingled that they could only be husband and wife. They walked arm in arm with amused expressions. She wore an elegant green dress, while he wore a tightly fitted black suit. Their attachment to one another told me they were the vampires Yasmir and Sing. The pair hadn't been seen since they razed the city of Hasprin to the ground.

I bowed to acknowledge their presence and to thank them for

gracing me with their presence. Demons had their own etiquette. Ignoring this would tip them off to the fact that I was not like them.

"I am the Vampire Vincent. And I am here to discuss terms."

Lusor gave me an amused grin. "I am the Vampire Lusor, and I can smell my blood on your lips. I'm going to enjoy teaching you what happens to those who steal from me."

There was something thrilling about engaging and competing with my own kind. My instincts pushed me to order Angelica to compel him and make him kneel. I kept those instincts in check. I needed to determine whether Yasmir or Sing was weaker before we fought.

I returned his amused smile with my own. "Consider your blood the price of being rude. You knew Darksmith was mine, and yet you invaded anyway."

"Yes, your little necromancer project." Lusor looked around. "I'm afraid we might have ruined your plans."

I chuckled. "That makes two of us. How is capturing the Darklord's daughter going for you, and how many students did you manage to turn in the end? Was it a tenth of those you came for, or even less? It was petty of me to take your prize, but I was in a petty mood before I left."

His smile turned ugly. "The students were of little consequence."

"Was the Darklord's daughter of little consequence?"

He showed his fang as he balled his fists. "No."

Yasmir released his wife's arm as he stepped forward and bowed. "Gentlemen, we all have reasons enough to want to drain each other dry, but this is neither the time nor the place, as none of us have sufficient advantage. I am the Vampire Yasmir. I am willing to discuss terms with you."

I returned his bow. "Do you speak on behalf of those in Necropolis?"

Sing stepped forward, caught the edge of her dress, and curtsied. "I am the Vampire Sing. I can confirm that my husband Yasmir speaks for us, much to Lusor's irritation."

I returned the curtsy with a bow before turning to Yasmir. "What terms do you offer?"

Yasmir smiled. "Why should we offer any? You can't stop us."

"Perhaps, but why waste your time when a simple agreement would tell you everything you wish to know?"

Sing cackled as she caught Yasmir's arm and leaned in. "He's so fresh and innocent. I remember when we trusted our instincts so blindly. And our shock when they failed us."

She stepped toward me, releasing her husband.

"Show me that face, child. Show me your disbelief as you realise your instincts and thoughts have led you to your demise. As you recognise what we all realise if we live long enough, that the instincts that make us so dangerous, the thoughts that make us so sharp, do not allow us to consider other options. That we walk only one path until that path leads us to our doom."

My mind automatically tried to prove her claim wrong and devise a second plan for what I could do next—not a contingency for if something happened, but a true second plan. Only one plan came to mind. The original.

Since becoming an ancient vampire, my mind had never encountered a problem it couldn't solve with brute force, so it automatically tried again. And again. And again. My mind kept trying to think of a second plan, but kept returning to the first, which caused it to try to think of a second plan, which returned it to the first, which caused it to try to think of a second plan. On and on this went, spiralling out of my control, until my body locked up tight, unable to spare a though to move a muscle.

My mind was caught in a loop that wouldn't stop.

I don't know how to explain it, but it was like my brain was a computer, and something had short-circuited. I couldn't move, reason, or do anything other than try to think of another plan.

I was caught in a loading window.

"There's the face," Sing whispered as she walked toward me. "The face of someone lost in their own thoughts, unable to comprehend their own inability, lost to the world because they are trapped in their mind. How long will it take you to find your way out? A season? A year? A decade? A century? Would you like a hint?"

Sing placed her hand on my shoulder as her fangs descended.

Davina and Angelica stood to the side, waiting for a signal that would never come. I was aware of everything around me but unable to react.

I'd lost control of my body.

I'd made a grave mistake.

Sing walked around me to whisper in my ear. "I'm going to drain what we need to know from your veins. You won't be able to stop me, and when I'm done, I will deliver you to our queen so she can play with you. You're going to wish you had let Lusor kill you at Darksmith."

I felt her tilt my head back, before her fangs entered my throat. My vampiric soul touch skill automatically kicked in as she began to feed, slowing my death, but it didn't stop me from being helpless.

Davina finally realised something was seriously wrong and took the initiative. "Angelica, command Lusor to fight Yasmir."

One of the compulsions I had Angelica under forced her to obey Davina during dangerous situations or when someone's life was in danger.

Angelica didn't hesitate, turning to Lusor as she slapped her visor closed. "Serve me. Kill Yasmir."

The force of her compulsion reverberated through my mind, locking my muscles tighter, and making Sing stop and turn to Angelica with concern.

Lusor's eyes glazed over as he leapt at Yasmir, transforming into a half-man, half-beast hybrid with claws for fingers. His mutated hands tore into Yasmir's body as Yasmir tried to keep Lusor's mouth from reaching his throat.

Davina flicked her hand in their direction and unleashed a holy wave of blinding white light. She was a lot faster than she used to be, and so was her magic. Yasmir's skin blackened, under the combined assault, weakening him and creating an opening for Lusor to get his teeth into Yasmir's throat.

Sing snarled as she leapt at Davina in a blur, only to collide with an Angelica-shaped blur mid-air. Death fire ignited Sing's dress as Angelica let loose, immolating her body and staff with black, smoky flames. Sing sensed the change as Yasmir rapidly began to grow weaker, and she kicked Angelica through a dozen gravestones to leap onto Lusor's back and sink her fangs into his neck.

Davina saw how conveniently they were arranged, raised her hand above her head, and then brought it down, summoning a holy fist of light that crashed into all three. We weren't inside the dungeon, so her mana regeneration only let her throw spells at the weak end of the expert-tier magic. It wasn't enough to kill ancient vampires of their strength, only weaken them.

Angelica exploded from the rubble and blurred to the fight, stopping just short. She raised her staff and released her dragon's breath from the tip as Davina brought her holy fist back down on them. It was the wrong move, but I couldn't move my mouth to tell them.

The holy strike temporarily disabled their regeneration, allowing Angelica's death fire to burn through their flesh. Yasmir's body partially dissolved, freeing him from Lusor's grasp.

A pair of burning streaks shot out of the inferno in a blur, racing through the streets in a desperate escape. Lusor stepped outside Angelica's dragon's breath and stopped as his body healed. He was under her control, but not mindlessly under her control, interpreting the order to fight as an order to fight here.

Angelica turned to Davina. "What the hell is wrong with him?"

Language!

"I have no idea," Davina replied. "We need to get out of here before they return with reinforcements."

"He's in a mind loop," Lusor said as Davina picked me up and started running.

A CROWD SHOUTED questions outside the building as Davina, Angelica, and Lusor stood over me. Davina had carried me all the way to the complex, ordered Gregory to let them in, and then dumped me on a table in the nearest building.

As I lay limp and immobile, she glanced at Lusor. "You said he's in a mind loop. What does that mean?"

Angelica had layered more compulsions over him while they ran, but not enough. Lusor didn't answer.

Davina realised the problem. "Angelica, make him answer me."

"Answer her questions, Lusor."

Lusor paused, fighting the compulsion before losing a few seconds later. "His mind is trapped, solving an impossible problem. This problem consumes all his thoughts, leaving him trapped in his body. It's one of our few weaknesses, before we learn how to overcome it."

"How do you overcome it?"

"You solve the problem."

"How does he solve the problem?"

"This problem is solved by splitting your mind in two."

Angelica came up with the solution first. "Lusor, feed him your blood and transfer the memories he needs to understand what to do."

Lusor gritted his teeth as he fought the compulsion. After several seconds of silence, Davina and Angelica took a step back. Lusor was beginning to break free from her compulsion. At the thirty-second mark, he finally lost.

He opened my mouth with one hand and moved his wrist above the opening. The skin over his wrist parted as he shapeshifted his flesh, making his artery exit his skin and split open. Blood flowed from the artery in a slow, steady trickle as he glared at me, fighting the compulsion.

Sickly cold blood touched my tongue, bringing with it a flood of memories. Lusor was trying to buy himself time by transferring his full experience. It was as informative as it was frustrating. He'd lain in his grave for decades contemplating this problem.

His mind worked identically to mine, suffering from the same inability to make multiple plans for the same scenario. His memories showed me how thoroughly trapped he'd been by the same thought that had me trapped.

He'd solved the problem by separating his mind into two unequal Lusors, like he'd said. It was almost like split personalities. One version knew everything he did, and the other one didn't. This meant they came to different conclusions, offering different solutions. This workaround allowed him to develop multiple solutions and freed his mind from the endless loop of trying to make a second plan.

Now that my mind knew how, it could split itself in two.

Except for my morals, everything I knew went into my second mind as my mind walled off my thoughts the way I would want it to. My second mind was a cold, calculating mind capable of doing anything. With its creation, there were now two Vincents in my head, with two different capacities.

That change was all it took to snap me out of my comatose state.

My mind had the two answers it wanted. They were no longer relevant, but I was free from that trap I'd walked into. The first thing I did with my new freedom was destroy the second mind I'd created, so it couldn't try to take control.

I then rolled off the table and stepped behind Lusor.

Davina sighed with relief.

Letting Lusor live was too great a risk. He would be free in the next few minutes. I sent a telepathic message to Angelica as I jumped on his back and felt the drain of his vampiric touch. I extended my fangs as I cancelled his vampiric touch with my vampiric soul touch.

Angelica stepped in front of Lusor and unleashed a new command. "Lusor, while Vincent feeds on you, transfer your memories on shapeshifting, then your soul-strengthening knowledge, then your knowledge of vampires and your abilities, and anything you know about making yourself stronger."

Lusor was not like other vampires. Binding his aura to his flesh had fundamentally changed him. A vampire's blood normally only held their power. For Lusor, it held everything he was. Centuries of knowledge and soul energy flowed into me as I bit into his throat with my vampiric soul bite. With each second, a decade passed as I absorbed the mountain of knowledge he possessed.

Lusor was a brute, a savage, a predator in human skin. He was obsessed with his flesh, with his strength, and with his power. He hadn't become a vampire by chance but by design. His pursuit of the ultimate form had followed him from life into death. It was his only passion, his only driver, and what kept him from succumbing to the Curse of Sloth.

In the end, Lusor was a simple creature. Powerful. Dangerous. But simple.

As he crumbled to dust, I came away from the experience with his understanding of shapeshifting; his superior hand-to-hand fighting ability; his more advanced understanding of how to assess his opponents, which was fundamentally flawed; his knowledge of soul strengthening and aura control; and his knowledge of vampires and how to make us stronger.

It didn't make up for my failure to kill Yasmir or Sing, but our encounter wasn't a complete loss.

Vampires were undead, and Lusor had discovered how to enhance us. My research into the subject had been an utter failure. His wasn't.

With his knowledge, I shapeshifted, making small changes to my body by rearranging muscles, tendons, and bones to perfect my proportions. Lusor's memories showed me there were many changes I could make, but I didn't have time or soul energy to change more than the basics, so I just improved my muscles, bones, organs, nervous system, and senses.

Sight, sound, taste, touch, and smell all became sharper, showing the world with more details. My bones lengthened, along with my muscles and tendons, altering my range of motion to make me more graceful. The changes to the structure of my nervous system and my muscle density increased my reaction time and strength.

It was a form of genetic adaptation, an evolution of human form that my demonic parasites made stronger. However, it was also a form of undead enhancement, so it required mana to maintain.

I pulled my character sheet.

Race: Ancient Royal Vampire Variant
Class: Hero
Level: 37
Strength: 437
Agility: 673

Endurance: ∞
Constitution: ∞
Cunning: 327
Perception: 574
Recovery: ∞
Mana Regeneration: 478 (-129)

My strength had increased by 33, agility by 98, endurance by 56, constitution by 81, cunning by 47, perception by 94, and recovery by 38, at the cost of 129 mana regeneration. Lusor had been able to triple the attributes our race offered us, but it would take me time to replicate his results. Time I didn't have.

There was a ritual we had to stop.

I turned my attention to my familiars and the poor performance I'd seen above. "Davina, what made you think it was wise to cast a holy spell that includes kinetic force? Lusor had Yasmir trapped, and you tried to knock them apart. You should have hit them with a spell that dealt pure, holy damage, allowing Lusor to kill him faster."

Davina dropped her gaze. "You were incapacitated."

"That's no reason to lose your objectivity. I didn't state it, but you knew we were there to kill them."

"You're in trouble," Angelica said, grinning.

"Don't start, Angelica. You're part of the reason they got away. Your dragon's breath burned off Lusor's fingers and enough of Yasmir's flesh to free him so they could escape. You both screwed up."

Angelica remained unphased. "My dragon's breath only burned off their flesh because of Davina's spell. It's not my fault."

"I didn't say it was. You both screwed up. But I screwed up first. I'm the reason they got away. Not you. And now a lot of good people are going to die because of that."

Angelica lost her grin. "What do you mean?"

"My plan was for you to command Lusor with your armour because he's weak-willed. With his help, we were going to kill at least one of the others. That would have let us retreat back here with Lusor so I could kill him, leaving us with only two or three ancient vampires to face. Now we have to fight all four with a vampire army backing them up."

"If we knew—"

"—These aren't liches, Angelica. The excitement in your scent would have given us away if you knew they were walking into a trap. I had to keep you in the dark. It was the only way."

"But."

I met Angelica's gaze. "What comes next isn't your fault. I had a chance to change the odds. I failed. Now, we have to do this the hard way."

40

WAR COUNCIL

Based on the information gathered by the spirit callers, we had forty-five minutes at most before the chosen enacted the true harvest ritual. This wasn't about the children anymore. It couldn't be. Once they succeeded, the chosen would become immortals and strong enough to prevent our escape.

We had to act now.

My failure and Lusor's death meant I had to speak with the high council. Hundreds of Old Monsters were hiding in the facility and throughout Necropolis, and we needed their help. There was an undead army between us and the cultists, and I didn't have enough people to tie the vampires down while we went after the chosen.

This would be a bloodbath, but since our only options were bloodbath or death, we had to choose bloodbath.

At the back of the warehouse, Harlin managed his family of spirit callers, continuing to track the enemy's movements, supplying me with up-to-date information. The rest of the high council sat on the first two rows of chairs, shivering in their robes due to the extreme cold. Behind them were Salic, Baris, Lidia, and Titus, with anyone else of importance who represented the necromancers of Necropolis.

Further back were the strongest survivors we'd brought with us. This included the faculty, students, merchants and guards from town, and anyone who had taken my oath. Heather Winterton sat with her boyfriend, Damian Black, holding hands. They had been some of the first to take my oath and were popular enough that other Southerners would follow them if they asked. They weren't powerhouses, but they one day would be if they survived long enough.

Carolyn sat to the side with Marin, surrounded by their guards. Mother and Father were nearby, with their leadership. Anyone who mattered was here. And they all knew a fight was coming. They just didn't realise how bad it would be.

A hush fell over the crowd as I walked up to the podium and swept my gaze across the room. "Salic has informed me that the mana batteries powering this facility's shields will be empty before the end of the day."

The crowd began muttering among themselves, trying to think of a way out of this that didn't involve them risking their lives. I couldn't spare the time to let them come to their conclusions.

"I see a lot of sceptical faces, so let me put this another way. Vampires cannot sleep outside their graves. Their graves are always found close to wherever they were turned. That means Necropolis is now home to the largest collection of vampire graves in the modern age, which means Necropolis will be the vampires' stronghold for their war in the North. If we do nothing and the cultists finish their harvest ritual, everyone in this facility will either be turned or fed upon. We cannot fight four ancient vampires and thirteen immortals at once, so our only option is to attack before this happens."

Gwen glanced at the other high council members, received several nods that showed she could speak for them, and stood up. "Won't the vampires know we have to attack?"

"Undoubtedly, but it doesn't stop this from being our only option."

"What about the Abyss?"

It was a good question, considering we'd arrived through the Abyss.

"Mana sickness will kill everyone I brought here before we reach a dungeon in South Murdell. There is also the risk of encountering the ancient vampires who attacked Darksmith down there. Our best option is to fight here and rush to the border."

Gwen paused. "You want us to fight beside you."

"Yes."

"Why should we?"

"Normally, I would appeal to your conscience and tell you that it's the right thing to do. I don't have time for that. So, instead, I'll say that I'm willing to destroy your barrier and use your families as bait to split their focus if you don't. Let me make this clear. I prefer your willing participation, but I will settle for using you as tools if you don't offer it."

Gwen stood there stunned, unsure how to reply to such a blatant disregard for her people.

Sometimes, it was easier to get things done by playing the villain everyone expected me to be.

I raised an eyebrow as I pressed my lips together and smirked. "You seem to expect me to treat your people better than you treated the rest of Necropolis? You left them to their fate because it was your only option. If you refuse to help me, using your families as bait is my only option for helping my people escape this country. You made the rules. I'm just playing by them."

I had no intention of using their families as bait, but they didn't know that, and better yet, they wouldn't believe me if I told them. All I had to do was plant the idea in their heads. Once it was there, it took over. Fight, or die like cattle. They weren't cowards. They would make the right choice.

Gwen slumped into her seat.

That one action took the fight out of the high council. One by one, I watched them come to the same conclusion that this was going to happen and that all they could do was figure out how to keep their people alive.

Salic raised his hand. "If you're drafting people, what's the minimum level for participation?"

"Level 80 for those with combat skills and level 100 for those without them. Anyone lower than that has to volunteer and be above level 40."

A wave of relief passed through the high council as they realised I wasn't sending their families in as cannon fodder, only those who stood a chance.

Salic nodded. "How will the battle proceed?"

"I'll lead our strongest people through the city to the harvester cultists. In the unlikely event that the ancient vampires don't try to engage us along the way, we will kill the cultists and return to the city to assist in hunting down the vampires."

Salic paused. "If that happens, we'll all be dead when you arrive."

"This is the start of a war, Salic. Your deaths are worth removing thirteen potential immortals from the battlefield. Feel free to disagree?"

Salic considered my words before nodding. "It's a good trade. Too good, if I'm being honest with myself. It's unlikely that the vampires will be willing to let you kill them. What will the rest of us be doing while you fight them?"

"The vampires have enough elders to overwhelm my force, but their primary goal is to build an army. Anyone who isn't strong enough to join me will be placed into teams to hunt down the vampire army. This will draw the elders away from the ancient vampires, so I'll send one of my people with each team to ensure this isn't fatal. If your teams do your job right, my force won't face overwhelming odds."

Salic pushed himself to his feet. "My family will fight with you, vampire." Having heard what he needed and stated his position, he turned and started walking to the door. His family were already dismantling their industrial plant at Baris's suggestion, getting ready to flee with as much as they could carry. Getting them to change task would take time.

Time we didn't have.

Gwen watched him leave, before reluctantly standing to face the high council. "It seems our only choices are fight or die. I propose the Grave Diggers' Society fight."

"Seconded," Harlin called from the back of the room. "The council will vote. A majority of eleven is required. All opposed." Three members raised their hands. "All for." The sixteen remaining members raised their hands. "Motion passed. The Grave Diggers' Society is going to war."

41

A NEW KING RISES

Subterfuge and ruthlessness come naturally to vampires. There's no line we won't cross to achieve our goals, so making an opponent think they have time to prepare their counterattack, only to then kill thousands of children to begin a harvest ritual fifteen minutes early makes perfect sense to us. The only reason we might hesitate to kill so many innocent victims is that human sacrifice is a messy business. The malevolence of the action can be felt from miles away by those who know what to look for, revealing our actions sooner than we might want.

Yasmir didn't care.

He knew we were coming. And because of the changes to the harvest ritual, he knew when we would arrive. And because of where we were hiding, he knew where we had to enter the city from. Timing, location, and firepower are what win battles, and Yasmir planned accordingly.

He'd filled the memorial grounds outside the dungeon entrance with hundreds of elder vampires and because he had the upper hand, he'd stopped them from repressing their auras. They were old and experienced, and more than capable of bombarding our defences with powerful spells the moment we left the tunnel. Further back were the oldest of the elder vampires, ready to take advantage of any gaps in our defence their scourge could make.

It was a meatgrinder.

One we weren't supposed to survive.

By accelerating the harvest ritual, Yasmir hadn't just forced our hand, drawing us into his trap. He'd ended any chance of saving the children. They were already gone. There were no lives left to save, no tethered souls to draw back to their bodies to resurrect them with.

The welcome party waiting at the memorial was his way of letting me know that fighting was pointless. That it was better to turn around and cower in the dark. To accept what was coming like a good little ancient vampire.

Yasmir didn't understand me at all.

Even though I only had three minutes to stop the cultists from performing the harvest ritual that would allow their chosen to ascend to immortality by casting the children's souls into Hell to pay for that immortality, I found it amusing that Yasmir and his companions were taking me so seriously and even more amusing that they had overlooked Gorgath. Yes, they had better timing and a better location to fight from, but we had more firepower.

It was going to be a costly mistake.

As the entrance to the memorial came into view, the team I had selected to confront the ancient vampires at the entrance to the Abyss moved aside and let Gorgath rush through. The runes on Gorgath's bone staff burned with small blue flames, charged with mana, ready to unleash utter destruction on the city above. The excitement and fear that infused the air made me grin, as Gorgath skidded to a stop in front of everyone and shoved his staff forward like he was thrusting a spear.

Rupert raised his hand from the front of our formation beside me and released a flash of blue light. Our formation halted their charge, coming to a complete stop a hundred yards from the entrance. The weaker archsorcerers, acting as Gorgath's bodyguard, lifted wands and staffs as they released their spells. Dozens of barriers appeared across the tunnel, shielding everyone from the coming backlash.

"Inferno," Gorgath roared as he released the same spell cast at Darksmith.

Blue flames exploded from the end of his staff in a swirling vortex with a napalm consistency. It crashed into the side of the tunnel with the strength of a typhoon and blinded the world with light. The flames spun to the surface, twisting and tearing into the tunnel walls, trying to expand. The tunnel didn't let them, focusing the torrent of fire into pressure that continually searched for a means to escape.

Gorgath was a level 320 elemental sorcerer with numerous new skills and levels. In the past day, he'd upgraded all of the magical skills I'd told him to, including his fire elemental skill. His ability to manipulate and control mana and magic was on an entirely different level than when we left Darksmith.

As Gorgath's spell reached the end of the tunnel, it burst across the surface, engulfing the world in flames. I felt the auras of the elder vampires waiting outside the tunnel to ambush us vanish. The masters of these scourges, who were further back, turned and fled, running as fast as they could, trying to outpace the inferno. Many didn't make it, overrun by the sticky flames surging through the surrounding city.

No human sorcerer could replicate what Gorgath had done with that spell. The kid worked on a scale far beyond human limits. The amount of mana he released made his weakest spells comparable to the greatest master-tier magic humans were capable of. And what he'd just cast was not a basic spell.

Based on what I felt, a fifth of the elder vampires that had invaded the city were now dead.

It was a good start.

I ran forward, through the smell of fire and ash, and punched the kid's ankle to get his attention. "Gorgath, phase two!"

Phase two involved our team overrunning the ambush site, entering the city and charging through the streets towards the main gate. While we did that, Gorgath would use his inferno spell to destroy several sections of the nearby city so the teams hunting vampires wouldn't be overwhelmed.

With the harvest ritual now in play, with a countdown measured in less than three minutes, I was the only one with a reasonable chance of intervening. Sir Trent and Rupert were now in command of the distraction. They didn't serve me, but they had the most experience in high-level combat. Their only objective was to engage the ancient vampires and lock them down so I could slip away and disrupt the harvest ritual before it ended.

A lot of people were going to die to achieve that.

Gorgath lowered his staff, making a mystical motion with his empty hand. The blue flames clinging to the tunnel vanished as he cast the counter-spell. The barriers disappeared a second later, releasing a wave of hot air that could flash-fry chicken.

"Phase two formation," Sir Trent roared.

Everyone reacted to the order and broke into a run, shifting positions to a holy running turtle formation. There were three rings to the formation. The melee fighters were in the outer ring, the archsorcerers were in the middle ring, with the clerics in the centre.

Archsorcerers rose ten feet into the air with magic, lifting the clerics with them to escape the frying pan heat of the tunnel floor. The warriors ignored the heat. Their constitution was so high that it didn't bother them. With the ability to fly, those in the air could match the speed of those running, and we surged forward, leaving the other forces to catch up when they could.

The flying spells were a necessary expenditure of mana to move quickly, but it would cost lives later. We were no longer in the dungeon, and it would be harder to replace any mana spent.

The formation blurred out of the tunnel and charged through the ash-coated memorial, with its melted headstones and scorched earth. Sir Trent and Angelica rushed ahead as we approached what was left of the iron gate and kicked it off its hinges, clearing our way into the burning city.

For a quarter of a mile in every direction, buildings and bodies burned, clogging the air with smoke and ash. Wraith wisps surged toward the flames from every direction, flying through the air, drawn by the vampires' deaths and the abandoned life force saturating the city.

I sprinted through Necropolis's burning city centre, filled with wide, twisting and turning streets and tall buildings. The city's main industry was the dungeon, and people wanted to live close enough to commute easily. It made the two miles around the dungeon a dense urban environment. Once we got through it, there wouldn't be so many directions to be attacked from.

We wouldn't get that far, though.

As burning structures gave way to ransacked homes, I moved to the front of the formation, beside Sir Trent, to act as a scout and an early warning system, pointing out buildings that held elder vampires. "There. There. There."

Sir Trent relayed what I told him to those under his command, calling names and sending warriors to deal with the threats. Running through a barrage of expert or master-tier spells would overwhelm us before we engaged our target. They needed to save as much mana as possible to deal with the real fight, so sending high-level warriors to deal with them was the most efficient way to do that, even if it cost lives.

As we ran, I heard elder vampires relaying orders they'd telepathically received from one of the four ancient vampires. In the beginning, they were cut down while speaking, but as we moved further into Necropolis, more and more of them were waiting for us. They weren't ready to deal with someone as strong as Angelica or Gregory, though.

When Yasmir realised that he was losing people without gaining anything in return, the elder vampires along our path retreated, shadowing our formation from several streets away, building up the numbers they needed to confront us.

"They're shadowing us now," I said, twenty seconds into our blind charge for the city wall.

Sir Trent grunted, signalling he'd heard.

From behind us, blue light suddenly illuminated the night sky as Gorgath reached the surface and began throwing spells. Unlike before, he didn't counter-spell his efforts, and the blue light continued to provide light as the city burned.

Being able to sense elder vampires' auras let me know what was going on by paying attention to their movements. Twenty seconds after Gorgath threw his second spell, our enemy realised we weren't the only threat. The distant elder vampires converging on our location began changing directions to intercept the teams hunting their army.

Without slowing, Rupert lifted a communication crystal to his forehead to receive a message from Harlin. His family members were tracking the ancient vampires for us. Before Rupert could share his update, I heard the elder vampires converge on us.

"Incoming attack!" I shouted. "All directions!"

The entire force stopped in three steps. Archsorcerers dropped everyone out of the air and cast barriers, protecting the clerics, while warriors spread out to engage an enemy they couldn't hope to match.

Sir Trent took control of the situation, shouting orders as the four ancient vampires blurred through our lines, cutting my weaker deathlords apart, sending limbs and heads flying. They overran the outer ring in a violent blur and leapt over the archsorcerers' barriers to pass above the clerics together, releasing eight master-tier destruction spells simultaneously.

The first pair of spells created a hole in the barrier above Davina as they targeted the biggest threat to their existence. Davina was just as fast as they were and managed to counter-spell the first destruction spell heading for her. The defences of her holy robe blocked the second.

Mother and Father weren't so lucky. The archbishops' robes blocked the first spells, but not the second, and the two of them dissolved into dust, vanishing like a dream upon waking.

Hellfire exploded from Professor Firebrand's hand, engulfing Yasmir's legs in unholy red flames that hurt to look at, filling the air with the smell of brimstone. At the same time, Angelica tackled Sing out of the air, dragging her to the ground through the hole in the barrier and landing in the middle of the clerics as the barrier reformed over them.

"Stay still," Angelica commanded, throwing everything she had into the command.

The force of the command washed over me and the other ancient vampires, causing all of us to pause for half a second as we fought the backlash of her compulsion. Sir Trent, Gregory, and Helen used the opening to attack the other two ancient vampires, while Professor Firebrand threw a second ball of hellfire at Yasmir.

Sing froze in place, unable to immediately fight off the compulsion directed at her. Archsorcerers and clerics got out of the way as Professor Lan pivoted and rushed to the momentarily helpless ancient vampire, weaving a master-tier banishment spell.

Angelica leapt aside, right before Professor Lan touched Sing. The ancient vampire and the cobblestones under her disappeared from this reality.

As I regained the ability to move, Yasmir released a primal scream of rage, quickly casting three destruction spells fuelled by the pain of his loss. The first opened a hole in the unstable barrier. The second was countered by Davina. And the third turned a triumphant Professor Lan to dust.

Professor Firebrand hit Yasmir's chest with a third ball of hellfire right as Angelica threw her staff through his shoulder like a spear, severing the limb. His arm fell to the ground as the hellfire cauterised his wound, stopping him from being able to regenerate. Yasmir ignored his burning body and backhanded Angelica through a building as she leapt towards him.

His strike left him open as I blurred towards him and swung Slaughter, forcing my aura into my cleave skill. An aura blade exploded from Slaughter and cleaved through his stomach, introducing hellfire into his core. The raw mana in his core behaved like gasoline for the hellfire.

Yasmir exploded, covering everything with hellfire for twenty feet. There was no way to escape. Hellfire engulfed my Day Walker set from head to toe, burning and corrupting any exposed flesh. My face melted beneath my hood as my soul screamed and my skin sizzled.

I blurred to the edge of the archsorcerers' barrier with my eyes shut, navigating through the world by auras. I needed a cleric to extinguish the flames before they burned through my eyelids and blinded me.

Necrotic bolts and fingers of destruction began to strike my back as the elder vampires entered the battle. The ring of deathlords thinned as they spread into the surrounding buildings to engage the vampires in close combat.

Dalin came to my aid, bathing me in holy purifying magic to extinguish the hellfire. He smiled at me through the barrier as I opened my eyes and leapt back into the fight, chasing after the elder vampire I could feel fleeing with Yasmir's severed arm.

Holy magic bombarded the ground where the rest of Yasmir's body lay as Davina did her best to purge him from existence and prevent him from regenerating here. Her magic wouldn't kill him without all of him here, and it wouldn't take him long to recover from his hellfire injuries once the hellfire burned out.

I ducked down an alleyway and leapt over a fence, ignoring the pain coming from the hellfire burns, knowing that my ancient royal vampiric soul regeneration would heal the burns shortly. The skill might have mutated with my parasites, but it should still have the underlying capabilities, and with it mastered, I wouldn't be injured for long.

A deathlock barrier appeared across the mouth of the alleyway I ran through. I cut down the barrier with Slaughter and used the mana from the spell to cast a finger of destruction at the vampire who had cast it.

He exploded in a cloud of dust.

I turned right at the end of the alleyway, seeing the three elder vampires fleeing down the street. In the space of two steps, I shapeshifted into a creature that resembled a cheetah, merging my Day Walker set and Slaughter into my body. A notification appeared.

Your Ancient Royal Vampiric Physique skill has increased to level 19.

I dismissed the notification.

Such a transformation was only possible because Lavire had specifically built the ability into the equipment he made, and I had

Lusor's understanding of shapeshifting. Changing shape did nothing for my pain, as the hellfire wound continued to fester, healing much more slowly than my other wounds.

I finished the transformation on all fours, killing the sound and scents from my body with my mastery of death magic. Lusor wouldn't have denied that attributes mattered, but he would have strongly argued that form mattered just as much. In a foot race, a longer stride and more efficient technique mattered just as much as attributes. Four legs are always faster than two, in his opinion. Wings were even better, but that would expose me to too many spells.

I was much faster in my new form, covering the distance like a speeding bullet. Without scent, sound, or an aura to give me away, the elder vampires trying to escape didn't notice my presence in time to react.

With a swipe of my paw, I broke the neck of the elder vampire carrying Yasmir's charred arm, used my teeth to snatch the charred limb that was already expanding in his grasp, and darted down another alley, being chased by spells.

Yasmir's cold, sickly blood ran down my throat as I fed on what was left of him with my vampiric soul bite. His flesh fought back, automatically using his vampiric touch to slow his death as I raced through side streets and alleyways, drawing as many elder vampires as I could away from my people.

Memories flashed through my head as I consumed Yasmir's knowledge of the harvest ritual. An ancient vampire named Belva was the one who had compelled the chosen and helped them acquire the demon king's greater orb for the ritual. Beyond the involvement of a greater demon orb, my impression was that Yasmir didn't know anything about the ritual that I didn't already know. That didn't stop me from continuing to absorb his memories.

Moving on all fours was so much faster than two legs, and I was several streets away with his arm in only a few seconds, heading for Necropolis's outer wall. I passed a heavily warded building full of survivors who had received Harlin's ghost message and saw a dozen exhausted necromancers outside the buildings, fighting vampires in the street.

Having a ghost deliver a message to fight was not the most effective way to gather support, so only one in three groups of survivors were participating in the fight. They added to the chaos, drawing more attention away from my people. I watched more than one necromancer die as I wove through the streets, passing down alleys and over fences, unable to stop and finish off Yasmir quickly. Stopping would allow those chasing me to catch up and with enough spells, they could potentially pull me out of the fight.

The tall, apartment-style buildings gave way to large, walled manors, exposing the ritual in the distance. Beyond the city wall, thirteen figures hovered far above the city. They held hands around a glowing orb of red and gold energy. With each passing second, the orb grew brighter, syphoning off the last of the life force and attributes of the children trapped below.

Above the orb was the soul vortex, a spiralling vortex of golden light. It was feeding on the same children, tearing their souls from their bodies to pay for the chosen's immortality. From the vortex, a funnel began to descend towards the orb.

I was out of time.

I was out of options.

I slipped into the Deadlands, ready to face Death.

CONTESSA TALKED about her many encounters with Death in her research journals. Death was the apex predator of the Deadlands, a form of spiritual entity that preferred to consume the undead over the living. It was immaterial, fast, powerful beyond reason, could exist in multiple places simultaneously, and had no weakness to anything the undead could throw at it.

Contessa described Death as a nomadic entity, so the chance of coming into contact with it in the Deadlands was low, except under two conditions. Massacres and anywhere undead congregated in large numbers always drew its presence. Wherever she set down roots with her undead horde, Death would follow, cutting her off from the Deadlands.

Contessa had no idea what the creature was, nor why it existed. She'd theorised that it was a spiritual construct, something created to prevent the undead from merging the Deadlands into reality. I didn't buy her theory, but I did buy that Necropolis was not the sort of place I wanted to enter the Deadlands.

I was right.

Within seconds of entering the Deadlands, Death stalked me, tracking me through alleyways and side streets like a bloodhound. The weight of its spiritual presence pulled at my life force, draining me and hastening Yasmir's demise.

I would never have risked travelling through the Deadlands without Yasmir's arm. Even as just an arm, his undead aura was stronger than mine, making him the perfect bait to reach my destination safely.

Yasmir's arm was tossed in one direction, and I went in another, using the time dilation of the Deadlands to reach the cultists before they could finish their ritual.

Using a levitation spell inside the Deadlands, I floated in a black and white sky behind the leader of the chosen. The thirteen Unseen archsorcerers still held hands in a circle, but they had thrown back their heads as they chanted the last words of the ritual.

Below them sat the harvest ritual circle. It was filled with hundreds of thousands of dead and dying soulless children, and surrounded by thousands of cultists who were powering the spell. There was nothing I could do for the children anymore. Their souls had already been harvested by the soul vortex above, waiting to be sent to Hell to pay for the chosen's immortality.

Their bodies were batteries, feeding what was left of their life force into the unholy greater orb floating among the chosen. With the tornado of power descending from the vortex, to the orb and ropes of life force extending from the orb to the chosen, there were only seconds left before they ascended, before they became immortal, before they damned all those children's souls to Hell for power.

That wasn't going to happen.

With my first glimpse of the children came rage, an anger so deep and primal that it would see worlds burned to ash and clay. What I was about to do was not sane. But in this moment, I was not sane. I was a father, watching other fathers' children suffer for power, and I would do anything to stop it.

I felt Yasmir's aura vanish as I floated out of the Deadlands, behind the cult leader, and swung Slaughter, cleaving her down the middle. My vampiric soul touch turned her to dust as I floated forward and took her place, sheathing Slaughter, and holding the hands of the chosen who stood beside her.

The rope of life force continued to snake towards my chest, unconcerned by the cult leader's death. I smelled the neighbouring chosen's fear as they noticed my presence and realised all was lost.

I tightened my grip.

The ritual had gone too far for me to just kill them. The only way to free the children's souls trapped in the vortex was to *void the contract* they'd made with the demon king.

The funnel of souls descending from the vortex touched the demon king's orb as the ropes of life force connected everyone's in the circle. The greater orb that was about to open a gateway to Hell and transfer the power the chosen craved, recognised that one of the chosen was not like the others.

The contract was voided.

The greater orb shattered, unleashing all the magic, life force, and soul energy it contained in a divine explosion that vaporised everything in its path. A true harvest ritual was not a master-tier spell, but a *divine* spell. It required life force and soul energy, and its power was far beyond what mana could offer.

The Curse of Sloth and the impulses that had turned me into a monster vanished as my flesh was stripped from my soul in a blinding flash of light. A notification appeared and disappeared so quickly that I barely caught sight.

You have mastered your Royal Vampiric Aura skill.

Time slowed as my soul was left floating in the air, watching as the explosion passed me by and destroyed everything around me.

My soul's ghostly, immaterial form refused to let me turn my head, as power flowed into me and my soul underwent a transformation. First, my immaterial form became as solid as flesh. Once it had become material, it swelled in size, growing larger, until I was as large as Lusor, before a pair of magnificent wings sprouted from my back.

There was no pain.

No discomfort.

I could feel myself growing stronger. I could feel the power swelling within me as the changes occurred, but the mind that perceived these changes were not the mind I'd become used to. There were no instant answers or vampiric instincts that could tell me what was happening to me.

I was Vincent.

Without my vampiric cunning or instincts, it took me longer to understand what was happening to me, even with time moving so slowly. I knew the changes I'd made to my soul to heal Kathrine caused my soul to grow stronger when I had access to excess life force and soul energy, and because of the nature of the explosion that had destroyed my body, my soul now had access to more life force and soul energy than ever before. It was absorbing the torrent of life force and soul energy released by the explosion, but why did it give me wings?

I watched, unable to move, as the explosion vapourised the earth beneath me, leaving a crater that extended a tenth of the way into the city, with no trace of the cultists, nor the children who had been below. Beyond the crater, the concussive force of the blast flattened everything in its path, leaving the city in ruins.

Chunks of earth and stone the size of houses were tossed into the air and began to rain from the sky as I felt a powerful spiritual presence appear behind me.

The presence placed one hand on my shoulder and struck. Pain exploded across my lower back as the creature cut through my soul to take hold of the nexus of magic that was my core and mana network.

"Stop fighting me," Shadow, my shade, spat into my ear. "If you regenerate with this inside you, you'll explode. That might be fatal in your condition."

I gritted my teeth, fighting against the pain, and felt control of my body returned to me as I shouted through my teeth. "Stop!"

Shadow ignored my order and gave a violent tug, tearing my core and mana network from me. The life force and soul energy I was still absorbing from the explosion went to work, repairing the hole in my back, lessening the pain and repairing the damage.

Shadow tightened his grip on my shoulder. "Don't move. Your soul is shielding a handful of demonic parasites that managed to survive the blast."

The pain receded as I looked over my shoulder to see a translucent copy of myself. Shadow now possessed all my features, including a ghostly version of my Day Walker set and Slaughter. Until now, he wasn't powerful enough to sustain his existence, surviving on a connection to me that fed him life force, mana, and soul energy. The explosion that had strengthened my soul must have done the same to him, through that connection.

He gave a grunt of discomfort as he shoved my core into his ghostly form.

"Put it back," I commanded.

Shadow gritted his teeth through the pain as he forced my core to merge with his new body. "You're not technically my master. You're just a part of him. I don't have to do what you say."

"You're not supposed to be able to harm me."

Shadow gave me a very predatorial grin, which twisted my face in a way I didn't like. "I'm not harming you. The changes to your soul are significant enough that I truly believe you have a chance to cast holy magic. If I'm right, this would cause your core to explode as your body tries to reform. In your disembodied state and with your mana capacity, that would be fatal."

My mind couldn't work as quickly as it could under my vampiric parasites' influence. There was no instant solution that came with his statement. I had to think it through. What he said sounded plausible. My wings did give a holy magic vibe.

"Why did you put my core inside you?"

Shadow continued to grin. "It's compatible with my transformation. Also, it's free loot, and it will make what comes next much easier." He grinned and patted my shoulder. "Remember, don't move, if you want to *live*."

Shadow dropped to the ground, in the middle of the crater. He raised his ghostly hand, the same way I would, if I was going to cast a master-tier spell.

This wasn't good.

Snap!

The sound reverberated through the city, as Shadow emptied his stolen core, weaving a spell even Contessa wouldn't cast. A wave of death magic crashed through the city with the speed of a nuclear explosion, momentarily breaking the barrier between the Deadlands and this reality. In its wake stood the ghosts of the city's inhabitants, the imprint they left behind when their souls moved on.

Shadow had woken the dead from their slumber, given them clarity and purpose, power without restriction, and set them free to act as they wished. The ghosts of the dead children and cultists filled the crater, and the ghosts of the thirteen dead chosen trembled in the air around me.

Shadow didn't lower his hand.

Snap!

There was no magic behind his second snap, only a force of will. In the blink of an eye, every ghost in and around Necropolis appeared beside the children in the crater. The temperature instantly plunged so far below freezing that the ground began to crack. The weight of so many spirits warped the world.

Shadow looked at the ghosts with open sorrow and rage, expressing the same anger I felt over what had been done here, and I understood what he intended to do.

He was going to give them justice.

"You didn't deserve this," he said, voice carrying far beyond what his soft-spoken words should have allowed. "Let me set this right."

With his words came his will, and I had to restrain myself from bending my knee. In his words were the promise of retribution. The promise of justice. The promise of peace, if I only bent my knee and offered my power to him.

The ghosts of Necropolis bent their knees without hesitation, giving up their existence for a chance at revenge. As their knees hit the ground, they vanished.

A crown grew from the dirt at Shadow's feet, containing all their spiritual power. It had a physical presence that matched the spiritual, and I felt the anger radiating from it. I'd seen a crown like it in the vault at the adventurers' guild in Hellmouth. And I knew what it would do to him, if he put it on.

Shadow reached down without ceremony and picked up the crown, holding it between his hands. He understood the burden he was about to place on himself. The sorrow vanished from his expression, leaving only rage as he looked at the ghosts of the cultists and placed the crown on his head.

His spiritual weight deepened, as the spiritual strength of Necropolis's dead flowed into him. His translucence faded as he grew solid, cementing his transformation into a ghost king. With a flick of his wrist, he asserted his new authority, and the ghosts of the cultists and chosen crumbled under his spiritual power.

Shadow raised his head, met my gaze, snapped his fingers, and broke the bond between us. Then he set his sights on the broken city and vanished.

I released a disembodied sigh.

Shadow's transformation into a ghost king was surprisingly low on my list of problems.

42

THE GRAVE CALLS

Shadow hadn't lied. It required a little soul-searching, but I managed to find thirteen absurdly strong demonic parasites that had survived the explosion. They must have mutated more than the rest, allowing them to absorb the mana, soul energy, and life force from the explosion, rather than being destroyed by it. They were spread across my soul like ticks, reinforcing their small sections of my soul in a way that made my soul act like a protective barrier.

With the transformation my soul had undergone, I could sense each one, and feel exactly what they were doing. Which is how I knew they were all dormant, waiting for the right conditions to begin regenerating my body, conditions that wouldn't occur without active intervention.

Without my vampiric cunning, it took a frustrating amount of effort to gather them together, manipulating my soul to push them into a single place. It took a bit more prodding after that, but they eventually realised that they weren't alone anymore.

Over the next ten seconds, they began to regenerate a drop of blood. When the weight of the drop grew too much to remain airborne, it fell to the crater below, pulling my soul with it. A secondary force began trying to pull at my soul, attempting to draw it inside my flesh.

With the strength my soul possessed after its transformation and my knowledge of astral projection, it was easy to resist being pulled in.

I might not have had my vampiric cunning anymore, but my soul's memory was flawless.

I let the blood pull me to the ground. Without a body to come back to, going walkabout would be a mistake. My feet collided with compacted earth, before the weight of the blood yanked me onto my back, leaving me lying face up, looking at the night sky.

For a moment, I froze. The beauty of the stars caught me off-guard, so did the alienness. They weren't my constellations, reminding me I was so very far from home.

So very far from the man I had been.

The vampiric instincts that had plagued me for so long were gone, but so were my emotions. I didn't feel anger or bitterness, nor any horror over the actions I had taken or that had been done to me. I was cold, almost logical in nature.

I knew who I was, and that wouldn't change.

Stars twinkled overhead as thunder cracked in the distance. It was quickly followed by dozens of other identical cracks of thunder, reminding me I was in a warzone, and no matter how good it felt to be away from my impulses and instincts, people needed me.

I forced myself to ignore the sky and pushed my focus inward, scanning each parasite and assigning a number. Lucky Number 7 got his name because he was doing half the work. The little guy was creating muscle like a steroid-drunk bodybuilder. However, even with Number 7's efforts, it was safe to say my regeneration was no longer measured in milliseconds and seconds, but minutes and hours.

The research Contessa conducted by torturing me had taught me that the parasites had some awareness of their surroundings. When she'd separated a few parasites from the other parasites inside my body, they'd refused to spawn new parasites but continued to create new flesh, as long as they weren't entirely alone. When the separated parasites and new flesh were reintroduced to my body, the two immediately merged, and the parasites returned to spawning new parasites.

After discovering this mechanism, Contessa tried to clone me. She took a sample of parasites and let them regenerate flesh away from my main body, unimpeded. The parasites threw everything they had into rebuilding me, killing themselves in the process. Contessa ran the experiment four times just to calculate the minimum number of parasites needed to clone me, but she didn't live long enough to see if she was right.

My thirteen mutated parasites were much stronger than the ones she worked with, but I highly doubted they would be enough for a full recovery, not when it took ten seconds to regenerate a single drop of blood. I was effectively out of this fight, which was a problem because my people needed all the help they could get.

Despite experiencing an explosion that destroyed most of this side of the city, the vampires had picked themselves up to continue fighting. I could sense the flow of the skirmishes and wider battle through my bonds, as those who had taken my oath, didn't adapt to the new situation as fast as their enemy.

The next few minutes continued the bloodbath the explosion had triggered, before everything fell into a new rhythm. My bond continually sent me warnings, trying to make me intervene. There were times when I knew I would have been able to save people, if I only had my body. Other times, like with Sir Trent, there was nothing I could do. One moment he was alive, healthy, and in danger, and the next he was dead.

A few seconds after he fell, Angelica was at death's door, fighting for her life. Thirty minutes went by without any changes to her condition, but there were changes to mine.

I felt the first signs of weariness enter Number 7.

I could tell he wanted me to return to my grave and rest. He was tired from regenerating half a pound of flesh and making the other twelve look bad.

By any definition, the twelve's ability to regenerate half a pound of flesh together was impressive. Except in a situation where they were sitting next to Number 7, who had achieved the same results alone. Then they looked like slackers.

By the hour mark, I was certain that if I didn't stop my recovery, the surviving parasites would kill themselves trying to save me. The pressure my soul was under to merge with my flesh was growing stronger by the minute, but I couldn't give in to it. Giving in would be a death sentence. Without a brain, I would be in perpetual agony, unable to think or act to save myself.

I was still lying there when the sun began to rise thirty minutes later. As I lay there, I saw thick, black clouds rise from the city, creating a doom of darkness that blocked out the light. There were holes in the doom, which suggested the effect wasn't from a spell, but from enchanted objects. Having some of their devices destroyed in the explosion would explain the gaps.

The sunlight didn't bother my thirteen surviving parasites. They were the type of parasites only ancient vampires had. They weren't affected by sunlight, continuing to regrow flesh unimpeded as the sunlight grew brighter.

Thirty minutes later, I was in a position to do something. I had four pounds of flesh, with enough control over that flesh through my soul to shapeshift it into another form. I knew I needed three pounds to build a functional brain, so I'd waited until I had another pound to get me airborne. My attributes would hopefully make up for the disparity.

Having more flesh to work with would have been better, but the grave was calling, and I couldn't wait.

I took my last glimpse of the sunrise, enjoying the feeling of being closer to my old self, and then rearranged the glob of flesh, blood, and bone into a fat crow. There were no internal organs, just a framework to house my brain, with enough muscle to flap my wings and keep me airborne. It was a fragile form. A single spell would kill it. And my parasites wouldn't be able to regenerate this much flesh a second time. But if nothing went wrong, it would be enough to save my life.

I let my soul merge back into my flesh and opened my eyes as the Vampire Vincent. My mind shifted gears as vampiric instincts reasserted themselves. I immediately noticed the flaws I'd incorporated into my new form. My foolish soul had been too cautious, too safe. I'd had more than enough flesh to have left this crater thirty minutes ago.

I shapeshifted again, harnessing the excess flesh, to create a form that was faster and stronger. The moment my avian form stabilised, I leapt into the air and flapped my wings, heading for the field hospital that I sensed had been set up in the city.

My attribute-enhanced strength and agility propelled me through the air like a rocket as I navigated around battles inside half-destroyed buildings, necromancers fleeing south on foot, and all the other chaotic elements that come with warzones. Getting to the city centre in one piece was my only goal. The field hospital was the only secure location outside of the dungeon, and enough of my people were there that I knew they could get Davina for me.

The smell of blood and pain tantalised my senses as I approached the building. It left me salivating as I glided closer. A deep, primal thirst was clawing at the back of my throat and the grave was calling me.

It wasn't as bad as when I'd kidnapped Carolyn, but it would continue to grow worse until Davina bound my parasites and commanded them to stop trying to regenerate me. Even if she were successful, it would still be three months until we reached my grave, so we would be cutting it close.

I circled the warehouse three times, evaluating the dozen guards, while I waited for my people to tell them not to attack me. I was closer to death than I'd ever come, and I wasn't willing to take any risks.

My fight was definitely over.

As the guards stood down, they opened the barrier. I flew through the hole in the roof of the warehouse and landed on Gregory's naked chest. The armour he'd borrowed from Titus was gone, taken by someone who needed it more. Gregory didn't react to my landing, staring at the ceiling, close to catatonic.

With my skin touching his and the changes my soul had undergone, I could sense the poor state of his soul. Yes, both his legs had been cut off and were sitting on the ground beside him, rotting and waiting to be reattached, but they were a minor issue compared to his missing left arm.

I could smell the hellfire clinging to the stump, infecting his soul, and preventing him from healing properly. The infection was eating at his soul, leaving him smelling depressed and defeated, like a man at the end of his rope, ready to jump off the cliff if he could only get the strength to take that last step.

I needed Gregory functional. Everything would go smoothly if the orders came from him.

I drew on the new reservoir of soul energy that sat within me where my core had been and poured it into his body, using the same healing palm technique I had used to heal Kathrine. What had taken me months of effort for her, only took seconds for him, giving me insight into the scope of the transformation my soul had undergone.

Gregory took a deep breath as his soul recovered, and he blinked. A few seconds passed as his body rebalanced his neurochemicals and returned to its normal state, utilizing his high agility. His hellfire injuries continued to damage his soul, but for a moment, that damage had been undone.

Gregory released a sigh filled with pain as he continued to blink. "Thanks, Boss."

I ignored his thanks and surveyed the room.

There were dozens of hellfire-injured deathlords and archsorcerers groaning in their sleep. The clerics and paladins were all off fighting, so no one was taking care of them. The only treatment they'd received was a potion or two to close their natural wounds and let them rest. Gregory's injuries were some of the worst, but they were nothing compared to Angelica's.

She was covered from head to toe in hellfire burns, giving her a charcoal complexion and an odour close to burnt barbeque. Her flesh had melted into her armour, fusing them together, likely saving her life. I could feel her armour's vampiric aura feeding her life force to slow down her decline. It was slowly killing the other patients, but there wasn't anything I could do about that.

Gregory saw me looking at Angelica and gave her a weak pride filled smile. "The vampires were overwhelming us with numbers, throwing spells without caring about their mana reserves, blocking us from finishing off their masters whenever we got the upper hand. We were desperate and dying, losing people left and right. Then she saved us."

"Angelica saved you?"

"I think it was Sir Trent's death that made her do it. She recognised that ancient vampire was going to kill him and went completely berserk, tackling her right as she was turning him to dust. Angelica then screamed at that hellfire professor to burn them both."

Sir Trent had spent months teaching Angelica how to fight, teaching her how to protect herself, so no one would ever harm her again. He was one of the few people she respected, but I doubted that she had ever told him that. It made sense that she would react so strongly to his death. Angelica might have been self-centred, but she was extremely protective of people she felt had shown her kindness.

"It was one of the bravest things I've ever seen," Gregory added.

"She probably thought her armour would protect her." My words came out clear, but they sounded strange, due to my beak.

"You wouldn't say that if you'd heard her screams." Gregory pointed at his charred stump with his good hand, wincing as he did. "Hellfire isn't just physical pain. It burns away your will and strength to fight. I know a fraction of what she felt, and I know I wouldn't have been able to hold on to that vampire the way she did. Your girl didn't falter. She didn't let go. She sacrificed herself, so the rest of us could make it out. Everyone in this warehouse and those still fighting are only here because of what she did. She turned the odds in our favour and scared the last ancient vampire enough to run away. I don't know if Rupert and Davina managed to put her down, but it doesn't matter. Angelica gave us the breathing room we needed to *win*."

I should have felt pride. I should have felt joy and happiness over her actions. But I couldn't. The closest I could come was a feeling of contentment that *my monster* had finally made the right choice. The demonic part of me hated her for that.

"Why are you here, sir?"

"I need you to get Davina for me. She's on the east side of the city."

"Why not go to her yourself?"

"I don't like my chances of reaching her."

"What?"

"I'm dying."

Gregory tilted his head forward to stare at me, before giving me a weary grin. "Welcome to the party, sir. I'll send someone to find her for you."

"I need protecting."

"I think that's mentioned in our employment contract somewhere."

I chuckled.

As Gregory called over the senior most deathlord, I flapped my wings and flew off his chest to land on Angelica's. A crackling sound came from her charcoal skin as I landed. Potions didn't heal hellfire. A cleric needed to purify her wounds for them to heal, but it wasn't something you could do quickly, so they'd left her to her fate.

Only a Dragon, a child of the reaping ritual, the owner of the Crypt Keeper set, and my familiar would survive what she had. That was just enough of an advantage to give her a slow and painful death.

As I stood on her chest, I used the healing palm technique. Seconds ticked by, stretching into minutes, as I repaired the thin sliver of her soul that survived her hellfire baptism. Angelica's injuries made Kathrine's injures look like a sprained ankle. It would have taken me years to repair all the damage, if my soul hadn't changed.

I was glad it had. Spending so long healing her would have been tedious.

I stared at her melted, blackened features, which barely looked human anymore, as I finished healing her soul. Angelica's breath remained shallow, despite the repairs.

"I command you to live, Angelica."

Her next breathing was a little deeper, but her features contorted in pain from so much movement.

The monstrous part of me wanted to continue placing compulsions on her. It couldn't feel fear, but it did understand concern, and it was concerned what Angelica would do to us now that she understood her equipment's control undead ability worked on ancient vampires. It wanted to wrap her in compulsions so she couldn't wrap us in compulsions.

I didn't listen.

Angelica had earned her freedom.

She'd earned her chance to discover how monstrous she'd become, to see if she could live without me keeping her impulses in check. I hoped that giving her this chance wouldn't cost me or others their life, but if it did, so be it.

I'd done enough harm to her already.

I wouldn't do more.

I hopped off her chest and flew back to Gregory, landing on his chest. The four deathlords he'd assigned to guard me followed.

Gregory opened one eye, fighting to remain awake through the pain and injuries. "You need me to do something else?" He knew I'd heard him send the messenger, so I wasn't asking for an update.

"No. I'm just seeing how quickly the hellfire burn is damaging your soul."

Gregory closed his eye. "How bad is it?"

"You'll start to fall apart again by the end of the day."

"I can live with that. How's Helen?"

I focused on my bond with her. "She's fighting on the west side of the city with a dozen of our people. I'll tell you if she falls."

"And the rest of my people?"

"It's too early to tell."

Gregory gave a weak smile. "The vampires know we're deathlords. They know most of us are resistant to death magic. They're throwing necrotic magic at us. We both know our people aren't coming back."

"Some are."

"I bet any that do always come back quickly."

He wasn't wrong.

"How many have been gone for a while?"

"Close to half. But the rate we're losing people has slowed."

Gregory gave me a grim nod and fell asleep, giving in to pain and exhaustion.

I turned to the other patients.

Healing Angelica had barely tapped my new reservoir of soul energy, so I moved down the line, checking each patient's soul and healing them if they needed it. If their souls grew too weak, they would depart this world, which—unlike for the children used in the harvest ritual—would instantly be fatal.

With each passing minute, I continued to grow bigger, and the call of the grave grew stronger. I had an hour at most before I would be in the same shape as I was after the church had finished testing me. But those estimates only applied if my condition continued to deteriorate in a linear way.

Thirty minutes after Gregory fell asleep, Davina blurred into the warehouse. Her robes were coated with ash and blood, and they radiated a holy light as numerous curses tried to harm her.

She skidded to a stop before me, and a radiant smile stretched across her face.

I was close to five pounds now, and I wasn't happy about it. "What are you smiling about?"

"You got your wings."

The way she said it told me she wasn't talking about me being a crow. "We can talk about that later. I need you to bind my demonic parasites. Only thirteen survived the explosion, and if you don't stop them from regenerating my body, they're going to kill themselves and take me with them."

Davina got to work, pulling ritual items from her storage pouch to create a binding circle. Items appeared on the ground in a feverish blur, as she simultaneously swept the stone floor clean with a spell.

I didn't bother asking her how we were doing. She wouldn't be here unless the situation had turned in our favour. "Have you seen Shadow?"

Davina nodded. "He tried to compel me to help him."

That was concerning.

"Did it work?"

"He might be a ghost king, but he's not you. I played along and helped him attack one of the better-defended vampire strongholds, but I think you need to keep him on a shorter leash."

"He's acting independently."

Davina knew almost as much about the undead as I did. Her gaze snapped towards me. "*How* independently?"

"I'm not sure. The explosion destroyed my body, leaving me as a disembodied soul that was much stronger than before the explosion. Shadow went through a similar transformation and used the opportunity to steal my core and insert it into himself, under the pretext that my core might no longer be compatible with the changes that had taken place. I can't fault his logic."

Her eye's widened as she understood what I was saying. "You weren't the one who woke the dead?"

"No. That was him. He used them to become a ghost king, which made him strong enough to break our bond."

"You don't sound surprised."

"I would have done the same, if I had been in his place. He knows I won't trust him, now that he's so powerful, which means I will keep him on a shorter leash, which will interfere with his ability to protect my family and serve my interests. The only reasonable action he could take under those circumstance was to free himself from my control while he had the chance, and grow strong enough that I couldn't summon him back and bend him to my will."

Davina looked over again. "You almost make it sound like nothing about his transformation concerns you?"

"Everything about his transformation concerns me, but creating a ghost king to stop thirteen immortals from coming into existence is a small price to pay. With everything that's happening, Shadow is low on my list of priorities and smart enough not to cause the kind of trouble that will move him up the list."

"What if he fulfils the obligations of his crown?"

"He's strong enough to kill elder vampires, but he can't fulfil his obligations unless the last ancient vampire is also dead. Gregory said you went after her."

"Rupert went after her, even though I told him not to. He led his people into an ambush and had lost half of them before I arrived. I would have died with him, but the matriarch of a necromancer family that had been surviving in the city, showed up with a void tear. She'd heard my call and killed the ancient vampire for us."

Shadow had just moved slightly higher up my priority list, but he still wasn't an immediate concern. He could only cause a fraction of the trouble that I could.

I changed the subject.

"If we survive this, I want you to devote yourself to practicing life and holy magic. You need to master those skills and form a core. This is just the beginning of a very long war."

Davina finished creating the binding circle and gave me a sad smile. "I know. I wish I had listened to you back at the academy."

I fluttered my wings and hopped into the circle. "If I thought it was necessary back then, I would have compelled you to practice. What happened here and at Darksmith isn't your fault. Now, hurry up. They need you out there."

"Yes, your Dark Eminence."

JUST BEFORE MIDDAY, I felt the last elder vampiric aura disappear from the city and turned to Gregory. He was sitting at a battered desk his people had found among the rubble, looking at a map of the city. With Shadow's actions, Harlin's family no longer had access to ghosts, so Gregory had to track the battle the old-fashioned way, using sorcerers, runners, and messengers to follow everything as best as he could.

The elder vampires had fought to the bitter end. Obviously, they were under some form of compulsion, because even with the chances of being chased down and exposed to daylight, running made more sense. Tracking them down and killing wasn't ideal, but it was the only way to evacuate the city without the survivors being ambushed by the newly turned vampires who were still hiding among the rubble.

"They've finished," I said.

Gregory looked up. "You're certain?"

"There isn't an elder vampire left in the city to organise a counterattack. Order the evacuation."

Gregory sighed with relief and closed his eyes. “We won.”

“You can celebrate after we reach the Bo Empire. Until then, we’re still in hostile territory.”

Gregory eyes snapped open. “Yes, sir.”

Gregory began shouting orders, calling for clerics and wagons to be found to begin the evacuation. He was out the door in seconds, ignoring the pain of his missing arm to take care of his people.

Fifteen minutes later, Davina showed up with a dragon hide cushion, into which Baris’s mother had stitched a permanent binding circle. Davina bound my parasites again with the same instructions not to regenerate my body, before beginning to heal the other patients.

After binding me the first time, she had reattached limbs and closed wounds before leaving. This time she was working on the hellfire injuries. The vampires that had been hit by Professor Firebrand’s hellfire had been commanded to jump on our people to take us with them. Most hadn’t survived the experience. These were the lucky few who had.

Davina was going to be busy for a while.

I turned as Helen walked through the door, scanning the room for threats.

Besides Davina, Helen was the person I trusted the most. I could instinctively sense that she would protect me with her life. It had something to do with her becoming Dalin’s successor.

The old cleric been killed by a destruction spell during the first ambush, right after he extinguished the hellfire that covered me. As his successor, his power had gone to Helen, turning her into a holy paladin and the head of his order, resulting in a transformation of her oath.

The armour she’d borrowed from one of Davina’s paladins and her husband’s spare kilij resting on her left hip had transformed upon Dalin’s death. I couldn’t identify what metal they were made from or any of the tightly packed runes they were enchanted with, but I could feel how potent they were. She was a very dangerous individual now.

Despite the new equipment, she carried a staff that had seen better days. She might not have been able to cast holy magic anymore, now that she was a paladin, but she still had access to her other branches of magic, and she was far more familiar with how to utilize those than she was with her new abilities.

"Helen, would you mind carrying my cushion?"

She continued to scan the area for threats. "Why me?"

"I trust you."

She paused her scan to frown. "You do?"

"I do."

She sighed, walked over to me, and picked up the cushion, bringing me to eye level to meet her gaze. "Let me make this clear. Our order doesn't serve you. That's not our purpose. We've committed ourselves to helping you and those like you to walk in the light, and we will challenge your decisions when we believe it's necessary."

"I understand."

"Good. Princess Carolyn wishes to speak with you."

Thirst was clawing at the back of my throat, and the grave was calling me. The last thing I wanted to do was talk to anyone.

"About what?"

"She didn't say, but I believe she means to inform you that the survivors of Necropolis are not welcome in Arcadia."

The field hospital was far from the main road, so I'd been cut off from what was going on. I didn't know anything about any survivors wanting to travel with us.

"Why do they want to come with us?"

"They don't want to come with us."

Helen was too used to being at odds with me and didn't elaborate.

"Why does Carolyn think they want to come with us?"

"There has never been a necromancer blessed by Heaven to the degree that Davina is. Many of the necromancers heard Davina's call during the battle and accepted. Hundreds of their family heads have become acolytes of her order."

I could see why Carolyn was upset.

I turned to my familiar. "Davina, are you taking them with us?"

Davina didn't look up as she continued working on her patient. "Do I need to dignify that with an answer?"

I turned back to Helen. "Take me to the princess, but make sure I've got enough guards."

Helen raised an eyebrow. "Her bodyguards can't harm you."

"She can."

"You're that weak?"

"Yes."

"I'll find more guards."

Helen collected only four more deathlords, because most were still off fighting vampires, and then she carried me through the city to the edge of the crater. Archsorcerers and sorcerers were working together, to reshape the crater into a road that wagons could ascend and descend through, so everyone could flee without having to run through the parts of the city the vampires still controlled. A long line of wagons loaded with necromancer families were already waiting for them to finish, with more arriving from the dungeon and other parts of the city. There were tear-streaked and frightened faces everywhere, and the monstrous part of me found the atmosphere quite pleasant.

The perpetual cloud of darkness still hung over the city, cutting off most of the sunlight, making the newly turned vampires a serious threat. Explosive cracks of thunder could be heard in the distance as the fighting continued. The surviving vampires had dug in and were on the defensive, but only until sunset.

Staying to finish them off would be a mistake. Reinforcements would show up at some point. Maybe not today, but definitely by tomorrow. There wasn't enough time to kill them all and get away. We had to leave while we had the chance.

Carolyn was down a side road with Gorgath and anyone who wanted to travel with us. Most of the survivors who had taken my oath were with her. The only ones that were missing were the students who had fled. I could sense some of them flying north and south, trying to escape the ancient vampires, who were still compelled to pursue them.

Baris nodded to me as I passed him. The wagons everyone were using held his family crest and carried industrial equipment and storage chests, showing they didn't intend to come back. I didn't need to ask his intentions. I could see it in his tear-streaked eyes. He was coming with us, and he was bringing the Undead Enhancement Club with him.

They would be useful in the future.

Rupert stepped in front of my guards as we approached Carolyn's wagon. His eyes were bloodshot, and he was suffering from mana exhaustion, leaning on his staff to stop himself from swaying. He couldn't throw a spell, but he didn't back down. Every deathlord guarding our group turned to look at him, instinctively ready to throw down.

Rupert gritted his teeth and leapt back, jumping into the wagon. His thirty-three Old Monsters who had survived our escape were outnumbered four to one, and most were off helping build the road. Most of mine were fighting, but I still had twice as many people here as he did, and that wasn't even counting those who had taken my oath.

He couldn't stop us.

And he certainly wasn't in charge.

Helen carried me to the edge of the wagon Carolyn was sharing with Amelia's family and Riza. My daughter's best friend was exhausted and stressed, but at least she was alive. So many weren't.

"I'm told you wish to speak with me, Princess."

Amelia smiled and waved, no worse off from the ordeal everyone had gone through. "Hi, Vincent."

"Hello, Amelia."

"I like your wings. They suit you."

I knew which ones she was referring to and chose not to bring it up.

Carolyn raised a disapproving eyebrow at her handmaiden for her casual conversation, before turning to me. "Is Luke alive?"

Rupert cleared his throat, giving Carolyn the same disapproving look she'd given Amelia.

Celest was still travelling away at the same rate she'd been traveling for the past day. Nothing had stalled my children's escape. If everything continued to go to plan, they would reach their destination late tomorrow evening.

"Luke's fine. He should arrive safely tomorrow evening."

She smiled. "Thank you for the update." She straightened her back.

"Now, I need to inform you that Arcadia cannot house the survivors of Necropolis."

She was exhausted and worried, but that was still a poor lie.

"The entire province of Hellmouth is under-populated, so we both know that's not true. You're concerned I already have too much power and influence in your kingdom, and you don't want me gaining a bunch of necromancer followers on top of what I already have."

She winced. "Can't you be a little more diplomatic?"

"Only when it suits me—and right now, it doesn't suit me, Princess. Besides, it doesn't matter. Soon, I'll be the Duke of Hellmouth."

"Excuse me?"

Her surprise was expected, becoming the Duke of Hellmouth had never interested me before. "Your family does a passable job on managing your kingdom, but an *appalling* job of managing Hellmouth."

"And you believe that's a good enough reason for making you the Duke of Hellmouth?"

"No. I'm saying I'm not giving you a choice."

Rupert gave a low growl, trying and failing to fill Sir Trent's enormous shoes.

Carolyn scowled at him. "Stop it, cousin. Vincent never acts without reason." She turned back to me. "Why do you suddenly want to control Hellmouth?"

"I've kicked the hornet's nest here in North Murdell. Killing five truly ancient vampires in a day is no small feat. That's enough to warrant retaliation from their queen. The obvious target is the hellmouth in Hellmouth. Opening it would cause me all sorts of problems for me, with my grave so close."

Rupert went pale. "Fuck."

"Language."

Carolyn considered my words. "Can you protect the province and hellmouth from them?"

"I think my chances are better than yours. All of your people who took my oath are dead."

Her expression went cold. “Don’t disrespect my people’s sacrifice.”

If I could have smiled, I would have. She’d misinterpreted my words, but that was the right response for a good future queen. “I’m not making light of their deaths, Princess. I’m simply pointing out that your strongest guards are still under level 200, while none of mine are. I have the power to protect the hellmouth. Your kingdom doesn’t.”

I wasn’t happy about her losing people. I’d made plans for using Sir Trent’s talents to make my people stronger, and now, I would have to figure out how to do everything without him. Finding someone to continue training my people was high on my priority list, now that they were so strong. It was just under getting them new equipment. Titus had survived the battle, so he might be able to help if he decided to come with us, but I knew for a fact he didn’t have the combat skill that Sir Trent did.

Carolyn accepted my explanation. “I don’t have the authority to make you the Duke of Hellmouth.”

I knew that.

“Write to your father.”

“He’ll say no.”

“He will, but your conscience will be clear when I decide to force the matter.”

“Please don’t kill him.” She blurted out so quickly that it was obvious that she understood how weak her family’s position now was.

“I don’t need to kill him. Waltzing through his security and taking him hostage will be enough to make my point. Now, back to our original topic. I have no objections to you stopping the Necropolis’s survivors from following us.”

“You don’t?”

“They aren’t your people, and you’re not obligated to help them. However, many of them have heard the necrosaint’s call and become acolytes. Arcadia’s treaty with the church allows their members to migrate to your kingdom with their families, so they’re coming whether you like it or not. You’re welcome to bring that up with the church if you have a problem with it.”

Rupert leaned forward and whispered in her ear. “Anyone who hears the call of a saint is no danger to Arcadia. Accept the small victory. We can discuss the duke issue later.”

“Thank you for sharing your position. I won’t keep you any longer. I imagine it’s going to be a long road home, and you have much to organise.”

I ignored the dismissal. “The families of those who took my oath will also be coming with us.”

Any other time, I would have turned and walked away in a dramatic fashion, leaving her no room to argue back, but I was stuck sitting on a pillow. Carolyn was already opening her mouth to protest.

I turned to Helen. “That was the moment to leave.”

Amelia giggled as Carolyn began to protest.

43

THE LONG ESCAPE

We only made one detour as we fled through South Murdell to the Bo Empire border fortress, and that was to visit the city of Draga, where Riza's family lived. The city was five days from the North Murdell border, and two days out of our way, close to the capitol and the bulk of South Murdell's strongest archsorcerers, who had an understandable problem with Gorgath not only being in their nation but being so close to their capitol. If Kathrine hadn't asked me to make sure Riza got home safely, I wouldn't have risked agitating them.

News of the destruction of Darksmith reached Draga before we did, and Riza turned up at her parent's door, just in time to attend the end of her funeral. No one was more surprised than her elderly great grandmother, who suffered a catastrophic heart-attack. I heard the commotion from down the street in the ruins of Kathrine's former home and sent one of my guards to get Davina to take care of the elderly woman.

I owed Riza that much.

Kathrine's childhood home was nothing but a burnt husk. Polite questioning of the locals by my people informed us that the building had burnt down due to improperly stored potions. The magical fire occurred a month after Kathrine disappeared, killing everyone inside and leaving no bodies. A quick check of the building showed no trace of burnt human remains.

Not being able to experience the life Kathrine lived without me left me with a hollow feeling. I'd hoped that visiting here would give me a glimpse into the years I'd missed. Instead, I found ash and ruin. A history from which I was completely cut off.

I didn't know what to do. Between the exhaustion and thirst clawing at my throat, time began to slip away. The Curse of Sloth took hold, and I just sat on my binding cushion letting the world roll by.

Riza came to find me after sunset, in what had once been Kathrine's bedroom.

Gregory and Helen leaned against the burnt stone walls, acting as bodyguards. Gregory was still missing his arm, showing ugly, twisted scar tissue, but he was no longer exhausted or pained from his ordeal.

Davina's healing skills lay in repairing injuries and resurrection. Cleansing unholy injuries like those from hellfire was an entirely different branch of study that she'd chosen not to pursue because Mother had already mastered it. With Mother no longer around to help her, Davina had only been able to partially cleanse the hellfire wounds. Everyone except Angelica was given a choice, regain full functionality, or live without pain.

Waiting to have your limb regrown to escape the constant agony that hellfire wounds caused wasn't a hard choice. Like everyone else, Gregory had chosen to live without pain.

Riza paused at the doorway, glanced over the blackened stone remains of the room, and began to smell sad. "Kat's going to be heartbroken. The Azurins were kind people."

"They're not dead."

Riza's frowned. "My parents believe they're dead."

"There are no traces of human remains."

Riza smiled. "They faked their deaths?"

I nodded.

"They hid her escape."

"Or ran away from the ramifications of losing your nation's hero."

"They aren't that sort of people. They love Kat like a daughter. They were the ones who taught her magic, even though they weren't supposed to."

"I didn't know that."

"Kat was afraid you'd go after them if she told you about them."

I knew that, and it wasn't an unreasonable concern.

"It's hard enough for me to focus on the things I care about in this state, and you don't fit that definition Riza, so stop stalling. Say what you want to say."

Riza sighed. "My family won't leave."

"I overheard your conversation."

Helen raised an eyebrow at her husband, wordlessly asking if he knew if I could hear conversations that far away.

Gregory shook his head.

Riza paused, afraid of what would come next. "Do we still have to come with you?"

"I never said you had to come with me. I said your family will be *safer* if they do, and that hasn't changed. Blood can make my kind obsessive. They'll go after your family to get to Kathrine if they think it's the easiest way."

Risa took a deep breath, gathering her courage. "You once told me that if I ever needed anything, you would help me. Is that still true?"

"Always."

Riza dropped her gaze to the floor. "Please, take my family to safety," she said in a small voice.

"Do you understand what you're asking me to do?"

"I'm asking you to kidnap them."

"Thank you for being clear." I turned to Gregory. "Operation Relocation is now in play. Make sure your people have her family out of the city by dawn."

Gregory pushed himself away from the wall he was leaning against. "Yes, sir."

Five days later, our convoy stopped for the night outside the Bo Empire's border fortress. The fortress guarded a trade tunnel that the Bo Empire had carved through the mountains to connect the two nations. Night-time entrances weren't permitted, but we were far enough from North Murdell that I didn't feel we needed to force the matter. If the vampires were going to come after us, they would have done so by now. They might retaliate in the future, but that wouldn't happen until after they had dealt with their current problems.

Throughout the night, those who had taken my oath stopped by to speak with me. Everyone was now aware they had sworn their oath to a vampire, and many who had tried to return to their nation had discovered they were no longer welcome.

With North Murdell at war with vampires and South Murdell bordering a nation that was at war with vampires, no one trusted someone who had sworn an oath to a vampire, even a hero's oath. With each passing day, more and more of those who had left returned to the convoy, following their bond to find their way back. There was never any doubt in their minds that I would take care of them. But now that we didn't seem to be in a rush, they wanted to know where we were going, and how they would survive when we arrived.

The conversations drained what little energy and focus I had left. The call of the grave was growing stronger by the day, and without my children around, it was getting the better of me. Davina sensed my struggle and moved Angelica to my wagon to get them to leave me alone. The sight of Angelica's scarred and injured body made most realise that their questions weren't that important, but the more persistent only stopped approaching after Davina called Gorgath over.

The kid lay beside our wagon with a large smile on his face, his hand folded behind his head while he looked at the night sky. He was constantly mesmerised by everything he saw on the surface. He loved trees, mountains, and lakes, but his favourite wonder was the sky. Its vast nature called to him and made him forget his problems.

Like the fact that the South Murdell government had repeatedly denied Arro's request for him to visit her home. They considered him a national threat, and if he didn't leave the country immediately, they would kill him. It was a reasonable position to have.

The kid was incredibly dangerous.

Their fear opened the door to me offering him the opportunity to visit Arcadia and finish his sorcerer studies. Most of the surviving faculty were coming with us, so his experiences at Darksmith wouldn't change too much, and I'd even agreed not to raise his tuition. It hadn't taken much convincing. He was in love with the surface world and jumped at the opportunity to stay.

Davina broke the silence, muttering to herself while she worked. Angelica was not like her other patients. Every inch of her body had been damaged by hellfire. Until a few days ago, stabilizing her was all Davina could do. But her experimentation with her other patients had finally borne fruit, teaching her how to cleanse the residual contamination more effectively.

Davina's healing spells still only had one-thousandth of their usual potency, but at least they now had an effect. Davina had spent the last two days healing Angelica enough to begin removing her armour. Each piece had to be cut away from her flesh. The flesh then had to be healed, while the armour was quickly scrubbed clean. Then the armour had to be put back in place. Even with her physical injuries gone, Angelica couldn't survive without her armour. The lingering effects from the hellfire would leave her in constant agony without its vampiric aura.

Davina never stopped channelling mana into her healing spell, or stroking Angelica's warped, wrinkled, bald scalp, even when one of her surviving clerics returned with Angelica's helmet. The scar tissue faded with each stroke of her hand, slowly returning Angelica's skin to pale, healthy flesh. Soon, she would put the helmet back on and wake her.

Davina looked over to me as the cleric walked away. "Can we talk about your wings now, or are you still avoiding me?"

I slowly turned my head, barely finding the energy to reply. "I was never avoiding you. I was avoiding distracting you from your work."

Davina smiled. "I appreciate that, but can we talk about them?"

"Will it change anything?"

"It might."

"Fine, but make it quick. What do think happened to me?"

"Your soul ascended."

That meant nothing to me, which caught my attention, and pulled me into the world of the living. "I've read multiple libraries, including everything Father had on strengthening and manipulating the soul, and I hold Lusor's memories from when he ransacked the Dancing Crane Sect nearly four thousand years ago. None of that knowledge mentions *ascension*. How do you know about it?"

I smelled no grief from Davina as I mentioned Father, only a slight longing that she wouldn't be seeing him for a while. Father was favoured by Heaven, and without the presence of soul reapers, there was no doubt in her mind of where he now was.

Davina continued healing Angelica. "My knowledge of ascension doesn't come from soul-strengthening. It comes from church doctrine. Knowledge only saints, archbishops, holy paladins, and popes are privy to."

"What's the doctrine?"

"The souls of those favoured by Heaven are not the same as those Heaven shelters from Hell. They can ascend to become *angels.*"

"How?"

"The church doesn't know, but they believe there are three stages. The first is any mortal soul favoured by Heaven. The second is a divine soul, which looks as real as anyone else and can interact with the world as we do, though they are substantially bigger than most people. The third stage is when a divine soul gains their wings and becomes an angel."

That was awfully vague.

"Is there any evidence to back up this doctrine?"

"The most compelling evidence was overheard during a battle between a demon and an angel. The angel told the demon to leave its descendants alone while fighting above a household. The family in the household were the only remaining descendants of a former archbishop known to be favoured by Heaven, and the angel's likeness matched an old painting of her."

"Do you believe them?"

Davina considered my question. "What happened to you proves that the soul is able to ascend. Even everything you have done to your soul wouldn't explain this transformation."

"That might be true, but it doesn't prove I've become an angel in a Heavenly sense."

"Why would you say that?"

"Angel blood is toxic to demons."

Davina tilted her head to the side, looking at me like I was speaking a different language. "What does that have to do with anything?"

"Only thirteen demonic parasites survived the explosion. That number hasn't changed. If my soul had truly ascended and become an angel, the angels' blood in my body would have destroyed them by now. Instead, they sit side by side without any issues."

Davina's frowned. "That certainly complicates matters."

"Not necessarily. Perhaps the term, 'angel' is a qualification for those from Heaven, like how we use the term Old Monster. It's not like this has ever been explained to humanity, beyond them occasionally introducing themselves as angels while they're hunting a demon. That is, unless you have church knowledge that contradicts my assumptions?"

"I don't know anything that contradicts what you just said, but it feels wrong *in here*." Davina touched the part of her heart where she claimed the angel's grace lived. "What I feel here says your soul is as worthy of walking into Heaven as he was."

"That could merely be because I'm favoured by Heaven?"

Davina paused. "True."

"Then we agree I'm not an angel."

"Not in the Heavenly sense, but you likely have access to most of their abilities. You seem to be able to effortlessly repair souls now. Does your soul still require life force to sustain itself?"

"I'm not sure. My soul is currently feeding on my new soul energy reservoir. Once that's depleted, it will likely draw on my life force, but that's just an educated guess."

"How high are the demands?"

"Less than before. The excess life force I consume also no longer strengthens my soul. Instead, it's converted to soul energy and joins the soul energy in my reservoir."

"If the demands are lower, why are you having Amelia hunt Unseen for you in every city we pass?"

I used my wing to emphasise my form, annoyed she had to ask.

Davina caught my meaning. "Oh, you can't store much life force in your current form."

"It's one of the many issues I face."

"Let me help with that."

Davina didn't give me a chance to reject her offer, reaching over and engulfing my head with her hand. With an effort of will, she manipulated my emotions and made the hunger, exhaustion, and pain disappear. The foul mood I'd been in since I attacked Kathrine went with it.

For a moment, I was able to accept that I had no control over that situation and forgive myself for what I'd done. I knew it wouldn't last. The monster in me wasn't capable of forgiveness. He needed control, and he wouldn't have that until he could be certain that it wouldn't happen again.

Davina moved her hand to my back, without releasing her hold over me. "Is that better?"

It was.

"Thank you."

Davina smiled. "I have something to confess."

I sighed. "What did you do?"

Davina turned to Angelica. "I gained the skill transfer skill while we were in the Abyss."

Skill transfer was considered a deathbed skill. It allowed you to permanently transfer any skill, at its current level, to someone else, so long as the skill was the same level or above skill transfer's current level. Occasionally, people would gift skills willingly, but that was rare. Unless you were as selfless as a saint.

"Which skills did you transfer to Angelica?"

Davina was wise enough not to smile. "Willpower, emotional control, self-reflection, self-awareness, happiness, forgiveness, inner healing, and inner peace. They were all level 20."

Emotional control, self-reflection, and self-awareness were all skills people only got after level 200. Happiness, forgiveness, inner healing, and inner peace were in the same level bracket but reserved for members of the church or monks. Willpower appeared randomly.

The skills she had transferred weren't a bad combination, and they would do a lot of good for Angelica at level 20, but it did raise a question.

"Why are you helping Angelica so much?"

Davina gave Angelica a sad smile. "Kathrine explained how much you regret what you did to her. How hard you're trying to undo your mistake. I wanted to help you."

They must have talked about it while they were in town or while I was training behind the barrier in my training hall, because I had no memory of such a conversation taking place at Darksmith, and I remembered every conversation that took place at Darksmith.

Now that she'd explained her actions, I understood why she was manipulating my emotions. She wanted me to care about her as much as I cared about Angelica and thought this might be the key.

It wasn't.

At best, she would make me care *less* about Angelica. None of these skills would immediately fix her, but they would equip her with what she needed to heal from her lifetime of abuse, helping her control what I'd done to her. In time, this might be the solution. And if it was, *my monster* would no longer be someone I thought about.

"This won't give you what you want. I'm still incapable of caring about you."

Davina gave me the same sad smile as she lifted Angelica's head and slid her helmet back on with the visor open. "Then I'll keep trying."

Angelica's eyes flew open, as Davina tightened her helmet strap, and then her hand blurred toward Davina's throat. Davina leaned back and slapped Angelica's hand aside, causing her to scream and pull her hand to her chest, cradling it like she had just been hit with a sledgehammer. The pain layered through her scent told me Angelica wasn't being dramatic, despite the strike not being hard enough to harm her.

Anger joined pain as Angelica got her bearings and recognised who was kneeling over her. "Did you have to hit me so fucking hard? You broke my wrist."

"Your wrist is fine," Davina replied. "The pain's coming from your hellfire injuries."

Angelica scowled. "Hurry up and heal me, then."

"I can't."

"Then get me somewhere safe so you can. They need me out there. Wait…why are we in a wagon?"

Davina patted Angelica's armoured shoulder. "You've been unconscious for ten days."

Angelica stared at Davina for several seconds as her words sunk in, and then her face lit up. "We won!"

"We *survived*," I corrected.

"It's the same fucking thing. That shit was crazy."

"Language, Angelica."

She leaned forward to glare at me but ended up wincing in pain. "I should be able to say 'fuck' when you make me fight ancient vampires."

"No, you shouldn't."

"Why are you a crow?"

"I'm injured."

She paused, began to run her gaze over me, the way a predator would size up another predator, but then tried to move her head more than two inches and wound up wincing. "*How* injured?"

"If I leave this binding circle for an extended period of time before we return to my grave, I'll die."

Angelica glanced in my direction, confused, but no longer hostile.

She'd worked out that she was too injured to pick a fight. "How are you that injured?"

"I was next to the explosion."

Her eyes widened. "The big one?"

"The big one."

"I can't believe you survived that."

"*Barely* survived."

Angelica stopped trying to look at me and lowered her head with a loud groan. "Why does everything ache?"

Davina blushed. "I'm not skilled enough to fully cleanse hellfire injures."

"I can tell."

Davina turned a brighter shade of pink. "Your equipment is numbing the pain you're feeling, so don't try to take it off."

"You call this numbing the pain?"

"I'm working on it."

"Work faster."

"I don't know how."

"Get someone who does, then."

"There *isn't* anyone else," Davina whispered, voice a little sullen.

Before Angelica could firmly put her foot in her mouth and be any more obnoxious, I explained what Davina meant. "Mother and Father didn't survive the battle."

"That would be a problem if she wasn't a saint," Angelica snapped back, in too much pain to be cordial.

"Half-saint," Davina corrected.

"Half-saint, whole saint, definitions don't really matter when you can walk into any cathedral, ask for help, and watch the archbishops fall over each other to do whatever you need them to do. It should have been the first thing you tried."

"His Dark Eminence felt it wasn't safe to stop until after we reached the Bo Empire."

"Well, that's just great. At least tell me we got them all. I'd hate to be in this much pain for no reason."

Davina smiled. "We did."

Angelica lifted her head, releasing another groan as she force a weak grin in my direction. "I don't owe you any money now."

"No, you don't, and you can collect your six sharn cores once you've recovered."

"What about my share of the loot?"

"I didn't get any loot."

"*You didn't get any loot*!"

"I didn't see anything that was worth risking my life for."

"Wow, you *are* injured."

"Almost as badly as you."

Angelica lowered her head and hissed. "Does recovering count as my time off?"

"No."

"Good. What happens now?"

"Now, we cross the border, find someone who can heal you and the others, and then go home and train like our lives depend on it."

Angelica groaned. "Just kill me."

44

THE ROAD TO GOODBYE

The Bo Empire's clergy reacted to Davina's arrival with as much enthusiasm as Angelica predicted. Clerics and paladins fell to their knees as she passed through their hallowed halls on her way to speak with their leaders, kissing the hem of her robe and renouncing their oaths to follow her wherever she might lead them. Archbishops and holy paladins smiled fondly when they met her, bowing low and apologising that they did not hear her call, before asking how they could help.

The clergy of the Bo Empire and Arcadia might not have recognised Davina's status as the necrosaint or her authority within their power structure because she'd been excommunicated for being my familiar, but that didn't stop them from lending her aid if they felt it was appropriate, which is how our convoy found itself moving from one training facility to another as we searched for an archbishop or a high-level cleric with enough skill to heal Angelica and the others.

The fact that their hellfire wounds originated from a cursed constitution instead of from a demonic attack made treating our people more complicated than they expected, which is why we were forced to use trial and error as the convoy headed east through the Bo Empire's

Southern Province, travelling around Arcadia's northern mountain border to the eastern border it shared with the Vorm Republic.

It was slow progress, and the call of the grave grew stronger with each passing day, but without the threat of running into vampires, there was little reason to rush, and many reasons to maintain our pace. Princess Carolyn's father had likely spent the majority of my absence from his kingdom creating a trap near my grave. I needed to give him time to learn how powerful my people had become, so he could remove whatever he'd created.

A one-sided defeat would ruin him politically and terrify the aristocracy in a way that would turn the entire nation upside down. The fallout could destabilize the kingdom so thoroughly it might not recover, which wasn't productive considering the threat the vampires posed. It also wouldn't help to make the world safer for my family.

Six weeks after entering the Bo Empire, I watched the sunrise from cleric Worton Linon's balcony, which overlooked the monastery's vineyards, enjoying the genius healer's discomfort over my unannounced appearance at his breakfast table. The monastery was normally a place of spiritual retreat, an out-of-the-way location, where clerics and paladins could meditate in peace, searching for guidance as to where their path should take them. It currently held the highest concentrations of archbishops and high-level clerics anywhere in the Southern Provence, a province that was larger than Arcadia, Murdell, and the Vorm Republic combined, as the healers all tried to expand their skills under Worton's tutelage to assist with the demon lord the empire was fighting in the North.

Worton was in his late twenties, with short blond hair and plain features, average height, and a gentle smile, yet he was already one of the empire's leading experts on hellfire injuries. That sort of growth and experience were only possible when you threw a teenaged genius into a demon lord war, and they survived. He'd grown up fast. He'd developed his skills faster. And he'd survived the demon lord's first assassination attempt, giving the church the rare chance to hide him on the opposite side of the empire to teach others his skills.

None of that was enough to pull me from the Curse of Sloth, or from the grave that was calling me, but last night he'd promised Angelica he'd help her escape being my familiar. The past few weeks in the Bo Empire had strolled by without me noticing the world around me, but his declaration was enough to pull me back to the world of the living.

The early morning air was crisp and foggy, filled with the chirping of birds and the sounds of the monastery starting its day, as Worton shakily placed his breakfast tray on the outdoor table and took a seat across from me. His hands trembled as he lifted his teacup and tried to sip his drink.

Tea soaked his blond moustache as he failed to swallow the hot liquid. Judging by his scent, Worton experienced more fear than most, but that hadn't stopped him from doing the right thing and offering to help Angelica, making him braver than most.

His Heaven's-blessed gaze watched me as he accepted the consequences of his actions and the early demise he thought was coming for him. He wasn't the only one Angelica had asked for help, but he was the only one to say yes.

He was a good man.

Better than those who had turned her away.

I peered down my beak at him, letting his emotions play out, enjoying his fear, which allowed the Curse of Sloth to remain at bay.

Traveling through the Bo Empire had given my people access to skilled craftsmen, so my dragon hide binding cushion was a thing of the past. A binding ring sat around each of my legs, with another around my neck, with even smaller and more numerous binding orbs housed within my flesh. Only one of the items had to survive to keep my demonic parasites in check and stop them from trying to restore my body, and I could power these items with my own mana if necessary. Most considered it overkill, but I wasn't sure if it would be enough.

The seconds ticked by as Worton's fear made the world around me come into focus, and the willpower I required to maintain my interest began to wane.

I took a slow breath to fill my tiny lungs and relaxed my gaze, bowing my head in acknowledgement for what he had done. "Thank you for offering to help Angelica."

Worton froze, tea dribbling down his chin, looking at me like a deer caught in headlights.

I loosened my posture as I rose. "Angelica hasn't said as much, but I know she's planning to wait until I reach my grave before she compels me to free her from my service. As my familiar, she knows it's when I'll be at my weakest. The only thing which could give her the courage to change her plan is if you have something that will give her a larger advantage. Before you ask, you don't have anything like that here. I checked. Which is why I want you to ask her to return here once she is free and offer her the church's protection."

The church's protection was a little like Witness Protection. The people who went into their system disappeared. Angelica wouldn't be able to disappear. She was too powerful, and without my compulsion, she would need to fight frequently to blow off steam. But the church would be able to move her around, so I couldn't find where she *was*, only where she *had been.*

Worton stared at me, gripped by fear, trying to understand my angle, before he realised the truth. "You really *did* make her your familiar to protect her from what you did to her, like the necrosaint claims."

I nodded. "It was my only option at the time."

Worton's hands stopped trembling, and he released a resigned sigh, placing his teacup down. "Why do you sound like you want her to get away?"

"Because you're reading subtext that isn't there. Angelica's freedom is going to cause her more suffering than she can imagine. I would prefer that she trusted me enough to stay by my side, where she didn't have to experience that suffering, but she's grown too strong too quickly for that to be possible."

Worton scowled for the first time, glaring down at me. "You should have brought her to us to begin with. The church can reduce the side effects of the reaping."

I shook my head. "You can, but only at great cost, which is a cost the church wouldn't have been willing to pay back then, as neither I nor Angelica had a reputation that would have encouraged the church to help us."

Worton sighed and then nodded, admitting I had a point. "Why do you want me to make sure you can't find her?"

"It's the only way for Angelica to feel safe, for her to let her guard down, for her to begin to heal from what those monsters did to her."

Worton frowned. "Why not release her yourself, then?"

"I can't."

His frown deepened. "Can't? Or won't?"

"I can't. For once in her life, Angelica needs to escape the monsters on her own. She needs to feel powerful. She needs to know that the monster she made a deal with to escape the other monsters in her life is something she doesn't need to fear anymore. That the monsters which terrorized her all her life are something she doesn't need to be afraid of anymore. I won't deprive her of that revelation or the chance to know she doesn't need to live in fear of others."

Worton relaxed his expression. "You care about her?"

"No. Not in a way you would understand. But I'm trying to do right by her."

Worton wiped his chin, lifted his teacup, and took a long drink, before placing it back down and meeting my gaze, showing his resolve. "Then, I'll do the same."

I looked deeply into his Heaven's-blessed eyes and began manipulating his mind. "What makes you think I'm giving you an option? And a cleric should know better than to meet the gaze of an ancient vampire, especially one that has something to protect."

Angelica didn't know the monastery couldn't offer her anything to help her escape, but that didn't stop Worton from telling her that the amulet he was giving her would leave me at her mercy once I compelled him to. The truth was, Angelica was now so powerful, and I was so weak, that there was nothing I could do to stop her. But she lacked confidence and didn't believe in herself, so she needed her magic feather to let her think she could fly. Anything would suffice, so long as she believed it would help her be free.

Until Winton offered to help her, I had always planned for Angelica to escape when we reached my grave. My recovery would give her the time she needed to get away. The time she needed to understand the horrors of what I'd done to her, offering me a small chance to convince her to return to me.

Winton's offer had changed that plan. If there was a chance for *my monster* to live an almost normal life free from my influence, I had to give her that chance.

I owed her that much.

A week after we left the monastery, Angelica caught me by the neck in the busy tavern as Davina finished reading aloud the letter that had been left by the convoy we'd spent the past week trying to catch up with, telling us we were now less than a day behind them. With her armour on, Angelica moved far too fast for any of my guards to intercept, and she was in and out of my protective circle before they could react.

Helen, Gregory, and everyone else who had been injured by hellfire stared at her incomprehensibly as she leapt through the nearest window to make her escape. As the glass shattered around us, she raised me to her face and started running.

"Release me from your service," Angelica commanded.

Her words reverberated through my skull, pounding against my psyche, crushing my will with their weight. I was at my very weakest, utterly defenceless to her compulsion. Yes, this world had skills, skills that would not allow my capabilities to fall below those skill's level, but they could only do so much. Angelica was now beyond the limits of my willpower. The gulf between her strength and mine was too great.

I let go of my power over her, releasing our bond, taking back everything I'd given her, as my guards watched her run away, staring after us dumbfounded. Tears of blood began to pour from her eyes.

With each tear our bond grew weaker, taking every compulsion I'd laid upon her with it.

The fingers around my neck and shoulders tightened as our bond vanished, breaking every bone, shattering the binding ring I wore around my throat, and turning my muscles to goo. Sensing the sudden threat to my life, Davina finally reacted. Davina blurred through the broken window, chasing us down the street as Angelica face lit up with excitement. My goo reformed in Angelica's grip, as my guards came rushing out of the building behind Davina.

Davina glared at Angelica as she sprinted after us, raising her staff. She couldn't keep up this pace for long. None of them could. With her armour, levels, and the effects of the reaping, Angelica's attributes were too high. "Release him, Angelica!"

"Release Davina from your service," Angelica commanded, no longer under a compulsion to listen to Davina, as she ran away.

The words reverberated through my skull, and all I could do was obey. Tears of blood began to pour from Davina's eyes as I released my hold over her and our bond grew weaker. Davina didn't stop running.

Davina wiped the blood away with her sleeve to clear her vision as she ducked down streets and side alleys, falling further and further behind. "Put him down, Angelica! I'm not going to warn you again."

"But we're free!" The excitement and joy in her voice would have broken my heart, if I'd had one.

Davina gritted her teeth, taking in where we were and not liking the idea of how many people would have to die for her to stop Angelica in such a crowded space, even if Angelica didn't go all out—and that might happen. "That doesn't change anything."

Angelica slapped her visor closed as she ran, ready to fight if she had to. "It changes *everything*."

"Does it? His Dark Eminence might not be able to kill you, but *Luke* can!"

Angelica stumbled as she heard Luke's name, shocked by the realisation that I wasn't the only threat. As Davina's words sank in, Angelica began to hyperventilate. Her heartrate sped up, and her confidence and jubilation disappeared as she began to panic.

She hadn't thought this through *at all.*

Typical.

"I can take him," Angelica called back without slowing.

"He's got more skills than both of us combined."

"I can take him."

This time it sounded like she was trying to convince herself. Angelica was incredibly powerful, but she wasn't on my son's level.

"You know you can't," Davina called as she fell out of earshot without ever releasing a spell.

ANGELICA RAN for three days and nights, through rugged wilderness and farmland, crossing rivers and streams that would have killed me if anything other than my thirteen demonic parasites had survived the explosion in Necropolis. She didn't care about my survival. She was too scared and panicked, unsure what she should do now that she was free. Fuelled by that fear and anger, all she could think to do was run. She ran without stopping, without slowing. She had no clue where she was going. She wasn't following a road. She was just running as if her life depended on it.

And she took me with her every step of the way, commanding me to be silent, to not move a muscle, interfere, or try to escape.

She only stopped when the mountain forest she was travelling through suddenly gave way to a five-thousand-foot drop that stretched as far as the eye could see. There she skidded to a stop, barely catching her momentum before running off the edge.

Angelica turned her head as she caught her breath beside the edge of the cliff, trying to decide where she would go, where she would run to next. She had no clue where she was, or how she had arrived there, but I knew where we were. It was a place called The Edge of the World. It was named that because far below us lived an environment that had evolved separately from the rest of the world. It was cut off from everywhere around it. It was a violent place, a dangerous place, where even the plants would try to kill you.

As Angelica stood at The Edge of the World trying to decide where she would go, exhaustion caught up with her. She had pushed her body too hard. She'd gone too long without rest. She'd reached the end of what even her endurance could sustain, and now she had nothing left in the tank, nothing she could use to run away from her problems. All she could do was rest and face the reality of her actions to decide what would happen next.

Angelica flopped to the ground, dangling her legs over the edge of the cliff, as she swayed and panted for breath, while pulling jerky and water from storage pouches. The forest stretched far below her, and the mountains she had passed through rose above, casting her into shadow.

There in the shadow of the mountain, lost in the wilderness, while trying to gather her strength, she broke down, releasing the emotions she'd been running from. As the tears flowed, exhaustion and fear welled up inside her, but also loneliness.

She had gotten what she wanted.

She was no longer my familiar.

But now she was alone and afraid, in the middle of nowhere, with no one to turn to.

I watched *my sad little monster*, knowing she might kill me now, and I was okay with that.

Angelica was so alone and hurt by the world. Unable to face the reality that was her life. She had been mistreated for so long, that being strong enough to protect herself left her distraught. It left her distraught because the change was too late to save her from the suffering of her childhood. Too late to save her from the nightmares she'd endured. The monsters were gone, and she couldn't vanquish them to give her soul peace.

I was the only monster left.

The last one to have enslaved her.

Even though it was for her own good.

Angelica turned her head and glared at me through the tears behind her visor, before dropping me on the ground beside her. Her anger intensified as she continued to glare at me, washing away her other emotions and the smell of earth and stone around us.

Slowly, she lifted her visor to see me clearer and her anger reached its peak. "I want you to stay there and hurt yourself as much as you hurt me."

Her command slammed into my mind, breaking what little willpower I had in my current state. She began to frown as I continued sitting without moving.

"Do it." The command hit me again, just as intensely, but had the same effect. "Tell me why this isn't working."

This command worked.

"I've never hurt you," I said calmly. "Not in the way you want me to hurt myself."

Angelica's face turned bright red as she gritted her teeth with indignation. "You tried to kill me the day you made me your familiar."

"I tried to make you strong enough to survive the lich."

"And that hurt like hell."

"Language, Angelica."

She glared at me. "I don't have to do what you say, not now, not ever again. *I'm* the one with the power here. Now tell me why this isn't working."

"Those were growing pains. They didn't hurt you. They were just uncomfortable."

"Fine," she said through gritted teeth. "Punish yourself as much as you punished me."

I continued to sit there.

"You've punished me plenty of times," Angelica whined petulantly, losing some of her anger to annoyance. "You can't say you haven't."

"I've never punished you in a way that harms you. Whenever you do something that's wrong, I try to teach you that it's not right. I don't try to hurt you or make you less than you are. I only try to help you see that it's not right while you grow."

Her fist crashed through my skull, creating a cloud of feathers, mangling my flesh, and leaving my body an unrecognisable mess. There was no magic behind her punch, so my flesh wasn't destroyed, letting my demonic parasites and my ability to shapeshift quickly reform the mess she left behind into a crow. Restoring my body this way increased my hunger and weakened me further, but at least it wasn't a death sentence.

However, the handful of my demonic binding items that were destroyed by the strike did concern me. If I somehow survived this, I would need at least one of those binding items to survive. She punched me again, pulverized me into mincemeat, destroying a few more items, while others went flying. This continued to happen as I reformed as quickly as she destroyed me.

Through the violence and pain, I heard her sobbing.

"You didn't try to *help* me. No one ever tries to help me. They just lie and hurt me. You're a monster. You're just like them. Why would you help me?"

Her unconscious command, driven by her emotion, slammed into me as she continued to pummel me, striking me for every abuse and injustice she had ever suffered. "Because. I. Saw. That. No. One. Else. Had."

Her fists stopped falling, but her tears didn't. "What did you say?"

I looked up as I reformed, but did not meet her gaze, because it wouldn't make her feel safe. "Because I saw that no one else had."

Angelica stared at me confused, hot tears running down her cheeks. "What?"

"When we took the other sacrifice, Salina, home after the ritual where we met, I realised that she wasn't your friend. She was just a girl who had been kind to you. Your scent wasn't among her things, and hers wasn't among yours. But the small kindness she had shown you was worth more to you than your freedom. You wanted someone to help you so badly, that even though no one had ever helped you the way that you needed, you helped her. I saw then how badly you needed help, so I helped. I'll always be sorry I couldn't see that sooner."

Angelica's face transformed with rage as her fist flew through my head. "You're not a hero! You're a monster!" She punched me again. "You didn't save me. You made me your slave." She spent the next few seconds making more mincemeat. "All I wanted was to be safe, and you made me your familiar so you could use me, too."

"I will always be sorry that I *had* to do that."

Her face had turned a bright shade of red as emotions burst through her without restraint. "You're not sorry. You're just afraid of me. Tell me the truth!"

Her command hit me like an anvil, and I told her the truth. "I've spent every day since we met trying to show you how sorry I am, because words are not enough to make up for what I did to you. Outside of my family, you are the only person I care about in this world, and I've never been afraid of you."

"You don't care about me. Tell me the truth."

The command slammed into me again. "I care for you as much as my nature will allow, and I can't care about you more than I already do." I projected the truth of my words to her, using the open-heart technique.

She froze, staring down at me. "You're not lying."

"I may have withheld information, but I've never lied to you."

She sniffed. "You *were* trying to help me."

"Yes."

"If you were trying to help me, why did you force me to become your familiar?"

Answering this question would crush Angelica's hopes and dreams. It would hurt her so deeply that she might never recover, but I had no way to stop myself from doing as she asked. My willpower and attributes weren't strong enough. So, instead of fight to remain silent, I used what little willpower I had to soften what she was about to hear.

"Why did you hit me just now?"

Angelica dropped her gaze to the forest far below, smelling embarrassed. "You made me angry."

Her emotions were all over the place now that she was no longer under my compulsions, which didn't surprise me. Her fear had been masking the problem, but that couldn't have lasted.

"You get angry a lot, don't you."

"Everyone gets angry."

"But you want to hurt people when you get angry."

"So what?" she replied indignantly. "Lots of people want to hurt people when they get angry."

“Yes, but most people don’t tear someone apart when they’re angry, do they?”

“No.”

“That’s not your fault, though. It’s mine.”

“Because you made me your familiar.”

“No. It’s because I put you through the reaping ritual. The ritual is evil, and it infects you with evil. I knew the side effects going in, and I was willing to let you bear them because I thought you were evil, too.”

“What?”

“The compulsions I put on you not to hurt innocent people were never there because you were my familiar. They were there because you went through the reaping. With them, you could live a normal life. Or as close to normal as possible. Without them, you’re emotionally erratic.”

“That’s just because you’re pissing me off.”

“I’ve made you this angry in the past, but this is the first time you attacked me or anyone else. If I wasn’t a vampire, you would have killed me.”

“I know that. That’s why I wouldn’t hit someone else.”

“You’re *lying* to yourself, Angelica. You know you couldn’t have stopped yourself from hitting me just now even if you wanted to.”

Angelica’s fist crashed through my skull and didn’t stop. It took her nearly a minute to regain control and thirst began to bite at the back of my throat when she finally finished. It was a warning that I was getting into very dangerous territory.

As I reformed, I looked up to see tears flowing down Angelica’s cheeks as she sat there in shock, finally beginning to realise what I’d done to her. “I made you my familiar so you couldn’t hurt people you didn’t believe deserved to be hurt, and to teach you to be better. I made you my familiar because it was the only way I could limit the harm from what I’ve done to you.”

With the open-heart technique, my words pierced through her anger, making her reexamine everything she had felt since the day we met. Until now, Angelica had always associated these impulses with being my familiar, not with what I’d made her do, or with what she had become. Horror replaced shock as she realised what I'd done to her. As she recognised, she was never going to truly escape me.

Her hand went to her mouth as her stomach turned. She swallowed the rising bile and dropped her gaze to me as reality came crashing down. "I'm a monster."

There was no accusation, no question in her tone, just a realisation of what I'd done to her.

I looked up at her and nodded. "*My monster*."

"Why do you always say that?"

"Because it's always true. You're the monster I made. My greatest regret."

Angelica sat there stunned for several seconds, and then the tears truly began to flow as she realised the implications of what I'd told her. Without being my familiar with the compulsions that came with it, she *couldn't* be around her brothers and sisters. She couldn't be around normal people. She was too dangerous, too violent, too easily upset.

Her freedom would cost her everything she cared about.

I didn't say anything as she quietly wept. No words would make what I had done to her any better. No apology would ever be enough. So, I let her cry, knowing that tears might turn to anger, and anger might lead to my death.

Because if anyone had a right to take my life, she did.

Angelica eventually cried herself out and pulled a handkerchief from her storage pouch, blowing her nose. She wiped her face, caught her breath, and stared out at the expanse that lay before us. "You let me believe these impulses came from being your familiar."

"I wanted to spare you this pain."

Angelica's lips trembled, but she didn't break out in tears this time. "I can't be around people without hurting them, can I?"

"Not without my compulsions or something similar."

"Will the urges get worse?"

"They can if you do evil. They can also get weaker if you do good. The further you turn from evil, the less it can influence you. It was always my goal that by the time my familiar bond began to fade, you would have more mental fortitude and be a better person."

"And if that didn't happen?"

"Then I would be there to help you."

"For how long?"

"For as long as it took."

"What if I never got better?"

"Then when you were old and frail and too weak to walk and lying on your deathbed angry and afraid, I would be next to you holding your hand helping you move peacefully from this life into the next."

A shadow of a smile touched her lips. "Then you would turn me into the most powerful zombie every created, so I could continue helping you make the world safer."

"It's only practical."

She giggled as she wiped more tears from her face, understanding my humour after being together for so long. "You would bury me, wouldn't you."

"In the most beautiful and peaceful place I could find. Then I would tell that stupid dracolich of yours to keep you safe forever."

"She would do it, too."

"She would."

"Why didn't you compel me not to use my armour to command you?"

"We were always going to have this conversation. If we didn't have it now, then we would have had it in five years when my compulsions were much weaker. If I had compelled you not to use your armour on me, you would have resented me more than you already do. It would have been another five years of you feeling trapped without any way out, and that would have made it impossible for us to talk like this."

"And that wouldn't have helped me," she replied, sceptically.

"No. Not at all."

"You're more focused than you normally are?"

"You're dangerous enough right now that my nature allows me to give you my full attention."

"How long will that last?"

"Until you become my familiar again or get far enough away not to concern me."

“I can become your familiar again?”

“If you want to.”

“I need time to think about that.”

“I can give you time, if you pass me that binding ring over there. Without it, I won’t live long enough for us to end this conversation.”

Angelica reached out and picked up the binding ring, placing it in front of me. I slid my foot into it and wove ambient magic through it to reactivate the spell that stopped my demonic parasites from trying to regrow my missing flesh.

The injuries Angelica had given me were not superficial, and if I wasn’t in existential danger, the call of my grave and the Curse of Sloth would have overwhelmed me by now.

We stayed on the side of the cliff for the next few hours. Angelica had dozens of questions for me. Sometimes, she asked them one after the other, and sometimes ten minutes would pass in between. She attacked me frequently, unable to restrain herself. She cried just as frequently. She was *my sad little monster*, and she was only just seeing how much I had been helping her survive the horrors of what I’d done to her.

We watched the sunset together.

Angelica dangled her legs off the side of the cliff as she processed what I’d done to her.

She sighed as the fading light warmed her face. “I can hear your call now. It’s asking me if I want to be a better person. If I want to devote myself to making the world safe for people like me. If I answer, I think I’ll be able to get past my fears and become your familiar again. The call is telling me that it will give me the strength I need to keep the world safe *from me*. Is that how you feel? That you have to not only make the world safe, but keep it safe from you?”

“I was once a good man. Now, I’m a monster. But the man I was is stronger than the monster I’ve become. I want to make the world safe for my family, and that starts with keeping the world safe from the monster that resides within me.”

“I’ve heard a lot of people talk about your call. None of them hear what I hear.”

"None of them are like us: good people, who were turned into monsters by others. So, they hear the call that applies to them, and you hear the call that applies to you."

She closed her eyes as the sun began to fall below The Edge of the World. Angelica didn't open her eyes until long after the sun had set. Stars filled the night sky when she turned to me, her mind made up.

"When I was little, I used to think that every family was like ours. That everyone pretended to be different when they were outside their homes. When I learned what heroes were, I dreamed about a hero coming to make my parents be nice to me, to make them be like the parents in the children's stories my teacher read. I didn't understand that the stories she read were meant to be scary, because they sounded like fairy tales to me. My parents were so much worse."

"You aren't them."

"But I *could* be, after what you did to me. And that scares me as much as being at someone's mercy."

"You can choose to be better. You can choose to trust me, to let me restrain your impulses."

"I just have to be brave." Angelica gave me a sad smile. "I'm not that brave, though." She pulled her legs back from the edge of the cliff and rose to her feet. "I've always thought you were only kind to your family. I was wrong. You're only *obvious* about your kindness when it comes to them. So let me be kind to you in return and spare your life. But just this once. If I see you again, I'm going to kill you."

"Thank you…It's better than I deserve."

Angelica gave me the same sad smile. "I know."

Angelica disappeared into the forest without looking back, leaving me alone at The Edge of the World.

As her presence vanished, the grave began to call me.

The Curse of Sloth made the world fall away.

My monster was free.

And I was dying.

45

THE LONG WALK HOME

Father mentioned to me before his passing that Rena's mother stopped by to visit her daughter's grave while I slept. After nearly a week of indecision, she settled on leaving her daughter's remains with me, but only after changing the sarcophagus I'd placed Rena in for one she felt her daughter would have been more comfortable with. The new sarcophagus lay to the left of mine and was made from spotless white marble that was so clean and unblemished it hurt to look at. There was an inscription near the base that read: Beloved daughter, sister, and hero of Arcadia.

Denton's wife didn't know what to do about her husband's body either, as his resting place was close to his family cemetery and ancestral home, along with being the site of his greatest accomplishment as an adventurer. So, he also rested in a new rose granite sarcophagus to the right of mine. His inscription simply read: The good Denton.

The ominous, glowing, blood red crystals in the chamber had been swapped with pleasant yellow ones. The rough brick walls had been replaced with black granite. Benches had been added for those who guarded my rest, and every defensive enchantment my people could create was installed to keep me safe.

It sounded lovely, relaxing, like a place where I could let the worries of the world drift away.

Thoughts of my grave and the absent bliss it would offer churned through my mind in an unending stream as I waited at The Edge of the World to be rescued.

I'd done the math. I was too weak, too small, too driven by thirst to make it back to my people with absolute certainty. And if making it to my people wasn't assured, then making it to my grave wasn't either, so all I could do was wait and trust that my people would come for me.

Two days after Angelica disappeared, Davina stepped out of the petrified forest and approached me slowly, gauging me for signs of hunger and madness. She was no longer my familiar, no longer protected from my appetites. And I looked like a tired, hungry vampire crow, so anything could happen.

She didn't need to worry.

Between attracting the animals that lived here and consuming the life force of the forest, I wasn't being driven mad by thirst. If she had taken any longer, it would be a different story, as I'd already destroyed the local ecosystem to satiate my hunger, but for now I could control my appetites.

Davina struck her staff against the ground with each step forward, a casual and clear warning to my instincts that she was not prey. Growing up surrounded by undead meant she understood our impulses and instincts better than anyone. She knew exactly how to behave to keep us in check.

The world came into focus as Davina crouched beside me like a tiger standing over a mouse. She was no longer my familiar. No longer under my control. And she was someone my instincts did not want me to be near while she was free to do as she pleased.

It was easy enough to ignore those instincts.

Davina gave me a gentle smile as she looked down at me, without lowering her guard. "You got away."

I shook my head. "No…Angelica spared me."

Her smile grew as pride and happiness entered her scent. "Do you think it was because of the skills I transferred?"

I was not in the mood for a happy reunion, or to feel proud of Angelica for becoming a better person, or to pat Davina on the head for a job well done. I was too tired, too hungry, too weak for pleasantries.

My gaze narrowed, and I ignored her question. "What took you so long? I expected you here this morning."

Davina sighed, accepting I wasn't in the mood for casual conversation. "Tracking a dark aura isn't easy, your Dark Eminence."

"It should be. You're the necrosaint. What happened?"

"I lost her trail a few times."

"That's something you are going to work on when we get to my grave."

Davina rolled her eyes as she picked me up and held me in the crook of her arm like a baby. "Are you going to be this grumpy the entire way back?"

"Most likely," I snapped back. "My instincts won't let me rest while I'm near you, since you aren't my familiar anymore, and that's affecting my mood."

"Because you're dying."

"Obviously?"

"Then I'll do my best to get you to you grave as soon as possible, Mr Grumpy Pants."

That was something my wife used to call me when I got home from working overtime. It always used to make me laugh.

I didn't laugh.

"Did Luke tell you to call me that?"

"No. Kathrine did. She said it might cheer you up. Did it work?"

"No. But it made me remember a happier time for a moment. Now, if you are done wasting time, let's go home."

Our journey from Edge of the World to our convoy took five days. Despite being exhausted, Davina stopped just long enough to gather the stronger half of my personal guard and then we set off for my grave, moving faster than the convoy but slower than when she was alone.

The fear of what we encountered in North Murdell had faded from the front of everyone's thoughts. News of their ongoing war had been sporadic, but the Bo Empire was taking the threat seriously, repositioning the southern army along Murdell's border and expanding their local training and recruitment. It was clear to everyone that they would invade the moment the darklord fell. They couldn't allow a vampire nation to exist on their border.

In my exhausted opinion, it was a mistake to wait.

But the Bo Empire were not conquerors. They liked to be welcomed into the nations and kingdoms they took over. The vampires also weren't the only catastrophic threat to the empire, and their strongest people were tied up dealing with those problems. Holding off made tactical sense to them, but it gave the vampires more time to grow their numbers, allowing them to become a bigger threat.

The days blurred together, and my exhaustion and hunger continued to grow. By the time we arrived at the town built around my grave, the call of the grave was nearly too strong to fight, even to pay my respects to the families of my fallen guards, so I asked Davina to bolster my strength as we arrived.

Davina held me in her arms, removing my pain, hunger, and the call of my grave the way only a saint could. Giving me the strength I needed to do what was right, in a time when I couldn't do so alone.

What was left of the disgruntled instructors from the kingdom's adventurer's guilds still studying at my academy walked through the street around us. Until two weeks ago, there had been ten times as many. In my absence, Princess Carolyn's father had flooded my town with foreign adventurers under false names and credentials, paying their tuition to attend my academy to setup an ambush for my return.

To maintain their cover, the adventurers had to go to classes, learning better ways to fight evil and make the world safe, which was why my academy existed. The king's plan to stop me had ultimately helped me further my goals; and after the events that took place at Necropolis, Carolyn had warned him against making a move, informing him of exactly how powerful my children, familiars, and guards had become.

I was a little surprised he listened.

I'd expected a fight.

Our group ended our short walk down the sparsely populated street, stopping outside a three-storey townhouse filled with children's laughter, laughter which would soon come to an end. Davina's grip tightened around me, searching for comfort from what came next.

Commander Taylor stepped forward and knocked on the front door, before lowering her hand to the urn she carried, steeling herself for what she had to do. A fully restored Gregory stood behind her with Helen. They both wore grim expressions, ready to do their duty. Commanders Erin and Masters waited beside us with pensive faces, knowing what was about to happen, knowing there was nothing they could do to stop it.

They'd all fought evil.

They'd all killed evil.

They'd all survived evil.

But others hadn't.

Now they had to tell the families of those under their command what doing the right thing had cost them.

Silvia Absten opened the front door with a baby on her hip. A fresh vomit stain sat on her right shoulder, and flour dusted the cuffs of her sleeves from the pancakes she'd made her children for lunch. All that was forgotten as she realised who stood at her door and what she carried.

"Please, no," Silvia's words were spoken softly, a request so small and deeply felt that it cut right to the gates of Heaven and Hell.

Gregory winced.

Commander Taylor took a deep breath and held out the urn. "I regret to inform you that your husband died under my command in a battle against an army of vampires led by no less than five ancient vampires 73 days ago. His bravery and sacrifice in the city of Necropolis allowed thousands of the inhabitants to flee to safety and put to rest five ancient evils, along with many others. It was my honour and privilege to have him serve under my command."

Silvia turned to Davina as tears formed at the edge of her eyes, searching for her last shred of hope. "Bring him back."

Helen stepped forward and gently took the Silvia's baby from her before the grief overwhelmed her, knowing what was about to happen.

Davina bowed to the widow. "It wasn't within my power."

Commander Talyor placed the urn in Silvia's hands and then squeezed her shoulder. "Your husband didn't suffer. He died instantly, killed by a powerful necrotic spell. There was no body left behind for the necrosaint to resurrect. Otherwise, I promise you she would have."

Silvia pulled the urn to her chest as her world fell apart, cradling what was left of her husband in her arms, crumbling to her knees like so many before her. And like so many others before her, she asked the same question, searching for meaning in her misery. "Did he make the world safer for our children?"

"*With everything he had*," we replied without hesitation.

The End

Final Stats
(This is without temporary changes)

Race: Ancient Royal Vampire Variant
Class: Hero
Level: 37
Strength: 404
Agility: 575
Endurance: ∞
Constitution: ∞
Cunning: 280
Perception: 480
Recovery: ∞
Mana Regeneration: 478

ALSO BY BENJAMIN KEREI

UNORTHODOX FARMING

Oh, Great! I Was Reincarnated as a Farmer

Oh, Great! I Discovered How to Cultivate a Farmer in 52 Easy Steps

THE VAMPIRE VINCENT

Death Loot & Vampires

Magic, Academies & Vampires

FIRST LINE OF DEFENSE

First Line of Defense 1

First Line of Defense 2

www.ingramcontent.com/pod-product-compliance
Lightning Source LLC
Chambersburg PA
CBHW030827310726
48980CB00006B/672/J

* 9 7 8 0 4 7 3 7 3 5 9 1 3 *